About the author

A graduate of the University of Mississippi, Greg Iles performed in a musical group for several years before writing his first novel. Now the author of five internationally-acclaimed bestselling thrillers, he lives in Natchez, Mississippi with his wife and two children.

D1494841

Also by Greg Iles

Dark Matter
Sleep No More
Dead Sleep
24 Hours
The Quiet Game
Mortal Fear
Black Cross
Spandau Phoenix

Greg Iles

THE QUIET GAME/ 24 HOURS

NEW ENGLISH LIBRARY

Hodder & Stoughton

This collected volume first published in Great Britain in 2003
by Hodder and Stoughton
A division of Hodder Headline

A Coronet Paperback

10 9 8 7 6 5 4 3 2 1

A CIP catalogue record for this title is available from the
British Library

ISBN 0 340 83080 8

Typeset in Baskerville by
Phoenix Typesetting, Ilkley, West Yorkshire

Printed and bound in Great Britain by
Clays Ltd, St Ives plc

Hodder and Stoughton
A division of Hodder Headline
338 Euston Road
London NW1 3BH

For
Madeline and Mark
Who will always be in my best work.

Anna Flowers
Who taught me about class in every sense.

AND

FOR GEOFF ILES
who has been there for me from the beginning
(almost).

ACKNOWLEDGEMENTS FOR THE QUIET GAME

Aaron Priest, for taking me to the next level.

Phyllis Grann, for faith and vision.

David Highfill, for a wonderful editorial experience.

Clare Ferraro, Rich Hasselberger, and the gang at Dutton for first-rate work.

Courtney Aldridge, the best buddy a writer could have.

Senior Special Agent Ronald Baughan, BATF, Certified Explosives Specialist, Retired.

Field Research, weapons: Keith Benoist, force recon marine and budding writer.

Historical expertise: Ron Miller.

Legal advice: Michael Henry, District Attorney Ronnie Harper, Kevin Colbert, Chancery Judge George Ward, Circuit Judge Lillie Blackmon Sanders.

Medical advice: Dr. Jerry W. Iles, Dr. Michael Bourland.

Cultural Perspective: Mildred Lyles, Georgia Ware, Peter Rinaldi.

Advance readers: Ed Stackler, Natasha Kern, Courtney Aldridge, Mary Lou England, Betty Iles, Michael Henry, Dianne Brown.

To those I omitted through oversight, my apologies.

All mistakes are mine.

ACKNOWLEDGMENTS FOR
24 HOURS

Aaron Priest, the Man.

Phyllis Grann, for paving the way.

David Highfill, for bearing with the writer's obsessive-ness.

Louise Burke, for her hard work and support.

MEDICAL ADVICE: Jerry Iles, M.D., William Daggett, M.D., Noah Archer, M.D., and Michael Bourland, M.D.

AVIATION: Mike Thompson, Justin Cardneaux, and Stephen Guido.

MISCELLANEOUS: Lisa Erbach-Vance, Glen Ballard, Jon Wood at Hodder, Michael MacInnis, Rush and Leslie Mosby, Ken and Beth Perry, Susan Chambliss, Simmons Iles, Robert Royal, Brent Bourland, Caroline Trefler, Carrie, Madeline, and Mark.

READERS: Ed Stackler, Betty Iles, Michael Henry, and Courtney Aldridge.

To those I have omitted through oversight, my sincere apologies. As always, all mistakes are mine.

THE QUIET GAME

Chapter 1

I am standing in line for Walt Disney's It's a Small World ride, holding my four-year-old daughter in my arms, trying to entertain her as the serpentine line of parents and children moves slowly toward the flat-bottomed boats emerging from the grotto to the music of an endless audio loop. Suddenly Annie jerks taut in my arms and points into the crowd.

'Daddy! I saw Mama! Hurry!'

I do not look. I don't ask where. I don't because Annie's mother died seven months ago. I stand motionless in the line, looking just like everyone else except for the hot tears that have begun to sting my eyes.

Annie keeps pointing into the crowd, becoming more and more agitated. Even in Disney World, where periodic meltdowns are common, her fit draws stares. Clutching her struggling body against mine, I work my way back through the line, which sends her into outright panic. The green metal chutes double back upon themselves to create the illusion of a short queue for prospective riders. I push past countless staring families, finally reaching the relative openness between the Carousel and Dumbo.

Holding Annie tighter, I rock and turn in slow circles as I did to calm her when she was an infant. A streaming mass of teenagers breaks around us like a river around a rock and pays us about as much attention. A claustrophobic sense of futility envelops me, a feeling I never experienced prior to my wife's illness but which now dogs me like a malignant

1

shadow. If I could summon a helicopter to whisk us back to the Polynesian Resort, I would pay ten thousand dollars to do it. But there is no helicopter. Only us. Or the less-than-us that we've been since Sarah died.

The vacation is over. And when the vacation is over, you go home. But where is home? Technically Houston, the suburb of Tanglewood. But Houston doesn't feel like home anymore. The Houston house has a hole in it now. A hole that moves from room to room.

The thought of Penn Cage helpless would shock most people who know me. At thirty-eight years old, I have sent sixteen men and women to death row. I watched seven of them die. I've killed in defense of my family. I've given up one successful career and made a greater success of another. I am admired by my friends, feared by my enemies, loved by those who matter. But in the face of my child's grief, I am powerless.

Taking a deep breath, I hitch Annie a little higher and begin the long trek back to the monorail. We came to Disney World because Sarah and I brought Annie here a year ago – before the diagnosis – and it turned out to be the best vacation of our lives. I hoped a return trip might give Annie some peace. But the opposite has happened. She rises in the middle of the night and pads into the bathroom in search of Sarah; she walks the theme parks with darting eyes, always alert for the vanished maternal profile. In the magical world of Disney, Annie believes Sarah might step around the next corner as easily as Cinderella. When I patiently explained that this could not happen, she reminded me that Snow White rose from the dead just like Jesus, which in her four-year-old brain is indisputable fact. All we have to do is *find* Mama, so that Daddy can kiss her and make her wake up.

I collapse onto a seat in the monorail with a half dozen Japanese tourists, Annie sobbing softly into my shoulder. The silver train accelerates to cruising speed, rushing through Tomorrowland, a grand anachronism replete with *Jetsons*-style rocket ships and Art Deco restaurants. A 1950s incarnation of man's glittering destiny, Tomorrowland was outstripped by reality more rapidly than old Walt could have imagined, transformed into a kitschy parody of the dreams of the Eisenhower era. It stands as mute but eloquent testimony to man's inability to predict what lies ahead.

I do not need to be reminded of this.

As the monorail swallows a long curve, I spy the crossed roof beams of the Polynesian Resort. Soon we will be back inside our suite, alone with the emptiness that haunts us every day. And all at once that is not good enough anymore. With shocking clarity a voice speaks in my mind. It is Sarah's voice.

You can't do this alone, she says.

I look down at Annie's face, angelic now in sleep.

'We need help,' I say aloud, drawing odd glances from the Japanese tourists. Before the monorail hisses to a stop at the hotel, I know what I am going to do.

I call Delta Airlines first and book an afternoon flight to Baton Rouge – not our final destination, but the closest major airport to it. Simply making the call sets something thrumming in my chest. Annie awakens as I arrange for a rental car, perhaps even in sleep sensing the utter resolution in her father's voice. She sits quietly beside me on the bed, her left hand on my thigh, reassuring herself that I can go nowhere without her.

'Are we going on the airplane again, Daddy?'

'That's right, punkin,' I answer, dialing a Houston number.

'Back home?'

'No, we're going to see Gram and Papa.'

Her eyes widen with joyous expectation. 'Gram and Papa? Now?'

'I hope so. Just a minute.' My assistant, Cilla Daniels, is speaking in my ear. She obviously saw the name of the hotel on the caller-ID unit and started talking the moment she picked up. I break in before she can get rolling. 'Listen to me, Cil. I want you to call a storage company and lease enough space for everything in the house.'

'The house?' she echoes. 'Your house? You mean "everything" as in furniture?'

'Yes. I'm selling the house.'

'Selling the house. Penn, what's happened? What's wrong?'

'Nothing. I've come to my senses, that's all. Annie's never going to get better in that house. And Sarah's parents are still grieving so deeply that they're making things worse. I'm moving back home for a while.'

'Home?'

'To Natchez.'

'Natchez.'

'Mississippi. Where I lived before I married Sarah? Where I grew up?'

'I know that, but–'

'Don't worry about your salary. I'll need you now more than ever.'

'I'm not worried about my salary. I'm worried about you. Have you talked to your parents? Your mother called yesterday and asked for your number down there. She sounded upset.'

'I'm about to call them. After you get the storage space, call some movers and arrange transport. Let Sarah's parents have anything they want out of the house. Then call Jim Noble and tell him to sell the place. And I don't mean list it, I mean *sell* it.'

'The housing market's pretty soft right now. Especially in your bracket.'

'I don't care if I eat half the equity. Move it.'

There's an odd silence. Then Cilla says, 'Could I make you an offer on it? I won't if you never want to be reminded of the place.'

'No . . . it's fine. You need to get out of that condo. Can you come anywhere close to a realistic price?'

'I've got quite a bit left from my divorce settlement. You know me.'

'Don't make me an offer. I'll make you one. Get the house appraised, then knock off twenty percent. No realtor fees, no down payment, nothing. Work out a payment schedule over twenty years at, say . . . six percent interest. That way we have an excuse to stay in touch.'

'Oh, God, Penn, I can't take advantage like that.'

'It's a done deal.' I take a deep breath, feeling the invisible bands that have bound me loosening. 'Well . . . that's it.'

'Hold on. The world doesn't stop because you run off to Disney World.'

'Do I want to hear this?'

'I've got bad news and news that could go either way.'

'Give me the bad.'

'Arthur Lee Hanratty's last request for a stay was just denied by the Supreme Court. It's leading on CNN every half hour. The execution is scheduled for midnight on Saturday. Five days from now.'

'That's good news, as far as I'm concerned.'

Cilla sighs in a way that tells me I'm wrong. 'Mr Givens called a few minutes ago.' Mr Givens and his wife are the closest relatives of the black family slaughtered by Hanratty and his psychotic brothers. 'And Mr Givens doesn't ever want to see Hanratty in person again. He and his wife want you to attend in their place. A witness they can trust. You know the drill.'

'Too well.' Lethal injection at the Texas State Prison at

Huntsville, better known as the Walls. Seventy miles north of Houston, the seventh circle of Hell. 'I really don't want to see this one, Cil.'

'I know. I don't know what to tell you.'

'What's this other news?'

'I just got off the phone with Peter.' Peter Highsmith is my editor, a gentleman and scholar, but not the person I want to talk to just now. 'He would never say anything, but I think the house is getting anxious about *Nothing But the Truth*. You're nearly a year past your deadline. Peter is more worried about you than about the book. He just wants to know you're okay.'

'What did you tell him?'

'That you've had a tough time, but you're finally waking back up to life. You're nearly finished with the book, and it's by far the best you've ever written.'

I laugh out loud.

'How close *are* you? You were only half done the last time I got up the nerve to ask you about it.'

I start to lie, but there's no point. 'I haven't written a decent page since Sarah died.'

Cilla is silent.

'And I burned the first half of the manuscript the night before we left Houston.'

She gasps. 'You didn't!'

'Look in the fireplace.'

'Penn . . . I think you need some help. I'm speaking as your friend. There are some good people here in town. Discreet.'

'I don't need a shrink. I need to take care of my daughter.'

'Well . . . whatever you do, be careful, okay?'

'A lot of good that does. Sarah was the most careful person I ever knew.'

'I didn't mean—'

'I know. Look, I don't want a single journalist finding out where I am. I want no part of that deathwatch circus. It's Joe's problem now.' Joe Cantor is the district attorney of Harris County, and my old boss. 'As far as you know, I'm on vacation until the moment of the execution.'

'Consider yourself incommunicado.'

'I've got to run. We'll talk soon.'

'Make sure we do.'

When I hang up, Annie rises to her knees beside me, her eyes bright. 'Are we really going to Gram and Papa's?'

'We'll know in a minute.'

I dial the telephone number I memorized as a four-year-old and listen to it ring. The call is answered by a woman with a cigarette-parched Southern drawl no film producer would ever use, for fear that the audience would be unable to decode the words. She works for an answering service.

'Dr. Cage's residence.'

'This is Penn Cage, his son. Can you ring through for me?'

'We sure can, honey. You hang on.'

After five rings, I hear a click. Then a deep male voice speaks two words that somehow convey more emotional subtext than most men could in two paragraphs: reassurance, gravitas, a knowledge of ultimate things.

'Doctor Cage,' it says.

My father's voice instantly steadies my heart. This voice has comforted thousands of people over the years, and told many others that their days on earth numbered far less than they'd hoped. 'Dad, what are you doing home this time of day?'

'Penn? Is that you?'

'Yes.'

'What's up, son?'

'I'm bringing Annie home to see you.'

'Great. Are you coming straight from Florida?'

'You could say that. We're coming today.'

'Today? Is she sick?'

'No. Not physically, anyway. Dad, I'm selling the house in Houston and moving back home for a while. What comes after that, I'll figure out later. Have you got room for us?'

'God almighty, son. Let me call your mother.'

I hear my father shout, then the clicking of heels followed by my mother's voice. 'Penn? Are you really coming home?'

'We'll be there tonight.'

'Thank God. We'll pick you up at the airport.'

'No, don't. I'll rent a car.'

'Oh . . . all right. I just . . . I can't tell you how glad I am.'

Something in my mother's voice triggers an alarm. I can't say what it is, because it's in the spaces, not the words, the way you hear things in families. Whatever it is, it's serious. Peggy Cage does not worry about little things.

'Mom? What's the matter?'

'Nothing. I'm just glad you're coming home.'

There is no more inept liar than someone who has spent a lifetime telling the truth. 'Mom, don't try to—'

'We'll talk when you get here. You just bring that little girl where she belongs.'

I recall Cilla's opinion that my mother was upset when she called yesterday. But there's no point in forcing the issue on the phone. I'll be face to face with her in a few hours. 'We'll be there tonight. Bye.'

My hand shakes as I set the receiver in its cradle. For a prodigal son, a journey home after eighteen years is a sacred one. I've been home for a few Christmasses and Thanksgivings, but this is different. Looking down at Annie, I get one of the thousand-volt shocks of recognition that has hit me so many times since the funeral. Sometimes Sarah's face peers out from Annie's as surely as if her spirit has temporarily possessed the child. But if this is a possession, it

8

is a benign one. Annie's hazel eyes transfix mine with a look that gave me much peace when it shone from Sarah's face: *This is the right thing*, it says.

'I love you, Daddy,' she says softly.

'I love you more,' I reply, completing our ritual. Then I catch her under the arms and lift her high into the air. 'Let's pack! We've got a plane to catch!'

Chapter 2

One of the nice things about first-class air travel is immediate beverage service. Even before our connecting flight lifts out of Atlanta's Hartsfield Airport, a tumbler of single-malt Scotch sits half-empty on the tray before me. I never drink liquor in front of Annie, but she is conveniently asleep on the adjacent seat. Her little arm hangs over the padded divider, her hand touching my thigh, an early-warning system that operates even in sleep. What part of her brain keeps that hand in place? Did Neanderthal children sleep this way? I sip my whisky and stroke her hair, cautiously looking around the cabin.

One of the bad things about first-class air travel is being recognized. You get a lot of readers in first class. A lot of lawyers too. Today the cabin is virtually empty, but sitting across the aisle from us is a woman in her late twenties, wearing a lawyerly blue suit and reading a Penn Cage novel. It's just a matter of time before she recognizes me. Or maybe not, if my luck holds. I take another sip of Scotch, recline my seat, and close my eyes.

The first image that floats into my mind is the face of Arthur Lee Hanratty. I spent four months convicting that bastard, and I consider it time well spent. But even in Texas, where we are serious about the death penalty, it takes time to exhaust all avenues of appeal. Now, eight years after his conviction, it seems possible that he might actually die at the hands of the state.

I know prosecutors who will drive all day with smiles on their faces to see the execution of a man they convicted, avidly anticipating the political capital they will reap from the event. Others will not attend an execution even if asked. I always felt a responsibility to witness the punishment I had requested in the name of society. Also, in capital cases, I shepherded the victims' families through the long ordeal of trial. In every case family members asked me to witness the execution on their behalf. After the legislature changed the law, allowing victims' families to witness executions, I was asked to accompany them in the viewing room, and I was glad to be able to comfort them.

This time it's different. My relationship to death has fundamentally changed. I witnessed my wife's death from a much closer perspective than from the viewing room at the Walls, and as painful as it was, her passing was a sacred experience. I have no desire to taint that memory by watching yet another execution carried out with the institutional efficiency of a veterinarian putting down a rabid dog.

I drink off the remainder of my Scotch, savoring the peaty burn in my throat. As always, remembering Sarah's death makes me think of my father. Hearing his voice on the telephone earlier only intensifies the images. As the 727 ascends to cruising altitude, the whisky opens a neural switch in my brain, and memory begins overpowering thought like a salt tide flooding into an estuary. I know from experience that it is useless to resist. I close my eyes and let it come.

Sarah lies in the M.D. Anderson hospital in Houston, her bones turned to burning paper by a disease whose name she no longer speaks aloud. She is not superstitious, but to name the sickness seems to grant it more power than it deserves. Her doctors are puzzled. The end should have come long ago. The diagnosis was a late one, the prognosis poor. Sarah weighs only eighty-one pounds now, but she fights for life with a young mother's tenacity. It is a pitched battle, fought minute by minute against physical agony and emotional despair.

Sometimes she speaks of suicide. It is a comfort on the worst nights.

Like many doctors, her oncologists are too wary of lawsuits and the DEA to adequately treat pain. In desperation I call my father, who advises me to check Sarah out of the hospital and go home. Six hours later, he arrives at our door, trailing the smell of cigars and a black bag containing enough Schedule Two narcotics to euthanize a grizzly bear. For two weeks he lives across the hall from Sarah, tending her like a nurse, shaming into silence any physician who questions his actions. He helps Sarah to sleep when she needs it, frees her from the demon long enough to smile at Annie when she feels strong enough for me to bring her in.

Then the drugs begin to fail. The fine line between consciousness and agony disappears. One evening Sarah asks everyone to leave, saying she sleeps better alone. Near midnight she calls me into the bedroom where we once lay with Annie between us, dreaming of the future. She can barely speak. I take her hand. For a moment the clouds in her eyes part, revealing a startling clarity. 'You made me happy,' she whispers. I believe I have no tears left, but they come now. 'Take care of my baby,' she says. I vow with absolute conviction to do so, but I am not sure she hears me. Then she surprises me by asking for my father. I cross the hall and wake him, then sit down on the warm covers from which he rose.

When I wake, Sarah is gone. She died in her sleep. Peacefully, my father says. He volunteers no more, and I do not ask. When Sarah's parents wake, he tells them she is dead. Each in turn goes to him and hugs him, their eyes wet with tears of gratitude and absolution. 'She was a trooper,' my father says in a cracked voice. This is the highest tribute my wife will ever receive.

'Excuse me, are you Penn Cage? The writer?'

I blink and rub my eyes against the light, then turn to my right. The young woman across the aisle is looking at me, a slight blush coloring her cheeks.

'I didn't want to bother you, but I saw you take a drink and realized you must be awake. I was reading this book and . . . well, you look just like the picture on the back.'

She is speaking softly so as not to wake Annie. Part of my mind is still with Sarah and my father, chasing a strand of meaning down a dark spiral, but I force myself to concentrate as the woman introduces herself as Kate. She is quite striking, with fine black hair pulled up from her neck, fair skin, and sea green eyes, an unusual combination. Her navy suit looks tailored, and the pulled-back hair gives the impression that Kate is several years older than she probably is, a common affectation among young female attorneys. I smile awkwardly and confirm that I am indeed myself, then ask if she is a lawyer.

She smiles. 'Am I that obvious?'

'To other members of the breed.'

Another smile, this one different, as though at a private joke. 'I'm a First Amendment specialist,' she offers.

Her accent is an alloy of Ivy League Boston and something softer. A Brahmin who graduated Radcliffe but spent her summers far away. 'That sounds interesting,' I tell her.

'Sometimes. Not as interesting as what you do.'

'I'm sure you're wrong about that.'

'I doubt it. I just saw you on CNN in the airport. They were talking about the Hanratty execution. About you killing his brother.'

So, the circus has started. 'That's not exactly my daily routine. Not anymore, at least.'

'It sounded like there were some unanswered questions about the shooting.' Kate blushes again. 'I'm sure you're sick of people asking about it, right?'

Yes, I am. 'Maybe the execution will finally put it to rest.'

'I'm sorry. I didn't mean to pry.'

'Sure you did.' On any other day I would brush her off. But she is reading one of my novels, and even thinking about *Texas* v. *Hanratty* is better than what I was thinking about when she disturbed me. 'It's okay. We all want to know the inside of things.'

'They said on *Burden of Proof* that the Hanratty case is often cited as an example of jurisdictional disputes between federal and state authorities.'

I nod but say nothing. 'Disputes' is a rather mild word. Arthur Lee Hanratty was a white supremacist who testified against several former cronies in exchange for immunity and a plum spot in the Federal Witness Protection Program. Three months after he entered the program, he shot a black man in Compton over a traffic dispute. He fled Los Angeles, joined his two psychotic brothers, and wound up in Houston, where they murdered an entire black family. As they were being apprehended, Arthur Lee shot and killed a female cop, giving his brothers time to escape. None of this looked good on the resume of John Portman, the U.S. attorney who had granted Hanratty immunity, and Portman vowed to convict his former star witness in federal court in Los Angeles. My boss and I (with the help of then president and erstwhile Texas native George Bush) kept Hanratty in Texas, where he stood a real chance of dying for his crimes. Our jurisdictional victory deprived Portman of his revenge, but his career skyrocketed nevertheless, first into a federal judgeship and finally into the directorship of the FBI, where he now presides.

'I remember when it happened,' Kate says. 'The Compton shooting. I mean. I was working in Los Angeles for the summer, and it got a lot of play there. Half the media made you out to be a hero, the other half a monster. They said you – well, you know.'

'What?' I ask, testing her nerve.

She hesitates, then takes the plunge. 'They said you shot him and then used your baby to justify killing him.'

I've come to understand the combat veteran's frustration with this kind of curiosity, and I usually meet it with a stony stare, if not outright hostility. But today is different. Today I am in transition. The impending execution has resurrected old ghosts, and I find myself willing to talk, not to satisfy this woman's curiosity but to remind myself that I got through it. That I did the right thing. *The only thing*, I assure myself, looking down at Annie sleeping beside me. I drink the last of my Scotch and let myself remember it, this thing that always seems to have happened to someone else, a celebrity among lawyers, hailed by the right wing and excoriated by the left.

'Arthur Lee Hanratty vowed to kill me after his arrest. He said it a dozen times on television. I took his threats the way I took them all, *cum grano salis*. But Hanratty meant it. Four years later, the night the Supreme Court affirmed his death sentence, my wife and I were lying in bed watching the late news. She was dozing. I was going over my opening statement for another murder trial. My boss had put a deputy outside because of the Supreme Court ruling, but I didn't think there was any danger. When I heard the first noise, I thought it was nothing. The house settling. Then I heard something else. I asked Sarah if she'd heard it. She hadn't. She told me to turn out the light and go to sleep. And I almost did. That's how close it was. That's where my nightmares come from.'

'What made you get up?'

As the flight attendant passes, I signal for another Scotch. 'I don't know. Something had registered wrong, deep down. I took my thirty-eight down from the closet shelf and switched off my reading light. Then I opened the bedroom door and moved up the hall toward our daughter's room. Annie was only six months old, but she always slept through the night. When I pushed open her door, I didn't hear breathing, but that didn't worry me. Sometimes you have to get right down over them, you know? I walked to the crib and leaned over to listen.'

Kate is spellbound, leaning across the aisle. I take my Scotch from the flight attendant's hand and gulp a swallow. 'The crib was empty.'

'Sweet Jesus.'

'The deputy was out front, so I ran to the French doors at the back of the house. When I got there, I saw nothing but the empty patio. I felt like I was falling off a cliff. Then something made me turn to my left. There was a man standing by the French doors in the dining room. Twenty feet away. He had a tiny bundle in his arms, like a loaf of bread in a blanket. He looked at me as he reached for the door handle. I saw his teeth in the dark, and I knew he was smiling. I pointed my pistol at his head. He started backing through the door, using Annie as a shield. Holding her at centre mass. In the dark, with shaking hands, every rational thought told me not to fire. But I had to.'

I take another gulp of Scotch. The whites of Kate's eyes are completely visible around the green irises, giving her a hyperthyroid look. I reach down and lay a hand on Annie's shoulder. Parts of this story I still cannot voice. When I saw those teeth, I sensed the giddy superiority the kidnapper felt over me, the triumph of the predator. Nothing in my life ever hit me the way that fear did.

'He was halfway through the door when I pulled the trigger. The bullet knocked him onto the patio. When I got outside, Annie was lying on the cement, covered in blood. I snatched her up even before I looked at the guy, held her up in the moonlight and ripped off her pajamas, looking for a bullet wound. She didn't make a sound. Then she screamed like a banshee. An anger scream, you know? Not pain. I knew then that she was probably okay. Hanratty . . . the bullet had hit him in the eye. He was dying. And I didn't do a goddamn thing to help him.'

Kate finally blinks, a series of rapid-fire clicks, like someone coming out of a trance. She points down at Annie. 'She's that baby? She's Annie?'

'Yes.'

'God.' She taps the book in her lap. 'I see why you quit.'

'There's still one out there.'

'What do you mean?'

'We never caught the third brother. I get postcards from him now and then. He says he's looking forward to spending some time with our family.'

She shakes her head. 'How do you live with that?'

I shrug and return to my drink.

'Your wife isn't travelling with you?' Kate asks.

They always have to ask. 'No. She passed away recently.'

Kate's face begins the subtle sequence of expressions I've seen a thousand times in the last seven months. Shock, embarrassment, sympathy, and just the slightest satisfaction that a seemingly perfect life is not so perfect after all.

'I'm sorry,' she says. 'The wedding ring. I just assumed—'

'It's okay. You couldn't know.'

She looks down and takes a sip of her soft drink. When she looks up, her face is composed again. She asks what my next book is about, and I give her the usual fluff, but she isn't listening. I know this reaction too. The response of most women to a young widower, particularly one who is clearly solvent and not appallingly ugly, is as natural and predictable as the rising of the sun. The subtle glow of flirtation emanates from Kate like a medieval spell, but it is a spell to which I am presently immune.

Annie awakens as we talk, and Kate immediately brings her into the conversation, developing a surprising rapport. Time passes quickly, and before long we are shaking hands at the gate in Baton Rouge. Annie and I bump into her again at the baggage carousel, and as Kate squeaks outside in her sensible Reeboks to hail a taxi, I notice Annie's eyes solemnly tracking her. My daughter's attraction to young adult women is painful to see.

I scoop her up with forced merriment and trot to the Hertz counter, where I have to hassle with a clerk about why the car I reserved isn't available (although for ten dollars extra per day I can upgrade to a model that is) and how long I'll have to wait for a child-safety seat. I'm escalating from irritation to anger when a tall man with white hair and a neatly trimmed white beard walks through the glass doors through which Kate just departed.

'Papa!' Annie squeals. 'Daddy! Papa's here!'

'Dad? What are you doing here?'

He laughs and veers toward us. 'You think your mother's going to have her son renting a car to drive eighty miles to get home? God forbid.' He catches Annie under the arms, lifts her high, and hugs her to his chest. 'Hello, tadpole! What's shakin' down in Disney World?'

'I saw Ariel! And Snow White hugged me!'

'Of course she did! Who wouldn't want to hug an angel like you?' He looks over her shoulder at me. For a few uncomfortable moments I endure the penetrating gaze of a man who for forty years has searched for illness in reticent people. His perception is like the heat from a lamp. I nod slowly, hoping to communicate, *I'm okay, Dad*, at the same time searching his face for clues to the anxiety I heard in my mother's voice on the phone this morning. But he's too good at concealing his emotions. Another habit of the medical profession.

'Is Mom with you?' I ask.

'No, she's home cooking a supper you'll have to see to believe.' He reaches out and squeezes my hand. 'It's good to see you, son.' For an instant I catch a glimpse of something unsettling behind his eyes, but it vanishes as he grins mischievously at Annie. 'Let's move out, tadpole! We're burning daylight!'

Chapter 3

My father served as an army doctor in West Germany in the 1960s, and it was there he acquired a taste for dark beer and high-performance automobiles. He has been driving BMWs ever since he could afford them, and he drives fast. In four minutes we are away from the airport and roaring north on Highway 61. Annie sits in the middle of the backseat, lashed into a safety seat, marveling at the TV-sized computer display built into the dashboard while Dad runs through its functions again and again, delighting in every giggle that bursts from her lips.

Coronary problems severely reduced my father's income a few years ago, so last year – on his sixty-sixth birthday – I bought him a black BMW 740i with the royalties from my third novel. I felt a little like Elvis Presley when I wrote that check, and it was a good feeling. My parents started life with nothing, and in a single generation, through hard work and sacrifice, lived what was once unapologetically called the American Dream. They deserve some perks.

The flat brown fields of Louisiana quickly give way to green wooded hills, and somewhere to our left, beyond the lush forest, rolls the great brown river. I cannot smell it yet, but I feel it, a subtle disturbance in the earth's magnetic field, a fluid force that shapes the surrounding land and souls. I roll down the window and suck in the life smell of hardwood forest, creek water, kudzu, bush-hogged wildflowers, and baking earth. The competing aromas blend into a heady gestalt you couldn't find in Houston if you grid-searched every inch of it on your hands and knees.

'We're losing the air conditioning,' Dad complains.

'Sorry.' I roll up the window. 'It's been a long time since I smelled this place.'

'Too damn long.'

'Papa said a bad word!' Annie cries, bursting into giggles.

Dad laughs, then reaches back between the seats and slaps her knee.

The old landmarks hurtle by like location shots from a film. St. Francisville, where John James Audubon painted his birds, now home to a nuclear station; the turnoff to Angola Penitentiary; and finally the state line, marked by a big blue billboard: WELCOME TO MISSISSIPPI! THE MAGNOLIA STATE.

'What's happening in Natchez these days?' I ask.

Dad whips into the left lane and zooms past a log truck loaded from bumper to red flag with pulpwood. 'A lot, for a change. Looks like we've got a new factory coming in. Which is good, because the battery plant is about dead.'

'What kind of factory?'

'Chemical plant. They want to put it in the new industrial park by the river. South of the paper mill.'

'Is it a done deal?'

'I'll say it's done when I see smoke coming from the stacks. Till then, it's all talk. It's like the casino boats. Every other month a new company talks about bringing another boat in, but there's still just the one.'

'What else is happening?'

'Big election coming up.'

'What kind?'

'Mayoral. For the first time in history there's a black candidate with a real chance to win.'

'You're kidding. Who is it?'

'Shad Johnson. He's about your age. His parents are patients of mine. You never heard of him because they sent him north to prep school when he was a kid. After that he went to Howard University. Another damn lawyer, just like you.'

'And he wants to be mayor of Natchez?'

'Badly. He moved down here just to run. And he may win.'

'What's the black–white split now?'

'Registered voters? Fifty-one to forty nine, in favor of whites. The blacks usually have a low turnout, but this election may be different. In any case, the key for Johnson is white votes, and he might actually get some. He's been invited to join the Rotary Club.'

'The *Natchez* Rotary Club?'

'Times are changing. And Shad Johnson's smart enough to exploit that. I'm sure you'll meet him soon. The election's only five weeks away. Hell, he'll probably want an endorsement from you, seeing how you're a celebrity now.'

'Papa said another bad word!' Annie chimes in. 'But not too bad.'

'What did I say?'

'H-E-L-L. You're supposed to say *heck*.'

Dad laughs and slaps her on the knee again.

'I want to stay low-profile,' I say quietly. 'This trip is strictly R-and-R.'

'Not much chance of that. Somebody already called the house asking for you. Right before I left.'

'Was it Cilla, my assistant?'

'No. A man. He asked if you'd got in yet. When I asked who was calling, he hung up. The caller-ID box said "out of area".'

'Probably a reporter. They're going to turn the South upside down trying to find me because of the Hanratty execution.'

'We'll do what we can to keep you incognito, but the new newspaper publisher has called four times asking about getting an interview with you. Now that you're here, you won't be able to avoid things like that. Not without people saying you've gone Hollywood on us.'

I sit back and assimilate this. Finding sanctuary in my old hometown might not be as easy as I thought. But it will still be better than Houston.

Natchez is unlike any place in America, existing almost outside time, which is exactly what Annie and I need. In some ways it isn't part of Mississippi at all. There's no town square with a lone Confederate soldier presiding over it, no flat, limitless Delta horizon or provincial blue laws. The oldest city on the Mississippi River, Natchez stands white and pristine atop a two-hundred-foot loess bluff, the jewel in the crown of nineteenth-century steamboat ports. For as long as I can remember, the population has been twenty-five thousand, but after being ruled in turn by Indians, French, British, Spanish, Confederates, and Americans, her character is more cosmopolitan than cities ten times her size. Parts of New Orleans remind me of Natchez, but only parts. Modern life long ago came to the Crescent City and changed it forever. Two hundred miles upriver, Natchez exists in a ripple of time that somehow eludes the homogenizing influences of the present.

In 1850 Natchez boasted more millionaires than any city in the United States save New York and Philadelphia. Their fortunes were made on the cotton that poured like white gold out of the district and into the mills of England. The plantations stretched for miles on both sides of the Mississippi River, and the planters who administered them built mansions that made Margaret Mitchell's Tara look like modest accommodations. While their slaves toiled in the fields, the princes of this new aristocracy sent their sons to Harvard and their daughters to the royal courts of Europe. Atop the bluff they held cotillions, opened libraries, and developed new strains of cotton; two hundred feet below, in the notorious Under the Hill district, they raced horses, traded slaves, drank, whored, and gambled, firmly establishing a tradition of libertinism that survives to the present, and cementing the city's black-sheep status in a state known for its dry counties.

By an accident of topography, the Civil War left Natchez untouched. Her bluff commanded a straightaway of the river rather than a bend, so Vicksburg became the critical naval choke point, dooming that city to siege and destruction while undefended Natchez made the best of Union occupation. In this way she joined a charmed historical trinity with Savannah and Charleston, the quintessentially Southern cities that survived the war with their beauty intact.

It took the boll weevil to accomplish what war could not, sending the city into depression after the turn of the century. She sat preserved like a city in amber, her mansions slowly deteriorating, until the 1930s, when her society ladies began opening their once great houses to the public in an annual ritual called the Pilgrimage. The money that poured in allowed them to restore the mansions to their antebellum splendor, and soon Yankees and Europeans traveled by thousands to this living museum of the Old South.

In 1948 oil was discovered practically beneath the city, and a second boom was on. Black gold replaced white, and overnight millionaires again walked the azalea-lined streets, as delirious with prosperity as if they had stepped from the pages of Scott Fitzgerald. I grew up in the midst of this boom, and benefited from the affluence it generated. But by the time I graduated law school, the oil industry was collapsing, leaving Natchez to survive on the revenues of tourism and federal welfare money. It was a hard adjustment for proud people who had never had to chase Northern factories or kowtow to the state of which they were nominally a part.

'What's that?' I ask, pointing at an upscale residential development far south of where I remember any homes.

'White flight,' Dad replies. 'Everything's moving south.

23

Subdivisions, the country club. Look, there's another one.'

Another grouping of homes materializes behind a thin screen of oak and pine, looking more like suburban Houston than the romantic town I remember. Then I catch sight of Mammy's Cupboard, and I feel a reassuring wave of familiarity in my chest. Mammy's is a restaurant built in the shape of a Negro mammy in a red hoop skirt and bandanna, painted to match Hattie McDaniel from *Gone With the Wind*. She stands atop her hill like a giant sculptured doll, beckoning travelers to dine in the cozy space beneath her domed skirts. Anyone who has never seen the place inevitably slows to gape; it makes the Brown Derby in L.A. look prosaic.

The car crests a high ridge and seems to teeter upon it as an ocean of tree-tops spreads out before us, stretching west to infinity. Beyond the river, the great alluvial plain of Louisiana lies so far below the high ground of Natchez that only the smoke plume from the paper mill betrays the presence of man in that direction. The car tips over on the long descent into town, passing St. Stephens, the all-white prep school I attended, and a dozen businesses that look just as they did twenty years ago. At the junction of Highways 61 and 84 stands the Jefferson Davis Memorial Hospital, now officially known by a more politically correct name, but for all time 'the Jeff' to the doctors of my father's generation, and to the hundreds of other people, both black and white, who worked or were born there.

'It all looks the same,' I murmur.

'It is and it isn't,' Dad replies.

'What do you mean?'

'You'll see.'

My parents still live in the house in which they raised me. While other young professionals moved on to newer subdivisions, restored Victorian gingerbreads, or even ante-bellum palaces downtown, my father clung stubbornly to the ash-paneled library he'd appended to the suburban tract house he bought in 1963. Whenever my mother got the urge to move to more stately mansions, he added to the existing structure, giving her the space she claimed we needed and a decorating project on which to expend her fitful energies.

As the BMW pulls up to the house, I imagine my mother waiting inside. She always wanted me to succeed in the larger world, but it broke her heart when Sarah and I settled in Houston. Seven hours is too far to drive on a regular basis, and Mom dislikes flying. Still, the tie between us is such that distance means little. When I was a boy, people always told me I was like my father, that I'd 'got my father's brain.' But it is my mother who has the rare combination of quantitative aptitude and intuitive imagination that I was lucky enough to inherit.

Dad shuts off the engine and unstraps Annie from her safety seat. As I unload our luggage from the trunk, I see a shadow standing motionless against the closed curtain of the dining room. My mother. Then another shadow moves behind the curtain. Who else would be here? It can't be my sister. Jenny is a visiting professor at Trinity College in Dublin, Ireland.

'Who else is here?'

'Wait and see,' Dad says cryptically.

I carry the two suitcases to the porch, then go back for Annie's bag. The second time I reach the porch, my mother is standing in the open door. All I see before she rises on tiptoe and pulls me into her arms is that she has stopped coloring her hair, and the gray is a bit of a shock.

'Welcome home,' she whispers in my ear. She pulls back, her hands gripping my upper arms, and looks hard at me. 'You're still not eating. Are you all right?'

'I don't know. Annie can't seem to get past what happened. And I don't know how to help her.'

She squeezes my arms with a strength I have never seen fail. 'That's what grandmothers are for. Everything's going to be all right. Starting right this minute.'

At sixty-three my mother is still beautiful, but not with the delicate comeliness that fills so many musket-and-magnolia romances. Beneath the tanned skin and Donna Karan dress are the bone and sinew and humor of a girl who made the social journey from the 4-H Club to the Garden Club without forgetting her roots. She could take tea with royalty and commit no faux pas, yet just as easily twist the head off a banty hen, boil the bristles off a hog, or kill an angry copperhead with a hoe blade. It's that toughness that worries me now.

'Mom, what's wrong? On the phone—'

'Shh. We'll talk later.' She blinks back tears, then pushes me into the house and takes Annie from Dad's arms. 'Here's my angel! Let's get some supper. And no yucky broccoli!'

Annie squeals with excitement.

'There's somebody waiting to see you, Penn,' Mom says.

I pull the suitcases inside. A wide doorway in the foyer leads to the dining room, and I stop dead when I see who is there. Standing beside the long table is a black woman as tall as I and fifty years older. Her mouth is set in a tight smile, and her eyes twinkle with joy.

'Ruby!' I cry, setting the bags on the floor and walking toward her. 'What in the world . . . ?'

'Today's her day off,' Mom explains from behind me. 'I called to check on her, and when she heard you were coming, she demanded that Tom come get her so she could see you.'

'And that grandbaby,' Ruby says, pointing at Annie in Peggy's arms.

I hug the old woman gently. It's like hugging a bundle of

sticks. Ruby Flowers came to work for us in 1963 and, except for one life-threatening illness, never missed a single work-day until arthritis forced her to slow down thirty years later. Even then she begged my father to give her steroid injections to allow her to keep doing her 'heavy work' – the ironing and scrubbing – but he refused. Instead he kept her on at full pay but limited her to sorting socks, washing the odd load of clothes, and watching the soaps on television.

'I'm sorry about your wife,' Ruby says, "Cept for losing a child, that the hardest thing.'

I give her an extra squeeze.

'Now, let me see that baby. Come here, child!'

I wonder if Annie will remember Ruby, or be frightened by the old woman even if she does. I should have known better. Ruby Flowers radiates nothing to frighten a small child. She is like a benevolent witch from an African folk tale, and Annie goes to her without the slightest hesitation.

'I cooked your daddy his favorite dinner,' Ruby says, hugging Annie tight. 'And after tonight, it's gonna be your favorite too!'

At the center of the table sits a plate heaped with chicken shallow-fried to a peppered gold. I've watched Ruby make that chicken a thousand times and never once use more than salt, pepper, flour, and Crisco. With those four ingredients she creates a flavor and texture that Harland Sanders couldn't touch with his best pressure cooker. I snatch up a wing and take a bite of white meat. Crispy outside and moist within, it bursts in my mouth with intoxicating familiarity.

'Go slap your daddy's hand!' Ruby cries, and Annie quickly obeys. 'Ya'll sit down and eat proper. I'll get the iced tea.'

'I'll get the tea,' Mom says, heading for the kitchen before Ruby can start. 'Make your plate, Ruby. Tonight you're a guest.'

Our family says grace only at Thanksgiving and

Christmas, and then almost as a formality. But with Ruby present, no one dares reach for a fork.

'Would you like to return thanks, Ruby?' Dad asks.

The old woman shakes her head, her eyes shining with mischief. 'I wish you'd do it, Dr. Cage. You give a *fine* blessing.'

Thirty-eight years of practicing medicine has stripped my father of the stern religious carapace grafted onto him in the Baptist churches of his youth. But when pressed, he can deliver a blessing that vies with the longest-winded of deacons for flowery language and detail. He seems about to deliver one of these, with tongue-in-cheek overtones added for my benefit, but my mother halts him with a touch of her hand. She bows her head, and everyone at the table follows suit.

'Father,' she says, 'it's been far too long since we've given thanks to you in this house. Tonight we thank you for the return of our son, who has been away too long. We give thanks for Anna Louise Cage, our beautiful grandchild, and pray that we may bring her as much happiness as she brings to us each day.' She pauses, a brief caesura that focuses everyone's concentration. 'We also commend the soul of Sarah Louise Cage to your care, and pray that she abides in thy grace forever.'

I take Annie's hand under the table and squeeze it.

'We don't pretend to understand death here,' Mom continues softly. 'We ask only that you let this young family heal, and be reconciled to their loss. This is a house of love, and we humbly ask grace in thy name's sake. Amen.'

As we echo the 'amen,' Dad and I look at each other across the table, moved by my mother's passion but not its object. In matters religious I am my father's son, having no faith in a just God, or any god at all if you shake me awake at four a.m. and put the question to me. There have been times I would have given anything for such faith, for the belief that divine justice exists somewhere in the universe. Facing Sarah's death without it was an existential baptism of fire. The comfort that belief in an afterlife can provide was obvious in the hospital waiting rooms and chemo wards, where patients or family members often asked outright if I was saved. I always smiled and nodded so as to avoid a philosophical argument that would benefit no one, and wondered if the question was an eccentricity of Southern hospitals. In the Pacific Northwest they probably offer you crystals or lists of alternative healers. I have no regrets about letting Sarah raise Annie in a church, though. Sometimes the image of her mother in Heaven is all that keeps my daughter from despair.

As Dad passes around the mustard greens and cheese grits and beer biscuits, another memory rises unbidden. One cold hour before dawn, sitting beside Sarah's hospital bed, I fell to my knees and begged God to save her. The words formed in my mind without volition, strung together with strangely baroque formality: *I who have not believed since I was a child, who have not crossed a church threshold to worship since I was thirteen, who since the age of reason have admitted nothing greater than man or nature, ask in all humility that you spare the life of this woman. I ask not for myself, but for the child I am not quali-fied to raise alone.* As soon as I realized what I was thinking, I stopped and got to my feet. Who was I talking to? Faith is something you have or you don't, and to pretend you do in the hope of gaining some last-minute dispensation from a being whose existence you have denied all your life goes against everything I am. I have never placed myself above God. I simply cannot find within myself the capacity for belief.

Yet when Sarah finally died, a dark seed took root in my mind. As irrational as it is, a profoundly disturbing idea haunts me: that on the night that prayer blinked to life in my tortured mind, a chance beyond the realm of the temporal was granted me, and I did not take it. That I was tested and found wanting. My rational mind tells me I held true to

myself and endured the pain as all pain must be endured –
alone. But my heart says otherwise. Since that day I have
been troubled by a primitive suspicion that in some cosmic
account book, in some dusty ledger of karmic debits and
credits, Sarah's life has been charged against my account.

'What's the matter, Daddy?' Annie asks.

'Nothing, punkin.'

'You're crying.'

'Penn?' my mother says, half rising from her chair.

'I'm all right,' I assure her, wiping my eyes. 'I'm just glad
to be here, that's all.'

Ruby reaches out and closes an arthritic hand over mine.
'You should have come back months ago. You know where
home is.'

I nod and busy myself with my knife and fork.

'You think too much to be left alone,' Ruby adds. 'You
always did.'

'Amen,' Dad agrees. 'Now let's eat, before my beeper goes
off.'

'That beeper ain't gonna ring during this meal,' Ruby says
with quiet certainty. 'Don't worry 'bout that none.'

'Did you take out the batteries?' Dad asks, checking the
pager.

'I just know,' Ruby replies. 'I just know.'

I believe her.

My mother and I sit facing each other across the kitchen
counter, drinking wine and listening for my father's car in the
driveway. He left after dinner to take Ruby home to the black
section north of town, but putting Annie to bed took up most
of the time I expected him to be away.

'Mom, I sensed something on the phone. You've got to tell
me what's wrong.'

She looks at me over the rim of her glass. 'I'm worried about your father.'

A sliver of ice works its way into my heart. 'Not more blockage in his coronary vessels?'

'No. I think Tom is being blackmailed.'

I am dumbfounded. Nothing she could have said would have surprised me more. My father is a man of such integrity that the idea seems utterly ridiculous. Tom Cage is a modern-day Atticus Finch, or as close as a man can get to that Southern ideal in the dog days of the twentieth century.

'What has he done? I mean, that someone could blackmail him over?'

'He hasn't told me.'

'Then how do you know that's what it is?'

She disposes of my question with a glance. Peggy Cage knows more about her husband and children than we know ourselves.

'Well, *who's* blackmailing him?'

'I think it might be Ray Presley. Do you remember him?'

The skin on my forearms tingles. Ray Presley was a patient of my father for years, and a more disturbing character I have never met, not even in the criminal courts of Houston. Born in Sullivan's Hollow, one of the toughest areas of Mississippi, Presley migrated to South Louisiana, where he reputedly worked as hired muscle for New Orleans crime boss Carlos Marcello. He later hired on as a police officer in Natchez and quickly put his old skills to use. Brutal and clever, his specialty was 'vigorous interrogation.' Off-duty, he haunted the fringes of Natchez's business community, doing favors of dubious legality for wealthy men around town, helping them deal with business or family troubles when conventional measures proved inadequate. When I was in grade school, Presley was busted for corruption and served time in Parchman prison, which to everyone's surprise he survived. Upon his release he focused exclusively on 'private security work,' and it was generally known that he had murdered at least three men for money, all out-of-town jobs.

'What could Ray Presley have on Dad?'

Mom looks away. 'I'm not sure.'

'You must have some idea.'

'My suspicions have more to do with me than with your father. I think that's why Tom won't just tell Presley to go to hell. I think it involves my family.'

My mother's parents both died years ago, and her sister – after two tempestuous marriages – recently married a wealthy surgeon in Florida. 'What could Presley possibly know about your family?'

'I'm not sure. Even if I knew, Tom would have to be the one to tell you. If he won't–'

'How can I help if I don't know what's happening?'

'Your father has a lot of pride. You know that.'

'How much is pride worth?'

'Over a hundred thousand dollars, apparently.'

My stomach rolls like I'm falling through the dark. 'Tell me you're kidding.'

'I wish I were. Clearly, Tom would rather go broke than let us know what's going on.'

'Mom, this is crazy. Why do you think it's Presley?'

'Tom talks in his sleep now. About five months ago he started eating less, losing weight. Then I got a call from Bill Hiatt at the bank. He hemmed and hawed, but he finally told me Tom had been making large withdrawals. Cashing in CDs and absorbing penalties.'

'Well, it's going to stop. I don't care what he did, I'll get him out of it. And I'll get Presley thrown under a jail for extortion.'

She laughs, her voice riding an undercurrent of hysteria.

'What is it?'

'Ray Presley doesn't care about *jail*. He's dying of cancer.'

The word is like a cockroach crawling over my bare foot.

'Which is almost convenient,' Mom goes on, 'but not quite. He's taking his sweet time about it. I've seen him on the street, and he doesn't even look sick. Except for the hair. He's bald now. But he still looks like he could ride a bull ragged.'

I jump at the sound of the garage door. Mom gives me a little wave, then crosses the kitchen as silently as if she were floating on a magic carpet and disappears down the hall. Moments later, my father walks through the kitchen door, his face drawn and tired.

'I figured you'd be waiting for me.'

'Dad, we've got to talk.'

Dread seems to seep from the pores in his face. 'Let me get a drink. I'll meet you in the library.'

Chapter 4

All my life, whenever problems of great import required discussion – health, family, money, marriage – the library was the place it was done. Yet my positive feelings about the room far outweigh my anxieties. The ash-paneled library is so much a part of my father's identity that he carries its scent wherever he goes – an aroma of fine wood, cigar smoke, aging leather, and whiskey. Born to working-class parents, he spent the first real money he made to build this room and fill it with books: Aristotle to Zoroaster and everything in between, with a special emphasis on the military campaigns of the Civil War. I feel more at home here than anywhere in the world. In this room I educated myself, discovered my gift for language, learned that the larger world lay not across oceans but within the human mind and heart. Years spent in this room made law school relatively simple and becoming a writer possible, even necessary.

Dad enters through a different door, carrying a bourbon-and-water brown enough to worry me. We each take one of the leather recliners, which are arranged in the classic bourgeois style: side by side facing the television. He clips the end of a Partagas, licks the end so that it won't peel, and lights it with a wooden match. A cloud of blue smoke wafts toward the beamed ceiling.

'Dad, I–'

'Let me start,' he says, staring across the room at his biographies, most of them first editions. 'Son, there comes a time in every man's life when he realizes that the people who raised him from infancy now require the favor to be returned, whether they know it or not.' He stops to puff on the Partagas. 'This is something you do not yet have to worry about.'

'Dad—'

'I am kindly telling you to mind your own business. You and Annie are welcome here for the next fifty years if you want to stay, but you're not invited to pry into my private affairs.'

I lean back in the recliner and consider whether I can honor my father's request. Given what my mother told me, I don't think so. 'What's Ray Presley holding over you, Dad?'

'Your mother talks too much.'

'You know that's not true. She thinks you're in trouble. And I can help you. Tell me what Presley has on you.'

He picks up his drink and takes a long pull, closing his eyes against the anesthetic fire of the bourbon. 'I won't have this,' he says quietly.

I don't want to ask the next question – I'd hoped never to raise the subject again – but I must. 'Is it something like what you did for Sarah? Helping somebody at the end?'

He sighs like a man who has lived a thousand years. 'That's a rare situation. And when things reach that point, the family's so desperate to have the horror and pain removed from the patient's last hours that they look at you like an instrument of God.'

He drinks and stares at his books, lost in contemplation of something I cannot guess at. He has aged a lot in the eighteen years since I left home. His beard is no longer salt-and-pepper but silver white. His skin is pale and dotted by dermatitis, his joints eroded and swollen by psoriatic arthritis. He is sixteen years past his triple bypass (and counting) and he recently survived the implantation of two stents to keep his cardiac vessels open. All this – physical maladies more severe than those of most of his patients – he bears with the resignation of Job. The wound that aged him most, the one that has never quite healed, was a wound to the soul. And it came at the hands of another man.

When I was a freshman at Ole Miss, my father was sued for malpractice. The plaintiff had no case; his father had died unexpectedly while under the care of my father and five specialists. It was one of those inexplicable deaths that proved for the billionth time that medicine is an inexact science. Dad was as stunned as the rest of the medical community when 'Judge' Leo Marston, the most prominent lawyer in town and a former state attorney general, took the man's case and pressed it to the limit. But no one was more shocked than I. Leo Marston was the father of a girl I had loved in high school, and whom I still think about more than is good for me. Why he should viciously attack my father was beyond my understanding, but attack he did. In a marathon of legal maneuvering that dragged on for fourteen months, Marston hounded my father through the legal system with a vengeance that appalled the town. In the end Dad was unanimously exonerated by a jury, but by then the damage had been done.

For a physician of the old school, medical practice is not a profession or even an art, but the abiding passion of existence. A brilliant boy is born to poor parents during the Depression. From childhood he works to put food on the table. He witnesses privation and sickness not at a remove, but face to face. He earns a scholarship to college but must work additional jobs to cover his expenses. He contracts with the army to pay for his medical education in exchange for years of military service. After completing medical school with an exemplary record, he does not ask himself the question every medical student today asks himself: what do I wish to specialize in? He is ready to go to work. To begin treating patients. To begin living.

For twenty years he practices medicine as though his patients are members of his family. He makes small mistakes; he is human. But in twenty years of practice not one complaint is made to the state medical board, or any legal claim made against him. He is loved by his community, and that love is his life's bread. To be accused of criminal negligence in the death of a patient stuns him, like a war hero being charged with cowardice. Rumor runs through the community like a plague, and truth is the first casualty. His confidence in the rightness of his actions is absolute, but after months of endlessly repeated allegations, doubt begins to assail him. A lifetime of good works seems to weigh as nothing compared to one unsubstantiated charge. Smiles on the street appear forced to him, the greetings of neighbors cool. Stress works steadily and ruthlessly upon him, finally culminating in a myocardial infarction, which he barely survives.

Six weeks later the trial begins, and it's like stepping into the eye of a hurricane. Control rests in the hands of lawyers, men with murky motives and despicable tactics. Expert witnesses second-guess every medical decision. He sits alone in the witness box, condemned before family, friends, and community, cross-examined as though he were a child murderer. When the jury finds in his favor, he feels no joy. He feels like a man who has just lost both legs being told he is lucky to be alive.

Could the present-day blackmail somehow be tied to that calamitous case? I have never understood the reason for Leo Marston's attack, and I've always felt that my father – against his nature – must have been keeping the truth from me. My mother believes Ray Presley is behind the blackmail, and I recall that Judge Marston often hired Presley to do 'security work' when I was in high school. This translated into acting as unofficial baby-sitter for Marston's teenage daughter, Olivia, who was also my lover. I remember nights when

Presley's truck would swing by whatever hangout the kids happened to be frequenting, its hatchet-faced driver glaring from the window, making sure Livy didn't get into any serious trouble. One night Presley actually pulled up behind my car in the woods and rapped on the fogged windows, terrifying Livy and me. I still remember his face peering into the clear circle I rubbed on the window to look out, his eyes bright and ferretlike, searching the backseat for a sight of Livy unclothed. The hunger in those eyes . . .

'Does this have anything to do with Leo Marston?' I ask softly.

Dad flinches from his reverie. Even now the judge's name has the power to harm. 'Marston?' he echoes, still staring at his books. 'What makes you say that?'

'It's one of the only things I've never understood about your life. Why Marston went after you.'

He shakes his head. 'I've never known why he did it. I'd done nothing wrong. Any physician could see that. The jury saw it too, thank God.'

'You've never heard anything since? About why he took the case or pressed it so hard?'

'To tell you the truth, son, I always had the feeling it had something to do with you. You and Olivia.'

He turns to me, his eyes not accusatory but plainly questioning. I am too shocked to speak for a moment. 'That . . . that's impossible,' I stammer. 'I mean, nothing really bad ever happened between Livy and me. It was the trial that drove the last nail into our relationship.'

'Maybe that was Marston's goal all along. To drive you two apart.'

This thought occurred to me nineteen years ago, but I discounted it. Livy abandoned me long before her father took on that malpractice case.

Dad shrugs as if it were all meaningless now. 'Who knows why people do anything?'

'I'm going to go see Presley,' I tell him. 'If that's what I have to do to–'

'You stay away from that son of a bitch! Any problems I have, I'll deal with my own way.' He downs the remainder of his bourbon. 'One way or another.'

'What does that mean?'

His eyes are blurry with fatigue and alcohol, yet somehow sly beneath all that. 'Don't worry about it.'

I am suddenly afraid that my father is contemplating suicide. His death would nullify any leverage Presley has over him and also provide my mother with a generous life insurance settlement. To a desperate man, this might well seem like an elegant solution. 'Dad–'

'Go to bed, son. Take care of your little girl. That's what being a father's all about. Sparing your kids what hell you can for as long as you can. And Annie's already endured her share.'

We turn to the door at the same moment, each sensing a new presence in the room. A tiny shadow stands there. Annie. She seems conjured into existence by the mention of her name.

'I woke up by myself,' she says, her voice tiny and fearful. 'Why did you leave, Daddy?'

I go to the door and sweep her into my arms. She feels so light sometimes that it frightens me. Hollow-boned, like a bird. 'I needed to talk to Papa, punkin. Everything's fine.'

'Hello, sweet pea,' Dad says from his chair. 'You make Daddy take you to bed.'

I linger in the doorway, hoping somehow to draw out a confidence, but he gives me nothing. I leave the library with Annie in my arms, knowing I will not sleep, but knowing also that until my father opens up to me, there is little I can do to help him.

Chapter 5

My father's prediction about media attention proves prescient. Within forty-eight hours of my arrival, calls about interviews join the ceaseless ringing of patients calling my father. My mother has taken messages from the local newspaper publisher, radio talk-show hosts, even a TV station in Jackson, the state capital, two hours away. I decide to grant an interview to Caitlin Masters, the publisher of the Natchez *Examiner*, on two conditions: that she not ask questions about Arthur Lee Hanratty's execution, and that she print that I will be vacationing in New Orleans until after the execution has taken place. Leaving Annie with my mother – which delights them both – I drive Mom's Nissan downtown in search of Biscuits and Blues, a new restaurant owned by a friend of mine but which I have never seen.

It was once said of American cities that you could judge their character by their tallest buildings: were they offices or churches? At a mere seven stories, the Eola Hotel is the tallest commercial structure in Natchez. Its verdigris-encrusted roof peaks well below the graceful, copper-clad spire of St. Mary Minor Basilica. Natchez's 'skyline' barely rises out of a green canopy of oak leaves: the silver dome of the synagogue, the steeple of the Presbyterian church, the roofs of antebellum mansions and stately public buildings. Below the canopy, a soft and filtered sunlight gives the sense of an enormous glassed-in garden.

Biscuits and Blues is a three-story building on Main, with

a large second-floor balcony overlooking the street. A young woman stands talking on a cell phone just inside the door – where Caitlin Masters promised to meet me – but I don't think she's the newspaper publisher. She looks more like a French tourist. She's wearing a tailored black suit, cream silk blouse, and black sandals, and she is clearly on the sunny side of thirty. But as I check my watch, she turns face on to me and I spot a hardcover copy of *False Witness* cradled in her left arm. I also see that she's wearing nothing under the blouse, which is distractingly sheer. She smiles and signals that she'll be off the phone in a second, her eyes flashing with quick intelligence.

I acknowledge her wave and wait beside the door. I'm accustomed to young executives in book publishing, but I expected something a little more conventional in the news-paper business, especially in the South. Caitlin Masters stands with her head cocked slightly, her eyes focused in the middle distance, the edge of her lower lip pinned by a pointed canine. Her skin is as white as bone china and without blemish, shockingly white against her hair, which is black as her silk suit and lies against her neck like a gleaming veil. Her face is a study in planes and angles: high cheek-bones, strong jawline, arched brows, and a straight nose, all uniting with almost architectural precision, yet somehow escaping hardness. She wears no makeup that I can see, but her green eyes provide all the accent she needs. They seem incongruous in a face that almost cries out for blue ones, making her striking and memorable rather than merely beautiful.

As she ends her call, she speaks three or four consecutive sentences, and a strange chill runs through me. Ivy League Boston alloyed with something softer, a Brahmin who spent her summers far away. On the telephone this morning I didn't catch it, but coupled with her face, that voice trans-forms my suspicion to certainty. Caitlin Masters is the woman I spoke to on the flight to Baton Rouge. Kate . . . *Caitlin.*

She holds out her hand to shake mine, and I step back. 'You're the woman from the plane. Kate.'

Her smile disappears, replaced by embarrassment. 'I'm surprised you recognize me, dressed like I was that day.'

'You lied to me. You told me you were a lawyer. Was that some kind of setup or what?'

'I didn't tell you I was a lawyer. You assumed I was. I told you I was a First Amendment specialist, and I am.'

'You knew what I thought, and you let me think it. You lied, Ms. Masters. This interview is over.'

As I turn to go, she takes hold of my arm. 'Our meeting on that plane was a complete accident. I want an interview with you, but it wouldn't be worth that kind of trouble. I was flying from Atlanta to Baton Rouge, and I happened to be sitting across the aisle from you. End of story.'

'And you *happened* to be reading one of my novels?'

'No. I've been trying to get your number from your parents for a couple of months. A lot of people in Mississippi are interested in you. When the Hanratty story broke, I picked up one of your books in the airport. It's that simple.'

I step away from the door to let a pair of middle-aged women through. 'Then why not tell me who you were?'

'Because when I was waiting to board, I was sitting by the pay phones. I heard you tell someone you didn't want to talk to reporters for any reason. I knew if I told you I was a newspaper publisher, you wouldn't talk to me.'

'Well, I guess you got your inside scoop on how I killed Hanratty's brother.'

She draws herself erect, offended now. 'I haven't printed a word of what you told me, and I don't plan to. Despite appearances to the contrary, my journalistic ethics are beyond reproach.'

'Why were you dressed so differently on the plane?'

She actually laughs at this. 'I'd just given a seminar to a group of editors in Atlanta. My father was there, and I try to be a bit more conventional when he's around.'

I can see her point. Not many fathers would approve of the blouse she's wearing today.

'Look,' she says, 'I could have had that story on the wire an hour after you told it to me. I didn't tell a soul. What better proof of trustworthiness could anyone give you?'

'Maybe you're saving it for one big article.'

'You don't have to tell me anything you don't want to. In fact, we could just eat lunch, and you can decide if you want to do the interview another time or not.'

Her candid manner strikes a chord in me. Perhaps she's manipulating me, but I don't think so. 'We came to do an interview. Let's do it. The airplane thing threw me, that's all.'

'Me too,' she says with a smile. 'I liked Annie, by the way.'

'Thanks. She liked you too.'

As we step into the main dining space of the restaurant, a smattering of applause starts, then fills the room. I look around to see whose birthday it is, then realize that the applause is for me. A little celebrity goes a long way in Mississippi. I recognize familiar faces in the crowd. Some belong to guys I went to school with, now carrying twenty or thirty extra pounds – as I did until Sarah's illness – others to friends of my parents or simply well-wishers. I smile awkwardly and give a little wave to cover the room.

'I told you,' says Caitlin. 'There's a lot of interest.'

'It'll wear off. As soon as they realize I'm the same guy who left, they'll be yawning in my face.'

When we arrive at our table, she stands stiffly behind her chair, her eyes twinkling with humor. 'You're not going to pull my chair out for me?'

'You didn't look the type.'

She laughs and takes her seat. 'I wasn't before I got here. Pampering corrupts you fast.'

While we study the menus, a collection of classic Cajun dishes, I try to fathom how Caitlin Masters wound up in the job she has. The *Examiner* has always been a conservative paper, owned when I was a boy by a family which printed nothing that reflected negatively upon city worthies. Later it was sold to a family-owned newspaper chain which continued the tradition of offending as few citizens as possible, especially those who bought advertising space. In Natchez the gossip mills have always been a lot more accurate than anything you could find in the *Examiner*. Caitlin seems an improbable match, to say the least.

She closes her menu and smiles engagingly. 'I'm younger than you thought I'd be, aren't I?'

'A little,' I reply, trying not to look at her chest. In Mississippi, wearing a blouse that sheer without a bra is practically a request to be arrested.

'My father owns the chain. I'm doing a tour of duty down here to learn the ropes.'

'Ah.' *One mystery cleared up.*

'Okay if we go on the record now?'

'You have a tape recorder?'

'I never use them.'

I take out a Sony microcassette recorder borrowed from my father. 'The bitter fruit of experience.'

Our waitress appears and takes our orders (crawfish beignets and iced tea for us both), then stands awkwardly beside the table as though waiting for something. She looks about twenty and, though not quite in Caitlin Masters's league, is quite lovely. Where Masters is angles and light, the waitress is round and brown and sultry, with the guarded look of the Cajun in her eyes.

'Yes?' Caitlin says, looking up at her.

'Um, I was wondering if Mr. Cage would sign a book for me.'

'Sure,' I tell her. 'Do you have one with you?'

'Well – I live over the restaurant.' Her voice is hesitant and terribly self-conscious. 'Just temporarily, you know. I have all your books up there.'

'Really? I'd be glad to sign them for you.'

'Thanks a lot. Um, I'll get your iced tea now.'

As she walks away, Caitlin gives me a wry smile. 'What does a few years of that do for your ego?'

'Water off a duck's back. Let's start.'

She gives me a look that says, *Yeah, right*, then picks up her notebook. 'So, are you here for a visit, or is this something more permanent?'

'I honestly have no idea. Call it a visit.'

'You've obviously been living a life of emotional extremes this past year. Your last book riding high on the best-seller list, your wife dying. How–'

'That subject's off limits,' I say curtly, feeling a door slam somewhere in my soul.

'I'm sorry.' Her eyes narrow like those of a surgeon judging the pain of a probe. 'I didn't mean to upset you.'

'Wait a minute. You asked on the plane if my wife was traveling with me. Did you know then that she was dead?'

Caitlin looks at the table. 'I knew your wife had died. I didn't know how recently. I saw the ring . . .' She folds her hands on the table, then looks up, her eyes vulnerable. 'I didn't ask that question as a reporter. I asked it as a woman. If that makes me a terrible person, I apologize.'

I find myself more intrigued than angered by this confession. This woman asked about my wife to try to read how badly I miss her by my reaction. And I believe she asked out of her own curiosity, not for a story. 'I'm not sure what that makes you. Are you going to focus on that sort of thing in your article?'

'Absolutely not.'

'Let's go on, then.'

45

'What made you stop practicing law and take up writing novels? The Hanratty case?'

I navigate this part of the interview on autopilot, probably learning more about Caitlin Masters than she learns about me. I guessed right about her education: Radcliffe as an undergrad, Columbia School of Journalism for her master's. Top of the line, all the way. She is well read and articulate, but her questions reveal that she knows next to nothing about the modern South. Like most transplants to Natchez, she is an outsider and always will be. It's a shame she holds a job that needs an insider's perspective. The lunch crowd thins as we talk, and our waitress gives such excellent service that our concentration never wavers. By the time we finish our craw-fish, the restaurant is nearly empty and a busboy is setting the tables for dinner.

'Where did you get your ideas about the South?' I ask gently.

At last Caitlin adjusts the lapels of her black silk jacket, covering the shadowy edge of aureole that has been visible throughout lunch. 'I was born in Virginia,' she says with a hint of defensiveness. 'My parents divorced when I was five, though. Mother got custody and spirited me back to Massachusetts. For the next twelve years, all I heard about the South was her trashing it.'

'So the first chance you got, you headed south to see for yourself whether we were the cloven-hoofed, misogynistic degenerates your mother warned you about.'

'Something like that.'

'And?'

'I'm reserving my judgment.'

'That's kind of you. Do you like Natchez?'

'I do. It's not sterilized or Disneyfied like Williamsburg. It's still funky. Gossip, sex, whiskey, and eccentricity, all behind a gossamer veil of Southern gentility.'

I chuckle. 'A woman I grew up with decided to move back

here after working ten years as a film producer in Los Angeles. When I asked why, she told me she was worried that she was losing her mind, and knew that if she did it in Natchez, no one would notice.'

Caitlin laughs. 'That's exactly it! What about you? Do you like it?'

'That's like asking someone if they like their mother. I've been away for years, but no one who grows up here ever really leaves this town behind.'

She makes a note on her pad. 'I was surprised it's such a haven for gays. But the contrasts are disturbing. You've got a real race problem here.'

'So does Los Angeles.'

'But this is a purely white–black race problem.'

'And your paper contributes to it.'

She reddens. 'Would you care to elaborate on that?'

'Sure. The *Examiner* has never dug beneath the surface, never urged people toward their better natures. It was always too afraid to upset the white elite.'

'You think I don't know that?'

'You talk like you don't.'

'Trust me, I do. Let me ask you something. I've been following local politics pretty closely, and there's something funny going on.'

'Like?'

'You'd think Shad Johnson, the black candidate, would be making race a major issue, trying to mobilize every black vote.'

'How's he playing it?'

'He's not even mentioning race. He's in the former money capital of the slaveholding South, thirty percent of the black population receives some form of public assistance, and he acts like he's running for mayor of Utopia. Everything is New South, Brotherhood of Man. He's running as a *Republican*, for Christ's sake.'

'Sounds like a shrewd guy.'

'Will African Americans vote for him if he sucks up to the white vote like that?'

I can't help but laugh. 'If Johnson is the only black man in the race, local blacks will vote for him if he buggers a mule at high noon on the courthouse lawn.'

Two pink moons appear high on Caitlin's cheeks. 'I can't believe you said that. And I can't believe Johnson would stand for the way things are. The things I hear around here . . . sitting in restaurants, riding in cars with people. I've heard the N-word a thousand times since I've been here.'

'You'd hear it in Manhattan if you rode in the right cars. Look, I'd really rather not get into this. I spent eight years in the Houston courts listening to more bullshit about race than I ever want to hear.'

She shakes her head with apparent disgust. 'That's such a cop-out. Racism is the most important problem in America today.'

'Caitlin, you are a very rich, very *white* girl preaching about black problems. You're not the first. Sometimes you have to let people save themselves.'

'And you're a very white *guy* putting black men on death row for state-sanctioned murder.'

'Only when they kill people.'

'Only when they kill white people, you mean.'

A surge of anger runs through me, but I force myself to stay silent. There's nothing to be gained by pointing out that Arthur Lee Hanratty is a white supremacist, or that I once freed a black man who had been mistakenly put on death row by a colleague of mine. You can't win an argument like this. We stare at each other like two fighters after a flurry of punches, deciding whether to wade in again or rest on the ropes.

'Hanratty's an exception,' Caitlin says, as though reading my mind.

This lady is dangerous. It may be a cliché, but her anger has brought color to her cheeks and fire into her eyes, and I am suddenly sure that a string of broken hearts lie in the wake of this self-assured young woman.

'I want to understand this, Penn,' she says with utter sincerity. 'I need to. I've read a hundred books by Southern writers, Southern journalists, everything. And I still don't get it.'

'That's because it's not a Southern problem.'

'Don't you think the answer must be wrapped up in the South somehow?'

'No. Not the way you think, anyway. It's been thirty years since the last vestiges of segregation were remedied under the law. And there's a growing feeling that blacks have done damn little to take advantage of that. That they've been given special breaks and blown it every time. That they don't want an even playing field but their turn on top. White America looks at the Vietnamese, the Irish, the Jews, and they say, "What's the problem with the blacks?" The resentment you hear around this town is based on that, not on old ideas of superiority.'

'Do you feel that way?'

'I used to. I don't anymore.'

'Why not?'

'The Indians.'

'Indians? You mean Native Americans?'

'Think about it. Indians are the only minority that's had as much trouble as blacks. Why? Both races had their cultures shattered by the white man. All the other groups – Irish, Italians, Vietnamese, whatever – may have come here destitute, but they brought one thing with them. Their national identities. Their sense of self. They congregated together in the cities and on the plains, like with like. They maintained their cultural identities – religions, customs, names – until they were secure enough to assimilate. Blacks had no chance to do that. They were stolen from their country, brought here in chains, sold as property. Their families were split, their religion beaten out of them, their names changed. Nothing was left. No identity. And they've never recovered.'

'And you parallel that with Native Americans?'

'It's the same experience, only in reverse. The Indians weren't stolen from their land, their land was stolen from them. And their culture was systematically destroyed. They've never recovered either, despite a host of government programs to help them.'

Caitlin stops writing. 'That's an interesting analogy.'

'If you don't know who you are, you can't find your way. There are exceptions, of course. Bright spots. But my point is that whites don't look at blacks with the right perspective. We look at them like an immigrant group that can't get its shit together.'

She takes a sip of tea as she processes this perspective. 'Does Shad Johnson have the right idea, then? Should Natchez simply sweep its past under the rug and push ahead?'

'For Johnson, it's the smart line to take. For the town . . . I don't know.'

'Please try to answer. I think it's important.'

'If I do, we go off the record.'

She doesn't look happy, but she wants her answer. 'Okay.'

'Faulkner thought the land itself had been cursed by slavery. I don't agree.' I pause, feeling the writer's special frustration at trying to embody moral complexities in words. 'Have you ever read Karl Jung?'

'A little, in college. Synchronicity, all that?'

'Jung didn't try to separate good and evil. He knew that both exist in every human heart. He called the propensity to evil the Shadow. And he believed that trying to deny or repress the Shadow is dangerous. Because it can't be done. He believed you have to recognize your Shadow, come to grips with it, accept it, and integrate it.'

'Make friends with the evil in yourself?'

'Basically. And the South has never done that. We've never truly acknowledged the crime of slavery – not in our collective soul. It's a bit like Germany and the Holocaust, only slavery is much further in the past. Modern generations feel no guilt over it, and it's easy to see why. There's no tangible connection. Slave owners were a tiny minority, and most Southerners see no larger complicity.'

'How does the white South acknowledge the crime?'

'It'll never happen. *That's* what's scary about what Shad Johnson is doing. Because the day of reckoning always comes, when everything you've tried to repress rears up in the road to meet you. Whatever you bury deepest is always waiting for the moment of greatest stress to explode to the surface.'

'You're the only white person in this town who's said anything like this to me. How did you turn out so different?'

'That's a story for another day. But I want you to be clear that I think the North is as guilty as the South when it comes to blacks.'

'You don't really believe that.'

'You're damn right I do. I may criticize the South when I'm in it, but when I'm in the North, I defend Mississippi to the point of blows. Prejudice in the North isn't as open, but it's just as destructive. Most Yankees have no concept of living in a town – I mean *in* a town – that is fifty percent black. No idea of the warmth that can exist between black and white on a daily basis, and has here for years.'

'Oh, come *on*.'

'What happened in Boston when they tried busing?'

'That's a different issue.'

'Watts. Detroit. Skokie. Rodney King. O.J.'

She sighs. 'Are we going to refight the Civil War here?'

'How long have you lived here, Caitlin?'

'Sixteen months.'

'You could live here sixteen years and you'd still be on the outside. And you can't understand this place until you see it from the inside.'

'You're talking about the social cliques?'

'Not exactly. Society is different here. It's not just tiers of wealth. Old money may run out, but the power lingers. Blood still means something down here. Not to me, but to a lot of people.'

'Sounds like Boston.'

'I imagine it is. The structure is concentric circles, and as you move toward the center, the levels of knowledge increase.'

'Were your parents born here?'

'No, but my father's a doctor, and doctors get a backstage pass. Probably because their profession puts them in a position to learn secrets anyway. And there are a thousand secrets in this town.'

'Name one.'

'Well . . . what about the Del Payton case?'

'Who's Del Payton?'

'Delano Payton was a black factory worker who got blown up in his car outside the Triton Battery plant in 1968. It was a race murder, like a dozen others in Mississippi, only it was never solved. I'm not sure anybody really tried to solve it. Payton was a decorated combat veteran of the Korean War. And I'll bet you a thousand dollars we're sitting within five miles of his murderers right now.'

Excitement and awe fill her eyes. 'Are you serious? Did the *Examiner* cover the murder?'

'I don't know. I was eight years old then. I do know Dan Rather came down with a half dozen network correspondents. The FBI was up in arms, and two of their agents were shot at on the road between here and Jackson.'

'Why was Payton murdered?'

'He was about to be hired for a job that until then had been held exclusively by whites.'

'The police must have had some idea who did it.'

'Everybody knew who did it. Racist cowards motivated by the tacit encouragement of white leaders who knew better. A year before, they bombed another black guy at the same plant, but he survived. My father treated him. This guy was on the hospital phone with Bobby Kennedy every day, had guards all around his room, the works.'

'This is great stuff. My aunt went to school with Bobby.'

Her self-centered dilettantism finally puts me over the edge. 'Caitlin, you're so transparent. You want to hear the same thing every other Northern journalist wants to hear: that the Klan is alive and well, that the South is as Gothic and demonic as it ever was. Terrible things did happen here in the sixties, and people who knew better turned a blind eye. As a boy I watched the Klan march robed on horseback right out there on Main Street. City police directed traffic for them. But that has nothing to do with Natchez as it is today.'

'How can you say that?'

'You want to assign guilt? The *Examiner* printed the time of that Klan march but refused to print the time or location of a single civil rights meeting. Is the *Examiner* the same newspaper it was then?'

She ignores the question. 'Why haven't I heard people talking about the Payton case before? Even the African Americans don't talk about it.'

'Because if you live here, you want to make the best life you can. Stirring up the past doesn't help anybody.'

'But cases like this are being reopened every day, right here in Mississippi. The Byron de la Beckwith case. The retrial of Sam Bowers, the Klan Wizard from Laurel. You must know that the state recently opened the secret files of the Mississippi Sovereignty Commission?'

'So?'

'The Sovereignty Commission was like a racist KGB. They

kept files not only on African Americans but on hundreds of whites suspected of liberal sympathies.'

'So?'

Caitlin looks at me in bewilderment. 'So? *Newsweek* just ran a big piece on it, and Peter Jennings's people have been calling around the state, trolling for stories. The Payton case could be reopened at any time.'

'Glad to hear it. Justice should be better served than it was in Natchez in 1968, but this isn't some old trial with an all-white hung jury. This is an unsolved murder. A capital murder. No defendant. No suspects, as far as I know. No crime scene. Old or dead witnesses—'

'Nobody said winning a Pulitzer is easy.'

A light clicks on in my head. 'Ah. That's the plan? Winning a Pulitzer before you're thirty?'

She gives me a sly smile. 'Before I'm twenty-nine. *That's* the plan.'

'God help this town.'

Her laugh is full and throaty, one I'd expect from an older woman. 'Did you know that some of the Sovereignty Commission files are going to remain sealed?'

'No.'

'Forty-two of them. Some of them on major politicians. I heard Trent Lott's was one of them, but that turned out to be wrong.'

'That's no surprise. A lot of the most sensitive files were destroyed years ago.'

'Why haven't you explored any of this in your novels?'

'A sense of loyalty to the place that bore me, I suppose. A lot of people would have to die before I could write a book like that.'

'So, until then you write fluff and take the easy money?'

'I don't write fluff.'

She holds up her hands in contrition. 'I know. I did a Nexis

search on you. *Publishers Weekly* named *False Witness* the
fourth-best legal thriller ever written.'

'After what?'

'*Anatomy of a Murder, The Caine Mutiny,* and *Presumed
Innocent.*'

'That's pretty good company,' I murmur, painfully aware
that *False Witness* was four books ago.

'Yes, but it just seems so obvious that you should be writing
about all this. Write what you know! You know?'

Caitlin picks up the check and walks over to the cash
register, her movements fluid and graceful despite the
phenomenal energy that animates her. The restaurant is
empty now but for the cashier and our waitress, who chooses
this moment to come forward with her copy of *False Witness.*
I take the book, open it to the flyleaf, and accept the pen she
offers.

'Would you like me to personalize it?'

'Wow, that would be great. Um, to Jenny. That's me.'

'No last name?'

'Just Jenny would be cool.'

I write: *Jenny, I enjoyed meeting you. Penn Cage.*

She blushes as she takes back the book, then glances at
Caitlin, who stands waiting for me. 'I'd love to talk to you
sometime,' she says in a quavering voice. 'Ask you some
questions, maybe.'

I recognize the nervous tones of an aspiring writer. 'I'll be
in again. A friend of mine owns the place.'

'Wow, okay. Thanks.'

I join Caitlin as she walks out onto the brightly lit street.

'Did you get enough for your piece?'

'More than enough.' She tucks her copy of *False Witness*
under one arm and buttons her jacket. 'AP will probably pick
it up, and it'll be reprinted all over the South. They like fluff
as much as anybody.'

I sigh wearily.

'I'm joking, Penn. God, take it easy, would you?'

'I guess I'm a little tense.'

'A little?' She takes *False Witness* in both hands, then bends at the waist and touches the book flat against the sidewalk, displaying a limberness that makes my back hurt and draws looks from several passersby. 'Mmm, I needed that.'

'If I tried that, they'd hear tendons popping across the river.'

She smiles. 'Not if you practiced. We should do this again. You can be deep background on Southern crime and psychology.'

I start to decline, then surprise myself by saying, 'I might be able to help you with that.'

Her eyes sparkle with pleasure. 'I'll call you. And I'm sorry again about the airplane. Tell Annie I said hello.'

She holds out her hand and I take it, not thinking anything of it and so being all the more surprised by the shock I feel. When our eyes meet, we recognize something in each other that neither expects and both quickly look away from.

'The story will probably run Wednesday in the Southern Life section,' she says in a flustered voice, and awkwardly releases my hand. 'I'll mail some copies to your parents. I'm sure your mom still clips everything about you.'

'Absolutely.'

Caitlin Masters looks at me once more, then turns and walks quickly to a green Miata parked across the street with its top down. I am acutely aware of her physical presence, even across the street, and inexplicably glad that she suggested another lunch. With that gladness comes a rush of guilt so strong that it nauseates me. Seven months ago I was standing at my wife's deathbed, then her coffin. Seven seconds ago I felt something for another woman. This small and natural response causes me more guilt than sleeping with a woman out of physical necessity – which I have not yet done. Because what I felt was more than physical. A glacier consumes whole forests by inches. As small as it was, that glimmer of feeling is absolute proof that someone else will one day occupy the place Sarah held in my life.

I feel like a traitor.

Chapter 6

My father wakes me by slapping a newspaper against my forehead. After I rub the sleep from my eyes, I see my own face staring up from the front page of the Natchez *Examiner*, above the fold. They've scanned my most recent author photo and blown it up to 'this man assassinated the president' size. The headline reads: *PRODIGAL SON RETURNS HOME*.

'The goddamn phone hasn't stopped ringing,' Dad growls. 'Everybody wants to know why my son is disparaging his hometown.'

Beneath the author photo is a montage of smaller shots, like a family album: me as a lanky kid with Dad's arm around my shoulders, printed in a Father's Day issue in 1968; as a high school baseball player; as the flag runner in the annual Confederate pageant; my Ole Miss graduation photo. I quickly scan the columns, recognizing most of what I said yesterday, laid out in surprisingly faithful prose.

'I don't get it,' I say. 'What's wrong with this?'

'Have you been in Houston so long you've forgotten how things are here? Bill Humphreys said you set back thirty years of good race relations.'

'I didn't say anything you haven't said a hundred times in our kitchen.'

'The newspaper isn't our kitchen!'

'Come on, Dad. This is nothing.'

He shakes his head in amazement. 'Turn the page, hotshot. You'll see something.'

When I turn the page, my breath catches in my throat.

The banner headline reads: *30 YEARS LATER 'RACIST COWARDS' STILL WALK STREETS*: My stomach flips over. Underneath the headline is a photo of a scorched Ford Fairlane with a blackened corpse seated behind the wheel. That picture never ran in the Natchez *Examiner* in 1968. Caitlin Masters must have dug up an old crime-scene photo somewhere.

'Jesus,' I whisper.

'Harvey Byrd at the Chamber of Commerce thinks you may have single-handedly sabotaged the chemical-plant deal.'

'Let me read the thing, okay?'

Dad plants himself in the corner, his arms folded.

The story opens like a true-crime novel.

> *On May 14, 1968, Frank Jones, a scheduling clerk at the Triton Battery plant, walked out to his car in the middle of the third shift to run an errand. Before he could start his engine, he heard a boom 'like an artillery piece,' and a blackwall tire slammed into his windshield. Thirty yards away, a black man named Delano Payton sat burning to death. Jones was the sole eyewitness to the worst race crime in the history of this city, in which a combat veteran of the Korean War was murdered to prevent his being promoted to a 'white-only' job. No one was ever arrested for the crime, and many in the black community believe that law enforcement officials of the period gave less than their full efforts to the case. Best-selling author and Natchez native Penn Cage characterized the killers of Delano Payton as 'racist cowards,' and stated that justice should be better served than it was in Natchez in 1968.*
>
> *Former police chief Hiram Wilkes contended that leads were*

*nonexistent at the time, and said that despite exhaustive efforts
by law enforcement, and a $15,000 reward offered by Payton's
national labor union, no suspects were turned up. The FBI was
called in to work the case but had no more success than local
police. Former Natchez police officer Ray Presley, who assisted
on the case in the spring of 1968, stated, 'It was a tough murder
case, and the FBI got in the way more than they helped, which
was par for them in those days—'*

I reread the last sentence, my heartbeat accelerating. I had
no idea Ray Presley was involved in the Payton case. I want
to ask my father about him, but with the blackmail issue –
and my mother's suspicions about Presley – hanging like a
cloud between us, I don't.

'You've been dealing with the media for twelve years,'
Dad grumbles. 'That publisher must have shown you a little
leg and puréed your brain. I've seen her around town. Face
like a model, tits like two puppies in a sack. I know what
happened. It took her about five seconds to get Penn Cage
at his most sanctimonious.' He grabs the newspaper out of
my hands and wads it into a ball. 'Did you have to dredge
up the goddamn Payton case?'

'I just *mentioned* it, for God's sake. I thought we were off
the record.'

'She obviously didn't.'

I try to remember the point at which I asked to go off the
record. I can check my tape, of course, but I already know
what Caitlin Masters will say: she thought I wanted the
Jungian analysis and the comparison between Germany and
the South off the record, but not the Del Payton remarks,
which were an extension of our earlier conversation on
racism. At least she honored my request not to mention the
Hanratty execution.

'What about that Klan rally stuff?' Dad mutters.

'You took me to that rally!'

'I know, I know . . . damn it. I just wanted you to see that wasn't any way to be. But you didn't have to drag it all back up now, did you?'

'I made it clear that stuff was all in the past. And she printed my qualifications, I'll give her that.'

'God almighty, what a mess. Do you think—'

The front doorbell rings, cutting him off.

'Who the hell could that be?' he asks. 'It's only eight-thirty.'

He walks out of the bedroom, taking the wadded-up newspapers with him.

My thoughts return to Caitlin Masters. Despite her assurances, I was foolish to say anything to her that I didn't want printed. Maybe she did show me a little leg and lull my usually vigilant defenses. Am I that easy to manipulate?

'Get some clothes on,' my father says from the door, his face grave. 'You've got visitors.'

'Who? You look almost scared.'

He nods slowly. 'I think I am.'

Uncertain what to expect, I hover in the hall outside my mother's living room. The hushed sibilance of gracious women making polite conversation drifts from the wide doorway. I walk through the door and stop in my tracks. Two black women sit primly on the sofa, delicate Wedgwood cups steaming before them on the coffee table. One is in her eighties, if not older, and dressed in an ensemble the like of which I have not seen since the Sundays I drove past black churches as a teenager. The skirt is purple, the blouse green, the shoes a gleaming patent black. Her hat is a flowered concoction of black straw and varicolored silk. Beneath the hat is a shining black wig, beneath the wig a raisin of a face with watery eyes that glisten amid the wrinkles.

The woman beside her looks thirty years younger and wears a much more subdued outfit, a pleated navy skirt with a periwinkle blouse. She looks up, and her gaze disconcerts me. Most black people I grew up with rarely made direct eye contact, locking their feelings behind a veneer of humility. But this woman's gaze is unveiled, direct, and self-confident.

'You keep a fine house, Mrs. Cage,' the older woman says in a cracked voice. 'A *fine* house.'

'You're so kind to say so,' my mother replies from a wing chair on the other side of the coffee table. She wears a house-coat and no makeup, yet even in this state radiates a quiet, stately beauty. She turns to me and smiles.

'Son, this is Mrs. Payton.' She gestures toward the elderly woman, then nods at her younger companion. 'And this is Mrs. Payton also. They've come to thank you for what you said in this morning's paper.'

I flush from my neck to the crown of my head. I can only be looking at the widow and mother of Delano Payton, the man bombed and burned to death in 1968. Barefoot and unshaven, I make a vain attempt to straighten my hair, then advance into the living room. Without rising, the elder Mrs. Payton enfolds my right hand in both of hers like a dowager empress. Her palms feel like fine sandpaper. The younger Mrs. Payton stands and shakes my hand with exaggerated formality. Her hand is moist and warm. Up close, she looks older than I first guessed, perhaps sixty-five. Because she has not gone to fat, she projects an aura of youth that her eyes cannot match.

'Althea works in the nursery at St. Catherine's Hospital,' Dad informs me from the door. 'I see her all the time. And I've treated Miss Georgia for thirty-five years now.'

'Yo' daddy a good doctor,' the elder Mrs. Payton says from the sofa, pointing a bony finger at me. 'A *good* doctor.'

My father has heard this ten thousand times, but he smiles graciously. 'Thank you, Miss Georgia.'

'I remember you makin' house calls *late* at night,' Georgia Payton goes on, her voice reedy and difficult to follow as it jumps up and down the scale. 'Givin' shots and deliverin' babies. Had you a spotlight back then to see the house numbers.'

'And a pistol in my black bag,' Dad adds, chuckling.

'Sho' did. I seen it once. You ever have to use it?'

'No, ma'am, thank God.'

'Might have to one of these days, with all this crack in the streets. I told the pastor last Sunday, you want to find Satan, just pull up to one of them crack houses. Sheriff ought to burn ever' one to the ground.'

We all nod with enthusiasm, doing our best to foster a casual atmosphere. Blacks visiting socially in white homes – and vice versa – is still as rare as snowfall in Natchez, but this is not the reason for the general discomfort.

'Mr. Cage,' Althea says, focusing her liquid brown eyes on me, 'we really appreciate you speaking out like you did in the paper.'

'Please call me Penn,' I implore her, embarrassed by thanks for a few lines tossed off without any real feeling for the victims of the crime.

'Mr. Penn,' says Georgia Payton, 'ain't no white man in thirty years said what you said in the paper today. My boy was kilt outside his job in nineteen hundred and sixty-eight, and all the po-lices did was sweep it under the rug.'

Her statement hangs suspended in crystalline silence. I sense my father's reflexive desire to answer her charge, to try to mitigate the behavior of the law enforcement figures of the period. But the murder remains unsolved, and he has no idea what efforts were made to solve it, if any, or how sincere they might have been. Althea Payton looks momentarily disconcerted by her mother-in-law's frankness, but then her eyes fill with calm resolution.

'Are you still a lawyer, Mr. Cage?' she asks. 'I mean, I know you're a writer now. Can you still practice law?'

I incline my head. 'I'm still a member of the bar.'

'What that mean?' asks Georgia.

'I can still practice law, ma'am.'

'Then we wants to hire you.'

'For what?'

'I think I know,' Dad says.

'To find out who murdered my baby,' the old woman says, 'The po-lice don't want to do it. FBI don't want to. The county lawyer neither.'

'The district attorney,' Althea corrects her.

'You've spoken to the district attorney about this?'

Althea nods. 'Several times. He has no interest in the case.'

Dad emits a sigh easily interpreted as, *Big surprise.*

'We hired us a detective too,' Georgia says. 'I even wrote to that man on *Unsolved Mysteries*, that good-looking white man from that old gangster TV show.'

'Robert Stack?' asks my mother.

'Yes,' Althea confirms. 'We got back one letter from the show's producer expressing interest, but after that nothing.'

'What about this detective?' I ask. 'What happened with him?'

'We hired a man from Jackson first. He poked around downtown for an afternoon, then told us there was nothing to find.'

'White man,' Georgia barks. 'A no-good.'

'Then we hired a detective from Chicago,' Althea says in a tense voice. 'He flew down and spent a week in the Eola Hotel—'

'Colored man,' the old woman cuts in. 'A *no-count* no-good. He stole all our money and went back to Chicago.'

'He was very expensive,' Althea concedes. 'And he said

the same thing the first detective told us. The pertinent records had been destroyed and there was nothing to find.'

'NAACP say the same thing,' Georgia adds with venom. 'They don't care about my baby none. He wasn't a big enough name. They cry about Martin and Medgar every year, got white folks makin' movies about Medgar. But my baby Del in the ground and nobody care. Nobody.'

'Except you,' Althea says quietly. 'When I walked out in my driveway this morning and picked up that paper – when I read what you said – I cried. I cried like I haven't cried in thirty years.'

Dad raises his eyebrows and sends me one of his telepathic messages: *You opened your damn mouth. See what it's got you.*

'I still gots some money, Mr. Penn,' Georgia says, clutching at a black vinyl handbag the size of a small suitcase.

I envision a tidal wave of one-dollar bills spilling out of the purse, like money at a crack bust, but Mrs. Payton has clutched the bag only to emphasize her statement. I cannot let this go any further.

'Ladies, I appreciate your thanks, but I don't deserve them. As I said in the paper, I'm here for a vacation. I'm no longer involved in any criminal matters. What happened to your husband and son was a terrible tragedy, but I suspect that what the detectives told you is true. This crime happened thirty years ago. Nowadays, if the police don't solve a homicide in the first forty-eight hours, they know they probably never will.'

'But sometimes they do,' Althea says doggedly. 'I've read about murder cases that were solved years after the fact.'

'That's true, but it's rare. In all my years with the Houston D.A.'s office, we only had a couple of cases like that.'

'But you had them.'

'Yes. But what we had more of – a hundred times more of – was distraught relatives pleading with us to reopen old cases. Murder is a terrible thing, and no one knows that better than you. The repercussions reverberate through generations.'

'But there's no statue of limitations on murder. Is there?'

Statue of limitations. I see no point in correcting her grammar; I've heard attorneys make the same mistake. Like congressmen referring to *nucular* war. 'Everything hinges on evidence,' I explain. 'Has any new evidence come to light?'

Her desolate look is answer enough.

'That's what we were hoping you could do.' Althea says. 'Look back over what the police did. Maybe they missed something. Maybe they *buried* something. I read in a book that sixty percent of the Natchez police force was Klan back then. God knows what they did or didn't do. You might even get a book out of it. There's a lot nobody knows about those times. About what Del was doing for his people.'

I fight the urge to glance at my parents for assistance. 'I'm actually in the middle of a book now, and I'm behind. I–'

'I've read your books,' Althea breaks in. 'All of them. In paperback, of course. I read them on the late shift, when the babies are resting well.'

I never know what to say in these moments. If you say, *Did you like them?* you're putting the person on the spot. But what else can you say?

'I liked the first one the best,' Althea offers. 'I liked the others too, but I couldn't help feeling . . .'

'Be honest,' I urge her, dreading what will follow.

'I always felt that your gift was bigger than the stories you were telling. I don't mean to be critical. But that first book was so real. I just think if you really understood what happened to Del, you'd have a story that would take all the gift you have to tell it.'

Her words are like salt on my soul. 'I truly wish I could help you. But I can't. If some new evidence were to come to light, the district attorney would be the proper man to see.' I look at my father. 'Is Austin Mackey still the D.A. here?'

He nods warily.

'I went to school with Mr. Mackey. He's a good man. I could–'

'He nothing but a politician!' scoffs Georgia Payton.

The old woman gets slowly to her feet, using her huge handbag as a counterweight. 'He don't care none. We come here 'cause we thought *you* did. But maybe you don't. Maybe you was talking free in the paper 'cause you been gone so long you ain't worried 'bout what people thinks around here. I told Althea, you must be like your daddy, a hardworking man with a good heart. But maybe I told her wrong.'

I flush again, suddenly certain that the men of the Payton family are intimately familiar with the guilt trip as a motivational tool.

Althea stands more slowly than her mother-in-law, as though lifting the weight of thirty years of grief. This time when she speaks, she looks only at the floor.

'I loved my husband,' she says softly. 'After he was killed, I never remarried. I never even went with another man. I raised my boy the best I could and tried to go on. I don't say it was hard, because everybody got it hard, some way. You know that, Dr. Cage. The world's full of misery. But my Del got took before his time.' Her lower lip is quivering; she bites it to keep her composure. 'He wanted us to wait to have children. So we'd be able to give them the things they needed. Del said our people hurt themselves by having too many children too quick. We just had one before he died. Del was a good boy who grew into a good man, and he never got to see his own baby grow up.'

The mournful undertone in her voice pierces my heart. All I can see is Sarah lying in her casket at age thirty-seven, her future ripped away like a cruel mirage. Althea Payton breaks the image by reaching into her purse and taking out a folded piece of paper, which she hands to me. I have little choice but to unfold it.

It's a death certificate.

'When the ambulance men got to Del, he was already burned up. But they couldn't get him out of the seat. The springs from the seat had blown up through his thighs and pinned him there. That's why he couldn't get out, even though he was still alive after that bomb went off.'

I stare at the brittle yellowed paper, a simple form dated 5-14-68.

'Look in the middle,' Althea says. 'Under cause of death.'

I push down a hot wave of nausea. Thirty years ago, on the line beside the printed words CAUSE OF DEATH, some callous or easily cowed bureaucrat had scrawled the word *Accidental.*

'As long as I live and breathe,' Althea whispers, 'I'll do what I can to find out the truth.'

I want to speak, to try to communicate the empathy I feel, but I don't. Sarah's death taught me this. In the face of grief, words have no power.

I watch the Payton women follow my mother into the hall. I hear Georgia repeat her compliment about the fine house my mother keeps, then the soft shutting of the front door. I sit on the sofa where Althea sat. The cushion is still warm. My mother's slippers hiss across the slate floor of the foyer, the sound like a nun moving through a convent.

'The neighbours are standing out in their yards,' she says.

Wondering at the sight of black people who aren't yard men or maids, I reflect. *And tomorrow the maids and the yard men will return, while the two Mrs. Paytons sit or work in silent grief, mourning a man whose murder caused no more ripples than a stone dropped into a pond.*

'I know that was hard,' my father says, laying a hand on my shoulder. 'But you did the right thing.'

I shake my head. 'I don't know.'

'That boy's long dead and gone. Nothing anybody can do will help him now. But it could hurt a lot of people. Those two poor women. The town. Your mother. You and Annie most of all. You did the right thing, son.'

I look up at my father, searching for the man Georgia Payton said he is.

'You did,' my mother insists. 'Don't dwell on it. Go wake Annie up. I'm going to make French toast.'

Chapter 7

The couch in my father's medical office has heard many terrible truths: revelations by the doctor (you're sick; you're dying; they couldn't get it all), confessions by the patient (my husband beats me; my father raped me; I want to die), but always – always – truths about the patient.

Today the truth about the doctor will be told.

I can imagine no other reason for the sudden summons to his office. It requires a conscious effort to control my anxiety as I sit on that worn leather couch, waiting for him to finish with his last patient of the day.

After the Payton women left our house this morning, Dad took his old pickup truck to work so that Annie and I would have the BMW. Having no desire to endure the glares of the local citizenry, I spent the morning in the pool with Annie, marveling at how well she moved in the water and fighting a losing battle to keep her skin covered with sun block. Mom and I had tuna sandwiches for lunch, Annie a bowl of SpaghettiOs. When the two of them drove downtown to buy Annie new shoes, I retired to the library and read T. Harry Williams's *Huey Long* on the sofa until I fell asleep.

The telephone woke me at four-thirty p.m. I hated to chance answering it myself, but I thought it might be my mother.

'Penn?' said my father. 'Can you drop by my office about five? Alone?'

'Sure. What's up?'

'I think it's time we had a talk.'

'Okay,' I said, trying to sound casual. 'I'll see you at five.'

I went to the bathroom and showered off the chlorine from the pool, then dressed in chinos and a polo shirt. Dad's office is only a couple of miles from the house, so I read another twenty minutes in *Huey Long*. When I fell asleep, the Grand Imperial Wizard of the Ku Klux Klan, speaking from the 'imperial klonvocation' in Atlanta, had just announced that he was going to Louisiana to campaign against Huey because of his pro-Negro policies. The Kingfish stormed into the press gallery of the state senate while the legislature was in session and announced that if that 'Imperial bastard' crossed the Louisiana state line, he would shortly depart 'with his toes turned up.' The Klan leader wisely elected not to test the Kingfish's sincerity. As humorous as it seemed in retrospect, Long could all too easily have backed up his threat. I could see how dictatorial power might be an asset in solving sticky problems like racism. Of course, that road also leads to the crematorium ovens.

When I got to my father's office building, I used his private door. I'd known Anna, his chief nurse – an attractive black woman – for most of my life, but I was too curious to spend even ten minutes reminiscing about old times. I sat on the couch opposite his desk and waited in the lingering haze of cigar smoke.

During his first fifteen years in Natchez, Dad practiced in a sprawling downtown house. This was the era of separate waiting rooms for 'colored' and white, but his only nod to this convention was a flimsy wooden partition set up in the middle of the room. On any day you could find whole families – white and black – camped out in that great room, kids playing on the floor, parents eating from bag lunches and waiting to see the doctor on a first-come, first-served basis. His new office, convenient to both hospitals and sterile as a hypodermic needle, runs like any other doctor's – almost. He has rigidly scheduled appointments, a gleaming laboratory, and modern X-ray facilities, but he still routinely brings everything to a standstill by spending whatever time he feels a patient needs for examination, commiseration, or just plain conversation.

At last his strong baritone filters around the door. The volume tells me he is bidding farewell to a geriatric patient. Old people comprise the bulk of his practice now, as his 'patient base' has aged with him. Anna leans in and gives me a smile, then closes the door behind Dad. He squeezes my shoulder as he walks past and sits in the big chair behind his desk.

This is how I picture him in memory: white lab coat, stethoscope hanging loosely around his neck, ensconced behind mountains of incomplete medical records, drug samples, and junk mail. He reaches into a small refrigerator behind his desk and takes out a Dr Pepper, which he offers to me. When I decline, he pops the top and takes a long pull from it, his eyes watering from the sudden shot of carbonation.

'I'm in a bad spot, Penn,' he says in a frank voice. 'I apologize for being an ass the other night. It's not easy for a father to admit weakness to his son.'

I nod awkwardly, imagining a future when I am certain to fall short of Annie's idealized image of me. 'Dad, there's nothing you can tell me that will change my opinion of you. Just tell me what's going on so we can deal with it.'

He clearly doubts my statement, but he's made up his mind to talk. 'Twenty-five years ago,' he says, 'your Aunt Ellen got into some trouble.'

My mind is spinning. When he said 'twenty-five years ago,' I thought he was going to start talking about Del Payton. But Payton was killed thirty years ago. The shift to my mother's younger sister, Ellen, throws me completely.

'She was divorced and living in Mobile, Alabama. Ellen

was about your age now, I guess. Dating a guy there. He was a year or two younger than she was. Name was Hillman. Don Hillman. Your mother and I didn't know it at the time – at least I didn't – but Hillman was abusing Ellen. Beating her, controlling every word and action. Your mother finally convinced her that the relationship was going to end badly no matter what she did, and Ellen tried to break it off. Hillman didn't take it well. I advised Ellen to go to the police. Then I found out Hillman was the brother of a cop over in Mobile. A detective. This was 1973. Nobody'd heard of stalking laws.'

'I hope you brought her here.'

'Of course. She stayed with us for a summer. You remember, don't you?'

I do. For most of one summer our hall bathroom became an exotic world of hanging stockings, lacy underwear, cut-glass perfume bottles, and blue Noxema jars.

'Hillman called the house a few times after the breakup. Late, drunk out of his mind and railing, or else hanging up. One night when he didn't hang up, I told him if he came to Natchez making trouble, he'd be a long time getting back to Mobile. The calls stopped. After a while Ellen wanted her own place, so I rented her an apartment at the Windsor Arms and got her a job at the Jeff Davis.'

He takes another slug of Dr Pepper. 'As soon as she got her own place, strange things started happening. Slashed tires, eggs on her door, more juvenile crap. One morning she found her cat at her door with its throat cut. I called the Natchez police, but they couldn't find Hillman anywhere in town.' He closed his eyes and sighs. 'Then he raped her.'

A shudder of horror accompanies my amazement. Families are mazes of secrets, and none of us ever knows them all.

'Hillman was waiting inside her apartment when she got home from a date. He beat the hell out of her, raped her, sodomized her. Then he disappeared. Ellen was too shaken up to swear out charges. I had to sedate her. I got the Natchez

D.A. to call the Mobile D.A. and make a lot of noise, but Ellen would have been a shaky witness at best, even if I could have gotten her to press charges. And Hillman's brother was a cop, remember? The Mobile D.A. didn't sound excited about making trouble for him.'

I nod in sympathy. The old-timers in Houston told me a thousand times how tough it was to get rape convictions before feminists changed public perception of the crime. And the cop angle was a serious complication. Nothing is more incestuous than Southern law enforcement. Everything is personal relationships.

'Needless to say, things were pretty bad at home,' Dad goes on. 'We tried to keep it from you and your sister, but your mother and Ellen were at the end of their rope. Peggy was driving her to Jackson every three days to see a psychiatrist.'

I remember this too. Mom taking Aunt Ellen to the doctor all the time. 'We thought it was her ovaries or something.'

'That's what we told you. Anyway, two weeks after the rape, Hillman started calling again.' Dad is clenching and unclenching his right fist on the desk. 'I never felt so god-damn impotent in my life.'

I don't know what's coming, but the hair on my forearms is standing up.

'About this time, Ray Presley happened to come to see me about his blood pressure. You know how I get to talking to patients, and Presley always had a good story. He saw that I wasn't myself. He asked what was bothering me, and I told him. He'd been a cop, after all. I thought he might have a suggestion.'

He'd also done a hitch in Parchman prison, I think, but now does not seem the best time to bring that up.

'Ray heard me out, and he didn't say much. Grunted a couple of times in the right places. You never know what he's thinking. So we're both just sitting there, saying nothing.

After a while he says, "So what's this shitbird's name, Doc?" I didn't say anything for a minute. Then I told him. We shot the bull for a few more minutes, and Ray left. Three weeks later, the Natchez D.A. called and told me Hillman was dead. Somebody'd shot him in the head and taken his wallet outside a topless bar in Mobile.'

'Jesus Christ.'

'At first I was relieved. But somewhere in the back of my mind I was worried about Ray. He'd always appreciated me taking care of his mother, and some part of me wondered if he hadn't taken it into his head to get rid of my problem for me.'

'Oh, man.'

'A month later he came back in to get his pressure checked. I told the girls I was too busy to talk, but he slipped into my office and waited for me. When I went in, I asked him point blank if he knew anything about Hillman's death.'

'And?'

'He told me right out he'd killed the guy.'

'Shit.'

Dad shakes his head. 'Just like saying, "I fixed that flat for you, Doc." He gave me this funny smile and told me not to give it another thought. Said I didn't owe him anything. Just get back to doctoring and living. Those were his exact words.'

'Tell me you reported this to the police.'

'I didn't.'

Having watched my father make moral choices that cost him money and friendships for years, I am stunned by this answer. 'That's accessory after the fact, Dad. Five years in the pen.'

'I realize that. But the situation was more complicated than you know.'

'You hadn't committed any crime until you kept Presley's confession from the police.'

'Listen, damn it! Ray must have seen how he upset me. Because twenty minutes after he walked out, he came back and handed me a zipper pouch. Inside it was a pistol I'd lent him about six months before, a forty-five.'

My heart slaps against my chest wall. 'He killed Hillman with that pistol?'

'No. But he was always borrowing things from me back then. Guns, books, my Nikon for a stakeout, that kind of thing. You know I can't say no to anybody. Anyhow, I'd lent him another pistol about a year before, a little feather-weight thirty-eight. So, when he handed me the forty-five, I asked about the thirty-eight.' Dad takes a deep breath and exhales slowly. 'He told me it had been stolen.'

I close my eyes as though to shield myself from what is coming.

'He told me not to worry about it, that he'd get me another thirty-eight. But he was really telling me that reporting the murder wasn't an option. He'd killed Hillman with my thirty-eight, and he still had the gun. If I tried to report him, he could tell the police that I'd asked him to commit the crime and had given him the gun to do it.'

'How soon did he start blackmailing you?'

'He didn't mention it again for twenty-five years.'

'What?'

'He had no intention of blackmailing me, Penn. Ray Presley idolized me back then. Still does, I think. But last year he got prostate cancer, and he doesn't have health insurance. He needed money, so he started getting it wherever he could. For all I know, he's blackmailing ten other people besides me. The point is, he had me over a barrel. I couldn't see any option but to pay him.'

'Why didn't you call me when he first came to you?'

'Do you really have to ask? I was ashamed. Because of me, a man was murdered.'

'You had nothing to do with that! You didn't solicit the

thing, for God's sake. You couldn't know Presley would kill the guy.'

Dad dismisses this rationalization with a wave of his hand. 'Do you remember *Becket*?'

'The movie or the historical archbishop?'

'The movie. After Becket makes his moral stand against King Henry, the king is alone in the palace with his nobles. These so-called nobles are a nasty bunch, greedy, violent, and drunk. And though King Henry loves Becket, he says out loud: "Will no one rid me of this meddlesome priest?" And of course they do. They go to Canterbury and murder him with swords.'

Sometimes I wish my father had less rigorous moral standards.

'Henry knew what he was saying, Penn. He knew the company he was in. And that made him guilty of murder. That's why he submitted to the lashing by Becket's monks.'

'You're not a king. You couldn't know what Presley would do.'

Dad is too wracked by guilt for me to get through to him. 'I've spent years thinking about this. I didn't know Presley would kill the man, but when he asked for the name, I knew he might do *something*. I'd treated his parents for free, and he felt indebted to me. He'd just gotten out of prison. From the moment I told Presley that name, Hillman was bound to get hurt, maybe killed. There's no getting around that.'

I know what it has cost my father to admit this. He may even be right. But that's not my primary concern at this point. 'That's not how the law would see it. Technically, your only crime was accessory after the fact. And the statute of limitations ran out on that in 1975.'

'What about the gun?'

'That's another story. If Presley will lie to the D.A. and say you asked him to kill Hillman, and that you gave him the gun – and if he still *has* the gun – that adds up to capital murder.

It puts you in line for what I've got to witness in two days. Lethal injection.'

'That's what I thought.'

'Why did you decide to tell me this today?'

'You want to find out who killed Del Payton. I know you do, and you're right. Maybe you even have an obligation to do it. But the road to Payton's killers runs right through Ray Presley, because he worked on the case. I knew you'd eventually go see him, and if you did, you'd probably find out about this. He might even hit you up for money. I wanted you to hear the truth from me.'

'The hell with Del Payton. There's only one thing to do.'

'What?'

'Go to the D.A. before Presley can. Tomorrow morning we're going to walk in there, tell the whole story, and demand that Presley be arrested for murder and extortion.'

Dad raises both hands like a supplicant. 'I've thought of doing that a hundred times. But why should the D.A. believe me?'

I think of Austin Mackey, district attorney and former schoolmate of mine. Not my first choice for a sympathetic confessor, but we go back a lot of years. 'The D.A. has a lot of discretion in a case like this. And it's possible we could sting Presley. Wire you before meeting with him. Videotape a blackmail payment.'

'You're underestimating Ray. Since he started this, he's talked and acted as though we were partners from the beginning.'

'Damn.'

'Mackey would probably insist that you drop the Payton business, Penn.'

'I dropped it the second you told me about this. We don't have any options. We've got to come clean, and Mackey's the man we have to see.'

Dad seems to sag behind his desk. 'If that's what you think, I'm prepared to do it. It'll be a relief, no matter what happens. But even if Mackey decided not to prosecute, wouldn't I still be subject to prosecution in Alabama?'

He has a point. 'Yes. Anywhere that an element of the crime took place. But I can get Mackey to talk to the Mobile D.A. for us.'

'Hillman's brother still lives in Mobile. The cop. I checked two months ago.'

Wonderful. Even if Mackey does his best to convince the Mobile D.A. to lay off, my father's life will be in the hands of the Alabama authorities. And that comes pretty close to unacceptable risk. That's why Dad has not come forward before now.

'Presley has cancer,' I say, thinking aloud. 'How long does he have to live?'

Dad shrugs. 'His oncologist thought he'd be dead before now. But he's still ambulatory. Ray is one tough son of a bitch. One of those I always say is too damn stubborn to die. He could live another year.'

'A year isn't so long. We could keep paying him till he dies. Pay his medical bills.'

'That's what I've been doing so far. It's getting damned expensive.'

'How much have you paid him?'

'A hundred and sixteen thousand dollars to date.'

I shake my head, still unable to believe the situation. 'Over how long?'

'Seven or eight months. But he wants more. He's talking about needing to provide for his kids now.'

'That's the way it is with blackmail. It never stops. There's no guarantee it would stop with his death. He could give the gun to one of his kids. He could leave documentary evidence. A videotape, for example, A dying declaration.

You know. "I've got cancer, and I've got something to get off my chest before I stand before my maker." That kind of thing is taken very seriously by the courts.'

My father has turned pale. 'Good God.'

'That leaves us only one option.'

Something in my voice must have sounded more sinister than I intended, because Dad's eyes are wide with shock. 'You don't mean kill him?'

'God, no. I just told you his death wasn't necessarily a solution.'

Relief washes over his face.

'Everything depends on that gun.'

'What are you suggesting? That we steal it?'

'No. We buy it.'

Dad shakes his head. 'Ray will never sell it.'

'Everybody has a price. And we know Presley needs money.'

'You just said it could be a meal ticket for his kids for years.'

'Presley knows me. By reputation at least. I'm a nationally known prosecutor, a famous author. If I stand for anything, it's integrity. Same as you. I'll show Presley a carrot and a stick. He can sell me the gun, or he can watch me go to the D.A. and stake my reputation on convincing the authorities that you're innocent. I have contacts from Houston to Washington. You and I are pillars of our communities. Ray Presley's a convicted felon. At various times he's probably been suspected of several murders. He'll sell me the gun.'

A spark of hope has entered Dad's eyes, but fear still masks it, dull and gray and alien to my image of him. 'Buying evidence with intent to . . . to destroy it,' he says. 'What kind of crime is that?'

'It's a felony. Major-league.'

'You can't do it, Penn.'

His hands are shaking. This thing has been eating at him

every day for twenty-five years. Long before Presley's black-mail began. God, how he must have sweated during the malpractice trial, worrying that Leo Marston would learn about Hillman's murder from Presley, his paid lackey. I saw this situation a hundred times as a prosecutor. A man lives morally all his life, then in one weak moment commits an act that damns him in his own eyes and threatens his liberty, even his life. Seeing my father in this trap unnerves me. And yet, to get him out of it, I am contemplating committing a felony myself.

'You're right,' I tell him. 'We've got to take the high road.'

'Talk to Mackey?'

'Yes. But I want to feel him out first. I'll call him tonight. Maybe stop by his house.'

'He won't be home. There's a party tonight, a fund-raiser for Wiley Warren.' Riley Warren – nickname 'Wiley' – is the incumbent mayor. 'Your mother and I were invited, but we weren't going to go.'

'Mackey will be there?'

'He's a big supporter of Warren's. You're invited, by the way.'

'By you?'

'No. By Don Perry, the surgeon hosting the party. He stopped me at the hospital after lunch and asked me to bring you along.'

'Why would he do that? Especially after the story in the paper?'

'Why do you think? It's a fund-raising party, and he thinks you're loaded.'

'That's it, then. I'll talk to Mackey there. If he sounds amenable, I'll set up a formal meeting, and we'll figure a way to sting Presley.'

Dad lays his hands on his desk to steady them. 'I can't believe it. After all this time . . . to finally *do* something about it.'

'We've got to do something about it. Life's too short to live like this.'

He closes his eyes, then opens them and stands up. 'I feel bad about the Paytons. I feel like we're buying me out of trouble by burying the truth about Del.'

This is true enough. But weighed against my father's freedom, Del Payton means nothing to me. Blood is a hell of a lot thicker than sympathy. 'You can't carry that around on your shoulders.'

'Back during the sixties,' he says, hanging his stethoscope on a coat rack, 'I was tempted to ask some of those Northern college kids over to the house. Give them some decent food, a little encouragement. But I never did. I knew what the risks were, and I was afraid to take them.'

'You had a wife and two kids. Don't beat yourself up over it.'

'I don't. But Del Payton had a wife and child too.'

'Mom told me you patched up two civil rights workers from Homewood after the doctor over there refused to do it. They were beaten half to death, she said.'

He looks disgusted. 'I did take the Hippocratic oath, goddamn it.'

'I guess that Homewood doctor forgot it.'

Anger and shame fill his eyes. 'It wasn't enough. What I did was not enough.'

I stand and take my keys out of my pocket. 'Nobody white did enough. Payton's killers will pay sooner or later. It just won't be me who makes them do it.'

Dad takes off his lab coat and hangs it on the rack. 'If you don't Penn, I don't think anybody else will.'

'So be it.'

Chapter 8

Dad and I are dressing for the Perry party – me in a sport jacket borrowed from his closet – when the phone rings beside his bed. He reaches for it without looking, the movement as automatic as scratching an itch.

'Dr. Cage,' he says, waiting for a description of symptoms or a plea for narcotics. His face goes slack, and he presses the phone against his undershirt. 'It's Shad Johnson.'

'Who's that?'

'The black candidate for mayor.'

'What does he want?'

'You. Want me to say you're not here?'

I reach for the receiver. 'This is Penn Cage.'

'Well, well,' says a precise male voice in the middle register, a voice more white than black. 'The prodigal son himself.'

I don't know how to respond. Then a fragment of Dad's thumbnail sketch of local politics comes to me: Shad Johnson moved home to Natchez from Chicago specifically to run for mayor. 'I hear the same could be said of you, Mr. Johnson.'

He laughs. 'Call me Shad.'

'How can I help you, Shad?'

'I'd like you to come see me for a few minutes. I'd come to you, but you might not want the neighbors thinking we're any closer than we are. News travels fast in this town. Like those Payton women coming to see you this morning.'

A wave of heat rolls up the back of my neck. 'I have no

intention of getting involved in local politics, Mr. Johnson.'

'You got involved the second you talked to the newspaper about Del Payton.'

'Consider me uninvolved.'

'I'd like nothing better. But we still need to talk.'

'We're talking now.'

'Face to face. I'm over at my campaign headquarters. You're not afraid to come to the north side of town, are you?'

'No.' My father is straining hard to hear both sides of the conversation. 'But I've got to be somewhere in an hour.'

'Not that fund-raiser for Wiley Warren, I hope?'

Shad Johnson obviously has the town wired. I'm about to beg off when he says, 'You and your family are in danger.'

I fight the impulse to overreact. 'What are you talking about?'

'I'll tell you when you get here.'

'Give me your address.'

'Martin Luther King Drive. It's a storefront setup, in a little strip mall.'

'Where's Martin Luther King Drive?'

'Pine Street,' Dad says, looking concerned.

'That old shopping center by the Brick House?' I ask, recalling a shadowy cinder-block bar I went to once with two black guys I spent a summer laying sewer pipe with.

'That's right. But it's not the Brick House anymore, just like it's not Pine Street anymore. Times change, counselor. You on your way?'

'Give me fifteen minutes.'

'What the hell did he want?' Dad asks, taking the phone from me and hanging it up.

'He said our family's in danger.'

'*What?*'

I tie my tie and walk to the bedroom door. 'Don't worry. I'll be back in forty-five minutes. We'll make the party in plenty of time.'

He gives me his trademark stern-father look. 'You'd better take a pistol with you.'

The north side looks nicer than it did when I was a boy. Back then it was a warren of shotgun shacks and dilapidated houses separated by vacant lots and condemned buildings, their walls patched with tin or even cardboard. Juke clubs operated out of private houses surrounded by men drinking from paper bags, and paint-and-body shops sagged amid herds of junk cars, looking like sets for *The Road Warrior*. Now there are rows of well-kept houses, a sparkling video store, a state-of-the-art Texaco station, good streetlights, smooth roads.

I swing into the parking lot of the strip mall and scan the storefronts: a styling salon, a fish market, an NAACP voter-registration center, a Sno-Cone stand thronged by black kids, and one newly painted front hung with a bright banner that reads, SHAD JOHNSON – THE FUTURE IS NOW.

An open-air barbecue pit built from a sawn-in-half fifty-five-gallon drum smokes like a barn fire outside the NAACP center, sending the aroma of chicken and pork ribs into the air. A knot of middle-aged black men stands around the pit drinking Colt .45 from quart bottles. They fall silent and watch with sullen suspicion as I get out of the BMW and approach Johnson's building. I nod to them and go inside.

A skinny young man wearing a three-piece suit that must be smothering him sits behind a metal desk, talking on a telephone. Behind the desk stands a wall-to-wall partition of whitewashed plywood with a closed door set in it. The young man looks up and motions me toward a battered church pew. I nod but remain standing, studying the partition, which is plastered with posters exhorting the public to vote for Shad

Johnson. Half show him wearing a dark suit and sitting behind a large desk, a model of conservatism and rectitude; the other half show a much younger-looking Johnson sporting a Malcolm X-style goatee and handing out pamphlets to teenagers on an urban playground. It isn't hard to guess which posters hang in which parts of town.

A voice rises over the partition. It has anger in it, but anger communicated with the perfect diction of a BBC news reader. As I try to get a fix on the words, the young assistant hangs up and disappears through the door. He returns almost instantly and signals me to follow him.

My first impression of Shad Johnson is of a man in motion. Before I can adequately focus on the figure sitting behind the desk, he is rising and coming around it, right hand extended. A few inches shorter than I, Johnson carries himself with the brash assurance of a personal-injury lawyer. He is light-skinned – not to a degree that would hurt him with the majority of black voters, but light enough that certain whites can reassure themselves about his achievements and aspirations by noting the presence of Caucasian blood. He shakes my hand with a natural politician's grip, firm and confident and augmented by a megawatt of eye contact.

'I'm glad you came,' he says in a measured tenor. 'Take a seat.'

He leads me to a folding chair across from his spartan metal desk, then sits atop the desk like a college professor and smiles. 'This is a long way from my office at Goldstein, Henry in Chicago.'

'Up or down?'

He laughs. 'Up, if I win.'

'And if you lose? Back to white-shoe law in Chicago?'

His smile slips for a nanosecond.

'You said my family is in danger, Mr. Johnson.'

'Shad, please. Short for Shadrach.'

'All right, Shad. Why is my family in danger?'

'Because of your sudden interest in a thirty-year-old murder.'

'I have no interest in the murder of Del Payton. And I intend to make a public statement to that effect as soon as possible.'

'I'm relieved to hear you say that. I must have taken fifty calls today asking what I'm doing to help you get to the bottom of it.'

'What did you tell them?'

'That I'm in the process of putting together the facts.'

'You didn't know the facts already?'

Johnson examines his fingernails, which look professionally manicured. 'I was born here, Mr. Cage, but I was sent north to prep school when I was eleven. Let's focus on the present, shall we? The Payton case is a sleeping dog. Best to let it lie.'

The situation is quickly clarifying itself. 'What if new evidence were to come to light that pointed to Payton's killer? Or killers?'

'That would be unfortunate.'

His candor surprises me. 'For local politicians, maybe. What about justice?'

'That kind of justice doesn't help my people.'

'And the Payton family? They're not your people?'

Johnson sighs like a man trying to hold an intelligent conversation with a two-year-old. 'If this case were to be dragged through the newspapers, it would whip white resentment in this town to a fever pitch. Black people can't afford that. Race relations isn't about laws and courts anymore. It's about attitudes. Perceptions. A lot of whites in Mississippi want to do the right thing. They felt the same way in the sixties. But every group has the instinct to protect its own. Liberals keep silent and protect rednecks for the same reason good doctors protect bad ones. It's a tribal reaction. You've got to let those whites find their way to the good place. Suddenly Del Payton is the biggest obstacle I can see to that.'

'I suppose whites get to that good place by voting for Shad Johnson?'

'You think Wiley Warren's helping anybody but himself?'

'I'm not Warren's biggest fan, but I've heard some good things about his tenure.'

'You hear he's a drunk? That he can't keep his dick in his pants? That he's in the pocket of the casino companies?'

'You have evidence?'

'It's tough to get evidence when he controls the police.'

'There are plenty of black cops on the force.'

Johnson's phone buzzes. He frowns, then hits a button and picks up the receiver. 'Shad Johnson,' he says in his clipped Northern accent. Five seconds later he cries 'My brother!' and begins chattering in the frenetic musical patois of a Pine Street juke, half words and grunts and wild bursts of laughter. Noticing my stare, he winks as if to say: *Look how smoothly I handle these fools.*

As he hangs up, his assistant sticks his head in the door. 'Line two.'

'No more calls, Henry.'

'It's Julian Bond.'

Johnson sniffs and shoots his cuffs. 'I've got to take this.'

Now he's the urbane attorney again, sanguine and self-effacing. He and Bond discuss the coordination of black celebrity appearances during the final weeks of Johnson's mayoral campaign. Stratospheric names are shuffled like charms on a bracelet. Jesse. Denzel. Whitney. General Powell. Kweisi Mfume. When the candidate hangs up, I shake my head.

'You're obviously a man of many talents. And faces.'

'I'm a chameleon,' Johnson admits. 'I've got to be. You know you have to play to your jury, counselor, and I've got a pretty damn diverse one here.'

'I guess running for office in this town is like fighting a two-front war.'

'*Two*-front war? Man, this town has more factions than the Knesset. Redneck Baptists, rich liberals, yellow dog Democrats, middle-class blacks, young fire eaters, Uncle Toms, and bone-dumb bluegums working the bottomland north of town. It's like conducting a symphony with musicians who hate each other.'

'I'm a little surprised by your language. You sound like winning is a lot more important to you than helping your people.'

'Who can I help if I lose?'

'How long do you figure on sticking around city hall if you win?'

A bemused smile touches Johnson's lips. 'Off the record? Just long enough to build a statewide base for the gubernatorial race.'

'You want to be governor?'

'I want to be president. But governor is a start. When a nigger sits in the governor's mansion in Jackson, Mississippi, the Civil War will truly have been won. The sacrifices of the Movement will have been validated. Those bubbas in the legislature won't know whether to shit or go blind. This whole country will shake on its foundations!'

Johnson's opportunistic style puts me off, but I see the logic in it. 'I suppose the black man who could turn Mississippi around would be a natural presidential candidate.'

'You can thank Bill Clinton for pointing the way. Arkansas? Shit. Mississippi is fiftieth in education, fiftieth in economic output, highest in illegitimate births, second highest in welfare payments, the list is endless. Hell, we're fifty-*first* in some things – behind Puerto Rico! I turn that around – just a *little* – I could whip Colin Powell hands down.'

'How can you turn this town around? Much less the state?'

'Factories! Industry! A four-year college. Four-lane highways linking us to Jackson and Baton Rouge.'

'Everybody wants that. What makes you think you can get it?'

Johnson laughs like I'm the original sucker. 'You think the white elite that runs this town wants industry? The money here likes things just the way they are. They've got their private golf course, segregated neighborhoods, private schools, no traffic problem, black maids and yard men working minimum wage, and just one smokestack dirtying up their sunset. This place is on its way to being a retirement community. The Boca Raton of Mississippi.'

'Boca Raton is a rich city.'

'Well, this is a mostly poor one. One factory closed down and two working half capacity. Oil business all but dead, and every well in the county drilled by a white man. Tourism doesn't help my people. Rich whites or segregated garden clubs own the antebellum mansions. That tableau they have every year, where the little white kids dance around in hoop skirts for the Yankees? You got a couple of old mammies selling pralines outside and black cops directing traffic. You see any people or color at the balls they have afterward? The biggest social events in town, and not a single black face except the bartenders.'

'Most whites aren't invited to those balls either.'

'Don't think I'm not pointing that out in the appropriate quarters.'

'Mayor Warren doesn't pursue industry?'

'Wiley Warren thinks riverboat gambling is our salvation. The city takes in just over a million dollars from that steamboat under the hill, while the boat drains away thirty million to Las Vegas. With that kind of prosperity, this town will be dead in five years.'

I glance at my watch. 'I thought you brought me here to warn me.'

'I'm trying to. For the first time in fifty years we've got a major corporation ready to locate a world-class factory here. And you're trying to flush that deal right down the toilet.'

'What I said in the paper won't stop any company serious about locating here.'

'You're wrong. BASF is a German company. They may be racists themselves, but they're very sensitive to racial issues in foreign countries.'

'And?'

'They have concerns about the school system here.'

'The school system?'

'The public school is eighty percent black. The population's only fifty percent black. BASF's management won't put their employees into a situation where they have to send their kids to expensive and segregated private schools for a decent education. They have to be convinced that the public schools are safe and of excellent quality.'

'And is that the case?'

'They're safe enough, but the quality's not the best. We've established a fragile consensus and convinced BASF that the public school is viable. We've developed all sorts of pilot programs. Those Germans are damn near committed to build here. But if the Payton case explodes in the media, BASF will crawfish so fast we'll finally hear that giant sucking sound Ross Perot always whined about.'

I hold up my hands. 'I have no interest in the case. I made a couple of comments and attracted the attention of Payton's family. End of story.'

As Johnson smiles with satisfaction, my defensive tone suddenly disgusts me. 'But I'll tell you this. The harder people try to push me away from something, the more I feel like maybe I ought to take a look at it.'

He leans back and eyes me with cold detachment. 'I'd think long and hard before I did that. Your little girl has already lost one parent.'

The words hit me like a slap. 'Why do I get the feeling *you* might be the danger you warned me about?'

He gives me a taut smile. 'I'm just trying to do you a favor, brother. This town looks placid, but it's a powder keg. Drop by McDonald's or the Wal-Mart deli and watch the black workers serve blacks before whites who got there first. Blacks are angry here, but they don't know how to channel their frustration. What you've got here are blacks descended from those who were too dumb to head north after the Civil War or the world wars. No self-awareness. They take things out on whitey however they can. A while back, some black kids started shooting at white people's cars. Killed a young father. There's a white backlash coming, and when it comes, there's enough resentment among black teenagers to start a war. That's what you're playing with. Not to mention whoever killed Del Payton. You know those cracker bastards are still out there somewhere.'

'Sounds to me like Del Payton died in vain.'

'Payton was a paving stone in the road to freedom. No more, no less. And right now he's best honored by leaving him lie.'

I stand, my face hot. 'I've got to be somewhere.'

'When you get to your party, tell Wiley Warren I'm going to whip his lily-white ass.'

I pause at the door and look back. Johnson already has the phone in his hand.

'I think you're underestimating blacks in this town,' I tell him. 'They're smarter than you give them credit for. They see more than you think.'

'Such as?'

'They can see you're not one of them.'

'Don't kid yourself, Cage. I'm Moses, cast onto the waters as a child and raised by the enemy. I *prospered* among the mighty and now return to *show my people the way*!'

In an instant the candidate's voice has taken on the Old

Testament cadence and power of a young Martin Luther King.

As I gape, he adds in his mincing lawyer's voice: 'Next time come over to campaign headquarters south. It's on Main Street. The atmosphere's more your style. Genteel and Republican, the way the old white ladies like it. Over there I'm a house nigger made good.'

Johnson is still laughing when I leave the building.

The sky is deep purple, the warm night falling to a soundtrack of kicked cans, honking horns, shouting children, and squealing tires. The smell of chicken sizzling on the open pit pulls my head in that direction. Two black teenagers on banana bikes whizz toward me as I stand beside the BMW. I'm about to wave when one spits on the hood of my car and zips past, disappearing into a cloud of dark laughter. I start to yell after them, then think better of it. I did not bring the pistol my father advised me to, and I don't need to start the riot Shad Johnson just warned me about. I get into the BMW, start it, and head south toward the white section of town.

I've hardly begun to reflect on Johnson's words when I notice the silhouette of a police car behind me. Blinding headlights obscure its driver, but the light bar on the roof leaves no doubt that it's a cop. As he pulls within fifteen yards of my rear bumper and hangs there, it hits me. I'm driving a seventy-five-thousand-dollar car in the black section of town. Some eager white cop is probably running my father's plate right now, checking to see whether the BMW has been reported stolen. As we pass in tandem under a street lamp, I notice that the vehicle is not a police car but a sheriff's cruiser. A sickening wave of adrenaline pulses through me as I wait for the flare of red lights, the scream of a siren.

Somewhere along here, this road becomes Linda Lee Mead Drive, named for Natchez's Miss America. As I top the hill leading down to the junction with Highway 61, the cruiser pulls out and roars past me. I glance to my left, hoping to get a look at the driver.

The man behind the wheel is black.

He is fifty yards past me when both front windows of the BMW explode out of their frames, shattering into a thousand pieces. I whip my head to the right, trying to shield my eyes. My eardrums throb from sudden depressurization, and I instinctively slam on the brakes. As the back end of the car skids around, something hammers my door, sending a shock wave up my left thigh. The car comes to rest facing the right shoulder, blocking both lanes of the road. In the silence of the dead engine, the reality of my situation hits me.

Someone is shooting at me.

Frantically cranking the car, I notice the brake lights of the sheriff's cruiser glowing red at the bottom of the hill, a hundred yards away.

It's just sitting there.

As my engine catches, two bullets smash through the rear windshield, turning it to starred chaos. I throw the BMW into gear, stomp the accelerator, whip around, and start down the hill. Before I've gone thirty yards, the sheriff's cruiser pulls onto the highway and races off toward town.

'*Stop!*' I shout, honking my horn. '*Stop, goddamn it!*'

But he doesn't stop. The rifle must have made a tremendous noise, though I don't remember hearing it. Maybe the exploding glass distracted me. But the black deputy in the cruiser *must* have heard it. Unless the weapon was silenced. This thought is too chilling to dwell on for long, since silenced weapons are much rarer in life than in movies, and indicate a high level of determination on the part of the shooter. But if the deputy didn't hear the shots, why did he stop so long? There was no traffic at the intersection. For a moment I wonder if he could have fired the shots himself, but physics rules that out. The first bullet came through the driver's window, while the deputy was fifty yards in front of me. The last two smashed the back windshield after the skid exposed it to the same side of the road.

My heart still tripping like an air hammer, I turn onto Highway 61, grab the cell phone, and dial 911. Before the first ring fades, I click End. Anything I say on a cell phone could be all over town within hours. The odds of catching the shooter are zero by now, and my father's blackmail situation makes me more than a little reluctant to bring the police into our lives at this point.

Shad Johnson's words echo in my head like a prophecy: *A while back, some black kids started shooting at white people's cars. Killed a father of three.* But this shooting was not random. This morning's newspaper article upset a lot of people – white people exclusively, I would have thought, until Shad Johnson disabused me of that notion. What the hell is going on? Johnson warns me that my family is in danger but gives no specifics, and ten minutes later I'm shot at on the highway? *After* being followed by a black deputy who doesn't stop to check out the shooting?

Whoever was behind that rifle meant to kill me. But I can do nothing about it now. I'm less than a mile from my parents' house, and my priority is clear: within an hour I will be talking to the district attorney about my father's involvement in a murder case, and deciding how best to sting Ray Presley, a known killer.

Chapter 9

'Tom Cage, you dog! I can't believe you came!'

In small towns the most beautiful women are married, and Lucy Perry proves the rule. Ten years younger than her husband – the surgeon hosting the party – Lucy has large brown eyes and a high-maintenance muscularity shown to perfection in a black silk dress that drapes just below her shapely knees. She also has suspiciously high cleavage for a forty-year-old mother of three, which I know she is, having been given a social update by my father on the way over to the party. Lucy uses the sorority squeal mode of greeting, which is always a danger in Mississippi. She flashes one of the brightest smiles I've seen off a magazine cover and throws her arm around my father.

'I'm here for the free liquor,' Dad says. 'Not for Wiley Warren to pick my pocket.'

Lucy has a contagious laugh, and Dad has drawn it out. He's one of the few people honest enough to use the mayor's nickname within earshot of the man himself. Now Lucy looks at me as though she's just set eyes on me.

'So *this* is the famous author.'

I offer my hand. 'Pleased to meet you, Mrs. Perry.'

'Mrs. Perry? For God's sake, *Lucy*.' She steps inside my proffered hand and draws me to her in a one-armed hug that lasts long enough for me to learn that she's been drinking gin without much tonic and that her breasts are not original architecture. 'I've *forbidden* anyone to mention that awful newspaper story. No one believes anything they read in the *Examiner* anyway.'

The house is full of people, and it's some house. Though not one of Natchez's premier mansions, it would easily fetch nine or ten million dollars in Los Angeles. A brass plaque announces that it is on the National Register of Historic Places. The interior has been meticulously restored at a cost of countless gall bladders and appendices. A wide hallway bisects the ground floor, with arched doorways leading to capacious rooms on both sides. Of the fifty or so faces in the hallway I recognize about a quarter. People I went to school with, friends of my parents, a half dozen doctors I know. I give a broad wave to cover the group. Many nod or smile in acknowledgment, but no one approaches. Caitlin Masters's article has done its work. I stick close to Dad as we work our way toward the bar table at the end of the hall.

As Shad Johnson predicted, the only black faces in the house belong to white-jacketed bartenders and maids, who circulate with heaping platters of hors d'oeuvres.

'Bourbon and water, Roosevelt,' Dad tells the bartender. 'Easy on the water. Penn?'

'Gin and tonic.'

The bartender grins. 'Good to see you, Dr. Cage.'

Dad and I jump as a boom rattles the windowpanes behind the bar table. Terror grips me until a trombone, trumpet, and double bass join the thundering drum kit and reorient me to normalcy. A black Dixieland jazz band is performing on the patio. There are no dancers. It's too damned hot to dance on a patio. It's too damned hot to be playing music out there too, but Lucy and her hubby aren't worried about the musicians.

Dad squeezes my arm and leans toward me. 'Think they were gunning for you again?'

I try to laugh it off, but both of us are nervous as cats. He agreed with my decision not to report the shooting to the police, but he insisted on bringing a pistol to the party. He's wearing it in an ankle holster.

I turn and pan the hall again. At the far end, beyond the talking heads, Lucy Perry opens the front door and pulls a young woman inside. I feel a little jolt when I recognize Caitlin Masters. She's wearing a strapless jade dress with sandals, and her black hair is swept up from her neck. As she steps aside for Lucy to close the door, I spy the rebellious flash of a gold anklet above one sandal. How do I feel about her? Angry that she printed something I considered off the record. But I can't help admiring her for shaking up our complacent town a little.

A blustering male voice pulls my attention to the staircase, where Wiley Warren stands dispensing political wisdom to seven or eight smiling listeners. Warren is a natural bull-shitter, an ex-jock with enough brains to indulge his prodigious appetites within a younger group that admires his excesses and keeps his secrets like JFK's press corps. Dad says he's done a fairly good job as mayor, but nothing he's accomplished thus far would compare to getting the BASF plant, a deal which would secure his political future.

'The reason Shad Johnson isn't making race an issue,' Warren crows, 'is that he's damn near white as I am.'

This is vintage Wiley. The crowd chuckles encouragement.

'Ol' Shadrach went off to prep school with the Yankees when he was eleven, and didn't come back till he was forty and ready to run for mayor. He's no more a representative of his people than Bryant Gumbel!'

'Who *does* he represent?' someone calls.

'Himself, of course.'

'So he's just like you,' says a gastroenterologist whose name I can't recall.

Warren laughs louder than anyone, tacitly admitting the self-interest that drives all politicians and which Southern voters prefer to see in the open rather than cloaked in hypocrisy. Brutal honesty in such matters is part of the mayor's charm.

I am about to go in search of Austin Mackey, the district attorney, when I spot him at the edge of the group listening to the mayor. He motions for me to follow him to some chairs in an empty corner. Mackey was a year ahead of me in school from kindergarten through college. A perennial middle-of-the-class kid, he managed to make most athletic teams but never the first string. His grades were unremarkable, and I'm pretty sure he chose Ole Miss Law School so he wouldn't have to pass the bar exam in order to practice in Mississippi, a rule they changed the year after he went into practice.

'Any particular reason you came home and shat in our little sandbox?' he asks as we sit.

This is not a fortuitous beginning. 'Good to see you again, Austin.'

'Skip the sentiment, Cage.' He keeps his eyes on the mayor.

Watching Austin Mackey play the tough throws me a little. But Natchez is his legal fiefdom now, and if he chooses to behave like George Raft in a bad film noir, he can.

'Look, Austin, about that article. Caitlin Masters didn't exactly–'

'Earth to Cage, give me a fucking break. By now every jig in this town is bitching about how Austin Mackey never lifted a finger to help Mrs. Payton find out who killed her poor baby.'

I don't know how to segue from this to warm reminiscences of our shared history. Mackey seems to have forgotten we have one. 'I just mentioned the Payton case as an example of a local mystery. Because it was an unsolved murder.'

Mackey's eyes glint with superiority. 'Don't be so sure about that.'

'What do you mean?'

'The FBI worked the Payton case. You think they tanked it? Just because no one went to jail for that particular crime doesn't mean the perp didn't go down for something.'

'If that's the case, why not tell the family? Give them some peace.'

'I can't tell them what I don't know for sure. Listen, when I ran for D.A., I knew the blacks might ask me about past civil rights cases. So I asked the Bureau for their files on the Payton murder. I was assistant D.A. then, and I requisitioned them in the name of the office.'

'And?'

'They said that unless we'd developed a suspect and had new evidence, they wouldn't be showing our office any files.'

'Why would they say that?'

'Can I read the mind of J. Edgar Hoover?'

'Hoover? He's been dead twenty-five years.'

'Well, his spirit's alive and well. Hoover made the final decisions on the disposition of those civil rights cases. And he worked them hard, especially the murders up in Neshoba County. But it's no secret that his personal agenda had nothing to do with advancing civil rights. He hated Martin Luther King and the Kennedys. Cases like Payton's were nothing to him but chips in a political game.'

'What about your office file?'

'There isn't one. No one was ever charged with the crime.'

'Have you looked?'

'I don't need to.' He finally meets my eyes. 'Let's get this straight right now. Unless you're the attorney of record for a member of the Payton family, you'll receive zero assistance from my office. And since you're not licensed in this state, that pretty much settles things.'

Actually, I am licensed to practice in Mississippi, but I see no reason to point this out now. And though my combative instincts urge me to tell Mackey that a single phone call could secure my position as attorney for the Payton family, concern for my father stops me.

'You really get to me, Cage,' Mackey goes on before I can change the subject. 'Mr. St. Stephens, law review at Texas, big-time author. You've got nothing better to do than come back here and make your old schoolmates look like assholes?'

Bitterness and envy literally crackle off the man. I am so surprised that I can do little but apologize. 'That wasn't my intention, Austin.'

'I'd hate to see what would happen if you really meant some harm.'

'What would you say if I told you I was shot at by a sniper less than an hour ago?'

His head snaps up. 'Were you?'

'Yes.'

'Did you report it?'

'Not yet.'

His eyes are like signs reading, *Thank God for small favors.* 'Where did this happen?'

'The black section, Linda Lee Drive.'

'What the hell were you doing over there?'

'Shad Johnson wanted to talk to me.'

'Jesus.' The muscles in Mackey's jaw tighten. 'What did he say?'

'He warned me off the Payton case.'

An ironic smile. 'Shad's no fool. The election's five weeks off, and the polls have him and Warren neck and neck.'

'That's all you have to say about an attempt on my life?'

'You're back in Mississippi, bubba. You piss people off, they're going to hit back. Anyway, it's pretty obvious which side you're on.'

I sip my drink. Melting ice has drowned the gin. 'I'm not on any side.'

'Then you've forgotten the primary political reality of your home state.'

'Which is?'

'There's no middle ground. Whatever's there gets crushed to powder by the sides. I'd pick one quick if I were you.'

Mackey stands abruptly and drifts back into watchful orbit around his candidate. The conversation couldn't have gone any worse if I'd set out to make him hate my guts. This is the man upon whose mercy I advised my father to throw himself?

I stand and walk into the hallway, half looking for Dad and half aiming for the bar. I'm almost to the alcohol when a powerful hand closes on my shoulder and a voice whispers in my ear: '*Don't move, you outside agitatin' son of a bitch.*'

I whirl, ready for anything, only to find the laughing bearded face of Sam Jacobs, whom I've known since we were five years old.

'A little nervous, are we?' Sam wiggles his black eyebrows up and down. 'Wishing we'd been a little less candid with the fourth estate?'

I punch him in the chest, then hug him hard.

When Sam and I were tenth-graders at St. Stephens, an assistant football coach invited the varsity football team to establish a chapter of the Brotherhood of Christian Athletes at the school. While the rest of the team lined up to get the necessary applications, two boys remained in the otherwise empty bleachers: Penn Cage and Sam Jacobs. As a Jew, Sam was barred from membership. And I – ever since walking out of Episcopal communion at age thirteen – was a devout agnostic. Under the suspicious gaze of teammates and coaches, Sam and I left that meeting joined in a way that had more to do with manhood than football ever would. Now a petroleum geologist, Jacobs is one of only three non-family members who flew to Houston for Sarah's funeral.

'It's great to see you, Sam. What are you doing at this tight-ass function?'

He grins. 'I've sold Don Perry enough Wilcox production to qualify him as a certified oil maggot.'

'So, that's how he paid for this palace. You must be doing well.'

'I ain't complaining. When the bottom dropped out of the drilling business, I slid over into production. Bought up old wells, worked them over, got them running full bore, and sold out at an obscene profit. It's getting harder to find wells, though. Everybody's into it now.'

'I'm sure whatever happens, you'll be the guy sitting on top of the pile.'

'The last guy clinging to the limb, more like.' Sam sips his drink. 'How does it feel?'

'What?'

'Having everybody in the place stare at you.'

'I'm pretty used to the fishbowl lifestyle now.'

'Natchez is a lot smaller bowl than Houston. Even small waves seem big here.'

'Come off it. A week from now, who'll give a damn about that article?'

'Everybody, ace. How much do you know about the BASF deal?'

I shrug. 'A little.'

'That chemical plant means salvation to a lot of people. Not just blue-collar either. These doctors need patients with private insurance to keep the gravy train running. Everybody's on their best behaviour, trying to sell Natchez as a Southern utopia. We're pushing our opera festival, the literary celebration, the hot-air balloon race. And this morning you tossed a toad right into the punch bowl.'

I glance around the room and instantly find what I'm looking for: Caitlin Masters, deep in conversation with two older men. 'You see that girl?'

Sam cranes his neck. 'Caitlin Masters?'

'You know her?'

'I know she's fine as wine and worth a few million bucks.'

'She printed a little more than I intended her to.'

'Fess up, man. You were just being you. At your pompous best.'

'That's what Dad said.'

'Speaking of your old man, I'm surprised he came.'

Before I can ask what Sam means, someone taps me on the shoulder. Sam hides a smile behind his drink. I turn and look into the luminous green eyes of Caitlin Masters.

'Are you going to slug me?' she asks.

'If you were male, I might consider it.'

'I know I angled that story in a way you didn't expect.'

'*Angled* it? Try sensationalized it. Remember the words "off-the-record"?'

Her lips part slightly in surprise. 'I honoured that request.'

'About the Hanratty execution. But as for Del Payton—' I force myself to shut up, not wanting to argue the point in front of a crowd.

'Why don't we have lunch tomorrow?' she suggests. 'I'd like to help you understand why I did what I did.'

I want to say no, but just as yesterday, something about Caitlin Masters makes me want to see her again. The jade dress is linen, and it lies against her skin like powder. She is a study in elegance and self-possession.

'Is that a no?' she asks.

'Once burned, twice shy,' Sam chimes in.

'I like Wilde's quote better,' Caitlin rejoins.

'What's that?' I ask.

'The burnt child loves the fire.'

She winks at me, then turns on her heel and walks away, ignoring the gazes of half the people in the room, who have watched our exchange with intense interest.

'You sure know how to liven up a town,' Sam says, his eyes glued to Caitlin's retreating form. 'And she knows how to fill out a dress. A *shiksa* from dreamland, that one.'

I step hard on his toe. 'You already married one of those, remember? What were you saying about my dad?'

'I'm surprised he came, is all.'

'Why?'

'Because I'm pretty sure Judge Marston is on the guest list.'

I feel a sliding sensation in my stomach. A quick survey of the room yields no sign of either Marston or my father. Squeezing Sam's shoulder, I push off through the crowd. Natchez is a funny town. People involved in running feuds frequently socialize together. Men who've gutted each other in business disputes leave their rancor at the doors of certain seasonal soirées, and it's not unheard of to see a woman who has caught her husband in bed with someone else pouring punch for that woman – or man – at a party.

Leo Marston and Tom Cage are different. The judge once made it his mission to try to ruin my father's medical career, and Dad hates him with a fury that will brook no false bonhomie. He behaves, in fact, as though the judge were dead. Since Dad rarely goes anywhere other than his office or the hospitals, he rarely crosses paths with Marston, making that illusion easy to maintain. But if Sam Jacobs is correct, that might change tonight. Dad has already drunk one bourbon, probably two by now. If Marston provokes him, Dad is capable of swinging on him. With that thought my blood pressure plummets, because with it comes the memory that my father is carrying a gun tonight.

Catching sight of a silver head a few inches taller than the others near the bar, I move quickly forward, take Dad's arm, and pull him into the kitchen. It's empty save for a black maid, who smiles and nods when she sees us.

'What's going on?' He takes a sip of his bourbon and water *sans* water.

'Judge Marston's on the guest list. He may already be here.'

Dad blinks. Then his cheeks turn red. 'Where is he?'

'Dad, this isn't the time or the place.'

'Why not? I've avoided that SOB too many years already.' His breathing is shallow, and his motions have a jerky quality that might be the result of anger or alcohol.

'That's the whiskey talking. You're a hundred percent right about Marston, but if you talk to him now, you're going to hit him.' *Or shoot him.* 'And I'll have to spend all my time at home defending you on a battery charge. That's after I bail you out.'

'What do you want me to do? Leave?'

'Considering what we have to do in the next few days, I think you should.'

That brutal reminder of the blackmail situation gets his attention.

'What about talking to Mackey?' he asks.

'I already did. And this isn't the place to discuss it.'

His eyes flit back and forth; then he dashes his plastic cup against the stainless steel sink. 'Goddamn it. Let's go.'

'Stay close to me.'

I take his forearm, lead him into the hallway, and freeze. Twenty yards away, in the open front door, stand Judge Marston and his wife, Maude. The odds of getting through that door without anyone making a smart remark are zero. I drag Dad back toward the kitchen.

'Where the hell are we going now?'

'The back door's closer to where I parked.'

'You saw Marston, didn't you?'

He tries to pull free. I tighten my grip and hustle him toward the back door, knowing that if he really tries to resist me, I won't be able to stop him.

'Goddamn it, I'm not running!'

'That's right, you're not. You're taking the advice of your lawyer.'

'You're not licensed in this state.'

'Actually, I took the Mississippi bar exam when I

graduated, and I've paid the licensing fee every year.'

He is so distracted by this information that he allows himself to be pulled through a side garden to the street.

'Here's the car.' I unlock my mother's Maxima – the damaged BMW having been consigned to the garage – and practically push him into the driver's seat.

He looks up at me, eyes anxious. 'You felt Mackey out?'

'Yes. It was like feeling out a porcupine. We're going to have to go the other way.'

'What other way?'

'We're going to have to buy the gun.'

He blinks in disbelief. 'Christ. Are you sure?'

'It's the only way. I want you to call Ray Presley at ten in the morning. Tell him I'll be at his place at ten-thirty. That doesn't give him enough time to get the police involved.'

Dad looks down at the steering wheel. 'Goddamn it, if anyone has to do this, it should be me.'

'You've been under Presley's thumb too long. He'd never buy your bluff. Do you have a hundred thousand dollars liquid?'

He looks up, helpless with rage. 'It'll cost a fortune in penalties, but I can get it. And I won't have a damn cent to pay the IRS in January.'

'Don't worry, I'll pay you back. But there's no point in creating a paper trail to me yet. Have the money at your office as early as you can. I'll pick it up. I may not offer Presley the whole hundred grand, but I need to be able to go up to that.'

He looks too dazed to keep track of this. 'Well . . . get in. We'll get it all figured out.'

'I'm not coming, Dad.'

'What?'

'I want to talk to Sam Jacobs about Presley. Sam knows everything that goes on in this town. Have you got everything straight?'

He takes a deep breath and nods slowly. 'I'll have the money waiting. Ray too.'

'Good. Now, go home and get some sleep. And don't speed. The last thing you need tonight is a DWI.'

He gives me a somber salute, then shuts the door, starts the engine, and pulls slowly away. I stand at the curb and watch the taillights wink out as he hooks around the block to get headed home on the downtown streets, which are all one-way.

After years of putting men into prison – even into their graves – for committing crimes, I am about to cross the legal line myself. Tomorrow morning I am going to risk prison, forced separation from my child, to try to spare my father the same fate. That knowledge simmers in my stomach like a bad meal, acid and portentous. Is it the right thing to do? Is it stupid? Ultimately, it does not matter.

It's the only thing I can do.

Chapter 10

As I pass through the wrought-iron gate of the Perry garden, I see a figure standing at the foot of the steps leading to the side door of the mansion, and the orange eye of a cigarette burning in the dark.

The shrubs and trees in the garden are lighted with white Christmas lights, like little stars. Nearing the steps, I realize that the figure is Caitlin Masters. She's rocking slightly to the rhythm of 'Don't Get Around Much Anymore' wafting from the back of the house. I stop a few feet from her.

'I didn't know you smoked.'

She blows a stream of smoke away from me. 'I don't. You're hallucinating. Is your father okay?'

'He had an emergency call. So, you only smoke at parties?'

'Only when I'm bored.'

She doesn't look bored. She looks like she's been waiting for me. 'Are there many people in town your age?'

She cuts her eyes at me. 'You mean men?'

'I guess I did.'

'*Nada.* It's a desert.' She stubs out the cigarette with her sandal and takes a sip of her drink. It looks like white wine, but it's not in a wineglass, and in the dim light has a tinge of green.

'Is that Mountain Dew?'

'God, no. It's a gimlet. Gin and Rose's lime juice. Raymond Chandler turned me on to them.'

The Chandler reference surprises me. I'm starting to suspect that Caitlin Masters is full of surprises.

'You know the book?' she asks.

'*The Long Goodbye.*'

'Very good. For that, I'll tell you a little secret I learned today. Interested?'

'Sure.'

'Remember I told you about the Sovereignty Commission files? How forty-two of them are sealed for security reasons?'

'Yes.'

'One of my reporters requested a Sovereignty Commission file today, and I was more than a little surprised to learn that it was one of the forty-two.'

I think for a minute. 'Not Del Payton?'

She nods. 'I thought you'd be interested.'

'Surprised, anyway.'

'I saw you talking to the D.A. inside. Anything I should know about?'

'He's just an old school friend.'

'He didn't look too friendly.'

Caitlin Masters doesn't miss anything. I wonder what she would do if she knew her story had got me shot at tonight. Probably tear into the story like a bulldog.

'You're dangerous, aren't you?'

She laughs softly and pulls a loose thread of linen from the front of her strapless dress. Her shoulders are lean and ghostly white in the shadows, accenting the long, graceful lines of her neck.

'I try to be. You're sure you won't reconsider lunch tomorrow? I promise to show a little remorse about the articles.'

Her tone is casual enough, but there is more in it than hunger for a story. Her steady gaze has nothing to do with the words she spoke. Whatever I felt when we touched after the interview yesterday, she felt too. Between us floats a curious longing to feel that shock again, that aliveness. Without preamble she reaches out with her free hand and takes my right, her eyes unwavering. Her hand is cool, but a rush of warmth runs up my arm.

She smiles. 'Feels good, doesn't it?'

It's only her hand, but the intimacy of her touch is undeniable. It's been so long since I've had any physical contact with a woman that it almost paralyzes me. Sarah's illness made it impossible at the end, and in the months since her death I've felt no response at all to the flirtations of the women I've met. It's as though the sexual component of my personality, once dominant, has been wrapped in so many layers of guilt and grief that the prospect of having to work through them with someone new discourages me from even trying. But with one simple gesture Caitlin Masters has cut through all of that.

'I suppose I'm being forward,' she says. 'By Southern standards anyway.'

The urge to kiss her is a living thing inside my chest, and with it returns the guilt I felt yesterday, magnified a hundredfold. I close my eyes and squeeze her hand, fighting and savoring the pleasure at the same time. As though bidden by my thoughts, her lips brush mine.

When I open my eyes, hers are only inches away, green and wide, full of curiosity. She closes them, rises on tiptoe, and presses her lips to mine, sending another thrill of heat through me. From the first moment it is a knowing kiss, not the timid tasting of strangers, but the self-assured encounter of lovers who recognize each other. Her tongue is warm against mine, her lips cool. My senses read every curve and valley beneath the linen, and my arousal is immediate. Immediate and obvious. I slip my hand into the small of her back and for a moment kiss her as I truly want to, and the passion of her response explodes the boundaries I had perceived around us. As she kisses me, I feel something shift deep in my soul, a heavy door, and whatever stirs behind that door is too powerful to set free here, in this place. I break the kiss.

'Well,' she says with a laugh, 'I guess that answers that question.'

'Which question?'

'Did we really feel something yesterday.'

Her cheeks are flushed, and part of her hair has fallen around her neck. She points at the edge of the flower bed beside us, where her gimlet glass lies in the monkey grass. 'I dropped my drink.'

'I'm sorry, Caitlin.'

'I can get another one.'

'I mean for getting so . . . you know.'

She shakes her head. 'I liked it. Hey, you didn't break any laws here. You look like you saw a ghost.' Her smile vanishes. 'You did see a ghost, God, I'm such an ass sometimes.'

'It's all right.'

She takes my hand again. 'This just happened, okay? Nobody's fault. We'll just be friends, if you want.'

'This is unfamiliar territory for me.'

'We're the only ones out here, Penn. Everything's fine.' She reaches behind her neck to pin her hair back up. 'Do you need a ride home?'

'No. I need to talk to Sam Jacobs. He'll give me a ride. Thanks, though.'

She releases my hand and gives me the kind of encouraging smile you give a sick friend, then walks up the steps ahead of me. As she turns the doorknob, I reach out and touch her elbow. 'I do think that lunch would be nice, though.'

She turns and smiles. 'Same place?'

'Works for me. Twelve?'

'I'll meet you there.'

She opens the veneered door and goes inside, and I follow, watching her wend her way through the crowd in the hall, drawing looks from most of the women and all of the men. A woman that beautiful and perceptive hasn't been seen in these precincts for quite some time. Not since Livy Marston came back from the University of Virginia to serve as Queen of the Confederate Pageant.

At Caitlin disappears into one of the great rooms, I detour out of the hallway to search for Sam. The first room I enter is relatively empty, but the arched proscenium leading to the next is completely blocked by a semi-circle of men and women. I move closer to the line of backs, then freeze.

The focus of their attention is Judge Leo Marston.

The mere sight of him raises my temperature a couple of degrees, from anger mostly, but also – though I hate to admit it – from a residue of fear. Most of the men I knew as a boy I outgrew during high school, and they seem small to me now. Leo Marston still has three inches on me, and age has not diminished his physical presence. He must be nearly seventy by now, but he looks as though he could outfight any man here. With bulk in proportion to his height, he dwarfs the men standing in his audience. He masks his rawboned body in bespoke suits shipped to him once a year from London, but his outsized hands betray the power beneath. Like my father, Marston has kept his hair through the years, and he wears it in a steel-gray brush cut reminiscent of the leading men of the 1950s. When I was younger, I thought of him as an oversized Lee Marvin with a patina of Southern refinement. But no amount of refinement can conceal the animal alertness of his eyes. The irises are ice blue with gray rims, giving him a wolfish aspect, and they never settle anywhere for long. In moments they will pick me from the crowd.

I step behind a tall man to my right, removing myself from Leo's line of sight. Still, his mellifluous basso carries to me without losing any volume to distance. It's one of his most formidable weapons as an attorney, second only to his intellect. The timbre of that voice is graven forever in the circuits of my brain. Twenty years ago I listened to it accuse my father of negligence bordering on murder, first indirectly, as Marston tried to draw out testimony from reluctant nurses and technicians, then directly, like an inquisitor, as he cross-examined Dad on the stand. I took two weeks off from college to attend the trial, and by the second Friday I was ready to confront Marston on his way home from court and put a bullet through his heart.

'My point,' Marston is saying, 'is that the Germans are either at your feet or at your throat. We have to let BASF know that while we *want* them to locate here, we won't grovel.'

'But we will,' someone says. 'And they know it.'

Everyone laughs, then stops abruptly when they see that Marston does not share their humour.

'It all comes down to dollars,' he says in a cold voice. 'That's when you find out who needs whom. And that remains to be settled.'

He continues in this line, tantalizing the men with his inside knowledge and the women with his references to money. When people speak of 'old Natchez families,' they mean the Marstons. Leo's great-great grandfather, Albert Marston, owned a massive cotton plantation in Louisiana, which he administered from an Italianate mansion in Natchez called Tuscany. During the Civil War, Albert paid lip service to the Confederate cause while lavishly entertaining the Union officers occupying the city. He was the first Natchez planter to sign the loyalty oath to the Union, which enabled him to maintain his assets and continue to do business while prouder men lost everything. Many called Marston a traitor, but he laughed all the way to the bank.

People say Leo is the reincarnation of Albert, and they're

right. I often saw the grim ancestral portrait in the hall at Tuscany when I picked up Olivia in high school, a canvas enshrining a virtual twin of the man who warned me without subtlety to have 'his angel' home by eleven 'or else'. By the time Leo graduated law school nearly a century after Albert's death, the family appetites for power and profit had expressed themselves as forcefully as the genes for those chilling blue eyes. Leo Marston knew the secret and immutable laws of Mississippi politics the way a farmer knows his fields. The state's eighty-two counties function more or less as feudal domains, each with its closed circle of power, and Leo was born into one of the richest. Yet despite the relative wealth of Adams County, its elected officials cannot help but be swayed by admiration, envy, or outright fear of men like Leo Marston. Add to these the appointees whose hirings Marston has assured, and the result is a local political network that allows the judge to grant or quash things like building permits and zoning variances with a single phone call.

And Marston's power is not limited to the city. During his judicial career – first as a circuit judge, then a justice of the state supreme court – he did so many favors for so many people that his capital reserves of influence are impossible to estimate. Nor did he idly spend his time as state attorney general or chairman of the agriculture board. He has like-minded friends in every corner of Mississippi, and owns financial stakes in business all over the state, including the two biggest banks. He can sway the trials of friends and enemies from Tupelo to Biloxi, and put fear into newspaper editors as far away as Memphis and New Orleans. He is a vindictive son of a bitch, and everybody knows it.

On the other hand, he is easy to like. A man doesn't attain that kind of power without being able to play the social game with flair. Marston can discuss the finer points of obscure wines with vintners vacationing in Natchez, and an hour later put a crew of roughnecks on the floor of an oil rig with jokes that would make a sailor blush. In the company of women he becomes whatever the mood and situation require. With a priggish society wife he fancies, he tells off-color stories in a quiet, bourbon-laced voice, flustering her with the idea that a man in the judge's exalted position could be so down-to-earth. With a buxom barmaid he plays the cultured Southern aristocrat for all he is worth. I've seen Leo Marston play so many roles that I'm not sure anything lies at the center of the man other than a burning compulsion to increase his dominion over people, land, and money.

As I contemplate him, his words begin to lose their rhythm, then falter altogether. He has spotted me. The blue-gray eyes hold mine, unblinking, searching, revealing nothing. A few heads in the audience turn to me, wondering who could possibly have upset the equilibrium of the judge. Noticing this, Leo resumes speaking, though without the ease he earlier displayed.

He focuses on the women in his audience, lingering upon the prettiest. That his weakness was women I discovered in high school, when his sexual escapades almost destroyed his family. Leo's wife found a way to live with his flagrant infidelities, but his youngest daughter could not. When Olivia Marston learned at sixteen that her father had left a wake of brokenhearted and pregnant women behind him (which clarified the mystery of her mother's chronic alcoholism), she turned the strength she'd inherited from Leo against him, shaming and threatening him into changing his ways. It worked for a while, but appetites on that scale can't be suppressed long. What I found fascinating – and Livy disgusting – was that she was the only woman who ever challenged him. Not one of Leo's cast-off paramours ever tried to bring him down. The single ones he paid off with abortion money and more, frequently enough to send them back to college or get them started in a new town. The married ones nursed their broken hearts in silence, or, if they confessed to their husbands, were surprised by the nonviolence of the reaction. Such male passivity was unheard of in the South, but by virtue of his power, Leo Marston enjoyed a sort of modern-day *droit du signeur*, and he used it. As far as I know, he's paid only one price for his sexual adventures. Though his name has been floated more than once as a potential candidate for governor, each time party officials quietly let the suggestion die. No one feels confident about exposing Leo Marston's past to the scrutiny of a modern election.

'You're not carrying a gun, are you?'

Startled from my reverie, I find Sam Jacobs standing beside me. He looks as though he's only half joking.

'Am I that obvious?'

'You look like you're ready to tear Leo a new one.'

'I can dream, can't I? Look, I need to talk to you. Can you give me a ride home?'

'I'm ready now. Let's hit the bar before we go. Don's got a bottle of Laphroig over there.'

Sam leads the way. I shake hands with several people as we move through the crowd, accepting compliments on my books and answering polite questions about Annie. The alcohol has loosened everybody up, though thankfully not too much. As Lucy Perry promised, no one mentions the newspaper article. When I catch up to Sam at the bar, he's chatting with two other men waiting for drinks.

'Hell's bells!' cries a gravelly female voice behind me. 'If it ain't the Houston representative of the *N-Double-A-See-P*.'

Dread fills me as I turn, certain that I'm about to endure a public dressing-down for my comments in the paper. The speaker is Maude Marston. Leo's wife is obviously drunk, as she has been for as long as I can remember. In response to the judge's amorous adventures, Maude developed a sort of battleship manner, charging through her daily social round with prow thrust forward and guns primed for combat.

Anyone who whispers malicious comments within her hearing risks a withering broadside salvo or, worse, depth charges dropped with stealth and unerring aim, that detonate days or weeks later, leaving the offender shattered and forever outside the inner social circle. I hate to guess what she has in store for me.

'Whassa matter, hotshot?' she drawls. 'Cat got your tongue?'

I force myself to smile. 'Good evening, Maude. It's nice to see you.'

She stares with blank rage, as though the synapses behind her eyes have stopped firing. Maude was once a great beauty, but her two daughters are the only remaining testament to that fact. Her hair should be gray, but it has been bleached and hennaed and sprayed so often that it has acquired a sort of lacquered-armor look. The cumulative effect of that hair, the gin-glazed eyes, combative stance, and scowling avian face stretched taut by various plastic surgeries is enough to send any but the most stalwart running for the exits.

She pokes a grossly bejeweled finger into my chest. 'I'm *talking* to you.'

'You're drunk,' I say quietly.

She blanches, then pokes me again, harder.

'That's assault.'

'You gonna have me arrested, hotshot?'

Over Maude's shoulder I see Caitlin watching from the hall, her eyes flickering with curiosity. 'No. I'm going ask your husband to take you home.'

A harsh cackle bursts from Maude's lips, and she wobbles on her feet. 'You appointed yourself special protector of the nigras in this town or what?'

Sam Jacobs reaches between us and takes hold of my forearm. 'Got the drinks! Let's roll! Great to see you, Maude!'

As Sam pulls me away, Maude speaks softly but with a

venom that makes me pause. '*You ruined my daughter's life, you bastard.*'

Then she throws her drink in my face.

A collective gasp goes up from the nearby guests. The drink is mostly ice. It's Maude's words that have stunned me. I have no idea what she's talking about. It has to be Livy, but that makes no sense at all. Before I can gather my thoughts for a question, Lucy Perry appears and gentles Maude away from the bar the way a trainer gentles a wild mare.

'Let's blow this joint before somebody gets killed,' Sam whispers.

As we depart, Caitlin leans toward me. 'I can't wait to hear the story behind that.'

Perfect.

Chapter 11

Sam Jacobs drives a royal blue Hummer, the civilian version of the military Humvee. He claims it's the only way to travel in the oil fields. I cling to the window frame as the huge vehicle rumbles like a tank down State Street.

'Talk about a babe magnet!' he says, trying to hold his drink steady with his left hand. 'More women come on to me in this thing than when I had my Mercedes.'

I nod absently. Maude Marston has popped the cork on a dark vintage of memory.

'Did you give Caitlin Masters a tour of the garden?' Sam asks, giving me a bemused smile. 'You two had that *couple* look when you came in.'

'Did you hear what Maude said before she threw the drink in my face?'

'About ruining her daughter's life?'

'Yes. She had to be talking about Olivia, right?'

'Had to be.'

'When did Livy's life get ruined? Isn't she still married to that sports lawyer in Atlanta?'

'Definitely fartin' through silk, on the money side.'

I laugh, wondering whether the Jewish crowd in Manhattan would believe the Southern accent coming from Sam Jacobs's mouth.

'How*ever*,' Sam adds, cutting his eyes at me. 'My wife's sister was in Atlanta last month for some kind of Tri-Delt alumni ball, and Livy showed up without her husband.'

'So?'

'The gossip of the party was trouble in paradise.'

'Not exactly a reliable source. Do they have any kids?'

'Don't think so.' He glances at me again. 'It would be pretty strange, the two of you being available at the same time. It's like fate. Maybe history's reversing itself.'

Not wanting to continue in this line, I stick my head out of the window as the Hummer roars up the bypass toward my parents' neighborhood. The wind is warm and wet in my hair. The downtown bars and riverboat casino will still be going great guns, but this part of town looks like Mayberry, R.F.D.

'Have you seen anybody?' Sam asks. 'You know . . . since Sarah died?'

I pull my head back inside and look him in the eye. 'Lunch with Caitlin Masters tomorrow is my first date since the funeral. If you call that a date.'

'Shit. I know it's tough, Penn. I joke about fooling around, but if I ever lost Jenny, I wouldn't know what to do.'

I take his cup from his hand and gulp a sweat-inducing shot of Laphroig.

'That's the ticket,' he says, slapping me on the knee.

The Hummer jerks as Sam hits the brakes, then lets off slowly. 'Would you fucking look at this?'

'What?'

'A cop. Looks like a sheriff's deputy.'

I turn slowly. A sheriff's department cruiser just like the one that tailed me from Shad Johnson's headquarters has settled in twenty yards behind the Hummer. The sight throws me back to the shooting, glass exploding inches from my face.

'Sam, what do you know about Ray Presley?'

'Ray Presley? He's sick, I heard. Bad sick.'

'What's he been up to the last few years?'

'Same thing he was always up to. Being a sleazy coonass who'll do anything for money.'

'Presley's no coonass. He's from Smith County. Who did he work for?'

'Old Natchez people, mostly.' Sam's eyes keep flicking to the rearview mirror. 'He did some things for a driller I know. Strong-arm stuff. I think Marston kept him on his payroll as a security consultant, if you believe that.' Sam accelerates, as if daring the deputy to pull him over. 'You know what? I'll bet the BASF deal is what set Maude off on you.'

'What does Maude Marston care about a chemical plant? She has more money than God.'

'But does she have *enough*? That chemical plant means more to the Marstons than anybody. Short term, anyway.'

'Why?'

'The industrial park isn't big enough for the projected facility. You want to guess who owns the land contiguous to the park site?'

'Leo?'

'Yep. He'll squeeze blood out of BASF for every square foot of land, or kill them on usage and access fees.'

'But that's got nothing to do with Livy.'

Sam nods, then turns and looks hard at me. 'Caitlin Masters's article said Ray Presley worked the Payton murder when he was a cop. Is that what this is about?'

'It's nothing to do with that.'

Sam slams his hand against the Hummer's steering wheel. '*Look* at this asshole! I hate it when they follow you like that.' He cranes his neck around and looks through the back windscreen. 'You gonna stop me or what!'

'I don't think he is. I think it's the same guy who followed me from Shad Johnson's headquarters earlier tonight.'

'Shad Johnson's headquarters?' Sam shakes his head. 'I'm riding with a crazy man.'

'Ten seconds after he passed me, somebody shot up my car with a rifle.'

'*What?*

'I'm just saying that if this guy passes us, watch him close.'

Sam reaches under the seat, pulls out a holstered Colt .45 and sets it in my lap. 'He's fucking with the wrong vehicle if that's his plan. This Hummer will drive right *over* that Crown Vic he's in.'

'Take it easy. He's just tailing us.'

'Why the sudden interest in Ray Presley?'

'I'll tell you in a couple of days. Do you think we could find anybody who could testify that Presley has committed murder for money?'

'A lot of people could. *Would* is another question.'

Sam turns into my parents' neighborhood, watching his rearview mirror through the turn. 'There goes our shadow. Bye, bye.'

A minute later he pulls the Hummer into our driveway and leaves it idling. 'I feel bad about mentioning Sarah. I guess time is the only thing that can get you past something like that.'

I swallow the last of the Scotch. 'I'll never get past it, Sam. I'm a different person now. Part of me is lying in that grave in Houston.'

'Yeah, well. Most of you is sitting right here. And your daughter needs that part.'

'I know. I keep thinking about Del Payton's widow. Race doesn't even come into it for me. For thirty years part of her has been buried wherever her husband is. We're both wounded the same way. You know?'

Sam shuts off the engine. 'Listen to me, Penn. Whoever blew up Del Payton was in their twenties then, thirties max. Kluckers full of piss and vinegar. Those guys have got wives and grown kids now. And if you think they're gonna let some hotshit, nigger-lovin' *writer* take all that away, you're nuts. That's who shot at you tonight. And if you keep pushing, they'll kill you.'

Sam has the Jew's special fear of fanatics. During the civil rights era this anxiety caused many Mississippi Jews to keep as low a profile as possible. Some gave heroic support to the Movement; others, primarily in the Delta, actually joined the White Citizens' Councils, for fear of the consequences if they didn't. Sam's parents chose the difficult middle ground.

'Don't worry, Sam. Caitlin Masters has given everybody the idea I'm a crusading liberal, ready to drag the town through the mud. Nothing could be further from the truth.'

'Bullshit. I know you when you sound like this. You'll pull down the temple to find the truth.'

'I remember you sounding like this once. That time in junior high, when your dad hired us to clean out his attic?'

Sam gives no sign that he's heard, but I know he has.

'Going through all those boxes,' I remind him. 'We found that list. Two hundred names, all handwritten.'

He reaches out and toys with the Hummer's ignition key. The papers we found had listed most members of Natchez's Ku Klux Klan and White Citizens' Council. The Jewish community had maintained the list as a security measure, and more than a few names on it belonged to fathers of kids we went to school with.

'You remember how you felt when you saw those names?'

He picks up the drink cup and nervously shakes the ice. 'Scared.'

'Me too. But it pissed me off more. I wanted to expose those assholes for what they were. So did you. Have you ever done business with anybody on that list?'

He looks up, his eyes hard as agates. 'Not a fucking one. And I spiked them where I could.'

A side spill of headlights washes across my parents' house.

'Would you look at this?' Sam mutters, looking over his shoulder. 'It's the same car.'

The sheriff's cruiser sits idling in the street, fifteen yards behind us.

Bolstered by the confidence of being on my father's property, I set the .45 in Sam's lap, climb out of the Hummer, and walk toward the car. The passenger window whirs down into the door frame. It's the black deputy who followed me before. I put my hands on the door and lean into the window.

'Can I help you?'

The deputy says nothing. He has a bald, bullet-shaped head dominated by black eyes set in yellow sclera shot with blood. He's at least fifty, but he fills out his brown uniform like an NFL cornerback. Even at rest he radiates coiled energy.

'You were following me earlier tonight, right?'

The black eyes burn into mine with unsettling intensity. 'Could have been,' he said in a gravelly voice.

'Ten seconds after you passed me, somebody shot up my car. You stopped. Why didn't you help me?'

'I didn't hear no shots. I saw you stop. I waited to make sure you started again. Why didn't you report it if you was shot at?'

'What the hell is this about, Deputy? Why are you following me?'

He purses his lips and taps the steering wheel. 'Get rid of your friend. Tell him I warned you off the Payton case, then go inside. After he leaves, meet me back out here.'

'Look, if this is about Del Payton–'

'This is about *you*, Penn Cage.' He spears me with a chilling stare. 'And unfinished business.'

Unfinished business? A needle of fear pushes through my gut. Could he be talking about Ray Presley? Could he know something about what happened in Mobile in 1973? 'Do you know a man named Ray Presley, Deputy?'

His jaw muscles flex into knots. 'I know that motherfucker.'

'Does this have anything to do with him?'

'It might. You just be out here when I get back.'

He presses the accelerator, spinning me away from the car. After regaining my balance, I watch the cruiser disappear, then walk back to the driver's window of the Hummer.

'What the hell was that about?' Sam asks.

'How many black sheriff's deputies are there?'

'Nine or ten, I think. That was one of them?'

'Yeah. Fiftyish, but tough. Bald-headed.'

'Had to be Ike Ransom. You know him.'

'I do?'

'Ike the Spike. Remember?'

I do remember. Ike 'the Spike' Ransom was a legendary football star at Thompson, the black high school, in the mid-sixties. He was so good that his exploits were trumpeted in the pages of the *Examiner* despite his skin color, and the records he set had held until Sam and I played ball ten years later.

'What the hell did Ike Ransom want here?' Sam asks.

'Same as everybody else. Warned me off the Payton case. I can't believe Ike the Spike is a deputy. I figured he played pro football or something.'

Sam shrugs. 'He was a cop first. After he put in his twenty there, he went to the sheriff's department. He's a bad son of a bitch, Penn. Even the blacks don't like him.'

'What do you mean? He was a hero.'

'Ransom was one of the first black cops. I heard those guys had to prove they'd be tough on their own people to keep their jobs. Some people say Ransom was worse than white cops.'

'Great.'

Sam cranks the Hummer. 'Forget Del Payton. Take care of your own. And if somebody fucks with you, give me a call. I can still pull your slack if you need me.'

I squeeze his shoulder. 'Sounds like a plan. Thanks.'

He backs out of the driveway and roars away, the echoes reverberating off the houses on the silent street.

I walk into the garage and lean against the trunk of my mother's Maxima. The high whistling *cheeep* of crickets rises to a manic drone, overpowering the buzz of the streetlight overhead and giving me a strange sense of peace. Our street looks almost exactly as it did thirty-five years ago, when we moved in. A few houses have changed color, some trees have disappeared, others have grown. But for the most part it's the same.

In the corner of our yard stands a huge oak. When I was a boy, a wisteria vine grew around its trunk, spiraling around and around until it reached the high branches. My friends and I used to splay our bare feet on that vine, spread our arms wide around the trunk, and see how high we could work our way up and around the tree before we fell. I never won those contests; I had too much imagination to success-fully block out my fear. Back then the vine was the thickness of a boy's wrist. Now it's thicker than my thigh and looks as though it will soon strangle the old oak like a boa constrictor.

The drone of an engine cuts through the hot night air. As promised, Ike the Spike's cruiser turns the corner and rolls to a stop at the end of our driveway.

I push off the Maxima and walk toward the street.

Chapter 12

The inside of the cruiser smells like a black man sweating. I know the odor from summer jobs digging ditches and riding in trucks with men who gave off a different scent than I did – no worse but harder somehow, distinctive enough for me to know it forever. I pull the door shut, closing myself into an oppressive square completed by the dashboard, a wire mesh screen, and Deputy Ike Ransom.

'Let's take a ride,' he says.

'How about you tell me what I'm doing here?'

'You want the neighbors asking everybody what the sheriff's department was doing at your folks' house?'

I look up the street. There are still lights in a few windows. 'How do I know you're not in with whoever shot at me tonight?'

'If I wanted you dead, your mama would be at the funeral home right now.'

This is easy enough to believe. 'Okay. Ride.'

Ike Ransom drives up to the bypass and heads south. Most of the traffic is eighteen-wheelers bound north for the interstate junction sixty miles away, or west for the bridge over the Mississippi.

'What's this about, Ike?'

He glances at me. 'You know me?'

'My friend did. What's the big secret?'

'It's about Del Payton.'

'I told you I didn't want to hear about that.'

'It's about you and Del both.'

'Me and Del? I was only eight years old when the guy died.'

He looks at me again, the yellow sclera of his eyes washed white by oncoming headlights. 'He didn't *die*, college boy. He was murdered. There's a difference. You and him tied together, though. Ain't no doubt about that.'

'How do you figure that?'

'First tell me why you said what you said in the paper.'

'I was talking through my hat. I wasn't thinking.'

'That newspaper bitch didn't pick Del's name out of the blue.'

'I mentioned him.'

'There you go.'

I sigh in frustration. 'I'm lost, Ike.'

'That's for damn sure. Can't you see? Del died thirty years ago and nobody paid for it. His soul ain't never been at rest. It's been wandering 'round here all this time, looking for peace. But it can't *get* no peace. Not while his killers walk free.'

Maybe Ike the Spike is some kind of religious nut.

'Now, here you come, thirty years later, and in one day you got more people talking about Del's killing than they was the day he died.'

'That wasn't my intent.'

'*That* don't matter. Don't you see? What goes around comes around! You just an instrument. An instrument of a higher power."

'I'm a guy with a big mouth. I'm not an instrument of anything.'

Ransom shakes his head and laughs with eerie certainty. 'You just sit tight. You gonna understand everything in a minute. You gonna thank old Ike for this one.'

He turns right at the Ford dealership and crosses Lower Woodville Road near the paper mill, which glows fluorescent in the dark like a small city, churning white smoke into the night sky.

'Where are we going? The river?'

'Battery plant.'

'The battery plant? What for?'

'Privacy. They closed right now. Asian market's down. They crank back up in thirty-six hours.'

There are few lights on this road. Beneath the sulfurous odor of the paper mill drifts the thick, ripe smell of kudzu, sweetened by a breath of honeysuckle. The river is only six hundred yards away, and just a few feet below our present elevation.

The dark skeleton of the Triton Battery plant materializes to our right as Ike turns onto Gate Street, then right again into a parking lot lightened by the pink glow of mercury vapor. The Triton Battery Company came to Natchez in 1936 to build batteries for Pullman rail cars. In 1940 they retooled the line to manufacture batteries for diesel submarines. After the war it was truck batteries, marine batteries, whatever fit the changing market. The last I heard, Triton was using its ancient equipment to produce motorcycle batteries for European manufacturers.

Ike stops the cruiser on the far side of the parking lot. We're sitting on an acre of gravel packed into dirt by years of hard use, bordered on three sides by trees and unkempt grass. The west side faces the main gate of the battery plant, with Gate Street running between. I used to bring girls out here in high school.

'Is this where Del Payton died?'

'This is it,' Ransom says. 'Come on.'

'Where?'

He laughs harshly. 'You a nervous son of a bitch, ain't you? Come on.'

I get out of the cruiser and follow him across the gravel. A massive old pecan tree grows out of a clump of grass at the center of the lot. The spaces in its shade are probably coveted by everyone who uses the lot.

Ransom stops ten yards short of the tree, his back to me.

'Thirty years,' he says. 'Thirty years ago Del Payton parked his Fairlane right in this spot. When he came out of the plant, the bomb was in his car.' He half turns to me and spits on the gravel. 'I seen car bombs go off, man. It's a motherfucker. That fire burned forty minutes before they got it out. Del was sitting behind the wheel all that time.'

I stand silent in the buzzing of the lights, wondering where Ike Ransom has seen car bombs go off. He squats on his haunches and picks up a piece of gravel.

'A man's soul left this earth right here.'

I walk a few steps closer. 'Look, Ike . . . I know what happened that night. And I'm damn sorry it did. But I don't see any connection to me.'

He stands and points at me, his black eyes smoldering. 'I'm gonna say two words, college boy. After that you gonna be in this thing up to your neck.'

'Okay.'

'Leo Marston.'

He watches me as though waiting for me to guess a riddle.

'Leo Marston? I don't get it. What–'

'*Judge . . . Leo . . . Marston.*'

My palms tingle. 'Are you saying Marston was somehow involved in the Payton murder?'

'Involved?' Ike the Spike laughs quietly in the dark. 'Oh, yeah.'

'That's impossible. What could Leo Marston possibly have had to do with Del Payton?'

'He was D.A. back then, wasn't he?'

My head is swimming. 'Leo Marston was district attorney in 1968?'

131

'You didn't know that? It was in the article this morning.'

I see my father jerking the paper from my hands and wadding it up. 'I didn't read the whole thing.'

'That wasn't too smart, was it?'

'You're saying Marston covered something up? Buried evidence while he was D.A.?'

Ike fires his rock across the street like a major league outfielder. It flies over the cyclone fence bordering the plant and strikes something metal, silencing the crickets for a few seconds. 'I'm saying all these years that motherfucker been handing out jail time and making millions, he should have been rotting at Parchman Farm.'

A dark thrill ripples through my chest. 'You're saying Marston was involved in the actual *crime*?'

'I done said all I got to say.'

'You can't drop a bomb like that and then shut up! How do you know any of this?'

'You a cop in this town for twenty years, even a black cop, you get to know some things.'

The hair on my arms is standing erect. I cannot interpret my emotions. Fear? Excitement? I walk the ten yards to the pecan tree, unzip my pants, and urinate on its trunk as I try to get my mind around what Ransom has told me.

'Shook you up, huh?' he says, laughing.

I zip up and turn back to him. 'You've known for thirty years that Leo Marston was guilty of a felony and you've done nothing about it?'

'Who says I knew for thirty years? I wasn't on the job thirty years ago. What I'm gonna do anyway, man? A nigger cop on the bottle gonna go up against the judge? That's why you here, man. Takes somebody like you to do it.'

'Like me?'

'You're white, famous, and you make your money someplace else. They can't hurt you much here.'

'Who's they?'

'That's what you got to find out.'

'Christ. Just tell me what you know. I'll take it and run with it.'

Ike gives me a knowing smile. 'You want Marston's ass bad, don't you?'

'Tell me, goddamn it!'

'That don't play, college boy. You gotta work your way to it. Then you'll understand.'

'Why tell me this, Ike?'

'*Why me, Ike?*' he mocks in a woman's voice. 'Don't play that shit with me! Everybody knows the judge went after your old man. Damn near got him too.'

This stings me to the quick. 'That's bullshit. My father was unanimously exonerated by a jury.'

'I ain't talking 'bout that. I'm talking about *damage*. Doc Cage had a heart attack while he was waiting for that trial, didn't he?'

I nod slowly.

'Hey, I love your daddy, man. He took care of me when I was a kid. Took care of my mama till she died. That's why I'm telling you this. It's what the hippies used to call karma. What goes around comes around. That's what brought you back here. You the chicken coming home to roost. Right on Marston's ass.'

'So give me what I need to nail him.'

Ike shakes his head. 'Gimme, gimme, gimme. I told you, it don't play that way. I can point you in the right direction. But that's it.'

'I don't like playing games.'

Ransom snickers. 'That's what they do here, college boy. You ain't been gone so long you forgot that yet. Right now they playing their favorite game of all.'

'What's that?'

'The quiet game.'

'The quiet game?' Memories of Sarah flood into my brain,

of her trying to trick Annie into being silent long enough for us to eat dinner in peace, by seeing who could go the longest without talking. 'Who's playing the quiet game, Ike?'

'Everybody, man. White and black both. Everybody keeping quiet, making like things is sweet and easy, trying to fish that new plant in here. Nobody wants nobody digging into Del's killing. Nobody 'cept you. You got a reason.'

'What about you? What's your reason?'

His grin vanishes as though it never existed. Hatred comes off him like steam. He extends his forefinger and taps his powerful chest with it. 'That's between me and me. Del's killers is playing the quiet game too. They been playing it thirty years. Not even sweatin'. You got to make people *nervous* to win the quiet game. And I got a feeling you pretty good at that.'

Something is coiling within my chest, something I have not felt for years. It's the hunter's tension, wrapped like the armature of an electric motor, tight and copper-cored, charged with current and aching for resolution, for the frantic discharge of retribution.

'A lot of people think poking into this case would be damned dangerous,' I tell him.

Ike the Spike closes the distance between us and squeezes my right shoulder, his grip like the claw of a wild animal, like he could close his hand a little tighter and snap the bone.

'That's where I come in. Boy, you lookin' at dangerous. Ask anybody.'

We do not speak as Ransom drives back towards my parents' house. I watch the dark streets drift by, lost in memory. I think mostly of the malpractice trial, of Marston's savage cross-examination of my father just five weeks after his triple coronary bypass surgery. It required a supreme concentration of will on my part not to jump up in the court-room and attack the man. In all my years as a prosecutor, I never stooped to the tactics Marston used that day.

'You got any FBI contacts?' Ike asks.

'A few. Why?'

'You might not want to use them on this.'

'Why not?'

'Free advice. Take it or leave it.'

'You know Ray Presley worked the Payton case, don't you?'

Ike glances away from the road long enough to give me a warning look. 'Presley was dirty from the day he was born. That motherfucker crazy as a wall-eyed bull and mean as a snake. You don't talk to him unless I'm somewhere close.'

This does not bode well for my meeting tomorrow morning.

The radio chatters over a low background of static. There's a domestic-violence call in the southern part of the county, followed by a disturbance at the gangplank of the riverboat casino. As we roll into my parents' neighborhood, I glance over at Ransom. The man is too old to be doing the job he has.

'Can I ask you a question, Ike?'

He takes a Kool Menthol from his shirt pocket, lights up, and blows a stream of smoke at the windshield.

'How'd you wind up a cop?'

'That's what college boys ask whores. How'd a girl like you end up here?'

'I remember the stories about you playing ball. Ike the Spike. You were a hero around here.'

He sniffs and takes another drag. 'Like the man said, that was my fifteen minutes.'

'You must have played college ball.'

'Oh, yeah, I was the BNOC.'

'What's that?'

'The Big Nigger On Campus.' His voice is laced with

bitterness. 'I got a full scholarship to Ohio State, but I went to Jackson State instead. First quarter of the first game, a guy took out my shoulder. Back then doctors couldn't do shit for that.'

'You lost your scholarship?'

'They gave me my walking papers before I even caught my breath. I was good enough for the army, though. I'd been drafted in early sixty-six, but I had a college deferment. When I lost my scholarship, I couldn't afford to stay in school. Next thing I knew, I was landing at Tan Son Nhut air base in DaNang.'

I am starting to perceive the twisted road that led Ike Ransom to this job. 'I'd like to hear about it sometime.'

Another drag on the Kool. 'You one of them war junkies?'

'No.'

'You get off on other people's pain, though. That's what writers do, ain't it? Sell other people's pain?'

'Some do, I guess.'

'Well, this is your big chance. There's a heap of fucking pain at the bottom of this story.'

I try to gauge Ransom's temper, but it's impossible. 'Sam says you've got a bad rep. Even with black people.'

He stubs out his cigarette and flips it out the window. 'I was the third black cop on the Natchez P.D. Back then a lot of the force was Klan. I didn't take that job to make no civil rights statement. I'd been an M.P. in Saigon, and that was the only thing I knew how to do. The first time I got called to a black juke, I had to go alone. When I walked in the door, everybody thought it was a big joke. Patting me on the back and laughing, handing me beer. But this big field nigger named Moon had a machete in there. He'd already cut the guy who was dicking his old lady, plus the first nigger who said something about it. He was sitting by hisself at a corner table. I'd seen lots of guys lose it overseas, and this guy was like that. *Gone.* I told him he had to give up the blade. He wouldn't do it. When I held out my hand, he jumped up and charged me. I shot him through the throat.'

'Jesus.'

'I didn't want to waste that brother. But I didn't have no backup. And that pretty much set the tone for the next twenty years. I had the white department on one side, watching me like a hawk, making sure I was tough enough, and my people on the other, always fucking up, always begging for a break. I cut slack where I could, but goddamn, it seemed like they never learned. It got where I hated to pull a nigger over, knowing he'd be drunk or high. Hated to answer a domestic call. Couple of years of that, I was an outsider. It fucked with me, man. That's what got me on the bottle.'

'Why didn't you resign?'

Ransom rolls down his window, hawks and spits. 'I didn't come here to give you no Jerry Springer show.' He pulls something out of his shirt and hands it to me. It's a card. On it are printed Ransom's name and rank, and the phone numbers of the sheriff's department. 'My cell phone's on the back. When you call, don't use names. I'll know you, and I'll pick a place for a meet.'

'You're the only person not named Payton who seems to want the truth told.'

The radio crackles again, this time about a theft of guns from a hunting camp in Anna's Bottom. Ike picks up the transmitter and says he'll respond to the call.

'You gonna do this thing?' he asks, putting the transmitter back in its cradle.

I think of my father and his trouble, of Ray Presley and the gun I hope to have in my possession by tomorrow. 'I don't know yet.'

His eyes flash with dark knowledge. 'You know you lying. Get out of my fucking car.'

Before I can close the door, the cruiser screeches off into the night.

*   *   *

My father is waiting in the kitchen with a bowl of melted ice cream in front of him, smoking the last of a cigar in his boxer shorts and a tank T-shirt. Beside the ice cream lies the pistol he wore to the party, a 9mm Beretta.

'Everything okay?' I ask.

'Are you sure you want to try to buy that gun from Ray? I'd rather throw myself on the mercy of the court than get you involved in this.'

I shake my head. 'It's the only way. You just call Presley in the morning and set up the meeting.'

'You'll have to go to his trailer. He lives out toward Church Hill, past the Indian mound. It won't be pretty. He's a bitter son of a bitch.'

'You say he gets around okay?'

'Yeah. The home-health people see him a good bit. And I hear he's got a private nurse now. I've made a couple of house calls to give him shots for pain. Trailer calls, I should say.'

'Fifteen-mile house calls for Ray Presley?'

'I've treated the man for thirty years, Penn. He doesn't call unless he's hurting bad. And if Ray says it's bad, it's bad.'

This is vintage Tom Cage, making house calls on a man who is blackmailing him, not out of fear but because he feels he should.

'Prostate cancer was about the worst thing for Ray to get,' he reflects. 'He's got the biggest dick I ever saw on a white man, and he likes to brag about it. I think the surgery probably made him impotent. He says no, but he's twice as surly as he ever was. More dangerous, if anything.'

'Worrying won't help. Come on. We both need some sleep.'

He stubs out his cigar, then stands looking at me, his eyes unreadable. I long to tell him what Ike Ransom said about

Leo Marston, but this isn't the time. *Get the gun first.* Without quite meaning to, I step forward and put my arms around him. The embrace surprises him, and he stiffens. Age has changed the shape of him, this body that once lifted me as though I weighed nothing.

'Dad, tomorrow you're going to find out what being born again really means.'

He pulls back and looks me in the eye. 'I'll let you go see Ray. But by God, you're going armed.' He picks up the Beretta. 'And if he gets squirrelly, you shoot first and ask questions after, okay?'

'Okay.'

My mother is curled up in bed beside the smaller lump of Annie in my old room. My old baseball trophies gleam in the dark on the shelves above them, like little watchmen. I creep in and touch Mom on the shoulder, and she stirs in the shadows.

'Tom?'

'It's Penn, Mom. Go on to bed. I'll sleep with her.'

She rubs her eyes. 'All right, honey.'

I reach out and stroke Annie's hair. Mom is already asleep again. I gently push her leg with my knee. 'Mom?'

She opens her eyes again and smiles blankly, then gets up and sleepwalks toward the hall.

I quickly brush my teeth, strip to my shorts, and climb into bed beside Annie, who is already stirring. In seconds her hand finds my shoulder, reestablishing her early-warning system.

As I lie in the dark, her shallow breathing troubles rather than soothes my heart. Sleeping with Annie always brings memories of Sarah. After the funeral I had to move Annie's bed into my room because she couldn't fall asleep alone, and still she wound up in my bed most nights. The pulse of her life so near always stirs my dreams. I dream of Sarah before the diagnosis, before fear entered our lives and took away the most precious gift, which is not hope but youth. Immortality. The sense of unlimited possibility. It's an illusion, of course, the most precious illusion of life.

Sometimes my dreams are linear, like movies, other times disconnected, like fragments of film snatched at random from an editing room floor. As Annie breathes steadily beside me, fatigue deadens the signals flashing through my brain, the anxiety about meeting Presley, the delicious prospect of revenge on Leo Marston. Consciousness tries to hold me with the terrifying jerk of a perceived fall, but I catch myself. Soon the darkness above me tunnels into light, and I see the silver surface of a pool surrounded by lush ferns and massive cypress trees. The wind-rippled surface slowly stills to glass, opening the water to my gaze. There are plants below the surface, green fronds reaching up from unknown depths, gently waving in an invisible current. Among the fronds something moves, pale against the green. A person. A woman. She turns lazily, gracefully among the water plants, like a swimmer synchronized to unheard music. Her hair floats around her head in a bright corona, obscuring what must be extraordinary beauty. Ceasing her languid motion, she lifts her arms and pulls toward the surface. I recall the Lady of the Lake, who gave Excalibur to Arthur. This woman is like that. She has something to give me. But even as she fights her way to the surface, she somehow recedes, like reality rewinding. I reach down to help her, but I am far too high. Slowly the storm of hair parts and reveals her face, and she opens her mouth to speak. I cannot hear her words, but her face nearly stops my heart. Something pure and cold courses through me as the translucent eyes seek mine in mute desperation. That face once haunted me like an inner shadow, a secret sharer watching, judging, holding me in thrall until at last the light of Sarah and Annie shone into the hidden chambers of my heart, and it receded into memory. Receded but did not die. Once, long ago, that face taught me what it was to be alive.

That face . . .

Olivia Marston.

Chapter 13

Driving through rural Mississippi with a hundred thousand dollars cash in your trunk can make you nervous. Ray Presley's trailer is fourteen miles north of town, situated between Emerald Mound and the tiny rural community of Church Hill. The second-highest ceremonial mound in North America, Emerald Mound rises from the forest like a Maya temple of earth. When I was a boy, we sledded down its great slope on pizza pans, on those biannual occasions when Natchez got its inch of snow. As teenagers we gathered there to watch the sun rise while we drank beer and cheap wine and howled over the treetops in the ecstatic tongues of adolescence.

The wooded road between Emerald Mound and Church Hill is dotted with trailers and small houses, but as I near the two-hundred-year-old Episcopal church that marks the settlement, the woods recede, and the landscaped grounds of splendid plantations stretch away from both sides of the road. Beyond moss-hung cedar trees and white fences, swans glide majestically across ponds that might be in England. But the only cathedrals near these estates are cathedrals of kudzu, arsenical green spires and buttresses which construct themselves at a terrifying rate, using oaks and pecans and elms as scaffolding, encroaching upon the old cotton fields with the stealth of new jungle.

The history here is not all antebellum. Andrew Jackson married Rachel Robards at the end of this road in 1791, but of late the neighborhood has entertained more eccentric visitors. When I was in high school, the actor George Hamilton purchased one of these homes and lived there for a while in opulent planter style. The fall of the Marcos regime in the Philippines brought to light the strange revelation that the 'Hamilton' house was actually owned by Imelda Marcos. It then passed for a time into the hands of Hare Krishnas, a separatist faction which morphed into the Southern Vedic Life Association, stirring up the county with fears of brainwashing. Even in rural Mississippi nothing is what it seems.

Ray Presley's trailer is set a little way back from the highway, beneath a stand of pine trees, and beside an algae-covered pond that might be an oil sump. The trailer has seen better years, but there's a gleaming new satellite dish hammered onto the southwest eave, like a ribbon on a pig's ear. A shining Ford pickup and a rusted Chevy Vega sit out front.

I pull my mother's Maxima beside the Vega, set the burglar alarm, and walk up to the door, leaving the Wal-Mart briefcase holding the extortion money in the trunk. Before I can press the bell, the door is opened by a thin young woman I assume is Presley's nurse, though she is wearing a denim work shirt, not a uniform. Blonde and lank-haired, she could be twenty-five or thirty-five. She has the indeterminate look of hill people everywhere: sallow skin and hard angles, though she is pretty in the way waitresses at the Waffle House can be pretty at four a.m. She doesn't speak but leads me into the den of the trailer, which is a time capsule of blue shag carpet and dark, seventies-era paneling.

Presley himself sits on a sofa opposite a large color television tuned to a soap opera, a TV tray before him and a stainless steel intravenous drug caddy standing beside. He looks surprisingly fit for a fifty-six-year-old man with metastatic carcinoma. He has the stringy toughness of a laborer, the long, ropy muscles you see on men working shirtless on highways, shrimp boats, and oil rigs. He wears blue cotton pajama pants and a white tank T-shirt. A grease-stained John Deere cap covers his head, which has been burned bald by chemotherapy, the green bill shading brow-less eyes that smolder in their sockets.

I glance around the room so that he won't feel I'm staring. The walls are decorated with plaques and photos commemo-rating a career in law enforcement: certificates from various police societies, a couple of trophies sporting a man aiming a pistol. There's also the usual complement of stuffed deer heads and mounted largemouth bass, along with a fearsome compound bow hanging from a hook. Sliding glass doors open onto a small deck behind the sofa, where a gas grill and a smoker sit rusting in the sun.

'So you're Doc Cage's boy,' Presley says. His voice is deep and rough as a wood rasp. 'I recognize you from the paper. Excuse me if I don't get up.'

'Please don't.' It's odd how we revert to the basic courtesies, even when talking to killers, especially if they are ill. My seating choices are a cracked Naugahyde recliner and a pillowy velour monstrosity that looks like a Kmart special.

'Take the La-Z-boy,' Presley advises.

I sit on the edge of the chair so that I can keep my forward attitude. With men like Ray Presley, the critical subtext of any conversation is animal. Even in the silences, everything is territory and dominance, a battle for advantage.

'So you're the one shot his mouth off about Del Payton in the paper,' he says, a half-humorous light in his eyes.

'That's right.'

'You looking to make a name for yourself?'

'I already have that.'

He leans back and regards me with disdain. 'I guess you do. But you'd have to go a long way to outdo your daddy.' He reaches down and eats a crust of toast from the egg-stained plate on the TV tray. 'How come you didn't go to medical school? Grades not good enough?'

This is the ultimate baiting question for any doctor's son who didn't follow his father into the profession. 'They were too good. The medical school thought I'd be bored there.'

I let Presley chew on this a minute, and it takes him about that to finally decide I am joking. His primitive instincts are finely honed, but his grasp of the larger world is limited.

'I remember you in high school,' he says. 'You was porking Livy Marston.'

I keep my face impassive.

'That was one fine bitch,' he goes on, watching my reaction. 'Had too much of everything, that was her trouble.'

The skin of my face seems to stretch and burn, but I say nothing, unwilling to be drawn into this game. After an interminable wait, he ways, 'You here to ask me about Del Payton?'

'I'm here because I heard you had a gun for sale.'

He picks up a remote control and flips through several channels, finally settling on a fishing program. 'You heard wrong.'

'I don't think so.'

'What kind of gun did you hear it was?' His eyes remain on the screen. 'This gun you're talking about, I mean.'

'A featherweight thirty-eight. Smith and Wesson.'

'That's a damn good piece. Good for close work. How much would you be looking to spend on a gun like that?'

I take a piece of paper from my wallet, write *50,000* on it, then lean forward and pass it to him.

He studies it for a few seconds. 'That's a piece of money.'

'Cash.'

He hands the paper back to me. 'Too bad I don't have what you're looking for. I could use a piece of money like that.'

'I think you need some air. Why don't we step outside?'

'I don't get around so good anymore.'

'I didn't realize you'd lost so much strength.'

His pride thus goaded, Presley puts down the remote and stands almost as easily as he must have at age twenty. He walks to the double glass doors, slides one open, and steps onto the little square redwood deck.

I follow.

Presley stops at the rail, surveying the modest lot left him in life: a few weed-choked rows of exposed earth where a garden once grew; a small barn stripped of its walls, rotted, and collapsed inward, leaving a modernist sculpture of rafters and tin. The wall boards were probably bought by some itinerant New England artist. Beyond the barn the land falls abruptly into the woods.

'Take your shirt off,' Presley says in a peremptory tone he probably used with prisoners in the days before he was one himself.

Had he not demanded this ritual, I would have, but it irks me that he beat me to it. 'I'll show you mine if you show me yours.'

He actually grins at this. We pull off our shirts and turn in a circle. My body is lean but smooth as a lamb's, the legacy of my generation, which was never shipped overseas to do battle and has done less manual labor than any generation before it. Presley's torso is marked by multiple knife scars, at least two bullet wounds, and what might be the scar of a central veinous line for chemotherapy.

'Pants too,' I tell him.

We both strip our pants halfway down our thighs. Like me Presley still wears jockey briefs, and my father's comment about his anatomy is readily borne out. Satisfied that neither of us is wired, we button and zip back up.

'I don't like bullshit,' I tell him. 'So I'll get right to it. You killed a man named Don Hillman in 1973 in Mobile, Alabama. You did that on your own hook, no matter what you thought. I'm prepared to offer you a substantial price for the pistol used in that crime, but it's a one-time offer. An outright purchase. You can take what I'm offering, or we can go to Plan B.'

'You fixing to threaten me, sonny?' Presley sounds more amused than angry.

'If we don't come to terms over this, I'm going to go straight to the district attorney – whom I went to school with – and use every bit of influence at my disposal to have you indicted for capital murder and extortion. That's a risk for my father, but it's one he's prepared to take. He's been more than generous with you, and he's tired of living in fear.'

Presley looks off into the trees.

'He deserves better. And you know it.'

'I can't help the way things turned out,' Presley says bitterly. 'Fact is, Doc has money and I don't. And I need some.'

'My father treated your family free for years, just like he did a lot of others. What he's got now is patients who think he's a saint and not much else. He's in bad health himself. He deserves to retire in peace.'

Presley scratches his ratty pajamas. 'The way I figure, that gun's worth a lot more than fifty thousand.'

'Or nothing. It could simply be evidence sitting in the D.A.'s office.'

'A hundred grand. Cash money.'

Relief trickles through my veins like cool water. 'You've committed other murders in the past. I suspect you're blackmailing other people as we speak. Right now I haven't the slightest bit of interest in those crimes. But that could change. You could spend what little time you have left in jail. And you know what that's like, Ray.' I spit off the deck. 'Sixty-five thousand.'

He doesn't like me using his first name. And though he hasn't moved, something changed in him at the mention of prison. 'Eighty,' he says in a taut voice.

'Is the gun here?'

'Could be.'

'If you get it now, I'll go seventy-five. That's all I brought with me.'

Presley's facial muscles flex. He's grinding his teeth. He wants that money. But as badly as he does, he hates to give up the gun. He's like a miser sitting on his last nickel. His eyes burn beneath the bill of the cap, hating me for who I am, for the life I've had. He rolls his tongue around his inner cheek, wanting to tell me to fuck myself. But at last he breaks eye contact and walks toward the glass doors of the trailer. His growl floats back to me on the humid air.

'Get your money, boy.'

I hurry down the dry-rotted stairs of the deck and around the trailer to the Maxima. I parked so that I could open the briefcase in the trunk without being seen from the trailer. Popping the trunk, I move the sack of quick-setting cement behind which I concealed the case and count out twenty-five thousand dollars, which I stuff into the spare tire well. Then I snap the case and shut the trunk.

Before going back to the trailer, I get in the car. Inside the glove box is Dad's 9mm Beretta. I slip the automatic into my waistband at the small of my back, tuck my shirt over it, and head up the front steps.

Presley is waiting for me on the sofa. The sallow blonde is attaching a plastic saline bag to the IV stand, and her back is to me. Her motions are quick and efficient. Presley points at the TV set. Lying atop it in a Ziploc bag is a small .38-caliber revolver, Smith & Wesson. I take a card from my wallet. On it is written the serial number of the pistol my father has not seen for twenty-five years. I remove the .38 from the Ziploc and compare its serial number to the one on the card.

They match.

Resealing the pistol in the bag, I slide it into my trouser pocket and toss the case containing the money onto the sofa. Presley tugs it onto his lap, unsnaps it, and counts the packets with methodical care. As the blonde waits, she glances over her shoulder at me, her eyes vaguely accusatory. Presley finally snaps the case shut, drops it on the floor, leans back on the sofa, and extends his right wrist toward the blonde woman, dorsal side up.

'Time for my poison,' he says, the corners of his mouth turned up with black humor.

The girl removes a heparin-lock catheter from its packaging, swabs Presley's wrist with Betadine, and pops it through the skin in the time it would take most lab techs to locate a vein. As she tears off some white tape and fixes the catheter in place, Presley leans up and slaps her on the rump with the familiarity of a lover. The blonde does not complain or make any move to stop him. She doesn't even look embarrassed.

'You'd best get going, sonny,' he says. 'Crystal's gonna take the edge off the nausea for me.'

The girl half turns to me, a resentful gleam in her eye. The top three buttons of her work shirt are unbuttoned, revealing the clasp of a black bra beneath. She's at least twenty years Presley's junior – probably thirty – and for some reason this offends me. My Puritan morals, I suppose, I'm not one to deny a dying man what pleasure he can get, but something about this arrangement seems wrong. The woman doesn't strike me as a hooker, but Presley is paying her in some way. Probably not much, either. When you're poor, a little money looks like a lot. Or maybe he's not paying her. Maybe she's here because she wants to be here – or needs to be. That bothers me even more.

'I didn't know nurses could administer chemotherapy at home.'

Presley laughs darkly. 'This is my Mexican cocktail. They

UPS it up here from Tijuana. My New Orleans cancer doc says it'll kill me, but I've outlived that bastard's prediction by a year already.'

Bootleg chemotherapy. Is that what's keeping him alive? Or is it just brute redneck stubbornness?

'They cut out my damn prostate,' he mutters, 'but I made 'em leave the nerves in. I can still go like a Brahma bull.'

The blonde sits on the floor at his feet, waiting for me to leave.

'Just remember something, Ray. You've got all you're going to get from this particular well.'

'Nice doing business with you, son. Let me give you a piece of advice before you go.'

'What's that?'

'Leave Del Payton in the ground. You start messing with business that old – especially nigger-business – it makes a lot of people nervous.'

'I figured that out already.'

'You're a smart boy, ain't you?'

The blonde checks Presley's IV line for bubbles, then leans back against his legs.

I walk to the door, but something makes me turn. 'Let me ask you something, Ray. How did Judge Marston get involved in Payton's murder?'

Presley goes as still as a snake poised to strike, his eyes locked on mine. 'Maybe you ain't so smart after all.'

'There's a lot of guys on death row who think different.'

I shut the door, leaving him to his bootleg chemo and his blonde. My stomach is fluttering like the wings of a hummingbird, but the Smith & Wesson is a hard bulge in my left front pocket. I have the gun. *I have the gun.* Seventy-five thousand dollars is a small price to pay to have a spike removed from your heart.

Chapter 14

As soon as I hit the highway, I dial my father's office and wait for him to come to the phone.

'Dr. Cage,' he says finally.

'It's me.'

'What happened?'

'I have the package.'

A long exhalation. An expression of relief I can only guess at. He's been waiting with the same anxiety his patients suffer through when awaiting a call from him about test results. 'Jesus,' he breathes. 'Son, you don't know—'

'Forget it, Dad. It's all over. We'll talk tonight, okay?'

'I can't believe it.'

'Believe it. It's a new world. I'll see you tonight.'

I punch off and zoom south toward Natchez, profoundly aware of the gun in my pocket. I feel like a character from Poe, the symbol of guilt attached to my body and screaming for atonement. But there's no danger. Ray Presley is happy with his seventy-five grand. He isn't calling anybody about that gun. Not today, anyway. With every mile I put between myself and his trailer, the burden of my father's anxiety falls away, and my mind returns to its own selfish concerns.

Ike Ransom awakened a sleeping giant within me. The giant is anger. Anger so profound, complex, and deeply buried that I have never fully plumbed it. I have, in fact, spent years not thinking about it, which required that a constant portion of my life energy be devoted to denial. Yet the anger was always there, pulsing quietly beneath my surface life, affecting my judgment, my decisions, my very concept of justice and morality. For years I thought it was based on Leo Marston's attack on my father, but this was self-delusion. My anguish was not for my father's pain but for my own. The most devastating result of Marston's merciless legal persecution of my father was the end of any possibility that Olivia Marston and I would have a future together. And that altered *my* life in ways beyond measuring. Ultimately, it weakened my character, like a crack in the steel of a bridge. Because always, at the periphery of my existence, the unwalked road of my life with Livy stretched tangentially to infinity, to be reflected upon only in sadness, frustration, and regret. Last night Ike Ransom offered me a chance I never thought I would get: a chance to settle up with Leo Marston for all he did to me and my family. To put paid to two decades of resentment and confusion.

The sheer power of my desire to destroy the man disturbs me. As a prosecutor I tried to divorce myself from the concept of revenge. Justice, not punishment, was my ideal. I didn't always succeed, but I tried. This is different. I have no idea *how* Leo Marston could be involved in Payton's murder, but he is a complex man of vast appetites, and he has rarely been thwarted in his desires. I can easily envision a situation in which he let his temper get the best of him. Great wealth does not confer immunity to violent impulses.

I lift the cell phone and punch in the number of my Houston office, which occupies nine hundred square feet of our house. At least it did until I instructed my assistant to store my furniture and sell the place.

'Penn Cage's office,' says Cilla Daniels.

Relief floods through me. 'I'm glad to know I still have one.'

She laughs. 'I let the movers take everything but the office furniture and equipment.'

'Good instinct. Leave it all set up for now.' I swing the Maxima into the left lane and goose it around a pulpwood truck.

'What about the Hanratty execution?' Cilla asks. 'Mrs. Givens called this morning. She's decided to witness the execution without her husband, and she wants you there.'

'Any last-minute filings? Likely stays?'

'The usual desperation tactics, but they won't stop it this time. And George W. Bush isn't about to grant a pardon. Midnight tomorrow night, Hanratty gets the needle.'

'Damn. Tell Mrs. Givens . . . tell her I don't know yet whether I can make it.'

'Please try, Penn. That woman needs you. You walked her family through the whole trial.'

'Message received. Listen, do you remember Peter Lutjens?'

'Sure. The FBI analyst who helped on *Presumption of Guilt*.'

'I need his phone number at the Bureau.'

'Hang on . . . I think the FBI switchboard is the best I can do on Lutjens.'

'That'll do.' I scrawl the number on my wrist. 'Thanks, Cil. I've got to go.'

'Not so fast. What are you up to? Have you resurrected the manuscript?'

'Just some research.'

'That's what you always say when you're on to something.'

'Bye, Cil.'

I hang up, dial the Hoover Building, and ask for Peter Lutjens, giving my name as Special Agent Jim Gates. During my time with the D.A.'s office, I became friends with several Houston-based field agents, one of whom was Jim Gates. Most of those friends are now stationed around the country and globe, and occasionally prove excellent sources for my books, despite a standing order from FBI Director Portman to give me no assistance. Peter Lutjens is better at research and analysis than chasing bank robbers, and because the FBI knows this as well as I do, they keep him buried in the massive archive of past Bureau case files.

'Gates?' asks a surprised voice. 'What are you doing in Mississippi?'

Lutjens is obviously looking at some sort of caller-ID readout. 'This isn't Jim Gates, Peter. It's Penn Cage.'

'Penn Cage? Jesus, you've got some nerve. What kind of trouble do you want to get me into now?'

'Did I get you into trouble before?'

'Well . . . the acknowledgment in your book made me semi-famous up here. And the new director is no fan of yours, as you well know.'

'The new director's an asshole, Peter, as you well know.'

'No comment. What's going on?'

'I need a favor. It's right up your alley, historical stuff.'

'Save the Vaseline. What is it?'

'I'm looking into a thirty-year-old murder case in my old hometown. A civil rights murder. I know the Bureau worked the case. Somebody took a shot at a couple of your agents on Highway 61 during the same time frame.'

'You've sure got piss-poor timing.'

'Why?'

'Since the opening of the Mississippi Sovereignty Commission files, we've been deluged with requests for records from that period. I'm talking about requests by law enforcement, i.e., *legitimate* requests.'

'I really need this, Peter. It's personal.'

Lutjens doesn't reply. There's no reason for him to bend any rules on my account – other than the goodwill resulting from a few enjoyable lunches, the easy rapport of kindred spirits – and all the reason in the world for him not to. 'I know a guy who's processing those requests,' he says in a cautious voice. 'We worked together on the internal history of the Bureau.'

'Peter—'

'Give me the victim's name.'

'Delano Payton. Killed Natchez, Mississippi, fourteen May 1968.'

'Was anyone convicted of the crime?'

'No one even arrested.'

Lutjens clucks his tongue in admonishment. 'You'll never get a file on a case that's technically open. Not under the Freedom of Information Act.'

'I just want names. The agents who originally worked the case.'

'These guys worked for J. Edgar Hoover, Penn. They're not the talkative type.'

'Somebody always wants to talk. Nobody'll ever know how I found them.'

'Portman would boil my balls for this.' He hesitates a moment longer. 'Stay by your phone. I'll know all I'm ever going to know within five minutes.'

'I'm at—'

'I've got the number.'

I hang up and hit the accelerator, feeling a burst of adrenaline as I eat up the miles between Emerald Mound and the city limits. Lutjens's willingness to help me says a lot about the success – or lack of it – that John Portman has had since taking over the Bureau. When he was appointed to the directorship seven months ago, great things were expected from the former field agent, both within the Bureau and without. But according to the reports I've heard, Portman has displayed the same traits in the Hoover Building that brought him into conflict with me when he was a U.S. attorney. He masks coldness as competence, manipulation as management, and megalomania as superachievement. The simple fact that he still carries a grudge against an ex-assistant district attorney from Houston tells me that he is a pygmy in his soul.

Lutjens calls back as I pull into the drive-through line at Hardee's Hamburgers for some breakfast.

'Call me back from a land line,' he says.

Two pay phones stand at the edge of the gas station lot next to Hardee's. 'Give me thirty seconds.'

I pull out of the line of cars and use my credit card to call Lutjens back. He answers his line in a near whisper.

'This is the only conversation we're going to have on this matter. Don't use names.'

'Okay.'

'You're not the only interested party. A request for the same file came in forty-five minutes before you called. From your local D.A.'s office. An A.M. made the request. You know him?'

Austin Mackey. 'Yes. This case is political dynamite down here. He's probably got the mayor pushing him, trying to cover their asses. Is there any way you can–'

'No copy of the file. No way, no how. Anyway, it's forty-four volumes.'

'Forty-four volumes! How many pages in each?'

'Two to three hundred.'

'Jesus, I wish I could get a look at that.'

'You're not alone in your disappointment. A.M. won't be seeing the file either.'

'Why not?'

'It's sealed.'

'Sealed how?'

'There are several exceptions to the Freedom of Information Act. Reasons we can refuse to release documents. The most common ones exist to safeguard the lives of informants or to protect the privacy of citizens involved in investigations–'

'I know all that. But A.M. is a law enforcement official.'

'We can also refuse to release documents that pose a risk to national security. Under this exception we can refuse to release documents to *anyone*, even other law enforcement agencies.'

'This is a thirty-year-old Mississippi murder. It's got nothing to do with national security.'

'Nevertheless, the file was sealed on grounds of national security in May 1968. The order was signed personally by the director.'

A faint buzzing has started in my head. 'J. Edgar Hoover?'

'The man himself. The file can't be opened for nine more years. Not without a vote by Congress. There's no telling what you've stepped into. Hoover used the rubric of Vietnam to conceal a multitude of sins during the sixties.'

I'm so lost that I don't even know what question to ask. 'What about the names? The agents.'

'I'm going to send a fax to your office. A list of agents working out of the Jackson, Mississippi, field office in the summer of sixty-eight. I don't know how complete it is, but it's the best I can do. Personal memoirs from the period might help you narrow it down.'

'I owe you big-time for this.'

'Yes, you do. Listen, the Bureau has been very supportive of Mississippi prosecutors this year, providing files on these old civil rights cases. Even if the files embarrassed us a bit. This file is obviously different. I'd think long and hard about pursuing it.'

'I will.'

'Watch your back, buddy.'

And with that he is gone.

I pull back onto the highway, heading toward my parents' house. I suddenly have a lot to do today, but I can't do it with a murder weapon in my car. Accelerating through the bypass traffic, I punch in my office number and get Cilla, who tells me Lutjens's fax is already coming through.

'No cover page. It looks like a list of some kind. Sixty or seventy names. Social Security numbers too.'

I say a silent thank-you to Peter Lutjens.

'There's a handwritten note at the bottom. It says, "If you telephone anyone on this list, you've announced your interest to Washington." Penn, what's going on?'

'You don't want to know. Those names belong to FBI agents, probably all retired. Find phone numbers for every one you can. Then start calling them. Give them the usual line: you're working for me, researching a novel. I need to know which agents worked in Natchez, Mississippi, in the summer of 1968. Particularly on the Delano Payton case. Okay?'

'Delano Payton. No problem.'

'Fax a copy of the list to my father's medical office.'

'Right.'

'And, Cil?'

'Yes?'

'Use a fake name on these calls.'

'I will. I'll – My God, a KHOU truck just pulled into the driveway. Got to be about the Hanratty execution.'

'You can handle them.'

'You got that right. I'll call you.'

She rings off.

As I punch End on the cell phone, I see my hand shaking. I am crossing a line I have crossed only a few times previously, and always with sense of euphoria mingled with dread. In the great train of cases that crossed my desk as a prosecutor, a few engaged not merely my mind or my talents or even my heart. A few penetrated the deepest springs of my being: my fears, my prejudices, and my desires. When that happened, I became more than a lawyer. I became a personification of justice. And not justice as the law defined it, but as *I* did.

That is how I feel now.

Last night, when Ike Ransom told me Leo Marston was involved in a thirty-year-old capital murder, I wanted to believe it, but some part of me refused. I could see no possible connection between Marston and his supposed victim. But when Peter Lutjens said the words 'J. Edgar Hoover' and 'national security,' a circuit closed somewhere in my brain, sparking the faintest glimmer of understanding. Leo Marston is a political man from a political family, and if the Delano Payton murder had a political angle sensitive enough for the file to be hidden from public view, then a connection to Leo Marston no longer seems impossible.

Twenty years ago, that ruthless bastard wronged my father, hurt my mother, and stole my future. He did not suffer one moment for doing that. He lived as men of his kind always have: exempt from justice, untouchable. But now, far in the distance, he has come into sight, like a buck on a high ridge line. And this time I have a weapon in my hands. That weapon is a dead man.

Del Payton.

Chapter 15

The district attorney's office is in a three-story building near the courthouse, and there are open parking spaces out front. I take one, then trot up the stairs beside the brass plaque with Mackey's name on it. There is no receptionist, only a long hall with offices on both sides and a black custodian working in a broom closet at the far end. I walk past partly open doors until I see Mackey sitting behind a desk, wearing one of those striped oxford shirts with a white collar that I always found a little too precious.

Pushing open the door, I see a heavyset woman sitting across from Mackey's desk. 'I'm sorry. I'll wait.'

As I close the door, I hear Mackey say, 'Excuse me just a moment, ma'am.' He steps into the hall, looking put upon by the unannounced visit. 'What do you want, Cage?'

'I came to see if you have any files on the Del Payton murder.'

His fair-skinned face goes red, making him look like a pissed-off fraternity boy. 'Do you have wax in your ears? I told you last night there was no file. I also said I'd give you no assistance unless you're the attorney of record for a member of the Payton family.'

'Let's say I am.'

He swallows, brought up short. 'Are you or aren't you? I checked with the bar association this morning. They told you you're licensed to practice in Mississippi.'

'Put it this way, Austin. If you insist on being a pain in the ass, I'm a lot more likely to be.'

His lips disappear into a tight seam.

'What about the file?'

'There *is* no file. After the party last night I stopped by here and checked, just to be sure. All the records from 1966 through 1968 were destroyed in a fire when you and I were still in grade school.'

This throws me. My first instinct is to ask whether Leo Marston was still district attorney during that fire, but I don't. Mackey isn't Clarence Darrow, but if I appear too interested in Marston, he'll zero in on my real motive quickly enough. And Marston will instantly hear about it.

'What about the police department?'

'The chief won't show you files on an unsolved murder case.'

'Is he actually investigating the case?'

'What do you think?'

'I think he may be investigating it before the week is out, whether he wants to or not. What about the sheriff?'

Mackey reaches backward and pulls his door completely shut. 'Why do you have a bug up your ass about this? I don't remember you as a flaming liberal.'

'I'm not. I'm a flaming humanist. I happen to care that some poor son of a bitch was blown to pieces and his family never saw justice done.'

A strange light comes into Mackey's eyes. 'I've got it now. You don't give two shits about Del Payton or his family. You want a best-seller out of this. Maybe get yourself on Oprah's book club? Penn Cage, whitebread crusader for justice.'

'Yeah, that's it.'

Mackey draws himself to his full height, positive that he's divined my true motive. Greed is something he can understand. 'You may be willing to drag this town through the mud for a dollar. I've got more loyalty than that. Don't come back here unless you've got new evidence in your hands.'

He goes back into his office and softly closes the door.

As I turn toward the stairs, I hear footsteps closing quickly on me from behind. I whirl and find myself staring at the black custodian who was standing at the broom closet before. He's over sixty, with bluish skin and pink blemishes like freckles below his eyes, and he reeks of cigarettes.

'Keep walking,' he says.

I move toward the staircase, the custodian on my heels.

'I heard you ask about Del Payton. Mackey tell you all them files burned up in a fire?'

'Yes.'

'Some did, some didn't. Everything that's left is down in the basement. Five, six boxes.'

I stop on the landing. 'Is the basement locked?'

'Yep.' He looks up and down the empty stairwell. 'The door's out back. If you was to check there in about five minutes, you might find a key. When you done, leave it where you found it.'

He shuffles down the stairs without another word.

I wait a few moments, then walk out onto the street and stare across at the oak-shaded courthouse. Sifting through old legal files could take some time. I need to move my father's car in case Mackey comes out before I'm done. When I stopped at my parents' house to take care of the Smith & Wesson, I found that the glass in the BMW had been repaired. I gave the Maxima back to Mom, so that if anyone targeted the BMW again, it would be me, and not my mother and daughter, who took the risk. I also transferred the remaining $25,000 into the trunk of the BMW, meaning to get it back to my father before the end of the day. Climbing inside the car, I pull around the corner, call directory assistance for the number of the *Examiner*, and have them connect me.

'Caitlin Masters, please.'

'Ms. Masters is in a meeting. Would you like me to transfer you to her voice mail?'

'Tell her Penn Cage is on the phone.'

'Sir–'

'Please just do it.'

Thirty seconds later, Caitlin says, 'You'd better not be standing me up for lunch.'

'I do need to postpone. Something's come up.'

'What could be more important than me?'

'Actually, I was going to suggest dinner tonight.'

'Who says change is bad? Does eight o'clock work for you?'

'Yes. Thanks, Caitlin.'

'You can repay me with information.'

I hang up laughing, then lock the car and hurry into the inner square of the block. It harbors parked cars, dumpsters, and fire escapes, but thankfully no people. At the rear of Mackey's building, eight concrete steps and a green handrail descend to a steel door. There's no key in the lock. I go down the steps and feel beneath the crack of the door. Nothing. In the lee of the bottom step lies a broken, rust-colored brick. I bend and lift it.

The key is there.

The basement is lighted by bare hanging bulbs, and it stinks of mildew. I feel like I'm breathing fungus. What I first perceived as walls are stacks of boxes, hundreds of them, old bellied cardboard things that look like they were stolen from a grocery store trash pile. Thankfully, there are dates scrawled on them in black magic marker.

There seems to be no organizing concept. Files from the 1920s have been stacked next to files from the 1970s. I scan the wall of dates as though searching for my size in a display of blue jeans. No luck. But after twenty minutes of digging through rat droppings and dust, I find a short stack of boxes labeled '73 FIRE.

Dragging the stack into the nearest pool of light, I open the top box and riffle through its contents. The files inside are charred, stained, and mildewed, and all date from 1966. I set that box aside and open the next one. My pulse quickens. The files inside are dated 1968.

Starting at the front of the box, I examine the first page inside each folder. Marston's name is all over the files, but none deals with Delano Payton. When I get to the end of the box, I go back to the beginning and flip through every sheet in every folder, but again I find nothing. One by one I go through each folder in the boxes dating from the fire with painstaking care, but I find nothing related to Del Payton.

It looks like Mackey was telling the truth.

After restacking the boxes, I lock the door, put the key back under the brick, and climb back into the sunlight. The custodian is standing thirty yards away, smoking a cigarette in the shadow of a nearby building. I walk straight up to him like a tourist asking for directions.

'Mackey was right.'

He spits on the concrete. 'Shit.'

'You don't happen to clean the police station, do you?'

He shakes his head.

'I guess that's it, then. I appreciate your help.' I start to leave, but he reaches out and touches my elbow.

'You know, we had a couple of black police chiefs. The first one was back in 'eighty-one. I knew him pretty good. He didn't mind stepping on toes to get the job done, so they fired him after a few months. He might know something.'

'What was his name?'

'Willie Pinder.'

'Does he still live in town?'

'He stay over to Gaylor Street. Blue house. Drives a old Dodge pickup.'

'Would he be home during the day?'

'I believe he 'tired. You could see.'

'I'll call him. Hey, I never got your name.'

'That's right. You watch your ass, Penn Cage. And tell your daddy Zoot say hello.'

He grinds his cigarette beneath the heel of a cheap work boot and walks back toward the D.A.'s office.

As soon as I reach the car, I dial directory assistance again. There's a listing for a Willie Pinder on Gaylor Street. This time I dial the number myself.

'Yeah?' says a coarse voice.

'Is Willie there?'

'This Willie.'

I hang up.

Gaylor Street is in a black neighborhood off the road that leads up to the city cemetery. It takes several trips through blocks of small, brightly colored houses, but I finally find the ex-chief's Dodge pickup parked on the street. A cracked pad of cement leads to the rear of the house. I drive around and park near Pinder's back porch. It's fully screened, with rust eating the black wire in big orange patches.

'Who the hell are you?' shouts a hostile voice. 'You just call me on the telephone?'

I wave broadly at the dark screen. For all I know, I'm looking into the barrel of a shotgun. 'I'm Penn Cage. I'm looking for the former chief of police, Willie Pinder.'

'Who you work for, chump?'

The screen door opens with a screech of protesting springs, and a big black head appears in the opening. The sleepy-eyed face says late fifties, with some rough years on the back end.

'Car like that, you ain't no process server. Must be a lawyer. You work for my ex-old lady?'

'No. My name's Penn Cage. If you're Willie Pinder, I want to ask you about the Del Payton murder.'

At the words 'Del Payton' the sleepy eyes wake up. 'I'm Willie,' he says, looking closely at me.

'You got my name, right?'

'Trouble. That's your name.'

'Will you talk to me?'

'Sure.' Pinder laughs. 'I might be hearing your last words. Come on up.'

He holds the door open for me. Three steps lead up to the porch, the kind of weed-grown slat steps that snakes like to lie under in the heat. In one bound I am up and through the door, which slaps shut behind me with a bang like a pistol shot.

'Porch is far enough,' says Pinder. 'Hotter inside anyway. AC's busted. You want a beer?'

'Sure.' I try not to glance at my watch; it can't be eleven a.m. yet.

Pinder goes inside and returns with two sweating cans of Schaefer. He hands me one, then sits beside me in a green iron lawn chair, pops the top off his can, and drinks.

'So you're retired now?' I say, opening my beer.

He laughs again. 'That don't quite seem to say it. I'm fucked now. How about that?'

I'm not sure how to proceed. I don't want the man's life story, but neither do I want to offend him. Thankfully, Pinder spares me.

'You the crazy man who popped off about Del Payton in the paper?'

'I mentioned the case.'

'Case? Ain't no *case* on Del Payton.'

'What about a file, then? There must have been a police file.'

He takes another long swig of Schaefer. 'I was pretty busy back then. It was all I could do to hold the goddamn place together.'

'I'm sure. Still, I'd think you might have wanted to check some things the white chiefs had let slide for too long.'

Pinder sniffs and looks through the rusted screen. 'I worked in that department eleven years, and I never saw no Payton file. Didn't think there was one. But when the old chief gave me the combination to the station safe, and I opened it up, there it was. Sitting on the bottom of a stack of insurance policies. Just like that. First day on the job.'

'Did the police seriously investigate the case in sixty-eight?'

He smiles. 'In 1968 the city slogan was "Natchez, Where the Old South Still Lives." It *looked* like they investigated. There was lots of confidential-information reports, rumors tracked down, stuff like that.'

'Any suspects?'

'A couple.'

'Who?'

He smiles enigmatically. 'You know, I might ought to check the file. My memory ain't what it used to be.'

Something quivers in my chest. 'How can you check the file?'

'Easy. I got it inside.'

Jesus. 'You made a copy?'

'Nope. I got the original. Took it when they screwed me out of my job.'

I feel like hugging him. 'May I see it?'

'I ain't no loan library, boy. I think we're talking about a rental situation here.'

'How much?'

Pinder's face goes blank as he computes a price. 'Five

hundred,' he says finally, a note of challenge in his voice. 'And you read it right here in front of me.'

When I think of what I just paid Ray Presley for my father's .38, I feel like laughing. 'A thousand,' I counter. 'But I take the file with me. I'll photocopy it and get the original back to you within twenty-four hours.'

Pinder has lost a little of his studied calm. 'How 'bout two thousand?'

'What's in the file? How long is it?'

'About twenty-five pages. Plenty of names in there, if that's what you're after.'

'Any mention of Judge Marston in it? He was D.A. back then.'

Something ticks in the ex-chief's face. 'That motherfucker in there.'

'Two thousand it is.'

His head slides back on his neck, his eyes full of suspicion. 'I don't want no check, now.'

'You get the file, I'll get the cash.'

'You got it here?'

'Oh, yeah. Get the file.'

While Pinder goes inside, I go to the car and open the spare tire well, count two thousand dollars from the remaining twenty-five, and return to the porch. Shuffling and sliding sounds come from inside the house, as though Pinder is moving furniture. Then the door bangs open and he reappears with a worn manila folder in his hand. I hand him the cash, and he takes it, but he doesn't pass me the file. He sits down again and drinks from his beer can.

'You ain't asked me if I solved the case or not.'

'Did you?'

'No.' He looks at me out of the corner of his eye. 'But not because it ain't solvable. I kept that file close to my vest, man. Didn't tell no white officers nothin' 'bout it. Told a couple of black ones I trusted I was gonna be working the case real quiet. One week later somebody sent me a message.'

'What kind of message?'

'They sent a man to talk to me. A man I hated but wasn't about to ignore.'

'Who was he?'

'Ray Presley.'

I try to keep my composure, but Pinder cannot fail to notice the thunderous effect the name has on me. 'I know Presley,' I say carefully. 'He was somehow involved in the original case.'

'That's right. And that son of a bitch'll kill a man like picking off a scab. He's killed for less than what you just give me.'

'Did he threaten you over the Payton case?'

'Not the way I expected. If he had, I'd have thrown him in a cell. He'd been to Parchman by then, and I was still riding my high horse. He didn't say, "Stay out of this or you might wind up dead." No, he said, "I hear you're thinking about looking into the Del Payton murder, Willie. I worked that case myself in sixty-eight, worked it hard, and just about the time I thought we was getting somewhere, somebody told me to leave it alone. And I did. I left it alone. I was white and I wanted to solve that bombing, but I let it go. You ought to think about that."'

'What do you think he meant? Who was he talking about?'

'Don't know.' Pinder's voice softens, becomes vulnerable. 'But anybody who could put fear into Ray Presley scared me plenty. My kids was still living with me then, and I wasn't about to watch them die for my pride. Or black pride, or whatever you want to call it. I couldn't even trust the brothers in my own department. How far was I gonna get? Del Payton was gonna be just as dead either way.'

'Was it the Klan, you think?'

'The Klan? Shit. Klan wouldn't scare Ray Presley. Those

kluckers scared of *him*. He did shit them crackers only talked about.'

'Could it have been the FBI?' I ask, recalling Lutjens's story of the sealed file.

A funny gleam comes into Pinder's eyes. 'Why you ask that?'

'Is it possible?'

'Anything's possible. The feds and the local cops didn't get on too good then. Not much better now, really. But why they'd warn Presley off . . . don't make no sense. Hoover hated Martin Luther King. But Del didn't have nothing to do with no big-time peoples like that.' Pinder stands suddenly and drops the file in my lap. 'We finished here.'

Despite this strong hint to leave, I open the file. The first page is headed: SUPPLEMENTARY INVESTIGATION REPORT, and dated 5-15-68. Beneath this is typed: *Delano Payton Murder Bombing*. Then come four handwritten paragraphs that appear to detail an anonymous phone call. The signature beneath them reads, *Patrolman Ray Presley*.

'You can do your reading at home,' Pinder says. 'I'm goin' fishin'. Gonna spend the afternoon forgettin' I ever saw you.'

I stand and shake his hand. 'I appreciate the help, Chief. Don't spend it all in one place.'

He chuckles. 'Hey, I got an old bulletproof vest I can sell you. Wanna take a look?'

'I don't plan to need it.' I push open the screen door and walk quickly down the steps. 'I'll drop the original back tomorrow.'

'Keep it. I don't want no part of that no more.'

'I never saw you.' I put one leg into the BMW. 'Hey . . . if you really gave up on the case, why'd you steal the file when you left?'

Pinder stands motionless in the open doorway. 'Get a little of my own back, I guess. I knew I'd be the last black chief for a long time.' He smiles oddly, as though he has just seen something in a new light. 'Maybe that file's been waiting here for you all this time. Mysterious ways, right? Maybe the bastards won't get you after all.'

I give Pinder a salute. 'Hope they're biting today, Chief.'

He winks at me. 'They biting every day, if you know where to look.'

Chapter 16

The Payton house is a typical rural home, built with cheap materials on concrete blocks, but better maintained than most. Lovingly tended flower beds border the front, concealing the dark crawl space beneath the structure. The cars in the driveway are probably worth more than the house, but at least the nearest neighbor is fifty yards up the road.

Georgia Payton sits beneath a large pin oak, rocking slowly in a white cotton dress. She lifts a hand as I pull into the driveway, but she does not get up.

I walk over to say hello before going to the front door. 'Hot one, isn't it?'

She cackles at me. 'I lived three-quarters of my life without no air conditioning. The Lord's breeze be good enough for me.'

'Mr. Cage?'

Althea Payton is beckoning to me from the door. She wears navy shorts and a red blouse tied at the waist. She looks like she's been gardening.

'Come in out of that heat!' she calls. 'Georgia's fine out there.'

I smile at the old woman, then cross the drive and follow Althea into the house.

'Georgia's like an old loggerhead turtle sunning herself on a rock,' she says. 'I asked her to stay outside while we talk. She can be a little hard to handle. Have a seat.'

I sit on a flame-print love seat, and Althea takes a cloth-covered easy chair to my right. The living room holds old but clean furniture, all of it arranged around a new television set. Dozens of framed family photos hang on the wall behind the TV. I look away when I realize I'm staring at a wedding photo of Del and Althea. They look young and happy, destined for anything but what happened to them in the spring of 1968.

'On the phone,' she says hesitantly, 'you said it was about my husband.'

'Yes, ma'am.' My next words are an irrevocable step. 'I've decided to look into Del's death after all. I've already taken some steps in that direction.'

She seems not to have understood. Then her eyes well up and her voice spills out in a reverent tone. 'Sweet Lord Jesus, I can't believe it.'

'I don't want us to get ahead of ourselves. There may not be anything to find out.'

She nods, her hands clasped over her chest. 'I realize that. I just . . . it's been so many years. Do you have any idea what you need to charge me?'

'Yes. I'm going to need a retainer of one dollar. And I'll bill you for my time at the rate of one dollar per day.'

She shakes her head in confusion. 'You can't be serious.'

'I'm deadly serious. Althea. Don't give it another thought.'

She wipes tears from her eyes, and I look away. The wall to her left holds the sacred trinity of photographs I've seen in the homes of many black families: Martin Luther King, JFK, and Abraham Lincoln. Sometimes you see Bobby, or FDR. But the Paytons have only the big three. A plastic clock hangs above the photographs, its face painted with a rather bloated likeness of Dr. King. The words *I HAVE A DREAM* appear in quotes beneath him.

'Georgia bought that clock from some traveling sales-man in May of 1968,' Althea says. 'It stopped running before that Christmas, but she never let me get rid of it.'

'Maybe it's a collectors' item.'

'I don't care. Those clocks probably put a million dollars in some sharpie's pocket.' She grips her knees with her palms and fixes her eyes on me. 'Could I ask you one thing?'

'Why did I change my mind?'

'Yes.'

'I have a personal stake in the case now. I want to be honest with you about that.'

'Are you going to write a book about Del? Is that it?'

'No. But if anybody asks you what I was doing here, that's what you tell them. And I mean anybody, police included. Okay?'

'Whatever you say. But what is your personal interest, if not a book?'

'I'd prefer to keep that to myself, Althea.'

She looks puzzled, then relieved. 'I'm glad you've got a stake in it. You having a child like you do. It would be too hard if I thought you were taking this risk only for me.'

'I'm not. Rest assured of that.'

'Thank you.' She leans back in her chair and looks at me with apprehension. 'What can you tell me? Have you learned anything yet?'

'We won't be getting any help from the district attorney. The police either, if my guess is right. I've managed to obtain some documentary information dating back to 1968 that could be helpful, but that's between us and God.'

'Can you tell me what it is?'

'No. I won't expose you to potential criminal charges.'

She nods soberly. 'Just tell me this. Do you think there's any hope? Of finding out the truth, I mean.'

I fight the urge to be optimistic. A lawyer has to make that mistake only once to learn what it costs. You give people hope; then the pendulum swings the wrong way and they're left shattered, as much by false hope as by misfortune.

'I wouldn't take the case if there wasn't hope. But I want to proceed cautiously. I promise to contact you if and when I learn anything of value. I understand that you've waited a long time for justice.'

Althea's hands are clenched in her lap, the knuckles white.

'If you feel up to it, I'd like you to tell me what you can about what Del was doing at the battery plant before he died. For civil rights, I mean.'

She takes a deep breath and closes her eyes, as though striving to remember with perfect accuracy. 'Del wasn't any big civil rights worker. He was a workingman. He just saw things he thought were wrong and did what he could to change them. When he was a young man, he was carefree. You never saw a smile so full and happy. When he went to Korea, something changed in him. He still had that smile, but it didn't fill up his eyes the way it used to. He was different inside. He got shot over there, and I think he saw some pretty bad things. When he got back, he told me life was too short to spend it standing at the back of the line.'

'When did he go to work at Triton Battery?'

'A couple of years after the war. He put in his time and saved his money back then. Said he didn't want to marry me till he could afford to take care of me like I deserved.' Althea's voice cracks a little, but she smiles. 'I sure got tired of waiting. Del bought this house in 1959, for cash money. Not many black men could do that back then.'

'You got married in fifty-nine?'

She nods. 'It was right around then that Del met Medgar.'

'Medgar Evers?'

'Yes. Medgar heard how good Del was doing at the plant, and wanted to meet him. Medgar was building up the NAACP back then, pushing voter registration. Del *loved* Medgar. Loved his quiet way. Said he'd known men like Medgar in the army. Quiet men who worked hard and wouldn't back down for anything. Medgar took to Del too.

He saw that Del didn't hate the white man. Del believed if we could help white people see inside us, see past the color, their hearts would change.'

'So Medgar got Del into civil rights work?'

'Lord, yes. Medgar ate right in this house whenever he came through town.' Althea shakes her head sadly. 'When Beckwith killed Medgar in June of sixty-three, Del changed again. He said the war had come home to America. Then President Kennedy was shot that November. Del had joined the NAACP by then, of course, and by 1965 he was in charge of voter registration for this area. Del was the highest-ranking black man at the battery plant. Even the white men liked him. They knew he knew his job.'

'Who do you think planted that bomb, Althea?'

'Well . . . the Klan, I guess. There were a lot of beatings out at the paper mill around then, Klan workers beating black workers. You know. Scaring them off. There was some Klan at the tire plant, and at the battery plant too.'

'A car bomb is quite an escalation from a beating. Did Del have any personal enemies you know of?'

'Del didn't have an enemy in this world.'

He had at least one, I say silently. But it's certainly possible that Payton was chosen at random, to send a warning to someone. 'Did he seem any more worried than usual about going to work near the time of his death?'

She shakes her head. 'We had some death threats, but we got those with every promotion Del had. He just kept on keeping on. He'd say, "Thea, we can't let 'em get us down."'

I remember the nightmarish weeks of the Hanratty trial, when death threats arrived almost daily. What courage it must have taken for Del Payton to get up every morning of his life and go to work with men he knew wanted him dead.

'He was depressed,' Althea adds. 'Over Dr. King's death. Martin was assassinated just five weeks before Del was killed.

And Del was so saddened by that, because already he saw the Movement being taken over by advocates of violence. Men with bitterness in their hearts. Stokely Carmichael and the rest. Black racists, he called them.'

The more I learn about Del Payton, the more I feel that his murder was a terrible loss to the community in which I grew up. 'Does anything else stand out?'

'No. The FBI asked me all this back when it happened, and I told them the same thing. One day Del went to work and just didn't come home.'

I looked helplessly around the room. Del Payton has been dead for thirty years, but he is as alive here as a dead man can be. When Annie is a grown woman, will this large a piece of my heart still be reserved for Sarah?

'Do you remember the names of any of the FBI agents who talked to you?'

'I remember one, very well. Agent Stone. He was about Del's age, and he'd served in Korea too. Agent Stone really tried to help me. But he was the only one. He had a younger man with him who never said much. He didn't care nothing about us. Like all the rest.'

'Do you remember his name?'

'No. Just a stuck-up Yankee. Agent Stone came by the house before he left town the last time. He apologized for not having gotten justice for Del. He was a good man, and I got the feeling he knew there was some dirty work at the crossroads on Del's case.'

'Did he say anything specific?'

'No. He just seemed like he wanted to say more than he could.'

'Do you know a deputy named Ike Ransom? Some people used to call him Ike the Spike.'

A strange stillness comes over Althea. 'They still call him that. Ike was a good boy who turned out bad. He got on that dope over in Vietnam and drank all the years after that. He hurt a lot of black people to impress his bosses. Why you asking about Ike Ransom?'

'It's not important.' I stand. 'I think that's enough questions for now.'

Althea studies me for a few moments, then stands and presses her shorts flat against her thighs. 'Come out to the garden and let me get you some tomatoes.'

'Oh, no. But thank you.'

'Nonsense. Your daddy *loves* my tomatoes. I been paying him in tomatoes for years.'

I follow her to the kitchen, where she picks up a Piggly Wiggly sack and goes out the back door.

The backyard is bordered by woods, and most of the yard is taken up by a vegetable garden laid out with architectural precision. The vines along the ground are bursting with squash and rattlesnake watermelons, and the tomato plants stand four feet tall. Toward the back rows I see butter beans, corn, collards, and pole beans. The only eyesore is a rusted, weed-grown husk of a car sitting up on blocks on the near side of the garden.

Althea pulls a red bandanna from her back pocket, ties it around her head, and walks between two rows of tomato plants. I check the junker for obvious wasp nests, then climb onto its trunk and watch Althea pick prize specimens for her sack.

'This is some garden,' I call after her.

'Daddy always had a garden. Drove mama crazy. We had mason jars stacked to the ceiling at canning time.'

The low rumble of a truck passing on the road breaks the stillness, then fades. I wish Annie was here to see the garden.

'I don't know why I keep that old wreck,' Althea says from among the plants. 'It makes me sad more than anything. But sometimes it reminds me of the times me and Del went riding out by the river, when we were young. We'd roll down the window and cruise up the levee road, listening to Nat Cole. Del would have his arm around me, and it was like nobody could touch us. We could do anything we wanted, you know? Go anywhere. It was just a dream, but it was a good one.'

I feel a strange heat at the back of my neck. For the first time I really look at the car I am sitting on. It's a Ford Fairlane. A white sedan, maybe a '61. I slide off it slowly.

'Is this . . . ?'

'I thought you recognized it when you first saw it,' Althea says, stepping out of the rows. 'From the newspaper picture.'

'I guess it's the rust,' I say distractedly.

The Fairlane's hood is lying crossways over the engine compartment. I put my hands under the hot metal and flip the hood off the car. Several desiccated wasp nests cling to the fender wells, but it's not the wasp nests that send a chill through me. The Ford's engine is a mass of mangled metal. The bomb that killed Del Payton was set between the engine block and the firewall. The explosion blew the motor forward, breaking the mounts, tore the transmission away from the bell housing, and cut a fissure through the lower part of the firewall. I can't believe Payton survived two seconds after that blast. Even the engine block shows signs of shearing, and the whole compartment is littered with tiny metal fragments. The exhaust manifold was sliced in two like a length of salami. This image tickles something at the back of my mind.

'It sat rusting behind the jail for a year,' Althea says. 'I thought they were keeping it in case they got a clue about the bombing, but they'd just forgot about it. So I had my father tow it out here. Nothing but a home for birds and wasps now.'

As I bend over the wrecked engine, something else strikes me. This car burned. I knew that, of course, from Caitlin's article, and also from the picture, but it never really registered. Rust has eaten away the charring on the exterior of the car, but the passenger compartment is a nightmare of blackened metal and melted plastic. This too has hidden significance.

'What do you see?' Althea asks.

'I'm not sure.'

Alarms are ringing now. I don't know the significance of what I am seeing, but I know with utter certainty that it *is* significant. And I know a man who can tell me why. While researching my third novel, I spent two days with a BATF explosives expert named Huey Moak. Huey showed me a lot of photographs and even more pieces of stretched and twisted metal. What I'm seeing now, I saw in some of those photos.

'Do you mind if I borrow a piece of this engine?'

'Take the whole car if it will help.'

Reaching down into the mass of metal debris, I pull out a flat piece about two inches square, sheared off as cleanly as if it had been cut by a blowtorch. I slip this into my pocket, then rake a handful of tiny shrapnel off the top of a smashed and corroded Triton battery. Like his coworkers, Del Payton got his batteries at a sixty percent discount from the company.

'May I borrow your bandanna?'

Althea unties the red cloth from her head and hands it to me. I lay it on the roof of the Fairlane, set the shrapnel in it, and tie the cloth into a tight sack.

'Thanks. I'd better get going.'

'You've seen something,' she says. 'You're excited. I can tell.'

'Yes, but I don't know what it means. I'll let you know as soon as I do.'

She looks into my eyes, then nods. 'All right. I'll walk you to your car.'

As we round the house, a battered pickup pulls into the drive. Three black kids stand in back, looking over the roof of the cab. Two girls and a boy. The truck wheezes to a stop, and a black man a few years younger than I gets out wearing a grease-stained jumpsuit. As he approaches, I see a white patch on his breast pocket. The word DEL is stenciled on it in red. Over his shoulder, Georgia Payton continues her purposeful rocking.

'Penn,' says Althea, 'this is my son, Del Junior. Del, this is Mr. Penn Cage.'

I offer my hand, but the man makes no move to shake it.

'*You shake this man's hand*,' Althea snaps in a voice crackling with maternal authority. 'This the man who's going to find out who killed your daddy.'

Del Jr. grudgingly holds out his hand, and I shake it. You'd have to cut a quarter inch into his palm to draw blood.

'Take the kids inside,' Althea tells him.

Del Jr. jerks his head toward the house, and the children walk backwards to the front door, staring at me as they go. Del looks at my father's BMW, and it's painfully easy to read his face. The money that car cost would keep his family fed and sheltered for five years. He turns and follows his kids into the house.

'He's got a lot of bitterness in his heart,' Althea says.

'He's got reason to. I sure thank you for the tomatoes.'

'Any time, Penn.'

I get into the car and lay the bandanna on top of the police file, then wave at Georgia Payton as I drive away. She doesn't respond.

As I clear the first turn, the significance of what I saw in Del Payton's charred Fairlane bursts into my conscious mind with the brilliance of a flare. I pull onto the shoulder, park, and with shaking hands pick up the file I bought from Willie Pinder. Caitlin's article said Del's car was destroyed by dynamite. That fit with the story I'd heard all my life. But if I remember Huey Moak's drawled lectures correctly, much of what I saw five minutes ago contradicts that version of events.

For one thing, dynamited cars almost never burn. Payton's did. But it's the shearing that's important. Whatever exploded in that Fairlane attacked both engine and firewall with tremendous cutting force, like an acetylene torch completing its job in a fraction of a second. It left shrapnel no bigger than thumbtacks. And it created a flash hot enough to set fire to a car constructed with only a fraction of the plastic used in modern vehicles. I can still hear Huey's voice in my mind: *Those are characteristics of a uniquely stable, versatile, and powerful explosive that the Army calls C-4. The Russians call it Semtex. The French, plastique.* Civilians call it good old plastic explosive . . .

Fifteen pages into the Payton file, I find the crime-scene report. Near the middle of the page a handwritten sentence reads 'Bomb constructed of unknown material' in black ink. But a blue line has been drawn through the words 'unknown material' and the words 'commercial-grade dynamite' written above them. At the bottom of the page, a note in blue reads, 'One day following the initial scene investigation, Patrolman Ray Presley discovered fragments of civilian blasting caps and wire fragments in the wooded area one hundred feet from the vehicle. Subsequent lab analysis showed traces of nitroglycerine.' Nitroglycerine is one of the main ingredients in dynamite. Beneath that final note are two signatures: *Detective First Grade Henry Creel* and *Detective Ronnie Temple.*

One day after a bomb destroyed Del Payton's Fairlane, Ray Presley discovered 'proof' that the bomb was made of dynamite. Thirty years later I glance into the same car and find evidence that seems to indicate something quite different. I could be wrong, of course. I know of no reason why Presley should lie about the type of bomb that destroyed Del Payton's car. And speculation is pointless until I know that he did. But that's the beauty of physical evidence. I'll get my answer. All I have to do is get that sheared fragment and sack of shrapnel to Huey Moak, then convince the BATF agent that it's in his interest to help me. And the surest way to do that is to let him know that a quick analysis could put a great deal of egg on the face of the FBI.

Though I can't see how, I am strangely certain that I've taken one step closer to Leo Marston.

Chapter 17

'Daddy, look at the crawdads! They've got humongous claws!'

Annie races across the patio and leaps into my arms like a thirty-pound bullet. Though petite for her age, she is wiry and strong, like her mother.

'You'd better not let one get your nose!' I warn her. 'It'll thunder seven times before he turns loose.'

'Your daddy's lying to you, girl,' Ruby calls from beside the pool. 'That's a snapping turtle he talking 'bout. Crawfish can't hurt you none.'

'One already pinched my finger!' Annie cries. 'It didn't even hurt.'

Dad is tending a five-gallon boiler near the house, and the roar of burning propane makes my stomach rumble, a Pavlovian response that remains automatic even after twenty years away. A cooler full of live crawfish sits beside the boiling water.

'Sam Jacobs brought these by,' he explains. 'He went over to Catahoula Parish to look at a stripper well and brought them back. They're good-sized. Pretty too.'

'Did you ask him to stay?'

'He said he had to get home, but that you should call him one night and go get a beer.'

'I could use one now.'

'There's a six-pack of Corona in the fridge. Limes too. Bring me a Heineken while you're at it.'

'On the way.'

I walk over and hug Ruby, then go inside. My mother's in the kitchen, washing corn and potatoes for the crawfish pot. She asks how my day went, and I say something inane about how little the town has changed. During the past hour I photocopied the Del Payton police file, rented a safe deposit box and stored the original inside, bought packaging material at Fred's Dollar Store, and delivered the fragments of Del's engine to the UPS office five minutes before they closed. I also spoke to Huey Moak, whom Cilla tracked down in Lexington, Kentucky, where he is investigating an explosion at the university. Huey could not conceal his pleasure at the prospect of solving a bombing case the FBI had bungled, even if it was thirty years old. The engine fragments will arrive before noon tomorrow at the Holiday Inn where he and his BATF team are staying. All that activity left me only one task to complete: the felony I started this morning.

I carry a Heineken out to my father and sit in a lawn chair at the edge of the pool. Annie has taken two crawfish from the cooler and is trying to make them race across the patio. She quickly learns that the only direction crawfish will move under duress is backward. I sip the Corona and watch the crustacean derby while Dad purges the mudbugs in the cooler by dumping salt water over them. Mom brings out a huge bowl of new potatoes, corn, and onions, which she dumps into the steaming pot along with three bags of Zatarain's crab boil. The sharp aroma of spices fills the air, making my mouth water, and Annie stares with saucer eyes as Dad loads the wire-mesh inner boiler with brown crawfish and submerges them in the boiling water. When he hauls them out twenty minutes later, they are a flaming red-orange.

'Wow!' Annie marvels.

'Time to eat 'em!' Dad says.

Mom covers the wrought-iron patio table with newspaper,

and Dad dumps the steaming crawfish onto the center, making a small mountain. I spear some potatoes and corn with a fork and make a plate for Annie, assuming she likes the look of crawfish better than she'll like the taste. But I'm wrong. She isn't strong enough to crack the tails efficiently, but with Dad peeling for her, she goes through a half pound of tails before she's done. As I watch her joyful eyes, the Payton case recedes in my mind. I should have brought Annie here right after the funeral. My mother's matter-of-fact attitude toward the mysteries of life has already brought her out of her melancholia. When Annie announces that her tummy is full, Mom leads her over to the faucet to wash the hot spices from her hands.

'Annie wants ice cream,' Mom calls from the faucet. 'Anybody else?'

'Y'all go ahead,' Dad shouts back. 'We'll clean up this mess and be inside in a minute.'

He slides a cigar from his pocket and puts it in his mouth, but doesn't begin the ritual of lighting it. 'You want another beer?'

'I'd better skip it. We need to take a ride.'

He raises an eyebrow. 'We do?'

I raise my hand and make a mock pistol with my thumb and forefinger, then drop my thumb like a hammer.

'I see. Let's clean this mess up for your mother first.'

As he begins wrapping the crawfish shells in newspaper, I carry the heavy boiler to the edge of the yard to dump the water. The gun is only twenty feet away from me, in the pool house, preparing for its final journey.

I am standing in the stern of a rusty green johnboat, poling it across a cypress swamp south of town. The sky is aflame with orange and purple light, the dying sun turning the hanging moss into long black beards on the cypress limbs. The johnboat belongs to a pumper who monitors an oil well that stays underwater for much of the year. The well has been pumping for over twenty years, and the johnboat has been sitting in a thicket nearby for most of that time. Sam Jacobs pointed it out to me one summer during college.

Dad sits forward, facing me, smoking his cigar and keeping watch on the receding shoreline. Between us stands a five-gallon plastic paint bucket filled with rock-hard cement. Embedded somewhere inside it is the Smith & Wesson .38 I bought from Ray Presley this morning. Dad flips some ash into the water and speaks in a casual voice.

'A patient told me she saw my car over at Willie Pinder's house today. She asked if the ex-chief was having heart trouble again.'

'God can take a rest from watching sparrows fall in Natchez,' I reply. 'Nothing gets by anybody here.'

He laughs mirthlessly. 'And a rather strange fax arrived at my office this morning. A list of names with a note at the bottom saying something about Washington.'

I forgot all about the fax. 'I'm sorry about that. Where is it now?'

He takes a folded piece of fax paper from his pocket. 'What's it about? This list?'

'Those are FBI agents who worked out of the Jackson field office in 1968. Did you see the name Stone on it?'

He unfolds the paper and scans it, then shakes his head. 'No Stone. Where'd you get that name?'

'Althea Payton remembered a sympathetic FBI man.'

'And the visit to Willie Pinder?'

'Pinder had the original police file on the Payton murder. He stole it when he lost his job as chief. I bought it from him.'

My father looks out over the dark water. Already the ranks of cypress trunks screen us from anyone on shore. 'I know what I said yesterday. About how justice needs to be done.

God knows black people have had a shitty deal for a long time. I saw things growing up in Louisiana that I'd never want to say out loud. I understand why your blood is up. You and Althea Payton have experienced one of the worst tragedies there is. Losing a spouse, I mean. But I don't think you fully appreciate the danger of what you're doing.'

'I think I do. Everybody I talk to tells me to watch my back.'

'That's not what I'm talking about. I'm going to be candid, son. You're not my main concern here. If a man wants to risk his life for something noble, that's his lookout. But Annie's life is something else.'

The undercurrent of fear in his voice gives me pause. 'Do you really think whoever killed Payton would hurt Annie or Mom?'

'Anybody who'll hide in the shadows and bomb a man is capable of anything. They're scum. Dogs. And they have the dog's pack mentality.' He gives me the cold eye. 'You've already been shot at. You put these people at risk for the death house at Parchman, they'll come for you the way they're surest to get you. And that's through your family.'

'Who is this "they" you're talking about? Do you have any idea?'

My father sighs and looks at the bottom of the boat, then picks up a red and white plastic fishing bob and starts working the line mechanism with his thumb. 'Natchez is a good town. I've practiced here thirty-five years, and I know. But towns are like people. Even the best of us has dark places in his soul. Fears, prejudices, appetites. The capacity for sin, I suppose. Whoever's behind this Payton business is an expression of that. It could be some white-trash asshole, or our next-door neighbor. The point is, you'll never see them coming.'

'Dad, if you'll listen to me for one minute, I think you'll understand why I have to do this.'

'Nothing to do out here *but* listen.'

'Do you know a deputy named Ike Ransom?'

'Sure. Ike the Spike. I treated his mother for years.'

'He followed me home last night after the party. He wants Payton's killer punished. And he knows who it is.'

'Why doesn't he do something about it, then? He was a cop for twenty years.'

'He's scared.'

Dad shakes his head wearily. 'Over the years at least three men I know of have claimed they killed Delano Payton. Drunk rednecks like to take credit for that kind of thing. Ransom probably overheard something like that and believed it. Who does he say did it?'

'Leo Marston.'

Dad's mouth drops open. 'Leo Marston? That's crazy. Marston's a lot of things, but he's no racist.'

'That's what I thought too. But how do you know he's not?'

'Well . . . I've seen pictures of him with Bobby Kennedy, for one thing. With Charles and Medgar Evers too. I think I even saw a shot of him with Martin Luther King.'

'How do you know that wasn't just public relations?'

'In the sixties? A white man posing with the Evers boys and King?' Dad shakes his head again. 'Is Livy Marston a racist?'

'No. But that doesn't prove anything.'

'Sure it does. Apples don't fall far from the tree.' He draws thoughtfully on his cigar. 'Ike Ransom's a bad alcoholic, son. Has been for years. I think he's playing you. He knows Marston hurt our family, so that makes Marston the best way to suck you into the Payton case. He figures once you're into it, you'll go for the throat of whoever turns out to be guilty. That's what the blacks in this town want, and I don't blame them.'

'I don't think blacks want that at all. Shad Johnson sure doesn't. They want that new chemical plant in here as much as anybody. I can't believe you're defending Marston.'

He slaps himself like a madman as a horsefly the size of a small fighter plane attacks him, refusing to give quarter. Fearing that this battle will overturn the boat, I scramble forward and smash the insect against his shoulder.

'Thanks,' he mutters. 'I'm not defending that bastard. But Leo Marston destroys people. He doesn't murder them.'

'You're thinking in a business context. What if it was personal? Maybe Payton and Marston had business dealings of some kind. Or maybe Payton was in a position to know something about Marston's personal affairs.'

He dismisses this with a flip of his hand. 'No way, no how. Different universes.'

'Ike's anger felt personal to me. He *hates* Marston.'

'That's a big club. Look, for all we know, Marston sent Ike Ransom's brother to jail. He could have any kind of grudge against Marston, and we wouldn't know it.'

'But if Marston's *not* involved in the Payton case, how would putting me on it hurt Marston? You see? You can't have it both ways.'

He groans in exasperation.

'You're looking for logic,' I continue. 'But Marston went after you for malpractice in 1979, and we never learned why. Motives aren't always obvious.'

Now he's listening.

'Leo Marston was D.A. when Payton was killed. I think that's how he's tied into it. When Willie Pinder became police chief, he started looking into Payton's murder. Very quietly, using only black officers. But before he got far, somebody warned him off the case.'

'Who?'

'Ray Presley.'

Dad tosses his cigar into the water, where it hisses and sputters out. 'Why am I not surprised?'

'Ray told Willie that he'd tried to solve the case in sixty-eight, but that *he'd* been warned off too. He wouldn't say by whom, but it was enough to scare him off.'

'That would take some doing.'

'That's what Willie said. He dropped it. Didn't Presley do a lot of work for Marston in the seventies?'

'I believe he did.'

'Think about it. We've got Ray Presley, a blatant racist, investigating a politically sensitive race murder while Leo Marston is D.A. I don't think it's outside the realm of possibility that Marston could have committed criminal acts under those circumstances.'

'But *why*? That's what I can't see.'

'I don't know.'

'Wouldn't the statute of limitations have run out on anything short of murder?'

'That's right. Anything short of murder.'

He looks like a sculpture in the bow of the boat, frozen in contemplation. We're two hundred yards from shore now, far enough that even a severe drought would be unlikely to uncover the swamp bottom. Even if it did, there would only be the cement-filled pail lying in the baking mud among the dead fish and loggerhead turtles. A lost anchor. Nothing else.

I lift the long pole out of the water and lay it along the gunwale of the boat. Dad starts to get up, but I motion for him to stay seated. The last thing we need is to capsize in water teeming with water moccasins, and perhaps even alligators.

I drag the heavy bucket toward the stern and lift it onto my seat, then sit beside it, flex my arms, and roll it over between my legs. After a deep breath, I slip my hands under it and stand up, using my legs for power. In seconds my arms are quivering from the weight.

'Throw it!' Dad cries.

I heave the bucket to my left and into the black water, heeling the boat hard to starboard and almost losing my balance. The splash sounds like a cannonball and showers both of us with slimy water.

'God almighty!' Dad exults. 'I thought we were going over!'

'That gun is history,' I say quietly. 'Let's go to the house.'

I pick up the pole, plunge it to the muddy bottom, and work the bow back around until it points to the dirt road where we parked Dad's pickup. High above us, a hawk circles over unseen prey. As it sails through the falling dusk, Dad says: 'Could it have been the feds who warned Ray off the Payton case?'

Despite the heat, I feel a shiver deep in my chest. Willie Pinder's remarks are playing in my head. 'What makes you ask that?'

'I remember a picture from somewhere. It showed Marston and J. Edgar Hoover together. Both of them glaring into the camera like junior G-men. Marston always claimed to be a personal friend of Hoover's. That's not fashionable now, of course. But thirty years ago it was quite a coup.'

I had thought I might be able to keep my father on the periphery of this case, but that's simply not practical. The fact is, I need his help. 'Dad, the guy who sent me that list of FBI agents is Bureau himself. He told me a couple of disturbing things.'

'Like?'

'This morning Austin Mackey requested the FBI file on Del Payton, and he was turned down. The Payton file was sealed by J. Edgar Hoover in 1968 on grounds of national security.'

His eyes narrow in disbelief. '*What?*'

'Now you tell me Marston was a personal friend of Hoover's. I've already determined that Presley probably lied about the bomb that blew up Payton's car. The FBI had to know that. I don't know how it all adds up, but as district attorney, Marston had to be right in the middle of all this.'

He looks toward the shore, as though trying to spot his truck against the darkness of the trees. When he answers, his voice is so soft it seems to drift out of the lap of water against the bow.

'Leo Marston put our family through hell for a year and a half. The stress damn near killed me, and it changed your mother forever.'

I say nothing, wondering if he's talking to me or himself.

'The things he's done to other people . . . compromised them, bullied them. You don't know half of what he's done. I'm not a vindictive man. But to make that bastard pay for some of that . . . God, that would be justice.'

He is taking himself where I wanted to take him all along.

'We'd have to find a way to protect Annie and Peggy,' he says. 'Around the clock.'

'We can do that.'

He looks back at me. 'You're not in Houston anymore. You have no authority here. You can't investigate secretly. Half the town already knows what you're doing.'

'The more people who know, the safer we'll be.'

'Marston can apply pressure from angles you never dreamed of. But physical safety is the first priority. I know a couple of good men. Cops. Patients of mine.'

'Do you really think you can trust them? Cops, I mean. Ray Presley was a cop.'

Dad chuckles softly in the shadows. 'They're both black. What do you think?'

Chapter 18

Caitlin Masters has the corner booth in Biscuits & Blues. She smiles and waves when she sees me walking through the tables. I speak to a couple of people I know, but there's no applause tonight. The restaurant is packed with diners absorbed in their own affairs.

'I'm sorry,' Caitlin says, pointing at a shrimp cocktail before her. 'I was starved. I couldn't wait. Have one.'

'No, thanks,' I reply, sitting down opposite her. She's wearing a white button-down oxford shirt and emerald drop earrings that bring out the color in her eyes. Each time I see her, I'm shocked by the way those green eyes are almost wrong for her face. The fine black hair and porcelain skin seem to call for something else. And yet the final result is a remarkable beauty.

The young waitress who asked me to sign *False Witness* the other day hurries over and asks if she can get me something to drink.

'Jenny, right?'

She blushes and nods.

'What happened to my waiter?' Caitlin asks.

'I switched tables with him. I'll take much better care of you guys.'

Caitlin gives her a sidelong glance. 'I'll bet you will.'

'Jenny, I'd love a Corona with a lime.'

'On the way.' She disappears like a dark-complected elf.

'Jenny has the hots for you.'

'A little starstruck, maybe. She's probably got a novel in progress upstairs.'

'I don't think that's it. She watches you in a strange way.' Caitlin drinks from a sweating martini glass. 'Trust me. I have lethal instincts.'

'You're not drinking gimlets tonight?'

'They're out of Rose's lime. So, how'd you spend this lovely day?'

'I'll tell you later. First, you owe me an explanation.'

She gives me a wry look. 'Why did I make such a big thing of Del Payton?'

'Yes.'

'It's simple, really. My father.'

'The one you grew up without?'

'That's him. When he took over the chain from *his* father, it was five dailies, all in Virginia. In twelve years he built that into thirty-four papers across the Southeast.'

'I'm impressed.'

She raises a cynical eyebrow. 'Do you know how he did that? He went into small cities that had only one or two newspapers. If there were two, he'd buy the dominant one, then institute John Masters's Commandments, the cardinal one being, "Don't piss off the advertisers." He printed every detail of little league games, weddings, society parties, high school graduations – everything but controversy. It didn't make for very informative newspapers, but it kicked profits into the stratosphere.'

'Is it a public company now?'

Caitlin makes a fist and thrusts it toward the ceiling with mock fervor. 'Never! Family-owned, down the line. Starting to get the picture?'

'You want to shake up Daddy's world.'

'Yes. But not for some Freudian reason. Hard news is going unreported in every town where we have a newspaper. I'm instituting a new policy. At *one* paper, anyway.' She takes another swallow of her martini, and her eyes flash with conviction. 'From now on, hard news leads.'

'The Payton murder wasn't news until you made it news.'

'So, sue me. My gut tells me it's a big story, and I'm going with it.'

'Good for you. It is a big story.'

She freezes with a shrimp in midair.

I take my Corona from Jenny the waitress before she can set it down. 'How would you like an exclusive on the solution?'

'Is that a trick question?'

'There's one condition. You print absolutely nothing until I give you the okay.'

'You know who killed him?'

'Maybe. But even if I do, proving it could be difficult.'

She pops the shrimp into her mouth and chews for a few moments. 'I don't get it. If you don't want me to print anything, why bring me in at all?'

'Because I need your help.'

'For what?'

'Research that I don't have the time or resources to do.'

'What do you need to know?'

'You haven't agreed to my condition yet.'

She mulls it over some more. 'Why should I muzzle my paper to help you? How do I know you'll solve the case any faster than I could?'

'Do you have a copy of the original police file?'

'No. But I'm working on a request for his FBI file under the Freedom of Information Act.'

'Don't bother. You won't get it. J. Edgar Hoover sealed the Payton file in 1968 for reasons of national security.'

She shakes her head in disbelief. 'I smelled a Pulitzer the minute you told me about this case. Okay, deal. Tell me what you want, I'll get it. Fast. But I want in on everything.'

'Fair enough,' I say, wondering if I mean it. A half hour

ago Cilla called from Houston. After spending hours tracing the names on Peter Lutjens's list, and finding most retired or dead, she lucked into a fan of mine. He hadn't worked the Payton murder, but he remembered it. More important, he numbered Special Agent Dwight Stone, the field agent Althea Payton recalled so fondly, among his old friends. Stone is retired and living outside Crested Butte, Colorado. Cilla called him and found him friendly enough until she mentioned Del Payton, at which time Stone bluntly stated that he would not discuss the Payton case with me or anyone. I intend to test his resolution very soon.

'So, what do you want to know?' Caitlin asks.

'I need everything you can get on Leo Marston. You know who he is?'

'Sure. A big-time attorney everybody calls Judge because he served on the state supreme court. I tried to get a comment from him for my Payton story, but I couldn't get through. His secretary's a cast-iron bitch.'

'You should meet his wife.'

'The woman who baptized you at the cocktail party?'

'That's her.'

'No, thanks. Why Marston?'

'You don't need to know that yet.'

She doesn't like this response. 'Who else?'

I'd like a detailed bio of Ray Presley, but Caitlin can't access the kind of information I need on him. 'Just start with Marston. Companies he owns, whole or in part. Personal and political connections. His tax returns if you can get them.'

Jenny reappears at our table, her dark eyes watching me with a disconcerting intensity. 'Have you decided?'

'I'm not really hungry,' I confess, handing her my unopened menu. 'I had to eat before I came. My daughter helped cook.'

'How old is she?'

'Four.'

'That's a fun age.'

'Are they working on my ribs back there?' Caitlin asks.

'They'll be out in a minute.' Jenny gives her a curt smile and heads back to her station.

'You owe me an answer too, remember?' says Caitlin. 'You're the most liberal person I've met here, as far as race goes. You're fascist on the death penalty, of course, but we'll skip that for now. How did you wind up so different from other people here?'

'It's simple, really. My father.'

She puts her last shrimp into her mouth and chews slowly, her green eyes luminescent in the soft light. 'Let's hear it.'

'This never sees print. It's no big deal, but it's personal. That's something we need to get straight right now. If we're going to work together, some things *never* see print.'

'No problem. It's in the vault.'

'I remember three defining moments with my father when I was growing up. The first had to do with race. Most kids I grew up around used the word "nigger" the same way they used "apple" or "Chevrolet." So did their parents and grand-parents before them. One night, at home, I used it the same way. My father got out of his chair, turned off the television, and came and sat beside me. He said, "Son, I grew up working in a creosote plant right alongside colored people. And they're just like you and me. No better, no worse. We don't say that word in this house." Then he turned the TV back on. And I stopped saying nigger.

'A couple of years later, the thing to be was a hippie, and I tried my best. Grew my hair down my back, smoked grass, the whole bit. I heard hippies on TV saying the "pigs" this, the "pigs" that. The cops, you know? So, one day, riding in the car, I said something about the pigs. My father pulled onto the shoulder, turned around, and said, "Son, if we had to go three days in this country without police, it wouldn't be a place you'd want to live. We don't use that word." And I never used it again.'

Caitlin's eyes shine with fascination. 'And the third moment?'

'I was fifteen, and I'd been sleeping with this older girl from the public school who went off to junior college. I stole the family car a couple of times to go to see her. In the kitchen one night my mother told me I couldn't do that anymore. In my hormone-intoxicated state, I said, "Mom, why are you being such a bitch about this?"'

'Oh, my God.'

'My dad clocked me. This man of reason who had never lifted a finger to me slapped me an open-handed blow that damn near blacked me out. I was spiritually stunned. But it was the right blow at the right moment. The only one I ever needed. It drew the line for me.'

Caitlin nods slowly, a smile on her lips. 'Thank you for telling me that. You're lucky to have a father like that.'

I wonder what she'd say if she knew that an hour ago my wonderful father and I sank a murder weapon in a swamp.

Her barbecued ribs finally arrive, and we run through a half dozen other subjects while she eats. Journalism, my law career, publishing. She grew up with money but worked hard to make her own mark. She did internships with the *New York Times* and the *Washington Post*, traveled extensively overseas, and worked a year for the *Los Angeles Times*. When she asks obliquely about the Hanratty execution, I change the subject.

'Where do you live? I don't picture you in an apartment.'

She smiles and wipes her mouth with a napkin, knowing I'm evading her question. 'I pretty much live at the paper. But I did buy a house on Washington Street.'

'Roughing it, huh?' Washington Street is old Natchez; most of the town houses there sell for over three hundred thousand dollars.

'I need my space,' she says frankly. 'You should come

see it. It was completely restored just before I bought it.'

A wave of warmth passes over my face. Is she hinting that I should go to her house after dinner? I've been out of circulation for years, and she's only twenty-eight. In the realm of dating, she is the expert, not me.

'Do you need to get home?' she asks. 'I'll bet Annie's waiting up for you.'

That is what she's suggesting. I look at my watch to conceal the fact that I'm blushing. 'Annie's falling asleep about now. I'm okay for a bit.'

'Well . . . would you like to see it? We could have some tea and talk. Or we could just take a ride. You could show me the real Natchez.'

In the dark? But the automatic rejections I've practiced since Sarah's death don't come to me. 'A ride might be fun.'

My answer surprises her. More than that, it makes her happy. With a smile of anticipation she signals Jenny over, asks for two go-cups, and passes her a company credit card. Jenny meets us at the front door with the ticket, and while Caitlin signs it, I say hello to a couple of people at the bar. It's strange to be back in a place where I know someone every place I go.

Stepping from the air-conditioned restaurant to the streets is like putting on a mildewed coat in the jungle. October in Mississippi. In Crested Butte they're skiing right now.

'We could take my Miata,' Caitlin says, 'but I don't advise it. I thought a convertible would be perfect for the South, but it's too damn hot down here to use it.'

'My car's right down there.'

I lead her across the street, then turn right on the sidewalk, heading toward the small parking lot where I left Dad's BMW. A country dance bar is going strong on this side, and knots of people line the sidewalk for the length of the block. The club draws mainly from the Louisiana farmland across the river, hard-shell Baptist country that birthed Jimmy

Swaggart and Jerry Lee Lewis. Caitlin and I weave carefully through boots and hats and clouds of cigarette smoke.

As we near the parking lot, I see four men who look a little rougher than the rest, passing around a bottle of Jack Daniel's. They're wearing oil-stained denim and caps instead of hats. Roughnecks who drove straight from the oil field to the bar, most likely. Lean, hard-muscled, burned brick red by the sun, they wear thin mustaches and suck dips of snuff while they drink. As Caitlin and I approach, one points at me.

'You oughta keep your goddamn mouth shut about the niggers in this town, Cage.'

The use of my name surprises me, but I have no intention of stopping to discuss the issue. Feeling Caitlin slow down, I squeeze her arm and keep walking.

'You're fucking up the chemical plant deal,' says another.

Now that we're closer, I recognize the man who spoke first. His name is Spurling. A year older than I, he attended the White Citizens' Council school on the north side of town. Spurling has the sullen expression of a man for whom life holds few happy surprises. He will fight me on the slightest provocation, and probably on none. These guys have never gotten past the emotional age of fifteen. They brawl over disputed calls at little league games, beat up homosexuals for fun, and shoot each other over marital infidelities.

'*Keep walking*,' I whisper to Caitlin, and we pass them with only a brush on the shoulder.

'I'm talking to you, cocksucker,' Spurling calls after me.

'That was the newspaper chick,' says a slurred voice. 'That stuck-up Yankee bitch.'

Caitlin stops and turns. 'Why don't you dickless Neanderthals find a gun to play with? Maybe you'll do the world a favor and shoot each other.'

They hoot and run after us. This is exactly what they wanted. I admire Caitlin's courage, but she is writing verbal checks that I might have to cash with blood. In seconds the four of them have formed a line between us and the parking lot.

'She's a bitch,' says the one with the slurry voice. 'But she's a fine bitch.' He jabs a finger toward Caitlin's crotch. 'I'd sure like to get in those pants.'

'I already have one asshole in my pants,' she retorts in a voice like a saber's edge. 'Why would I want another?'

The roughneck blinks, thrown off balance by the ricochet comeback. But Spurling has his Academy Award-winning line ready. 'How about sitting on my face when you say that?'

'If I thought you'd know what to do once I sat down, I might.'

Spurling sticks out his tongue and flicks it up and down like a snake. He's trying to force me to throw a punch, which I do not especially want to do, considering the odds. Chivalry is a wonderful concept, but just now it doesn't seem the most prudent of options.

Spurling is still wiggling his tongue when Caitlin pops him across the mouth with a closed fist. He's most surprised than hurt, but he must have bitten his tongue, because he's spitting blood on the concrete.

'*You thucking cunt!*' he gurgles.

'Let's all take it easy!' I say, holding up my hands. 'We were minding our business, walking along a public street—'

'Nobody wants you on this fucking street!' yells the one with the Jack Daniel's bottle. 'Go back to Beverly Hills or wherever the fuck you live. We gotta make a living here, unlike you.'

A few club patrons have noticed our exchange and are moving toward us, but they don't look like ready sources of aid. I take Caitlin's arm, spin her around, and walk her toward the BMW. She hisses something indignant, but I'm not listening to her. I'm listening for the scuff of boots on gravel.

Soon enough, I hear it.

I shove her to my right and dart left, feeling a breeze as the whiskey bottle arcs through the space my head occupied a split second ago and smashes on the gravel of the parking lot. Guessing that someone will follow the bottle forward, I whirl and throw a blind punch.

Luck is always better than skill. I hear bone crack, or maybe nasal cartilage, then a strangled scream of agony as someone hits the gravel. Throwing the car keys at Caitlin, I yell, 'The black BMW!' then whirl to face the other three, who jump me simultaneously.

We're wrestling more than fighting, but once they get me on the ground, they'll remove my teeth two at a time.

'*She bit me!*' someone screams. '*She bit my fucking ear off!*'

I would probably laugh had not serious blows begun landing on my skull. My thoughts instantly evaporate into survival instinct as I cover my head and try to keep my feet.

A wallop to my right temple obliterates my sense of balance, and I drop to my knees, glimpsing the silver toe cap of a boot just before it savages my ribs. Another head blow puts me on my back, and the fists come down in a steady hail. I see white flashes of light, and my ears are roaring. You hope you black out at a time like this, but I'm not that lucky. Every fist feels like I walked into a steel pole.

Suddenly a new sound breaks through the fog in my jiggling brain. A brief, percussive *pock*. Again: *pock-pock*. At first I think it's the sound of something hitting my skull, but no one is hitting me anymore, yet the sound goes on. *Pock! Pock-pock!*

Rolling onto my side, I see three men cowering against a brick wall. A large uniformed man stands over them, hammering them mercilessly with a stick.

Deputy Ike Ransom.

Ike the Spike is beating Spurling and his redneck posse like willful dogs, his baton cracking shins, shoulders, elbows, and skulls with surgical precision. The flashing lights I saw must have been the arrival of his squad car.

'Penn? Penn, can you hear me?'

It's Caitlin. Soft hands try to pull me to my feet, but they haven't the strength to lift my frame.

'Count to five!' she orders, her voice electrified by fear.

'Is that what they teach you at Radcliffe?' I croak, wobbling to my feet. 'I'm surprised you're not over there screaming about police brutality.'

'Screw them. They need to learn some respect for women.'

Two roughnecks have fallen facedown, but Ike shows no inclination to stop what he's doing. Spurling makes the mistake of lunging at the deputy and screaming 'nigger,' which earns him a sweeping baseball-style lick that lays him out flat on the ground.

'*Ike!*' I yell. '*Stop it, man!*'

Caitlin and I run toward him, but I'm not about to try to grab his baton. In his present state he might not be able to distinguish between white faces quickly enough to spare me a concussion. Caitlin isn't so timid. She steps between Ike and his targets and holds up both hands, creating a sight arresting enough to paralyze the deputy. Ike lowers his baton and turns to me, his eyes filled with sweat.

'You'd best get out of here quick. Police won't be long.'

Now isn't the time for extended thank-yous. I take Caitlin's arm and hobble toward the driver's door of the BMW.

'You're not driving,' she says. 'Give me the keys.'

'I'm fine.'

'You took at least ten blows to the head. Your nose is bleeding. I'm driving you to the hospital.'

'My father can check me out when I get home. Get in the car!'

She scrambles over the driver's seat to the other side. I crank the car and pull slowly out of the lot. Ike's cruiser is already gone.

One circuit of the block takes me to Caitlin's green Miata, and I park in the street beside it. Double-parking is an old Natchez tradition.

'I can't believe you bit that guy,' I tell her, rubbing the back of my skull. 'You fight more like a bar girl from Breaux Bridge than a blueblood from Boston.'

'When in Rome, right?' She slaps her thighs and yells, '*Whoooooo*, what a rush! That's the most fun I've had with my clothes on in a long time.'

'Yeah, loads of fun,' I mutter, but her excitement is contagious. Her face is flushed like a sprinter's, and her breath comes in short gasps.

'I assume that deputy was a friend of yours?'

'I'd say he's a friend of ours.' I give her a hard look. 'We still have a deal, right? No story about that little altercation in tomorrow's paper?'

'Absolutely. No story.' She pokes me in the shoulder. 'I told you I could hold my own.'

'I'm afraid that was just the first round. It'll get a lot worse.'

Her smile doesn't waver. 'We can handle it.' She gets out of the car and closes the door, then leans into the open passenger window. 'Would you be furious if I asked a personal question?'

'Go ahead.'

'Have you thought much about our kiss since last night?'

I'm glad for the dark. The black veil of her hair gleams in the window, framing her porcelain face, setting off her lips and eyes.

'Please tell me to drop dead if I'm out of line,' she says quickly. 'It's just . . . I've been thinking about it. It literally curled my toes. And I wanted you to know that.'

A pulse of pure pleasure spreads outward from my heart. How do I answer? *Yes, I've thought about it a hundred times, in a way that's not even thought but a constant awareness of how your mouth opened to mine, the coolness and knowingness of it—*

'Would you like to go to Colorado with me tomorrow?'

She opens her mouth but makes no sound.

'I'm flying up to talk to the lead FBI agent on the Del Payton case in 1968. But part of your job will be baby-sitting Annie. She's coming along.'

Caitlin is shaking her head in confusion. 'Is this trip business or pleasure? Or a baby-sitting job?'

'I'm sorry – I didn't put that very well. It's business, but I'm taking Annie along for her safety, and we have a stop to make on the way. A place I can't take her.'

'Where?'

'Huntsville, Texas. The Hanratty execution.'

Her eyes go wide. 'Are you serious?'

'Yes. You can be there when I interview the agent, but I need you to stay at the hotel with Annie during the execution.'

'The hottest ticket in journalism this week, and I'm going to be baby-sitting?'

'They wouldn't let you in the witness room anyway. It's your call.'

She purses her lips in thought. 'I'm still not sure how to think of this. Do you *want* me to come?'

'Very much.'

'Then I will. But what if Annie won't stay in the hotel without you there?'

'Then I'll skip the execution. I don't really want to see it anyway.'

'She'll be fine with me. We got along great on the plane. Hey, what's this FBI agent's name?'

Caitlin's mention of that flight makes me remember her deception about her identity, and this makes me hesitant to confide Stone's name. I wipe my bloody nose on my shirt-sleeve and look through the windshield.

'Penn, I could have the guy's life story before we ever talk to him.'

She has a point. 'Dwight Stone. Crested Butte, Colorado.'

'That wasn't so hard, was it?' Her eyes are almost mocking, but they hold more understanding than I have seen in a long time.

'The answer to your earlier question is yes. I've thought about it since last night.'

A serene smile lights Caitlin's face.

'And I'd like to kiss you again.'

Her smile broadens.

'May I?'

She leans through the window and across the passenger seat, her eyes not closed like last night but open, inviting me into them. Our lips touch, and a perfect echo of the warmth I felt last night rolls through me. This kiss is passionate but more intimate, the crossing of another boundary together. She pulls back and peers into my eyes, then closes hers and kisses me once more.

When she pulls away this time, she has a Charlie Chaplin mustache.

'You've got blood on your lip.'

'My first war wound.' She laughs. 'It'll wash off. What time do we leave?'

'Seven-thirty for the drive to Baton Rouge Airport.'

She touches her forefinger to my nose, then pulls back through the window. 'Pick me up at the paper. I'll be ready.'

Chapter 19

The trip to Baton Rouge airport takes eighty minutes, just enough time for Annie to adopt Caitlin as a big sister. Caitlin seems to know every TV character Annie does, outlandish names I can never keep up with but which Caitlin rattles off like the names of old friends. When I asked my mother if she thought Annie was ready for a trip to Colorado with Caitlin and me, she said, 'Annie's ready. Just make sure you are.' When I asked what this meant, she gave me one of her looks and said, 'Am I wrong, or is this the first extended time you've spent with a woman since Sarah died?' I told her she wasn't wrong. 'Just don't rush it,' she advised. 'Even chitlins smell good to a starving man.' Caitlin Masters is a long way from chitterlings, but there's no point in trying to explain this to my mother.

The short-term parking lot is easy walking distance from the Baton Rouge terminal. I carry the suitcases, Caitlin the carry-ons, and Annie her pink backpack. We check our bags at the door and go straight to our gate, only to find that our plane, which is parked at the gate, is running twenty minutes behind schedule. As irate passengers began to deplane, Annie announces that she has to tee-tee, and Caitlin escorts her off to the ladies' room. I'm absently watching the gate when Olivia Marston walks through it.

I know it's Livy because of the sudden tightness in my chest. Also because the plane just flew in from Atlanta, her home for the past thirteen years. As soon as she clears the gate, she steps out of line and starts past the other passengers, not rushing but somehow overtaking businessmen who have five inches on her. Southern belles are notorious for traveling heavy; Livy travels light. Yet the single overhead-sized suitcase rolling behind her will contain a color-coordinated ensemble versatile enough to get her through every social event from a luau to a formal ball.

A belle by birth, Livy matured into something altogether different. The beauty of belles is a soft beauty: pliant curves and shapely baby fat. Livy is leaner, with enough sculpted cheekbone to separate her utterly from the peach-skinned debutantes who fill the ranks of the Junior League below the Mason-Dixon line. Her eyes are a deep and brilliant blue, and the tailored jacket and skirt she's wearing bring out their color just as she intended.

Her name is actually Livy Sutter now, but I live in such denial about her marriage that the name Sutter never really registered. I remember it only on those rare occasions when I pass through Atlanta on business and in the tipsy midnight of a lonely hotel room pick up the phone book and flirt with the idea of calling her. Of course, I never have. *Oh, John, that was Penn Cage, the writer. He's an old friend from Natchez . . .* I'd rather die than be another 'old friend' of Livy Marston's. Have good old John think of me with pity, knowing that every heterosexual man who ever met his wife fell in love with her to some degree. As far afield as Montreal and Los Angeles, I've had lawyers – upon learning that I'm originally from Natchez – come alive with questions about the fantastic Livy Sutter. Do I know her? Isn't she remarkable? Unique? Different somehow? That was certainly the opinion of the Pulitzer prize-winning writer-in-residence who made a fool of himself (in his sixties, no less) and ruined his marriage over Livy when she was a junior at UVA.

Twenty yards away from me, Livy slows and pans the

concourse. She has her father's survival instincts. Her eyes pass over me, then return.

'Penn Cage,' she says, without the slightest doubt that it's me.

'Hello, Livy.'

She walks toward me with a smile that cuts right through resentment and regret. Her hair is the color of winter wheat in summer and just touches her shoulders, looking much as it did during high school. The last time I saw her (at Sarah's funeral) she had a short, severe, lady-lawyer cut. She must have been growing it out ever since. I like it much better this way. Probably because it fits the images that haunt my dreams.

'My God, what happened to you?' she asks.

For a moment I'm confused, but it's the bruises she's noticed. Last night's altercation left me looking quite a bit worse for wear.

'I ran into the welcome wagon.'

She shakes her head as though this is about what she would expect from me, then leans forward. Livy is a big hugger, but I have never submitted to this. Her hugs somehow put you at a remove even as they seem to pull you in. Remembering my aversion, she drops one hand and squeezes my wrist with an intimate pressure, her eyes already working their subversive spell upon me, blurring my critical faculties, creating a juvenile desire to please her, to make those blue eyes shine.

'What are you doing here?' I ask.

'I'm on my way home. To Natchez, I mean. My mother's having health problems. Dad's been after me to come visit, so when he called this time, I decided to spend a few days with them.'

Her health was good enough to toss a drink in my face two nights ago, I think. Maybe 'health' is a euphemism for alcoholism. If they intend to try an intervention with Maude, I don't want to be within a hundred miles of it. In fact, I'd recommend Kevlar body armor to the participants.

'What about you?' Livy asks.

'I'm on my way to Huntsville Prison.'

'Oh, God, the Hanratty thing. It's all over the news. Midnight tonight, right? Are you required to be there?'

'No. The victim's family wants me there.'

She shakes her head. 'You always were one for duty.' In a lighter voice she says, 'I still see your books in all the airports. And it still makes me jealous.'

'Come on.'

'I mean it. I make great money, but I'm compromising every day for it. You're living the life you always talked about.'

'You talked about that kind of life too.'

She blushes, but before she can reply Annie is tugging my trouser leg. I reach down and scoop her into my arms. 'Hey, punkin! You remember Miss Livy?'

Annie solemnly moves her head from side to side. I was stupid to think she'd remember anyone from the funeral.

'My hair was shorter then,' Livy tells her. Like Caitlin, she makes no attempt to talk baby talk. 'I sure remember *you*, Anna Louise.'

I can't believe she remembers Annie's full name. The female memory defies explanation.

Suddenly something brushes my shoulder. It's Caitlin, holding out her hand to Livy.

'Caitlin Masters,' she says, cutting her eyes at me as she gives Livy a professional smile.

'I'm sorry,' I apologize, far too late.

'Liv Sutter,' Livy says, giving Caitlin's hand a firm shake.

Liv Sutter. Another thing I'd forgotten: Livy's name metamorphosed as she progressed through life. She wasn't like a Matt who suddenly insisted on being called Matthew to be taken more seriously. Her name actually got shorter with each incarnation: 'Olivia' in grade school; 'Livy' in high school; and just plain 'Liv' in college and law school. And there was never any question of people not taking her seriously – Livy Marston Sutter is as serious as a garrote.

'You two obviously know each other,' says Caitlin.

'Oh, we go way back,' Livy explains, laughing. 'Too far back to think about.'

'We only go back a couple of days,' Caitlin replies. 'But we're looking forward to Colorado.'

There's nothing quite like the meeting of two beautiful women of the same class. I would never have guessed that Caitlin had a catty side. Livy is ten years older but gives up nothing in any department. The friction is automatic.

'How's John?' I ask as Livy studies me with new interest. 'Her husband,' I add for Caitlin's benefit.

'We're separated. Six weeks now.'

So, Sam Jacobs's gossip was accurate. 'I'm sorry.'

'Don't be. I should have gotten out of it five years ago.'

This bombshell leaves me tingling with a sense of un-reality. We all stand around feeling awkward until Caitlin takes Annie from my arms, points at the broad picture window, and says, 'Let's go look at those big airplanes!'

They're quickly swallowed by the crowd, but not before Caitlin gives me a reproving look over her shoulder.

'Who was that?' Livy asks.

'The new publisher of the *Examiner*.'

'You're kidding.'

'Her father owns the chain.'

'Ah.' Livy feels comfortably superior again. 'Nepotism run amok. She doesn't seem your type.'

And what's my type? Dead saints and ghosts from my youth? 'I think my type is changing. Rich heiresses seem like a good place to start.'

Livy gives me a look intended to make me feel guilty, but we share too much history for me to be taken in by that.

212

'How long will you be in Colorado?'

'A couple of days.'

'Call me when you get back. We should get together and talk.'

We should? 'Why don't you call me? Then I can skip speaking to your father.'

She lets this pass. 'I will. Wait and see.'

'I'd better find Annie. We'll be boarding soon.'

She reaches out and takes my hand. 'It's strange, isn't it?'

'What?'

'Twenty years after high school, and suddenly we're both free.'

I can't believe she said it. Gave voice to something I would not even allow myself to think. 'There's a difference, Livy. I didn't want to be free.'

She pales, but quickly recovers and squeezes my hand. 'I know you didn't. I'm sorry. I didn't mean to put it that way.'

I take back my hand. 'I know. I'm sorry too. I've got to run.'

I turn to go in search of Annie and Caitlin, but after ten steps I stop and look back. I don't want to. I have to.

Livy hasn't moved. She's looking right at me with a provocative expression of both regret and hope. She holds up her right hand in farewell, then turns and disappears into the crowd.

'Daddy, was that lady a movie star?'

Annie and Caitlin have reappeared at my side.

'No, punkin. Just someone I went to school with.'

'She looks like somebody on TV.'

She probably does. Livy is a living archetype of American good looks: not a Mary Tyler Moore but a warmer, more accessible Grace Kelly. A *Southern* Grace Kelly.

'*I* didn't think she looked like a movie star,' Caitlin announces.

'What do you think she looks like?' I ask, not sure I want to hear the answer.

'A self-important B-I-T-C-H.'

'Hey,' Annie complains. 'What's that spell?'

'*Witch*,' says Caitlin, tickling her under the arms, which triggers explosive giggles. 'The Masters intuition never fails,' she adds, looking up at me. 'You've got it bad for her, don't you?'

'What? Hell, no.'

'Daddy said a bad word!' Annie cries.

'Daddy told a fib,' says Caitlin. 'And that's worse.'

'I think I need a drink.'

The ticket agent announces that first class will begin boarding immediately.

'First love?' Caitlin asks in a casual voice as we move through the mass of passengers funneling toward the gate.

'It's a long story.'

She nods, her eyes knowing. 'If short stuff here goes to sleep on the plane, that's a story I wouldn't mind hearing.'

Perfect.

Airplanes work like a sedative on Annie. After drinking a Sprite and eating a bag of honey-roasted peanuts, she curls up next to Caitlin and zonks out. At Caitlin's suggestion, I move her across the aisle to my seat and, when she begins to snore again, move back across the aisle beside Caitlin.

'You're going to make me drag it out of you?' she says.

I say nothing for a moment. Certain relationships do not lend themselves to conversational description. Emotions are by nature amorphous. When confined to words, our longings and passions, our rebellions and humiliations, often seem melodramatic, trivial, or even pathetic. But if Caitlin is going to help me destroy Leo Marston, she needs to know the history.

'Every high school class has a Livy Marston,' I begin. 'But

Livy was special. Everyone who ever met her knew that.'

'Marston? She said her name was Sutter.'

'Her maiden name was Marston.'

'Marston . . . *Marston*. The guy you asked me to check out? The D.A. when Payton was killed? Judge Marston?'

'He's Livy's father.'

'God, it's so incestuous down here.'

'Like Boston?'

'Worse.'

Caitlin calls the flight attendant and orders a gimlet, but this is beyond the resources of the galley. There seems to be a nationwide shortage of Rose's Lime Juice. She orders a martini instead.

'So,' she says, 'what made her so special?'

'How many people were in your graduating class?'

'About three hundred.'

'Mine had thirty-two. And most of those had been together since nursery school. It was like an extended family. We watched each other grow up for fourteen years. And those thirty-two people did some extraordinary things.'

'Such as?'

'Well, there's high school, and then there's life. Out of thirty-two people we had six doctors, ten lawyers, a Grammy-winning record producer, a photographer who won the Pulitzer last year—'

'And you,' she finishes. 'Best-selling novelist and legal eagle.'

'Every class thinks it's special, of course. But in a town as small as Natchez, and a school as small as St. Stephens, you have to have something like a genetic accident to get a class like ours. Our football team had eighteen people on it. Everyone played both ways. And we were ranked in the top ten in the state in the rankings of public schools. That's ranked against schools like yours, with seventy players on the squad. Our baseball team was the first single-A team in the history of Mississippi to win the overall state title.'

She rolls her eyes. 'So you were big-time in Mississippi sports. Let's call CNN.'

'Sports means a lot in high school.'

'What about academics?'

'Second-highest SATs in the state.'

'When do we get to Miss Perfect?'

'Livy was the center of all that. The star everyone revolved around. Homecoming queen, head cheerleader, valedictorian . . . you name it, she was it.'

Caitlin groans. 'Gag me with a soup ladle.'

'If you plop most high school queens down at a major university, they'll disappear like daisies at a flower show. Not Livy. She was head cheerleader at Virginia, president of the Tri-Delts, *and* made law review at the UVA law school.'

'She sounds schizophrenic.'

'She probably is. She was born to a man who wanted sons, in a decade when the cultural dynamic of the fifties was still alive and kicking in the South. She was a brilliant and beautiful girl with a mother who thought in terms of her marrying well and a father who wanted her to be president. She killed a ten-point buck when she was eleven years old, just to prove she could do anything a boy could.'

'Spare me the body count. I suppose she graduated, won the Nobel prize, and raised two-point-five perfect kids?'

I can't help but laugh at the animosity Livy has inspired in Caitlin; it can only be based on the degree to which Livy has intimidated her. 'Actually, she sold out.'

Caitlin cringes in mock horror. 'Not the head cheerleader of the law review?'

'She took the biggest offer right out of law school and never looked back. Chased money and power all the way.'

'Who did she marry?'

'This is the part I like. She had this Howard Roark fixation. You know, the architect from Ayn Rand's *The Fountainhead*?

She wanted the absolute alpha male, an artist-logician who wouldn't take any shit off her or compromise once in his life.'

'Did she find him?'

'She married an entertainment lawyer in Atlanta. He represents athletes and rap singers.'

'There is justice,' Caitlin says, laughing. 'Though I guess he made a lot more money than a Houston prosecutor.'

'Twenty times more, at least.'

'Why did you stay in the D.A.'s office so long? I thought most lawyers only did that for a couple of years to prep themselves for private defense work.'

'That's true. Most people who stay are very different from me. Zealots, moralists. Jesuits, I call them. Military types who like to punish criminals. My boss was a lot like that.'

'So, why did you stay?'

'I was accomplishing something. I felt I was a moral counterweight to those people. Some liberals said I had an overdeveloped sense of justice. And that may be true. I convicted a lot of killers, and I don't apologize for it. I believe evil should be held accountable.'

'Whoa, that was *Evil* with a capital E.'

'It's out there. Take my word for it.'

'An overdeveloped sense of justice. Is that why you're investigating the Payton case?'

'No. I'm doing that because of Livy Marston.'

Caitlin looks like I hit her in the head with a hammer. 'What the hell are you talking about?'

I lean into the aisle and signal and flight attendant; it's time for a Scotch. 'Twenty years ago Livy's father used every bit of his power to try to destroy my father. He didn't succeed, but he separated Livy and me forever. And I never knew why.'

'And you think Marston is involved in the Payton murder?'

'Yes.'

217

'God, I'm trapped in a Southern gothic novel.'

'You asked for it.'

She finishes off her martini in a gulp. 'I hope nobody's going to ask me to squeal like a pig.'

I laugh as she orders another martini, amazed by how quickly the age difference between us has become irrelevant. I wonder how far apart we really are. Does she know that John Lennon and Paul McCartney were the greatest songwriters who ever lived? That the pseudo-nihilism of Generation X was merely frustrated narcissism? That I, at thirty-eight years old, am as trapped in my own era as a septuagenarian humming 'Don't Sit Under the Apple Tree With Anyone Else But Me' and dreaming of the agony of Anzio is trapped in his?

'Back up,' Caitlin says. 'You and Livy were high school sweethearts?'

'No. For most of high school we were competitors. She only dated older guys, and no one steadily. She was her own person. She never wore a boy's letter jacket or class ring. She needed nothing external to define her or make her feel accepted. But at some point we both realized we were destined for bigger futures than most people we knew. We were going to leave that town far behind. That awareness inevitably pulled us together. We both loved literature and music, both excelled in all our classes. We dated for four months at the end of our senior year. We were both going to Ole Miss in the fall, but she was going to Radcliffe for the summer—'

'Oh, my God,' Caitlin exclaims. 'That magnolia blossom actually darkened the door of Radcliffe?'

'Aced every class, I'm sure. She wouldn't let Yankees feel superior to her for a second.'

Caitlin makes a wry face, then sips her martini and looks out her window. 'Was she good in bed?'

'A gentleman never tells.'

She turns and punches my shoulder. 'Jerk.'

'What would you guess?'

'Probably. She has the intensity for it.'

Yes . . .

'How did her father split you up?'

'He took a malpractice case against my father and pressed it to the wall. My dad was exonerated, but the trial was so brutal it nearly broke him. There was no way Livy and I could work through that.'

Caitlin is watching me intently. 'You're leaving a lot out, aren't you?'

Of course I am. How do we explain the abiding mysteries of our lives? 'Livy never showed up at Ole Miss,' I say softly. 'She disappeared. Fell off the face of the planet. Her parents told people she'd gone to Paris to study at the Sorbonne, but I called to check, and they had no record of her. A year later word filtered out that she'd just entered the University of Virginia as a freshman. I have no idea where she spent the previous year, and neither does anyone else.'

'Maybe she got pregnant. Went off and had the baby somewhere.'

'I thought about that. But this was the late seventies, not the fifties. Her older sister had gotten pregnant a few years before, and she had an abortion, even though they were Catholic. Livy would have done the same thing. She wouldn't have let anything slow down her career.' There's another reason I'm sure pregnancy is not the answer, but there's no point in getting clinical about it.

'Why did she go to the University of Virginia?'

'I think because it was far from Mississippi but still the South. She got an unlisted number, cut herself off from her old friends. By the time my father's trial got going, I didn't care anymore.'

'You didn't ask her why her father was going after yours?'

This memory is one of my worst. 'I flew up to Charlottesville a week before the trial, to try to get her to make Leo drop the case. My dad had already had a heart attack from the stress. She said she thought it was just a normal case, and that her father wouldn't listen to her opinion anyway. She was back in her high school queen mode, winning hearts and minds at UVA. It was like talking to a stranger.' I take a burning sip of Scotch. 'I wanted to kill her.'

'Yes, but you loved her. You're still in love with her.'

'No.'

Caitlin smiles, not without empathy. 'You are. You always will be.'

'That's a depressing thought.'

'No. Just recognize it and move on. Livy's not the person you think she is. Nobody could be. And you'd better be careful. She just separated from her husband, and you're still grieving over your wife. She could really mess you up.'

'I'm no babe in the woods, Caitlin.'

Her smile is timeless. All men are babes in the woods, it says. 'You're trying to destroy *her* father now. How do you think she'll react to that?'

'I don't know. She has a love–hate relationship with him. It's like something out of Aeschylus. She knows he's done terrible things, but in some ways she's just like him.'

'You should try very hard to keep that in mind.'

'Why?'

She takes a pair of headphones from her lap, plugs them into the seat jack, and starts flipping through her channel guide. 'How long has it been since you've seen her?'

'She came to my wife's funeral. We only spoke for a moment, though.'

'Before that.'

'A long time. Maybe seventeen years.'

'You pull the lid off something that might get her father

charged with capital murder, and suddenly she shows up like magic?'

'What are you saying? That her father called her to Natchez to . . . to influence me somehow? Because of your newspaper story?'

Caitlin shrugs. 'I don't want to upset you, but that's what I'm saying.'

She gives me a sad smile and puts on the headphones.

Chapter 20

I thought I was the last person to arrive in the witness room at Huntsville Prison until FBI Director John Portman walked in, flanked by two field agents who shadowed him like centurions guarding a Roman emperor. Up to that point the preparations for the execution had proceeded with the tense banality that characterizes them all.

I had arrived to find the room nearly full. My old boss, Joe Cantor, motioned me to the empty chair beside Mrs. Givens, the closest relative of the victims. The curtain was drawn over the window of the extermination chamber, but I knew Arthur Lee Hanratty was already strapped to the gurney behind it, while a technician searched for veins good enough to take large-bore IV lines.

I hadn't seen Mrs. Givens for eight years, but the smell of cigarettes on her clothes brought back everything, a nervous woman who chain-smoked through every pretrial meeting and rushed for the courthouse door at every recess. She had a Bible in her lap tonight, open to Job. When I touched her hand, she clenched my wrist and asked if I'd seen many executions before, and if they were difficult to watch. In a quiet voice, I explained the procedure: sodium thiopental to shut down Hanratty's brain; Pavulon to paralyze him and stop his breathing; potassium chloride to stop his heart.

'You mean they put him to sleep before they give the bad chemicals?'

'Yes, ma'am.'

'Will he be able to say anything?'

'I'm afraid so. He'll be allowed to make a final statement for the record.'

She patted the leather-bound book in her lap. 'I'm not going to listen. I'm going to read the Good Book then.'

'That sounds like a good idea.' Killers often asked forgiveness at the end, but that wasn't Hanratty's style.

That was the moment that the door at the back of the room opened. Some reporters in front of me turned around, and recognition and amazement lit their faces. I turned and froze, confronted by the most unlikely vision I thought I would see at midnight in Texas.

John Portman looks like a walking advertisement for Brooks Brothers: thin and strong but a bit stiff, handsome with a longish face framed by hair gone gracefully gray. He was fifty-five when he and I crossed swords over Arthur Lee Hanratty, but he looked forty. He scarcely looks older now. I've always sensed a Dorian Gray aura about him, as though he were committing secret sins that never registered on his countenance.

I can't imagine what he's doing here. There's no upside for him. None I can see, anyway. Maybe it's as simple as revenge. His experience with Hanratty almost derailed his juggernaut career, and Portman definitely knows how to carry a grudge. Watching Hanratty die might give him a great deal of satisfaction.

While his guards take up positions against the wall, he walks straight to the front row and sits in the empty chair next to Joe Cantor, who looks as surprised as the rest of us. I half expect Portman to turn and give me a grim smile, but he stares straight ahead at the curtain beyond which Arthur Lee Hanratty will soon take his last breath.

As we wait in silence, I realize I'm listening for the ring of a telephone. Conditioned by movies – and by a couple of real-life experiences – I run through the dramatic possibilities: the last-minute pardon, the hard-won stay courtesy of some crusading young lawyer from the ACLU. But that won't happen tonight. Even the mob of placard-bearing demonstrators outside the walls looked smaller and more subdued than usual as I passed through it. A few hundred people chanting dispiritedly in the Texas rain. Arthur Lee Hanratty is a poster boy for capital punishment.

Suddenly the curtain is drawn back, revealing a man in an orange jump-suit on an execution gurney, which looks like a medical exam table that has been welded to the floor. Strapped to the gurney with IV lines running saline into his arms, Hanratty doesn't look much like the madman I remember – a killer with the bunched and corded muscles of the convict weightlifter – but like every other man I've seen on that table. Helpless. Doomed. He reminds me of Ray Presley, though Hanratty has the lamplike eyes of the fanatic, not the cold rattlesnake beads of Presley.

The warden retained a good venipuncturist tonight – or else Hanratty has good veins – because the execution is proceeding on schedule. The warden stands with two guards against the wall behind the gurney. At 11:58 he steps forward and asks Hanratty if he has any final words. I once watched a man sing 'Jesus Loves Me' with tears in his eyes at this point, and die with the song on his lips. But I don't think that's what's coming now.

Hanratty cranks his neck around and searches our eyes one witness at a time, like a brimstone preacher trying to put the fear of Hell into his congregation. I've always felt that the window here should be one-way glass, to prevent the killer from making eye contact with the spectators. But the families of murder victims don't want it that way. Many of them want their faces to be the last thing the condemned sees before he dies. When Hanratty finds my eyes, I give him nothing.

'Well, well, *well*,' he croons from the gurney, '*Everybody's* here tonight. We got Mr. Penn Cage, who got famous killing my brother and convicting my ass. We got Joe Cantor, who got reelected off Mr. Cage convicting my ass. And we got former U.S. Attorney Portman, head of the FBI. I'm flattered you came to see me off, Port. Ironic, ain't it? If you could have covered up me killing that Compton nigger like you wanted to, none of us would have to be here tonight.'

The reporters devour this unexpected windfall like starving jackals. Surely, Portman must have known something like this could happen. The warden takes a step closer to the gurney. The word 'nigger' has got him thinking about gagging Hanratty, though legally the condemned man is allowed to speak freely.

'After tonight,' Hanratty goes on, 'there'll only be one of us Hanrattys left. But that's all right. My brother knows what to do. Some of you folks are gonna get a visit real soon. Some warm night when you least expect it, a deer slug's gonna plow right through your brain. Or maybe through your kids' brain–'

The warden motions to his guards.

'I got a right to speak!' Hanratty shouts, neck muscles straining.

The warden raises his hand, stopping the guards. He'd like to avoid being branded a fascist by the media if he can avoid it.

'*Evening*, Mrs Givens,' Hanratty says in a syrupy voice. 'I'll be thinking 'bout your sister and your niece when they send me off to Jesus. I've thought about them many a night when I'm falling asleep. Yes, ma'am.'

Mrs Givens's shivering hand clenches my wrist like a claw.

'The black man is a mongrel creature,' Hanratty says with a tone of regret. 'But the good Lord knows a nigger wench is heaven between the sheets.'

'Gag the prisoner,' orders the warden.

'*All you motherfuckers gonna die worse than me!*' Hanratty shouts. '*This ain't nothing! Nothing!*'

Two guards seize Hanratty's head and fasten a black leather restraining device over his mouth and chin. The warden checks his watch and motions for the guards to follow him out of the room. Mrs. Givens isn't reading her Bible anymore. She's gripping my left wrist like it is the handrail on a cliff, her eyes riveted to the gurney.

'Are the chemicals going in?' she asks.

'Yes, ma'am. He's got about five minutes to live.'

Mrs Givens says something under her breath.

'I beg your pardon?'

'I said, he ought to be *awake* while it happens. My people was.'

Mrs Givens doesn't notice when I lift the Bible from her lap with my free hand and take up reading where her book-mark lies.

Now there was a day when the sons of God came to present themselves before the Lord, and Satan came also among them. And the Lord said to Satan, Whence comest thou? Then Satan answered the Lord and said, From going to and fro in the earth, and from walking up and down in it. And the Lord said unto Satan, Hast thou considered my servant Job, that there is none like him in the earth, a perfect and upright man, one that feareth God, and escheweth evil? Then Satan answered the Lord, and said, Doth Job fear God for nought? Hast Thou not made an hedge about him, and about his house, and about all that he hath on every side? Thou hast blessed the work of his hands, and his substance is increased in the land. But put forth thine hand now, and touch all that he hath, and he will curse thee to thy face. . . .

As God takes Satan's suggestion and puts forth his hand, I recall with soul-searing clarity the feeling of being singled out for suffering, of sitting in a plastic chair in the oncologist's office and hearing the white-coated doctor say to my wife that most terrible of words: *malignant.* Later I would learn more arcane terms, like *daughter cells* and *highly refractory*–

Suddenly everyone in the witness room is standing around me, shuffling, speaking in hushed tones. The prison doctor stands beside the gurney, listening to Hanratty's chest through a stethoscope, double-checking the leads that run to the EKG monitor. The reporters are wired – they always are at this point – unsure of their reactions even as they try to record them. No first-timer is ever ready for the banality of execution. Only we functionaries of the justice system know how depressing it really is. The doctor nods to the warden, and the warden motions for the curtain to be closed.

Mrs Givens thanks me for coming, then moves purpose-fully toward the door.

'You switched to prizefighting for a living?' Joe Cantor is standing beside me, a glint of humor in his eyes.

My hand instinctively goes to my bruised eye. 'I fell.'

'We still miss you at the office,' he says, shaking my hand with a grip reminiscent of Shad Johnson's. 'Nobody works a jury the way you did, Penn.'

'I wasn't working them, Joe. I was speaking from the heart.'

'That's what I'm talking about. They don't teach that in school. You were also the only assistant with the balls to argue with me. I kind of miss that too, believe it or not.' He leans closer. 'Watch out for Portman. That prick's had a hard-on for you ever since Hanratty's trial. And call me if you ever get tired of writing books.'

Then he is past me, shaking hands with someone else, working the crowd even here.

As I pass into the hall beyond the door, I find myself face to face with John Portman. His guards stand two feet behind him, their jackets unbuttoned to provide easy access to their weapons. Portman studies me with gray eyes set in his wind-burned face, a badge of privilege he has cultivated since youth. I decide to fire the first shot in this skirmish.

'I can't figure out what you're doing here, Portman. You must have known you were exposing yourself to something like what just happened.'

'I can absorb what just happened,' he replies, his voice edgier than I remember. 'It was worth it to see that genetic debris put down.'

A couple of reporters stop to question the FBI director, but the guards hustle them through the door.

'You're friends with Special Agent Peter Lutjens, aren't you?' Portman says.

A cold wind blows through my soul. 'Just tell me.'

'He's being transferred to Fargo, North Dakota. Lovely winters, I hear.'

'The guy is blameless, John.'

'Internal security is one of the hallmarks of the new Bureau,' he replies in a PR voice. 'Agent Lutjens didn't understand that.'

As I wonder how Portman learned of my contact with Lutjens, he says, 'Stick your nose into Bureau business, you get rhinoplasty. It's that simple.'

I usually try to avoid confrontations like this. They profit no one. But John Portman has a special place in my pantheon of dark spirits, and my guilt for what happened to Lutjens already weighs on me like a heavy stone.

'I go where the cases take me,' I tell him. 'And you'd do well to remember what happened the last time you went up against me.'

After years of near omnipotence as a federal judge, a man becomes unused to resistance. FBI directors must enjoy similar insulation from unpleasantness, because Portman's thin lips narrow to a white line, and his eyes blaze. Before he can threaten me further, I simply walk past him and down the hall. A rush of footsteps comes after me, and a hand jerks me around.

It's Portman, his face livid. 'You fucking dilettante–'

'You're not a judge anymore, Portman. You're a civil servant, serving at the pleasure of the President. And presidents are pretty sensitive to negative publicity.'

His grimace morphs into a twisted smile. 'You don't know what power is, Cage. But if you keep pushing, you're going to find out.'

'All this over a little Mississippi murder,' I murmur. 'I push in Natchez, you feel it in Washington. I find that very interesting. I think a lot of people will.'

This time when I walk away, Portman doesn't follow.

As I descend the staircase and cross the dark pavement outside the death house, I feel my pulse pounding in my temples. There's nothing quite like threatening the director of the FBI to get the blood circulating. I quicken my steps toward the parking lot, wanting to get out of the prison as swiftly as I can. Life is back at the hotel with Annie and Caitlin, not here at the Walls.

But Portman won't leave my thoughts. I can't shake the feeling that he came to Huntsville specifically to see me, and not Arthur Lee Hanratty. He knew he could speak to me here without appearing to have sought me out. His ruthless punishment of Peter Lutjens proves that my interest in the Payton murder has touched a bureaucratic nerve, at the very least. And at worst? I can't even guess. Anything is possible.

As I near my rental car, a couple of reporters from the witness room start shouting questions at me. Do I really believe the death penalty is a deterrent? Am I absolutely convinced of Hanratty's guilt? What were John Portman and I talking about? What was the FBI director doing here at all? I climb into the car, resisting the temptation to pour gasoline onto the fire of the Payton case. I need to think. I need to see Annie and Caitlin.

As I drive through the gate of the Walls, passing the now silent crowd standing their candlelight vigil in the rain-swept darkness, one thing comes clear to me. This is the last trip I will make to this prison. The yellow glow of the candles grows smaller in my rearview mirror. Three more men pass their days on death row because I put them here.

They will die without me present.

Chapter 21

When I reach the hotel, Caitlin is waiting for me with a cold can of Dr Pepper and a chicken sandwich. I'm starving. It took two hours to get back to Houston through the rain and traffic, but knowing that Annie might not go to sleep without me close kept me from stopping for food. I shouldn't have worried. She is sound asleep in one of the double beds, while the television plays CNN in muted tones. Caitlin is wearing silk pajamas that somehow look demure and sexy at the same time. I collapse at the table by the window and devour the sandwich, then drink the Dr Pepper in a few gulps. Her instincts are as accurate as always; she says nothing while I eat.

'Thank you,' I tell her, tossing the sandwich wrapper into the wastepaper can. 'Really.'

'I saw a clip of you coming out of the prison. Was it bad?'

'Bad enough. That's the last one I go to.'

'Let's change the subject, then. Annie only woke up once, and I rubbed her back till she fell asleep again.'

'I really appreciate you staying with her.'

'No problem. She's great.' Caitlin reaches out and touches my knee. 'You really look tired. You want me to go to my room so you can crash? Our flight to Gunnison leaves at eight-thirty.'

We're renting a Cherokee in Gunnison for the drive up to Crested Butte. 'I don't think I can get to sleep yet.'

'Okay.' She scoots back in her chair and folds her legs

beneath her. 'Let's talk business, then. Your assistant called. Your ATF friend called her and confirmed that Payton's car was destroyed by C-4 plastic explosive. They found traces of something called RDX in the shrapnel. He said there should be plenty more embedded in the metal of Payton's car. No problem to prove in court.'

Half my fatigue disappears into the shot of adrenaline this produces. 'So, Ray Presley planted the blasting caps and dynamite. And someone falsified the lab report.'

She nods. 'I've been studying your copy of the police report. It's mostly gossip really. Wild theories. The interesting thing is that there were rumored suspects the detectives never talked to, local guys who had done other race crimes. Almost as if Creel and Temple knew those suspects weren't guilty.'

'Presley may well have planted that C-4 himself. He's killed before. But for money usually. If he killed Payton, it wasn't on his own hook.'

'You think he killed Payton for Leo Marston?'

'Yes.'

'Where did you first get the idea Marston was involved?'

'From the deputy who saved us the other night. Ike Ransom.'

'Well . . . I hope you can trust him. Because I've got to tell you, everything my people have found on Marston indicates that he's a liberal, as far as race goes, anyway.'

'I know. I think the murder might not have been about race at all.'

Her mouth opens slightly. 'What else could it have been about?'

'I don't know yet. Have your people learned anything about Dwight Stone?'

'Yes. One of our reporters in Alexandria, Virginia, says Stone was dismissed from the FBI in 1972 for alcohol-related problems.'

'Anything else?'

'He was second-generation law enforcement. His father was a state trooper in Colorado. Stone himself served with the marines in Korea and won a handful of medals I don't know the significance of. He went to law school after he got out of the service, and joined the Bureau in 1956. He spent sixteen years in, and received several commendations before being dismissed.'

'Althea Payton told me Stone was sympathetic to her, that he really wanted to solve the case. I wonder if the fact that they both served in Korea was the root of that?'

'I guess it could be.'

'Something strange happened at the prison tonight, Caitlin.'

'What?'

'The director of the FBI showed up.'

'John Portman? Why would he show up at the Hanratty execution?'

'To warn me to stay out of the Del Payton case.'

'*What?*

'Portman and I have a history. When you asked about the Hanratty case on the plane, I left out some details. When Hanratty committed that first murder in Compton, he was seen by a dozen witnesses before he fled the scene, and they ID'd him from photographs under his real name. An LAPD detective remembered that Hanratty had been the star witness in a federal hate-crime trial a while back. His testimony put a half dozen white supremacists in jail and made a star out of the U.S. attorney of Los Angeles.'

'Portman,' Caitlin says softly.

'Exactly. The LAPD went to Portman, who told them Hanratty was under witness protection and couldn't have committed the crime. Political pressure started building. The next day Hanratty "escaped" from the program and wound up in Houston with his brothers. The rumor was, Portman tried to cover up the murder to keep his reputation clean. I'm pretty sure now that it's true. Hanratty referred to it tonight in his deathbed statement. Anyway, Portman wanted to neutralize the rumor by throwing the book at Hanratty in the L.A. courts.'

'And you stopped him.'

'Exactly. The guy hates my guts.'

'But what does that have to do with the Del Payton case?'

'I'm not sure. But Portman just killed the career of an FBI agent who gave me a little help on the phone. He's transferring him to Fargo, North Dakota. I don't think there's even a field office there. Just a resident agency. Whatever's in the Del Payton file must be embarrassing as hell to the Bureau. I want you to get your people working on Portman immediately. I want to know everything there is to know about him.'

'I'll call our Alexandria guy before we fly out in the morning.'

'I'm going to call that FBI agent right now. I owe him an apology.'

'It's the middle of the night. And it's later in Washington.'

'I doubt he's sleeping.'

I pull the phone over from between the beds, dial directory assistance, then use my credit card to call Peter Lutjens at his home in Washington. His phone rings five times before he answers, but his voice is wide awake.

'Peter, this is Penn Cage.'

Silence.

'I had no idea this thing would boomerang on you like this. I am so sorry.'

'Shit. I don't blame you. I gave you the list, didn't I?

'Peter, if there's anything I can do–'

'Can you get Portman fired?'

'I don't–' Suddenly an idea hits me. 'Maybe I can.'

'What?'

'Peter, have you wondered why Portman would punish you so severely for what you did?'

'He hates you, that's why.'

'It's the Payton file. Portman flew to Huntsville, Texas, tonight to warn me off the Payton case. And asking about the Payton file is what got you into trouble. Right?'

'Yes.'

'I think Portman is concealing some illegality about that case. If he is, and you can find out *what* it is—'

'Stop right there. Are you suggesting that I go back and try to look at that file myself?'

'Have they barred you from the building?'

'No, but—'

'When do you leave for Fargo?'

'Don't even say that word, goddamn it. And I'm not losing my pension for you. Cowboy time is over.'

'Peter, if that file is damaging enough, it might get Portman thrown out of the directorship. It might buy your old job back.'

'I've got a wife and kids. And I'm not out to trash the Bureau.'

'I'll shut up, then. I really called to apologize anyway.'

'That makes me feel so much better.'

The phone goes dead in my hand.

Caitlin puts the phone back between the beds for me. 'He wouldn't try it?'

'No.'

'Let's just forget it all for tonight, then.'

She picks up the remote control and flips through the channels, finally settling on a showing of *To Catch a Thief*. Grace Kelly and Cary Grant zoom across the screen in a vintage sports car.

'Okay with you?'

Staring at Grace Kelly, the coolly luminous Princess Grace, I recall my earlier thought that she and Livy Marston look more than a little alike. The similarities go deeper than looks too, for despite her cool exterior, Grace Kelly had a dark and promiscuous sexual history.

'It's fine,' I say absently.

Caitlin turns up the sound, and we watch from our chairs while Annie snores away on the bed. My mind is so full I cannot think clearly, but one image is predominant: Livy Marston in the Baton Rouge airport, seemingly as beautiful and untouched as she looked at seventeen. But when is anything ever what it seems? As beautiful as Livy was, she was not untouched. No girl that radiant survives adolescence without attracting the attention of every male in the three grades above her. And nature being what it is (and the seventies what they were), sex usually follows. I didn't understand this so clearly then, of course. At sixteen, though I was as perpetually and mindlessly horny as the rest of my compatriots, I was also ready to place some lucky (or unlucky) girl on a pedestal of mythic proportions. When, after a showing of *Looking for Mr Goodbar*, Livy tearfully confessed to me how she'd lost her virginity – a date rape by a senior with whom I played football – she installed herself on that pedestal with the permanence of a pietà.

Once she occupied this place of reverence in my psyche, it became impossible for me to see her clearly. Her public image was flawless. Queen of the elite private school in a city with five high schools, she was wanted by every male student in the city – not merely lusted after, but actually worshipped – and thus floated above the usual tortured angst of high school life. What I didn't understand then was that, to a girl like that, the most exciting company would be guys who didn't care what she said or thought, and who treated her accordingly.

Everyone knew Livy Marston occasionally went out with boys from the public schools – rough, handsome guys who straddled the line between 'hoods' and outright criminals –

some of whom were so dumb as to boggle the mind. It was hard to imagine what Livy could find to talk about with these guys. What I didn't understand then – or was too afraid to admit – was that she was not interested in talking to them.

It was something of a tradition for St. Stephens boys to sleep with girls from the public schools, who we thought to be 'looser' than the ones we saw in class every day. Whether this was true or not, I'm still not sure. Some public school girls defended their virtue like Roman vestals, while many St. Stephens girls led active romantic lives, to say the least. In any case, it was understood, according to a time-honored double standard, that boys slept around as a rite of passage into adulthood. When girls did it, they entered that unjustified but unforgiving territory known as sluthood. When Livy Marston did it, she confused everybody. To the point that no one really believed she was doing it. Everyone thought she was putting on a show. Acting wild. Driving her uptight father crazy. Now, of course, I understand it perfectly. In the time-honored tradition of Southern women of a certain class, Livy was taking her pleasures downward.

When she opened to me like a flower in the spring of our senior year, I accepted her attentions like a divine gift. For girls that age, having sex is usually so tied up in the desire to be accepted by peers that true motives are impossible to fathom. But for Livy Marston acceptance was not an issue. When she gave herself, it was because she wanted to, and that knowledge immeasurably dilated the experience. That her skills did not seem virginal I wrote off to her being as gifted sexually as she was in so many other ways. I submerged my self into hers, basked in the glow of being seen with her, of being known to be loved by her. I cared as little for what lay ahead of me as for what lay behind, and so set myself up for the fall of my life.

'Penn? Are you awake?'

I blink and look over at Caitlin. She's watching me

from her chair, her face flickering in the television light.

'What are you thinking about?'

'Nothing. Everything.'

An enigmatic smile. 'Livy Marston?'

'God, no,' I lie, thinking that Caitlin was absolutely right when she told me she had lethal instincts.

'I'm going to bed,' she says, rising from her chair. 'Tomorrow's a big day.'

I get up to walk her to her room, amazed by how tired I feel. Witnessing death up close saps you like a day under the sun. It also stokes the sexual fires, urging toward procreation. As we stand outside her door, Caitlin looks up at me, her face tilted perfectly for a kiss, and I realize again how beautiful she is. But I no longer see her as I did last night in the restaurant. I'm looking through the distorting memory of Livy Marston. Caitlin lowers her chin, and the moment passes.

'What do you think Dwight Stone knows?' she asks.

'More than we do. Maybe he knows everything.'

She opens the door and slips through without looking back, leaving me alone with my ghosts.

Chapter 22

Crested Butte, Colorado, is a tiny village nestled nine thousand feet in the Rocky Mountains, twenty-five miles from Aspen as the crow flies, three hours by car. The easiest way to get there is to fly into Gunnison and drive north up the valley for half an hour. But to get to former special agent Dwight Stone's cabin, you must leave the pastel storefronts of Crested Butte's old town behind and drive northwest into the mountains on a forest service road, past the summer homes of the rich, until the road turns into a jeep trail that follows the Slate River upstream between Anthracite Mesa and Schuylkill Mountain. A few hundred yards north of an eight-foot vertical drop in the river, situated in the thick fir and spruce between the jeep track and the narrow blue-black span of the Slate, stands a small but well-built cabin, facing southwest to catch the sun.

Dwight Stone likes his solitude.

When I called Stone from the Gunnison airport and asked if I could speak to him about the Payton case, he politely declined. I did not tell him where I was calling from.

That was an hour ago.

Now Caitlin and Annie and I approach his front porch like a lost family asking for directions. I'm glad we brought coats. When we left Natchez it was ninety degrees. Here it's less than fifty, and there are dark clouds glowering over the summit of Gothic Mountain to the east.

Before I can knock, a tall, fit-looking man in his late

sixties clumps around the side of the cabin wearing hip waders, a Black Watch flannel shirt, and carrying a fly rod.

'You folks lost?' he asks in a deep, resonant voice.

'That depends on where we are.' I've already recognized the voice, but I say, 'Are you former special agent Dwight Stone?'

Stone has the eyes of a combat veteran, and they narrow instantly, assessing threat. A man with a woman and a little girl can't seem like much danger, but I don't know what his anxieties are.

'You're on my property,' he points out, quite reasonably. 'Why don't you introduce yourself first?'

'Fair enough. I'm Penn Cage.'

His eyes relax, but he sighs wearily. 'You've wasted your time, son. Flying up here to get told no to your face instead of over the phone.'

'I hoped you might soften up a little when you saw us.'

He shakes his head, climbs onto the porch, and leans the fly rod against the cabin wall.

'I'm not a journalist. I have no interest in sensationalizing this story.'

'You're a writer, aren't you?'

'Yes, but that's not why I'm looking into this case.'

'Why are you?'

My gut feeling about Dwight Stone is that if you want to get anywhere with him, honesty is the best policy. 'I could say it was to help the victim's family. Althea Payton and her mother-in-law. And I do want to help them. But I also have a selfish reason. I'm trying to nail a man who hurt my father a long time ago.'

Stone studies me for several seconds. 'Who would that be?'

'Leo Marston. Judge Leo Marston. He was the district attorney back—'

'I know who he was.' Stone eyes Caitlin. 'This your wife?'

'No, a friend. Caitlin Masters. But this is my daughter. Say hello, Annie.'

Annie waves her right hand while clinging to Caitlin's leg with her left.

'You bring her along for the sympathy factor?'

'I brought her to keep her out of harm's way. I've already been shot at. Not many people want the Payton case reopened.'

A flicker of something in Stone's eyes. 'You convicted Arthur Lee Hanratty, didn't you?'

'That's right.'

'I saw you on CNN last night, at the Walls.'

I nod but say nothing.

'That'll buy you a half hour of my time, Mr. Penn Cage. How about some coffee?'

'Coffee would be wonderful,' Caitlin says, lifting Annie into her arms.

Stone takes a trout bag from his shoulder, then wipes his hands on his shirt and reaches for the cabin door. 'I don't get much company up here, but I think maybe we could rustle up some hot chocolate too.'

Annie breaks into a wide grin.

Stone settles Caitlin and me on a sand-colored leather sofa with Annie between us. Before us is a huge fieldstone fire-place, and Stone quickly builds a roaring blaze in it. The cabin is full of hunting and fishing gear, snowshoes hanging on the walls, rifles over the mantel, a fly-tying bench littered with bright feathers. A large double-paned window faces the Slate, which runs flat and smooth thirty yards from the cabin's back door. Only a large white propane tank mars the illusion of virgin wilderness, and when there's snow it's probably invisible.

After putting the trout in his sink, Stone brings us mugs of coffee and chocolate heated on an old woodstove, then sits opposite us in a rough handmade chair. His waders hang on a hook by the door, dripping into a brass bucket with the sound of men making use of a spittoon.

'You've got a nice place,' I tell him. 'No neighbors at all. How'd you manage that?'

He smiles. 'Everything you see around this place is government land. But this cabin sits on a mining claim that's been in my family for three generations. Grandfathered down to the present. The federal government can't do a thing about me.'

'I love it,' Caitlin says.

'Thank you. Now, I heard the story Mr Cage told me on the telephone. Tell me what you really know about the Payton case. And why you care.'

'We've read the original police file,' I begin. 'Informant reports, interviews, interrogations, theories.'

'What did you learn from that?'

'The report was wrong about the bomb that blew up Payton's Fairlane.'

If this rings a bell, Stone has one hell of a poker face. 'Wrong how?'

'It said the bomb was made of dynamite, based on a patrolman discovering fragments of blasting caps, plus lab analysis.'

'So?'

'I located Payton's car. It's still in decent shape, believe it or not. The damage looked more characteristic of C-4 to me. A lot of metal shearing, small shrapnel. I sent a fragment of the engine to an expert for analysis. Last night he confirmed it. C-4.'

Stone nods thoughtfully. 'C-4 was damn hard to come by in 1968. And your Klan boys didn't know shit about using it.'

He has not directly refuted my assertion. 'You're saying the expert is wrong?'

'It's happened before. But that's not what I'm saying.'

'Then you're saying the Klan wasn't behind the murder.'

'I didn't say that either. What kind of theories were in the report?'

'Mostly rumors. I thought one story was plausible. Someone thought Payton's death as a mistake. That the real target was the president of the local NAACP. He apparently rode to and from work with Payton a good bit.'

Stone nods with familiarity. 'What about the one where a black button man was hired from New Orleans to come up and pop Payton? Strictly a money hit.'

This scenario had been reported to the police by a Louisiana woman. Her story was given credence because she turned down the full fifteen-thousand-dollar reward rather than give more details. She claimed she'd never live to spend the money. No further information was recorded in the file.

'Is that what you think happened?' I ask.

Stone smiles. 'It *could* have happened. How old are you, Mr Cage? Thirty-five?'

'Thirty-eight.'

'Do you have any idea what things were like in 1968?'

'In Mississippi?'

'In America.'

'Well . . . the country was turning against Vietnam. LBJ was being ground down by the war. Civil rights hit its highwater mark, with Martin Luther King at his peak before he–'

'I'm glad you passed your civics course,' he interrupts. 'I'm talking about reality, son. Behind the scenes. In 1968 a few powerful and paranoid men were trying to hold their vision of this country together in the face of social revolution. It was a tide they had no prayer of stopping, but they didn't understand that, and they used every method at their disposal to try.'

As Stone speaks, I glimpse a furnace of anger seething behind his eyes. He has tight control over it, but he's been holding in that anger for years.

'The Constitution meant nothing to these men. Richard Nixon was one of them, but he was bush league compared to them.'

'You're talking about J. Edgar Hoover?'

'Hoover was one of the more visible.'

'How does this tie in with Del Payton?'

Stone looks from my face to Caitlin's, as though deciding whether we have earned the right to any of his hard-won knowledge. Now that I think of it, he's probably seventy years old, but his tanned, weathered face and soldier's eyes convey the strength of a much younger man.

'A lot of blacks were killed in Mississippi in the nineteen-sixties,' he says in a deliberate voice. 'Del Payton was one. But he was killed later than most. Have you thought about that? A lot of the race murders happened around sixty-four. Payton came later.'

'What's the significance of that?'

'Just something for you to think about.'

Everything's riddles with this guy. 'Martin Luther King was assassinated in 1968,' I point out.

He shakes his head. 'I'm talking about grassroots murders.'

Caitlin looks ready to pop; she obviously has a hundred questions, but I hope she won't ask them. The harder we push Stone, the more he'll resist us. From lawyerly instinct, I move away from Del Payton, and ask a question to which I already know the answer.

'Did you serve your full term of service with the Bureau? That is to say, did you retire at full pension?'

He takes a deep breath, and a little more anger spills through his eyes. 'I'm going to answer that because you're going to find it out anyway, if you don't already know. And because I'm not ashamed to answer. I was asked to resign in 1972. Officially for alcoholism.'

Caitlin nods with empathy. 'Did your drinking have anything to do with the Del Payton case?'

'That I won't answer. But I'll tell you this. If every alcoholic in the Bureau in 1972 had been asked to resign, Hoover couldn't have mounted a raid on a cathouse. You had to drink just to stomach what was going on back then.'

'What kind of thing are you talking about?' I ask.

'You ever read *American Tabloid*, by James Ellroy?'

'No.'

'Give it a look. Things weren't quite that crazy, but they were damn close.'

'How did you earn a living after leaving the Bureau?'

A sour look wrinkles his face. 'Worked as a private dick for a while. Big firm. That was sleazier than Hoover's Bureau, so I quit. Worked as an insurance investigator. I drank professionally for a few years. I was close to dying when my daughter pulled me back up to the light. I finally hung out my shingle here and started helping the locals fight the government and the big mining companies. That suited my temperament.'

'Were you in charge of the Payton investigation?'

'I was.'

'How did you like Natchez?'

'It wasn't much like the rest of Mississippi. Better in a lot of ways. More liberal, the people more educated. But in a way that made the things that happened there worse. You know? Because there were people there who knew better.'

Stone goes to the stove and returns with the coffeepot, talking as he refills our cups. 'When I was assigned to that case, I was only a couple of years younger than Payton was when he died. I had a wife and two kids, and I still had a few illusions. That case knocked them right out of me.'

He sets the empty pot on the stone hearth and takes his chair. 'Do you have any illusions left, Mr Cage?'

'Not many.'

He studies me as if judging the truth of my statement.

Caitlin takes this chance to jump in. 'How do you feel personally about J. Edgar Hoover?'

Stone examines his fingernails, a seemingly casual gesture calculated to hide inner turmoil. 'I don't care if the man wore Frederick's of Hollywood to bed every night. I don't care if he wanted to *marry* Clyde Tolson, that pompous ground squirrel. But the man presented himself to this nation as a paragon of law and order. A champion of right. And the son of a–' Stone winces like Humphrey Bogart– 'the *man* didn't know the meaning of the words. He stole from the government, misused agents for personal gain, colluded with mobsters, broke the securities laws . . . Human beings just weren't meant to have that much power. Jesus, I need a drink.'

'Go right ahead.' It's barely two p.m., but I feel like I could use one too.

Stone shakes his head. 'Four months sober. It's a daily battle.'

Watching him get control of his craving is like watching a man fight a malarial fever. As a younger man Dwight Stone did what most Americans never do – peered behind the curtain at the men running the machine – and he is a different man because of it. America isn't the same country now, of course. It's better in a lot of ways. But I can see how this wouldn't matter to Stone. We are, all of us, men of our own eras.

'You want to destroy Leo Marston?' he asks, his eyes hard.

The name flows easily from his lips. He has thought about Marston since 1968. 'Do you think that's possible?'

'Put it this way. I think it's a noble goal.'

Caitlin presses her knee hard against mine. I can feel her

excitement, but I don't look at her. It's suddenly as clear to me as the mountain air outside Stone's cabin: the man sitting across from us knows who killed Del Payton, and why, and probably why that knowledge was never made public.

'But it won't be easy,' he adds.

'That's what someone else told me.'

'Who?'

Stone is playing it so close to the vest that I decide to keep Ike Ransom's name to myself. 'You wouldn't know him. He came along after your time. But he's interested in the case, and he hates Leo Marston. What can you tell us about Marston's involvement?'

'Nothing more than I have already.'

'Will you help us with this case?'

A deep conflict is playing itself out behind the old agent's eyes, one only hinted at by the tension in his muscles and the tightness of his lips. 'I can't,' he says finally.

'Why not?'

'Because despite what you see here, I'm not alone in the world. There are people I care about. I'm thinking of getting married, believe it or not. And I won't put innocent lives at risk for something that can't make any difference now.'

'Do you really think there's that much danger?' asks Caitlin.

Stone rakes a hand along his jaw. 'Make no mistake about it. You are already swimming with sharks.'

His baleful eyes linger on mine, trying to impress his seriousness upon me. He reminds me of an old homicide cop I knew in Houston, a guy who'd been shot twice in the line of duty. When he told you to start worrying, it was time to put on the Kevlar.

'What about the Mississippi Sovereignty Commission files?' Caitlin asks. 'Payton's is sealed. Do you think we could learn anything significant from it?'

'Those were state files. I never saw them.'

'The FBI file is sealed as well. Does that surprise you?'

He barks a laugh. 'I'd be surprised if the damn thing exists at all.'

'It exists, all right,' I tell him. 'Forty-four volumes. The question is, what's in it?'

'Forty-three volumes of nothing, and my final report.'

'What was in your final report?'

He sighs and looks past us, to the front windows of his cabin. 'I can't tell you that.'

Caitlin glances at me, her lower lip pinned by her teeth, her gesture of concentration. 'The file was ostensibly sealed for reasons of national security,' she says. 'Can you give us any hint as to what the Payton case could have to do with national security?'

Stone taps his fingers nervously on the arm of his chair. 'Del Payton was killed five weeks after Martin Luther King was assassinated, and three weeks before Robert Kennedy. Have you considered that?'

Caitlin and I share a look.

'Are you saying Payton's death was somehow connected to those assassinations?' I ask.

'Kings climb to eminence over men's graves, Mr. Cage.'

'Who said that?'

'A very wise man.'

'Who is the king you're referring to?'

'I'm just quoting an old poet, son.'

'Last night I was threatened by the present director of the FBI. Why should John Portman be concerned with a thirty-year-old civil rights murder?'

'Why do you assume Payton's death was a civil rights murder?'

At this echo of Ike Ransom, my heart twitches in my chest. 'You're saying it wasn't?'

'I'm just thinking aloud.'

'Have you ever met Portman?' I ask, my pulse racing.

'I met him.' Stone's distaste is plain. 'He joined the Bureau a few years before I got out.'

'What did you think of him as an FBI agent?'

'He was a brown-nosing, manipulative, Ivy League rich boy with the moral sense of a cat. A good little German with obsessive ambition. After seven years in the field they promoted him to the Puzzle Palace.'

'The Puzzle Palace?' Caitlin asks.

'The Hoover Building. FBI Headquarters. The guys who work there call it SOG. For "Seat of Government." It is the perfect environment for devious, back-stabbing sons of bitches. I apologize for the profanity. I forgot about your little girl.'

Annie didn't hear him. She's busy examining a rock collection displayed in a glass-box end table. If she had heard him, she would have yelled, *Mr. Stone said a bad word!*

'Did you keep any personal notes from the Payton investigation?' I ask, recalling the habits of that cop Stone brought to mind a moment ago. 'Something you didn't turn in to your superiors, maybe?'

His gaze wanders to the rear window, where the stream rushes along the rocks. 'You want to learn what I learned back in 1968?' He looks back at me, his eyes burning into mine as though striving to communicate something he cannot say aloud. 'Do what I did. Talk to the eyewitnesses. Have you done that? Have you talked to the eyewitnesses?'

I admit that I haven't.

'You didn't convict Arthur Lee Hanratty by sitting in your office, did you? Pound the bricks. Talk to everybody who'll talk and pressure those who won't. That's what we did back then. And we learned the truth.'

This statement hangs in the air like a volatile gas.

'Then why didn't anyone go to jail?' Caitlin asks softly.

Stone's jaw muscles clench in an effort to control his

rage. 'For the same reason this country is going to hell in a handbasket. And don't ask me that again.'

'What was your partner's name?'

'We didn't have partners,' he says, his eyes still on me. 'Not like municipal police. I worked a lot with Henry Bookbinder. He died of cirrhosis back in seventy-four.'

'I know you're fond of quotes. Have you heard this one? "You yourself are guilty of a crime when you do not punish crime."'

Stone's right hand squeezes into a fist. 'I think your half hour's up, pardner.'

'May I ask you one more question?'

He stands and stretches his back muscles. 'What is it?'

'Do you remember a cop named Ray Presley?'

Just before Stone's eyes glass over, I glimpse an anger even more personal than that which I have seen to this point.

'I remember him,' he says in a flat voice.

'Do you think the police made an honest attempt to investigate the case?'

'That's two questions.' Stone turns to Annie, who's now touching a clay pot that looks like Pueblo work. 'How'd you like that hot chocolate, little darling?'

'Mmmm. It was great!'

He walks to the door, leaving us little choice but to follow. I take Annie's hand and lead her after him.

'Sorry you folks had to come all this way for nothing,' he says, opening the door to the dark vista of Gothic Mountain rising above the mesa. 'Rain coming. That's October for you.'

We're on the porch now. The sibilant sound of the Slate beckons from the edges of the cabin.

'I don't think it was for nothing,' Caitlin says, turning to Stone with a look of absolute frankness. 'I think something evil happened in Natchez in 1968. I think you know what it was. I realize we sort of ambushed you here, and I apologize for that. But we want justice for Del Payton. I think you do too.' She takes a card from her pocket and passes it to Stone. 'You're going to do a lot of thinking after we leave. You can reach us at this number.'

His jaw tightens as he examines the card. 'You're a goddamn reporter?'

'A publisher. An honest one.'

He looks at me, his eyes brimming with outrage.

'She won't print a word you said,' I assure him. 'She won't even print your name. She prints nothing at all until this whole mess is resolved.'

Stone shifts his gaze to Caitlin.

'I want the truth, she says. 'The truth, and justice. Nothing else. Thank you for your time, Agent Stone.'

As we walk to the Cherokee, he stands in his doorway looking – for the first time since we've seen him – a little unsure of himself. It strikes me that he liked Caitlin using his old rank. Despite all his deep-rooted anger, Stone is still proud to have been an FBI agent.

Unlocking the door, I hear the scuff of boots behind me. Stone has come down off the porch. He puts his right arm on my shoulder in a fatherly way and looks into my eyes.

'You've got too much to lose to dig into this mess, son. The world has already changed too much for it to make any difference.'

'I don't agree.'

A strange recognition lights his eyes, and I am suddenly sure that in me he sees a shadow of the man he was years ago. 'I'd like to give you one more quote,' he says. 'If you don't mind.'

'Whatever.'

'The hour of justice does not strike on the dials of this world.'

I look away from his sad eyes, wondering what could possibly have driven a man of his strength and experience into such a miasma of defeatism. 'No offense, Agent Stone, but I think you've been doing too much reading and not enough soul-searching.'

To my surprise, this does not anger him. He squeezes my shoulder. 'You have more illusions than you think. I wish you luck.'

'I wouldn't need it if you'd tell me what you know.'

He shakes his head and takes a step back. 'Whatever you do, you send that little girl someplace safe before you take another step. You hear?'

'That I'll do.'

As he retreats to his porch, I buckle Annie into her safety seat and join Caitlin in the front. She looks at me with fire in her eyes.

'Did you catch what he said inside?'

'About Payton's murder not being about civil rights?'

'No. When you asked him if he had any personal notes he kept from his superiors.'

Stone is still watching us from the porch.

'He said if he wanted to learn what he did, we should do what he did.'

She nods excitedly. 'Talk to the eyewitnesses, right? That was the first thing he said. He looked at you real hard. Remember?'

'Yes. Like he was trying to communicate something nonverbally. Do you know what it was?'

She gives me an almost taunting smile. '*Talk to the eyewitnesses.*'

'What is it, for God's sake?'

'Penn . . . he used the plural. According to all accounts, there was only one eyewitness to the Payton bombing.'

She's right. Frank Jones, the scheduling clerk. Had Dwight Stone tried to tell me – without telling me – that there was more than one witness in the Triton parking lot on the day Del Payton died?

'I told you I was good at this,' she says, smiling with triumph. 'Let's get out of here.'

I start the Cherokee and wheel it around until we're pointed back toward the jeep track. 'What did you think of Stone?'

'I think he's scared.'

'Me too.'

We spent the night in Gunnison. We might have rushed and made our flight, but none of us really wanted to race back to the heat of Mississippi. We took a suite at the Best Western and ate a long meal in a local steak house. Caitlin and I tried to list every possible reason Del Payton could have been murdered besides civil rights work, but Annie didn't cooperate with this effort, which made it virtually impossible.

Back in the suite, we rented *The Parent Trap* on the in-house movie channel and watched it from the big bed. Annie lay between Caitlin and me, facing the TV, while we leaned back against the headboard, the pillows from both beds padding our backs. When Annie allowed it, which wasn't often, we speculated about Stone and his cryptic statements. But watching TV with a four-year-old means *watching* it.

Lying in bed with Annie and Caitlin catapulted me back to a time so innocent and wonderful that I could hardly bear to think about it. Before Sarah got sick. Before the hospitals. Just us and our baby, laid up on Sunday mornings watching *Barney* with no fear of the future. When our biggest problem was deciding where we wanted to go for dinner.

When *The Parent Trap* ended, Annie said she wanted another movie. As I punched in the code for *Beauty and the Beast* and Caitlin called room service for ice cream, I wondered if Annie was experiencing the same memories

I was, or at least the safe warm feeling she once knew with her mother and me. I thought perhaps she was, because two minutes after she finished her ice cream, she began snoring at the foot of the bed.

With this background of Disney music and snores, Caitlin asked me about Sarah. I sat silent for a while, but Caitlin didn't apologize or ask if I was all right. When she interviewed me, I had told her this subject was off limits. But that interview seemed a long time ago. As I sat there watching Belle confront her beast, I felt Caitlin's hand close around mine, tentative at first, then firm and warm. After a few moments I looked over at her. She gave me a smile that asked nothing, assumed nothing. A sense of pure goodness flowed from her.

Sarah would like this woman, I thought. For the first time since the previous day, the ghost of Livy Marston receded in my mind. I began to speak, and I did not stop until I had told Caitlin all of it, the pleasure and the pain, the joy and the grief, the beginning and the end. She asked to see a picture of Sarah, and I showed her the snapshot I carry in my wallet. It could have been an awkward moment, but it wasn't. Caitlin made it natural.

After I put the picture away, I tried to be as natural as she but found it impossible. The sadness that had been accreting in my soul for the past seven months began to break loose, and I found myself doing what I never allowed myself to do in front of Annie. I remember Caitlin holding my head against her breast, speaking soft words that escape me now. I must have fallen asleep that way, for I awakened to find light streaming through the curtains and Annie lying beside me, with no idea how we got beneath the covers. Caitlin was not in the bed, but she had taken good care of us before she left it.

Chapter 23

When we reached Natchez the next afternoon, I found a fax waiting for me on my parents' kitchen table. It had been sent to my father's office just before lunch. There was no originating number at the head of the page, but the fax itself was a copy of a newspaper story clipped from the Leesville *Daily Leader*. Leesville, Louisiana, is a community located next to Fort Polk, a huge army training base, and a hundred and fifty miles from Natchez. Above the article was a copy of the paper's masthead, and it showed the date as May 19, 1968. Five days after Del Payton died.

The article recounted the capture of two men – a supply sergeant and a civilian – who one month previous had stolen armaments from a military arsenal at Fort Polk. While the troops were on maneuvers and the marching band was parading around the base in full dress uniforms, these two enterprising souls had filled a two-ton truck with M-16s, Claymore mines, hand grenades, and C-4 plastic explosive, then had driven off the base and sold most of the ordnance piecemeal throughout the southeast. The civilian half of this duo was named Lester Hinson. I noticed because his name had been circled, probably by whoever sent the fax.

There was also a note for me to call Althea Payton at St. Catherine's hospital. I tried, but someone in the nursery told me she couldn't come to the phone. I called Caitlin at the newspaper, explained the mystery fax, and gave her Lester Hinson's name so she could begin tracing him. She asked if

I thought Dwight Stone had sent the fax. My guess was Peter Lutjens, but I didn't say his name on the telephone. I did make a mental note to call him again and make a pitch for him to take a run at Payton's FBI file before he woke up in North Dakota. Caitlin asked if I'd gotten started doing what Stone had told me to do: talk to the eyewitnesses of the Payton bombing. She recalled from her research that Frank Jones – the 'sole' witness to the bombing – worked as a salesman at the local Pontiac dealership. Jones didn't know it yet, but he was about to take me for a test drive.

The Pontiac dealership is festooned with balloons and strips of colored foil, but the only customers are clustered around the service bay. The salesmen hover in a loose knot inside the air-conditioned showroom, watching for customers through the huge glass window like predators scanning a drought-burned plain. The sight of my father's BMW 740i brings them all to their feet, albeit with feigned aloofness. They probably know the car on sight, but hope that old Doc Cage has temporarily taken leave of his senses and decided to buy American for once.

After parking at the end of the main display line, I make a show of looking at price stickers as I walk toward the showroom door. I search the salesmen's faces through the glass, gambling that the oldest will be Frank Jones. It stands to reason, although in a tough economy retirees might be working jobs like this to supplement their Social Security. When I open the door, everyone is suddenly busy, as though I've blundered into a Labor Day blowout sale.

I nod to the nearest salesman, then walk over to a Trans-Am sitting on the display floor and study the price sticker. Twenty seconds of silence is all it takes.

'She's a beaut, ain't she?' A head has suddenly materialized from behind a wooden partition near the back wall. 'You want two, or just the one?'

The face on the head is over seventy, and it splits into the forced grin of a man who always supplies the laughs for his own jokes. He comes out from behind the partition, right hand extended in greeting, revealing a baby blue polyester sport coat over a blue plaid shirt and brown tie.

'Frank Jones, sales manager!' he barks, pumping my hand. 'What can we do you for today?'

'I want to take a test drive.'

'That's why we're here. Which car?'

I drop the flat of my hand on the roof of the Trans-Am. 'How about this one?'

'You bet.' He looks vaguely to his left. 'Open the big door, Jimmy Mac.'

'Sure,' says a young salesman by the window. 'Can I talk to you a second afirst?'

'I got a customer here, son.'

Jones has the gleam of money in his eye. He hasn't yet spotted the BMW, and he seems to have sized me up as an all-cash type. I sit in the passenger seat as he guides the Trans-Am out of the showroom and stops so we can trade seats. Once behind the wheel, I adjust the seat for my longer frame, then pull out to the edge of the highway.

'That looks like Doc Cage's car,' he says, finally noticing the BMW.

'It is.' I merge into traffic, make a U-turn, and head for the Mississippi River bridge. 'I'm driving it.'

He looks at me and starts to speak but doesn't.

'I'm Penn Cage.'

'Shit. You're the book writer.' He stares straight through the windshield for half a minute, then turns to me. 'Did you say all that crap they printed in the paper?'

'Some of it. They didn't exactly stick to what I said.'

Jones snorts. 'Don't I know it. You can't trust a damn thing you read in that rag. They did the same to me back in sixty-eight.'

'About your account of the bombing?'

'Not so much that. It was the little things. Hell, they misspelled my name. How the hell can you misspell *Jones*? By God, that takes some doing.'

When we top the hill that runs down to the cut in the bluff, I remember that there are two bridges spanning the Mississippi now. Throughout my childhood there was only one, and I can't seem to keep the new one in my mind. As the Trans-Am ramps onto the main span of the westbound bridge, the mile-wide tide of brown river opens seventy feet below us. The vistas to the north and south look much as they did to Sam Clemens a hundred years ago: muddy water swollen into the forest and sandbars on both banks, pale blue sky blanked out at the center by a relentless sun. Ahead of us, Vidalia, Louisiana, is laid out like a toy town behind its levee, some buildings no higher than the river itself, the personification of provisional existence.

'You want to ask me about that killing, don't you? Hell, I've told the story a thousand times. A dozen times a day since that article ran.'

'Did the police question you a lot about what you saw?'

Jones squints, his rather dull version of a cagey look. 'Everybody questioned me a lot. I was the only person who saw that Fairlane blow.'

This isn't the time to contradict him. 'Did you get the feeling the police really wanted to solve the case?'

'What do you mean?'

I let the silence speak for me.

He licks his lips and looked out his window. 'You writing a book about this?'

'No.'

'Well, if you was . . . it seems like my story might be pretty valuable to you.'

'I'm not. I just want to know about the police. Do you remember who investigated the case?'

'Henry Creel and Ronnie Temple. And you're goddamn right they tried to solve it. Those guys had a hundred-percent clearance rate back then.'

'They must be the only detectives in the world with that record.'

'These days maybe. Back then they didn't have the goddamn ACLU breathing down their necks.'

'But they didn't solve the case.'

Jones rolls down the window and spits into the wind. 'Somebody killed a nigger. Case closed.'

'What do you know about Ray Presley?'

'Enough not to say a word about him.'

I turn onto Deer Park Road, which follows the river south on the Louisiana side. Soon we're driving past cotton and soybean fields, the levee on our left, the monotony broken only by shotgun churches, house trailers, and tar-paper shacks.

'You seem to know a lot about Creel and Temple.'

'Creel was my wife's cousin.'

'Was?'

'Lou Gehrig's disease, over to Shreveport. Temple's dead too. Heart attack.'

I swing the car up onto the road that runs atop the levee. Between the levee and the river lie the perpetually flooded 'borrow pits' created by the dredging that built the levee. The blackwater pits teem with catfish, crawfish, gar, water moccasins, alligators, abandoned cars, and the occasional corpse.

'Good fishing down there this month,' Jones offers.

'Do you think Payton was killed for doing civil rights work?'

He shrugs. 'I don't know nothing from civil rights work. He was stirring up a pile of shit, I know that. He used the national union to get himself promoted to quality-control inspector, which was a white job up till then. That pissed off a lot of people. Then he started bucking for injection-mold foreman. What the hell did he expect? Wasn't nobody out there gonna tolerate a nigger foreman in sixty-eight. Next thing they'd be wanting the front office. Too far, too fast. It's that simple.'

'Did the Klan kill him?'

Jones's cheeks redden. 'I don't know nothing about no Klan. Payton just pissed off too many people. Anybody coulda killed him.' He snaps his fingers nervously. 'Turn this damn thing around. I gotta get back to work.'

'I noticed you guys were pretty busy.'

'Kiss my sanctified ass.'

He turns on the radio, selects a country station, and adjusts the volume so that further conversation will be impossible. I make a U-turn and head back toward the twin bridges. A couple of minutes later, he surprises me by yelling over the roar of the stereo: 'I can't stand this shit!'

'What?' I ask, turning down the volume.

'All this happy-ass, fake-rock, slicky-boy country shit. They don't play nothing good no more.'

'What's good? Hank Williams?'

'Hank's all right, sure. But Jim Reeves, boy, that's the prime stuff.'

I almost laugh. I'm no Jim Reeves fan, but whatever differences separate me from his redneck, he and I are bound together by manner, rites, and traditions imprinted deep beneath the skin. That's why Caitlin's newspaper story didn't stop him from talking to me. I am white and Mississippi-born, and at bottom Jones perceives me as a member of his tribe. I wonder how wrong he is. If push comes to shove, and I'm forced to choose between white and black, will I realize there is no choice at all?

'Did the FBI question you?'

'Shit. Federal Bureau of Integration, we called 'em back then.' Now that we're headed back, Jones has regained some of his old swagger. 'Had 'em an office up in the City Bank building. A dozen Yankees with blue suits and ramrods up their butts. Agents came down from Jackson special just to question me. I think Bobby Kennedy sent 'em. Hoover wouldna sent assholes like these were.'

'They were tough on you?'

'A pack of pussies, more like. They didn't do no better with the case than Creel and Temple did. And Kennedy got what he deserved a couple weeks later.'

Robert Kennedy deserved a bullet in the head? 'What about an agent named Stone? Special Agent Dwight Stone?'

Jones's face goes as dead as though someone zipped it shut. 'Never heard of him.'

'He was lead agent on the Payton murder.'

The ex-Triton man sets his jaw and stares straight ahead like an obstinate mule. He remembers Agent Stone, all right. And not fondly.

We're approaching the arched midpoint of the eastbound bridge. Above us, Natchez stretches across the horizon like a Cecil B. De Mille movie set, sweeping up from the cotton-rich bottomland to the spires and mansions on the great bluff, then back down again to the Triton plant and the sandbars where the river rolls on toward New Orleans and the Gulf. It's the first time in years that I've seen the city from this aspect, and it's breathtaking. Below us, two steamboats are docked at Under-the-Hill, grand anachronisms that now carry tourists rather than cotton merchants and gamblers. As we roll off the bridge and top the first long incline, the Pontiac sign appears in the distance. Jones's posture instantly relaxes. This will be my last chance to speak to the man with any hope of a candid answer.

'What were you doing out there in the parking lot by yourself at eight o'clock that night?'

Something in his reaction telegraphs that he is about to lie. He does not squirm in his seat or make a sharp exclamation. Rather, a new stillness settles over him, one that sits heavily on a man unaccustomed to it.

'My wife called me,' he says. 'She wanted me to get some bread and eggs and such. I was on night shift and the Pik Quick was about to close.'

This is the story recorded in the police report. But hearing Jones repeat it aloud, I sense the wrongness of it. 'You were coming back from getting groceries when you saw the explosion?'

'I never got to leave.' He shifts in his seat, finally giving release to his nervous energy. 'Had a problem with my battery. Or I thought it was my battery. Turned out to be my solenoid.'

A strange elation takes hold of me. Eight years of questioning hostile witnesses honed my intuition to a pretty fine point. Frank Jones is lying. He's been lying for thirty years. And any cop worth a damn would have seen it as easily in 1968 as I saw it today. Dwight Stone would have seen it a damn sight quicker.

I pull onto the edge of the Pontiac lot and stop, then catch Jones's left wrist and hold it tight. 'Who else was in that parking lot that night?'

His eyes go wide with surprise. 'What? Nobody.'

I squeeze harder. He tries to pull away, but he hasn't the strength.

'Nobody, I tell you!'

'You saw the killer.'

'That's a goddamn lie!'

'Then who was it? Who else was there that night?'

Jones jerks his arm free and rubs his wrist. 'You don't know shit!'

'I'm going to blow this case wide open, my friend. And the longer you lie, the harder it's going to go on you.'

He glances nervously at the showroom window. He actually looks like he wants to talk, but he has stuck with a lie for thirty years, and he won't abandon it easily now. He grabs the key from the ignition, killing the engine. 'Get out of this goddamn car.'

I start to get out, then stop. 'You don't mind if I call your wife to confirm that story, do you? About her calling you to go get groceries?'

'Do what you want. I divorced that bitch thirty years ago. Just get the hell out of this ride.'

I climb out and walk to my father's car. The other salesmen are lined up against the showroom window, staring openly now. As Jones switches seats and pulls the Trans-Am toward the building, I start the BMW and drive quickly off the lot.

One cell phone call to my mother tells me all I need to know. Frank Jones's ex-wife still lives in Natchez. After a messy divorce she married the president of a local oil company, quite a trade up from Frank Jones. The 'messiness' involved affairs Jones had trailed with several secretaries at the battery plant. I dial the oilman's home and ask for the ex-wife by her new name: Little.

'This is Mrs. Little,' says a rather prim voice.

'Mrs. Little, this is Penn Cage.'

'Dr. Cage's boy?'

'That's right. I—'

'I remember when you used to take the blood and Xrays at your daddy's office.'

At least she didn't hang up. 'Yes, ma'am. I wanted to ask you a couple of questions, if you don't mind.'

'What about?'

'The day Del Payton died.'

A hesitation. 'What about it?'

'I just talked to your ex-husband, and—'

'Sweet Jesus. What did that no-count say about me?'

Her anger sounds fresh, even after thirty years. 'He used you for an alibi, Mrs. Little. He said he went out to the Triton parking lot on the night Del Payton died because you asked him to pick up some groceries.'

'That's a damn lie, pardon my French. He was in that parking lot because he was diddling one of his floozies.'

This remarkable statement stops me for a moment. 'Are you . . . you're saying you think someone was in the lot with him that night?'

'Are you hard of hearing? That no-good tomcat came home that night and asked me to tell the police the same story he told you. And I did, numbskull that I was.'

I'm not sure I'm breathing.

'The next morning I took the car to the grocery store – for real that time – and as I was loading the bags into the back-seat, I found a pair of stockings. They weren't mine, and they were not in pristine condition – *if* you know what I mean. When I got home, I kicked that sorry sack right out of the house. For good.'

'Have you ever told this to anyone before today?'

'Sure. The police. I called them back and told them I hadn't been straight with them. That my husband made me lie.'

A car horn honks behind me. I pull into the right lane and accelerate to the speed of the cars around me. 'What did the police say?'

'Not to worry. That I wouldn't get into any trouble. Everything was under control.'

Under control. 'Do you remember which officer you told?'

'Yes. He came out to the house. It was that cop they sent to Parchman later on. Ray Presley.'

No account of this meeting made it into the case report. 'Was Presley alone when he came to see you?'

'Yes. He gave me the creeps, that Presley. Always did.'

'Did anyone from the FBI question you about this?'

Mrs. Little says nothing, but not because she has nothing to tell.

'Mrs. Little, do you remember an FBI agent named Dwight Stone?'

'Well, actually . . . I do, yes. But that's all I have to say. Good–'

'Please wait! Do you have any idea who your husband was with on that day? Which floozie, I mean? I know this is painful, but it's terribly important. The faster I get to the bottom of this, the less chance anyone is going to get hurt.'

'I don't like talking about this.' Her breaths are shallow, anxious. 'If you get to the bottom of it, my ex-husband is going to come out of it smelling like a cowpie, isn't he?'

'Probably.'

'Betty Lou Jackson.'

'Ma'am?'

'That's the slut's name. She's married to some electrical contractor now. Beckham, her name is. Acts like she's as good as anybody, but she's a tramp through and through.'

'Thank you, Mrs. Little.'

'Don't thank me, because I never told you anything.'

The phone goes dead.

The nice thing about small towns is that it's easy to find people. Directory assistance has only one Beckham listed. I'm starting to feel like I might solve the Payton case without ever leaving the car.

'Hello?' A woman's voice.

'Is this Betty Lou Beckham?'

'Yes. I don't use the "Lou" anymore, though. It's just Betty. Betty Beckham. Who is this?'

'This is Penn Cage, Mrs Beckham.'

Deafening silence.

'Mrs. Beckham?'

'I'm real busy right now, Mr.–'

'I just wanted to ask you a couple of quick questions.'

'I can't help you. I'm sorry.'

'You don't know what I'm going to ask you.' *Or do you?*

'I saw the paper the other day.' Her voice is so tight that her vocal cords must be near to snapping. 'It's about that, isn't it?'

'Mrs. Beckham, I realize this might be a delicate matter. I'd be glad to speak to you in person if you'd feel more comfortable.'

'Don't you come around here! Somebody might see you.'

'Who are you worried would see me?'

'Anybody! Are you crazy?'

'Mrs. Beckham, I really only have one question. Were you in that parking lot when Del Payton's car exploded?'

'Oh, my God. Oh, dear Jesus . . .'

'I have absolutely no interest in what you might have been doing there, Mrs. Beckham. I just want to know about the bombing.'

How stupid did that sound? If Betty Lou was doing what Mrs. Little suspected she was doing in that parking lot, it might end up on the network news.

'Don't call back,' she pleads. 'You'll get me in bad trouble. Yourself too. You don't know. You just don't know!'

She's hung up, but the fear in her voice was real enough to raise the hair on the back of my neck. She is afraid of more than memories. She's been living in dread ever since Caitlin's story ran in the paper.

As I turn into my parents' neighbourhood, the cell phone rings. It's Althea Payton.

'I tried to call you earlier, Althea, at the hospital. But you were busy.'

'I know. I got this number from your father.' She sounds out of breath. 'I think I've remembered something important.'

'Take it easy. I'm not going anywhere. What is it?'

'I was visiting an adult patient this morning, and his TV was tuned to CNN. I really wasn't paying attention, but then I heard your name. They were talking about that execution in Texas. How you were the lawyer who convicted that man.'

'Right . . .'

'They showed you walking into the prison. And then, right after that, they showed another man. They said he was the head of the FBI. I didn't hear his name, but I watched again an hour later to see if they'd run the same thing, and they did.'

'I don't understand, Althea. What did you remember?'

'I knew that man. Mr. Portman. John Portman.'

'You knew him? From where?'

'From here. Right here in Natchez.'

'You've seen John Portman in Natchez?'

'That's what I'm trying to tell you. Remember I told you about Agent Stone? How he was nice and really wanted to help us?'

'Yes.'

'And I told you some of them didn't. How Mr. Stone had another man with him, a young Yankee man, who was cold and never said anything?'

My chest feels hollow. 'Yes . . .'

'That was him. That John Portman on the TV was him.'

'Althea, you must be mistaken. John Portman would have been very young in 1968.'

'It's him, I tell you. His hair's a little grayer, but that's the only difference. The second time they ran the story, I watched close. Ain't no doubt about it. It was him. A young Yankee man, cold as February. Chilled me right to the bone.'

Somewhere in my mind Dwight Stone is saying, *I knew Portman. He came into the Bureau a few years before I got out . . .*

'Don't say anything else, Althea. I'm on a cell phone. I'm going to check on this and get back to you.'

'What do you think it means?'

'I don't want to speculate. Don't talk to anyone about this. I'll get back to you.'

'I'll be waiting.'

I hit End, then turn into my parents' driveway and park, leaving the engine running. Of all the things I could possibly have learned about this case, this is the most astonishing. If John Portman was in Natchez in 1968, a lot of things suddenly make sense. Dwight Stone's personal hatred of him. Stone's unwillingness to talk about the case. Maybe even the national security seal on the Payton file, although this is probably going too far. No one could have known in 1968 that Special Agent John Portman would wind up director of the FBI thirty years later. So that wasn't the reason Hoover sealed the file. But Portman almost certainly knows *why* the file was sealed, as does Stone. Given Stone's hatred of Portman – and Stone's dismissal from the Bureau while Portman rose through its ranks – that reason must have been something Stone could not stomach but which Portman went along with. *He was a good little German,* Stone had said of Portman. *He followed orders.* The question is, what was he ordered to do?

As I get out of the car, a middle-aged black cop in uniform walks around the corner of the house, one hand on the gun at his hip.

'Are you Penn Cage?'

'Yes, sir.'

He smiles and nods. He has the sad, drooping eyes of a beagle. 'I'm James Ervin. Just keeping an eye on things for you and your daddy.'

'I'm glad to see you, Officer Ervin.' I reach out and shake his hand. 'That gun loaded?'

He taps the automatic on his hip. 'You bet.'

'Good man.'

'You sure got a pretty little girl in there. Reminds me of my girls when they was little.'

'Thank you. Do you know what all this is about?'

Ervin sucks in his upper lip and looks at the ground. 'You trying to get whoever killed Del Payton, ain't you?'

'That's right. Did you know Del?'

'My daddy knew him.' He raises the beagle eyes to mine, and they are full of quiet conviction. 'Don't you worry none. You ain't gonna have no trouble. Somebody come messin' 'round here, they on the *wrong side*.'

Chapter 24

It takes less than ten minutes on my mother's computer to verify what Althea Payton told me on the cell phone. The FBI's official web page features a thumbnail biography of its new director. The bio boasts of Portman's first year as a field agent, one which he spent investigating race murders in Mississippi and Alabama. That year was 1968. A *Time* magazine writer hailed Portman's 'year in the trenches' and stated that his 'sterling civil rights credentials' were one of the major reasons the President had tapped the Republican federal judge to lead the FBI in a bipartisan gesture that shocked most Democrats. The Bureau had been wracked by racial problems for the past decade, having been successfully sued by both African-American and Hispanic agents. Portman's Deep South experience sat well with minority political interests.

By my calculations, Portman was twenty-five when he visited Althea Payton's house with Dwight Stone. Fresh out of Yale Law. Stone was probably ten years older. Beyond this my facts are few. Portman rose swiftly through the Bureau's ranks while Stone was fired five years later. In Crested Butte I sensed that Stone felt his dismissal was related to the Payton case. But if that was true, why would Hoover wait five years to terminate him? Or had whatever happened in 1968 haunted Stone, fueling his alcoholism, until Hoover was finally left no choice but to fire him?

Unable to answer this question, I list the names of main

players on the computer and stare at them a while. *Payton. Presley. Marston. Stone. Portman. Hinson.* One of the first things a writer learns is that the best way to solve a problem is to get out of the way of his subconscious and let it work. Following this dictum, I begin playing with the screen fonts and point sizes, switching from Courier to Bookman, from flowing Gothic to a tortured Algerian. As the fonts swirl and transform themselves before my eyes, it strikes me that men like Leo Marston and John Portman cannot be investigated by normal means, especially by a private citizen. Caitlin's status as a reporter lends us some theoretical authority under the First Amendment, but this means next to nothing in the real world. What is required is some creative thinking.

Kings and presidents can be brought down with the right weapons. The trick is to find their vulnerabilities. Men like Portman and Marston live for power. They hunger for it even as they wield more than most men will ever know. They act with certainty and dispatch, rarely allowing themselves the luxury of doubt. And so long as they operate from this fortress of psychological security, they are untouchable. Perhaps the way to bring them down is to breach that fortress, to turn their worlds upside down and force them into a *re*active mode. The way to do that seems obvious enough. Re-introduce them to an emotion they have not felt in a great while.

Fear.

My first thought when my father comes through the pantry door is that he looks ten years older than he did two days ago. He kisses my mother and Annie, then motions for me to follow him into the library. I shrug at my mother and follow.

He sits in his leather recliner and switches on the television, apparently to mask our conversation.

'Somebody just tried to kill Ray Presley.'

'What?' I exclaim, dropping onto the sofa to his left.

'His girlfriend was giving him the first few cc's of that Mexican chemotherapy he takes. He started complaining of angina and ripped the catheter out of his wrist. The girl called 911 and gave him CPR until the paramedics got there. He was having a coronary. He just checked himself out of the CCU against my orders.'

'What makes you think it was attempted murder?'

'The girl brought in the IV bag, and one of our lab techs ran a few tests. He thinks there's some potassium chloride mixed in with the cocktail.'

'Jesus. Did you call the police?'

'Ray told me not to. He was so goddamn mad he wouldn't let anybody but me close to him. He said he'd handle it himself.'

'I'll bet he will. How much damage did his heart sustain?'

'I don't have enough enzyme tests back to tell.' Dad drums his hands on the arms of the chair. 'We've got another problem.'

'What?'

'You talked to Betty Lou Beckham today?'

'How do you know that?'

'She showed up at my office at four o'clock, half in the bag. Said she had to talk to me.'

I should have expected this. For years my father has acted as a confessor to countless souls, particularly women, who have no outlet for their sorrows and anxieties other than their ministers or local psychologists, as Natchez has attracted only one or two psychiatrists over the past two decades, and none has stayed. In this vacuum, a compassionate M.D. fills the void as no one else can.

'Was she in that parking lot when Del Payton died?'

'Yes. She and Frank Jones were having sex in his car when the bomb went off, if you can believe it. She saw Payton walk out to his car. She actually saw the damned thing explode.'

'Christ. What else did she see?'

'When the bomb went off, Jones panicked. He started to take off, but Betty Lou reminded him that he was supposed to be working inside the plant. She was off that day, so she got into her VW to leave. When she was almost out of the lot, she looked up and saw somebody watching her from a pickup truck.'

'Who?'

'Ray Presley.'

A fist closes around my heart. 'Presley was there *when* the bomb went off?'

Dad nods once, very slowly.

'So . . . he was involved in the actual murder.'

'It looks that way.'

'Did Betty Lou tell anybody she'd seen him there?'

'Not at first. Presley came to see her and explained that might not be good for her health.'

This scene is all too easy to imagine.

'Then Frank Jones's wife found Betty Lou's stockings in his car and kicked Jones out of the house. I gather that Mrs Jones then told the police her husband had lied about why he was in the parking lot, because Presley came to see Betty Lou again. Gave her a harsher warning.'

'But she told the FBI, didn't she? Special Agent Dwight Stone.'

'Not at first. When Agent Stone found out Jones's wife had kicked him out the morning after the murder, he talked to the wife, and she led him to Betty Lou. Stone offered her money, but Betty Lou wouldn't talk. She was too scared of Ray. Then somebody shot at those FBI agents on the highway. Stone came back and told Betty that if she withheld evidence, he'd make sure she did time in federal prison. He convinced her. She's basically a good girl. She wanted to tell the truth all along.'

'She gave up Presley to Stone.'

'Yes.'

'Then what happened?'

'Nothing. Betty Lou kept waiting for Presley to be arrested, but he never was. Then the FBI pulled Stone out of town. Presley showed up again, beat the hell out of her, forced her to give him oral sex . . . she was a basket case. She was about to skip town when Presley was arrested on the drug-trafficking charges that sent him to Parchman.'

I sit back on the sofa, trying to process it all.

'She's still scared to death of Ray. She's been working herself toward a nervous breakdown since Caitlin Masters's article came out. When you called this afternoon, she lost it. I gave her a shot of Ativan and drove her home.'

'Ray is the problem you were talking about. He's directly involved in the murder, but if I push him, he'll push back. He doesn't have your gun anymore, but he could still raise a hell of a stink if he wanted to.'

Dad sighs and leans back in his chair.

'It doesn't matter,' I decide. 'Presley wasn't solely responsible for Payton's death. The fact that someone just tried to kill him proves that. Somebody's afraid he'll talk.'

We both look up as my mother slides open the library door. I assume she is summoning us to supper, but she says, 'You've got a visitor, Penn.'

'Who is it?'

'Caitlin Masters.'

I wasn't expecting Caitlin, so she must have news. 'Bring her in.'

'She's playing with Annie.'

When Mom disappears, Dad says, 'How much does Masters know?'

'Nothing about the blackmail.'

'Don't tell her what happened to Ray. Not yet.'

Caitlin comes to the door carrying Annie in her arms, then

passes her off to my mother and promises to be back in the kitchen in a few minutes. She's wearing black jeans, sandals, and a white pinpoint button-down with her sable hair spilling around the collar. She looks harried but also ready to burst with excitement.

Dad stands as I make the introductions, and as soon as Mom closes the door, Caitlin says: 'I just hit the jackpot.'

'What are you talking about?'

'I traced Lester Hinson. The guy in the article from the Leesville *Daily Leader*?'

'What's his story?'

'He's a small-time crook who spent most of his life in Angola Prison. He lives in New Orleans now.'

'You talked to him?'

Too excited to remain in one place, Caitlin begins pacing. 'More than that. I found out exactly how he ties in to the Payton case. In April of 1968 Lester Hinson and a supply sergeant named Earl Wheeler ripped off an arms depot at Fort Polk and started selling the stuff on the black market. A month later they were busted by the Army CID. That's what the article was about, right? Well, Hinson was a civilian, and he got a visit in jail from Special Agent Dwight Stone. Stone wanted to know if the pair had sold C-4 to anyone from Mississippi, particularly Natchez. They had. Stone had to get the charges pled down to find out who the buyer was, but he didn't mind that at all.'

'The buyer was Ray Presley,' I say in a monotone.

Her mouth drops open. 'You're not guessing, are you?'

'No. We just placed Presley at the crime scene when the bomb went off.'

'How did you do that?'

'You finish first. I can't believe Hinson just spilled his guts to you.'

'He didn't. I did what cops do.'

'What's that?'

She grins. 'I paid him. I told him what I wanted, then wired five hundred dollars to a Western Union office in New Orleans. I told him I'd wire him another five hundred if he told me what I wanted to know. He would have talked all day for that money.'

Dad gives Caitlin an admiring look.

'Forget that,' she says. 'How did you put Presley at the scene?'

'You were right about what Stone was trying to tell us. There was another witness to the murder. One who never made it into the police report.'

'Who?'

'Her identity isn't important right now. What matters—'

'Not important!'

Caitlin isn't going to like this. 'This witness can only implicate Ray Presley. Presley probably killed Payton, but he almost certainly did it for someone else. That's how he worked. And I don't want to move on Presley until we have the man who ordered the crime.'

Caitlin is shaking her head. 'But that's how you get to the top guy, isn't it? You squeeze the little fish until they talk.'

'Usually, yes. But Presley's a special case. He's never scared easy, and now he has terminal cancer. He doesn't have a lot of fear of earthly punishment. So, he bought some plastic explosive in 1968. The statute ran out on that long ago. The witness who saw him in the Triton parking lot is a terrified woman who's now married and respectable, but who happened to be committing adultery in a car when the bomb exploded. I seriously doubt she would make a statement to the police, much less testify in open court.'

'Penn, I can't believe I'm hearing this. We now have means and opportunity for Presley to have committed homicide. The motive could be racial prejudice. He's a lock for it. If we don't squeeze Presley, how can we get any further?'

'We've just been discussing that.'

She looks from one to the other of us, her green eyes probing. 'You guys know something I don't. Right? Something about Presley. Something that's keeping you from going after him.'

'Yes.'

'What is it?'

'I can't tell you. Not at this point.'

The familiar pink moons appear high on her cheeks. 'What kind of bullshit answer is that? Are we partners or not?'

I trust Caitlin implicitly, but I cannot trust her with my father's secret. 'If I could tell you, I would. But I have to ask you to trust me for now.'

'You ask me to trust you, but you don't trust me.' She looks at my father, who is staring pointedly at the floor, then back at me. 'You think Leo Marston hired Presley?'

'Don't you?'

'There's no evidence of that.'

'Ike Ransom says it's Marston, and Dwight Stone said the same thing in so many words.'

'But neither of them will go public.'

'There's been another development as well.'

She sighs and looks at the floor. 'I'm afraid to ask.'

'Stone lied to us in Colorado. He knew John Portman a hell of a lot better than he led us to believe.'

'How do you know that?'

I quickly explain Althea Payton's call about seeing Portman on CNN, and my subsequent verification that he worked in Mississippi in 1968.

Caitlin gropes backward for her chair and falls into it. 'Holy shit. Do you realize what this means?'

'Tell me.'

'This story just went national. This story is *huge*.'

'Remember our deal. You print nothing until I say so.'

'When I made that promise, I didn't know you were going

to obstruct the investigation for reasons you don't see fit to tell me.'

'There were no conditions on the promise. And I expect you to abide by it.'

She purses her lips. 'Could I please point out a couple of things? One, we have no real investigative power. Two, the files we need are under government seal, and we're unlikely to get that changed without a protracted court battle. Three, the Payton case somehow involves the director of the FBI, who has practically unlimited power to interfere with us. Four, the case also involves Leo Marston, the single most powerful man in this county, possibly in the state. Five, no one directly involved in the case wants to talk to us.' She holds up her hands in desperation. 'What do you want to *do*? I think the media is the only weapon we have.'

'I agree.'

'You do?'

'I simply want to use it in a different way than you.'

'How?'

'To scare the shit out of Portman and Marston, and see which way they jump.'

Now I have her attention. 'How can you do that?'

'By making them think we can prove they're guilty of Payton's murder.'

'And how do you propose to do that?'

'Simple. I state publicly that Leo Marston was responsible for the murder of Del Payton.'

'*What?*' my father cries.

'With no evidence?' asks Caitlin. 'Just slander him?'

'Exactly. I slander him.'

'But why?'

'Because by doing that, I leave Marston no option but to sue me.'

Dad snorts in amazement. 'What the hell does that accomplish?'

'The minute Marston sues me, I'll answer his charge by stating that truth will be my defense. I will then be free under the rules of discovery to request Marston's business records, personal papers, tax returns – all kinds of things from the years surrounding the crime.'

'A fishing expedition?' asks Caitlin. 'You think you'll find some documentary proof that Marston ordered Payton's murder?'

'Not really. My primary goal is psychological. Ike Ransom says everyone around here is playing the quiet game. He says the way you win that game is by making people nervous. So, that's what I'm going to do. Marston won't believe I'd make a public charge like that without hard evidence. He'll panic. His first thought will probably be Ray Presley. After Presley, who knows? Portman maybe. We don't know who else was involved. But Marston does.'

'You *think* he does. What if you're wrong? What if you have no evidence by the time the slander case comes to trial?'

'Then I'll lose a great deal of money. Maybe everything I have.'

'How long would that be? From the time of the slander till the trial?'

'Hard to say with someone like Marston. The deck would be stacked against me from the start. He'd want a quick trial, and he'd get one. Everybody in this town owes him favors, especially in the judicial system.'

'He's got his share of enemies too,' Dad points out. 'You might get some unexpected help.'

'I'll tell you what would scare the shit out of him,' I think aloud, feeling excitement building inside me. 'A jury trial. In this town the jury might be fifty percent black. We might even get a black judge.'

Dad actually cackles. 'Marston would be apoplectic! After a lifetime of moderation on race, he gets hauled before a black jury on a case like this?'

'How would you do it?' Caitlin asks. 'The slander, I mean. Walk into a bar, pound on a table, and accuse him of murder?'

'No. I'd have to make it impossible for him not to sue.'

'Talk radio?'

'Maybe. But the ideal medium is print. It carries the most authority.'

She blanches. 'You mean *my* newspaper? Not a chance in hell.'

I smile. 'Hey, are we partners or what?'

She stands and jabs her forefinger at me. 'Marston would sue the paper for libel. He'd sue my father!' She shakes her head violently. 'My father will tolerate a lot. But a libel suit? Do you know what kind of damages people have been awarded in libel cases? *Tens of millions of dollars.* He'd jerk my butt out of here so fast my feet wouldn't touch the ground.'

'Caitlin—'

She shakes her head again and walks quickly to the door. 'I'm going to forget I ever heard this. And I suggest you think long and hard before you put everything you have up for grabs. You have a daughter to raise.'

'Not a word in the paper about any of this,' I remind her.

She closes her eyes and sighs angrily.

'Unless you want to print my accusations of Marston's guilt. Then you can blow the story wide open. You can take it national tomorrow morning. The more noise, the better.'

She stands in the door with her hands on her hips, nostrils flared, eyes burning. 'Damn you, Penn Cage.' She glares at my father. 'If I were you, I'd try to talk some sense into my son.' Then she steps through the sliding door and shuts it with a bang.

Dad looks at me with a glint in his eye. 'That's some woman.' He takes a cigar from his shirt pocket, unwraps it, and sticks it between his back teeth. 'Desperate times call for desperate measures?'

'What choice do we have? Even if Betty Lou would go public, she might never get the chance. Presley could kill her. And even if we somehow turned Presley, Marston could have him killed. But as soon as I go public, any suspicious accidents make Marston look guilty.'

'I agree. Not only that, I like it.'

'There's only one problem,' I murmur, fighting the fear germinating in my gut.

'What's that?'

'Leo is one cool customer. What if I can't spook him?'

By nine p.m. I've pretty much decided to go forward without Caitlin's help. Finding a newspaper reporter or radio talk-show host who will let me spout off about Leo Marston and a race crime shouldn't be too difficult. In the current media climate, where celebrity and controversy are the benchmarks of ratings, they'll probably fight over the story. But Caitlin's apprehension still worries me. What I need now is positive confirmation that I'm right to go after Marston.

Dwight Stone answers his phone after five rings, but as soon as I identify myself, he hangs up. I try once more, in case he made a mistake, but the result is the same. More curious than discouraged, I take out my wallet and fish out the card with Ike Ransom's cell phone number. The deputy answers instantly.

'This is your buddy from the Triton plant,' I tell him.

He asks if I'm home, then says he'll call back from a land line. A minute later, he tells me to meet him at an abandoned warehouse by the river, in the industrial park. This doesn't strike me as a good way to spend the evening, so I suggest that he pick me up in the Wal-Mart parking lot. He reluctantly agrees.

Fifteen minutes later, I climb into his cruiser, the claustrophobic little world of anger and guns and cigarettes. He looks just as he did the other night, only more nervous. He looks, in fact, like he might be wired on speed.

'Where the hell have you been?' he demands.

'Colorado. I talked to an FBI agent who worked the case in sixty-eight.'

Ransom hits the brake, then catches himself and continues up the bypass. 'I thought I told you to stay away from the FBI.'

'You did. And I'm curious as to why.'

He ignores the comment. 'What's this guy's name?'

'Stone.'

He taps the wheel impatiently. 'Couple of people I talked to remembered him. They said it seemed like he really tried to solve the case.'

'He did more than try. He solved it.'

Ransom looks over at me, his speed-pinned eyes distant. 'He tell you that?'

'In so many words.'

'No details?'

'He won't talk about it.'

Ike laughs humorlessly. 'What did I tell you? The quiet game. Everybody's playing it.'

'What are they so scared of? Marston?'

'Judge Leo got some serious juice, man.'

'Is that all?'

'What you mean?'

'Did you know John Portman was here in 1968?'

'John who?'

I hesitate before answering. I have a feeling Ike knows

exactly who I'm talking about. 'The director of the FBI,' I say, watching him.

He accelerates and whips around the car ahead of us, but I can't tell whether he did it to buy time or not.

'What you mean, he was here?'

'It was his first year as an FBI agent. He was working the Payton case with Stone.'

Ike shrugs. 'That's the first I heard of it. But I told you to stay away from the FBI, didn't I? You can't trust no Feds, man.'

'Never mind. Look, I've thought of a way to go after Marston. But it's risky. I've got to know more than I know now. You understand? You've got to give me something more.'

'Like what?'

'How about some evidence?'

'Shit, man, if I had evidence, I'd get that motherfucker my own self. Finding evidence is your job.'

'Why do you think he was behind Del's murder?'

'I just know, okay?'

'It's not okay, damn it. It doesn't make sense. Why would Marston want Del Payton dead?'

'That's what you're supposed to find out.'

My father's original doubts about Ike's motives are coming back to me. 'Why do you hate Marston so much, Ike?'

He turns to me, his eyes smoldering. 'I done told you once. It's personal.'

'That's not good enough anymore.'

'Fuck you, then!'

I say nothing for the next mile. Ike's respiration is heavy and erratic, as though so much of his energy is consumed by his anger that he has to remind himself to breathe.

'Were you and Ray Presley cops at the same time?'

He keeps his eyes on the road. 'Presley was in Parchman when I joined the force. But I knew that motherfucker later on. We were like two bad dogs on a street. We always stayed on different sides. Still do.'

'Well, somebody just tried to kill him.'

An eerie stillness comes over Ike. Then he turns his head toward me, and the intensity in his eyes is frightening. 'Tried to kill him how?'

'Poison.'

'Take more than poison to kill that bastard.'

'I think Presley planted the bomb that killed Del Payton.'

Ike rolls his tongue around his cheek, his eyes moving on and off me. 'Why you think that?'

'I've got reasons. What do you think?'

'I think all the evidence in the world against Ray Presley ain't gonna get you no closer to Marston.'

'Why not?'

''Cause Presley don't know shit about the *reason*. You got to find the *why* of it.'

'Take me back to my car. You want me to fight your battles for you, but you don't give me shit for help.'

He spins the wheel and turns the cruiser back toward Wal-Mart, his anger making his knuckles pale. 'Marston fucked up my family,' he says through clenched teeth. 'Fucked up my whole life. That's all I'm gonna tell you. It's got nothing to do with Del Payton, but I knew you could bring Marston down behind the Payton thing. That's why I went that way. I want that bastard destroyed. In *public*. That's what'll hurt him the most. If it wasn't for that, I'd have killed his ass a long time ago.'

I settle back on the seat and let my eyes go out of focus, which turns the oncoming headlights into slow white meteors. 'Ike . . . I want you to swear on the soul of your mother that Marston ordered Del Payton's death.'

He doesn't hesitate. 'On the soul of my mother. If it

284

wasn't for Leo Marston, Del Payton would be alive today.'

I guess that's all the certainty I'm going to get.

When I get home, Caitlin's Miata is parked in the driveway. She is standing in the garage, talking to Officer Ervin.

'What's the matter?' I ask as she walks out to meet me.

'Dwight Stone just called me at the newspaper. He thinks his phone is tapped. He gave me the number of a pay phone and told me to get you to call him back. He said you should use a pay phone too. One far from your house.'

'Let's go.'

I drive us up to the bypass, then north to Highway 61. There's a pay phone at a convenience store, but I go a little farther to a grocery store parking lot, where there won't be so much noise. Caitlin stands beside me as I dial the number.

'Yes?' Stone says in a gruff voice.

'It's Penn Cage.'

'Listen to me, Cage. My phone is tapped. So are the phones at your father's house and medical office. Probably the lines at the newspaper as well. You should also assume physical surveillance. I'm being watched right now.'

'Jesus. Someone just tried to kill Ray Presley.'

Caitlin tenses beside me, but I ignore her.

'How?' asks Stone.

'Poisoned his IV bag. He had a coronary, but he's still ambulatory and mad as hell.'

Stone says nothing, but I can sense the conflict raging within him. 'I know you worked with Portman on the Payton case in sixty-eight,' I tell him. 'Why did you lie about that?'

'I was trying to protect people.'

'Who?'

'You, for one. Others too.'

'Well, I took your advice. I talked to the eyewitnesses, and I've placed Presley at the crime scene.'

'And?'

'I want Leo Marston, not Presley.'

'Squeeze Presley.'

'That's easier said than done.'

Stone laughs softly. 'Ray's not very squeezable, is he? Son of a bitch tried to kill us on the highway to Jackson.'

'You're the agent who got shot at on Highway 61?'

'Portman and me, if you can believe it. The world would be a lot nicer place if Presley had hit Portman that day.'

'Why? Goddamn it, what's the big secret? What was so terrible that Hoover had to bury it under a national security seal? What's Portman hiding? What could still scare you after thirty years?'

'Do you really expect me to answer that?'

'You're damn right I do. It's time you listened to your conscience, Stone.'

'Don't preach to me, son. You haven't earned the right.'

'If Ray Presley shot at you, why didn't he go to jail for it?'

'He did.'

'Presley went to Parchman for drug trafficking. That's a state prison.'

'Justice doesn't always happen in a straight line. You should know that.'

I grip the phone with exasperation. 'I've thought of a way to go after Marston without Presley's help, but it's a gamble. A big one. I can't afford to be wrong.'

'What are you asking me, counselor?'

'Am I wrong about Leo Marston being behind the murder of Del Payton?'

Just as I decide Stone is not going to answer, he says, 'You're not wrong.'

A wave of triumph surges through me.

'But that doesn't mean there's evidence lying around waiting to be picked up,' he adds. 'I don't know how much I'd gamble on being able to prove it.'

'Did you prove it in sixty-eight?'

'Yes.'

'Then why wasn't the son of a bitch prosecuted?'

'Oldest reason in the world. You just be damn sure about every step you take. This road doesn't end where you think it does.'

'Hold on. Why are you willing to warn me, but not to help me?'

'I thought I just did. Good hunting, counselor.'

When I hang up, Caitlin grabs my arm, her eyes furious. 'Why didn't you tell me someone tried to kill Presley?'

'No one knew but my father, and he asked me not to tell.'

She takes a deep breath and expels it slowly. 'What did Stone say?'

I glance around the dark parking lot, searching for suspicious vehicles. Would I even see surveillance if it was there? Surely the FBI is better than that. I pull Caitlin to me and put my mouth to her ear. She stiffens.

'What are you doing?'

'Stone says we're probably under surveillance. Act like we're lovers.'

After a moment her arms slip around me and her breasts flatten against my chest, but her eyes are anything but romantic.

'We've got to go with my slander plan,' I whisper. 'We don't have time for anything else, and the more public this is, the safer we are.'

She slides her cheek past mine and answers in my ear. 'I won't do that. Don't ask me to.'

'It's the only way.'

She pulls away from me, her eyes bright. 'Take me back to my car.'

'You told me you wanted to shake up your father's business.'

'Not like that. I have no right to put him in jeopardy that way.'

We get into the car, and I cross the highway to 61 South. 'You think Marston's going to stand on ethics?' I ask her. 'He'd kill us in a second if he thought he had to.'

She turns to me with a defiant look. 'As far as I know, the worst thing Leo Marston has ever done is sabotage your love life. And that's not against the law.'

'The danger is real, Caitlin.'

'Give me a break. Nobody killed Woodward and Bernstein.'

'They weren't working in Mississippi.'

Chapter 25

Einstein said the arrow of time flies in only one direction. Faulkner, being from Mississippi, understood the matter differently. He said the past is never dead; it's not even past. All of us labor in webs spun long before we were born, webs of heredity and environment, of desire and consequence, of history and eternity. Haunted by wrong turns and roads not taken, we pursue images perceived as new but whose provenance dates to the dim dramas of childhood, which are themselves but ripples of consequence echoing down the generations. The quotidian demands of life distract from this resonance of images and events, but some of us feel it always.

And who among us, offered the chance, would not relive the day or hour in which we first knew love, or ecstasy, or made a choice that forever altered our future, negating a life we might have had? Such chances are rarely granted. Memory and grief prove Faulkner right enough, but Einstein knew the finality of action. If I cannot change what I had for lunch yesterday, I certainly cannot unmake a marriage, erase the betrayal of a friend, or board a ship that left port twenty years ago.

And yet . . . today I am granted such a chance.

Livy Marston does not call as she promised she would. She shows up at our front door at nine a.m. wearing faded Levi's and a white blouse tied at the waist, sapphire earrings a shade darker than her eyes, and a silk scarf in her hair. On the street behind her, a midnight blue Fiat Spyder convertible idles like a resting cat.

'I'm kidnapping you,' she says. 'If it's all right with Annie.'

It takes a moment to center myself in the present. 'Kidnapping me to where?'

She smiles. 'It's a surprise. If you thought about it, you'd know. But don't think. Today is a right-brain day.'

Five minutes after I clear it with Mom and Annie, I'm clinging to the passenger door of the Spyder as Livy races up the highway, cutting in and out of traffic like a Grand Prix driver. She borrowed the car from a friend of her mother's, and we both know why. Our senior year in high school, after she received some honor or other, Livy was given a Fiat convertible much like this one by her father. The night they brought it back from the dealership in New Orleans, she and I drove across half the state with the top down, drinking beer and reveling in the promise of futures unbound by visible limits. We spent many of our best moments in that car, and she has apparently decided to relive some of them. I've fantasized about scenes like this more than once, but there is something eerie about tearing up the sun-drenched highway toward the edge of town twenty years after we did it the first time, and in the same car.

As the Spyder crosses the westbound bridge into Louisiana, Maude Marston's words echo in my mind: *You ruined my daughter's life, you bastard.* I want to ask Livy outright what her mother was referring to, but Livy always had a way of being elliptical where serious matters were concerned.

'What did you mean, today is a right-brain day?' I ask.

She laughs. 'I mean today everything is off limits.' Her voice has deepened slightly over the years. 'Everything except experience.'

'Livy, I have some questions.'

'You mean like why are my husband and I separated?

Why did you and I really split up in college? Why did my father try to destroy yours?'

'Yes. Little things like that.'

'We'll get to all that. I have questions too. But first we give ourselves a little of the past. A little innocence.' She grants me a brilliant smile. 'We owe ourselves that.'

At the foot of the bridge she pulls into the parking lot of the liquor store we patronized during high school. Joking that it's finally legal for us to shop here, she goes inside and returns with two chilled bottles of Pouilly Fuisse. Handing them to me, she takes a small ice chest from the trunk and sets it on the backseat. Inside, I see French bread, cheese, grapes, peeled shrimp, and chocolate chip cookies.

She crosses the four-lane and whips the Spyder onto Deer Park Road, the same route I drove yesterday with Frank Jones. Only Livy takes the gently curving blacktop at ninety miles per hour. She was always an excellent driver, aggressive but in control. When the road jumps onto the levee, she has to slow to seventy, but the wind still whips through our hair, keeping the sun from frying us. I serve her wine in a styrofoam cup, and when she drinks, the wine clings to the same fine golden down that dusted her upper lip when she was seventeen. But she is not seventeen now. And the questions hanging between us cannot be ignored.

She pulls a pair of Ray-Bans down from the visor and slips them on, snapping me straight back to Sarah's funeral. I didn't notice Livy at the church service, but later, at the graveside, I saw her standing at the edge of the crowd, a hauntingly beautiful apparition in a black dress and sunglasses, unmistakable even after twenty years.

'It meant a lot that you came to the funeral,' I say above the whine of the engine. 'I'm sorry I couldn't do more than say hello.'

She shakes her head and touches my arm. 'I had to come. And I didn't expect any more than that.'

At the end of the levee she stops, and we switch seats for the return leg. Somewhere in the middle of the empty cotton fields, she intertwines the fingers of her left hand in my right. I don't look at her, but I feel a sudden tingling, as though I've put my hand through a portal in time and felt a charge of energy pour through. On some level, acceding to this intimacy seems a betrayal of myself, but it also presages a deeper connection, one that might lead to meaningful conversation, so I leave my hand in hers.

As we climb the eastbound bridge, the Cecil B. De Mille panorama of Natchez rises above us as it did yesterday, when I crossed the bridge with Frank Jones. The whole grand stage seems laid out with such dramatic intent that I ask myself the question Caitlin asked at our first meeting: why haven't I written about this place?

'What are you thinking?' Livy asks.

'I thought questions were prohibited.'

She ignores this remark. 'I was thinking about this place. The town. The fact that it *is* a place, with a unique identity. Atlanta is so sterile that I literally can't stand being in it sometimes.'

'I've felt the same thing in Houston.'

Looking up from the bridge, I see Natchez as the tourist sees it: the high bluff where sun-worshipping Natchez Indians massacred the French soldiers of Fort Rosalie in 1729; where Aaron Burr was arrested as a traitor and set free to the cheers of crowds; where an African prince labored twenty years as a slave; where Jefferson Davis wedded Varina Howell in the halcyon days before the Civil War. But I see so much more. I see the city Livy Marston captivated with a beauty and poise not seen since P. T. Barnum brought Jenny Lind down the river in 1851. I see the thin edge of a universe of vibrant life and mysterious death, of shadowy secrets and bright facades, and of races inextricably bound by blood and tears, geography and religion, and above all, time.

'This is a good place to be from,' I murmur.

'Could you ever live here again?' Livy asks in a strange voice.

I sense a deeper question beneath the one she's asked. 'I don't know. Could you?'

She doesn't take her eyes from the bluff. From this place she left to conquer the world. How does it look to her now?

'Not while my parents are alive,' she says, so softly that I'm not sure she knows she spoke aloud.

Before I can ponder what she meant, she turns to me, her eyes languid, and says, 'Let's go to the Cold Hole.'

The tingling in my hand spreads up my arm and across my neck and shoulders. *The Cold Hole.* One mile from the spot where my father and I sank the pistol I bought from Ray Presley – in the midst of that slimy, sulfurous swamp – a cold spring bubbles up through the green water, creating a pool as clear as Arctic snowmelt. It is the pool from my dream, the one I had the night Ike Ransom first told me about Leo Marston's involvement in the Payton murder. The woman in my dream was Livy Marston, and she sits beside me now, asking me to take her to that pool. Only in the dream she had something to tell me. Today she says the past is off limits.

Her presumption offends me. The Cold Hole was the geographic center of our intimate life, the name alone a talisman of spiritual and sexual exploration. Does she really believe that the passage of twenty years has somehow de-activated the mines that lie between us? Surely not. But perhaps she feels that in that hidden place, surrounded by our secret past, we can speak of things too painful to broach anywhere else. If that's what it takes to get her to solve the riddle of our truncated history, I'm willing. As I point the Spyder south and let the motor out, she lays her head back on the seat and smiles into the sky.

This is not the first time since my father's trial that Livy has tried to bridge the gulf it opened between us. Three years after she disappeared from Natchez, she was asked to be Queen of the Confederate Pageant, the apogee of social recognition by old Natchez standards. She was at UVA then, and everyone who was anyone waited on pins and needles to see whether she would accept. No one had ever declined the invitation to be queen, but all her life Livy had vowed that, if asked, she would be the first. That she *would* be asked was never in doubt. Her grandmother had been queen in the nineteen-thirties, her mother in the fifties, and if Livy accepted, she would be the first third-generation queen in history. Yet for years she had denigrated the Confederate Pageant (the nightly highlight of the pilgrimage to Natchez's antebellum mansions) as a hobby for garden club ladies with nothing better to do, a celebration of the Old South without a trace of irony or racial awareness. A lot of 'new Natchez' people thought she was mostly right, and she earned points with them for flouting tradition. So, in the spring of my junior year, when it was announced to great fanfare that Livy Marston had agreed to sacrifice two weeks of college to serve as queen, I was stunned. For nine nights she would preside over the very pageant she had scorned, playing a generic Scarlett O'Hara for those Yankees and Europeans who journeyed thousands of miles to see the Old South reincarnated. This was vintage Livy Marston, the girl who liked to have things both ways.

The Pilgrimage season sparkles with evening parties, culminating in formal balls – the Queen's and King's – where liquor and champagne flow like water, and guests spanning four generations dance deep into the night. Nowadays the king's and queen's balls are often compressed into a single event, a telling commentary on the reduced fortunes of the city. But twenty years ago they were Gatsby-like orgies of conspicuous consumption, competitive arenas for the proud parents of young royalty. Livy's ball was the grandest in recent memory, and no one expected anything less. I was not invited, of course. But my date was: an 'old Natchez' girl with a wicked sense of humor and no great love for the Marstons. I initially declined her invitation, but she finally convinced me that it would be a crime to skip such a historic display of excess.

Fifteen hundred invitations were mailed, and more than two thousand people chose to attend. Leo chartered a jet to fly Livy's sorority sisters down from UVA, a plane packed with Tri-Delts that – had it crashed – would have sent the Virginia marriage market into an irrecoverable tailspin. Ice sculptures were trucked down from Memphis in refrigerated vans, wondrous fantasy figures that melted so fast they drew solemn crowds of matrons who looked near tears that such extravagant beauty would be allowed to perish. Livy herself wore an eighteen-thousand dollar gown hand-sewn by the woman who crafted the dresses for the Mardi Gras queens in New Orleans. It was made of candlelight silk, white brocade, and imported satin gathered tightly at the waist and spreading to a veritable landscape of snowy fabric embellished with alençon lace, pearls, iridescent paillettes, and jewels, and trailed by a seven-foot, three-paneled fan train to be carried by toddler pages during the pageant.

Traditionally, queens never wore their pageant dresses to the balls, but Livy Marston, as ever, decided to make her own rules. When she appeared in the entrance of the hotel ballroom – escorted by the quarterback of the University of Virginia football team – a thousand women sighed together, making a sound like a soft wind. All I could think of was Audrey Hepburn at the head of the staircase in *My Fair Lady*, a shimmering chrysalis transformed into the most beautiful creature in the world. Even when the ball began in earnest, you could sense where Livy was at all times, a center of social gravity around which everyone whirled in attentive, almost worshipful fascination.

My date and I danced at the periphery of the crowd. She

knew that, were I to come face to face with Leo Marston so soon after the trial, sparks would fly. I occasionally glimpsed Livy near me, spinning in the arms of her quarterback or her father, or passing in a glittering flock of Tri-Delts. But our eyes never met.

In the third hour of the ball, she suddenly appeared at my shoulder, touched my date on the arm, and said, 'May I borrow him for one dance?'

I don't know why I went with her, but I did. Livy led me off without even pretending to dance, whisking me through the crowd as though pursued by paparazzi. She stopped long enough to hug a sorority sister, who giggled and glanced at me during a strange flurry of arms and handbags. Then Livy pulled me on again, nodding regally to anyone who tried to stop her, floating through the tuxedos and store-bought gowns like the daughter of a tsar in the Winter Palace.

Suddenly we were outside, moving along a row of blue doors. In a brick alcove she stopped and pressed her lips to mine, her eyes flashing in the dark. She tasted like champagne. When we pulled apart to breathe, she said, 'I can't believe you came. My parents are livid.' Before I could answer, we were off again, passing door after numbered door until she stopped and opened one with a key. *That's what she hugged her sorority sister for*, I thought as she pulled me inside the room.

That was the last coherent thought I had for some time. Livy sat on the edge of the bed and held me before her, working at my belt, then freed me with an exhalation of satisfaction and enclosed me again in an infinitely warmer place. Receiving this sort of attention from a woman wearing an eighteen-thousand-dollar gown is quite an experience, enough to obliterate consciousness. As I felt myself crossing the point of no return, she drew back and said, 'My turn,' then pulled me down to my knees, kissed me, lifted the jeweled hem of that dress, and lay back on the bed.

Her undergarments were surprisingly simple considering the dress worn over them, and I removed them with a surreal sense of wonder. She tasted as she always had – clean and coppery – and she climaxed almost instantly, as though she'd been poised on a cliff, preparing for a long dive, with only a slight push needed to send her over. The ululations that escaped her throat drove me into a state of primitive arousal. I reared up over her, but she held me away and said, 'No. The dress.' While I stared in amazement, she stood, turned around, and guided my fingers to an invisible line of eyelets that ran along her spine. There must have been two hundred of them, and each had to be unhooked before the dress would free her. While I worked at the hooks, Livy reached back and worked at me, and after a seeming eternity, eighteen thousand dollars of Leo Marston's money hit the cheap hotel carpet with a haughty rustle.

She lifted the dress off the floor and laid it carefully across the table by the window. Then she stood before me with a pride I have seen in no other woman, supremely secure, elegant even without clothes. The bitterness that had tortured our families was nowhere in her eyes. There was only us. She reached past me and pulled the coverlet off the bed, then took both my hands and pulled me onto the sheet, kissed me deeply, and lay back, pulling me across her. I supported my weight on my arms and peered into her eyes, which were wide open and glowing with desire. She caressed my nipples with her fingers, the hint of a smile on her lips. When my breath went shallow, she slid her hands down to my waist, pulled me between her legs, and whispered, 'Make love to me.'

In that moment I became almost preternaturally aware of the ball in the next building, missing its queen now, the guests like hundreds of planets and moons whirling through space without their sun. I could feel the anxiety of the quarterback, the puzzlement of Livy's parents, the confusion of her sorority sisters. Their sun was here, in this dark room, unclothed, aroused, wanting me.

But she didn't, really. Not the way I wanted her to. She wanted me, yes, but she also wanted Virginia and her quarterback and her parents' admiration and a thousand things besides. She wanted me for those few minutes, in that context, while I filled some discomfiting space in the puzzle of how she saw herself in her sheltered little universe. The first glimmer of this knowledge cut me to the bone. Despite all that had happened between our fathers, I loved her. I wanted her in the way most women dream of being wanted. Till death do us part. She wanted me *for the night*. The way I'd wanted girls before. Utterly and completely until my passion was spent, and then not at all. She wanted me to fill her with myself, and by so doing, make myself less. She would own me then, in a way, without ever having to bother with me again. She would nullify the past and move on. She should have whispered 'Fuck me' – not 'Make love to me' – because that was what she meant. This realization terrified me, and it taught me more about what it was to be female than I would learn in all the rest of my life.

'I can't,' I said, looking down at her with secret horror.

She reached between us and squeezed the rigid evidence to the contrary, pressed me against her sex, her eyes triumphant. For an instant – for the only time in my life – I felt the urge to rape, to plunge inside her with all the violence I could muster and pound against her womb until she could stand no more. But even that would have been her victory. She would, I suspect, have enthusiastically endured my most violent onslaught, reached a slightly more intense orgasm than usual, and then subsumed my rage and sadness into her with my seed, leaving her serene and content. That is the superiority of a woman unencumbered by love.

I could do only one thing to save myself, and I did it. I climbed off of her and began to dress. From the expression on her face, I was the only man who had ever done this, at least for any reason other than performance anxiety. And I was doing it because I loved her. She stared wordlessly at me, unable to believe I was doing what her eyes told her I was, even when I buttoned my tuxedo trousers and walked to the door.

'What are you *doing*?' she asked finally, her voice hoarse with confusion.

I couldn't see her clearly at that distance, so I focused instead on the white dress, which lay across the table like a fallen battle flag in the darkness, an artifact of a secret engagement no one would ever record. 'Saving my soul,' I said.

'What about my dress?' she asked, hysteria creeping into her voice. 'I can't put it on by myself.'

'You'll think of something.'

And she did. She reappeared at the ball a half hour later, looking no worse for wear, and I'm certain that the UVA quarterback got the lay of his life later that night, without ever knowing why. I didn't tell my date what had happened, but when I took her home, she kissed me fervently and pushed my hands into her dress. I resisted at first, but she pressed me against her until I gave in to the moment. We spilled out of the car onto the grass and made love recklessly and fiercely beside her parents' house, until all I had withheld from Livy sluiced from me in an annihilating rush. I did not love that girl, but that was all right. She knew I didn't, and she wanted me anyway.

'Where are you, Penn?'

I blink myself to the reality of Liberty Road, startled to find Livy beside me, her hand in mine. She looks scarcely older than she did on the night of that ball.

'Nowhere good,' I reply, steering the Fiat around a hairpin turn. This road was old when Mississippi became a territory in 1798, and it has settled deep into the earth over the centuries. The dirt banks rise higher than the car, and in some places the limbs of oaks meet high above our heads.

'What are you really doing in Natchez?' Livy asks.

'I thought you said no questions.'

She refills my styrofoam cup and passes it to me. 'You don't have to answer if you don't want to.'

'Annie's having a tough time getting over Sarah's death. I couldn't help her. My mother has already worked wonders with her.' I sweep around another turn, passing a cement truck like it's standing still. 'What are *you* really doing here?'

'Visiting my mother. I told you that.' Livy points to our right. 'There's the turn.'

I swing the Spyder off the pavement and into deep gravel that quickly shallows to ruts as thick pine forest closes around us.

'The next turn's easy to miss,' she reminds me.

Twenty years ago, a dirt oil-field road led to the Cold Hole. Some lucky wildcatter hit a well not fifty yards from the pool, and while this damaged the aesthetic of the place, the pool itself remained pure and clear. Surrounded by a jungle of cypress trees, dense fern, and a carpet of lily pads, it remained an essentially secret place, where time and society held no sway. Summer after summer adolescents reenacted the eternal rites there, clothed and naked, drunk and sober, but always defiantly, totally alive. A plank walkway led across the lily pads to the edge of the clear water, and high in a tall cypress a diving platform had been built. Livy and I spent the most perfect day of our lives on that perch, lost in each other's eyes, talking of God and time and other imponderables, poised in that blessed state of awareness that has yet to comprehend its own mortality.

We were drinking white wine that day too, but we also had one bottle of red. The sun was so hot that we wanted to keep even the red cold. To this end, I climbed down the platform and swam to the bottom of the pool, into the waving fronds, so deep that my eardrums ached in the cold current welling up from the spring below. I wedged the bottle tightly among the stems of the water plants, then fought my way back to the surface and climbed up to the platform.

Hours later, when the sun began to fall, we carefully negotiated our way back down to the water, and I dove for the bottle of red that I'd cached at the bottom. I could not find it. Livy joined me, but we searched in vain, though we stayed until night descended over the swamp, and snakes and alligators became a real concern.

Many times since, I've thought of that bottle. Once I even considered donning scuba gear to salvage it, so that I could ship it to Livy as a gift. (I'm pretty sure I conceived this madness on the night I heard she was getting married.) I'm not much for symbolism, but that unopened bottle of red wine fills the bill if ever anything did. Inside it is a road unwalked, a life unlived. And today, I suspect, Livy means to find it. An impossible task, probably. But impossible is a word she never paid much attention to. Her attitude is simple: where Livy Marston goes, the rules do not apply.

'Stop!' she cries. 'I think you passed it.'

I hit the brakes, skid a few yards through the gravel, then back up until Livy says stop. An autumnal sadness suffuses me when I see the overgrown track, a desolate path through the trees that none would take but a killer looking for a place to dump his victim.

'Pull in,' orders Livy.

I nose the Spyder into the trees, and she climbs out without opening the door and starts through the waist-high weeds. I put up the top of the convertible as quickly as I can and follow.

Five minutes' hard walking brings us to the edge of the swamp. The old pumping unit is still here, its great black arm frozen in place like a broken limb, the oil-bearing sands beneath the swamp long since depleted. The smell of stale crude permeates the air, and the cypress trees have no tops, casualties of salt water leaking from the well. The swamp itself is a scummy greenish-brown, swarming with breeding mosquitoes and obscured by a head-high wall of swamp grass. Our enchanted pool is gone.

'Well,' I say philosophically. 'I guess it's true.'

'What?'

'You can't go home again.'

Livy stares at the mess as though willing it back to its former beauty. I stand mute, waiting for her to face reality. But she won't. Why should she? Reality never stopped her before. She strips off her shirt and jeans, revealing a white one-piece bathing suit underneath. Then she hops onto a fallen tree that angles off through the hissing grass and walks like a gymnast down the rotting trunk. I call out for her to stop, but she pays no attention.

I have little choice but to follow.

When I get to the end of the trunk, I find myself stranded in a snaky morass with Livy nowhere in sight.

'Penn?' she calls from a jungle of foliage to my left. 'Come here.'

'Where are you?'

'There's a stump just below the surface of water. That will take you to the next trunk.'

Sighting the half-submerged stump, I leap onto it, catching myself just before I tumble headfirst into the slime. From here I can jump to the next fallen tree. Landing on the end of that one, I find myself peering down a green tunnel of leaves.

Livy stands at the other end, a motionless figure silhouetted by dazzling sunlight. Her body is still remarkable, not in the willowy way of a model or the lush way of a pinup girl, but somewhere in between. Her breasts are small but beautifully shaped, her wrists and ankles slim, her hands graceful. Yet the predominant impression she projects is of strength. She could be Artemis, more at home in the forest than among people. In this moment I cannot imagine her in a courtroom.

'Here,' she beckons, stretching out her hand, her voice laced with mystery.

I teeter out to the end of the trunk like a drunken riveter working high steel, then perform the tightly pleasant maneuver of edging around Livy. She holds my waist from behind and whispers: 'Oh, ye of little faith.'

The Cold Hole sparkles like a diamond on brown velvet, a pristine world in the midst of decay. The swamp must have risen over the years, its edge creeping ever nearer the oil well, but our spring-fed pool is where it always was. You just have to work a little harder to find it. Livy points high into the trees, and I follow her line of sight. Even the diving platform has survived, though damaged by the growth of the cypress. Once we spent hours kissing and touching each other up there, quivering like dryads in the high branches.

Without warning, Livy dives off the tree trunk and swims to the foot of the ladder. She climbs four planks high, then turns and motions for me to follow. I strip to my underwear and dive after her. The climb requires the negotiation of many rotten and missing steps, but before long we are perched forty feet above the water, breathing hard and laughing. From here the pool looks translucent, bottomless, like a hole in the floor of the world.

'Do you think it's still there?' she asks.

'It can't be.'

'The pool is.'

'Storms . . . the current from the spring . . . that bottle could be a mile away by now.'

She shakes her head. 'It's down there in the mud and the plants. And I'm going to find it.'

'Livy—'

Before I can argue, she arcs down to the pool like a falling arrow, lands dead center with scarcely a splash, and surfaces laughing. She waves and submerges again. I consider going down to help her, but I don't think she wants that. She wants to prove to me that she can find the bottle alone.

She searches with systematic diligence, diving to the bottom and probing the mud and plants in ever widening circles, surfacing for air, then diving again, her movements supple and efficient. It's like watching a Japanese pearl diver, except that Livy looks as unlike a Japanese woman as one can get. She is archetypally Western – Aryan even – like a hawk that has plummeted a thousand feet to penetrate the water and seize its prey. After fifty minutes by my watch, she surfaces and begins treading water, her face lifted to mine.

'I can't find it!'

I hold up my hands in commiseration and call down to her. 'It doesn't matter. You can't resurrect the past with a bottle of wine.'

She gives me an insouciant smile and dives again, so deeply that I lose sight of her. When she surfaces, she is at the edge of the pool, holding something in her hand. Not the wine. Her bathing suit. She drapes the white lycra over a cypress knee, then with a graceful roll pushes away from the stump and, floating effortlessly on her back, drifts to the center of the pool. This vision is more potent than any wine; it is my dream made flesh: Livy's hair floating in a corona around her face, her arms loose at her sides, her breasts little rose-tipped islands, her abdomen a submerged reef stretched to the rise of her pubis with its twist of burnished gold. The sight of her heats the backs of my eyes. As I gaze down, she raises a hand to block the sun and calls out:

'Don't you swim anymore?'

I scoot to the edge of the platform and drop forty feet through space, plunging deep into the pool. When I float to the surface, I find Livy treading water beside me. She splashes me playfully and says: 'I really thought I could find it.'

'Even if you had, it wouldn't make things like they

were before. We have to talk about what happened.'

She looks off through the silver cypress trunks. 'I can't. Not yet.' She stops treading and lies back, half floating, gazing into the hazy blue sky. 'I've thought about that bottle sometimes. Over the years.'

'Me too. During low times. Four o'clock in the morning, wondering if I ever made a single right choice in my life.'

She seems amused by this. 'Not me. I thought about it during good times. Or times that were supposed to be good. I thought about it on my wedding night.'

'Your wedding night?'

She turns her head slightly, watching me as she floats. 'There I was, supposed to feel some profound completion as a woman, and all I could think was that I was closing off forever an option I'd always thought I had.'

'And you did.'

Her eyes narrow. 'You hadn't exactly made me feel wanted the last time we'd seen each other.'

I look away, unwilling to explain my actions on the night of the ball without reciprocal explanations from her.

'We should have drunk that bottle twenty years ago,' she says. 'The extra time it would have taken might have changed everything that came after.'

I shake my head, unwilling to grant her this easy revision of history. 'Then I wouldn't have Annie.'

For a moment she looks as though she might make some cruel remark, but her face softens. 'I didn't mean it like that. We're here now. I'm not complaining.' She brings herself upright in the water, flips a wet strand of hair from her eyes, then reaches out and touches my nose. 'Will you do one thing?'

'What?'

'Kiss me.'

Livy has given me nothing that I need, not a single answer. But I want to kiss her. Between the fatigue of treading cold water and the proximity of her naked body, I feel as though every capillary in my skin has dilated, magnifying sensation. She swims closer and slips a hand behind my neck. I lean forward and press my lips to hers, gently at first, then harder in response to her passion. Treading water is impossible now. I take a quick breath through my nose as we slide beneath the surface.

Undulating in the slow current of the spring, time is the oxygen remaining in our lungs and blood, but there is enough to remember her taste, the pressure of her breasts against me as we sink like a single creature, an incarnation of salt water, only slightly denser than the fluid surrounding us. As my chest begins to burn, I feel the soft roughness between her legs, pressing against my thigh, seeking more complete union, and I swell with unthinking eagerness. Then my lungs betray me, sending me fighting toward the shimmering surface. I smash through gasping for air, resenting the fact that I need it. Livy gently breaks the surface beside me, her neck and shoulders flushed the color of broken seashells. She pulls back her hair, then treads easily as her clear blue eyes search mine.

'I want you inside me.'

I shake my head.

'I love you, Penn. I always have. I just didn't have the courage to choose you.'

Her words are like needles thrust into my heart, triggering emotions too intense to withstand, much less interpret. Caitlin's warning on the plane sounds in my head: *She could really mess you up—*

'You don't have any right to say that, Livy.'

'I know. I won't say it again. But I had to let you know.'

I roll away from her and swim back to the fallen tree that leads to the shore. As I climb onto it, I turn and see her perched on the cypress knee where she left her bathing suit, slipping on the white Lycra as gracefully as she does everything else.

'Where next?' she calls across the water, making no attempt to cover herself.

'I think it's time we got back.'

'Home? but the day's not half over.'

'I need to check on Annie.'

She nods somberly. 'I understand.'

I turn and make my way carefully along the slippery log. For any other woman I would wait, but Livy Marston can take care of herself.

As I swing the Fiat back onto Highway 61, I realize with a dull shock that guilt is not among the torrent of emotions rushing through me. A moment's thought tells me why: my past with Livy predates my life with Sarah. Intimacy with Livy is not a new experience. It's like walking through a checkpoint to a country I visited long ago and to which I now return, older and – hopefully – wiser.

She doesn't speak as the Spyder thrums northward in the afternoon sun, but I feel her eyes upon me, trying to penetrate my thoughts. What really brought her back to Natchez? Caitlin's belief that Livy has returned to persuade me to leave her father alone is not impossible. But Livy would not declare her love for such a cynical reason. That is the one gift she's reserved through the years, if indeed she has given love to anyone. She certainly must have said the words more than a few times, probably while trying to believe them herself. But why did she want this reprise of a perfect day twenty years past? And why does she think she loves me? Is it some strange analogue of a man wanting to marry the only girl who wouldn't sleep with him?

As we pass St. Stephens Preparatory School and join the traffic heading into town, Livy touches my knee and says,

'After you check on Annie, let's do something else. We still have our picnic.'

Her voice is calm enough, but I sense anxiety beneath it. She is reluctant to let this day end. Tomorrow things will not be so simple. It's one thing to pretend for a few hours that we can evade the past, as this town somehow evades the future. But it will be quite another when I insist on asking the questions she didn't want to hear today. And what will happen after I tell the world that her father ordered the murder of Delano Payton? When I commence my campaign of attrition against him? How will she feel then?

'I think we've done a lot to think about already,' I say evenly.

She bites her lower lip and looks away.

The whine of a siren overtakes us from behind, and I glance at the rearview mirror. Traffic is parting on the highway behind us. We're at the turn for my parents' neighborhood, so I swing right off the bypass, clearing the way.

'Penn?' Livy says, her voice tinged with fear. 'Look.'

A column of gray smoke is roiling out of the treetops in the distance.

'Penn, that's a fire.'

I hit the accelerator hard, knowing that a neighbor could be in trouble. Most of them are older now, and it doesn't matter whose house it is: I've probably known the family all my life.

'Where is it?' she asks, her voice tight.

'Close to my parents.'

I press harder on the gas, roaring up the street, with every yard becoming more afraid of something my brain does not want to consider. It couldn't be our house burning. It couldn't be.

Fifty yards from the corner, I see that it is.

Chapter 26

I drive the Fiat right into the yard, where my mother stands with Annie and a dozen neighbors, all pointing helplessly at the burning house, all in various stages of shock. I jump out of the car, run to my mother, and take Annie from her arms.

'Daddy, the house is on fire!' she cries, more amazed than frightened.

'The fire engine's right behind me,' I tell Mom. 'Is everybody okay?'

She grabs my arms, her eyes wide with terror. 'Ruby's in there! We heard a boom and then smelled smoke . . . when we saw the flames we ran but Ruby fell. Pen, I think she broke her hip. I couldn't drag her out. I brought Annie out, and by then it was too bad to get back in. But that off-duty policeman – Officer Ervin – he went in anyway. He went after Ruby, but he never came out!'

'How long ago was this?'

My mother is close to hyperventilating. I put my hands on her shoulders and squeeze hard enough for her to feel pain.

'Five minutes . . . maybe more. I don't know.'

As I stare at the house, a runner of flame races up the roof shingles. That's no kitchen fire. The whole house is burning. The house I grew up in.

'Where was Ruby when she fell?'

'By the back bathroom.'

There's no exterior door anywhere near that bathroom. And going through the front door would be suicide. I wouldn't even make it to the bedrooms before being over-come by smoke. I hug Annie and pass her to Mom, then kiss them both.

'When the firemen get here, tell them to look for Ervin.'

My mother blanches. 'Penn, you can't go in there.'

'I'm not leaving Ruby in there to die.'

Livy grabs my arm from behind. 'Penn, it's too late. Wait for the fire truck.'

I yank my arm free and sprint toward the garage before either of them can say more. In the garage I grab a shovel, then race around to the back of the house. As I near it, I begin smashing windows, trying to give the trapped smoke as many outlets as possible. I may be feeding oxygen to the blaze, but if I don't get some smoke out of there, I'll never reach Ruby alive.

The back bathroom has no window, but the adjacent bedroom does. A high, horizontal one about five feet wide and eighteen inches tall. I smash the glass with the shovel and stand back as thick gray smoke explodes through the opening. After thirty seconds, the plume thins a little, and I put my hand through the window. The heat is intense, but when I stand on tiptoe and put my face to the opening, I see no flames.

Taking off my shirt, I soak it in water at the outdoor faucet, then tie it around my face. I am scraping the window sill clean of glass shards when the scream comes. The sound is an alloy of animal terror and human agony, a child's wail from the throat of an eighty-year-old woman. An eighty-year-old woman who showed me more love and kindness than anyone but my mother. I feel like someone stuck my fingers into a 220-volt socket.

'*Ruby! Ruby, it's Penn! I'm coming to get you!*'

Hooking both hands over the sill, I swing my right leg up into the window and pull myself into the frame. The smoke that looked thin from outside instantly scorches my eyes, throat, and lungs. Breathing is pointless until I get my face down to the floor. I roll off the window frame and drop to the carpet.

There's air here, but the smoke is still too thick to see through. Before I lose my nerve, I shut my eyes and crawl around the bed toward the door that leads to the hallway. If I hadn't lived in this house for fourteen years – and stayed here for the past few nights – I wouldn't have a chance of finding Ruby. That's why Officer Ervin didn't get out. He's probably lying unconscious in the hall, if he even made it past the den furniture.

At the doorway I pause and shout again.

'Ruby! *Rubee!*'

All I hear is a living roar, the sound of fire devouring wood and carpet, curtains and glass, photos and china, silver and books – *Books*. My father's library is burning. If Ruby was not somewhere in this house, I would probably risk my life to save those books.

The bathroom, I remember. *Ruby fell by the bathroom.*

Thankfully, the heat is more intense to my right, toward the central hall. I put my nose to the carpet, take a breath and crawl to my left, toward the bathroom. It's two rooms, really, a narrow dressing room and linen closet with the commode and bathtub in a smaller cubicle beyond. I go through the door on my belly, groping forward like a soldier clearing a minefield.

The dressing room is empty. As I crawl toward the commode, my nostrils start to whistle with each breath. Panic ambushes me, like a wild thing tearing around in my chest. *Maybe Ruby isn't here at all. Maybe Ervin got her out. Maybe the scream I heard was the sound she made as he dragged her out.* I can't search the whole house. That's how firemen get killed, trying to save people who aren't there. I grope around the commode and inside the bathtub, then scramble back to the bathroom door.

The roar is closer.

'RUBY! IT'S PENN! ARE YOU HERE?

At first there is only the roar. Then a whimper floats out of the noise like a leaf from a bonfire. It came from the central hall. My lungs feel near to bursting, but I alligator along the carpet toward the corner, my eyes shut tight. The heat is nearly unendurable. Forcing my stinging eyes open, I look down the hall.

Dancing tongues of red and orange caper out of the black smoke like laughing demons. Primal terror seizes my muscles, paralyzing me long enough to fully comprehend the danger. Then my reptile brain shrieks: *DEATH! RUN!*

But I don't run. I can't. When I was six years old, a German shepherd got out of a neighbor's backyard and trapped me in a corner of our carport. That dog weighed ninety pounds, and when it bared its teeth and lunged at my face, all I could do was throw up my arms. When its teeth ripped into my flesh, I was too panic-stricken even to yell for help. After a seeming eternity of gnashing teeth and blood, I heard a sound like a hatchet hitting a watermelon, and saw a black woman as tall as our house swinging a shovel like a broadsword, bludgeoning that monstrous animal within an inch of its life. Ruby Flowers was terrified of dogs, but when she saw 'her baby' in danger, she pressed down her fear and charged out of our house like the wrath of God.

Fixing that image in my mind, I shut my eyes and crawl toward the flames. The frantic reptile voice whispers that the orange demons are flanking me, racing across the roof to close off my escape. But I hold Ruby's face in my mind, keep inching forward.

My hand touches flesh.

Bone.

An ankle.

The smell of cooked meat fills my nose and lungs, and I vomit up the wine I drank with Livy. Retching in the darkness, I take hold of the ankle and pull with all my strength. Something gives, and Ruby screams. At least she's alive. A broken hip can kill an old woman, but not as quickly as fire.

Switching ankles, I pull with both hands, dragging her far enough to get clear of the flames. She's moaning now, the sound like that of a wounded animal. I press my nose to the floor, take another breath of smoke, then get to my knees and heave her over my shoulder. As I struggle to my feet, dizziness pitches me against the wall, but somehow I right myself and stagger back toward the bedrooms.

The smoke is dense here too, but at the center of it is a dim, cool flicker of blue. I lean toward that blueness, trying to keep Ruby on my shoulder as I go forward. *Move your feet*, I yell silently. *Move* . . . It's as though my nerve fibers are shorting out one by one, attenuating the signals firing from my brain. Again the stench of scorched meat gags me, but I'm almost to the light. With a last heave I lift Ruby onto the windowsill and hold her there.

I don't want to drop her, but I can barely stand, much less lower her the six feet to the ground.

Suddenly two bright yellow gloves appear and pull her from my grasp. Male voices are shouting through the window, but I can't make out the words. The world outside the window seems part of some other universe. More yellow hands reach out of the brightness, reaching for me, but they are too far away.

I am falling.

The sun is in my eyes, and the skin of my face is burning.

A teenager wearing a black fireman's hat is holding something over my mouth and nose, and something like cool ambrosia is laving the burning walls of my lungs. I try to suck in more of it, but the effort triggers a coughing fit, great wracking spasms like blades tearing at my ribs and trachea as smoke pours from my nose and throat.

'Penn, I'm here,' says a woman's voice.

'Mom?'

'Livy.'

I see her face beside the fireman's now, her hair still damp from the Cold Hole. She takes my hand and squeezes gently.

'Ruby?' I ask.

'She's right over there. Look to your left.'

As I turn, I see two paramedics rolling a gurney across the lawn. A third is holding an IV bag at shoulder level as it drains fluid into Ruby's arm.

'I want to see her,' I croak, rolling over and getting to my knees.

'Easy, sir,' says the fireman. 'You've been through a little hell in the past few minutes.'

He's not really a teenager. He's probably in his mid-twenties, with a thin blond mustache and a hank of straight hair spilling from under his helmet.

'The cop?' I ask, recalling Officer Ervin's droopy beagle eyes. 'The cop who went in after her?'

'We got him out. Take it easy.'

'I'm okay . . . really.'

Livy slides under my right arm as I get to my feet, supporting me with surprising strength. I've never felt so jittery in my life. All my muscles are quivering and jerking as though exhausted by an overexpenditure of adrenaline, and my heart is laboring noticeably in my chest.

'The library,' I remember. 'My dad's books.'

Livy shakes her head. 'It's too late. The whole house is going up. It's a miracle you got out alive.'

'That's a fact,' says the fireman. 'We pulled you out just as the flames came through the bedroom door.'

'Thank you. I know I could have died in there.'

He smiles and gives me a salute. 'You done pretty good yourself, buddy.'

With Livy's help I make my way around to the front yard.

It looks as though every neighbor for a square mile has come to watch the fire. The crowd fills the surrounding yards and much of the street. Two fire trucks have their hoses trained on the house, and a third on the old oak with the creeper vine.

My mother runs up to me, her face ashen. 'Penn! I can't find Annie!'

I jerk erect and shake my head clear. 'Where did you see her last?'

'After you went in. It was taking so long – I was looking for you. I just put her down for a second!'

'How long ago?'

'Three or four minutes!'

The area is so choked with people that Annie could be ten feet away and we'd still miss her. The only thing in our favor is that we know most of the people in the crowd. Within five minutes, everyone on the street is looking for her.

As I run shirtless through the throng, fighting down panic, all I can think is that this fire was no accident. The 'boom' my mother heard had to be some kind of fire bomb. This whole disaster was staged to draw the attention of the cop watching the house. And it did. Officer Ervin bravely charged into the inferno to save Ruby's life, and in the process left my mother and daughter unprotected. My similar effort completed the kidnapper's work, by breaking my mother's concentration.

After five minutes of searching in vain, I realize I have to call the police. I prosecuted several kidnapping cases in Houston, and I learned one thing from the FBI agents who worked them. The first hour is the best chance of finding the victim, and every lost minute can mean disaster.

As I run across the street to use our neighbor's phone, a

ripple of noise like the roar at a football stadium rolls through the crowd. I turn back to our house, expecting to see the roof collapsing, the spectacular climax of residential fires. But it's not the roof. The crowd parts like the Red Sea, and my mother comes running through the open space.

She's carrying Annie in her arms.

Relief surges through me with such force that I nearly faint for the second time. But I run forward and hug them both as tightly as I dare. Annie's face is white with terror, and her chin is quivering.

'Someone dropped her off at Edna Hensley's,' Mom gasps. 'Edna answered her door and saw Annie standing there crying.'

A heavyset, blue-haired woman I faintly recognize has appeared behind my mother, wheezing from her exertions. Edna Hensley.

'Where do you live?' I ask her.

'About a half mile away. You've been there before, Penn. When you were a little boy.'

'Who dropped her off?'

Edna shakes her head. 'I didn't see anyone. Not a car, not anything.' Her gaze darkens. She reaches into her pocket, pulls out a folded sheet of construction paper, and hands it to me.

I unfold the paper with shaking hands. Printed on it in magic marker are the words: *THIS IS HOW EASY IT IS. LAY OFF, ASSHOLE.*

Livy braces me from the side, making sure I keep my feet.

I am back in Houston, watching Arthur Lee Hanratty's brother carry Annie out of the house, a tiny bundle about to disappear forever. It's as though I missed him that night, and he has returned to try again. But he can't. He's been dead for four years. His youngest brother is alive, but this isn't his work. Whoever kidnapped Annie today could easily have killed her, and the last surviving Hanratty would have done so, taking his revenge for his two brothers. This is something else entirely. This is a warning. This is the Del Payton case.

'Mom, take this piece of paper to the Lewises' house and put it in a Ziploc bag. I'll take care of Annie.'

She is reluctant to go, but she does. I thank Edna Hensley, then carry Annie through the crowd to Livy's borrowed Fiat and sit in the passenger seat, hugging her against me, rocking slowly, murmuring reassurances in her ear. She is still shivering, and her skin is frighteningly cold. I need to find out everything she can remember about her kidnapper before she starts blocking out the trauma, but I don't want to upset her any more than she already is.

'Annie?' I whisper, lifting her away from me enough to look into her hazel eyes. 'It's Daddy, punkin.'

Tears spill down her cheeks.

'Everything's all right now. I love you, punkin.'

She opens her mouth to speak, but her quivering chin ruins the words before they emerge.

'Honey, who took you to the lady's house? Did you see?'

She nods hesitantly.

'Who was it? Did you know them?'

'Fuh . . . fire. Fire man,' she stammers. 'Fire man.'

'A fireman? With a red hat?'

She shakes her head. 'A black and yellow hat.'

'That's good, punkin. He was just making sure you were all right. Did you see his face?'

'He had a mask. Like a swimming mask.'

A respirator. 'That's good. Did he say anything to you?'

'He said he had to get me away. Get me safe.'

'That's right, that's right. He was just getting you away from the fire. Everything's fine now.'

Her face seems to crumple in on itself. 'Daddy, I'm scared.'

I crush her to my chest, as though to protect her from the threat that has already passed. 'I love you, punkin. I love you.'

She shudders against me.

'I said, I love you, punkin.' I pull her back and look into her eyes, waiting.

'I love you more,' she says softly, completing our ritual, and my anxiety lessens a little.

Livy climbs into the driver's seat, squeezes Annie's shoulder, then takes her silk scarf from the glove compartment and begins wiping soot from my face.

'Where do you want to go?' she asks.

'Let's just sit for a minute.'

'Do you think it's safe here? Your mom told me about the note.'

Instead of answering her question, I lift the Fiat's cell phone, call Information, and ask for the number of Ray Presley. Livy takes her hand from my knee and watches me with apprehension. Presley's phone ring twenty times. No one answers.

'Is he there?' she asks in a quiet voice.

'No.'

Her face is strangely slack. 'Penn, why did you call Ray Presley?'

'There's no time to go into it now.'

'Penn? Where are you, son?'

It's my father. 'Over here, Dad!'

Livy looks back over the trunk of the convertible. 'He's seen us. He's coming.'

'Olivia!' Dad cries, rushing up to the car. 'Are you all right?'

'I'm fine, it's Penn and Annie who need help. I'm so sorry about this, Dr. Cage. It's just unbelievable.'

Dad leans over the passenger door and hugs Annie and me. Annie keeps her head buried in my neck.

'Is she all right?'

'I think so. Considering what just happened. Somebody—'

'I already heard. The story's spreading like—' He laughs bitterly. 'Like wildfire. Where's your mother?'

'I told her to go across the street and put the note in a Ziploc bag. There might be fingerprints.' I reach up and take his hand. 'I should have listened to you. You told me they'd stoop this low.'

He squeezes my hand. 'It's just a house. We'll build another one.'

'I was crazy to get involved in this case.'

He shakes his head, his eyes on the great column of smoke rising into the sky. 'Gutless sons of bitches . . . laid hands on my granddaughter. If I find the man who did this, I'll flay him alive.'

'Do you know anything about Ruby's condition?'

He sighs heavily. 'They carried her to St. Catherine's Hospital. Peter Carelli's in the ER with her now. It doesn't look good. Massive third-degree burns, a broken hip. The helicopter's on its way from Jackson. I'm about to go over there.'

'We'll follow you as soon as Mom gets back.'

He nods absently, watching the water pour onto the ruin that sheltered our family for thirty-five years.

'Dad, the library—'

'I know. No point thinking about it now. Right now we worry about the living.' He looks down at me, his eyes flinty and cold. 'This is the crossroads, son. We back off or we go forward. It's your call. I'll back you either way.'

Go forward? After this? 'Let's just find Mom and get to the hospital.'

He nods. 'I'll see you there.'

The treatment room in the ER is crowded but quiet. The muted beeps of monitors punctuate the hushed voices like metronomes. Ruby lies at the center of the room, a technological still life surrounded by doctors, nurses, a respiratory therapist, and my father. I move closer, straightening the scrub shirt a nurse brought me to replace the shirt I lost in the fire. Two large-bore IV lines are pouring fluids into Ruby's arms, and oxygen is being pumped into her lungs through a mask. Her mostly nude body is exposed to the air, the parts ravaged by fire – her right arm, shoulder, trunk, and both legs – bathed in Silvadene ointment. She was apparently wearing some sort of synthetic dress that caught fire and melted into her skin. The helicopter ambulance summoned from Jackson is under orders to whisk her to the burn center in Greenville as soon as it arrives, but my father doubts she'll survive to make the flight.

'Let my son in here,' Dad says, and the white coats part for me.

My first reaction is horror. Ruby's dentures have been removed and this makes her face look like a sunken death mask. Her black wig is also gone, leaving a thin snowy frizz atop her head. Her eyes are closed, her respiration labored. She looks like a dying woman photographed in some plague-stricken African village.

'Is she conscious?'

'She was until a minute, ago,' Dad replies. 'She's in and out now. Mostly out. In her condition, it's a blessing.'

One of Ruby's hands is undamaged, and I move around the table and take it, squeezing softly. 'Did Mom talk to her?'

'A little. Ruby had a panic attack and Peggy calmed her down.'

The thought of Ruby in terror makes it difficult for me to breathe. As I look down at her, her lips tremble, then move with purpose. She's trying to speak. But what comes from behind the mask is only a ragged passage of air. I lean closer and speak into her ear.

'Ruby? It's Penn, Ruby. I hear you.'

At last the rasps form words. '. . . *fine blessing. You . . . give a fine blessing, Dr. Cage. You go on . . . go on, now.*'

A chill races over my neck and arms. 'Dad? I think she wants you to say something religious.'

'She's obtunded, son. She doesn't really know what she's saying.'

'She knows. She wants you to say something over her.'

My father looks around at the ring of expectant faces. 'Jesus. I don't remember much.'

'Anything. It doesn't matter.'

He takes Ruby's hand and leans over her.

'Ruby, this is Dr. Cage. *Tom*, by God, though you refused to call me that for thirty-five years.' He chuckles softly. 'You're the only one in the world who could get me reciting from the Bible. Haven't done it since I was a boy.'

Ruby's lips move again, but no sound emerges.

'The Lord is my shepherd,' Dad says quietly. 'I shall not want. He maketh me to lie down in green pastures. He leadeth me beside the still waters. He restoreth my soul. He leadeth me . . . he–' Dad stops and picks up further on. 'Yea, though I walk through the shadow of . . . through the *valley* of the shadow of death, I will fear no evil. For thou art with me. Thy rod and thy staff comfort me. Thy . . .' He looks over at me. 'Damn it, what's the rest of it?'

I lean down beside Ruby's ear and continue for him. 'Thou preparest a table for me in the presence of mine enemies. Thou anointest my head with oil. My cup runneth over. Surely goodness and mercy will follow me all the days of my life, and I shall dwell in the house of the Lord forever.'

Ruby has stopped trying to speak. Her face is placid.

Dad lays a hand on my shoulder. 'Well, between us we managed it. She's got two atheists praying over her. Pretty pathetic, I guess.'

'It was good enough.'

Looking around, I notice expressions of shock and awe on the faces of the assembled doctors and nurses. 'What's the matter?'

'They've never seen me do anything like that before.'

'She's trying to speak,' says a nurse.

Ruby's jaw is quivering with effort, her wrinkled, toothless mouth opening and closing behind the mask like that of a landed fish. Dad and I lean over her and strain to hear. At first there is only a lisping sound. Then three words coalesce from the shapeless sounds.

'*Thank you . . . Tom.*'

Ruby's eyes flutter open, revealing big brown irises full of awareness. She seems to see not only us but beyond us. I suppose this is the look of faith.

'Lord Jesus,' she says, as clearly as if she were talking to me across the breakfast table. 'Ruby going home today. Home to glory.'

Seconds later her eyes close, and the monitors that were so muted before begin clanging alarms.

'She's coding,' Dad says.

'Crash cart!' cries one of the other doctors.

A hurricane of activity erupts around us, everyone rushing to his appointed task.

'Cardiac arrest,' Dad says in a calm voice.

'Tom?' says Dr. Carelli, a lean dark man in his late forties. 'Clear, Tom.'

Dad holds up his right hand. 'Everyone listen to me. This case is DNR.'

The alarms go on ringing with relentless insistence.

'Do you know that for a fact?' asks Carelli, standing anxiously over the cart with a laryngoscope in his hand. 'Tom, you know the rules.'

'This woman is eighty years old, she's got third-degree burns over sixty percent of her body, and a broken hip.'

'Tom, for a DNR we need it on paper.'

'She also has carcinoma of the lung,' Dad says softly. 'No one knows that but me. There's nothing on paper, but she's discussed it with me on several occasions. No extraordinary measures. Do not resuscitate. Turn off those alarms.'

The whole apparatus of technology stands poised on the edge of action, and my father has ordered it to stand down.

'Tom, are you sure?' asks Carelli.

'I take full responsibility. Turn off those goddamned alarms.'

One by one the alarms go off. Dad looks at me, his eyes weary. 'Go on out, Penn. Check on Annie and your mother. You don't want to see this.'

'Not until she's gone.'

He nods slowly. 'All right.' He turns to the assembled staff. 'Thanks for the effort, everybody. We'd like to be alone with her.'

I squeeze Ruby's good hand, kiss her forehead, and wait for the end. Looking at this ravaged shell of a woman, I find it hard to believe that she was the towering figure who saved me from that German shepherd. But she was. She is. As the last nurse files out, the drumbeat of rotor blades descends over the hospital, announcing the helicopter that will return to Jackson without its scheduled passenger.

Ruby Flowers is leaving Natchez by another route.

Our family has gathered in the small chapel provided by the hospital for patients and their families. It's a small, dim room, with electric candles, two pews, an altar, and some 'new' Bibles full of undistinguished prose. I'm not a believer myself, but in time of death you can do a lot worse than the King James Bible for comfort.

My mother is praying quietly at the altar. Dad sits beside me in the front pew, with Annie on his lap. This is the first time we have been together in anything like a church since Sarah's funeral. My older sister was with us for that, but she's been teaching in Ireland ever since. Today was a good day to be there and not here.

I have never seen my father this angry. Not even during the malpractice trial. He is by nature a gentle and even-tempered man, and his medical experience has taught him to be calmer as situations deteriorate. But right this minute he has blood in his eye, and I understand the feeling. If I knew with certainty that Ray Presley set that fire, or that Leo Marston had ordered it, I would shoot them both without a second thought.

Mom rises to her feet, then walks over and takes Annie from Dad. 'We'd better check into a motel,' she says. 'And we need to think about getting some clothes. I'm sure everything is ruined.'

'The insurance will cover most of it,' Dad replies. 'The police are waiting to talk to me in the ER.'

Mom looks at him and shakes her head. 'The things I cared about in that house, no insurance can replace.'

'I know that, Peggy.'

'Mom, I'm sorry,' I say uselessly. 'I know this happened because of me.'

She reaches out with her free hand and squeezes my arm. 'Let's just get checked in somewhere. We need to take care of this little girl.'

Dad follows her to the door, then shuts it and comes back to me. 'We're going to need some protection, son. Real protection. Off-duty cops aren't up to this. Who do we call?'

'I know some people in Houston. Serious people. An international security company. I'll call the CEO right now.'

'I want them here tonight. I don't care what it costs.'

'They'll be here. And I'm paying.'

He sighs and looks at the altar. 'Who do you think set that fire?'

'First guess? Ray Presley. I called his trailer while the house was burning. He wasn't home. Could he have managed it after that poisoning attempt? After his heart attack or whatever?'

Dad nods. 'Physically, he could do it. He's a lot more able than I am. What about Marston?'

'Leo Marston knows everything that goes on in this town. He wouldn't dirty his hands with the actual deed, but he'd order someone to do it.'

'I hate to think Ray would go that far. Kidnapping Annie . . . my God. What do you want to do?'

'Let's get settled somewhere first, get the security in place. Then we'll talk about it.'

He opens the chapel door and nearly walks over Livy, who's standing in the hall. She backs up so that we can exit, and as we do I see my mother and Annie waiting at the end of the hall, by the wide ER doors.

'Tell me what I can do,' Livy says. 'Your mother said you're going to a motel.'

'For now. We need to get Annie settled. She—'

Suddenly the ER doors swing open, and Caitlin Masters runs up the corridor with a camera swinging around her neck and her black hair flying behind her.

'I just came from your house,' she says. 'Penn, I'm so sorry.'

'Caitlin—'

'I need to talk you and your father. Right now.'

'What is it?'

She looks at Livy. 'Could you excuse us for a moment, Mrs. Sutter?'

Livy bristles and looks at me, expecting me to tell Caitlin she can stay.

'Why don't we go in the chapel?' I suggest. 'We'll just be a minute, Livy.'

Livy starts to say something to Caitlin but doesn't. Instead she bites her bottom lip and watches us walk into the chapel.

Caitlin's energy is like a flame inside the little room. She can't remain still, and her eyes simmer with anger.

'Someone kidnapped Annie?' she asks. 'Is that right?'

'Yes.'

'And they brought her back? With a warning note?'

'Yes.'

'The same person who set the fire?'

'Almost certainly.'

'Okay . . . okay.' She nods furiously, then paces out a tight circle. 'That's all I wanted to know.'

'Caitlin, what's going on? Why are you so worked up?'

'I'll print the story.'

'The story. About the fire?'

She blinks in confusion. 'The fire? Hell, no. The slander. Marston being behind the Payton murder. You say it, I'll print it. In type big enough to give him a coronary over breakfast.'

I simply stare at her.

'Maybe that's the answer,' Dad says. 'Last night we thought it was.'

'Last night you had a house,' I remind him. 'What changed your mind?'

Caitlin stops pacing and looks me dead in the eye. 'Annie, for one thing.'

'This girl is good people,' Dad says, squeezing her shoulder.

'For another, my instincts have started humming. Don't ask me why, because I don't know. Maybe because this happened two days after we went to see Stone, and Stone says Marston was behind Payton's death. Maybe because John Portman threatened you, and we know he worked the Payton case in sixty-eight. And we know Marston and J. Edgar Hoover were friends. Maybe it's because I get a funny vibe from Marston's daughter. All I know is that I'm not sitting still while these bastards go after people I care about. They want to play hardball? They're going to get the game of their goddamn lives.'

My father looks like he wants to kiss her.

'What time is our deadline?' I ask.

'Just call me after you guys get settled somewhere. I'll come to you.'

'I don't know what to say. Just . . . thank you.'

When we leave the chapel, Caitlin walks past Livy without a word. She hugs my mother by the ER doors, kisses Annie, then slips through the doors and disappears.

Livy keeps pace with Dad and me as we walk down the hall and join my mother and Annie.

'Where do you think we should go, Tom?' Mom asks.

'The Prentiss Motel is right up on the highway. Let's stay there tonight. We'll worry about the long term tomorrow.'

As Dad opens the ER doors, Mom follows him through with Annie on her hip, leaving Livy and me alone on this side. The awkwardness between us is palpable. Two hours ago we were in each other's arms. Now . . .

'What can I do?' she asks. 'I'll help with Annie, go out for food. Whatever you need.'

'I think it better just be family tonight,' I say gently. 'Thanks for offering, though. Thanks for today too.'

Her eyes cloud with frustration and confusion. 'Penn, for God's sake . . . what's happening here?'

'Maybe you should ask your father.'

Chapter 27

When the *Examiner* hit the driveways at four this morning, it polarized the town. Caitlin's words entered the public consciousness like electrodes dipped into water, ionizing opinion to positive or negative with no neutral between, the opinions predictable in most cases by the simple indicator of skin color. The process took about three hours: from the time the insomniacs, farmers, and shift workers walked outside to read the front page by street lamp until the last Washington Street matrons toddled downstairs to read what the maid had laid out beside their morning coffee. By seven a.m. telephones were ringing all over town, and by eight every conversation from the sewer ditches and oil fields to the paper mill and the hospitals was centered on two men: Leo Marston and Penn Cage.

My only contributions to Caitlin's story were the actual accusations against Marston, slander per se if I ever heard it. Of course, my slanderous charges became libel per se – meaning that the libeled party would not have to prove damages – the moment Caitlin printed and distributed them. My phrases, preserved for the ages, ran as follows:

> *There is no doubt that Delano Payton was murdered on May 14, 1968. It is just as certain that former State Attorney General Leo Marston, known locally as 'Judge' Marston because of his stint on the state supreme court, was the man behind the conspiracy that resulted in Payton's murder. Under*

Mississippi law, that makes Marston as guilty of murder as the man who planted the bomb. Murder by explosive device is a capital crime in this state, and there is no statute of limitations. I urge the local district attorney to reopen the Payton case. If he does, he will quickly find enough proof to send Leo Marston to death row at Parchman.

Asked by 'the publisher' to describe the evidence on which I based my accusations, I stated:

I am in contact with certain members of the Justice Department who have long known of Marston's involvement in the crime. Conscientious citizens and law enforcement officers have also come forward with previously unknown facts about the Payton murder. I believe we would already have seen a prosecution of Judge Marston but for the fact that John Portman, the present director of the FBI and a former federal judge, was involved in the original Payton investigation in 1968. Some former FBI agents believe the Bureau itself may have been involved in a cover-up of certain facts of Payton's death, but this will be difficult to prove without the original FBI file on the Payton case, which is sealed until the year 2007, ostensibly for reasons of national security.

I was purposefully vague about Marston's possible motives for the crime, but on Caitlin's advice I hinted that Marston, heretofore considered a moderate on race, might secretly have been working in concert with members of the Mississippi Sovereignty Commission to prevent black workers from rising into 'white jobs.'

Because of my reference to John Portman, the wire services picked up the story before noon, and just before one Caitlin received a call from CNN in Atlanta. There were already two network stringers in town to cover the 'black–white' mayoral election, and they spent the morning outside my family's motel rooms, pleading for comment on the story.

But the morning paper had far more tragic consequences. Caitlin had written a separate piece about the fire and kidnaping. In it she vividly described the rescues of Ruby Flowers and Officer Ervin, and also Ruby's death in the ER. She quoted several citizens on Ruby's character, in particular the pastor of the Mandamus Baptist Church, of which Ruby had been a devoted member. She also quoted the fire chief, who pronounced the fire arson, based on the discovery of an incendiary device in the collapsed attic of our house. Caitlin concluded by saying that the arson and kidnaping were clearly attempts to stop my investigation into the Delano Payton murder. It was yellow journalism at its finest, and the consequences were immediate.

At a little after one, a seventy-four-year-old white man named Billy Earl Whitestone walked down his sidewalk to get his mail from the box. He got both barrels of a twelve-gauge shotgun instead, fired from a red Monte Carlo driven by two unidentified black youths. The gunmen stopped long enough to drop a copy of the *Examiner* on Mr Whitestone's shattered skull, but even if they hadn't, the shooting would have been recognized as a reprisal for Ruby's death. In his younger days Billy Earl Whitestone had achieved national notoriety as a Grand Wizard of the White Knights of the Imperial Ku Klux Klan. He had also enjoyed a brief renaissance of fame during the 1980s when, Wallace-like, he marched at the head of some black civil rights parades, but apparently this belated conversion had not sufficiently impressed certain members of the African-American community. At least not the two young men in the Monte Carlo.

A drive-by shooting in Natchez is the equivalent of a race riot in Los Angeles. Within the hour Mayor Warren went on the local country radio station to appeal for calm and to condemn the 'reckless and irresponsible charges' made against 'one of the city's finest citizens' by former Natchezian Penn Cage. He also blasted the 'Yankee editor' of the local newspaper. Shad Johnson also took to the airwaves – the black AM station – to urge restraint in the face of 'the deteriorating racial situation.' Unlike Wiley Warren, Shad urged the city authorities look into the charges printed in the morning paper and, if they were found to be substantive, to reopen the investigation into Del Payton's murder. Despite his wish that the Payton murder remain a non-issue, Shad could not in the aftermath of the fire and shooting afford to be seen as anything but a champion of the black community, his core of electoral support.

Three hours after Whitestone's death, I was invited to the police station to discuss the statements I'd made in the newspaper, particularly my reference to 'local law enforcement officers.' The police chief conducted the interview, and he seemed to labor under the misapprehension that I was subject to arrest if I didn't answer his questions. I calmly and courteously enumerated my rights under the Constitution, then explained that I had first contacted the district attorney about my suspicions and found him apathetic. I refused to answer any questions, and suggested that the chief talk to Austin Mackey instead. As I departed, he told me he considered the death of Billy Earl Whitestone my responsibility, and I didn't argue. He was mostly right.

I left my bodyguard outside during this interview. He and his three associates from Argus Security had arrived from Houston just after midnight, flying into Baton Rouge via Argus's Gulfstream V and driving up to Natchez in four separate rental cars. They checked into the Prentiss Motel, and by two a.m. my family was being protected by some of the finest bodyguards in the world. The total cost of this protection was staggering, but my memory of Annie's quivering chin was enough to make me ashamed for even thinking of money.

Three of the four guards were former FBI agents, and fit exactly the mental image I'd had before they arrived. Lean and tight-lipped. Late forties. Economical movements. Nine-hundred-dollar business suits specially tailored to conceal the bulges of various firearms. The fact that they were former FBI agents concerned me a little, but their boss had assured me that none of his men had worked under John Portman. The fourth Argus man was about thirty-five and blond, with the lean, confident look of a professional mountain guide. He wore jeans, a sweatshirt, and hiking boots. Daniel Kelly was a veteran of the army's Delta Force, and like the others, was billed at eight hundred dollars per day.

After hearing the details of our situation, the senior member of the detail suggested the following plan. One operative should remain with my mother and Annie at all times, another with my father, and one with me. The fourth would sleep at the hotel for six hours, then relieve one of the other men, beginning a continuous rotation. I agreed, and chose Daniel Kelly as my guard.

After my interview at the police station, Kelly and I stopped by the offices of the *Examiner*, where we found Caitlin doing her best to handle a barrage of phone calls from other newspapers. She stopped working long enough to tell me that her father had called from Richmond and demanded to know what the hell she thought she was up to, then ordered her aboard the first Virginia-bound aircraft leaving Mississippi. Caitlin told him he had better get ready to mount a libel defense, because she was sticking by her story, and if he fired her, he should prepare to read further instalments of the Payton story in the *Washington Post*. I didn't envy Mr. Masters. Caitlin had been preparing for this day for a long time.

Thirty minutes before the courthouse closed, Leo Marston filed suit against myself and the Natchez *Examiner* for a grand total of five million dollars, his complaint drafted in record time by his junior law partner, Blake Sims. Actually, they filed two separate suits – one for slander and one for libel – neatly severing my fate from that of the *Examiner*, which, as part of a media group, will have a battery of attorneys on retainer, many of them First Amendment specialists. A deputy served me with the papers just as our family was leaving the motel for dinner at the Shoney's Restaurant across the street.

I invited the Argus men to eat with us, but they took their jobs too seriously for that. Two stood in the front parking lot near their cars, like businessmen shooting the breeze after an early dinner, while Daniel Kelly covered the rear entrance. I hadn't felt that safe in a long time. The Argus men made quite an impression on Annie too. She'd spent most of her waking hours since the fire on my mother's lap, but during dinner she began to loosen up, using the Shoney's crayons to play each of us in games of tic-tac-toe.

Ruby's death hung over the adults like a pall, but we tried to focus on the good times we'd had with her, which were countless, as they spanned thirty-five years. My father had stopped by Ruby's house earlier to give her husband, Mose – a retired pulpwood cutter – a substantial check and a gallon of Wild Turkey. They talked for half an hour, shared some whiskey, and Dad left the house wondering how long the old man would survive without Ruby around to take care of him.

Caitlin's articles had upset my mother, but Marston's lawsuit terrified her. I tried to reassure her by explaining that my intent had been to force just such a lawsuit, but she refused to be mollified. Like most people who have lived any length of time in Natchez, my mother believes that Leo Marston is untouchable, and that anyone who tries to hurt him is doomed to failure or worse.

I kept the good news of the day to myself. Just after noon Special Agent Peter Lutjens had called the motel from a pay phone in McLean, Virginia, and asked me to call him back from a pay phone. When I did, he told me he'd been stewing about the Payton case and had decided to try to photocopy the sealed FBI file. He still had his security pass to the proper archive. The problem was the staff. The 'friend' who had reported his initial inquiry to Portman worked every day but Sunday, so Sunday was Lutjens's only shot. And he was due to report in Fargo on Monday. I thanked him profusely and tried to reassure him that what he was doing would ultimately serve the Bureau, not undermine it. He told me he'd call me Sunday if he wasn't in jail, and hung up.

When we got back to the motel after supper, I found two old-fashioned handwritten messages waiting: 'Call Livy' and 'Call Ike.' I had no idea what Livy could want, other than to curse me for vilifying her father in the newspaper, but I called Tuscany anyway. The number of the Marston mansion hadn't changed since we were kids, but the fact that it had remained in my memory for twenty years probably said something about my buried feelings for Livy. Butterflies fluttered in my stomach as the phone rang, but I resolved to tell Leo to kiss my ass if he answered.

'Marston residence.' A maid.

'Yes, could I speak to Liv, please?'

'Who's calling?'

'Her husband.'

'Just a moment, Mr. Sutter.'

After a few moments Livy came on the line and said, 'John?'

'It's Penn.'

'Oh. Just a minute.' Her voice was under tight control. I heard the clacking of heels on hardwood, then her voice again, more relaxed. 'I'm glad you called back. How's Annie doing?'

'Better. Look, I know you must be upset about the paper.'

A strange laugh. 'Things are pretty crazy around here. I don't know what you're trying to do. But I know *why* you're doing it.'

I said nothing.

'Penn . . . hurting my father won't make up for the years we lost.'

'I know that.'

'I hope so. Because I called to tell you that, as bad as all this is, I don't want to let him come between us again.'

We both waited in the vacuum of the open line, each hoping the other could somehow bridge the chasm my accusations had opened between us. I imagined her sitting alone in the Italianate palace that had sheltered her throughout her childhood. She had often portrayed it to me as a prison, but I never bought into this. She wouldn't have traded Tuscany for anything.

'Livy?'

'I'm here.'

'You haven't asked where I got my information about your father. You haven't protested his innocence.'

'Of course I haven't. It's ridiculous. My father murdering a black man? He's probably the least prejudiced man in this town.'

'Del Payton's death may not have been a race murder. Tell me something, Livy. What would you do if you found out your father ordered the burning of my parents' house?'

'That's insane.'

'Just pretend it was true. What would you do?'

'Well, obviously, I'd be the first one to call the police.'

Maybe she didn't even know she was lying. 'I need to go, Livy.'

'Can we see each other tonight?'

I couldn't believe she wanted to be within ten miles of me after the newspaper story. 'Not tonight.'

'Tomorrow, then?'

Images from the day before filled my mind: Livy floating naked in the pool, kissing me passionately as we sank slowly through the green water, her thigh pressing against me. 'We'd better play it by ear. There's a lot going on right now.'

'That's all the more reason to stay close. Just remember what I said about my father. I meant it.'

'I will.'

I hung up and dialed Ike's cell phone before thoughts of Livy could overwhelm me. I wanted to call her back and say, 'Pick me up in twenty minutes.' But the past had finally caught up with us, and Ike the Spike was growling in my ear.

'Meet me where I wanted to last night,' he said, meaning the warehouse in the industrial park by the river. 'One hour.'

'What about?'

'What *about*? About whatever the fuck it is you think you're doing, man. This town's going crazy. One hour.'

'I'll be there.'

'Damn straight you will.'

I've been sweating in the dark warehouse for twenty minutes, breathing the stink of fertilizer and wondering what could be keeping Ike. It's fully dark now, and the spotlight of a tugboat pushing barges upriver arcs through the night like a Hollywood klieg light, searching for sandbars and unexpected traffic. A slight breeze off the Mississippi penetrates the twenty-foot-wide warehouse door, where I stand watching the dark line of the levee, waiting for the headlights of Ike's cruiser.

I am unarmed but not unprotected. Daniel Kelly is covering me. After asking four times if I really trust Ike Ransom, Kelly parked his rental car behind the warehouse and told me to forget he was there. I parked the

BMW out front so that Ike would see it when he drove up.

What I take for the sound of another tugboat suddenly resolves into a car engine. A set of headlights descends the levee, pulls into the parking lot of the warehouse, and stops beside my car.

It's Ike's cruiser.

He gets out, his brown uniform looking black under the single security light, and walks towards the warehouse door. Halfway there he stops, turns, and watches the levee for nearly a minute. Maybe he senses Kelly's presence. Whatever the reason, he resumes walking toward me. When he's ten yards away, I step into the light, holding both hands in plain view.

Ike draws his pistol faster than I would have believed possible, recognizing me just as the barrel lines up with my chest. He quickens his step and shoves me back into the shadows.

'You ought to know better than that,' he mutters.

'Why are you so jumpy?'

The whites of his eyes flick left and right in the darkness. 'You ain't jumpy? After somebody burned down your house and took your kid?'

'Who set that fire, Ike? Who took my daughter? Ray Presley?'

'Could have been.' He holsters his pistol. 'But I don't know for sure. Not yet.'

'Why are we here?'

'So you can tell me what the hell you think you're doing in the paper. You crazy? Making statements like that?'

'You're the one who told me Marston was guilty.'

'Jesus. Is that the way you did it in Houston? Shoutin' shit in the papers before you got any proof?'

'Take it easy. Everything's under control.'

'Under control? Shooting your mouth off about local law enforcement coming forward?'

'I'm pursuing this the way I think best. As far as the

newspaper story goes, I wanted Marston to sue me, and the story accomplished that.'

'You what?'

'I wanted the right to request everything from personal papers to phone records from Marston under the rules of discovery.'

A gleam of recognition. 'That lawsuit means you can ask for Marston's personal shit? And *get it*?'

'That's right.'

'Okay . . . maybe you ain't crazy. You get the judge's legal files, you're liable to find all kinds of illegal shit.'

'Marston's legal files are protected under client confidentiality rules. But everything else is fair game.'

'How long you got to answer his suit? At least thirty days, right? That should give you plenty of time for fishing.'

'I'm going to file my answer tomorrow.'

His mouth drops open. 'Why you gonna do that?'

'By proceeding aggressively, I force Marston to conclude that I either have evidence in my possession or that I know people willing to come forward and testify against him.'

'But you don't.'

'Don't be so sure. I'm building a case.'

Ike's eyes narrow to slits. 'What you talking about? What kind of case? You holding back on me?'

'What if I am? You've been holding back on me from the start.'

He raises a warning finger but says nothing, and instead begins a staring contest. His bloodshot eyes are so jerky that he can't focus in one direction long, and he soon looks away.

'What are you taking, Ike? Speed? What?'

'I take me a drink now and then. So what? Have you talked to Stone again?'

'Yes, but he's just like you. Scared to tell what he knows.'

'I told you, man, I know Marston done it, but I don't know why.'

'*How* do you know, Ike? How can you know he did it if you don't know why?'

He grunts in the dark. 'I know what I know. Why'd you slam Portman in the paper? You go pissing off the head of the FBI, you're asking for some serious payback.'

'I did it to protect myself and my family. That newspaper story threw a lot of light on Portman. On me too. It makes it harder for him to retaliate.'

'Yeah? I heard somebody tried to poison Ray Presley. Who the hell you think did that?'

'I figured Marston ordered it. You think it was Portman?'

'Sure as hell wasn't the tooth fairy.' Ike scrapes the tip of a boot along the cement floor of the warehouse. 'Stone say anything about surveillance?'

'Why?'

'There's somebody watching me.'

A shiver runs along my forearms. 'How long?'

'I picked him up today, but he could have been there longer.'

'Stone's under FBI surveillance himself. He thinks Caitlin and I are too. Phones, the works. But why would the FBI be watching you?'

'Maybe 'cause of your damn newspaper article.'

'I didn't mention your name. Why did you warn me away from the FBI? Have you tried to talk to them about the Payton case before?'

'Say what?' He takes out a cigarette and taps it against his palm but does not light it. 'Why don't you focus on some shit that'll get you somewhere? Like Marston's papers. There's bound to be something in there to prosecute him on. He's had his hands in all kinds of shit for years. I mean, who cares what he goes down for, 'long as he rots in Parchman.'

'*I* care. To get out from under this slander charge, I've got to prove Marston guilty of murder. Not campaign finance fraud or any other bullshit. *Murder.* Do you comprehend that?'

Instead of answering, Ike flips open his lighter, ignites it, and puts the flame to the tip of his cigarette. As the orange glow illuminates his face, something incomprehensible happens. The flame reaches toward me as though sucked by a wind, and Ike slams his shoulder into my chest, punching the air out of my lungs and knocking me to the cement floor.

As he lands on top of me, gunfire erupts outside the warehouse and echoes through the metal building. Two shots, I think. Then a third, the sound quick and flat.

'Get *off*,' I grunt, unable to draw breath with Ike on top of me.

He rolls off and up into a kneeling position, his pistol pointed through the warehouse door.

'What happened?' I ask.

'There's two guns out there. One silenced.'

'I've got a man out there, Ike. Maybe one of the guns was his.'

He whips his head around. 'What man?'

'A private security guy. From Houston.'

He peers into the darkness the way he must have done in Vietnam, with absolute concentration. 'I can't see shit,' he hisses. 'But some lardass ex-cop ain't gonna help us one bit, I know that.'

'He's not what you think.'

After a minute of silence, he works his way toward the edge of the door.

'What do you see?'

'Shut the fuck up.'

A boom like a cannon shot shatters the silence, reverberating through the warehouse for at least four seconds. Ike hits the floor with his pistol still aimed at the door.

'That's a deer gun,' he says. 'Stay down. We got serious shit going down out there, and it ain't all got to do with us.'

'How do you know?'

'Ain't but one bullet come into this warehouse.'

As I lie facedown on the floor, breathing accumulated dust and oil, the seconds drag past. There are no more shots, but the instinctual voice that warned me during the fire that killed Ruby is not comforted by this fact. It knows that silence is the cloak of the approaching enemy.

'How long we gonna lie here?' I whisper.

'Till I tell you to get up.'

Another five minutes pass.

'Penn Cage!' yells a man from beyond the warehouse door. 'It's Kelly! Daniel Kelly.'

'That your guy?' asks Ike.

'It's Kelly!' shouts the voice again. 'Come out! And bring your friend. We need some law out here.'

I scramble to my feet and trot to the edge of the door.

Daniel Kelly stands forty feet away, an MP-5 submachine gun slung over his shoulder.

'What happened?' I ask, walking into the parking lot.

'Somebody tried to whack you. Or the cop. I couldn't tell which.'

Ike steps into the light, his pistol aimed at Kelly. 'Who shot who out here?'

Kelly holds up his hands. 'Take it easy, Deputy. I'm a friendly. I was out here covering your meeting when I saw a muzzle flash from over there.' He points at the levee, a dark silhouette fifty yards away. 'It was a silenced rifle, and it was firing subsonic rounds, because I didn't hear the bullet crack. I started running toward the flash, whipping out a spotter scope as I ran, trying to get within range and see at the same time. The shooter was firing from the prone position, already setting up for his second shot. I yelled just as he pulled the trigger, and as he swung around to deal with me, I double-tapped him on the run.'

'Is he dead?' Ike asks.

'Definitely. I put one through his head to be sure, and it's a good thing, because he was wearing a vest.'

'What about that deer gun I heard?'

Kelly points into the darkness south of the warehouse. 'The deer gun belonged to the guy over there. Who is also dead. The shooter on the levee took him out. That was the first muzzle flash I saw. He fired across my line of sight, at a right angle to you guys. The other guy must have fired off that deer slug as he was dying. Pure reflex, probably.'

'I don't get it,' I say. 'Why would they shoot at each other? A falling-out among hit men?'

Kelly shakes his head. 'I don't think these guys were together. They're dressed different, and their equipment's different. I think the guy with the deer gun was just in the way.'

'Who knew you were coming to this meeting?' Ike asks.

'My father and Kelly. That's it.'

'What about you?' Kelly asks Ike.

'Nobody knows where I'm at. How did these guys get so close if you were covering the meeting?'

Kelly scratches the side of his nose, as though to emphasize his calmness. 'First of all, they're not that close. Second, the curve of the levee blocked my line of sight to the guy with the deer gun, but not his line to you. Third, the sniper on the levee followed *you* in. He probably drove with his lights off and parked well back, then moved up on foot.' Kelly pauses, his cool blue eyes level with Ike's. 'And fourth, if I was in with those guys, you'd be bagged and tagged right now.'

Ike snorts and turns toward the levee. 'Show me the dead guys.'

Kelly unslings his MP-5 and starts jogging toward the levee. We follow him across the lot, trying to stay with him as he pounds up the spongy grass on the side of the levee. The odors of cow manure and bush-hogged grass weight the humid air. At the crest, Kelly points at a black shape lying at the edge of the gravel road that runs atop the levee.

'No wallet,' he says. 'No ID at all. Car's clean too. A rental.'

'That's risky,' Ike remarks. 'He gets stopped at random without ID, he's gonna get run in.'

'Unless he's willing to do the cop.'

Ike walks to the corpse, bends over, and takes a long look. 'Never seen him. Take a look, Cage.'

I walk over and glance at the dead sniper. He's dressed from head to toe in black, and looks like he stepped off a film set. His face is pale and placid in the dark, as though he were shot while sleeping. A dead face can be difficult to identify, so I give it long enough to be sure.

'I don't know him.'

'Here's his weapon.' Kelly holds out a long, bolt-action rifle to Ike. 'Rank-Pullin starlight scope. Fourth-generation passive amplification. Expensive toy.'

'Guy's definitely out of town,' Ike declares. 'Nobody around here uses shit like this. Caliber looks awful small.'

'It's a special twenty-two magnum. Chambers subsonic rounds. An assassin's gun.'

'Christ,' I whisper. 'Where's the other guy?'

Kelly points into the darkness south of the warehouse, then starts down the slope.

The second corpse is lying facedown in a thicket of weeds, dressed in jeans and a plaid flannel shirt. There's a red bandanna knotted around its head.

Ike bends down and pulls a rifle from the dead hand. 'An old Remington thirty-aught-six. Seen better days too.'

Kelly says, 'The shooter on the levee probably saw him moving up to get a shot. Poor bastard didn't have a chance.'

Ike puts both hands under the corpse and rolls it over. Below the dead man's left eye is a small black hole. Small but obviously fatal.

'I've seen a hundred shitkickers just like him,' says Ike. 'But I don't know this one.'

As I stare, the slack features suddenly coalesce into a coherent whole, and a feverish heat shoots through me. The dead man is a nightmare made flesh, a physical echo of the most terrifying night of my life.

'I know him,' I say, grabbing Ike's arm.

'Who is he?'

'His name's Hanratty. I convicted his brother of capital murder. He was just executed.'

'I'll be damned. That Aryan Brotherhood bastard?'

'Right. I also shot his other brother four years ago.'

'No shit,' says Kelly, with respect mingled with surprise.

'This one was the last.' The fever heat has disappeared, leaving a chill in its wake. 'The youngest.'

Ike kicks the corpse's leg. 'No more boom-boom for this Aryan *papasan.*'

He kneels and starts going through the dead man's pockets, quickly turning up a wallet. 'Hanratty, Clovis Dee,' he says, reading the driver's license.

'Brother of Arthur Lee,' I say absurdly.

'And white people make fun of African names,' Ike mutters, getting to his feet. ''Least we know what happened now. This shitkicker was out for revenge, and he picked the wrong night to try it. He was crowding that ninja assassin up on the levee, and he paid for it. The question is, who sent the assassin?'

'Portman?' I suggest. 'The hardware looked pretty sophisticated.'

'John Portman would definitely have access to people like that,' Kelly says quietly. 'Retired Bureau. Agency. Former CT operators.' He looks at Ike. 'In any case, I hope you appreciate this enough to take care of any problems that might arise.'

'Don't sweat it,' Ike replies. 'We're in the county here. Me and the sheriff understand each other. Although three killings in one day is big-time trouble for this town.'

'The district attorney could be a problem,' I tell them, thinking of Austin Mackey.

'Fuck that tightass,' Ike mutters. 'We got three witnesses telling it one way, dead guys got nobody. Mackey got no choice.'

'I was thinking of Kelly's submachine gun. It's illegal.'

Kelly smiles and draws a pistol from his holster.

'What you gonna do with that?' Ike asks, dropping his hand to his own gun.

Kelly fires three quick rounds into the night sky, then holsters the pistol. 'Browning Hi-Power,' he says with a smile. 'Chambers the same nine-millimeter cartridge as the MP-5. Very convenient, as long as they don't do a ballistics analysis.'

Ike nods as if noting this for future use. 'Well, let's get this over with. Let me call the sheriff.'

He starts back toward the warehouse, but I take his arm and stop him. 'Who sent the sniper, Ike? Who's trying to kill me?'

He looks back, his face indignant. 'How you know he was shooting at *you*?'

He pulls his arm free and walks on, but I stay where I am, breathing the cooler air blowing off the river. The stars are bright here, the water close. A few minutes ago a silent bullet passed within inches of my face. But I am still alive. And the last Hanratty brother is finally dead. My daughter is a lot safer than she was before Daniel Kelly did something not many men could have done.

'Thanks, Kelly,' I say softly.

He gives me a self-deprecating smile. 'Just doing my job, boss.'

Right.

Chapter 28

The sheriff's office looks like an armed camp when we arrive. It's a modern, fortress-like building, with a state-of-the-art jail occupying its upper floors. Uniformed deputies swagger through the halls like cowboys in a western, stoked by the air of incipient violence blowing through the city. Ike disappears for a few moments, leaving Kelly and me in the entrance hall.

Five minutes later, he returns and escorts us into the sheriff's office. I sense immediately that we're going to benefit from the jurisdictional rivalry that exists between the police department and the sheriff's office. Had we reported the levee shootings to the police, the chief would have kept Kelly and me all night, mercilessly grilling me as payback for the constitutional lesson I gave him earlier in the day.

The sheriff is tan and fit-looking, with the watchful eyes of a hunter. He seems to view the death of the youngest Hanratty as a fortuitous event, though the timing could have been better.

'When those black kids shot Billy Earl Whitestone,' he says, leaning back in his chair and folding his hands behind his neck, 'they turned this town into a powder keg. The Sports Center sold out of ammunition at four o'clock. They sold mostly to whites. Wal-Mart sold out of everything but paintball rounds. They sold mostly to blacks. We may have a world of trouble coming down on our heads tonight. And all because of that newspaper story.' He looks at me like a wise poker player. 'You think going after Leo Marston is worth all this trouble?'

'The built-up resentment in this town is none of my doing, Sheriff. What's happening now would have happened eventually, whatever the cause.'

'Maybe,' he allows. 'I sure hope you've got some evidence, though. Messing with Judge Leo ain't generally good for your health.'

'Any leads on the Whitestone shooters?' Ike asks.

'The P.D. has an informer working it. They're not telling me squat, of course, but the word is, it's some kids from the Concord Apartments. Nobody's been arrested yet, though. And we need an arrest. Jailing those two might go a long way toward calming people down. Maybe you ought to take a ride over to those apartments, Ike. See if you can shake something loose.'

'I'll do it.'

The sheriff smooths his thinning hair. 'Think you can give me some overtime tonight?'

'Glad to get it.'

'I want you to stick to the north side, try to keep everybody indoors.'

The sheriff is telling Ike to keep the black population inside their houses.

'I've given the white deputies the same orders for their parts of town,' he adds for my benefit. 'It's fear that drives all this nonsense. If we can get through this first night, we might just make it okay.'

The sheriff's phone starts ringing, and he leans forward to shake our hands. 'You boys try not to shoot anybody else, okay?'

Ike leads us out to the front steps of the building, where he takes a pack of Kool Menthols from the pocket of his uniform. He offers Kelly one, but Kelly declines. As Ike holds his lighter flame to the tip of his cigarette, his

347

hand trembles, and Kelly shoots me a quick glance.

'You sleep with this boy if you have to,' Ike tells Kelly, exhaling a long stream of smoke. 'He's doing some good, even if he is doing it the hard way.'

Kelly winks at Ike. 'No sweat, Sergeant.'

'How'd you know I was a sergeant?'

'It's like a sign around your neck, brother.'

Ike's laugh is good to hear, but as we move down the steps toward our cars, Kelly leans toward me and says, 'He's speeding like a racehorse, with bourbon underneath. Something's eating him. Bad. None of my business, of course.'

I slap him on the shoulder. 'You say whatever pops into your head, Kelly.'

'Will do.'

Since my mother's computer was destroyed in the fire, I planned to draft my answer to Marston's suit at the offices of the *Examiner*. They occupy an entire building in an old section of downtown, a long one-story structure with inadequate parking.

Even at this late hour the door is open, and we find Caitlin in the newsroom, sitting before a twenty-one-inch monitor, commanding her staff with a cell phone in one hand and a computer trackball in the other. She's dressed in jeans and a teal pinpoint button-down, which gives her the look of a college yearbook editor. She waves when she sees me but continues her phone conversation. The newsroom is forty feet long and twenty wide, with a half dozen computer workstations – all in use – and photos of distinguished Natchezians decorating the walls.

'Who's this?' Caitlin asks, sliding her cell phone into a belt holster as we approach.

'Daniel Kelly. Part of the security from Houston. Kelly, this is Caitlin Masters, fledgling muckraker.'

Caitlin sizes Kelly up as she leads us down a hall, noting his average size and easy demeanor. Falling back beside me, she whispers, '*Is he qualified?*'

Kelly chuckles softly.

'He just saved my life,' I say in a normal voice. 'I'm sold. Have you put tomorrow's issue to bed?'

Her eyes flash with excitement. 'Are you kidding? This town's about to pop.'

She pushes us into a glass-walled conference room screened with venetian blinds for privacy. 'We're pushing back the deadline as far as we can. Two in the morning if we have to.'

'Can you do that?'

'With computers we can reformat the whole paper and go to plate in thirty minutes. There's a rumor that the police are close to an arrest in the Whitestone killing. And we must have gotten a dozen calls about people carrying guns in and out of their houses. They're saying it's just like it was before the riot in sixty-eight.'

'That wasn't much of a riot. Everybody was scared to death, but nobody got killed. Just a bunch of broken store windows.'

'Let's hope that's all that happens this time.'

'I'm glad to hear you say that.'

She gives me an icy look. 'You think I want the town to explode so I can sell papers?'

'No.'

She doesn't look convinced. 'Three hours ago a CNN crew yelled a question at John Portman as he was leaving the Hoover Building. He walked over and told them on camera that the Del Payton case involved matters of national security, and that the FBI was looking into the question of whether you or I had violated any laws in our pursuit of the case.'

'The best defense is a good offense, I guess. Anything else I should know?'

'Leo Marston's attorney gave me a phone interview. He said your charges are ridiculous and they're going to cost both of us seven figures. I'm running it tomorrow.'

'I expected that.'

Caitlin smiles like a child hiding a cookie. 'I also have some good news. My father called back and told me that if I was sticking by my story, there must be something to it. He's going to help.'

'How?'

'By committing the full resources of the media group to investigating Marston and Portman. He's already spoken to Senator Harris from Virginia. Tomorrow, Harris is going to the Senate Intelligence Committee to ask for a special resolution authorizing the opening of the Payton file. Failing that, he'll ask that it be moved from FBI custody to a place where it can't be tampered with, at least until Director Portman's involvement in the case can be clarified. If that doesn't work, he'll stand up on the Senate floor and ask the same things on C-Span.'

I feel the relief of a man trying to push a car uphill when four strong backs join him in his effort. But the feeling vanishes quickly. 'Asking that the file be opened is good. But if he can't get that, it's best that the file stay where it is. At least until Sunday.'

For a moment Caitlin looks confused. Then she grabs my wrist. 'Lutjens is going to try for the file?'

'Sunday.'

'I'll tell my dad to call the senator back.'

'It's nice to have powerful friends.'

Her eyes twinkle with irony. 'Isn't it?'

Kelly laughs. He's not sure what he's gotten into, but he's clearly enjoying it.

'How did Mr. Kelly here save your life?' Caitlin asks.

'He killed two guys who were trying to kill me. One was Arthur Lee Hanratty's brother.'

'Jesus. Did this happen near the river? We heard some kind of call on the scanner, but it was coded.'

'That was it.'

'Can I print this story?'

'Absolutely. The more public this thing gets, the safer we are.'

'We ought to be very safe, then. I'm getting nonstop calls from the major papers, the networks, everybody.'

There's a sharp knock at the door, and Caitlin walks into the hall for a hurried conference. When she returns, her face is flushed pink with excitement. 'The police just trapped the Whitestone suspects in the Concord Apartments. I'm going over to cover the arrest.'

The Concord Apartments are a low-income housing development, and a center of drug and gang activity in Natchez. 'The residents over there aren't big fans of the police,' I warn her. 'They're probably as volatile as old dynamite right now.'

'That's why I'm going. You want to come along?'

'I can't take the time. I've got to file my interrogatories and requests for production along with my answer. That'll keep Marston off balance, make him think I'm ready to go to court on a moment's notice.'

'Speaking of Marston, where's your other friend?'

'My other friend?'

She give me a sidelong glance. She means Livy.

'Oh. I have no idea. With her father, I guess.'

Caitlin obviously wants to say more, but she's unwilling to do so in front of Kelly. 'I've got to get going, guys.'

'Wait. Go with her, Kelly.'

Kelly looks at Caitlin, then back at me. 'I think you're the one who needs protection, boss.'

'I'll have a photographer with me,' she protests. 'I'll be fine.'

'Kelly's worth ten photographers. I'll be here for at least two hours, then I'm going straight back to the motel. He can tell you how he saved my life on the way.'

Caitlin is wavering.

Kelly bends over, lifts a cuff of his jeans, and pulls out a small automatic, which he passes to me. 'Safety's on.'

I slip the gun into my pocket and look at Caitlin. 'Satisfied?'

'Okay, I'll take him. But you go straight to the motel from here. No side trips.'

'I need a computer. And coffee. Lots of coffee.'

'We've got plenty of both.'

Kelly and Caitlin still haven't returned when I leave for the motel. While typing my discovery requests, I overheard enough newsroom conversation to follow the situation unfolding at the Concord Apartments. The two teenagers who allegedly shot Billy Earl Whitestone had holed up in the apartment of their grandmother. Somehow, Caitlin managed to get them on the telephone, and during that conversation one of the boys admitted to the shooting. He claimed he'd shot Whitestone because Ruby Flowers's death had so upset his grandmother that he had to do *something*. He chose Whitestone as his victim because he'd often heard an uncle talk about how Whitestone had run the Klan during the 'bad times.' An hour after this confession, the grandmother talked the boys into giving themselves up, on the condition that Caitlin be allowed to accompany them to the police station to ensure their safety. I assume Caitlin is still at the station now, running the police crazy and keeping Kelly jumping.

Kelly's pistol is on my lap as I drive toward the motel. There's no traffic on the streets, or even the highway. Fear has worked its way into the fabric of the town.

A police car screams out of the empty darkness, siren blaring, going in the opposite direction. Halfway to the motel, a jacked-up pickup filled with white teenagers roars alongside me, pauses as its occupants peer in at me, then roars off again. Night riders looking for a fight? Or kids trying to figure out what all the excitement's about? I won't know until I read tomorrow's paper.

The single-story buildings of the Prentiss Motel remind me of the motor courts of my childhood vacations. But viewed without the kaleidoscopic lens of wonder, they are a mean and depressing sight. The thought of my parents forced to live here because of my actions is hard to bear. Yet they have not uttered one word of complaint since the fire, not even my mother, who urged me to avoid the Payton case from the beginning. Now that events have proved her right, what is she doing? Making the best of things. I feel like dragging some realtor out of bed and buying her the biggest goddamn house in the city.

Orienting myself by the greenish glow of the swimming pool, I park and start walking toward our rooms with Kelly's gun held along my leg. Halfway there, I feel a sudden chill.

There's someone sitting in one of the pool chairs. Fifty feet away, a dark silhouette against the wavering light of the water. As I walk down the long row of doors, the figure rises from the chair. I put my finger on the trigger of the pistol and quicken my steps.

'Penn?'

The voice stops me cold. It's Livy.

I slip Kelly's gun into my waistband and jog toward the pool fence. Livy opens the gate and waits just beyond it. She's wearing a strapless white evening dress that looks strangely formal beside the deserted swimming pool. The moonlight falls lustrous upon her shoulders but is somehow lost in her eyes, which look more gray than blue tonight.

'What are you doing here? What's the matter?'

'I wanted to see you,' she says. 'That's all. I had to see you.'

'Is everything all right?'

'That depends on what you mean by all right. Things are a bit tense at our house. More than a bit, really. But I'm sure your house was like that when my father went after yours.'

She has no idea how bad things got at our house during the year leading up to that trial. But soon she might. Before she can say anything else, I ask what I've been wanting to ask since I saw her at the airport in Baton Rouge.

'Livy, a few nights ago, at a party . . . your mother threw a drink in my face.'

'She *what*?'

'She told me I'd ruined your life.'

Livy's expression does not change. She holds her eyes on mine, attentive as a spectator at the opera. But I sense that she's expending tremendous effort to maintain this illusion of normalcy.

'What was she talking about?' I ask.

'I have no idea.' She looks away from me. 'Mom probably doesn't either. She's a hairbreadth from the DTs by five o'clock every day. Daddy's talking about sending her to Betty Ford.'

'She was referring to something specific. I saw her eyes.'

Livy turns and peers into the cloudy water. 'My divorce has upset her quite a bit. Divorce isn't part of the fairy tale. If it were, she'd have left my father long ago.'

'I thought you were only separated.'

'Pending divorce, then. It's just semantics.' She looks at me over her bare shoulder, an injured look in her eyes. 'You think I'd ask you to make love to me if there was a chance my husband and I would get back together?'

This is one of those moments where we make a heaven or

hell of the future, by choosing honesty or deception. 'I don't know. You weren't that discriminating in the past.'

She flinches, but she can endure much worse than this. 'The past, the past,' she says. 'The damned sacred past. Can't we try living in the present for once?'

'Yesterday was the only free ride we're going to get.'

She looks back into the depths of the pool. 'I have a room,' she says in a deliberate voice. 'It's two doors down from yours. Why don't we talk there?'

A room. Part of me wants to slap her for assuming so much. I move sideways so that I can see her face. 'Will you really talk?'

She pulls her hair back into a thick ponytail, as though to feel the breeze on her neck. Her collarbones are sculpted ivory, creating shadowy hollows at the base of her throat.

'About what?'

'About what? Everything. Why you did what you did twenty years ago.'

'What do you mean?'

This is Kafkaesque. Can she really have edited the past so completely that she no longer remembers how badly she betrayed our dreams? 'Why you disappeared for a year. Where you went. Why you ran off to Virginia. Why you treated me like a stranger when I flew up to ask you to get your father to drop the suit.'

She turns to me and lets her hair fall, and whatever mask she was maintaining falls with it. She looks more vulnerable than I have ever seen her, and when she speaks, her voice is stripped of all effect. 'Penn, I can't do it.'

'Livy, if I understood some of those things, I might . . . well – things might not have to happen the way they are.'

'What do you mean? If I answer your questions, you'll withdraw the charges you made against my father?'

I don't know what I mean. I started into the Del Payton case to destroy Leo Marston, but compared to understanding

the mysteries that shaped my life, revenge seems meaningless. Of course, there is still Del Payton. And Althea. And the
small matter of justice—

'I can't pull out of the Payton case now. It's too late for that.
But I can pursue it a different way. If your father's part was
only—'

'Stop,' she says, shaking her head. 'I can't talk about twenty
years ago. Not even to make things easier on my father.'

She takes a step toward me. I want her to stay back,
because the closer she gets, the more I want to go to her room
with her. She is achingly beautiful in the moonlight.

'How did I ruin your life?' I ask.

She shakes her head, absolving me of any possible sin.
'You didn't.' Another step. 'But you can save it.'

'Livy, listen—'

'Come with me,' she pleads. 'Right now.'

If she had kissed me then, I would have walked away. But
she didn't. She picked up her purse from the pool chair, took
my hand, and led me across the parking lot toward the motel,
a purposeful urgency in her stride.

The déjà vu of walking beside the numbered doors is
powerful enough to dislocate time. If I were to close my eyes
and open them again, I would see the eighteen-thousand-
dollar gown flowing behind her like a trail of mist. The
lifetimes of water that have passed under the bridge since that
night have all flowed back in a span of moments.

When she opens the door and closes us inside, I pull her
to me and kiss her with the thirst of a binge drinker returning
to the bottle. My questions fade to dying sparks, made irrelevant by the absolute connection of our lips and hands. I
don't even know I am backing her toward the door until she
collides with it, the unyielding wooden face holding her as I
continue forward, pressing against her, my hands groping at
her dress, searching for the hem.

'That's right,' she says hoarsely. 'That's right . . . that's—'

The moment my hand finds her sex, she is breathing like a sprinter in the last few yards of a race. She kisses me with almost desperate passion, then pushes down the front of the strapless dress and pulls my mouth to a breast. In seconds both her arms are outstretched, fingers splayed and quivering, discharging the frantic energy pouring from her core. Touching her this way is rapture, at once within her and without, needing no other thing, no friend, no thought—

The knock at the door reverberates through our bodies, stunning us from our trance. Yet still Livy presses herself down against my hand, unwilling to let the world back in. I jerk her away from the door and onto the bed, fearing someone might shoot through the thin metal.

The knocking comes again. This time, with the distance to the bed and with half my faculties restored, it sounds reasonably discreet.

'Who is it?' I call, digging in my pocket for Kelly's gun, hating the ragged edge of fear in my voice.

'Kelly.'

Relief cascades through me. I turn to tell Livy everything's all right and find her standing with both hands pointed rigidly at the door, a pistol clenched between them. She must have taken it from her purse.

'Whoa!' I say, holding up my hands. 'I know this guy. He's with me.'

She lowers the gun slowly, as though unsure whether to trust my judgement. I turn back to the door and open it a crack.

Daniel Kelly's sandy blond head leans toward mine.

'I saw you go in here as I pulled up. I just wanted you to know I'm back.'

I nod. 'I heard about what happened at the apartments. You must be tired. You can go ahead and get some sleep.'

'I'm fine. Wired, really.'

I hesitate to ask the next question, but I want to know. 'Is Caitlin with you?'

An ironic smile, there and gone. 'She's back at the paper, writing the story. She's a tough lady, man.'

Coming from Daniel Kelly, this is high praise indeed. 'Thanks for looking out for her. And thanks again for the levee thing.'

He nods, but there's a curious hesitancy in his face.

'What is it, Kelly?'

'Well, I thought maybe you and Caitlin were . . . you know.' He looks past me, through the crack in the door. 'I guess not, huh?'

'I guess not,' I reply, feeling hollowness in my chest.

He makes a clicking sound with his tongue. 'I'm gonna get some eggs over at Shoney's. One of the other guys'll be watching this door.'

'Thanks.'

'Oh, and your little girl is fine. No worries.'

His words hit me like a blow. Maybe he meant for them to. My cheeks burn with self-disgust.

''Night, boss,' he says, and disappears from the crack.

I shut the door and bolt it.

Livy is sitting on the bed, her face composed, the gun nowhere in evidence. Only her tousled hair hints at our brief encounter at the door.

'Why are you carrying a gun?'

She shrugs. 'The town's gone crazy, hasn't it? And Daddy insisted.'

Leo would.

Livy's shoes, hose, and panties lie on the floor beside her bare feet. She looks at me like she can't understand why I'm still standing where I am. Like what happened against the door was the opening movement of a symphony.

I glance at my watch. Twelve-twenty. Annie is almost certainly asleep, but Kelly's words have left me with a guilty longing, like an unresolved chord. I need to see my daughter sleeping.

'I need to check on Annie.'

Livy stands and takes my hand, pulls me toward her. 'I know.'

'I mean it.'

'I know.' She puts her arm around my waist and pulls me against her.

'Livy—'

She kisses my nipple through my shirt. The sharp edges of her teeth pull at flesh and wet cloth, sending a delicious current of pain through me.

'It'll only take a minute,' I tell her. 'I'll be right—'

With three or four quick movements she unbuckles my pants and pushes them far enough down to free me, then entwines her fingers behind my neck. When I try to speak, she takes my right hand and lifts it to my mouth, cutting off my words. Her scent on my fingers is overpowering.

'Me first,' she whispers.

Even as I despise myself for it, in one violent motion I reach beneath her dress, lift her into the air, and set her down upon me.

Chapter 29

I am parked in the alley between Wall and Pearl Streets, the legal center of the city. It's nearly dark and raining steadily, a drizzle with a breath of fall in it. The courthouse towers above me on its pedestal of earth, grayish-white and imposing amid the windblown oaks that surround it. Across the street, running down the block in a line, stand the offices of various law firms, all of them small, most very profitable. The most prestigious among them is Marston, Sims. Founded in 1887 by Ambrose Marston, Leo's great grandfather, the firm has handled everything from high-profile criminal cases to corporate litigation involving tens of millions of dollars. And I am parked in this alley to see whether the senior partner of the firm will commit a felony tonight.

I filed my requests for production this morning, and if Leo plans to hide or destroy any documentary evidence, the sooner he does it the better, at least from his point of view. I would like to be there when he tries. I've staked out his office because Tuscany – his fenced estate – does not lend itself to surveillance, Daniel Kelly is covering the back entrance for me, and we're in contact via handheld radios, which were among the toys he and his associates brought from Houston. Also among those toys was a Hi-8 video camera with a night-vision lens, which rests on the seat beside me. The rear entrance of the office is well lighted by a security lamp, so Kelly is using a standard camcorder borrowed from Caitlin

Masters. The pistol he lent me last night lies on the seat beside the Hi-8 camera, its safety off.

'*One-Adam-twelve, one-Adam-twelve.*' Kelly's voice crackles out of the radio. '*Sitrep, please.*'

I laugh and press Send on my walkie-talkie. 'Nothing out here but rain.'

'It's like fishing. That's what my butt's telling me, anyway.'

'Yeah. Maybe we'll catch something.'

As I set the radio back on the passenger seat, something bangs against my window, nearly stopping my heart. I grab for the gun, knowing I'll never bring it up in time to save myself if the person outside the car means me harm.

When my eyes focus through the rivulets of water on the window, I see Caitlin Masters, her hair soaked from the rain. I let out my breath with a sigh of relief and motion for her to come around to the passenger side.

'I'm glad I wasn't trying to kill you,' she says, sliding into the passenger seat. 'You'd be dead.'

She's wearing a windbreaker with *Los Angeles Times* stenciled on the chest. From the pocket she takes a barrette and puts the end in her mouth, then flips down the visor mirror above her seat. 'Nothing yet?' she asks through her teeth.

'Nope.'

She gathers her fine black hair and pins it in a loose bun behind her head. 'There. I should have done that before I left.'

She turns and gives me a dazzling smile. 'Well, are you up on the day's events?'

'I'm up on *my* events. The rest of the world I know nothing about.'

'Four TV vans covered the Whitestone suspects' walk to their arraignment. Jackson, Baton Rouge, Alexandria, and a Gulf Coast station. The courthouse looked like it was under siege. The wire services picked up all three of my stories, and they're being rerun in dozens of papers.'

'That Pulitzer's getting closer every day. Which judge did the kids get?' Natchez has two criminal court judges, a white woman and a black man.

'The black one. And he gave them bail.'

'On first-degree murder?'

'With a confession, no less. He set it at a million apiece, which is like a billion to those kids' families. But I heard the NAACP may put up the cash bond. Two hundred thousand.'

'They might as well paint targets on the kids' backs.'

Caitlin picks up the video camera, switches it on, and trains it on the polished mahogany door of Marston, Sims. It's set deep in a deep brick alcove; a brass plate on the street announces the presence of the office to the public.

'Night vision,' she murmurs. 'Nice. Where's Kelly?'

'Watching the back door.'

She zooms in on the door, then pans the rain-slickened street. 'How much are those bodyguards costing you?'

'Let's just say I'm going to have to hurry up and finish another book.'

She laughs. 'It's money well spent. That Kelly's been all over and done some wild things. He's cute too.'

An irrational prick of jealousy irritates me. 'I wouldn't know about that.'

'Don't get all homophobic on me.' She pokes my knee as she scans the street. 'Well . . . here comes a familiar face.'

'Where?' I turn the ignition key and flip on the windshield wipers.

'Our side of the street.'

Now I see. A woman is jogging up the sidewalk in tight lycra warm-up pants and a TULANE T-shirt.

'It's the waitress with the crush on you,' says Caitlin.

'Jenny?' I lean forward and watch the dark-haired young woman approaching through the rain. It is Jenny. 'Give me a break.'

'I mean it. That chick is fixated on you.'

Jenny jogs past the car at a good clip, not paying us the slightest bit of attention. The rain has soaked her T-shirt, leaving absolutely nothing to the imagination.

'She ought to wear a sign,' Caitlin says drily. 'Please stare at my tits.'

'I'm surprised you'd comment, after the blouse you wore the day you interviewed me.'

Caitlin takes her eye away from the viewfinder and gives me an elfin smile. 'That was different. I was trying to distract you.'

'It worked.'

'It always does. I'm really rather modest.'

'Modesty isn't what comes to mind when I think of you.'

Her smile changes subtly. 'You don't really know me very well, do you?'

She reaches over and switches off the engine, killing the windshield wipers. 'Any word on when Ruby Flowers's funeral will take place?'

Her quick segues are hard for me to follow. 'Mose – Mr. Flowers – is thinking of Sunday, but that's not set in stone.'

'Sunday? But that's . . . five days after she died.'

'That's how the blacks do it. Haven't you read your own paper's obituary column?'

'Why do they wait so long?'

'Well, they usually have to wait days for relatives who live up North to get back to Mississippi. Sometimes they have to ride the bus. Ruby has two sons in Detroit, a daughter in Chicago, and another boy in Los Angeles.'

'Can't you fly them in?'

'I'll do anything Mr. Flowers asks me to do, but he hasn't asked. My father already bought Ruby's coffin and head-stone, which probably cost more than the church the funeral will be held in. Personally, I think he overdid it. Ruby never wanted to stand out from her own people in life, and I don't think she'd want to in death. Why do you care when the funeral is, anyway?'

'I hate to be the bearer of bad tidings, Penn, but Ruby's funeral is going to be the epicenter of a media hurricane.'

'What?'

'Shad Johnson is going to speak, and there are bound to be TV trucks there–'

'Damn it, that's all wrong.'

'You should thank God for small miracles. Al Sharpton called Shad this morning and offered to come down and "help out with the Movement." Shad told him to stay in New York.'

Even as I say a silent thank-you to Shadrach Johnson, bitter gall rises into my throat.

'Take it easy,' Caitlin says, touching my arm. 'Tell me what you did today.'

'What I did? It's isn't what I did. It's what the judge did.'

'Which judge?'

'The white one. Franklin. Two hours ago she set our trial date.'

Caitlin goes still. '*Our* trial date? The libel trial?'

'Just my part of it. You don't have to worry. But my slander trial is set for next Wednesday.'

'Next *Wednesday*? That's only' – she counts swiftly on her fingers – 'six days from now!'

'Yep.'

'That's ridiculous.'

'I expected a quick trial date, but I thought I'd get at least a month. Simply going through the materials I've requested under discovery could take a month.'

'How can the judge set a date like that?'

'Easily. She's in Marston's pocket. Why do you think he picked her?'

'Picked her? I thought they assigned judges by drawing lots or something.'

'In this district they match cases to judges by simple rotation. Theoretically, whichever judge's name is up when a suit is filed gets that case. But all the clerk has to do to steer a case to a particular judge is hold on to it until that judge's turn comes up. One phone call from Marston to the clerk would do it.'

'How do you know he has Franklin in his pocket? Maybe he just has the clerk.'

'I talked to a local lawyer I went to school with. Marston was the heavy hand in getting Franklin elected. Big contributions, an endorsement, words in the right ears. That was eight years ago, but she won't have forgotten who put her on the bench.'

'But how can she possibly defend that trial date? No one could build a defense that fast.'

'In my answer to Marston's complaint, I stated that my defense would be truth. Truth is the oldest defense against a slander charge. By definition, truth cannot be slanderous. If Franklin is challenged about the trial date, she'll say, "The defendant doesn't dispute that he uttered the alleged slander. He claims that his statements are true. Therefore, let him prove that without delay Leo Marston's reputation should not suffer any more than it already has while Mr. Cage goes on a fishing expedition." She can also cite the racial violence in the community resulting from my charges.'

Caitlin is shaking her head. 'Shit. You're in a deep hole.'

'Will you help me wade through the materials I've requested in discovery?'

'Absolutely. I'll get my reporters and interns going through the stuff as soon as you get it.'

She digs into her windbreaker pocket, pulls out a Snickers bar, and tears open the wrapper. After two bites she freezes and looks guiltily at me.

'Sorry.' She offers me what's left.

'That's okay. You eat it.'

'Come on. It's not like we haven't already exchanged germs. Though that seems quite a while ago.'

I take it from her hand. 'Thanks. I haven't eaten for hours.'

The chocolate seems to be absorbed directly through the lining of my mouth, giving me an instant sugar buzz.

'Stakeouts are the worst,' Caitlin grumbles. She glances toward the law office, then looks back at me. 'Was your wife from a wealthy family?'

'Sarah? No. Why?'

'Well . . . Livy Marston is from a wealthy family.'

'So?'

'And *I'm* from a wealthy family. And I felt that you were attracted to me. Until Livy showed up, anyway. I just wondered if something about that background draws you in some way.'

'No. Sarah's father was a carpenter. That's probably how she stood the years when I was an assistant D.A. When we got rich, she wasn't sure how to react. At first she insisted that I put every penny in the bank, not spend any of it. Save it for the kids. But after my third book hit the list, she loosened up. When we bought our house in Tanglewood, she thought she'd died and gone to heaven.'

Caitlin is watching me with a strange intensity. I reach out and touch her wrist. 'Hey. I'm still attracted to you.'

She looks vulnerable, yet ready to withstand a hard truth. 'But you're sleeping with Livy Marston. Right?'

I know it's a mistake to look away, but I can't meet her eyes in this moment. 'Did Kelly tell you that?'

'No. I just felt it. I shouldn't say anything about it. I don't have any right to. But I care about you. And Livy is just trying to keep you from hurting her father.'

'She hasn't asked me to do anything like that. You don't really know her. In some ways she hates her father.'

'Some ways. But not all.' Caitlin's eyes hold wisdom far

beyond her years. 'And she's too smart to be overt. Maybe she just wants to distract you. Maybe she doesn't even admit her real motives to herself. But that's what she's doing. Protecting her father.'

'Message received, okay?'

'May I ask one more question?'

'All right.'

'Did your wife like her?'

A hollow feeling spreads from the pit of my stomach. 'No.'

Caitlin looks away as though embarrassed by forcing me to admit this. I am about to speak when she grabs the video camera, zooms in on the office door, and begins recording.

'What is it?'

'The object of your obsession is parking in front of her father's office.'

Peering through the rain, I see a silver Lincoln Town Car parked in front of Marston, Sims. A woman with shoulder-length hair sits behind the wheel. She could be Livy, but I'm not sure. Until she gets out. She walks briskly through the rain to the mahogany door, her regal carriage as distinctive as a fingerprint.

After Livy unlocks the door, Leo's huge frame emerges from the passenger door of the Town Car, his close-cropped hair gleaming silver under the light of the street lamp.

'What the hell are they doing?' Caitlin whispers.

'Let's wait and see.'

Livy holds the door open for Leo, scanning the dark street as she waits. I want to believe the best of her, but even from this distance her eyes look full of purpose. She lays a hand on Leo's shoulder as he passes through the door, then takes one more look up the street, seeing us but not seeing. I am suddenly back in the motel room last night, being led through a carnal labyrinth with Livy as my guide, dissolving and reforming inside her until I lay inert, my mouth dry as sand, my skin too sore to touch–

'*Shit*,' Caitlin hisses. 'We can't see anything now. We should call Judge Franklin.'

'Calm down. They could be doing legitimate work. Preparing his case. Livy is an attorney, you know.'

'I'll bet they're shredding the files you asked for right this minute.'

'Let's just sit tight, okay? See what happens.'

The seconds pass in tense silence, with Caitlin taping the door the entire time. My walkie-talkie crackles from the edge of Caitlin's seat.

'I've got lights in the building,' Kelly says.

'We've got visitors. We're not sure what they're up to. Just stay put.'

'I'm here if you need me.'

Suddenly the mahogany door opens, and Leo backs out of the alcove with two large file boxes in his arms.

'Would you look at that?' Caitlin breathes. 'The son of a bitch *is* guilty.'

'Is the time-date stamp working?'

'I think so. It's displayed in the viewfinder.'

As Leo loads his boxes into the backseat of the Town Car, Livy emerges from the office carrying another one.

'She's helping him!' Caitlin cries. 'You've got to call the judge.'

'We don't know what's in the boxes. They could be using those records to prepare Leo's case.'

She shakes her head with manic exasperation as Leo returns with another box. Livy soon does the same, and one more trip by Leo makes six. Livy locks the door behind them.

Caitlin takes her cell phone from the holster on her belt and shoves it at me. I push it back at her.

'No. Let's see where they're going first.'

'Jesus. She's got you wrapped around her little finger.'

'Enough!'

I start the car and wait for Livy to pull out.

'What about Kelly?' Caitlin asks.

I pick up the walkie-talkie and press Send. 'I'm following Livy Marston, Kelly. You keep watching the back. I'll call if I need you.' I drop the radio on the floor and glance at Caitlin. 'Less for them to notice.'

I stay several car lengths behind the Town Car, but I needn't have worried. Livy drives straight to Tuscany. The mansion is set far back from the road, with eight acres of trees shielding it from sight and sound of passing traffic. A motorized gate closes after the Lincoln passes through, leaving us locked outside.

Livy jumps out of the car even before I've stopped, video camera in hand. I shut off the engine and follow her, which requires some fast footwork, as she has already scaled the gate and run on by the time I reach it. My feet crunch on the wet pea gravel as I race after her up the long, curving drive.

Tuscany was built in 1850 by a retired English general who imported the Italianate craze to Natchez from London. Three stories tall, the mansion is a splendor of northern Italian design, with an entrance tower, front and side galleries, marble corner quoins, huge roundheaded windows with marble hood moldings, and balustrade balconies on the second floor. Yet despite its grandeur, the overall effect of this transplanted villa is surprisingly tasteful.

The great door of the mansion closes just as Caitlin and I come within sight of it. From where we stand – beneath a dripping oak with a trunk as thick as ten men – Tuscany looks like an epic film set, floodlit, surrounded by trimmed hedges, azaleas, moss-hung Southern hardwoods, and luxurious magnolias. The broad, waxy leaves of the magnolias glisten with beads of rainwater.

'Do you know your way around the house?' Caitlin whispers.

'I used to.'

'I'll bet. Come on.'

She starts toward the house in a running crouch. Soon our faces are pressed to the panes of a ten-foot-tall window, with spiky hedges pricking our backs. The window glass is more than a century old, full of waves and imperfections, but Caitlin is videotaping through it anyway. Through the distorting medium I see Leo Marston standing before an enormous marble fireplace. Above the fireplace is a portrait of Livy as a teenager, or perhaps Maude. Leo bends, obscuring part of the fireplace, then straightens up and puts his hands on his hips. Beyond his knees, yellow flames billow up from a gas jet.

'He's building a fire,' Caitlin says in a tone of disbelief. 'It's seventy-five degrees and he's building an effing fire.'

My last resistance crumbles. 'Give me your cell phone.'

I call directory assistance for Judge's Franklin's number, then let the computer connect me. The judge herself answers, and it sounds like cocktail hour at her house.

'Penn *Cage*, Judge Franklin. The lawyer Leo Marston is suing for slander.'

'Oh. Why are you calling me at home?'

Leo lifts one of the file boxes and sets it squarely on the andirons. The flames lick their way up the sides of the cardboard, burning it black.

'Judge, at this moment I am watching Leo Marston destroy what I believe is the evidence I requested today in my requests for production.'

A stunned pause. 'Is he in the room with you?'

'No, ma'am. A few minutes ago I observed him removing file boxes from his office in a surreptitious manner. I followed him home, and I am now watching him burn those file boxes in his fireplace. Watching through a window.'

'You mean you're trespassing on his property?'

'Is that really the point, Judge?'

I hear the clink of ice against glass, a hurried swallow.

'Judge, I have the publisher of the Natchez *Examiner* with me, and the events I described are all on videotape. She's taping right this minute.'

'Christ on a crutch. What do you want me to do, counselor?'

'Call the police and have them come straight to Marston's house and confiscate those files. And I'd like you to come with them. You might just prevent bloodshed.'

'I'll do it, Mr. Cage. But you get your tail off Leo Marston's property right this minute, before he puts a load of rock salt in your butt. Or worse.'

'Yes, ma'am.'

I click End and touch Caitlin's arm. 'She's sending the police.'

'They won't make it in time. The gate's closed, and they won't be able to get through.'

'What do you want to do?'

'Make Marston *want* them to get here.'

She pulls free of my grip and bulls her way through the hedge. Seconds later, the sound of shattering glass reverberates across the floodlit lawn.

Leo goes rigid before the fireplace, his ears pricked. Caitlin's rock smashed the window of another room, and he is unsure of what he heard.

Then another hundred-fifty-year-old pane smashes, this one less than ten feet from Marston. He stares at the broken window, looks back at the fireplace, then hurries out of the room.

Caitlin is standing in the drive like a pitcher on the mound, right arm cocked, a rock in her hand. She may not know what Leo is going after, but I do. And from the gallery Marston could pick her off firing from the waist.

I charge through the prickly hedge and run onto the lawn. 'Get your ass under cover!'

Her cocked arm fires, and another pane shatters into irreparable shards. I spring the last few yards and grab her arm, dragging her toward a thicket of azaleas. Just as we plow into the bushes, the front door of Tuscany crashes open and Leo bellows into the night:

'*Where are you, you gutless sons of bitches? Come out and fight like goddamn men!*'

I have to give him credit. At this moment most Natchezians are huddled in their houses, terrified of a race war. For all Leo knows, a gang of crazed rioters smashed his windows and is now waiting to pick him off from the bushes. Yet there he stands, shotgun in hand, defending his castle like Horatius at the bridge. He shouts twice more, then fires blindly into the night. I cover Caitlin with my body as the shotgun booms through the trees like a cannon. After five shots Leo shouts a final curse, then goes back inside, slamming the door behind him.

God only knows what Maude and Livy are thinking. Surely one of them must have called the police and opened the gate by now.

'*Get off,*' Caitlin groans from beneath me. '*I can't breathe.*'

I roll off and scrabble to my knees in the azaleas.

She smiles up at me, breathing fast and shallow. 'That wasn't exactly how I've pictured us getting horizontal together.'

'Me either.'

The smile vanishes. 'Marston can still burn those files before the cops get here.'

'There's nothing we can do to stop him.'

'Give me your gun.'

'No way, no how. You're a menace.'

She sighs in frustration and rolls over to watch the mansion while we wait for the police.

Before long, three uniformed cops come racing up the driveway on foot. They rap on the great door, which Leo answers shouting at full volume, condemning the police department as a useless bunch of fools and high school dropouts. From their body language, the responding officers do not appear to be reacting favourably to his words. As he continues his tirade, two squad cars roar up the drive and stop before the front steps, which are bookended by Negro lawn jockey hitching posts. A black patrolman gets out of the first cruiser and opens his passenger door.

Circuit Judge Eunice B. Franklin emerges, looking like hell warmed over. She's wearing boxy blue jeans, an Ole Miss sweatshirt, hair curlers tied beneath a blue scarf, and she looks pissed. I pull Caitlin to her feet and hurry toward the gallery. When we arrive, Leo is lambasting Judge Franklin in the same superior tone he used with the police. Franklin seems to be enduring it with remarkable equanimity.

When Leo recognizes me standing behind the judge, his face flushes bright red. There's murder in his eyes, and everyone on the gallery sees it.

'Did you smash my windows, Cage?' he yells.

'Don't say anything, counselor,' Judge Franklin orders me. She turns back to Marston. 'Leo, the issue tonight is files. Did you remove any files from your office tonight and attempt to burn them?'

At last comprehension dawns in Marston's eyes. 'Did that bastard tell you that?'

Caitlin aims the video camera at Leo's face. 'I have it all on tape, Judge Franklin. You can watch it right now, if you'd like.'

Franklin looks back at Marston. 'You want to rethink your answer, Leo?'

Marston draws himself up like a feudal lord being forced by a priest to deal civilly with serfs. 'I brought some files home from my office. Old junk. Tax records, bad-debt files.'

Franklin nods patiently, but her jaw is set. 'Then you won't mind if these officers take them down to my chambers for safekeeping. I'm sure this is all a misunderstanding, but it'll save you the trouble of hauling away the ashes.'

Leo blocks the door with his considerable bulk, his arms outstretched from post to post. 'Eunice, I think you and I should have a private word.'

Franklin glances at the video camera. 'Turn that off, Ms. Masters.'

'I'm sorry, Judge, but the First Amendment of the Constitution guarantees my right to do what I am doing now.'

Judges do not react well to defiance. Eunice Franklin reddens a shade, and for a moment I fear she is about to order Caitlin's arrest. To my surprise, she turns to Marston and says, 'Clear that door, Leo.'

Marston's hard blue eyes lock onto Franklin's. 'Eunice, you'd better think about what—'

'Officer Washington,' she cuts in, 'go in there and confiscate whatever files you find. Take them straight to my chambers.'

Two cops push past Marston, whose only choices are to stand aside or defy the orders of a judge by assaulting police officers. He stands aside, his face red with fury. Eunice Franklin will pay a heavy price for this, but my sympathy is limited. Dilemmas like these are the price of backroom politics. With a final savage glare in my direction, Marston stomps back into the dark reaches of his mansion.

Judge Franklin pokes me in the chest, her eyes cold. 'I want you in my chambers at nine a.m., mister.' She points to Caitlin. 'I want that videotape there as well.'

'Will Marston be there?' I ask.

'That's not your concern.'

'Destroying evidence is a felony, Judge.'

Franklin's lips tighten until all I can see is the spiderwork of lines around her mouth, the result of years of smoking cigarettes. As we stare at each other, a patrolwoman carries a charred box of files through the front door.

'Go home, Mr Cage,' orders Judge Franklin. 'And you will pay restitution for any physical damage to this property.'

I am about to follow her advice when Livy walks through the front door of Tuscany. In a voice that could shave a peach, she says, 'Judge, my name is Livy Marston Sutter. I'm here as counsel for my father, Leo Marston. Those boxes contain files of Marston, Sims clients, and thus enjoy the protection of attorney–client privilege.'

Judge Franklin is momentarily taken aback, but she recovers quickly. 'They'll be as safe in my chambers as they will anywhere.'

Livy looks past her to me. 'Penn? Would you please tell me what's going on here?'

I stand mute before her. Tonight's events have cast us as enemies, but even at this awkward moment part of me remains inside her, linking us in the most primitive way.

'You tell me, Livy.'

'Who broke our windows?'

'I did,' Caitlin says, as though she would welcome another lawsuit.

Livy gives her a glance of disdain. 'What's Lois Lane doing here?'

Caitlin holds up the video camera. 'Making home movies, sweet cheeks. I don't think you're going to like them.'

'That's it,' says Franklin. 'Get out of here, both of you. Go back inside, Ms. Sutter.'

'Your father was trying to destroy evidence, Livy. I couldn't let that happen.'

'Evidence? You mean those old tax records? Daddy told me the day I got back that he needed to clean out his old files. I helped him because of his bad back.'

Is she really trying to convince me that her motives are pure? Or is she using my presence as an opportunity to try to mitigate her culpability in the presence of Judge Franklin?

'I said this meeting is over,' snaps Franklin.

I take Caitlin's arm above the elbow and lead her away from the house. Soon we're in darkness, surrounded by the smells of wet grass and decaying leaves. The pulse in her brachial artery is pounding like a tom-tom.

'What do you think?' she asks.

Instead of answering, I turn back and gaze through the dripping trees at Tuscany. What was once a temple of memory is now alien to me. The gallery that once hosted so many lawn parties now creaks under the tramp of police boots, and the sweet air of the grounds carries the tang of gunpowder. After five generations of seclusion, the world outside the gates has crashed through to Tuscany with a vengeance.

My gaze drifts upward, to the third floor, where a solitary light glows in a high window. Framed in that window is an amorphous shape that confuses me at first, but at last resolves into something human. It's the harridan head of Maude Marston, once a celebrated beauty, now a wreck, ravaged by emotional pain and by the alcohol she uses to blunt it. As Caitlin takes my arm and pulls me along the drive, I remember Dwight Stone's penchant for quotes, and I think, *What havoc hath he wrought in this great house?*

Chapter 30

The two days after Judge Marston's attempt to destroy the files pass in a blur of work that reminds me what it is to be a working lawyer. At nine o'clock Friday morning, Judge Franklin and I agree to an unconventional compromise worthy of Solomon. Without giving reasons, she makes it clear that she prefers not to charge Leo with obstruction of justice or contempt of court. Before I can argue this point, she tells me she considered recusing herself from the case but rejected the idea because Marston played as big a part in getting the black circuit judge elected as he did Judge Franklin. We both know I can go to the judicial oversight committee to plead for relief, but I sense that Eunice Franklin intends to offer me something.

What she offers is the boxes Marston tried to destroy, one of which contains three legal files, as Livy indicated. Marston's blatant attempt to destroy them has convinced Judge Franklin that he was attempting to hide evidence of criminal activity. She feels that a case can be made to the court of appeal that Marston's act justifies giving me access to these records. Moreover, Leo himself has agreed to this arrangement rather than be charged with obstruction or contempt. This tells me that the files, while probably damaging to Marston's reputation, will not contain proof of complicity in Del Payton's murder.

This agreement accomplished, the judge and I spend a few minutes getting to know each other. Eunice Franklin is fifty-six years old, and graduated from the Ole Miss Law School a year before Del Payton was killed. I can only imagine what she must have endured during her three years at that temple of Southern male traditionalism. She is a bit defensive about her court, and my 'big-time' experience in Houston seems to be the cause of this. She warns me that she will run her courtroom with at least as much discipline I am accustomed to in 'the big city,' and perhaps more. She will tolerate no antics or theatrics, either from myself or from Marston's attorney.

Leo will be represented by Blake Sims, the son of Creswell Sims, his partner of forty years. Judge Franklin has already instructed Sims that, considering the early trial date his client requested and got, they should have all discovery materials in my hands by the close of the business day.

She expresses strong misgivings about my intention to represent myself at trial, but says she cannot stop me from sabotaging my case if that is my intent. She defends the trial date along the lines I predicted to Caitlin, and adds that the recent racial tensions and violence played a part in her decision. With the mayoral election only four weeks away, she wants my inflammatory statements about the Payton murder resolved and hopefully forgotten by the time the voters walk into the polling booths on November 3.

Leaving her chambers, I feel a little better about the situation than I did walking in. Judge Franklin owes Marston some favors, but Leo's attempt to destroy evidence has made her angry. Under the blaze of scrutiny this trial will draw, Eunice may stiffen her backbone and run a relatively impartial court.

The media frenzy is already underway. Tying men like John Portman and Leo Marston to a dead black man is like waving a red cape in front of a herd of bulls. Twenty-four hours after my accusations hit the paper, Mississippi resumed its role as whipping boy for the nation on race.

Celebrated authors and academics weighed in with windy and self-righteous op-ed pieces in every major paper from New York to Los Angeles. At the close of last night's newscast, a somber-faced Dan Rather recalled his days covering civil rights in Mississippi. Black media stars roundly condemned the state, speaking as though the lynchings of the distant past were still daily occurrences.

Contrary opinions were few, and the battle was becoming embarrassingly one-sided until this morning, when into the fray charged my old friend Sam Jacobs, the self-styled Mississippi Jew, who in a half-humorous letter to the *New York Times* pointed out that while Mississippi might seem behind the times to outsiders, it actually had its collective finger on the pulse of America. The Magnolia State, Sam opined, had given the world William Faulkner, Elvis Presley, and Tennessee Williams. And while this holy trinity of American culture ought to be enough for anybody, for skeptics there were also Robert Johnson, Richard Wright, Jimmy Rodgers, and Muddy Waters; Leontyne Price, Charley Pride, Tammy Wynette, and John Grisham; Howlin' Wolf, B.B. King, four Miss Americas, and Oprah Winfrey. And while boneheaded nuisances like the Ku Klux Klan had committed atrocities to shame the South Africans, and slavery had come near to breaking an entire people, you couldn't by God refine gold without a fire. The state of Israel was created from the ashes of the Holocaust, and Mississippi was on its way to redemption. Why, the legacy of blues music alone, declared Sam, which was jazz and rock 'n' roll, had done more to end the Cold War than all the thin-blooded diplomats ever minted at Harvard and Yale.

How the *Times* selected Sam's letter I'll never know, but it prompted my editor to telephone and read it aloud to me over breakfast, claiming that the list of artists only bolstered his theory that great suffering produces great art, and since I'd had my share of the former, I should now move north to more civilized environs. I declared myself a loyal Southerner to the last and headed out for Judge Franklin's office. I forgot the article during our conference, but after I loaded Marston's charred file boxes into my trunk, I heard a Jackson disc jockey reading Sam's letter on the air as I drove to the Natchez *Examiner* building. Sam Jacobs will be a household name throughout the South by nightfall.

Caitlin has offered me her glass-walled conference room as a work space, plus staff volunteers to help me wade through the files. After I lug Marston's boxes into the conference room, she gathers her reporters, photographers, and interns for a brief orientation. The *Examiner* is used as a training ground for the Masters media group; thus the staff hails from all points of the compass. Not one among them is over thirty, and all are rabid liberals. I view this as a positive, for when the Marston camp discovers I'm using these kids against them, they'll almost certainly try to bribe a few for inside information. Youth and left-wing politics may give my team an immunity to filthy lucre that I couldn't hope to find elsewhere.

Caitlin's speech is modeled on those given by army officers requesting volunteers for particularly dirty missions. She succinctly summarizes my reasons for provoking the slander suit, then in broad strokes describes what we'll be looking for in the mountain of paper that will arrive later in the day.

'This is an unusual situation,' she concludes. 'Some of you may think I'm stepping over an ethical line by involving the paper in a legal proceeding that we'll be reporting on. That's true enough. But I stepped over a harder line when I printed Mr. Cage's charges. We'll be reporting this story the way papers reported stories in the good old bad old days. We're throwing the full weight of our media group behind a cause.'

A buzz of approval runs through her audience.

'We are seeking the truth about a terrible crime, and I'll

publish the truth as I find it, whether it conforms to my pre-conceptions or not. I think that lives up to the truest spirit of objectivity.'

A burst of applause follows this. Two of the male reporters, whose goatees make them look like anarchists in a Sergei Eisenstein film, pump their fists in the air.

Caitlin brushes an errant strand of hair from her eyes and goes on. 'Anyone who feels uncomfortable about this, see me in my office. You'll be excused with no questions asked and no negative consequences.'

A blond guy in the back says, 'And go back to covering board of supervisors meetings?'

'At least there's comedy at the supervisor meetings,' squawks a dark-haired girl with a Brooklyn accent. 'Try covering the flower shows.'

Caitlin holds up her hands. 'Before we disperse, I want Mr. Cage to say a few words.'

Facing the ring of expectant young faces, I feel as I did addressing new assistant district attorneys in Houston, smart kids who concealed their idealism behind shells of aggressive cynicism. 'First of all, everyone here calls me Penn. No exceptions. Second, when I made those charges against Leo Marston, I had no intention of setting foot in a courtroom. But Marston is a powerful man, and there is going to be a trial. That trial is five days from now. I have *five days* to prove Leo Marston guilty of murder.'

Skeptical sighs blow through the conference room.

'The good news is, he's guilty. The bad news is, the people who know that won't testify. Your job is to wade through documentary evidence. You're looking for several things. First, illegal activity. You're not lawyers, but if it looks or smells dirty to you, it probably is. Second, any correspondence mentioning Ray Presley or the Triton Battery Company. Third, any reference to or correspon-dence with the federal government, particularly with FBI

Director John Portman or former director J. Edgar Hoover.'

'*Whoa*,' says one of the anarchists. 'This is like *X-Files*, man.'

A ripple of laughter sweeps through the group.

'This case may be more like the *X-Files* than any of us wants to believe,' I tell him. 'Just remember that none of you are Fox Mulder or Agent Scully, okay? People are dying in this town, and they're dying because of this case. I don't want anybody in this room trying to win a Pulitzer by going after Ray Presley. He's killed before, and he probably set the fire that killed Ruby Flowers. He wouldn't hesitate to kill any of you if he felt you were a threat to him. Is that clear?'

Grim nods around the room.

'Are there any questions?'

One of the goateed reporters raises his hand. 'This murder happened thirty years ago. It's gone unsolved all that time. Do we have a hope in hell of solving it in a week?'

'You're assuming that someone has been trying to solve it. This is a small town. In small towns there are sometimes truths that everyone knows but no one mentions. Open secrets, if you will. No one really wants to probe the details, because it forces us to face too many uncomfortable realities. We'd rather turn away than acknowledge the primitive forces working beneath the surface of society.'

'Amen,' someone murmurs.

'In the case of Del Payton, no one knew exactly who planted the bomb that killed him, but everyone believed they understood what had happened. An uppity nigger got out of line, so somebody stepped in and reminded the rest of them where the line was. Unpleasant but inevitable.' My easy use of the 'N-word' obviously shocks some members of the audience. 'I believe this crime was misunderstood from the beginning. Del Payton's death may have had nothing to do with civil rights. Or only peripherally to do with it. His death may be old-fashioned murder masquerading as a race crime. And understanding that could be the key to solving this case.'

Caitlin steps up beside me. 'Any other questions? We've got work to do.'

No more hands go up.

She sends everyone back to work with a two-handed 'scoot' gesture. After they've gone, she sits at the head of the conference table, a skeptical look on her face.

'Penn, do we have any hope of tying Marston to Ray Presley or the crime scene in time for the trial?'

'That depends on what we find in the discovery material.'

'Do you really believe Marston would send you anything incriminating?'

'I've found some pretty big surprises during discovery in my career. People make blunders.' I motion toward the boxes the police saved from the fireplace at Tuscany last night. 'And then there's that stuff. Maybe we'll get lucky.'

Caitlin nods, but she doesn't look hopeful. 'Do you realize that almost every witness who knows anything you need to tell the jury would have to embarrass themselves terribly by testifying? Frank Jones – Betty Lou Jackson. Not only that, they'll be putting themselves in the killers' sights. Your ATF pal will testify, and maybe Lester Hinson, if you pay him enough. But the rest? No way.'

'That's what subpoenas are for.'

'You're not that naive. Portman, Marston, and Presley know about all these people, or soon will. And they'll try everything from bribes to murder to keep them quiet.'

'That's why we have to crack Marston's nerve between now and next Wednesday.'

'And if you can't?'

'Then we pray our long shots come through.'

'And those are?'

'Peter Lutjens, for one. He's going for the Payton file in two days.'

'I've been thinking about that. What exactly is he going to try to do? The file is forty-four volumes long. He can't walk out with it under his coat. He can't even photocopy it unless he has all night.'

'He won't have to. Remember what Stone told us in Colorado? The file is forty-three volumes of nothing and his final report. That's all we need. Stone's final report.'

'Lutjens knows that?'

'I talked to him this morning.'

'What's the other long shot?'

'Stone himself.'

She shakes her head. 'Never happen. He's too scared. They've got something on that guy. Stone's not going to talk.'

'I disagree. Whatever dirt Portman has on Stone is a two-edged sword. And Stone's conscience is working on him. It's been working on him for thirty years. Guilt is a powerful thing, Caitlin. Stone needs to unburden himself, and I think he'll come through for us. Or for himself, rather.'

'What about Ike Ransom? What's his story?'

'I think Ike's got a personal grudge against Marston that has nothing to do with Payton. He knew I'd go after Marston if I had any kind of weapon, so he gave me the Payton case.'

'But has he given you any real information? Any idea of Marston's motive for the crime?'

'Not really.'

She drums her fingers on the table. 'Motive, means, and opportunity, right? The means and opportunity are Ray Presley, but we're stuck on motive. Marston actually made public statements supporting civil rights in the sixties. I found them in the morgue here.'

'I think it's money. Somehow Payton's death increased Marston's fortune or power.'

'I can't see that. Financially, Payton was a nonentity.'

'Maybe he was an obstacle to something. Some deal.'

'What about sex?' suggests Caitlin. 'Sexual jealousy. That's a common motive for murder.'

The photo shrine in Althea Payton's house flits through my mind, followed by images of Del Payton huddled over his dinner table with Medgar Evers, talking about changing the white man's heart. 'That's not it. Payton was a family man all the way.'

'That's what they all say until they're caught with their wee-wees in the wrong cookie jar.'

'It's not sex, Caitlin. It's money or power. That's what Marston lives for.'

She sighs and gets up, then drops her left hand on the charred box of files. 'I hope there's something in here.'

'You've got to remember one thing. I'm treating this like a murder case, but it's not. It's a civil case.'

'So?'

'So the standard of proof is lower. I don't have to prove Marston's guilt to twelve people beyond a reasonable doubt. I have to convince nine jurors that it's *more likely than not* that Marston was involved in the Payton murder. That means a fifty-one percent certainty. And the jury won't have to agonize over their decision the way a criminal jury would. Because their verdict won't send Marston to jail or to a gurney for lethal injection. Another jury will get that job.'

Caitlin moves toward the door. 'I think you're going to have a hell of a job convincing those nine people unless you figure out *why* Marston would want Payton dead. And prove it.'

When she opens the door, the goateed anarchists pop through it with their sleeves rolled up and smirks on their faces.

'Mulder and Scully reporting for duty,' says one.

Caitlin shakes her head and walks out, leaving me to deal with my new assistants.

*   *   *

In the forty hours between the end of my lecture on Friday and dawn on Sunday, we built a circumstantial case against Leo Marston. The only sleep I got was brief naps on the couch in Caitlin's office, taken while reporters, photographers, and interns worked in shifts over the boxes of Marston papers that arrived in desultory waves from storage rooms unknown. Only my anarchists – who did have actual names, Peter and Ed, prosaically enough – kept pace with me during this marathon. They seemed to see it as a holy mission, one in which iconoclasts could cheerfully take part.

Daniel Kelly moved through the building like the ghost at the feast, making wry observations, delivering coffee, and disappearing for brief reconnaissance patrols, which he called 'checking the perimeter.' Whenever Caitlin left the building to cover a story, Kelly went with her. The police scanner in her office enabled her to reach the scene of several racial altercations before the cops did. Most of these involved two or three individuals, and broke out in stores or restaurants, where inflammatory language was easily overheard. On two occasions these fights escalated into brawls, and Kelly proved his value both times by protecting Caitlin with his rather alarming skills.

Saturday morning, Ed the anarchist decided we needed fresh inspiration, so he sat down with a computer and inkjet printer and went to work. An hour later, he walked into the conference room wearing a T-shirt with NAIL BOSS HOG emblazoned across the chest in red. I found it hard to believe that Ed had ever watched an episode of *The Dukes of Hazzard,* but he assured me he'd followed it religiously as a child growing up in Michigan, and that most of his ideas about the South had been formed by this grotesque television show. By afternoon, half the *Examiner* staff was wearing NAIL BOSS HOG shirts, and their galvanizing effect was undeniable.

Even Caitlin popped into the conference room wearing one.

But the work itself was tedious and exhausting. The master map that guided us on our paper journey into Marston's past was his 1997 tax return. It listed most of his business holdings (the number of Schedule C's and E's was astounding), and I immediately began drafting a supplemental request for production using these as a guide. His form 1040 showed an adjusted gross income of over two million dollars for 1997, and the sheer variety of his holdings was staggering. Real estate, manufacturing, banking, timber. And despite the moribund oil business, he had recently struck a significant gas field in south Texas. What fascinated me was the variety of small enterprises in which he participated. Several fast-food franchises around town. A steam laundry. A Christmas tree farm. Hunting camps. Apartment buildings in the black sections of town. We even found a scrawled note listing income he had realized from arranging private adoptions over a period of twenty-five years.

In short, Leo Marston appeared to administer an empire of great and small dominions, all entirely above board. On closer examination, however, a dark underside began to show itself. One of the boxes Leo had planned to burn contained records of a collection agency wholly owned by him. Listed as an officer of that company was one Raymond Aucoin Presley. This was the first tangible proof of a connection between Marston and Presley. We found copies of letters sent to hundreds of local citizens, demanding payment of debts on everything from materials bought through Marston companies to personal loans made by the judge. It wasn't hard to guess what function Presley served when these letters failed to bring payment of the outstanding balances. Most important, he was operating in this capacity during 1968, while serving as a Natchez police officer and in the month Del Payton was murdered. Closer inspection of Marston's other companies revealed that Presley was listed as a paid 'security consultant' to several of them.

Another of the 'burn boxes' contained records of land transfers made to Marston or his business partners. I noted the disturbing frequency with which the parcels of land had been sold by recent widows whose estates Marston's firm had handled. Many other sellers could be cross-indexed to debtors listed in the 'collection-agency' box. It was a letter from this box that gave me my first glimmer of a possible motive for Payton's murder.

The letter pertained to a large parcel of land south of town, near the present industrial park. It was written in an oblique style, but from it I inferred that Marston had used a secret intermediary to buy this parcel of land. Thus, while Marston was not legally the owner, he controlled the parcel's future use and would receive all monies from such use, without anyone but the intermediary knowing about it. A related letter – this one from one Zebulon Hickson, the owner of several carpet factories in Georgia and Alabama – expressed interest in purchasing this land for use as a site for a new factory. Hickson also expressed concern about labor conditions in Adams County. He was aware that Natchez had long been a 'union' town, but what concerned him more was the 'wave of racial unrest' sweeping through Southern factories. This was clearly a euphemism for 'nigger trouble.' What made all this interesting was that the letters had changed hands in January 1968, a few months before Del Payton died. The situation was oddly similar to the present one, in which Leo Marston owns the land BASF needs to have adequate space for its projected facility.

On Saturday night, things began to turn our way. I had requested Marston's telephone records, but with the trial only a week away, I had little hope of getting them. Technically, phone records can be had at the touch of a computer key, but the phone company is a hidebound bureaucracy, and in actuality it can take weeks to get them. I'd put in a call to a Bell South executive in Jackson, who promised to try to expedite the process, and apparently he did. A local Bell South technician arrived Saturday night with a manila envelope containing Marston's phone records, logging all calls beginning the day before Caitlin's 'libelous' article ran.

I hurried to Caitlin's office, and we pored over the printouts together. On the day the article ran, there was a call from Marston's law office to a number in Washington D.C. at 1:45 p.m. Caitlin quickly confirmed this number as the main switchboard at the Hoover Building, headquarters of the FBI. The call lasted eighteen minutes. One hour later Marston's office had received a call from D.C., this one from a different number, which turned out to be John Portman's office in the Hoover Building. In all, six calls passed between Marston's office and the Hoover Building that day, and several more had since. We could now prove that a link existed between Leo Marston and the director of the FBI, who had worked the Del Payton murder as a field agent in 1968, when Marston was district attorney. And while we could not know what was said during those calls, their timing indicated that they were almost certainly related to the Payton case.

Caitlin's father faxed us a steady stream of information on both Marston and Portman. Marston's Mississippi history was familiar to me, but his national political activities weren't. He is not only a powerful force in the Mississippi Republican Party, but also has major influence in the national GOP. Like many Mississippians, Marston was a nominal Democrat for most of his life, voting Democratic in local elections and Republican in presidential races. But in the Reagan era he jumped ship and voted GOP straight down the line. A close friend and adviser of Senators John Stennis and 'Big' Jim Eastland – Mississippi Democrats whose seniority gave them unparalleled power on Capital Hill for decades – Marston became a major supporter of

Senator Trent Lott, who eventually rose to the position of Senate majority leader.

John Portman's thumbnail biography fascinated me. Born to old money in Connecticut while his father 'patrolled the coast' of Rhode Island for German U-boats in his yacht, Portman was raised in a cloistered world of governesses and squash courts. He attended Choate, then Yale, where he was tapped for Skull-and-Bones and graduated second in his class at Yale Law. He was the right age for Vietnam but did not serve (perhaps owing to a dearth of yacht units). And while the FBI seemed an odd choice for a blue-blooded lawyer, during the Reagan era these 'street' credentials fueled Portman's meteoric rise into the upper ranks of the Justice Department. His stellar legal career as a U.S. attorney and federal judge was crowned by the poetic symmetry of returning to the fields where he'd begun, no longer a foot soldier but a general, and the media ate this up. The Hanratty affair provided the only bump in the road to his confirmation as FBI director, and since nothing could be proved, that came to naught. Portman sailed through the hearings without further trouble, and he has ruled the Bureau without a public misstep ever since.

In short, John Portman appeared to be a Teflon-coated bureaucrat with no visible weaknesses. His evasion of Vietnam service might be fertile ground for tabloids, but that wouldn't help my case any, and there was probably nothing to it anyway, or it would have exploded during his confirmation hearings. The more I learned about him, the more I became certain that the only way I would uncover his secrets would be if Dwight Stone decided to break his silence, or if Peter Lutjens succeeded in stealing Stone's final report from the Payton file in the FBI archive.

As I waded through the mountains of paper, eyes blurring, pulse skipping from caffeine, the tragedies of the past few days began to weigh heavily upon me. I'd involved myself in the Del Payton case for essentially selfish reasons, and because of my actions my parents' house had been destroyed, my daughter terrorized, and Ruby Flowers murdered. The sad irony was that I had returned to Natchez to help heal my daughter, yet she had not received my full attention for many days, and had not even seen me for the past two. Yet something drove me on. Despite the selfishness that had initiated my quest, I sensed a new yet familiar energy stirring inside me. As I pored over the yellowed documents and musty ledgers, doing the sort of work I had done as a young lawyer, the sterile hollowness and free-floating anxiety I had felt in the months after Sarah's death began to fall away. I felt alive again. And I knew this: Annie would fare far better with a father who was fully engaged with the world than with one grasping at meaning while clinging to the past.

I was not laboring in a vacuum. I was surrounded by idealistic kids who had no doubt they were on the right side of a noble quest for justice. During the forty-hour marathon, rumors and snippets of information filtered into the *Examiner* building that opinions in Natchez were not as clear-cut or one-sided as I had imagined. Many whites interviewed about the Payton case stated on the record that if Del Payton's killer could be found, he should pay the maximum price, no matter who he might be or how much time had passed. They regretted that the battle between myself and Marston had generated such bad publicity for the town, but justice, they said, had to be served. A consensus was building that the rest of the nation had to be shown that Mississippi was not afraid to confront its old demons, if and when they could be dragged into the light.

The rumored riot of a few nights ago never materialized. On Saturday afternoon local black leaders staged a silent march to commemorate Ruby's death, and the hushed procession walked without incident from the bandstand on the bluff to the crossroads of St. Catherine Street and Liberty Road, where slaves had been auctioned before the Civil War. The symbolism of this destination was not lost on whites, but black restraint in the face of Ruby's murder was seen as a positive signal of black faith in Natchez's justice system.

The real whirlwind was taking place outside Mississippi. We stood in the eye of a media storm, quietly going about the business of justice while national figures raged and pontificated about our backwardness. I soon began to see this as a metaphor for the Payton case itself. Yes, Ray Presley was probably the man who planted the bomb that had killed Del Payton. And perhaps Leo Marston had ordered him to do it. But it was clear to me that they had not acted alone. J. Edgar Hoover had not sealed the Payton file because it could potentially embarrass the state of Mississippi. And John Portman was not threatening me or punishing Peter Lutjens because of the local implications of this case. Nor was the fearsomely equipped sniper who shot at me from the levee the type of hit man an angry Southern businessman like Leo Marston would typically hire. Still more disturbing, I had begun to recall Dwight Stone's comment about the timing of Payton's slaying. Del was killed five weeks after Martin Luther King and three weeks before Robert Kennedy. Could there possibly have been some connection between a black factory worker in Natchez, Mississippi, and the explosive national politics of 1968?

As I pondered this question, my motive, which had begun as a quest for revenge and evolved with Livy's arrival into an exorcism of my past, began to change again. Like a stubborn coal lying dormant in the ashes, a desire for truth flickered awake in my brain. Fanned to life, this glowing ember dimmed the baser motives that had brought me thus far. Revenge against Leo Marston is a hollow and perhaps even self-destructive goal. For by destroying him, would I not also destroy the second chance I've been granted for a life with Livy? And what of my hunger for explanations from Livy? Is it her fault that I've carried confusion and bitterness inside me for twenty years like shrapnel from some undecided war, a war that a more mature man would have put behind him long ago?

Ten years before Livy disappeared from my life, Del Payton was brutally murdered. That's what's important. That's what has brought death back to this quiet town, and put the lives of those I love in mortal danger. I have but one riddle to answer. Ike the Spike told me that from the beginning. Not *who* killed Del Payton, but *why*. Because the why of it is as alive today as it was in 1968, and therein lies the answer to all my other questions. The relief that accompanied this liberating insight put me into a dead sleep on the couch in Caitlin's office late Saturday night.

When Sunday dawned, this was the sum of our knowledge: a potential land deal in 1968 that involved Marston and a Georgia industrialist concerned with 'racial' labor problems in Natchez (a deal that, as far as we could determine, was never consummated); phone records, proving suspicious contact between Marston and John Portman; and proof that Ray Presley had worked as a 'security consultant' for Marston at the time of the Payton murder and while employed by the police department. It was a good harvest for forty hours' work, but with the trial only three days away, it wasn't nearly enough. All the NAIL BOSS HOG T-shirts in the world wouldn't put me one step closer to proving Marston's complicity in the murder. And without that I would never unravel the tangled skein of lies, corruption, and official silence that made Del Payton's unpunished murder such a travesty, and forced my native state to bear the sole guilt which by rights should have been shared with others.

I needed a witness.

A star witness.

I needed Peter Lutjens or Dwight Stone.

At eleven a.m. on Sunday, I was about to call Stone to set up a secure call when Caitlin stuck a cup of scalding coffee in my hand and told me to go home and get dressed for Ruby's funeral, which was scheduled to begin in three hours.

Chapter 31

There is no more moving religious spectacle than a black funeral. If you've been to one, you know. If you haven't, you don't. Grief and remembrance are not sacrificed to the false gods of propriety and decorum but released into the air like primal music, channeled through the congregation in a collective discharge of pain. Ruby's funeral should be like that, but it isn't. It's a ritual struggling under the weight of a political circus.

The church itself is under siege when I arrive, Annie in the backseat with my parents, Kelly in front of me, the other Argus men in a second car behind us. Sited on a hill in a stand of oak and cedar trees, the one-room white structure stands at the center of an army of vehicles, including a half dozen television trucks parked in a cluster beside the small cemetery. Lines of parked cars stretched down both sides of the church drive to Kingston Road, the winding old two-lane blacktop leading to the southern part of the county, where the Cold Hole bubbles up from the swamp.

A black-suited deacon waves us away from the drive, but Kelly ignores him and accelerates up the chute created by the parked cars, stopping only when he reaches the church steps. Camera crews instantly surround the BMW.

An old white-haired black man appears on the steps and jabs a finger at the human feeding frenzy around us. A wave of young men in their Sunday best rolls into the reporters, pushing them bodily away from the car, assisted by the three

Argus men who drove up behind us. The old man comes down the steps and opens the back door of our car.

'I'm so sorry about this, Dr. Cage. Afternoon, Mrs Cage. I'm Reverend Nightingale. Y'all come inside. One of these young men will park your car for you.'

Annie climbs between the seats into my arms, and I hurry up the steps with her as the camera crews close around us. A cacophony of shouted questions fills the air, but all I can distinguish are names: *Marston, Portman, Mackey, Mayor Warren* . . . As soon as we clear the church door, I turn and see my mother and father fighting their way through. A deacon slams the door behind them, leaving Kelly outside to help defend the entrance.

Two hundred black faces are turned toward the rear of the church, staring at us. People are jammed into the pews and packed along the walls like cordwood. The building seems to have more flesh in it than air. Only the center aisle is clear. Reverend Nightingale takes my mother's arm and leads her along it, through the silent staring faces. Dad and I follow, me carrying Annie in my arms. The rear pews hold a bright sea of color, oscillating waves of blue, orange, yellow, and green (but no red, never red) and like proud sails above the waves, the most stunning array of hats I have seen outside of a 1940s film. All the children are dressed in white, like angels in training. As I follow my mother, Ruby's voice sounds in my mind: *You never wear red to no funeral; red says the dead person was a fool.* The nearer we get to the altar, the darker the dresses get, until finally all are black.

At the end of the aisle Reverend Nightingale pulls my mother to the left, and I see our destination: a special box of pews standing against the wall, protected by a wooden rail. Despite the throng in the church, this box is empty. It's the Mothers' Bench, seats reserved for 'sisters' who have reached a certain age (eighty), I think) and accepted 'mother' status.

Today it has been reserved for us. As we take our seats behind the rail, I see an identical box against the other wall. The Deacons' bench. Behind its rail sits Ruby's immediate family: her husband, Mose; her three sons (all tall men with gray in their beards); her daughter, Elizabeth, wiping her eyes with a handkerchief; a handful of grandchildren (all in their twenties) and two infants.

A single camera crew has been allowed inside the church to tape the ceremony. The logo on the camera reads WLBT, the call letters of the black-owned station in Jackson. As I pan across the crowd, I see several familiar faces. In the first row sits Shad Johnson, wearing a suit that cost enough to buy any ten suits behind him. A few feet down the same pew sits the Payton family: Althea, Georgia, Del Jr., and his children. Althea nods to me, her brown eyes full of sympathy. In the second row sits the Gates family, the most powerful force in black politics in Natchez for forty years, now upstaged by the urban prodigal from Chicago. Several pews beyond them sits Willie Pinder, the former police chief. Pinder winks as I catch his eye. And in the last pew, sitting restlessly in the aisle seat as though prepared to make a quick exit, sits a man who looks very much like Charles Evers. The former mayor of Fayette and brother of Medgar looks like a man who does not intend to be bothered by anyone.

Suddenly the back door opens and two white faces float through it, Caitlin Masters and one of her photographers, escorted by Deputy Ike Ransom in his uniform. Ike remains just inside the back door, like a sentry, while Caitlin and her photographer slip through the crowd at the back wall and stop beside the WLBT camera.

In the shuffling, sweating silence the organist begins to play, and the purple-robed choir rises to its feet, beginning a restrained rendition of 'Jesus, Keep Me Near the Cross.' The rich vibrato of two dozen voices fills the building, making the church reverberate like the soundboard of a grand piano.

The whole congregation knows the words, and they join in softly.

As the last chorus fades, Reverend Nightingale makes his way slowly down the aisle and ascends to the pulpit. He is a small man, with fine white hair and frail limbs, but his voice has the deep, resonant timbre of the best black preachers.

'Brothers and sisters. Mothers. Deacons and officers. Visitors and friends. We are gathered here today to mourn the passing of Sister Ruby Flowers.'

A collective *Mm-hm* ripples through the church, punctuated by a couple of soft *Amens.* Reverend Nightingale touches the rim of his spectacles and continues.

'Everyone in this room knows how loyally Sister Flowers supported this church. She was born in 1917, and came to Jesus when she was nine years old. Reverend Early was pastor then. He was a godly man, but sparing with his praise. Yet as a boy I often heard him speak of how lucky he was to have womenfolk like Sister Flowers in his flock.'

Yes, Lord, comes the reply. *Yes, sir.*

'In the last few days a lot of reporters been asking me what Sister Flowers was like. Do you know what I tell them?'

Tell it.

'I say, "You know how when you got two people, and you got to carry something heavy for a ways? Like a big chest of drawers? There's different ways you can pick up on it. You can pick up on it straight and level, with your legs and your back, and take your share of the weight" – Reverend Nightingale pauses, letting the image sink in– "or you can kind of *fudge* it. Pick up with just your arms, or pick up a little *high,* puttin' most of the weight on the other person."'

Soft laughter, guilty recognition. But Reverend Nightingale's face is set in stone.

'That was *not* Sister Flowers,' he thunders.

No Jesus, comes the chorus. *I know that's right.*

'Sister Flowers picked up square and straight,' he declares.

'She picked up whenever she was asked to. And more than that, she picked up when she *wasn't* asked to.'

Praise Jesus.

'Sister Flowers was not a rich woman,' the reverend says in a conversational tone. 'But she gave unstintingly of the money she made. She had a generous heart. She bought flour and sugar and butter, and she baked cakes deep into the night to sell to raise money for the poor.' Nightingale raises his right hand, forefinger extended toward Heaven. 'During the Depression? Sister Flowers visited white families, collecting old coats and sweaters, hats, shoes, and mittens for the wintertime, bringing them out here to kids who didn't have *nothing* between them and the cold.' The finger descends, admonitory now, 'You children today smirk and turn up your nose when I say *old* coats and *old* shoes. But what you don't know – and you better thank God you don't know – is that when you're *cold*, you'll take *whatever* coat you can get, and praise Jesus for it.'

Lord, yes! Praise Jesus!

Reverend Nightingale turns to the Deacons' Bench and remarks on what fine children Ruby raised. My parents always felt Ruby's children didn't do enough for her after they were grown, considering the sacrifices she'd made for them. But they did what Ruby most desired that they do, went North and found good jobs, raised families. Part of the price of their success may have been embarrassment at their mother's humble position, or confusion at her unwillingness to leave Mississippi, a place they regarded as backward and evil.

'Sister Flowers was not seriously ill or afflicted,' Reverend Nightingale says soberly. 'She was taken before her time, by the hand of a stranger. The police don't know who set that terrible fire. But *I* know who it was.'

A gasp of shock from the pews.

'It was a man cut off from the Lord. That man is suffering

right now. Today. And I hope he'll soon see the only way to wash his soul is to come forward, confess his sins, and pay the price of justice.'

Reverend Nightingale grips the forward edge of the podium with both hands. 'And I know *why* this man killed Sister Flowers. Because he wanted to stop Mr. Penn Cage from finding out who killed Brother Delano Payton.'

Silence blankets the room. Every eye focuses on me.

'Now, some of you may feel anger toward Mr. Cage because of what happened to Sister Flowers. But not one soul in this room should blame him. Because Penn Cage is doing what no man – white or black – has done in the last thirty years. He is putting himself and his family on the line to find out who murdered Brother Del.

'And why was Del killed?' Reverend Nightingale slams a hand against the podium with a report like a pistol shot. 'To keep the black man in this community down! To keep honest black men from getting a leg up. To keep us from making a working wage at a good job. A job with some *dignity*.'

He removes a white cotton handkerchief from his coat pocket and wipes his forehead. The mass of bodies is turning the little building into a convection oven.

'You may wonder why Mr. Cage, a white man, is doing what he's doing. He must be gonna make some money some way, right? He must want to get on *Oprah* with a book or something. But that's not it. No, sir. I'll tell you why Mr. Cage is doing what he's doing. He's doing it because he was *raised* by Sister Flowers.'

My mother's hand closes around mine.

'And he wasn't raised by Sister Flowers alone. He was raised by Dr. Tom Cage. And Dr. Cage been takin' care of black people in this town for nigh on forty years. If you couldn't pay, did Dr. Cage turn you away from the door?'

A great tide of *No, sir! Lord, no!* issues forth from the congregation and rolls through the church, accompanied by shaking heads and murmurs of gratitude. When I turn to my left, I see a sight I have never seen in my life: my father sitting with his head bowed, staring resolutely at the floor, his jaw muscles clenched as tears run down his face.

'And *Mrs.* Cage,' says Reverend Nightingale. 'Mrs. Cage was one of the ladies who helped Sister Flowers gather up them old coats in the wintertime, and made sure they got where they needed to get.' He smiles at my mother and goes on. 'Thursday last, after that newspaper story ran about Del, I asked Sister Flowers about Penn Cage. You know what she said? She said, "Pastor, that boy was raised right, and he'll do whatever he's got to do to make things right about Del."'

Ruby and I never discussed the Payton case. But the realization that she knew I was working on it, and approved, eases my conscience in a way nothing else could.

'Some of you older members may remember,' says Nightingale, 'that Del Payton visited this church several times when he was a boy. Del was a member of Beulah Baptist, out to Pine Ridge. But that boy had too fine a voice to confine it to one house of worship. Several Sundays we were blessed to have Del solo here at Mandamus. And many a family' – Reverend Nightingale says *fambly* – 'requested Del for solos at funerals. I know right now Del is beatifying Heaven with that sweet voice, preparing the host of angels to receive Sister Flowers.'

'*Praise Jesus,*' answers the chorus.

'Right now we're going to have a solo by Sister Lillian Lilly. Sister Lilly is a gospel recording artist from Jackson, and she's come down to bless us with her talents. Afterwards, Brother Shadrach Johnson wants to speak to you for a few minutes. You all know Brother Johnson is running for mayor, and the election's getting close. He believes what's happened in the past few days is important to us all, and he's gonna talk to you about that. Sister Lilly?'

From the midst of the choir a woman in a flowing blue

gown rises, folds her hands before her, and begins singing 'Precious Lord' with such raw power and authentic faith that the initial cries of *Sing it! Sing it!* fade to awed silence, and many of the elderly members of the congregation weep openly. When she takes her seat again, the air is brittle with expectation, and it is then that Shad Johnson stands and walks up to the podium. How must he look to this audience, in his two-thousand-dollar suit that shines like a deuce-and-a-quarter on Saturday night? He must look, I believe, like a savior.

'Brothers and sisters,' he begins in a gentle voice. 'When I came into this church, I thought I was a stranger to Sister Ruby Flowers. But when I heard Reverend Nightingale's impassioned eulogy, I knew that I was wrong. I knew a hundred women like Sister Flowers when I was growing up here in Natchez. Five hundred, probably. Strong black women who sacrificed everything so that their children could climb one step higher up the ladder to a better life.'

Yes, Lord.

Shad nods to his left, and the assistant I saw at his headquarters hurries toward the back of the church, stops beside the WLBT cameraman and says a few words. The cameraman looks confused, but a moment later he shrugs and touches the controls on the tripod mounted camera.

'Brothers and sisters,' Shad resumes, 'I've asked that the camera be turned off, so that I can speak frankly to you. We all know what's happening in this town. Why there's so much agony in our hearts today. Sister Flowers died hard. She died scarred and in terrible pain. She died at the hands of a murderer. Undoubtedly at the hands of a *white* murderer. And the consequences of that act are tearing this community apart. At this moment two of our children are sitting in jail for taking the life of a man who once ordered the beatings and murders of African Americans. You feel anger over this. You feel *rage*. And that's only natural.'

Shad holds up his hands and brings them softly together. 'But I've come here today to ask you to set aside that rage. Because we are poised on the brink of a great victory. The plantation mentality that has paralyzed this town for so long is finally eroding from the inside out. Significant numbers of white people have grown tired of the self-aggrandizement and profiteering of men like Riley Warren. And those are the people who can put me into the mayor's office in two weeks. Not you, my good friends. Lord knows, I need every one of you. But without those good white people, all our work will have been for naught. The sacrifices of Ruby Flowers and Del Payton? All for nothing. Think about that. Del Payton died thirty years ago. He died for civil rights. But how much better off are you, really, than you were in 1968? You can drink from the public water fountain. You can go into a restaurant and eat next to white people. But can you afford to pay the check? How good a job can you get? If this violence escalates any more, I don't think we'll ever see those men from BASF in town again. There are too many towns where things are peaceful to put a good plant like that in a trouble spot.

'So.' Johnson lays his hands on the podium. 'What am I asking you to do? Only the same thing Jesus asked. It's the hardest thing in the world, brothers and sisters. Especially for you younger men. I want you to turn the other cheek. Keep cool. Because if you do, the meek are going to start inheriting a little of this Mississippi earth.'

Shad turns slowly, giving every person in the room a chance to look him in the eye, then stops, facing me. 'And I'm asking Penn Cage, right here and now, to withdraw his charges against Judge Leo Marston.'

A low murmur moves through the congregation. Even Reverend Nightingale looks caught by surprise.

'After the election,' Shad goes on, 'there'll be plenty of time to probe the death of Del Payton. And with me running the city, you can rest assured that will happen. But further pressure on Marston at this point could keep Riley Warren in the mayor's office for another four years. And we simply cannot afford that.'

Shad is staring at me as though he expects me to rise and answer him, here, at the funeral of a woman I loved like a second mother. Every eye in the church is upon me. As though pulled by the collective will of the congregation, I start to stand, but my mother's hand flattens on my thigh, pushing me back onto the bench. At that moment Althea Payton rises from the first pew and looks around the church. She speaks softly, but in the silent room every word rings with conviction.

'Thirty years ago my husband was taken from me. Murdered. For thirty years I've waited for justice. And no man alive has lifted a finger to help me get it, without I paid him money. Last week I went to Mr. Penn Cage and asked him to help me. And he *did*.'

Althea raises her eyes to the pulpit, from which Shad stares like an attorney facing a dangerously unpredictable witness, and points at him. 'That man there wants to be our mayor. He's come down from Chicago special to do it. And he might be a good one. He sure talks a good game. But I know this. He never came to my house and offered to help me find out who killed my man. And to stand up here like this . . . to use this poor lady's funeral to tell a good man to stop trying to do good so *he* can get elected . . . well, it don't sit right with me.'

'Mrs. Payton, I think you've misunderstood my motives,' Shad says in an unctuous voice.

'I understand more than you think,' Althea replies. 'Get me elected, you say. *Then* I'll do good. But like the man said a long time ago, "If not now, when?"'

'Tell him!' comes a shout from the back pews.

'*Yes, Lord!*' from the choir stand. '*If not now, when?*

Shad is about to respond when Reverend Nightingale eases him away from the pulpit with a forced smile. Althea retakes her pew as the reverend smooths his jacket and says, 'I thank Brother Johnson for that thoughtful comment. We sure have a lot to think about these days. Now, the service is almost over, but I think I'd be remiss if I didn't give our white friends a chance to speak today.'

This is unexpected, but in the silence that follows, my mother stands and turns to the congregation. Her voice is softer than Althea's, but it too carries in the church.

'Ruby worked for our family for thirty-five years,' she says. 'We considered her part of our family, and we always will.'

And she sits down.

The expression on Shad Johnson's face makes it clear that he views this statement as white paternalism at its worst, but the faces in the pews say something different.

Reverend Nightingale closes the funeral with a prayer, then directs the choir to sing 'Amazing Grace.'

The pallbearers carry Ruby's casket down the aisle and out the front door, preceded by the deacons, who act as an informal security force, hustling reporters away from the door with the help of Daniel Kelly and the Argus men. The congregation waits for our family to depart, then follows us out, and soon we are all gathered in the small graveyard beside the church while five camera crews film steadily from the perimeter of the crowd.

Ruby's coffin lies above the freshly turned earth, on straps that will lower her into the ground when the graveside service is done. As Reverend Nightingale begins his prayer, a horn honks loudly from Kingston Road, blaring again and again but thankfully dropping in pitch as the vehicle goes on down the road. While a cameraman runs off to try to get a shot of the heckler, Reverend Nightingale increases his volume and pushes right through the twenty-third psalm. When he finishes, he turns to the gathered mourners.

'The family will remain seated. The members will please turn away from the body.'

Though unfamiliar with this custom, I obey. From the air, this would look strange indeed, two hundred people gathered in a circle around a hole in the ground, facing away from it. I'm not sure of the significance of this ritual, but turning away from death is sometimes the best thing we can do. Reverend Nightingale recites another brief prayer, including the words, 'Ashes to ashes, dust to dust,' and the congregation walks away from the grave as one.

A half dozen younger black men remain behind, beside a loose stack of shovels, and I remain with them. After Ruby's children drop flowers into the grave, they start toward their cars with their own children. I shake hands with them as they pass, and express my condolences. I sense different reactions in each, but all are courteous.

When Ruby's casket reaches the bottom of the grave, I pick up one of the shovels, and spade it into the soft pile of earth. Dad starts to join me, but I touch his chest, reminding him of his heart trouble, and he rejoins my mother and Annie at the edge of the little cemetery.

I feel like it should be raining, but the sun is hot on the back of my suit jacket. As we shovel the diminishing pile of dirt over the gleaming casket, I think of the white funerals I have attended, how everyone walks away at the end of the graveside service, leaving the coffin to be covered by a backhoe or by a couple of unknown gravediggers. This way is better. We should be covered into the earth by people who loved us.

After the grave is full and tamped down, and the camera crews have shot all the footage they want, only a few people remain on the hill. My parents stand with Annie and Reverend Nightingale beside the BMW, which someone has brought from wherever it was parked. Kelly and his associates drift around the edge of the hill, looking for possible threats. Caitlin and the photographer sit on the church steps, fiddling with a camera as Ike Ransom watches.

After Reverend Nightingale toddles off toward his baby blue Cadillac, Ike beckons me to the side of the church, out of earshot of Caitlin and the photographer. I walk over and speak to my parents, then join Ike.

'What you got?' he growls, stepping around me so that I can see no one but him. The blood vessels in his eyes form a red network around the dark irises, and the smell of cheap whiskey blows past me with his every word. 'You got enough to nail Marston on Wednesday?'

'I'm working on it.'

'Working? The trial's three days from now!'

'You think I don't know that?'

'So, tell me what you got.'

I quickly summarize my case, from Frank Jones to Betty Lou Beckham and everyone in between.

'Will that bitch testify in open court?' Ike asks, loudly enough to be heard across the hill. 'Betty Lou?'

'I don't know. She's scared of Presley, and her husband doesn't want her to testify. I've got my father working on her.'

'What about tying Presley to Marston?'

'I've got something working,' I say grudgingly, thinking of Peter Lutjens, who at this moment may be risking prison to get a copy of Stone's original FBI report.

Ike grabs my wrist, his grip like a claw. 'What you talking about?'

I jerk my hand free. 'I'll let you know if it works out.'

His glare is disquieting. 'Is Stone helping you?'

'No.'

'You ask him to testify?'

'He won't. Look, I need to go. My family's waiting.'

'You ain't telling me shit, man!'

'You need to get some sleep, Ike.'

'Sleep? Let me tell you something. I been thinking. I been thinking I messed up coming to you. You may put Presley in jail, but that ain't nothing. He's dying anyway. Marston's laughing at you, man. Old Shad may be right about you leaving this alone, even though the nigger be a little *bright* for my taste.'

'I'm going now, Ike.'

He grabs my arm. 'You keep me posted, right?'

I nod slowly. 'Let go of my wrist.'

He looks down at the junction of our limbs as though unaware he has hold of me. As the hand relaxes, a question comes to me. 'Are you a member of this church, Ike?'

'Me? Baptist? I'm Catholic, man. Holy Family.'

'You've known more than you've told me from the start. Whatever you have, now's the time to tell me.'

His head moves forward, then back, like a man falling asleep at the wheel of a car. 'You think I'm playing the quiet game too?' A faint smile, as though at a private joke. 'I told you, man, everybody keeps something back. It's the only way to stay safe.'

'I'm gone, Ike. Be careful, okay?'

When I come around the corner of the church, everyone is waiting in the cars but Caitlin and Kelly. Caitlin says something to him, then breaks away and meets me halfway.

'What was all that about?' she asks. 'It sounded like he was yelling at you.'

'He's drunk. He's losing his nerve as the trial gets closer.'

'What about you?'

'Solid as a rock.'

She smiles. 'I couldn't believe Shad put you on the spot like that.'

'Are you going to report what he said?'

'He said it, he's responsible for it.'

'Good.'

'Have you heard anything from Peter Lutjens?'

'Not yet.'

'You think he really has the nerve to try for that file?'

'If he doesn't, he's going to spend a lot of winters shoveling snow in North Dakota.'

'God, I hope he gets it. If he doesn't—'

'There's still Stone.'

'Don't hold your breath. You want to come back to the paper and wade through some files? I'll help.'

'Not yet. I'm going to take a drive. My parents and Annie are riding back with the Argus guys.'

Caitlin takes my hand. 'Want some company?'

'Not this time.' I squeeze her hand. 'But thanks for offering.'

She looks off toward Kingston Road. 'You're taking Kelly on this ride, right?'

'No.'

She looks back at me, her eyes worried, then suspicious. She drops my hand. 'Tell Livy I said hello.'

'Livy? I have no intention of seeing Livy. Kelly can come if he wants, but in his own car. I just want to be alone for a while.'

Her eyes soften. 'I'm sorry. I understand. I'll tell him.' She rises on tiptoe and kisses me on the cheek. 'Keep your eyes open.'

'I will.'

Chapter 32

Sometimes we think we are moving randomly. But random behavior is rare in humans. We are always spiraling around something, whether we see it or not, a secret center of gravity with the invisible power of a black hole. As a teenager, most of my 'aimless' rides led me past Tuscany. Usually I would drive past the entrance, hoping to catch sight of Livy entering or leaving in her car. But a few times, at night, I would idle up the long driveway (it wasn't gated then) and look up at her lighted window, staring at it like a caveman at a fire, then turn around and continue my endless orbit, a ritual that left me perpetually unsatisfied but which I was powerless to stop.

After Ruby's funeral, I circumnavigate the county on its backroads, hurtling along gravel lanes with Kelly in my wake, driving his rented Taurus. Like a planet and its moon, we circle the town and the mystery that lies at the heart of it. Often the act of driving acts as a catalyst that allows the information banging around in my subconscious to order itself in a new way.

Today is different.

Today the emotional fallout from the funeral will not dissipate. Reverend Nightingale's portrayal of my 'unselfish' motives shamed me in a way I've never felt before. As he stood there praising me, I felt like a soldier who ran from battle being mistakenly awarded a Silver Star. At the other extreme was my anger at Shad Johnson, who hijacked

Ruby's funeral for his own political ends. And yet, if I were black, his suggestion that I retract my charges against Marston would make sense. My public statements may already have frightened liberal whites who might have voted for Shad into casting their ballots for Wiley Warren and the status quo.

After an hour of driving, the secret heart of my troubled orbit finally reveals itself. For the past week I've been acting like a writer. I was a prosecutor for twice as long as I've been a novelist, and I should have been thinking like one. At least my hands know where to take me, if my brain doesn't. I'm on the Church Hill road, less than a mile from Ray Presley's trailer. When I pull off beside the dilapidated structure, Kelly parks behind me, gets out, and jogs up to my window.

'What's up, boss? Who lives here?'

'The man who killed Del Payton. I think he killed Ruby too.'

Kelly winces. 'And what are we doing here?'

'What I should have done days ago.'

He squints and looks up the two-lane road. 'I didn't sign on to kill anybody. Or to watch it done.'

'I'm just going to talk to him.'

He gives me a skeptical look. 'That sounds an awful lot like, "I'm just going to put it in a little way."'

'I mean it. I'm here to talk. But this asshole is dangerous. I assume you won't stand on ceremony if he tries to kill me.'

'He makes the first move, I got no problem punching his ticket.'

'Come on, then.'

I get out and walk toward the trailer, Kelly on my heels. We're ten feet from the concrete steps when the front door bangs open and Presley yells from inside.

'That's far enough! What the hell you doing here, Cage?'

'I want to talk to you.'

'Who's that hippie?'

411

'A friend.'

'Is he carrying?'

'You bet your ass.'

A long pause. 'I got nothing to say to you. Except you're playing mighty fast and loose with your daddy's future, all that shit you're saying in the papers.'

'You haven't heard my proposition, Ray. You might just save your life by listening. However much you've got left, anyway.'

'Yeah? Fuck you. You could save your daddy from going to jail by shutting the hell up and going back to Houston.'

'My father will never go to jail for the Mobile thing, Ray. But *you* will if you open your mouth.'

A bluejay cries raucously in the silence, the sound like a rusty gate closing.

'You got two minutes,' calls Presley. 'But the hippie stays out there.'

I look back at Kelly, who walks casually past me and up to the open door, his hands held out to his sides. I can't hear what he says, but when he's done, he walks back to me and gives me the OK sign.

'What did you say to him?'

'I made sure he understood that hurting you would be a bad idea. He understands. Watch the girl in the corner, though. She looks shaky.'

Holding my hands in plain view, I walk up the three steps and into the trailer.

The stink of mildew and rotting food hits me in a wave, as though the trailer hasn't been opened for days. As my eyes adjust to the dimness, I see Ray standing by his wall of police memorabilia. He's dressed just as he was the other day: pajama pants, tank-top wife-beater T-shirt, and the John Deere cap pressed over his naked skull. He's also holding a shotgun, which is aimed in my general direction, and wearing a shoulder holster with the butt of a large handgun protruding from it. Deeper in the gloom, on the couch by the IV caddy, sits the pallid blonde I saw on my first visit. Her legs are folded beneath her, and she's clenching a rifle in her hands. She looks nervous enough to pull the trigger without provocation.

'So talk,' says Presley.

'I've got three days to prove Leo Marston conspired to kill Del Payton.'

He snorts. 'Maybe you can find out who killed the Kennedys before Wednesday too.'

'I know you killed Del, Ray.'

Not even a tremor in the narrow face.

'I know you lied about the dynamite. You planted those blasting caps. I also know the murder wasn't your idea.'

The eyes blink slowly in the shadows, like a snake's. 'You don't know shit.'

'You'll find out different on Wednesday.'

The shotgun barrel moves closer to me. 'You can't prove I killed that nigger, because I didn't kill him.'

'Come on, Ray. What's the point in lying now?'

He chuckles softly. 'You know how people say, "That boy don't know nothing"? Well, you don't even *suspect* nothing.'

'If you'll tell the D.A. how the Payton murder really went down – if you'll give up Marston – I'll get the D.A. to grant you full immunity.'

'Immunity for murder.'

'Your testimony would force Marston to plead guilty. If Leo cuts a deal, it saves the city the embarrassment of a public trial for a race murder. That's what the powers-that-be-want.'

'Rat out Judge Marston.'

'And John Portman.'

A short bark of a laugh. 'Boy, you're so goddamn stupid

413

I'm surprised you made it through law school. What you think Portman had to do with anything?'

'I don't know. But I know he's scared enough to try to kill you to keep you quiet.'

A nerve twitches in Presley's left cheek. 'That weasel. He wasn't shit in sixty-eight.'

'He is now. And he'll try again. He's got too much to lose. Cut a deal, you short-circuit the whole trial. It'll all be over before Portman knows what hit him.'

Presley waves the shotgun furiously. 'You think I give a fuck if that trial happens? What do I care if the niggers run wild in the streets? Let the goddamn bleeding hearts see what happens when there ain't nobody like me around to keep the jungle bunnies in line.'

He turns his head and spits through a narrow door, which I hope is the bathroom. Then he says, 'You're working with a nigger on this, ain't you?'

'You mean Althea Payton?'

'Shit, no. That nigger deputy, Ransom.'

'Don't know him.'

'Don't try to lie, boy. You ain't had the practice. That Ransom ain't right in the head. Never has been, since the army. He did dope and turned on his own people. He sucked that bottle like a tit for twenty years. The boy can't hardly function without a football in his hand. You ever ask yourself why he wants Marston so bad?'

I say nothing.

'I knew Ike when he was with the P.D. His old shit will drag him down quick as it will me.'

'You're not listening, Ray. If I'm forced to put on my case, you'll be indicted for murder before sundown Wednesday. I guarantee it.'

Presley squints at me as though measuring me for a shroud. 'You keep pushing for that trial, you won't live to see

Wednesday. And that fag bodyguard you got out there won't be able to help you none.'

'Who's going to kill me? You?'

'Me? I ain't leaving this trailer.'

'Do the deal, Ray. It's your only chance.'

'Me and the judge go back thirty years. I ain't no punk to roll over on my friends.'

'You think Leo Marston is your friend?'

He jabs the shotgun at me. 'I know *you* ain't.'

The blonde's eyes track me over the sights of her rifle, all the way to the door. I shouldn't say another word, but Ruby's blood is calling to me from the ground.

'Where were you Tuesday afternoon, Ray?'

He cuts his eyes at the blonde, then looks back at me, a smug light in his eyes. 'I believe I was delivering a message in town.'

'A message,' I repeat, recalling the flames eating through the roof of our house, the smell of Ruby's cooking flesh. My hands ball into fists at my sides.

'I don't think it got received, though,' he says.

I step within two feet of him. 'I'm going to settle that score, you piece of shit. You're going to die in the Parchman infirmary. They don't stock your Mexican cocktail there. And there aren't any blondes to take the edge off, as you like to put it. Not girls, anyway.'

His thin lips part in a predatory smile, revealing small white teeth. 'You'll be dead before I will. It's coming now, and you don't even see it.'

When I open the door, the sun hits my eyes like a flashbulb, but it feels good to get out of the stinking trailer.

Kelly is standing by the cars. 'Accomplish anything?'

'No.'

When I reach the cars, he pats me on the shoulder. 'Let's go back to town, boss.'

*   *   *

One of the things that has always separated Natchez from other Mississippi towns is that if you want a drink you can get it, no matter the day or hour.

Kelly suggests the Under the Hill Saloon (a national treasure of a bar), but a big crowd gathers there on Sundays to watch the sun set over the river, and they start celebrating early.

A crowd is not what I want right now.

The bar at Biscuits and Blues is oak and runs a good thirty feet down one wall, with a mirror behind it and glittering bottles and glasses stacked in front. The restaurant is empty but for a couple eating in a booth against the wall opposite the bar. Clanks and clatters filter through the heavy kitchen doors, but otherwise the atmosphere is perfect.

I order Scotch, Kelly the same. Our reflections watch us from the mirror behind the bar like solemn relatives visiting from a cold northern country. When the whisky comes, I swallow a shot big enough to steal my breath, then wipe my mouth on my jacket sleeve. Kelly sips with a deep centeredness, like a man who has known life without luxuries and wants to savor them while he can. He doesn't talk. He doesn't look at me. He stares through the bottom of his glass, as though pondering the grain of the wood beneath. Yet I am certain that every movement in the restaurant – even on the street outside – registers on his mental radar. Kelly is covering me even now.

'Kelly?'

'Mm?'

'Did you have a maid when you grew up?'

His head bobs once. Then I hear soft laughter, an ironic chuckle.

'Did you?'

'My mother was a maid.'

He glances at me from the corner of his eye, then looks back into his glass. Embarrassment is not exactly what I feel. It's more like mortification. I'm trying to think of how to apologize when he says, 'Nothing wrong with being a maid. It's honest work. Like soldiering.'

I want to hug him for that.

'How long did Ruby work for your family?'

'Thirty-five years. She came when I was three.'

'That's a long time.'

'And she burned to death. Because of what I'm doing, she burned to death.'

Kelly rotates his stool and puts his foot on a crosspiece of mine. 'Can I ask you something?'

'Sure.'

'Why are you doing what you're doing?'

'The truth? I don't know. In the beginning I wanted to nail a guy who hurt my father a long time ago. And me.' I take another shot of Scotch, and this one brings sweat to my skin. 'That's a bad reason, I guess.'

'Not so bad.'

'It's not worth Ruby's life.'

'No. But that's not the only reason you're doing it. You're trying to set a murder right. And from what I can tell, it needs setting right. I've watched you these last few days. You're a crusader. I knew some in the service, and you're one of them. I've got a feeling you saw some horrible atrocity when you were young. A race murder or something. Something that's weighed you down a long time.'

'No. I never saw anything like that. Not much of that happened around here, to tell you the truth.'

I swallow the remainder of my Scotch and signal the bartender for a refill. 'What I do remember . . . it probably won't sound like anything. I was in the fourth grade when integration started here. I was in the public school then. The first semester they sent twenty black kids into our school.

417

Five. Into an all-white elementary school. The black kid in my grade was named Noble Jackson. Nobody was horrible to those kids. Not overtly. But every day at recess, we'd be out there playing ball or whatever, and Noble Jackson would be standing off at the edge of the playground by himself. Just standing there watching us. Excluded. I guess he tried to play the first couple of days, and nobody picked him for anything. Every day he just stood there by himself. Staring, kicking rocks, not understanding. The next semester my parents moved me to St. Stephens.'

The Scotch has soured in my stomach. 'Now that I'm older, I know that kid's parents made a conscious decision to do something very hard. Something my parents wouldn't do. They risked their child's education, maybe even his life, put him into a situation where it would be almost impossible for him to learn because of the pressure. They did that because somebody had to do it. When I think of that kid, I don't feel very good. Because exclusion is the worst thing for a child. It's a kind of violence. And the effects last a long time. I think maybe Noble Jackson is part of the reason I'm doing this.'

'What happened to him? Where'd he end up?'

'I have no idea. I've often wondered. Wherever he is, I'll bet he got the hell out of the South as soon as he could.'

We return to our drinks, both lost in our own thoughts. As the bartender returns to refill his glass, Kelly says, 'Got a phone book, chief?'

The bartender turns around and takes one from beneath the telephone. The Natchez phone book is only a half-inch thick, including the yellow pages. Kelly flips through it, then runs his finger down a page. 'Here's your man. Noble Jackson.'

A strange tightness constricts my chest. 'That's probably his father.'

'Let me borrow that phone,' Kelly says to the bartender.

'Local call?'

'You bet.' Kelly takes the phone and dials the number, watching me in the mirror. 'Hello, I'm calling for Noble . . . It is? This is Sergeant Kelly, Noble. *Daniel* Kelly . . . You don't recognize my voice? From Bragg? . . . Fort Bragg. I'm trying to track down some members of our old unit . . . You're kidding me, right? . . . Never been in the service? You're *shining* me, man. Well, Noble always said he was going to get out of Mississippi as soon as he could . . . Yeah? How old are you? . . . Well, that's the right age. What you do for a living? . . . Ha. Noble sure didn't know nothing about engines. You married? . . . No kidding. Man, I'm sorry I bothered you. My mistake all the way. You have a good Sunday, chief.'

Kelly hangs up, and the bartender puts the phone back in front of the mirror.

'Noble Jackson works as a mechanic for Goodyear. He's thirty-eight years old, married with four kids, and he's lived in Natchez his whole life. He sounds happier about it than a lot of people would be.'

This knowledge, mundane as it sounds, somehow eases my grief over Ruby. 'Kelly, you're a funny guy.'

His eyes twinkle. 'That has been said.'

He looks past me, and I hear the restaurant door open behind me. His expression tells me that whoever came in is a woman, an attractive one. I find myself hoping it's Caitlin.

'Female inbound on your six,' he says. 'You know her?'

I rotate my stool and watch a tanned brunette walk toward me. It's Jenny, the waitress. She's wearing black jeans and a T-shirt that says LILITH FAIR. Her dark hair is swept back from her neck, and her large brown eyes are shining. She gives me a shy wave as she reaches us.

'Jenny, this is Daniel Kelly.'

She smiles and shakes Kelly's hand, then looks back at me. 'I'm surprised to see you here. Isn't the funeral today?'

'We just came from there.'

'Oh. Um, could I talk to you for a minute?'

'Sure.'

She looks furtively at Kelly. 'Alone, I mean?'

Kelly starts to slide off his stool, but Jenny takes his arm and holds him there. 'I didn't mean for you to leave.'

'How about one of those booths?' I suggest.

'Well . . . I was hoping you'd come upstairs. To my apartment. Just for a minute.'

My mental alarm is ringing now, soft but steady. Even modest fame can attract some strange people and propositions, and legal complications often follow. Caitlin pegged Jenny as having a fixation on me the first time she saw her. Maybe she's right.

'It's practically deserted in here,' I say. 'Let's just grab a booth.'

Jenny suddenly looks on the verge of tears. 'It's nothing weird, I promise. It's . . . personal. It has to do with what you're working on. Your case.'

Curiosity muffles the alarm in my head. 'The Payton case? What do you know about that?'

She glances at the bartender, who's totaling numbers on a calculator a few feet away. 'It has to do with the Marston family.'

I'm convinced. 'Okay. Upstairs it is. Have another on me, Kelly.'

'Glad to, boss. Keep your pants on.'

Jenny leads me to the rear of the restaurant, where a spiral staircase winds up to the second floor. We pass some long tables set up for a party, then climb a short flight of stairs to a small landing and a red door. Jenny takes a key from her pocket, opens the door, and waits for me to go through.

Her apartment is as spartan as the cell of a lifer. You could bounce a quarter off the bed, and the linens are surprisingly masculine. A tall set of shelves stands against the wall to my right, and it's filled from top to bottom with books. Literary novels mostly, though the familiar spines of my books are among them, along with Martin Cruz Smith, Donna Tartt, and Peter Hoeg. There's no television, but a boom box sits beside the bed, an Indigo Girls concert flyer tacked to the wall above it. Caitlin's suspicion that Jenny has a crush on me is looking less accurate by the second.

With careful steps Jenny crosses the room to the far corner, where a microwave oven and coffeemaker stand on a table beside a lavatory. She pours water from a Kentwood bottle into the coffee carafe, then from the carafe into the coffee maker. Her back is to me, but she appears to be concentrating on her movements.

'Is green tea okay?' she asks.

'It's fine.'

A spoon jangles loudly in a cup. Jenny's hands are shaking.

'Are you okay?' I ask.

She nods quickly, still facing away from me. 'Just nervous.'

'How do you know the Marston family? Are you originally from Natchez?'

'No.' She turns and faces me, revealing the anxiety in her eyes. I have a sudden intuition that she's about to tell me Leo Marston forced her to commit some sexual act, or perhaps got her pregnant. She's far too young for him, but if an impoverished killer like Ray Presley can rob the cradle, why can't Leo Marston?

'But you know the Marstons,' I press her.

'I know Olivia.'

Olivia. 'Does Livy have something to do with the Payton case?'

'I don't know.'

'Jenny, why don't you just tell me what you know? Start at the beginning, and let me decide how important it is.'

She shakes her head. 'You've got the wrong idea. I mean – I misled you a little. This isn't about your case.'

My alarm is ringing again, full volume now. 'Then what's it about?'

'This is so hard for me.' She wrings her hands and looks at the ceiling, then focuses her glistening eyes on mine. 'I think – I mean, I'm pretty sure – Mr. Cage, I'm pretty sure you're my father.'

Chapter 33

I'm pretty sure you're my father.

Jenny's words hang in the air like ozone after a lightning strike. My discomfort escalates to panic in a fraction of a second. This is the root of the strange fascination Caitlin picked up that first night. It's something I've heard about my whole life, orphaned or adopted children convincing themselves that the father who abandoned them is some famous man.

'Look, Miss—' I grope for her last name, then realize I never knew it.

'Doe,' she says. 'Isn't that pathetic? That's my last name. Jennifer Doe. It's on my birth certificate.'

I'm backing toward the door, which leads to the stairs and the second floor and the spiral staircase and the restaurant and sanity. 'I think we'd better go back down.'

She holds up her hands in supplication, pleading for my attention. 'I don't want anything from you. And I'm not crazy. Please believe me. I'm scared to death right now. I'm so scared. I just want to know who I am!'

Hot, clear water bubbles out of the coffeemaker, for tea that will never be made.

'I can't help you with that question, Jenny.'

'If you'll listen to me for two minutes, you'll know you can.'

My hand is on the doorknob.

'Livy Marston is my mother!'

423

This stops me.

'I was born in February of 1979.'

My brain is working backward to the point of conception. February, January, December – oh hell, just go back twelve months and add three. If Jenny is telling the truth, she was conceived in May of 1978. The month Livy and I graduated high school.

'My birth certificate proves it,' she says in a defensive voice.

I drop my hand from the knob. 'Let me see.'

She goes to the bookshelf, takes down my second novel, and opens it to the flyleaf. From there she removes a white sheet of paper, which she holds out to me. I don't look at her face as I reach for it. If I did, I know I would be searching for similarities to my own.

The birth certificate looks authentic. Issued by the State of Louisiana, the city of New Orleans. The child's name is listed as *Jennifer Doe.* What nearly stops my heart is what is printed on the line for *Mother.* Right there in black and white is the name *Olivia Linsford Marston.*

The line beside *Father* is blank.

'Jesus God,' I murmur.

'It was a privately arranged adoption,' Jenny says. 'Set up before I was ever born. The adopting parents wanted the name Jennifer on the birth certificate.'

My heart is skipping beats.

She rushes on, her voice shaky. 'I didn't know any of this until a year ago. I spent most of my life in foster homes. I wanted to know where I'd come from. Who my birth parents were. I didn't have anybody–'

'Jenny, slow down.' I hold up my hands. 'I'm going to listen, okay? Just calm down and tell me your story.'

She looks frozen, like a strip of film stopped in mid-motion. The relief in her eyes is heartbreaking. If she weren't so caught up in her own emotions, she might realize that after seeing that birth certificate, it would take a winch to pull me out of her apartment. Already thoughts that haven't meshed for twenty years are falling into place. Livy was pregnant our senior year. Or the summer following it, rather. And she carried the child to term. That *is* why she disappeared. I guess the assumptions I made about female reproductive biology in 1978 were about as accurate as my judgments of Livy's true nature.

'Pour the tea,' I say dazedly. 'That'll calm you down.'

'I don't want it.'

'Okay . . . you said you wanted to find out who your birth parents were. How did you go about doing that?'

'Well, like I said, it was a private adoption, which is big business in Louisiana, if you don't know. It took a lot of work, but I finally learned the name of the lawyer who handled the adoption. Clayton Lacour, from New Orleans. I did some checking on him, and I found out he was well connected. Mafia connected. I was afraid that if I just walked in and asked, Lacour wouldn't tell me anything about my birth parents. All the law required was that he ask my mother whether or not she wanted to be found by me. And I was pretty sure that whoever she was, she wouldn't be too happy about me showing up on her doorstep after twenty years.'

Jenny's voice is leveling out; the act of telling her story has distracted her from the fears bubbling inside her.

'I'd been around a little. I knew the street. So instead of marching in and asking my questions, I applied for a job at Lacour's office. P.A., gofer, answering the phone, whatever. I dressed like a college girl – a loose one – and made sure Lacour saw me when I went in. He practically licked me from head to toe. Took me into his office for a personal interview and hired me on the spot.'

She would have made a good D.A.'s investigator.

'It was a race between finding out what I wanted to know and Lacour getting up the nerve to jump me right there in the office. Whenever I was alone, I'd search the place. I brought my lunch every day, told them I was dieting. File room, computers, his personal cabinets, closets, everything. A lot of the stuff had combination locks. It took me five weeks to find out where everything was, and another week to copy it all.'

'What did you find?'

'Lacour handled a lot of adoptions. All privately arranged, always white babies. And for real money. Thirty-five thousand dollars changed hands when I was adopted. You believe that? I went through all his records and finally found the Jennifer Doe birth certificate. I'd always been called Jenny, every home I went to. So I copied the file and studied it at home. I found out I'd been adopted on the day I was born, by a childless rich couple from New Orleans. Lacour had made notes in the file. He thought the couple was trying save their marriage by adopting a baby. He turned out to be right. They divorced when I was two, and neither one wanted custody. I went into the state system. I was adopted by another family, but . . .' Her eyes glaze to opacity as she trails off. 'I don't really want to go into that. It was . . . an abuse situation. I ended up in the foster care system, and that's where I stayed until I was eighteen.'

She doesn't have to go into it. As a young district attorney in Houston, I handled cases arising out of foster care that are still burned into my heart.

'All that mattered,' she says, 'was that the file contained the name of my birth mother. Olivia Marston. It also contained the name of another lawyer, the one who'd brought me to Lacour's attention.'

'Leo Marston,' I say softly.

'Yes. Judge Marston and Clayton Lacour went way back. They'd done a lot of deals together. Oil leases, real estate, you name it. What had happened was obvious. Marston's daughter got pregnant when she was eighteen, and he arranged to get rid of the baby for her. I was that baby. What I couldn't figure out is why she didn't just have an abortion.'

'The Marstons are big Catholics.'

Jenny gives me the jaded stare of a runaway who has seen it all. 'What's your point?'

She's right, of course. Livy's sister had an abortion when she was in college.

'What did you do after you found that out?'

'I quit Lacour. But before I did, I stole everything pertaining to Marston. Most of it was files. The rest was tapes.'

'Tapes?'

'Lacour taped everything. He was connected, like I said. And totally paranoid. He'd worked for the Marcello family when he was younger. Carlos Marcello, the Mob guy? Anyway, he saved these phone tapes just like files. Sometimes when he was drinking, he'd talk about his "insurance." That was the tapes. There were twelve tapes coded for Marston's name. I took them all on the day I split.'

'What did Lacour say about you quitting?'

'I didn't stick around to talk. I'm sure he thought I left because he couldn't keep his hands off me. I'd used a fake name, so he couldn't trace me. He's bound to have noticed the missing files, but so what? I stole some other files relating to Judge Marston just to confuse the trail.'

'What did you do next?'

'I went to Atlanta to find my mother.'

'And?'

'She refused to see me.'

'At all?'

'When I called her home, she hung up on me. So, one day at her office, I sort of ambushed her. It's a big law firm. She was so afraid I'd make a scene that she took me into her private office. Acted like I was a client. She told me she didn't want anything to do with me. She had no interest in my life, nothing. She wrote me a check for twenty-five thousand dollars and told me to go away.'

Jenny is crying now, but she wipes away the tears with fierce determination. 'She broke my heart that day. I'd been through a lot in my life. I thought I was tough. But to have the woman who'd given birth to me offer me money to disappear . . . to pretend that I'd never even been born. I just couldn't stand it.'

She closes her eyes, takes a deep breath, and holds it.

'Why don't you sit down?' I suggest.

She expels the air in a long, steady exhalation. 'No, this is better. Really.'

'What did you do next?'

'I tore up her check. I probably should have kept it, because I really needed the money. But I couldn't. I tore it up and asked her to tell me my father's name. She turned white, Mr. Cage. That question scared her to death. I begged her to tell me, but she wouldn't. I told her I would never do anything to hurt her and asked her to please reconsider. Then I left.'

'I'm so sorry, Jenny.'

'After that I got stoned for three weeks. From the file, I worked out that my mother must have gotten pregnant at the end of her senior year of high school. Which meant she was probably living here at the time, right? And her father still lived here. I figured if I hung around here awhile, I might be able to find out who she was dating back then. Maybe figure out my birth father that way. So I got on a Trailways and came to Natchez. When I got here, I found out Livy Marston was practically a celebrity. Everybody remembered her. They talked about her like she was like a princess or something.'

'She was, in a way. Did you tell anybody that she was your mother?'

'No. I played it very cool. I'd hear people talking about

her sometimes, waiting tables or hanging out, and I'd ask about her. It didn't take long to find out that you were her boyfriend during her senior year. I even saw an old yearbook with a picture of you together. And you *were* a celebrity. I mean, you are. A real one. It freaked me out, honestly. I knew so many foster kids who made up those kinds of fantasies. But this fantasy was *real*.'

I am past the point of being able to respond.

'People said Olivia disappeared for nearly a year after she graduated, that she'd gone to Europe or something. That's when she was pregnant with me.'

The beginnings of nausea are welling in my stomach. The logic of Jenny's story – and its accordance with the known facts – is unassailable. In five minutes a waitress has supplied the missing piece of a puzzle that has haunted me for twenty years. Leo Marston went after my father because I got his daughter pregnant. Because I changed the course of her life and shattered the dreams he'd had for her. His dream that she would go to Ole Miss. That she would attend the same law school he'd gone to. Marry some suitable Mississippi boy and move back to Natchez to practice with her father. *That* was what Maude was talking about the night she threw the drink in my face. What I can't understand is why Livy wouldn't tell me she was pregnant at the time. Why keep it from me? And why hadn't her father called mine in a rage and demanded that I marry her?

But in that question lies the answer to the others. Livy's parents weren't white trash from the wrong side of the tracks, a family for whom a marriage to a doctor's son – even a shotgun marriage – would be a step up the social ladder. They were *Marstons*. Natchez royalty. The worst thing Leo and Maude could possibly imagine would be anything that might slow the momentum of their perfect daughter's perfect life. Marriage would never have entered their minds. They wouldn't want a single soul to discover that Livy was pregnant, and they would want the resulting child to disappear from the face of the earth. I can't believe Leo let Livy carry the child to term.

As for Livy keeping the pregnancy from me, her psychology was simple enough. She had ambitions, and marriage at eighteen wasn't one of them. When she thought of marriage, she envisioned someone who could not possibly be found in the backward and somnolent state of her birth. Yet for the past few days she has acted as though she'd like nothing better than to spend the rest of her life with me.

'She never told you anything about me?' Jenny asks in a small voice.

'Not a word. I never suspected that Livy had a child. No one did.'

'Well, she does. She may not want me, but she's my mother.'

'Jenny, I know this sounds pathetic, but . . . I don't know what to say.'

'I know I sprang this on you at a terrible time. I'm so sorry about your maid.'

'It's all right.'

She takes a tentative step towards me. 'Will you do me a huge favor, Mr. Cage?'

'If I can. What is it?'

'Will you get a blood test?'

My stomach flips over. 'A paternity test?'

'It's just one tube of blood. For a DNA test.'

'Jenny—'

'I know you feel like you've been hit with a ton of bricks. I don't want to creep you out or anything. But when I saw you sitting down there today, you looked so vulnerable. The way I feel all the time. I just knew you were more compassionate than – *her*. Even if you didn't want anything to do with me, I knew you'd be nicer about it.'

My mind has slipped away again. Livy's reaction to Jenny's appearance in Atlanta seems incomprehensible. I can understand her being shocked, or afraid of what her husband might think. But to be so cruel . . .

'It is possible, right?' Jenny asks. 'I mean, you were sleeping with Livy Marston in high school?'

'Yes.'

She shakes her head as though she still can't believe we're talking face to face. 'This is so scary. But it's liberating too. I really thought you were going to just run out of here. Straight to a judge to get a restraining order against me.'

'Jenny—'

'And you have a little girl,' she says excitedly. 'I mean, I could have a *sister*.'

Primal fear grips my heart. 'Jenny, we've got to take this one step at a time. You—'

'I know. I didn't mean to be pushy. I don't want to crash in on your life or anything. I'd never do that. I've just felt so alone my whole life.' In an instant her face seems to collapse in upon itself. 'You don't know the things that have happened to me, Mr. Cage.'

'I can guess. Look, the first thing I should do is talk to Livy.'

'She won't talk about it.'

'She'll talk to me.'

Jenny is wringing her hands again. 'I heard a rumour last night. Someone in the restaurant said you were seeing her again. They saw you out driving. I've been so weirded out by that. I thought you had a thing for the publisher of the newspaper.'

'Jenny . . . Livy may have been cruel to you, but she's not a monster.'

'I'm telling you, she's not rational about this.'

'Does Leo Marston know about you?'

'Oh, yeah.' She nods slowly. 'I talked to him once. He heard me out, then told me that he had to honor his daughter's wishes regarding me, and he expected me to do the same.'

'I'll bet he offered you fifty grand to disappear.'

'Ha. He told me it probably would have been better if I hadn't been born, but that I had been, so I had to do the best I could. Life is tough, he said. You believe that? Like his life was ever tough. That son of a bitch. But he scared me. He told me if I tried to make any public scandal, he'd have to take steps to "resolve the situation." And he wasn't talking about legal steps. God, I wish I'd taped that conversation. I'd seen mob guys in Lacour's office in New Orleans. They were basically okay guys, most of them. But Leo Marston . . . he's not a nice guy. He made me feel like I'd be doing the world a service if I slit my wrists.'

'I'm sorry, Jenny. That's all I can say right now.' Though I probably shouldn't, I walk to her and take her hands in mine. They're alarmingly cold. 'I don't know what the truth is. I honestly don't. But if I am your father, I'll take care of you. It's too late for me to be a father in the real sense. But you won't want for anything, and you won't be alone.'

To see a grown woman break into a child is a terrible thing, and I will not speak of it here.

The *Examiner* building is humming like a beehive, but I see no sign of Caitlin as I pass through the newsroom. I go straight to the conference room, which at the moment contains two female reporters poring over the Marston files, patiently separating wheat from chaff.

'Ladies, could I have the room for a few minutes?'

They looked up at me like graduate students disturbed in their library carrels, then blink and look at each other.

'Uh, sure,' says the one wearing glasses.

As soon as the door closes, I tear through the stacks of

paper on the table, looking for something that seemed trivial only two days ago: the scrawled note listing the income Marston realized from private adoptions. Yesterday it was just another scrap of paper among thousands. Now it's my personal Rosetta stone.

It's not on the table.

I drop to my knees and start working through the carefully stacked piles on the floor, shoving aside page after page, letting them fall where they will. In five minutes the room is awash in paper, and sweat is running down my face. In ten I am trying to suppress the furious panic of an Alzheimer's patient who sets down his car keys and can't find them five seconds later.

And then I am holding the damn thing.

One sheet of yellow legal paper, with a column of years beginning in 1972 and continuing to the present. Some years aren't listed, but beside each that is, an amount of money is noted. The highest figures correspond to the 1980s, and some of these are followed by a one-digit number in parenthesis, which probably indicates the number of adoptions handled in that year. Beside the year 1978 is written the figure $35,000.

Jenny Doe is telling the truth.

The weight of this knowledge is staggering, but before I can begin to absorb it, the door to the conference room opens a crack, and then Caitlin walks in, her face flushed with excitement.

'I just heard you were here. Listen to this. My father called twenty minutes ago. He found out why Dwight Stone won't testify for us.'

I fold the scrap of legal paper and slip it into my pocket. 'Why?'

'Stone has a daughter.'

'So? I have a daughter too.' *Maybe two.*

'Your daughter's not an FBI agent.'

The scrap of paper is momentarily forgotten. 'Dwight Stone has a daughter in the FBI?'

A triumphant smile lights Caitlin's face. 'Ten years in. John Portman can ruin her career with a single reassignment, and he can make it the same way.'

It had to be something like this. In Colorado I had gotten such an impression of integrity from Dwight Stone that I couldn't fathom what would keep him from helping me expose the truth of what happened here in 1968. But children make us all vulnerable. They're hostages to fortune, as the poet said.

'Hostages to fortune?' says Caitlin.

I must have spoken aloud. 'Nothing. It doesn't matter.'

'Penn, what's the matter? You looked zoned out.'

'I'm fine.'

'Bullshit. You look terrible.' She glances around the room, which is strewn with loose pages like leaves on a forest floor. 'What happened in here? What are you looking for?'

'I already found it.'

'What?'

'Something personal. Nothing to do with our case.'

Caitlin goes to the table and picks up a few pages, straightens them into a stack, and sets them back down. Then she turns those remarkable green eyes on me and speaks in a voice raw with hurt. 'It's Livy Marston, isn't it? Nothing else would get you so worked up.'

'It has to do with Livy, yes.'

'You can't tell me what it is?'

'Not yet. Not until I know something for sure. Right now I need a telephone.'

She waves her hand with disgust. 'Take any one you want.'

'It has to be private.'

'You can use my office.' There is something like pity in her eyes.

She escorts me through the newsroom, shrugging at Kelly

on the way. As soon as she shuts the door behind me, I dial Tuscany. Thankfully, Livy answers.

'This is Penn.'

'What do you want?'

'We need to talk.'

'You haven't thought so for the past three days.'

'I do now. It's important.'

'Important.' There's a long pause, but I don't jump to fill it. 'All right,' she says finally. 'Where?'

I close my eyes. 'I haven't eaten. I was thinking of getting a bite at Biscuits and Blues. That sound okay to you?'

Silence.

'Livy?'

'I'm not really hungry.'

'You could watch me eat,' I say, pushing it.

'Why don't we take a ride instead? It's nice outside.'

Sure, and why don't we ask our daughter to come along? 'Is your father home?'

'No. He's at his office with Blake Sims, preparing for the trial.'

'I'll pick you up in five minutes.'

'Five minutes?'

'It's important.'

'All right. I may look ghastly, but I'll be waiting on the gallery.'

Livy Marston has never looked ghastly in her life. 'Just have the gate open.'

I hang up and start through the newsroom, heading for the front of the building. Caitlin and Kelly are talking quietly in a corner. When she sees me, she breaks away from him and physically bars the door.

'Penn, you've got to tell me what's going on.'

'It's nothing to do with you. It's personal.'

She looks around the newsroom and realizes that her employees are staring at her. Taking my wrist, she speaks in a quieter voice. 'I consider your personal life personal to me.'

I have no response to this. Caitlin matters to me, but right now there is a motor spinning in my chest, driving me irresistibly toward Tuscany, the only place where the truth of my life can be found. 'It could be, someday. But it's not now. Let me by, Caitlin.'

She hesitates, then drops my wrist and moves aside.

Kelly starts to fall into step with me.

'Stay here,' I tell him. 'I don't need you for this.'

He stops, but before the main door closes behind me, I hear Caitlin say, 'Go with him.'

Tuscany is a magnificent mansion, but it would look incomplete without the indelible image of Livy standing on the gallery. She's wearing a royal blue sun dress, belted at the waist and falling just below her knees. The air is cool beneath the trees, and the freshly fallen leaves have been gathered into random piles by the wind. The scene looks staged, like a rich color shot from an ad in *Architectural Digest*. *Who is that beauty waiting for?* you wonder as you flip past it. *If only she were waiting for me.*

This beauty is waiting for me. Only she has no idea what a dreadful gift I bring. The last thing she wants to receive. A demand for the truth, and the means to compel her to speak it.

I park beside the Negro lawn jockeys and remain in the car. Livy comes down the steps, her tread light, her movements graceful. Her eyes are curious as they take me in. She walks around to the passenger door, clearly wondering why I haven't scurried around to open it for her. Unable to wait for the pretense of a drive to speak to her, I get out and address her over the gleaming black roof of the car.

'Do you know a girl named Jenny Doe?'

She freezes with her hand on the passenger door. Behind those eyes I know so well, have dreamed of for years, another pair of eyes is looking out. Frightened, hunted eyes.

'Who have you been talking to?' she asks, her voice oddly devoid of emotion.

'Does it matter? I want to know if you were pregnant in 1978.'

'That's none of your business.'

'Not my business. Is that girl our daughter, Livy?'

She takes a deep breath, recovering her composure with remarkable resilience. 'No,' she says simply.

'No, she's not my daughter? Or no, she's not yours either?'

She purses her lips, as though calculating the impact of various replies. 'Stay out of this, Penn. It's none of your affair.'

'Were you sleeping with someone besides me in the spring of seventy-eight?'

Her eyes flash. 'Weren't you?'

My heart feels suddenly cold. 'No. But if you were, how do you know for certain who the father was?'

'Maybe I don't care who it was.'

The steel in her voice cannot mask the fear and anguish in her face. 'Livy—'

'Listen to me, Penn. *You are not that girl's father.* I know that with absolute certainty. And if you thought hard about it, you would too.'

'What the hell does that mean? I worked out the months from her birth certificate. I could easily be her father. You got pregnant right before you disappeared.'

She studies me with cold objectivity, as though taking some life-altering decision. 'If you ever mention what I'm about to say, I'll deny I said it. Jenny Doe is my daughter. But she is not yours. She's twenty years old now, and I have no legal responsibility to care for her. As far as I'm concerned, she doesn't exist. Since she's not your child, you have no say whatever in the matter, and you should never mention it to me again.'

'Livy, where is this coming from? How can you be so cruel to this girl?'

'You're so naive. You don't know anything. You—'

She stops as the low purr of an engine murmurs through the trees. I assume it's Kelly until Leo Marston's silver Lincoln Town Car rounds the bend by the azalea bushes.

'Get out of here,' Livy says in a taut voice. 'Go. And don't come back. I was stupid to think we could ever make it work.'

I don't move. I can't.

Leo's face is masked by the glare of the sun on his windshield as he parks behind the BMW. When he gets out, his face is not mottled red with fury, as I expect, but calm. A smug smile curls his lips as he walks toward me. When he stops three feet away, I see that his upper cheeks are flushed, and when he speaks I smell the sweet odor of bourbon.

'Livy?' he drawls, glancing at her over the roof of the BMW. 'Does this person have your permission to be on our property?'

'He was just leaving.'

'That doesn't answer my question. I asked if he's a guest, or if he's a *trespasser*, like the other night.'

Livy looks at me with pleading eyes, the familiar eyes I once knew. 'He's my guest, but he's leaving. Let's go inside.'

'In a minute, in a minute.' Leo is grinning like a six-year-old boy with a secret. 'I'm glad I ran into you, Cage. I've got some news that you'll be interested in.'

'Is that right?'

'You're damn right that's right. A friend of yours was just arrested in the Hoover Building in Washington, D.C.'

Fear and guilt for Peter Lutjens clench my stomach.

'Seems this fellow was attempting to steal a file,' Leo drones on. 'A file sealed on national security grounds. He had a funny name. Foreign name. Dutch maybe. There's some question of treason, I believe. John Portman is person-ally investigating the situation.'

He turns to Livy. 'This boy's got no case, Livy. None at all.' He turns back to me, laughter rumbling low and deep in his chest. 'When Wednesday gets here, you're gonna wish you never opened your mouth about me. You're gonna *rue the goddamn day* you decided to fuck with Leo Marston.'

Confused images fire through the synapses of my brain. My father on the floor of his bedroom, felled by a heart attack. My mother in tears, unable to cope with the stress of the malpractice trial. Jenny Doe describing her meeting with the man who stands before me now, the man who made her feel she'd be doing the world a favor by committing suicide. Peter Lutjens being handcuffed while his wife and children wait for him at home in a clutter of U-Haul boxes.

Victory is written on Leo's face like blood after a hunt, and the wolfish blue eyes are laughing. I have not struck another human being in anger since I was fifteen years old, but my knee rises into his groin with preternatural speed and force. The air explodes from his lungs. As he doubles over, my elbow crashes into the side of his head, just the way a Houston police detective once taught me.

'Stop it!' Livy screams. *'Penn, stop!'*

She is running around the car to get between us. Some part of my brain knows I should stop, but I'm still moving forward, pursuing Leo as he staggers back. He shakes his head and raises his big left hand to his jaw. I draw back my fist, then freeze as a silver derringer appears before my nose as though by magic. He must have had it palmed all along, a little nickel-plated gambler's special.

'Go ahead, you little pissant,' he snarls. 'Go ahead.'

'Daddy?' Livy stands two feet behind her father, her voice riding a current of hysteria.

'Go inside, baby. You don't want to see this.'

'Daddy, I love him.'

The simple declaration hits Leo like an arrow. He actually flinches, like a bear struck between the ribs, and an expression of pure hatred comes over his face. 'Go inside, Livy! This boy's forgotten his place. He assaulted me on my property.'

But Livy doesn't go. The three of us remain locked in our positions, a pathetic standoff on the edge of tragedy that lasts until Daniel Kelly's rented Taurus rolls slowly up the drive.

Kelly parks alongside the cars, five feet from us, and rolls down his window like a tourist asking for directions. But what comes through his window is not a map but a Browning Hi-Power pistol, which he points at Leo's head.

'Please go inside the house, sir,' he says.

'Who the hell are you?' Leo asks, keeping the derringer in my face.

Kelly's suntanned face remains calm, as though he were listening to a soothing piece of music. 'I'm the man who's going to end your life unless you take that gun in the house.'

'Bullshit,' Leo grunts. 'Get the fuck off my property.'

'I'm here to do a job, sir,' Kelly says in the same lazy voice. 'Don't make yourself part of it.'

At last Leo really looks at Kelly, and the muscles in his jaw tighten. He has vastly multiplied his family fortune by accurately judging men's characters. And whatever he sees in Daniel Kelly's eyes convinces him that today is the wrong day to tempt fate. He lowers the derringer.

'You just made yourself part of *my* job, sonny.' He raises two fingers in a little toodle-loo gesture, then turns and walks up the broad steps of his mansion.

'Livy,' he says without turning around. 'Your mother needs you.'

'I'm coming.' She steps toward me and tries to take my hand, but I pull it away. 'Make a public apology, Penn,' she pleads. 'Please. Do that, and I'll convince Daddy to drop the suit.'

'It's too late for that.'

She looks at me sadly. 'You can't play my father's game and win. Not in this town. Not in this *state*. Nobody can. You could lose everything you have.'

'You've got a short memory, Livy. Your father lost his case against mine twenty years ago, and he's going to lose this one.'

'That was different. It was a weak case to start with.'

'Then why did he take it?'

Unreadable emotion flares in her eyes. 'I don't know. But I do know you nearly fainted when he told you that man had been arrested. He was your last hope, wasn't he? He was your case. If you walk into the courtroom Wednesday, you'll be like a lamb going to slaughter.'

I step back from her, trying not to think of Peter Lutjens. 'That's my problem. Your problem is a lot bigger than that. Your whole life is built around some secret tragedy whose real victim is a girl crying alone in a room three miles from here. What are you going to do about that?'

Her eyes go cold again. 'Nothing. And you'd better not either.' She turns and walks up three steps, then looks back at me. 'Don't say I didn't warn you about the trial.'

This time she goes all the way up and through the massive door.

I get into the BMW and start to leave, but Kelly pulls his Taurus in front of it, blocking my way. Then he gets out and comes around to my window.

'Boss? To an objective observer, it's looks like you're trying awful hard to get killed.'

'I've learned some upsetting things in the past half hour. I haven't even begun to understand them yet. All I know is that I want to nail that son of a bitch more than anything I've ever wanted in my life, other than to save my wife from dying. And that was beyond my power.'

'Maybe this is too,' Kelly says gently. 'I wouldn't mind

bringing that bastard down a peg myself. But things seem pretty seriously stacked against you. Sometimes you've got to pull back. Regroup. Fight another day.'

'No,' I say doggedly, perhaps stupidly. 'If I let the momentum die, Marston and Portman will never pay for whatever they did. Any evidence that exists will disappear.' Althea Payton's words sound in my head like a ghostly refrain. 'If not now, when. You know?'

A skeptical grunt. 'Yeah, maybe.'

'I've got one shot left, Kelly.'

'What?'

'Dwight Stone. He knows the truth. He could bring down the whole damn temple.'

'Caitlin says he won't testify.'

'He wants to help me. I know he does. But he's got a daughter in the FBI. That gives Portman total control of her life, and by extension, Stone's.'

'So, what can you do?'

'I'm going back to Colorado.'

The old Kelly smile returns to his lips. 'Well . . . I was ready for a change of scenery anyway.'

'Do we still have FBI surveillance covering us?'

'I've seen them three times today. They're good.'

'That's okay. You're going to keep them nice and busy for me.'

'Yeah, and . . . ? How do we lose them?'

'We don't. This time I'm going alone.'

Chapter 34

The American Eagle ATR plows into a trough of turbulence, drops like a stone, then catches an updraft from the Rocky Mountains below and settles out again. I and my fellow passengers are thirty miles from Crested Butte, Colorado, and I can't wait for the wheels to hit the runway. When I flew out of Baton Rouge, it was ninety degrees. When I changed planes in Dallas, it was sixty-eight. In Colorado there's two feet of snow on the ground, my plane is three hours behind schedule because of the unexpected storm, and the only thing I know about ATR aircraft is that they fly like hogs with ice on the wings. But that isn't the only reason for my anxiety. In less than an hour I will be face to face with former special agent Dwight Stone, the only man on earth who can give me what I need.

The desire for revenge I felt when I attacked Leo Marston at Tuscany yesterday seems trivial to me now. I am a different man than I was yesterday. The past I thought I knew is dead. Because last night I faced a truth so terrible I can hardly accept even now.

After Kelly and I left Tuscany, we drove straight to the motel. I felt an overwhelming desire to hug Annie, the daughter I knew beyond any shadow of doubt to be mine. After spending the evening watching television with her, I put her to bed and sent Kelly out for a bottle of Absolut. For the first time in years I drank with the sole purpose of getting drunk. It didn't take long, and drunkenness brought with it the blessed inability to ponder clearly the events of twenty years before. Who was sleeping with whom. And when. And why, if I 'really thought about it,' as Livy had told me to do, I would know that I could not possibly be Jenny Doe's father. I passed out in a chair, and if my mother hadn't knocked on my door to check on me, I might not have fathomed the truth until much later. As it was, I awakened in the midst of a nightmare, tortured by images I could not have conceived of the day before.

Livy told me the truth.

I am not Jenny's father.

I know this because the last time Livy and I ever made love – prior to this week – was one week after graduation, and she was just starting her period. She had been a couple of weeks late at the time, and we were both terrified she was pregnant. When her cycle resumed, we celebrated by going to a hotel – which we almost never did – and making love. At that point Livy had two weeks left in Natchez before leaving for the summer program at Radcliffe. I was miserable because earlier in the spring I had promised my father I would go to Shiloh with him after graduation. Of my two remaining weeks with Livy, I was going to give up one to tromp over a Civil War battlefield. I consoled myself with the knowledge that we would both be at Ole Miss in the fall, but when I got back from Shiloh, Livy had already left for Cambridge, and I did not see her again for more than a year.

During that time, I naturally considered the possibility that Livy could be pregnant. But I was fairly certain that, while it was possible for a woman to conceive while having her period, the odds against it were high. I later learned that a woman can have a period *while* she's pregnant, but by then I'd written off the possibility altogether. Given that Livy's sister had had an abortion, I was certain that Livy would have done the same in the event of pregnancy, and certainly not run off for a year like some 'girl in trouble' from *Peyton*

Place. But clearly I had been wrong to assume that. The question was, why?

At Tuscany, Livy had told me in no uncertain terms that I was not Jenny's father. If I wasn't, who was? Livy delivered Jenny nine months after leaving Natchez. The father had to be someone she'd slept with immediately after that last period. Given Livy's shadowy sexual history, that could easily be someone I did not know. But when I jerked awake last night in a clammy sweat of panic, I knew that Jenny's father was not unknown to me. This knowledge came to me even before I consciously apprehended it, announcing itself with a wave of horror that sent me running to the bathroom.

Jenny's father is Leo Marston.

As sickening as this idea was, I could not push it from my mind. Only this conclusion made sense of every incomprehensible action and statement that had followed, right up to the present. Livy's inexplicable promiscuity during high school. Her mother's chronic alcoholism. Not telling me about her pregnancy, then disappearing for a year, cutting herself off from family and friends. Starting life in Virginia as though her life in Mississippi had never existed. Settling in Atlanta. And most telling, her unwillingness to speak to Jenny even twenty years after her birth. What had seemed so cruel hours before suddenly made sense. Jenny was a living reminder of something so terrible that Livy simply could not face it. What had Livy said on the bridge, when I asked her if she could ever live in Natchez again?

Not while my parents are alive . . .

The idea that Leo had sexually abused his daughter from childhood on left me feeling hollowed out, like a wasting disease. Everyone in Natchez thought Livy Marston had enjoyed the most privileged and perfect childhood anyone could, free from want, full of love and adoration. But how many times had she told me that Tuscany was a prison, not a palace? How many times did I discount her laments as the

445

whining of a spoiled rich girl? The night we first began to get close, when she confessed the date rape by an older boy at school . . . had that been a fictionalized version of rapes by her father? Were they still going on even then? It was difficult to imagine Livy submitting to Leo's advances at that age. He outweighed her by more than a hundred pounds, but by eighteen Livy was a strong, athletic girl. Yet I know very little about abuse, and so much human strength springs from the mind, not the body. Was Livy's entire childhood a lie? Were her stellar performances in every facet of high school and college life part of some elaborate coping mechanism designed to conceal the awful reality she lived behind the walls of Tuscany?

Only two things argued against this interpretation of the facts. The first was Leo's persecution of my father. If I had gotten Livy pregnant, Leo's attack would be easy to understand: a quest for vicarious revenge. But if Leo had impregnated Livy, the malpractice case made no sense. The second was Livy's decision to carry the child to term. If her pregnancy had resulted from a rape by her father, her decision to keep the baby seemed unfathomable. Even the most dogmatic Catholic might consider abortion in those circumstances, and Livy wasn't dogmatic.

I reflected upon Marston's persecution of my father as I splashed water on my face from the motel lavatory and ate a handful of animal crackers Annie had left on the television. As soon as the sugar hit my bloodstream, I saw straight through to the truth of the malpractice lawsuit.

It was blindingly simple.

Maude Marston must have learned of her daughter's pregnancy. And that pregnancy somehow had to be explained. What more likely candidate for fatherhood could there have been than Penn Cage, Livy's most recent boyfriend? Whether Leo actually told Maude this lie or let her think of it herself did not matter. When the chance to persecute my father came, he jumped at it – his sole goal being to reinforce the initial lie about Livy's pregnancy. The question of whether Maude might – at some level – have known of the incestuous relationship was something I didn't even want to think about. But by trying to destroy my father as an act of 'vengeance,' Leo more deeply concealed his mortal sin from his wife, and perhaps even from himself. I suppose it's even possible that after twenty years of denial, he has convinced himself that I *am* Jenny's father, the man who 'ruined' Livy's life.

Truth always clarifies, but with clarification comes a whirl-wind of emotions no one can predict. My initial reaction was horror mixed with outrage. Suddenly even the murder of Del Payton seemed trivial. Payton burned to death in a few agonizing minutes. If I was right about Jenny Doe's parent-age, Livy had died a thousand times before she reached adulthood. She has been burning alive for more than thirty years.

I sat alone in the dark well of the night, pondering what to do with this terrible knowledge. After an hour I made some long-distance calls, irritating more than a few people. When dawn broke, I woke Kelly and spoke to him, and a few hours later we executed a ruse which left him surrounded by our FBI watchers at the Natchez Mall Cinema while Sam Jacobs drove me to the Baton Rouge airport in his Hummer. In Baton Rouge, I paid cash for a ticket to Dallas, where I changed planes for Albuquerque, and there boarded the ATR bound for the tiny airport at Crested Butte.

The pilot has begun his descent, plowing up the long valley from the southeast. The snowy majesty of the Rockies leaves me unaffected. At my core, in the moist and primitive darkness, a malevolent seed is germinating. A desire not to publicly humiliate Leo Marston, not even to destroy his career as a lawyer and judge by sending him to Parchman prison, but to end his very life. To remove him from the world. Not in Del Payton's name, but in Livy's. And in mine. For the life he stole from us.

I will soon be listening to former special agent Dwight Stone explain why he cannot tell a jury what he knows about Leo Marston and John Portman. He will soberly tell me about his daughter, the FBI agent. And he will expect me, as a father, to understand his position.

But I will not understand.

I have a surprise for Dwight Stone.

The snow has stopped when we touch down at Crested Butte, but thankfully the car rental company has fitted the tires of my Ford Explorer with chains. I am unaccustomed to icy roads, but it doesn't take me long to get the hang of it. The problem is that only the main roads have been plowed. The forest service road leading up into the mountains (and Stone's cabin) is plowed only to the summer houses by Nicholson Lake. The jeep track that breaks off from that is impassable, at least for someone of my limited mountain skills, so I have no choice but to abandon the Explorer near a large gravel pit and trek up between the mountains on foot.

It takes less than twenty yards to understand the necessity for snowshoes, a type of footwear I have never worn in my life. In my thinly padded windbreaker and tennis shoes, I am practically begging for frostbite, but Stone's cabin can't be more than three miles away. It's after three o'clock, but I should have plenty of light to make it. I rang Stone's phone from the airport to make sure he was there, and hung up as soon as he answered. I don't want him or anyone tapping his phone to know I'm coming until I arrive.

The jeep track is invisible in the snow, but by roughly following the course of the Slate River upstream, I must eventually strike on Stone's cabin, which is situated practically on top of it. Today the Slate, which was only ten or fifteen feet wide on my last trip, is a roaring flood of blue-black water sluicing down the valley like a logging flume. After a seeming eternity of slipping, falling, digging through drifts, and cracking my elbows and butt, I make my way past the entrance of an old mine, along the base of Anthracite Mesa, and up to the edge of a slot canyon, where the Slate is compressed into a raging chute that rockets over an eight-foot vertical drop. I pick my way along the edge of the canyon with care, knowing that a tumble into that water could easily kill me.

At last Stone's cabin comes into sight, nestled among the tall spruce and fir trees between the jeep track and the river. There's a welcome column of smoke rising from its chimney. I have not been this cold for many years. I stop to catch my breath and marshal my strength, then push on for the last two hundred yards like a climber going for the summit of Everest.

Stone answers his door with a pistol on his hip. The first words out of his mouth are, 'You damn fool.' Then he jerks me inside, slams the door, and darts to the front window, where he stands peering through the curtains.

A fearsome array of weapons lies on the coffee table before the sofa – a hunting rifle, two shotguns, several automatic pistols – and a huge fire crackles in the fieldstone fireplace. The curtains over the back windows are shut, blocking the view toward the Slate and the trees beyond.

Stone must be close to seventy, but his vitality is intimidating. He's one of those leathery guys who'll still be jogging six miles a day when he's eighty. The last time we met, he seemed charged with repressed anger. Now the whole interior of the cabin crackles with his fury, as though my first visit opened some channel to the past that made it impossible for him to hold in his rage any longer.

'What's out there?' I ask.

He keeps staring through the window, his eyes narrowed like those of a marskman. 'You didn't see them when you came in?'

'All I saw was mountains and snow. No cars. No skiers. Nothing.'

'They've been out there all day. Four of them.'

'Who are they?'

'FBI, I hope.'

'And if not?'

He glances at me. 'Then they only let you come in here for one reason.'

'Which is?'

'To make it easier to kill both of us.'

'Shit. Why are we standing here, then?'

'We'd be sitting ducks if we tried to make it out.'

'Call the police.'

Stone's taciturn face hardly moves when he answers. 'There's only the sheriff and a couple of deputies. If those men are here to kill us, they'll kill anyone who tries to interfere as well. And I happen to like the sheriff.'

'But they could be legitimate FBI agents. Right?'

'They could. But they don't *feel* legitimate.'

'What about the state police?'

'Take 'em too long to get here in the snow. And my phone's tapped. I have a cell phone, but whoever's out there will have those frequencies covered. If they mean to kill us, they'll move in the second I call for help.'

'Isn't it early for snow? It's ninety degrees in Mississippi.'

'Anything can happen in October. It rained four days up-country before it turned to snow. That's why the river's up like it is.'

I edge up to the other front window and peer out. I see nothing but spruce, firs, and snow. 'Why don't they move in now?'

'They're waiting for dark.'

'So, we just sit here?'

Stone takes one more look out the window, then walks over to the table holding his weapons. 'Look, you started all this. Now you've got to live with it. So just sit tight. I've been in spots like this before. It's a game of nerves.'

I came to Colorado alone knowing that I would be walking right into the men watching Stone. I did this believing that Stone – a good man with a guilty conscience – would be unwilling to add my death to that conscience by sending me back to Mississippi alone. I was sure that my obvious vulnerability would convince him that the only decent thing to do would be to accompany me back to Natchez to testify. I didn't reckon with the possibility that the men watching him would attempt to kill him outright – and me with him.

He lifts up a cordless phone from the coffee table, punches a button on it, listens, then hangs up and slips the phone into his pocket. 'You killed Arthur Lee Hanratty's brother, right?'

I nod.

'That makes me feel a little better.' He removes a pistol from the small of his back (I hadn't even noticed it), then takes the cordless phone from his pocket and sits on the sofa with both gun and phone in his lap. 'Well, what'd you come back for?'

'The truth. You know it, I need it. It's that simple.'

An ironic smile flickers over Stone's features. 'I suppose since you and I may die together soon, I could make you aware of a few facts. But I'm not going to testify for you. Voluntarily or any other way. And first you'd better show me you're not wearing a wire.'

It's a repeat of my visit to Ray Presley's trailer. I strip off my khakis and shirt, and Stone motions for me to remove my shorts and socks as well.

'Come over here,' he says.

'I'm not submitting to a rectal exam,' I tell him, walking toward the couch.

He chuckles then stands and runs his fingers through my hair, following the line of my skull. He sticks a finger in each of my ears. 'Sorry, but the transmitters are damnably small these days.'

'Now that we've got that over with,' I say, pulling on my pants, 'let's hear what really happened in Natchez in 1968.'

'How far have you gotten on your own?'

'I've got Presley nailed down for the actual murder. My witnesses are Frank Jones, his ex-wife, and Betty Lou Beckham. An ATF bomb expert will confirm C-4 as the explosive, proving Presley planted evidence at the scene. And one of the Fort Polk thieves will put stolen military C-4 in Presley's hands.'

Stone smiles. 'So, you got my fax.'

'Thanks.'

'How do you link Presley to Marston?'

'You.'

He raises his eyebrows. 'I hope you've got something else.'

'Well . . . I did have an FBI agent trying to copy your original report for me. But he was arrested yesterday.'

Stone gives a somber nod. 'I heard.'

Of course. His daughter told him.

'So,' he says, 'Marston orders Presley to do the hit. That's how you see it?'

'Well . . . there's Portman, of course. But I don't know what his role was. Are there more people involved?'

'Conspiracies are always complicated. But in this case, Presley and Marston make a nice package, so why complicate it? Of course, you don't even have Marston yet.'

'But you did.'

'Yes.'

'Tell me how.'

He picks up the cordless phone again, presses a button, listens, then hangs up and begins speaking to me in a low, clear voice, his right hand thumbing the gun in his lap.

'First of all, Portman wasn't my partner. Hoover foisted him on me, fresh out of Yale Law and the Academy. His father was a Wall Street lawyer with Washington connections. He thought the Bureau would be a good political incubator for his son. Like military service without the risk. So pal Edgar throws the kid into a high-profile assignment, safely under the wing of veteran agent Dwight Stone.'

Stone stops speaking for a few moments and listens. I hear only the crackle of the fire and, perhaps, the rush of the swollen Slate behind the cabin.

'Portman didn't give a shit about the Payton case,' he says finally. 'All he cared about was kissing ass and getting promoted to the Puzzle Palace.'

'But you cared. Althea Payton told me you did.'

He nods thoughtfully. 'Cage, in all the mountains of shit, sometimes one case gets to you. You know? For me, it was that one. Payton was a good guy who basically minded his own business and tried to better his lot in life. And he got killed for it. When I found out he'd served in Korea, it got personal. I'd known some black noncoms over there, and they were okay. Payton survived Chosin Reservoir only to get blown to shit by some gutless rednecks in his home town.' Stone slaps the cordless phone against his thigh with a percussive pop. 'Man, I wanted to nail those sons of bitches.

'My first steps were the same ones you've been taking. Frank Jones, his wife, then Betty Lou Jackson. Beckham now, I guess. Betty Lou knew something, but she wouldn't talk. Then Portman and me got shot at out on Highway 61. Hoover got irritated after that incident. Scumbags shooting at the FBI and getting away with it didn't fit his PR plan. He authorized a lot more money and muscle. I cracked Betty Lou, and that put Presley at the scene. Portman and I braced Presley at home, and he told us to stick it. That bastard didn't rattle easily, I'll give him that. Even when we got the Fork Polk thieves to admit selling him the C-4, Presley told us to go to hell.

'We put on the full-court press. On my request, Hoover authorized illegal wiretaps on Presley's home, plus all the nearby pay phones. We bribed local Klansmen, but they couldn't find out a thing about Payton's death. Whoever killed Payton had acted without Klan authority. We put intermittent surveillance on Presley, tight enough to annoy him but loose enough for him to shake. After a week he called Leo Marston from a pay phone near his house.'

'What did he say?'

'Nothing incriminating. Said he wanted to talk, somewhere private. Marston was D.A. then, of course. Nothing illegal about wanting to talk to the district attorney. I thought Presley might be trying to cut a deal with the state authorities to avoid any sort of federal prosecution. The Klan had a lot of influence in Parchman in those days, and they could have assured him an easy stretch. They also had influence over pardons.'

'But making a deal wasn't Presley's style.'

'No,' Stone agrees. 'Anyway, the second Hoover heard Leo Marston's name in connection with the case, the whole case changed. The director assumed personal control.'

'Why?'

'Hoover was a creature of politics. He demanded total control over every case that involved anyone who could do him good or harm down the road.'

'What happened next?'

'We did a black bag job on Marston's mansion. Bugged it top to bottom. Phones, the house, the garden, gazebo, the works. It was a beautiful job.'

'You and Portman?'

'Hell, no. Henry Bookbinder and me. The technology was primitive, but Henry was an artist with it, God rest his soul.'

'What did you pick up?'

Stone smiles with satisfaction. 'The mother lode. One day Presley drove up to the mansion and knocked on the door. Then he and the judge went out to the gazebo and had a long chat. They said enough in thirty minutes to put Marston in the gas chamber.'

I hear a faint ringing in my ears. 'Jesus. What did they say?'

Stone shakes his head. 'You haven't got anywhere on a motive for Marston?'

'That's been my problem all along. I know Leo secretly owned some property that an out-of-town company was thinking of buying. There was some kind of race angle to that. Labour problems. Beyond that, I don't have anything.'

'You were right on target, and you didn't know it. It was a carpet company from Georgia. Zebulon Hickson, the owner, was about a mile to the right of Attila the Hun. He thought slavery was the finest and most misunderstood institution this country ever had. When he opened new factories, he went into communities where what he called "the nigger problem" didn't exist. Of course, by 1968 towns like that were hard to find. Especially along the Mississippi River, which was where he wanted to be.

'Leo Marston stood to make a lot of money off that land. But the labor situation wasn't as stable as Hickson wanted it. Blacks were using the unions to push into white jobs. Hickson had the idea that if an example was made, it would calm the blacks down. Apparently he'd done this somewhere in Georgia, and it had worked.'

Marston's plan seems so obvious now. All it takes is a few facts.

'I honestly doubt Marston ever thought it would work,' muses Stone. 'He was too smart for that. But he didn't *care* whether it worked. He just wanted to sell Hickson his land.'

'So, he went to Ray Presley,' I fill in. 'He said, "We need to make an example of somebody."'

'You got it. Marston didn't care who died. It was just business.'

'Why didn't he use the local Klan? Put a word into the right ear and let the Klan take care of Payton? Why use a cop?'

'Marston was the D.A. He knew the Klan was riddled with federal informants. He wanted zero risk of the murder being traced back to him. He also despised the White Citizens' Council. He called them illiterate Baptist sons of bitches several times on the phone.'

'But he trusted Presley.'

'Yes. And he was right to. It's ironic as hell, really.'

'Why?'

'You'll see in a minute. So, Presley chose Del Payton as the victim. Why, I don't know. He was in charge of voter-registration drives for the local NAACP, but he was a quiet guy. Had a nice house and a pretty wife. Saved his money. He had a nicer house than Presley did, really. That by itself could have been the reason. Anyway, Zeb Hickson was all set to announce his plans for a Natchez carpet factory–'

'But you had Marston by the short hairs.'

'Yep.'

'But you didn't make any arrests.'

Stone sighs deeply. 'Right.'

'Why not?'

'As soon as Hoover heard the tape of Marston and Presley, he ordered me to forward every case note, transcript, surveillance report, witness interview, photograph, and audiotape to Washington. After he reviewed all that, he scheduled a visit to the Jackson field office. Good PR for the troops, he said. But the real reason for that trip was to meet Leo Marston.'

The ringing in my head is an alarm bell now. 'About what?'

'Politics. Clyde Tolson, Hoover's assistant, made the call. I still had the wiretap running, and I heard it. Marston thought he was going up to Jackson for a pat on the back for his performance as D.A. When he got there, Edgar read him the riot act, then laid the classic Hoover pitch on him.'

'Which was?'

'Work for me, or endure the punishment you so richly deserve for your sins.'

'Work for him how?'

A cynical smile thins Stone's lips. 'This is where it gets interesting. And dirty. Del Payton died in May 1968, five weeks after Martin Luther King. What else was going on then?'

'The Vietnam War?'

He waves his hand dismissively. 'The presidential primaries. Bobby Kennedy had jumped into the race as soon as Eugene McCarthy proved LBJ was vulnerable. After Kennedy came in, Johnson announced he wouldn't run for reelection. Del Payton was killed on the day Bobby won the Nebraska primary, and he'd won Indiana the week before. Kennedy was shaping up as the likely Democratic candidate in November.'

'I'm not following you. What's the connection?'

'*Hoover*, Cage. Compared to the presidential race, Hoover didn't give a damn what happened to some black factory worker in Mississippi. Why? Because the FBI director has always served at the pleasure of the President. Hoover had been director since 1924, and he meant to stay director until he died. Two of his least favourite people in the world were Robert Kennedy and Martin Luther King. King's assassination had thrilled him, literally. But Bobby's presidential campaign was giving him ulcers. Can you guess what Hoover's mission in life was in 1968?'

'Not to kill Robert Kennedy?'

'No, no. Forget that crap. He wanted to put Richard Nixon in office. And he was willing to do whatever was required to accomplish that. Hoover and Nixon went way back, to the

1960 election when Nixon lost to JFK. Bobby Kennedy, on the other hand, had treated Hoover like shit when he was attorney general. So, in May 1968 Nixon is making sober speeches about law and order to middle America, while Bobby Kennedy runs from ghetto to college campus preaching about racial equality, poverty in Mississippi, the evils of the Vietnam War, and reaching out to the Soviet Union.'

'I still don't see the relevance to Del Payton.'

Stone looks exasperated by my slowness. 'The relevance is to Leo Marston. And more important, to his father. Leo's father was a major Mississippi power broker, a former state attorney general, just like Leo turned out to be. He was close friends with Big Jim Eastland, a well-known segregationist, head of the Senate Judiciary Committee, and J. Edgar Hoover's number one cheerleader on Capitol Hill.'

At last the picture is coming clear.

'The sixty-eight presidential election was the second closest in history, Cage, after Nixon and JFK in 1960. In sixty-eight Nixon won by less than one percent of the vote. That's how close it was in November. Back in May, when Del Payton was murdered, anything was possible. Mississippi was a Democratic state, but it voted strangely in presidential elections. In 1960 her electors didn't vote for JFK or Nixon, but some guy named Byrd. In sixty-four they voted for Goldwater. In 1968 they were leaning toward–'

'Wallace,' I finish. 'George Wallace.'

Stone nods. 'The racist firecracker from Alabama. Wallace was running as an Independent. Leo and his father were Democrats, but they thought Bobby Kennedy was a communist. Wallace was too racist for them, and more important, they didn't think he could win. So, they cast their lot with Nixon. Old man Marston was doing all he could to sway the movers and shakers in Mississippi to forget Wallace and vote Republican.'

'Jesus.'

'You see it now? Into this mess rides Special Agent Dwight Stone, telling J. Edgar Hoover that the son of one of Nixon's biggest supporters is responsible for a race murder in Mississippi. Did that make the director happy? No, sir. Do you think Hoover wanted to tell his buddy Senator Eastland that the son of an old crony was going to jail for killing a nigger who got out of line? No, sir. And the thought of what Bobby Kennedy would do with that information was enough to give Hoover a heart attack. So . . . what do you think Hoover said to Leo at that meeting in Jackson?'

'I have no idea.'

'Sonny boy, you fucked up. You had the right idea, but you got caught. It's just a good thing you got caught by my people, or life would be getting very uncomfortable right now. In fact, it still could. Then Hoover talked to Leo's papa. It's a lot like *The Godfather*. Nothing formal, but everything understood. Fealty. Absolute loyalty.' Stone modulates his voice into a scratchy Marlon Brando impersonation: '"*Someday, I may ask you to perform a difficult service, but until that day, accept this favor as a gift.*" From that day forward, Hoover owned the Marston family. All their influence, everything.'

'Hoover buried your evidence?'

'All of it. Leo went back to his job and his future. The Payton investigation was allowed to die. Only Ray Presley paid a price.'

'Presley?'

'He'd shot at us on the highway, remember? Hoover wouldn't let that pass. It was part of the price he demanded from Marston. Presley had to go down for something. Didn't matter what.'

'Marston gave him up?'

'Didn't even hesitate. Presley had a dozen sidelines for making money. His police job was just a fulcrum for the rest of it. He fenced stuff, collected protection money–'

'And sold dope.'

'Right. Amphetamines mostly, for truckers. Interstate transportation of federally regulated narcotics. Marston gave us everything we needed to nail him, and we fed it to the state police. They busted him on possession with intent to distribute. I showed up at the arrest, just so Presley would know it was payback.'

'Did he find out it was Marston who gave him up?'

'Not as far as I know. That's the irony. Marston was right to trust Presley, but Presley was a fool to trust Marston. Presley's like a dog that way.'

'A pit bull maybe.'

Stone goes through his little phone ritual again.

'You waiting for a call?'

'No.' He picks up his pistol, stands, and walks back to the front window.

'They still out there?'

'Still there.'

'So, the national security seal was completely bogus?'

Stone chuckles dryly. 'Completely. Think about the Payton case. The Bureau had been tasked with destroying violent opposition to civil rights in the South. Instead, Hoover purposefully protected a race murderer for his own political ends. Normally, he would have added the Payton evidence to his personal files. The infamous blackmail files. But Payton's file was too big for that. We had agents in Natchez generating reams of useless crap. The national security seal was an impenetrable shield.'

'Do you think the audiotape of Marston and Presley is still with the main file?'

'I doubt it. That was the critical evidence. It was probably taken to Hoover's home when he died, with the other blackmail material. Shelves of books have been written about what might have happened to that stuff. You'll never find that tape.'

'So, Marston's motive was just—'

'Money,' Stone finishes. 'Greed. Bastards like him only care about one thing: grabbing everything within their reach. They think every dollar they get takes them one step closer to immortality, and every person they step on puts them one step above everyone else. I don't think other people really exist for people like Marston. They're just a means to an end.'

Including his daughter, I think with a shiver. 'When you had the bugs in his mansion,' I say hesitantly, 'did you ever pick up anything . . . unsavory?'

'Murder is pretty unsavory.'

'I'm talking about sexual stuff.'

'We heard him banging his wife's best friend one day.'

'I'm talking about abuse. Child abuse.'

He turns away from the window and looks at me. 'No. I had a daughter myself. If I'd heard anything like that, I would have gone in there and thrashed him within an inch of his life.' The corner of Stone's mouth twitches. 'The mikes were only in for a couple of weeks, though. And I can't remember if Henry covered the little girl's room.'

I force myself to push Livy from my mind. 'I need you to tell this story to a jury.'

'It'll never happen, son.'

'I think it will. I know about your daughter.'

In the midst of turning back to the window, he whips his whole head toward me, his eyes burning with anger.

I hold up both hands. 'I'm just telling you I know she's what's been keeping you from helping me.'

'Then you know it's pointless to ask me to testify.'

'Is it? I talked to her today, and she thinks different.'

Stone takes a step toward me. 'You talked to my daughter today?'

'Yes. Caitlin Masters found her for me.'

'You idiot. If you've put her life in danger.'

'She's all right! She's fine. And she agrees with me.

Portman started playing carrot and stick with her days ago. I didn't even have to tell her you could bring him down. She knew.'

'You had no right to put her in jeopardy, Cage.'

'I want justice. That's all.'

'You want revenge.'

'You're right. But I used to want it for myself. Now I want it for someone else. Marston has done things he should die for, Stone. Take my word for that.'

The old agent fingers the pistol in his hand. 'My daughter told me two days ago that I should testify. She thinks getting this thing off my chest would save my damned soul or something.' His face hardens. 'She's got no right to sacrifice her career for my guilty conscience. She doesn't know how things really work.'

'She knows.'

'It's not her choice, damn it!' His eyes flick around the interior of the cabin. 'God, I wish I had a bottle.' He paces over to the fireplace and pokes the logs, sending a storm of sparks up the chimney. 'You don't want me as a witness, Cage.'

'Why not?'

'I'm damaged goods.'

'Because of your drinking?'

'Drinking isn't one problem. It's a whole constellation.'

'Why were you fired five years after the Payton murder? It wasn't for drinking.'

He stirs the fire some more. 'No. Though I was drinking like a fish at the time. When Hoover cut the deal with Marston, I couldn't believe it. I don't know why. I'd seen him do it enough times before. But usually it was cases that were dirty all the way around. This murder had a real victim. An *innocent* victim. And the Korea angle really weighed on me. I started drinking to forget about it. Things were turning to shit in the Bureau. Hoover was using us to harass antiwar protesters, all kinds of constitutional stuff. Then we got

Nixon. Parts of the Bureau started to function like the goddamn KGB. It made me sick. The booze made it tolerable. For a while, anyway. It also made me impossible to live with. I drove my wife and baby away. I screwed up a dozen different ways. Then I topped them all. You'll get a kick out of this, because it involves your friend Marston.'

'What?'

'In 1972 I was in Washington, doing some shitwork Nixon had requested from Hoover. Something too boring for Liddy and his plumbers. I was walking through the lobby of the Watergate office complex, and there, bigger than life, stood Leo Marston. He was in town lobbying John Stennis for something or other. I was soused when I saw him, and I snapped. The Payton thing had been eating at me for four years. When Marston saw me, that smug bastard tried to make out like we were buddies from way back, in on the big joke. The dead nigger. I straightened him out quick. And everybody in the Watergate lobby heard me. Marston lost it. He took a swing at me, and I pulled my gun.'

I almost laugh, remembering the way I snapped and went after Marston yesterday.

'Henry Bookbinder had been outside parking the car,' Stone recalls. 'He ran in and backed me down. Nobody died, but Marston screamed blue murder to Hoover. One of Hoover's last acts before he died in seventy-two was firing me. I guess that's a distinction of sorts.'

'Where was Portman then?'

Stone goes still, the poker hovering above the crackling logs. 'Climbing the Bureau ladder. I didn't tell you everything before. When Hoover took over the Payton case, I started making copies of my case notes. I also copied the audiotape that incriminated Marston.'

The hair on my forearms is standing up. 'Do you still have that copy?'

He shakes his head. 'Portman saw what I was doing. He

463

started spying on me, reporting to Hoover as the case progressed. I can just imagine his reports. May be *ideologically unsound*, blah, blah, blah. Anyway, everything was stolen out of my apartment two days before I was fired. That was Portman, I guarantee it. On Hoover's orders.'

My heart sinks.

'You don't want me as a witness. They'd make me look pathetic on cross. Too many sins of my own.'

'What's Portman so afraid of now? From the story you told, his involvement was peripheral.'

'The Bureau's been under siege for ten years, in the public-relations sense. Its big Achilles heel is racism. The FBI has been sued by black agents, Hispanics, women, all claiming systematic discrimination. And these groups have *won*. Portman was appointed to correct these problems, to polish the image, and he was appointed by a Democratic president. If it were to come out that his "heroic civil rights work" in Mississippi consisted of helping to cover up a race murder, he'd be out on his ass in an hour. The President would have no choice.'

'So, let's make it known. Do the Bureau and the country a favor.'

Stone sets the poker in its rack and sits on the hearth, his face weary. 'I wish I could. Every trial decision Portman ever made as a federal judge would come into question, every decision as a U.S. attorney. He'd never work in the public sector again. And once the media got its nose into his past, God knows what they'd find. A guy like Portman doesn't cross the line once or twice. It's a management style with him.'

'Why didn't the media discover anything during his confirmation hearings?'

'The Bureau is a closed culture. It outlives presidential administrations, judges, even Supreme Court justices. If the leadership of that culture wants to keep Portman's secrets so he can be appointed FBI director, that's the way it'll be.'

Stone takes out his phone and checks the line again. 'I'd like to help you, Cage. But they've held my daughter over me for a long time. Since she was a kid.'

'What?'

'Oh, yeah. After he fired me, Hoover sent me a message. Portman delivered it. If I tried to air any dirty Bureau laundry, my kid wouldn't live to watch me on *Meet the Press*.'

'That's pretty hard to believe.'

He laughs bitterly. 'This was 1972. Worse things were happening every day, and the government was right in the middle of it.'

I pull the curtains away from the front window and squint through the gathering dusk. Beyond what must be the jeep track, the snow-covered wall of Anthracite Mesa climbs toward the sky, with spruce and fir trees marching up it in dark ranks. What I do not see is human beings.

'What did you mean about Presley and Marston making a nice package? You said, "Why complicate it?"'

Stone stands and walks toward me, telephone in hand. 'I didn't mean anything. Forget it.'

'You're holding something back, aren't you?'

He has the phone to his ear now, and his face has gone white. He throws down the phone and rushes me, holding out his pistol. 'Take it!'

'What?'

'The phone's dead! Take the gun!'

I take the gun, which looks like a Colt .45, and Stone snatches the hunting rifle up from the table. A Winchester 300, with a scope.

'Open the back door for me!' he orders. 'There's a sniper out there. Open it halfway, but stay well back.'

As I run to the back door, I decide that not bringing Daniel Kelly with me was about the stupidest idea I've ever had.

Stone kneels six feet back from the door, shoulders the

Winchester, and puts his right eye to the scope, as though preparing to shoot right through the door.

'Open it,' he says. 'Slowly. Then get clear, fast.'

I slowly turn the handle, then stretch as far away as I can from the door and pull it halfway open.

Stone quickly adjusts his aim, then fires. The report of the rifle inside the cabin is like a detonation.

'He's down!' shouts Stone. 'Follow me!'

'Where to?'

Before he can answer, the front window of the cabin explodes inward and a bullet ricochets off the hearth. Stone whirls, draws a small automatic from his belt, and empties half a clip through the broken window.

'Move!' he yells, grabbing my arm and jerking me toward the door.

'*Where?*' I ask, my throat dry as sand.

'Somewhere they can't follow!'

'Where's that?'

'The river.'

'The *river*? In what?'

'You'll see. Move your ass!'

Chapter 35

As Stone pulls me through the back door of the cabin, something explodes behind us. We fall facedown on the snow, stunned like cattle after being hit with an electric prod, but we scramble blindly backward for the cover of the cabin wall, knowing instinctively that exposure means death.

Hunched against the side of the cabin, I scan the swollen river and its banks in the dying light. I see no way to use that flooded stream as a means of escape. Stone's lips are moving, but I hear nothing. He turns and begins tugging at something beneath his cabin. It's some sort of inflatable boat, a long red plastic thing, like a cross between a canoe and kayak. Seeing that I can't hear his orders, Stone takes back the pistol he gave me, then motions for me to drag the kayak to the water, a distance of about eighty feet. He obviously means to cover me while I do this, but I'm not going to drag anything. If I have to cross that open space, I'm going to do it as fast as I can.

Dropping to my knees, I turn the kayak upside down and crawl under it, sliding it onto my back like an elongated turtle shell. Its coated fabric skin probably wouldn't stop a pellet gun, but at least I'll be able to run with the thing.

As I start toward the river, my Reebok-clad feet slip and crunch over the snow. The bow of the kayak bobs forward and back as I rush forward, obscuring my vision, making my gauntlet longer than it needs to be. I cringe at the stutter of an automatic weapon somewhere behind me, but the reassuring bellow of Stone's .45 pushes me on. At least I haven't completely lost my hearing.

The last half of my dash to the river has the terrible dream-like quality of pursuing a receding horizon, the shock of my feet hitting rocks under the snow the only tangible proof that I'm awake. The swiftly falling darkness is probably providing more protection than Stone's pistol, but it can't be long before someone sprays a clip at the fleeing kayak.

When my feet kick up the first splash, I leap forward and land in a bone-chilling current that pulls at the kayak like a giant hand. Fighting to my knees in the current, I flip the kayak upright and lie down in the shallows beside it, leaving only my head exposed. Muzzle flashes in the windows punctuate the flashes below them, where Stone must be firing. There's a brief lull, and then Stone comes charging out of the darkness toward the water, a two-bladed kayak paddle in one hand and his Winchester in the other.

He whirls and fires twice on the run, then breaks in my direction, using the white propane tank for concealment. He's halfway to the water when another flash lights up the interior of the cabin. Stone grabs his buttocks, lurches forward, then spins and returns fire as he goes down in the snow.

I start pulling the kayak toward the bank, but the bottom shallows quickly beneath me, forcing me into an exposed position. The water feels like glacial runoff, stealing my breath, making my teeth chatter uncontrollably. But it's better than what Stone is enduring. Every five seconds or so he lets off a .45 round back at the cabin windows, but he can't keep that up forever. Panic scrambles around in my chest like a crazed animal, urging me to flight. It wouldn't take anything, just a surrender to the current. I could float downstream for fifty yards, then climb into the kayak and be on my way.

As though sensing my panic, Stone holds the paddle and rifle along the length of his body and begins rolling across the snow toward the river. The old agent looks like a kid playing a game. Bullets kick up white powder in front of him, but he doesn't even slow down. When he is five yards away, I yell: 'Th-throw me the pistol!'

The .45 skids across the snow, but I manage to get my fingers around it before it disappears in the river. The steel feels warm compared to the water. It's too dark to aim accurately at the cabin from here, but two more muzzle flashes obligingly appear, and I let off three shots at the afterimage on my retinas.

'Into the current!' shouts Stone.

'What about the kayak?'

'Too easy to hit! Just hang onto the rope!'

He rolls into the shallows then hangs up on the rocks somehow. I fire twice more at the cabin, then grab his belt and drag him into the current while bullets spray water against my knees. The muzzle flashes are between the cabin and the river now. They're coming for us.

As I grope helplessly for the kayak, Stone rises to his knees in the water, the big Winchester braced against his shoulder. He fires once, then cycles the bolt, waits three seconds, and fires again.

A fireball the size of the cabin itself explodes out of the darkness, sucking up all the air around us. I feel the pull in my lungs and sinuses as a millisecond's image of a blazing man is seared into my brain and I tumble backward into the freezing water. *The propane tank*, marvels a voice in my head. *One shot to pierce its skin, the second to ignite the gas . . .*

Stone is already in the main channel of the river, trying to keep his head and the rifle above the surface. Wrapping the kayak's bow rope tightly around my wrist, I leap into the black water where the current is strongest and give myself to it. A couple of desultory shots ring out, but they could be loose rounds in the pistols of dead men, cooking off in the inferno Stone has made of his home. The river has us in its power now, and the assassins are but a burning memory falling behind us in the dark.

'Stone? Stone!'

'Ahead of you,' comes a faint reply. 'Did they hit the kayak?'

'I don't think so.'

'It's got three cells. Check it out.'

Since I'm hanging onto the kayak for dear life, it's not difficult to obey Stone's order. The strange craft seems intact, though its cells don't seem as fully inflated as they might be. Stone's two-bladed paddle is wedged between the seats and the starboard gunwale.

'It's okay.'

The water here is swift and smooth. The moon and stars shine with white brilliance, reflecting off the deep water like diamonds flung onto its surface. I kick with the current, hoping to ease my fear and aloneness by overtaking Stone.

A sharp cry comes from up ahead. I'm trying to place its direction when something smashes into my ribs, knocking the wind out of me. A rock. Stone must have hit the same one.

A white hand appears in the current. I grab it and pull, then wind the bow rope tightly around the wrist. Now at least we are riding the river together, and will share the same fate.

'Thanks,' says Stone, his face a gray blur beside mine.

'Are you h-hit bad?' I ask, trying to control my voice.

'Bad enough. I don't think it hit bone, though.'

'Shouldn't we get in the kayak?'

He shakes his head. 'We'll have to beach it to get in. Another forty yards or so.'

It's tough to judge distance in the dark, so I count to ten before I start kicking toward the left bank, watching for a suitable place to land. My kicks seem futile against the power of the river; we're like cars trapped in the center lane of an interstate, slaves to the main current.

'Get over!' Stone commands. 'Hurry!'

At last a broad shelf of rock rises out of the river like a ramp, and it's simple enough to float the kayak up onto it. Stone lets the current wash him up onto his back, then lies there, wheezing for air.

'What do we do?' I ask.

'G-get in. Keep going.'

'Where?'

'Town. Six miles south.'

'Six miles!'

'Listen, Cage. The river's at flood. We're moving faster than you think. And it's a good thing, because we've got to beat those bastards back to town.'

'But they can *drive*.' I clench my arms over my chest in a vain effort to stop shivering.

'They had to abandon their vehicles just like you. They've got to cover three miles on foot before they can drive. In the snow. We can beat them if we hurry. You ever been on white water?'

It's been ten years since I've been in a raft, and on that trip my guide went overboard and got crushed between the raft bottom and some rocks, breaking his leg in three places.

'A long time ago.'

'The Slate is easier to run at flood than at low water. But we've got two trouble spots. Both slot canyons. The first one's up ahead. It's a class-five vertical drop, but the floodwater should shoot us right over it.'

An image of an eight-foot waterfall flashes into my head, the one I saw while trudging up to the cabin this afternoon. In my desperation to escape the guns, I somehow suppressed this memory. But that's what Stone is talking about. Going over that falls in a plastic boat.

'Just grab the sides of the kayak,' he says, 'lean back, and pray. I'll handle the paddle. A mile farther on is the second one. Walls higher than you can reach, ending in a tight chute that's like a piledriver. People drive their fourwheelers out there to watch the kayakers crash.'

Jesus . . .

He grabs my windbreaker with a weak grip. 'If I was covering the river, that's where I'd wait. It'd be tough shooting, though. We'll come through that second chute like a runaway freight train, and if we clear it, we'll be okay all the way to town. They won't be able to find us in the dark.'

'This river goes through town?'

He grins. 'Right through it. Let's get this bus on the road.'

I slide the kayak down the rock ramp until the current is tugging it, then grab Stone by the belt buckle and man-handle him over the side near the stem. He goes rigid with pain when his buttocks hit the rock through the air-filled floor of the boat, but there's nothing to be done. I drag the kayak the rest of the way clear, then roll over the side and into the bow.

Immediately the main current has us, pulling us to its center, gathering speed as the rising banks constrict the water in its headlong flight to the first canyon. I get to my knees and try to obey Stone's barked orders – *Lean left! Lean right! Right again!* – as he expertly handles the paddle. Every twenty yards or so the bow lifts out of the water and slaps back down with a combative *thunk*.

'I hear the drop,' Stone says from the stem. 'Lean left. We've got to stay in the channel.'

I don't hear what Stone hears, but the black trough beneath us bears steadily left, and my forward line of sight has gone black. Then, slowly, the sound registers on my traumatized eardrums, like holding my ear to the biggest conch shell in the world. Fear balloons in my chest, pressing my heart into my throat.

I don't think Stone's paddle is affecting the course of the boat anymore. I feel like I'm trapped in a roller coaster as it tops its highest incline and tips slowly forward, headed for the long vertiginous fall. On both sides, walls loom out of the dark, near enough to touch.

Then we are airborne.

'Lean back!' yells Stone as the kayak is hurled forward into space. I obey out of pure instinct, my stomach flying up my throat as the bow plummets down a thundering pipeline of water and smashes into something I cannot see, then bounces up into a roiling mass of foam and spray.

'We're clear!' he cries. 'One down!'

We're back in the main current, riding as smoothly as a subway car on a scheduled run. The walls of the canyon have fallen away, and the sky above us has widened into a starry blanket that gives the snowy riverbanks a silver sheen.

For ten minutes we slide along as though on a Nile cruise, but every so often a stand of spruce near the river's edge reminds me just how fast we are moving. The farther we go, the more the valley widens around us, until it seems we are floating across a vast desert of snow. On another night this might seem an ideal time for Stone and me to talk, for him to tell me what to watch for ahead, or to discuss the eternal subjects like women and time. But tonight all we can do is shiver in the wind, chilled so deeply that if we don't find warmth and shelter soon, we could die from exposure.

Almost without our noticing, the banks begin to rise again. It feels like the river is cutting its way into the earth, carrying us with it on its darkening journey. The sound of the turbulent water grows as the walls rise, like the sound of a great beast waking from a long sleep.

'It's coming,' Stone says from behind me. 'Listen.'

Only the center of the stream is smooth now, a black torrent rushing through the narrow canyon, throwing off a mist of silver froth and spray. The kayak hurtles down this black tunnel like it's on rails, but of course it's not. If the bow gets turned around, we could spin out of control and be smashed on a rock, or capsize and be pinned by an inescapable hydraulic.

'Lean right!' Stone yells.

The kayak's nose pulls left, then slingshots around a bend, its fabric skin scraping the rock wall with a resilient wail.

'Shit! They're covering the chute!'

It's difficult to judge distance in the dark, but about a hundred yards ahead of us, a pair of headlights slices downward and across the narrow river, bright as a bonfire in the dark. And where those lights wait, guns are waiting too.

'We can't make it past that!' I shout toward the stern. 'We've got to get out!'

'Too late. We're in the canyon.'

A jet of fear flushes through my system. I feel like a steer being driven into a slaughter chute. 'We've got to get out of the kayak, then!'

'We can't run the chute without it.'

I turn in disbelief, but all I see is Stone's solemn face as he expertly wields the paddle.

The current continues to accelerate as the river is forced into an ever narrowing channel. The lights are only seventy yards away now.

'They won't see us until we're right on top of them,' Stone assures me. 'We'll be moving so fast, they'll only have a couple of seconds to fire.'

'What if they have automatic weapons?'

'We need suppressing fire. Can you handle a rifle?'

I don't bother to answer him. If we go through that chute in this kayak, we'll be cut to pieces by anyone sighting down the beams of those headlights.

'Cage? Are you listening?'

As the lights loom closer, a bowel-churning roar reverberates between the walls. One thing I remember my raft guide telling me – just before he broke his leg – was that some white-water guides train by floating rivers wearing only life vests. If they can do that in preparation for making a living, Stone and I can do it without vests to save our lives.

'*I said, take this rifle!*' he yells.

Without hesitation, I throw myself onto the right gunwale of the kayak and press down with all my weight. Stone screams like a madman, but I ignore him, leaning harder and farther forward until the first run of water surges over the side.

'*Stop it, you damn fool!*'

And then it is done. The inflatable tube that forms the right gunwale digs beyond the point of no return, and the river pours into the boat, swamping us in seconds. The shock of the cold water steals my breath again, but I roll over the side and into the main current.

The kayak is still floating upright – if mostly submerged – but Stone won't be able to get it above water without my help. At last he heaves himself over the rear gunwale and into the river. As soon as he's clear, the inflatable rises in the water. With a powerful wrenching move I flip it upside down in the current. When I let go, the buoyant craft rights itself as though nothing had happened.

'*You stupid son of a bitch!*' Stone appears beside me like a man in the last stages of drowning, his eyes furious points of light in the darkness.

I don't reply. The water is driving toward the chute with the momentum of a locomotive, Stone and me and the kayak bobbing along in it like fishing corks. I've got to slow us down a little, put us a few seconds behind the kayak—

A sledgehammer blow to the chest stops me dead in the water. Purely out of instinct, I grab whatever hit me and reach out for Stone with my legs. An explosive grunt sounds beside me as Stone collides with the object, and I lock my legs around his waist.

It's a tree trunk. A trunk the width of a man's thigh and smooth as glass, wedged into a crack in the ledge from which it fell. The river is trying to rip Stone's body from between my knees, but I hold him fast. With a supreme effort, I flex my stomach muscles and pull him higher in the water.

'Grab the tree!' I gasp. 'Grab the tree!'

He drapes one arm over it, loses his grip, then at last manages to get both arms over the trunk

'Can you hold yourself?' I ask, my legs burning from exertion.

He nods weakly, his face white.

As soon as I relax my leg muscles, the river sweeps both our bodies up onto the surface, holding us in near-horizontal positions. Forty yards away, halogen headlights illuminate a thirty-foot stretch of the chute like searchlights.

'*Boat! Boat!*' screams a voice from the roar at the end of the little canyon. A voice from the lights.

The illuminated water in the chute churns into boiling chaos as hundreds of bullets shred its surface. The kayak materializes in the headlights as though by magic and instantly explodes into confetti that sails through the bluish beams like the remnants of a child's balloon.

'Christ,' Stone coughs.

'Listen,' I hiss in his ear, hoping my raft guide knew what he was talking about. 'You go through feet first. On your back, feet first, okay? That cushions the rocks.'

He nods, his face looking bloodless in the dark.

'How long can you hold on?'

'Twenty seconds . . . maybe thirty.'

'Then we might as well go now. Save our strength.'

Stone nods, his eyes closed.

'Have you still got your pistol?' I ask.

'In my waistband.'

'Let's do it. On three. One . . . two . . . *three–*'

Letting go of the tree trunk is like surrendering to a god, so mighty is the force carrying us down the chute. Yet the water around us seems placid. At the center of the channel there is no white water, no churning froth or spray, just a great black mass of fluid driving forward with unstoppable power. Stone falls slowly behind me as we hurtle toward the headlights, but I can't worry about him now. I can't worry about anything. I suppose I should pray or vomit from fear or see my life pass before my eyes, but I do none of these things. At some point, terror becomes so total and control so minimal that you simply shed fear like a coat.

I lie back in the water as though going to sleep, only my face above the surface, my arms held out from my sides like Christ on the cross as I rush feet first toward the great black door at the end of the chute. The inverted bowl of sky sparkles with more stars than I have seen in years, and I feel a sudden and absurd certainty that whatever is about to happen happened a long time ago.

As the headlights white out the sky above me, I expel all my air and let my head sink beneath the torrent. I am nothing to those above me, a ripple of water sweeping beneath them, a piece of driftwood borne on the flood.

Suddenly, the black tide swells beneath me, lifting me toward the sky like a magic carpet. Thunder roars around me, atomizing the water to mist. There is no air here, only different states of water. I am suspended long enough to hear a burst of gunfire behind me. Then a great fist slams me to the bottom of a well and holds me there, trying with all its power to bludgeon me unconscious. My lungs scream as they did the day I dragged Ruby from our burning house, but I dare not breathe. To breathe here is to join the hammering darkness.

As suddenly as before, the great hand hurls me up out of the well and onto the surface, which feels land solid after the vaporous thunder of the chute. I feel as though some great beast had sucked me into its maw, chewed me for a few moments, and, finding me distasteful, spat me out whole.

The air feels warm against my face. I probe my arms

and legs, searching for broken bones. Remarkably, I seem intact. Turning back toward the thundering mist, I watch the exit of the chute, a white mouth of spitting foam between two rock walls like the jet of a great hose. Surely Stone has passed through by now, though not, I fear, as invisibly as I did. The gunfire I heard must have been directed at him.

I try to tread water, but my strength is gone. I can only lie back and float, nose and mouth above the surface, waiting for some sign that Stone survived. An image of his bullet-riddled body bobbing up beside me flits through my head, but I quickly banish it. My odds of surviving the night up here without him are very low.

Stone will come. If anything, the ex-FBI man is tougher than I. He is nearly seventy, yes. And he's wounded. But it's not as though physical prowess of any degree could affect one's fate while passing through that cataract. Stone's fate is in the lap of the gods.

'*Swim, goddamn it.*'

For a dazed moment I think I am talking to myself, but I'm not. Stone has kicked up beside me like a shipwrecked sailor, looking more dead than alive.

'Did they hit you again?'

His eyes are only half open. 'Kick your feet, Cage. We've got another half mile to go.'

'Why not get out here?'

'Too close . . . kick, damn you.'

I start kicking, and soon enough the current is carrying us along as steadily as it did behind Stone's cabin, though more slowly. The river has spread out here. Shrubs and boulders sail past us in the moonlight, while smaller rocks abrade our knees and elbows. Stone grips my windbreaker and speaks as we drift along.

'Crested Butte is three miles south. We can't stay in the river without the boat . . . too cold. And I can't run. I'm not dying, but I can't run. There's a campground up here. When we get close, you're going to get out on the south bank. Right now they're stuck north of the river. Follow the river south, running as fast as you can, hugging the bluff for cover. When you see the lights of town, circle to your right and come in from the south, in case they're waiting for you.'

'I'm not leaving you here. You—'

'We haven't got time for this! You want a bar called the Silver Bell. It's just off the main street, Elk Avenue. The bartender is a mountain of a guy called Tiny McSwain. In my drinking days we got pretty tight. Tell Tiny to take you to an airport. Any airport but the one you flew into. Still got your wallet?'

I grab my hip pocket. 'Still there.'

'Cash?'

I nod. I brought two thousand dollars in hundred-dollar bills for just this reason, so I couldn't be traced by credit card charges.

'You may have to hide out until you get a morning flight. Denver maybe. Do whatever you have to do, but stay out of sight.'

A yellow light appears from the darkness ahead, hovering in the air to my right, about fifty yards away.

'That's the campground,' Stone says. 'Come on.'

We separate and fight our way to the south bank. As my hands collide with cold rock, I hear a screech of brakes ahead. Crawling out of the water, I realize my legs are nearly numb.

'They must have driven like banshees to get here that fast,' Stone says through rattling teeth. 'Tear off a piece of your shirttail.'

'What?'

'Your *shirttail*.'

In my weakened state, tearing the soaked cotton is like trying to rip a phone book in half. As I struggle with the hem,

Stone jabs a stick through a stretched-taut place and rips off a long piece.

'What do you want me to do? Make a surrender flag?'

He hands me the fabric and rolls over on his stomach. 'Wad up a hunk of that and jam it into my wound.'

I tear off most of the shirttail and squeeze it into a tight wet tennis ball of cloth, then crouch over Stone's back. Garbled voices float to us from the direction of the campground.

'Where are you hit?'

'Left cheek of my ass. Took out a plug of muscle, I think.'

I feel along his left buttock until my fingers mush into a warm opening. Stone doesn't even flinch. The hole is ragged, but it runs across the buttock at an angle, like a deep grazing wound. The swelling below it is considerable, though, and it's bound to get worse now that he's out of the cold water.

'Hurry!' he grunts.

I squeeze the cloth into a tighter ball and hold it against the opening. 'Ready?'

'Do it.'

In one hard stroke I depress the cloth into the hole as he tenses beneath me. It reminds me of helping my father pack a decubitus ulcer when I worked for him in high school. Now I need something to hold the packing in the wound. Removing my soaked windbreaker, I pull off what's left of my shirt and slide it under Stone's left leg, then tie it over the hole.

'That's the best I can do for now,' I tell him, pulling my jacket back on.

'What's the name of the bar?' he asks, rolling over. His face is even whiter than before.

'The Silver Bell. Bartender's Tiny McSwain.'

'Good. Move your ass, kid.'

'What are you going to do?'

He drops one hand to his waist, where the butt of his .45

glints dully in the dark. 'Slow those bastards down for you.'

'I'll stay and help you, damn it.'

'You *can't* help me. You don't have a gun. You'll help me by getting your ass back to Mississippi and nailing Portman's hide to the barn wall.'

'Stone—'

The old agent grips my arm with more strength than I thought he could possibly have left. 'No matter what you hear, keep running. I mean that. If it sounds like the goddamn O.K. Corral up here, you keep running until you reach that bar.'

'There's only one way I'll go.'

'How's that?'

'If you promise to testify.'

His laughter is full of irony. 'Boy, if I survive this night, wild horses couldn't stop me from testifying. Portman gave the order for these sons of bitches to kill us because he thought I was going to testify. Well, now he's right. If I'm alive, I'll get to Mississippi. I'll drag Portman's ass down from the mountaintop if I have to tear the whole mountain down with him. Marston too. Now, get your ass out of here.'

I get to my knees and look through the trees to the south.

'Don't come back,' Stone says quietly. 'Not with Tiny or the sheriff. After you leave, everybody up here but me is a target. That's how I want it. The whole thing'll be over by the time anybody could get here, and if I don't come out on top, whoever came would die for nothing. If you come back, I'll shoot you myself.'

I grab his upper arm. 'The trial starts in thirty-six hours. You get your ass back to Mississippi. You owe it to Del Payton.'

He nods in the dark. 'That I do, Cage. That I do.'

*　　*　　*

My run to the town is a benumbed nightmare of falls and slides and collisions with trees, an endless march into a killing wind, but I never consider resting. Dwight Stone is offering up his life to cover my escape.

The first gunshot echoes down the valley behind me as the glow of Crested Butte appears like a mirage in the distance. All my instincts say turn around, go back, and help Stone. But the old soldier's tone of his last order keeps me going. Over rock. Through snowdrifts. Past a black mirror of a lake. Through thickets, thorns. Plodding forward into the relentless wind, ever forward, until at last I am sliding down a white slope toward a geometric heaven of lights and warmth.

When I reach the level of the buildings, I circle to my right in a broad arc that takes me around to the south entrance of town. Muted television dialogue drifts on the air, and the occasional sound of a car motor rumbles from between the buildings.

Crested Butte looks less like a cowboy town than a nineteenth century New England village plopped down in the mountains. The buildings along Elk Avenue have Victorian facades, and flowers line every street and window box. The windows are mostly dark, but as I move along the street, a shopkeeper backs out of a doorway, gives me a furtive glance, then locks his door and hurries to a truck parked across the street.

Twenty yards farther on, a yellow funnel of light appears down a side street to my left, illuminating a wooden bell painted silver. I turn down the alley and crunch through the snow as fast as my tingling feet will carry me.

The Silver Bell has old-fashioned swinging doors. It's a rustic place that caters to locals, not a 'ski bar' fluffed up for the tourist trade. There are three people sitting at the bar and two loners at the tables. All look like serious drinkers. Behind the bar stands a giant of a man with a gray-flecked black beard.

He has to be Tiny McSwain.

As soon as he sees me, he moves around the bar as though to throw me out. Before he can, I hold up my hands and croak:

'If you're Tiny McSwain, Dwight Stone sent me.'

He stops, his eyes narrowed. 'Who are you?'

'Better for you if you don't know. Stone told me you'd help me.'

'Somebody heard shots up near the Slate,' he says suspiciously. 'Was that Dwight?'

'It was the people trying to kill him. Him and me both.'

'I'll call the sheriff. Where's Dwight?'

'He's back by the creek. He told me not to call anybody. He said everything would be over by the time anybody could get to him, and if not, they'd get killed for nothing.'

'Those his words?'

'Near enough.'

Tiny nods. 'Then we don't call anybody.'

'There are at least two men up there, probably more.'

'Stone's a tough old boy. What did he tell you to do?'

'He said tell you to take me to an airport.'

'Which airport?'

'Denver. And he said do it quick.'

Tiny motions for a T-shirt-clad woman at a table to get behind the bar, then takes a set of keys from his pocket. 'Let's go, friend.'

'Hey,' calls the woman. 'Where are you going, if anybody asks?'

'If anybody asks, me and this guy went back up the Slate to help Dwight.' Tiny McSwain looks at his customers, who are staring indifferently at me. 'Nobody else says different.'

Blank nods from the drinkers.

'My Bronco's parked out back,' he says. 'Let's go.'

Chapter 36

I am standing at the Continental Airlines gate in Baton Rouge, searching the crowds of travelers for Daniel Kelly as fear slowly devours me from the inside. A week ago I stood a few yards from here, entranced by the sight of Livy Marston. Now I stand shaking from adrenaline and lack of sleep, wondering whether Dwight Stone survived the night, and whether I will live to defend myself at my slander trial, which is scheduled to begin in less than twenty-four hours.

Kelly should have been here hours ago, but I've seen no sight of him. A dozen businessmen who could be FBI agents have passed me, stared at me, even bumped into me, but none has tried to stop me. So far, anyway. If Kelly doesn't show in the next five minutes, I'm going to try to reach Natchez on my own.

Last night Tiny McSwain drove me all the way to Denver and dropped me at an airport motel. I paid cash and checked in under a false name, then lay in the chilly darkness, unable to sleep. Twice I lifted the phone to call the Colorado state police and send them up the Mesa after Stone. I had visions of him lying wounded beside the Slate River, his attackers dead, him dying but savable if he reached a surgeon in time. But Stone's orders came back to me, and each time I set the phone down.

Instead I called Sam Jacobs in Natchez, being fairly sure that his phone would not be tapped. The geologist promised to visit Caitlin Masters first thing in the morning and, through her, instruct Kelly to be at the Baton Rouge airport by ten a.m. and to meet every plane arriving from Dallas after that time. I know Jacobs well enough to know he followed through.

But Kelly isn't here.

When I did finally close my eyes last night, I saw nightmarish images of Leo Marston raping Livy as a child, forcing her into a conspiracy of silence, raising her in a schizophrenic world of material bounty and spiritual agony, somehow maintaining such a hold on her that she still allowed him sexual access at the age of eighteen. When I pondered the nature of that hold, I felt the dread and horror I felt the first time I saw Roman Polanski's *Chinatown*.

The dread came when Faye Dunaway told Jack Nicholson that the young woman she had been hiding was her daughter and her sister. The horror arrived with the next line when Jack, reaching for a thread of sanity, asked about her father: 'He raped you?' and Dunaway looked up and slowly shook her head. All sanity spun away with this terrible confession. I remember something similar from reading Anais Nin in college, that Nin had seduced her father several times; but Nin had been profligate in her sexual adventures, and besides, she was French. The idea of Livy Marston voluntarily having sex with her father simply would not set in my mind as reality.

'*Continental Airlines passenger Penn Cage, please pick up the nearest white courtesy phone.*'

It takes a moment for my name to sink in, but when it does, my fear escalates to alarm. The caller could be Kelly or Caitlin, but it could also be someone who means me great harm.

'*Continental Airlines passenger Penn Cage, please pick up the nearest white courtesy phone.*'

There's a white phone across the concourse from me, near a bank of pay phones, but I can't make myself walk over to it. What if Portman's people are waiting to snatch whoever walks up to answer that call? On the other hand, what choice do I have? The caller could be Daniel Kelly.

'This is Penn,' I say, picking up the phone.

'It's Kelly.'

'Jesus, are you in the airport?'

'Yes, but we can't meet. Listen to me, Penn, we only have a few seconds.'

Kelly's use of my first name rather than the facetious 'boss' brings my inner self to attention. 'What is it?'

'Portman's men are in the airport right now. You're going to have to get home on your own. I'm going to divert these guys, but you have to move fast.'

'I'm listening.'

'My Taurus is parked in sight of the terminal, in the short-term lot, space A-27. The keys are under the mat, and there's a cell phone under the seat. You got that?'

'A-27.'

'Right. Next: downstairs, near the baggage carousels, there's an Infiniti Q45 on display. I left a gun sitting on the left inside lip of the rear bumper.'

'Jesus—'

'*Listen.* You get that gun, get to the car, and haul your ass back to Natchez.'

'What are you going to do?'

'Buy you some time. But you've got another problem. I haven't been straight with you. Nobody at the company has. They've reported every move you've made to Portman.'

My chest goes hollow. 'How do you know that?'

'Because *we're* reporting every move you make back to the office. And we don't usually do that. Our CEO is former FBI, you know. And John Portman could swing a lot of corporate business to Argus any time he feels like it.'

The implications of Kelly's revelation ricochet through my mind. 'Is my family safe?'

'Argus doesn't kill people. Other than in defense of a client, like the other night. But I'd find myself some new security, just to be on the safe side. Local boys maybe. Buddies are good, family's better.'

'Kelly . . . how do I know I can trust you?'

'Because you're alive. And because I'm telling you this.'

'Why are you telling me?'

A brief silence. 'I think it's got something to do with the way you buried your maid. Now, get your ass out of here. Walk fast, but don't run. And if you hear shooting, don't look back.'

His order is an exact echo of Stone's. 'Kelly—'

'We'll be sharing a Scotch again before you know it. Move out.'

Reluctantly hanging up the phone, I scan the concourse like a tailback picking holes in an offensive line, then start through the crowds at a rapid walk looking back frequently for signs of pursuit. After clearing the metal detectors, I dodge a golf cart carrying a handicapped woman, then bound down the escalator to the baggage-collection point where Annie and I said goodbye to Caitlin Masters before we knew who she was.

Parked in the middle of the floor is the Infiniti Q45. Midnight blue. I look around once, then crouch and reach under the bumper, feeling along the inside lip for Kelly's gun. My fingers collide with something hard, but as I try to close them around it, the gun clatters to the floor. Glancing around at the people waiting for luggage, I drop to my stomach and sweep my hand across the tile, and the gun skitters into my chest.

It's Kelly's Browning Hi-Power.

I jam the pistol into my waistband beneath my shirt and trot past the rental car desks to the glass doors leading to the outdoor parking lot. I've heard no shots or even shouts since my conversation with Kelly, but this actually increases my anxiety. Did he manage to divert whoever was waiting for me? Or is he lying dead beneath a pay phone, the slug from a silenced pistol in his head?

The Taurus is parked sixty yards from the terminal. I can see it from the doors. Exiting the terminal with a group of LSU fraternity guys, I fall in with them until they stop near a Blazer thirty yards from the door, then break for the Taurus at a flat-out sprint. To my surprise, the wind cuts through my jacket with a cold bite. Maybe fall has come to Mississippi at last.

Laying Kelly's pistol on the seat beside me, I retrieve the keys, crank the engine, and force myself to drive normally as I leave the lot. In ten minutes I'm on Highway 61. Natchez lies eighty miles to the north, but much of the road is two-lane blacktop and heavily traveled by log trucks. The trip can be agonizingly slow during the day.

I reach under the seat for the cell phone, switch it on, and dial the Natchez *Examiner*. Caitlin has been handling the transportation of my out-of-town witnesses. Huey Moak and Lester Hinson are scheduled to arrive in Baton Rouge tonight, and we'd planned to have one of the Argus men pick them up.

'Penn?' Caitlin asks, after a minute of hold music.

'Yes. Remember, your phone's tapped.'

'What's going on? I've been freaking out here.'

'Have you asked any of the Argus guys to pick up the witnesses yet?'

'Not yet. I can call them now.'

'Don't.'

'Why not?'

'Just don't. Don't even mention it. I'll be there soon, and I'll handle it. Hang tight until then. Stay inside the newspaper building if you can.'

'Penn, Kelly was acting a little strange before he left. Like I might not see him again.'

You might not. 'Things are pretty fluid right now. I'm on my way.'

'Listen. An hour ago my receptionist told me I had a call from the editor of the *Rocky Mountain News*. When I got to the phone, he told me he was sending a reporter down to cover your trial, and he wanted to know if the guy could use our office facilities.'

'And?'

'He said the reporter's name was Bookbinder. Henry Bookbinder.'

Bookbinder. Stone's dead partner. And the *Rocky Mountain News* is based in Denver. I want to scream with joy, but I just say, 'Did he say when this reporter would arrive?'

'Only that he'd be here in time to cover the trial. And there's something else.'

'What?'

'CNN, Court TV, and some others have been pressing Judge Franklin to allow the trial to be televised.'

'Cameras aren't allowed in Mississippi courtrooms.'

'I know, but this is a civil case. Apparently if both parties agree, the judge could allow it.'

'But why would Leo agree? Portman would tear him a new one if he did.'

'CNN and the other networks have been saying publicly that if Marston and Portman have nothing to hide, they should have no problem with cameras. It's a PR nightmare for Portman. It's extortion, basically. I assume you'd have no objection to cameras?'

'Of course not.'

'Good, because I already told a CNN reporter that you didn't.'

'That's fine. Listen, if that "reporter" you mentioned shows up, keep him inside the building until I get there.'

'I will.'

'Thanks. I'll be there before you know it.'

As I hang up the phone, I yell, 'You tough old son of a bitch!' Though probably a thousand miles away right now, Dwight Stone is almost certainly alive. If he can reach Natchez by tomorrow morning without being killed, my slander trial will provide more fireworks than the city has seen in decades. And Leo Marston will be indicted for murder. Only now that prospect does not offer even a shadow of the satisfaction it would have two days ago. If I'm right about Leo being Jenny Doe's father, every judgment I ever made about Livy Marston was wrong. In my mind she has already been transformed from a privileged princess into a tragic figure, a lost girl trying to find her way.

I try to keep the Taurus under the speed limit. A state trooper has haunted this stretch of road for years, handing out tickets like confetti. As the hardwood forest drifts past, I lean back in the seat and force myself to ponder one of the connections that came to me last night in the darkness of the Denver motel. Sometime near dawn a remarkable and frightening idea struck me. A possible link between Del Payton and Leo Marston. Dwight Stone believes Ray Presley randomly chose Del Payton to be murdered. But if my theory of paternal incest is true, there could be a secret link joining the Payton and Marston families, one which Dwight Stone would have known nothing about.

Althea Payton.

Althea is a nurse now. She works in the hospital nursery. But where did she work in the 1960s? Could she have worked for a private physician? A pediatrician perhaps? Is it possible that she noticed some physical evidence of sexual abuse while handling Livy Marston and reported it to the doctor? If she had, what would have been the likely result? In the 1960s sexual abuse of children was grossly under-reported, and became public only in the most egregious cases. A man as powerful as Leo Marston would have had little to fear from a doctor, especially if the evidence was equivocal. And even if it wasn't, would the doctor have the nerve to confront Leo? To bring in the police to investigate the district attorney?

Of course, Leo Marston would never have been to the pediatrician's office. He wouldn't have taken time out of his day to carry his daughter to the doctor. Maude would have done that. A pediatrician might have been more comfortable bringing certain suspicious symptoms to the mother's attention. But if he wasn't, a compassionate nurse certainly might have. Mother to mother. I can see Althea Payton doing that. Pulling Maude aside and pointing out a couple of things. In the interest of the child.

What would Leo have done if Maude confronted him with such a thing? Denied it, of course. Deny, deny, deny. Then he would have demanded to know the source of Maude's suspicions. If she told him it was Althea, what then? Killing Althea would certainly silence her. But it was Del who had died, not his wife. Perhaps Leo had initially taken no action. But later, when the necessity arose to kill a black man to make an example for the Georgia carpet magnate, had Leo chosen Del Payton out of some perverse desire to strike back at the woman who had threatened him? A wild scenario perhaps. But Leo long ago demonstrated his penchant for holding grudges. Whatever the case, unraveling the truth of this low tragedy will be a nightmare for everyone involved. The idea of confronting Livy with my deductions leaves me numb.

A few miles before I reach town, I call Sam Jacobs at work, tell him my family might be in danger, and ask for his help. Jacobs is thirty-eight years old, with a wife and two kids, but by the time I arrive at the Prentiss Motel, he is parked outside with a .357 Magnum sitting on the front seat of his Hummer.

When I see that, I know I am looking at the Jewish boy who discovered the list of Klansmen and White Citizens' Council members in his father's attic with me twenty-five years ago.

With Sam beside me, I inform the three remaining Argus security men that their services are no longer required. It's an awkward moment, but they say little and leave the motel with expressionless faces. I'm tempted to tell them to pass a message to their boss when they get back to Houston – that he should look forward to a multimillion-dollar lawsuit – but I don't want to do anything that might hurt Daniel Kelly in the future.

My parents are stunned by my action, but as soon as I explain what Kelly told me, my father gets on the phone and speaks to two patients of his – avid hunters – and they promise to arrive within the hour, loaded for bear. Dad then makes my day by informing me that while I was in Crested Butte, he finally persuaded Betty Lou Beckham to take the witness stand tomorrow and tell the jury that she saw Ray Presley in the Triton Battery parking lot only seconds after Del Payton died.

What we need now is a new place to stay, a secure loca-tion, and it's my mother who solves this problem. When our house burned, a friend of Mom's offered us rooms in her bed-and-breakfast, which occupies the slave quarters of her home, Aquitaine, a massive Greek Revival mansion completed in 1843. Not wanting to impose on her friend's hospitality, Mom declined. But these are special circum-stances, and the fall Pilgrimage has just ended, so our staying there won't cost the chatelaine her peak-season fees. One phone call secures us lodgings in the slave quarters of Aquitaine.

Since the fire destroyed most of our things, moving from the motel to the mansion is relatively painless. The two-story slave quarters was sited across the ornamental gardens from the main house, which occupies most of a city block on the north side of town, near Stanton Hall. Once we're settled in our rooms, I order out for pizza and spend the forty-minute wait playing with Annie in the garden. She dances around the rim of the central fountain like a gymnast, oblivious to the anxiety mounting in the adults as the hours tick down to tomorrow's trial. That she does not pick up on our feelings shows me just how far she has come in her journey from the hypersensitive state that followed Sarah's death.

After devouring my share of pizza, I deal with the messages that came in while I was in Crested Butte. Althea Payton called several times, but the most persistent caller was Ike Ransom. Dad says Ike is desperate to talk to me, and that he sounded both angry and afraid during their conversations. I call Althea and give her an encouraging update, editing the violence into a less frightening picture. Nevertheless, she tells me that Del Jr. wants to help me any way he can, and that she's going to send him over to 'help keep the no-goods away' until the trial. In less than an hour, Del arrives carrying a sawed-off shotgun, and takes up a post on the balcony of the slave quarters, overlooking the street.

Which leaves me Ike.

I am not particularly anxious to talk to him after the way he acted at Ruby's funeral. Whatever the source of his hatred for Leo Marston, it has pushed him into unstable territory. Ike clearly has both a drug and an alcohol problem, and since he is unwilling or unable to provide me with any facts that will help prove Marston guilty of murder in a court of law, I see no urgent need to call him.

I call Ray Presley instead. Dwight Stone's revelation that Marston gave up Presley to the Feds as part of his deal with J. Edgar Hoover was music to my 'lawyer's ear.' Presley considers Leo Marston his friend, and loyalty is the supreme virtue to men of Presley's ilk. But if Ray were to learn that the five years he spent in Parchman came courtesy of Leo Marston, his attitude toward the judge might change fast. But whether he will or not remains a mystery, because Presley doesn't answer his phone.

I am working up the courage to call Livy when the telephone rings in my room. Somehow Ike Ransom has discovered that we've moved to Aquitaine and he wants to see me. He got my phone number from the main house. I start to beg off, but he stops me cold. He has, he says, what we've been looking for since day one. Hard evidence linking Leo Marston to Payton's murder. He will say no more, and he refuses to come to the B&B. He insists on a face-to-face meeting and says I must come alone. When I ask why, he tells me that no one can know he is the source for what he's about to tell me.

'Where do you want to meet?' I ask, recalling the feeling of being shot at in the warehouse by the river and not liking it too much.

'You're three blocks away from it,' he replies.

'Where are you talking about?'

'The old pecan-shelling plant.'

An image of a hulking brown brick building where I sold the pecans I collected as a boy comes into my mind. It is set right on the edge of the bluff, and as Ike said, it's only three blocks west of where I am now.

'What about the surveillance on me here?'

'Slip out the back alley on foot. They lookin' for that BMW. Or you could send your Jew buddy out first in the BMW, then come on in that Maxima your mama got.'

It's nearly dark, and I want to refuse, largely out of fear. But Ike is offering something of which I have precious little: hard evidence. Dwight Stone's testimony could be powerful, but without his FBI files to back him up, it will be his word against Marston's (and Portman's too, if the FBI director decides to honor my subpoena). Hard evidence is worth a three-block trip.

'When?' I ask.

'Thirty minutes. The place is an equipment-storage yard now. Drive around to the left side of the building. The chain on the gate'll be cut.'

'I'll be there.'

I hang up and speak to Sam Jacobs on the balcony, and Sam declares himself ready to draw off the surveillance long enough to get me clear of Aquitaine.

The old pecan-shelling plant stands on prime real estate in Natchez's old warehouse district, a sort of no-man's-land between the town proper and a sleepy residential area filled with Victorian gems. It has an unobstructed view of the river and one day will probably be the site of a luxury hotel. At the moment it is an eerily lighted compound surrounded by a high fence and razor wire, with the rigid arms of great cranes jutting against the night sky.

As Ike promised, the chained gate on the left side of the building has been cut open. I nose the Maxima through it without getting out, and negotiate my way through backhoes, draglines, and D-9 bulldozers parked like Patton's army marshaling for a campaign. I can't see the river, but forty yards to my left, the bluff drops away to a vast dark sky, leaving the impression that I'm driving along the edge of a mountain.

Out of the blackness to my right, a pink-and-blue light bar strobes like a carnival, then vanishes. I slow nearly to a stop, trying to place the location of Ike's cruiser.

There.

I turn right and idle toward the main building. As the black silhouette looms over me, the lights flash again. In their light I see that Ike has opened the old truck door of the plant and is parked in it. As I approach, he starts his engine and pulls forward, leaving me plenty of room to pull inside the building. I park the Maxima beside his cruiser and shut off the engine. Kelly's Browning is in the glove box, but I don't want to cause any kind of reflex reaction in Ike, especially if he's wired on speed.

Ike is standing by my passenger door, between his car and mine. I get out and walk around the trunk of the Maxima, extending my hand to shake his.

'What have you got, Ike?'

He holds out his hand, but instead of shaking he grabs my wrist and jerks me to my knees on the concrete floor. As I try to look up, something slams into the top of my skull. The blow drives every thought out of my head, leaving only white noise. My first coherent perception is of something cold and hard pressed against my hairline.

'That's a gun,' he says. 'Don't fucking move.'

The terror generated by the gun barrel is absolute, paralyzing. If any muscle in my body is moving, it's the sphincter of my bladder. 'Ike? What the hell are you doing?'

His breath is ragged above me, like a sick animal's.

'*Ike?*'

'Where the fuck you been?' he shouts, and the reek of cheap whiskey rolls over me like steam. 'Answer me, god-damn it!'

'Ike, what's wrong? Let's talk face to face, man.'

'*I said, where the fuck have you been?*'

'Colorado! I went back to see Stone.'

'I knew it! You sneaky son of a bitch. You been holding out the whole time. What that motherfucker tell you?'

'He told me what we want to know. He told me what happened here in sixty-eight. I've got Marston nailed, man.'

He twists around me and jabs the gun into my cervical spine. 'What did Stone say happened?'

'He told me why Marston wanted Payton dead. It was a land deal . . . Marston stood to make a lot of money off some land, but he had to make an example of a black union worker first. He paid Presley to do it for him. Presley chose Payton.'

'Bullshit!' Another fog of whiskey blows over me.

'What do you mean, bullshit?'

'Don't lie to me, goddamn it! *Don't you lie!*'

He jerks back the slide on the gun, and everything inside me goes into free fall. My thoughts, my courage, my blood pressure. 'Ike, please . . . I've got a little girl, man. Just tell me what the problem is and—'

The gun barrel rakes around my neck, under my jaw, up my right cheek to my eye. All I can see now is the taut belly of Ike's brown uniform.

'Get up,' he says coldly. 'Get up!'

The gun barrel stays screwed into my eye socket as I rise, but my terror abates slightly. The prospect of dying on my knees was as debasing as it was frightening.

Ike's gun is shaking. As he pulls it out of my eye socket and lays the barrel against my forehead, I see his eyes, bloodshot and jerky, the eyes of a man in agony.

'You a goddamn liar,' he says. 'I shoulda known a white boy wouldn't go against his own in the end. You been dicking that Marston bitch all along. You in with 'em all the way.' He shakes his head as though at his own stupidity. 'Setting up to get the nigger. Like always.'

'Ike, I have no idea what you're talking about. I'm setting up to get Leo Marston, and I'm going to use Ray Presley to do it. If I can find him. Dwight Stone and Ray Presley are going to send that bastard to the extermination chamber at Parchman.'

But Ike isn't listening. At the word Presley, his eyes glazed over with blind rage. 'That fucking Presley . . . he told you, didn't he?'

'Told me what? Talk to me, Ike! Something's been eating you up since we started this. What is it?'

He bites his lip and presses the gun harder against my forehead. Then suddenly he lets it drop to his side. 'I didn't know what I was doing, man,' he says in a desolate voice. 'Hadn't been back in the World but three months. Couldn't get no kind of job. I applied with the police three times. They wouldn't even talk to me. Had all the *Negro* cops they needed, they said. Didn't have but three. Same with the sheriff. I'd done more police work in Saigon than them motherfuckers done their whole lives, and they wouldn't even give me a *chance*.'

I'm more confused than I've been since the start of this mess, but I'm not about to interrupt him.

'What else could I do, man?' he almost wails. 'Wasn't gonna go on no welfare! I had to deal.' He slaps at a mosquito on his sweating face. 'Presley got me on a traffic stop. Just speeding, but he pulled his weapon and made me open my trunk. He found half a pound of white lady. Illegal search if I ever saw one, but you think that mattered back then? In them days he coulda sent me to Parchman for fifty years behind that much heroin.'

A dark perception is blooming in a corner of my brain. A fetid, cloying orchid of a thought. 'What did he want you to do, Ike?'

'Don't play that shit! You already know!'

The pain in his eyes is terrible to behold. I hold up both my hands. 'I know what you tell me. That's all.'

'What you *think* happened, man? Motherfucker put it to me right there on the side of the road. Said he had some-body needed killing. Said I'd been killing for Uncle for two years, what was one more? I knew what one more was. But what could I do, man? He had me. I didn't want to die on Parchman Farm. Presley took my dope and told me if I tried to back out, he'd plant it on me and bust me all over again.'

'He wanted you to kill Del Payton?'

'*What you think I been saying?*'

The nausea of a roller coaster that hurtles in only one

direction – down – sweeps over me as the whole sick plan falls together in my head.

'You asked Presley to get the C-4, didn't you?'

He stares at me with strangled emotion. 'Presley wanted the car blown up. I didn't know nothing about dynamite, but I'd worked with C-4 in 'Nam. I told him if he could get me some plastic, I could do the job.'

'Jesus, Ike. Did you know Del?'

'No. He was ten years older than me. Grew up out to Pine Ridge.'

'Did you know about his civil rights work?'

'Hell, no. I thought he was dicking a white woman or something. Didn't matter, though. I was so fucked up, I didn't know nothing 'bout nothing.'

'Ike, listen . . . what you did was terrible, but–'

'Don't you judge me!' he cries, the whites of his eyes making him look wild in the dark. 'Don't you cast no stone! I been torturing myself thirty years. After I realized the work Del was doing, I just about went crazy. The whole town was marching for him. I wanted to scream out what I'd done, what Presley made me do. But I didn't have the guts. I couldn't face my own sin.'

The diabolical irony of Ray Presley's plan leaves me cold. He actually blackmailed a black man into committing a civil rights murder. He and Marston must have laughed for weeks over that one. They've been laughing for thirty years.

'Does Stone know this? Or does he really believe Presley killed Payton?'

'Stone? 'Course he knows. He came to see me back then. He had the whole thing dogged out.'

'Why didn't he arrest you? Why didn't he tell me about you?'

Ike seems only partially aware of what I'm saying. 'I don't know why. He was different, I guess.'

'Why didn't you tell me all this at the start?'

'What could I tell you, man? I knew what I'd done. I knew about Presley. But that's all. I knew *what* happened, but I didn't know *why*. And that was the only way you were gonna get Marston.'

'But how did you know Marston was involved? Did Presley tell you?'

'He didn't tell me shit. A year after it happened, somebody called me on the phone. Wouldn't say nothing. I was about to hang up when they started playing this tape. It was Marston and Presley, talking about Del being killed. Talking about *me*. I figured it was Stone. Had to be.'

Stone must have called and played Ike Ransom the copy he'd made of the evidence tape he'd sent to J. Edgar Hoover. And his reason, I suspect, was a dark one. 'Thirty years, Ike. Thirty *years*. Couldn't you figure a way to trade what you knew for immunity, or–'

'*Who was I gonna go to, man?*' Spittle flies from his mouth. 'The FBI *already knew* what had gone down. And they didn't arrest nobody! A few years later I tried to find Stone, but the Bureau had fired his ass. Portman was a U.S. attorney, and I knew better than to trust that Yankee piece of shit. And Marston was on the state supreme court! What's a drunk nigger cop from Mississippi gonna do against people swingin' that kind of weight? You tell me.'

'Then why tell me? Why try at all after thirty years?'

His broad shoulders sag as though under a great weight, and he speaks toward the floor. 'I didn't have no choice. It ate at me so long . . . I thought it would get better over time, but it got worse. A few months back, I found myself going to church. Not wanting to . . . *needing* to. You know? Being raised Catholic, I guess. Don't matter if you stop goin'. You can give up on God, but it don't matter. 'Cause He don't give up on you.'

The tortured paths this man has pushed himself down are beyond any imagining. 'Ike, you came to me knowing you could go to jail for the rest of your life. That you could be executed. That means a lot. And I've figured a way to turn Presley against Marston. If you'll get on that witness stand tomorrow and tell the truth–'

'Is Stone gonna testify?'

'Yes.'

'Is he here in town?'

This isn't the time to lie. 'No. But he's on his way here. Some people tried to kill us last night. Portman's guys probably. We got split up.'

Ike starts pacing back and forth, patting the Sig-Sauer against his leg. 'But he's alive?'

'You can't let your decision be based on what Stone does. This thing's eating you alive because you know you did wrong. Terrible wrong. It's got nothing to do with you or me. You owe it to Althea Payton to tell the truth. You owe it to Del. You owe it to yourself, man.'

'I don't owe nobody but God!' The Sig jerks up again, aimed at my chest now. 'You don't know how close it's been. At first I thought maybe you could nail Marston without me having to go down. But that was stupid. Crazy. The closer you got to the truth, the more I saw I was gonna have to pay the piper, no matter what. One night I got so drunk I thought about killing you, just to stop it all. That night you left the newspaper by yourself . . . I was right behind you.'

My heart feels like a ball of lead.

'I couldn't do it, though. Part of me just wanted to pay, I guess. Father Tom says you got to. But I can't go to Parchman Farm. I done sent too many brothers there myself. I can't die in them cotton fields up there.'

'You won't have to, Ike. CNN will be covering that trial tomorrow. You get on the stand and tell the story you just told me, you'll have Johnnie Cochran down here begging to defend you. What you did was wrong, but you're the least guilty of the three by far. I think Stone believed that too. You know what the right thing is. That's why you came to me in the first place.'

He lets his gun fall again, then half turns from me and murmurs in the dark. 'I started out all right. But I turned off somewhere. That day my shoulder got hurt, everything started going down.'

He holsters his pistol and walks past me, toward the wide door, and looks out at the luminous clouds scudding over the river. Beyond him I can see a few stars, infinitely small on this first cool night. He turns back to face me, but since he's silhouetted in the door, I cannot see his features.

'I'll do it,' he says. 'Father Tom gonna think I'm the best man he ever knew. But he gonna be the only one. Every black man, woman, and child in this country gonna curse my name.'

He half turns again, and a dim shaft of light illuminates his face. In eight years as a prosecutor, I never saw a man look so lost.

Ike opens his mouth to say something, then flings an arm out as though to grab me, but he can't because he's flying backward, snatched like a puppet on a string. Before he hits the floor, a peal of thunder booms through the warehouse.

'*Ike!*'

He doesn't answer. He's lying facedown on the dirty floor, blood pumping from a fist-sized hole where his left shoulder blade used to be.

Chapter 37

I run to Ike, then drop to the cement floor as a second shot booms through the building. A third punches through the front and rear windshields of the Maxima, which is parked two feet to my left, and the concussion of the gun echoes around the old structure for three or four seconds.

The shooter is inside the building.

Inside, and probably at the front, shooting across the open floor. But he must not have a night-vision scope. He shot Ike as the deputy framed himself against the lighter background of the open loading door. Now that we're flat on the floor, his shots are far off the mark. Ike's face is less than six inches from mine, his eyes wide and glassy, like those of a wounded deer.

'Ike,' I whisper. 'Can you hear me?'

His eyelids blink once, slowly, but he doesn't speak. The man is dying before my eyes.

I need a gun.

Kelly's Browning is in the glove box of the Maxima, but I'm not about to try to reach it. If I rise off the ground, I will silhouette myself against the open door, just as Ike did. If I had walked to that door first, I would be dying now.

'Ike, I need your gun.'

As I reach down to his holster, something cracks through the air less than a foot above us, and the report that follows seems trivial compared to that supersonic passage of metal. Fighting down panic, I try to wrest the Sig-Sauer from Ike's holster, but it won't budge. He must have snapped the strap when he holstered it. Unsnapping it by touch, I yank out the Sig and take the safety off. As I aim it across Ike's back, a bullet crashes into his body, knocking us both a foot across the cold floor.

He doesn't make a sound.

Then, like a rising wind, a wail of inhuman agony escapes his throat. I shove my arm across his waist and fire three quick rounds into the darkness at the front of the building. Something sharp pricks the skin of my forearm.

Bone splinters.

The last shot smashed Ike's pelvis. He screams again, the sound sickeningly reminiscent of those Sarah made when the narcotics began to lose their race to keep up with the pain of her bone lesions.

Who is shooting at us? An anonymous sniper, like the one who shot at me on the levee that night? The one Kelly killed? With a strange rush of clarity I realize that the levee sniper wasn't shooting only at me, as I'd thought at the time. What did Ike say that night? *How you know he was shooting at you?* Ike had known from the beginning that he carried knowledge people would kill him for. As I cower behind his body, a voice calls out from the other end of the building.

'*Give it up! The nigger's dead!*'

Before I can process these words, another truncated wail bursts from Ike's lungs. '*Brrrraaaaaaah!*'

My instinct is to run for the door, run until my legs buckle beneath me. But that would be suicide. The moment I rise, I'll make myself a target. I could probably crawl out . . . but Ike isn't dead yet. I can't leave him. My next thought, born from rage, is to stand up and charge the darkness that shields the sniper, emptying Ike's automatic as I run.

With a defiant yell, I fire off two more rounds, then jump to my feet and grab Ike's legs. Two shots boom through the building as I drag him facedown and screaming behind his cruiser, but the bullets crack past without finding flesh or bone.

Kneeling beside him, I break the most fundamental rule of first-aid by turning him over onto his back. At this point it can't matter much. His eyes are still open. His jaw is moving, but no sounds come from his throat. I lean over his mouth.

'*Brrr–*' he groans.

I take one of his hands in mine and squeeze the cold flesh. 'Ike? What are you saying?'

'*Press me.*'

He must think I can stop the bleeding. 'Where? Your shoulder?'

'*Pressleee . . .*'

Press lee? *The nigger's dead–*

Son of a bitch. No sniper hired by John Portman would talk that way. He wouldn't talk at all. The man at the other end of this building is Raymond Aucoin Presley. The trial is tomorrow, and Presley has no intention of being indicted for murder. That's why he wasn't at his trailer when I called earlier. He's been following Ike around, laying for a shot.

'Ray!' I yell at the top of my voice. 'Stop shooting! I need to talk to you!'

Both windshields of Ike's cruiser star into chaos as safety glass rattles across the floor.

'*What you got to say I want to hear?*' comes the voice I recognize so easily now. '*You want it in the head or the heart?*'

I will live or die by my actions in the next minute. 'Listen to me, Ray! You want to hear this!'

'*I want to hear you choke on your own blood!*'

Every hair on my body is standing erect. Presley isn't nearly as far away as he was a moment ago. He's moving up for a kill shot. Crawling to the left side of the cruiser, I fire two quick rounds into the dark, then dart back to avoid return fire aimed at my muzzle flash.

'*Not even close, boy.*'

The tire beside my head explodes into ragged strips of rubber as Presley's next shot reverberates through the building. When the echo dies, I call: 'You want to know who sent you to Parchman, Ray? I think you'll be surprised.'

He fires again, smashing up a divot of cement beside Ike's head.

'Parchman, Ray! Didn't you ever wonder who ratted you out?'

Silence. Then: '*Talk fast, boy, I'm getting close!*'

He is close. It takes every bit of nerve I possess to hold my ground. 'It was Marston, Ray! Leo sent you up! Stone solved the murder, but Hoover didn't want Leo going down for it. Leo's old man had too much political clout. Hoover cut a deal to protect him, but he said you had to go down for shooting at Stone and Portman on the highway. It was Leo who gave you up!'

'*That's bullshit!*' For the first time the voice has come from more or less the same place.

'Stone said Marston didn't even hesitate! He fed the state police details of your drug business so they could catch you in the act. That's why Stone was at the bust!'

'*You lying piece of shit! You're just trying to save your own ass!*'

He's buying it. 'Leo didn't give a shit about you, Ray. How else do you think they got you? You must have had a lot of time to think about it. Five years, man!'

More silence.

'Ray?'

No sound at all. Nothing but the slow ticking of the two cars, barely audible through the ringing in my ears. The son of a bitch is probably moving up to kill me, and if I don't move, I'm going to die. But if I break for the door, I'm framing myself for a shot. Shivering against Ike's body, I realize that I no longer hear his breathing. His eyes are still open, but they are fixed and dilated.

Ike the Spike is dead.

'*Ray . . . ? Talk to me, Ray!*'

Nothing.

The loading door beckons. But as I gather my legs beneath me, Ruby Flowers's voice sounds in my head, an echo from childhood. *Broad is the gate that leads to destruction, but narrow the way that leads to salvation . . .*

To my left – in what must be a corner of the old shelling plant – is a pool of darkness so black it could be the bottom of the Marianas Trench. My legs are tensed beneath me like steel springs. Gripping Ike's gun in my right hand, I launch myself low and hard toward that black hole. As the darkness envelops me, a stroke of lightning flashes in my brain, and I know no more.

Consciousness returns like blood to a sleeping limb.

Pain is the first sensation.

Then light.

The pain radiates from my forehead. The light is faint but real, thirty yards away, illuminating a parked police car. Not a police car. A sheriff's cruiser.

Ike's cruiser.

I roll over slowly and feel along the cold cement for Ike's gun. My right wrist bangs into something cold and immovable. I touch it with my hand and feel along it. A steel rail. It's one loading arm of a forklift. That's what I slammed into when I ran into the pool of darkness. A goddamn forklift.

The gun is underneath the fork.

Closing my hand around its butt, I get to my feet and walk toward Ike's car. Strangely, I am unafraid. Unafraid because I know I'm alone. If I wasn't, I would be dead. Ray finally believed what I was telling him, and once he did, his priorities changed.

At the edge of the darkness I look at my watch. Eight

forty-five. I met Ike around eight. Ray started shooting about ten minutes after we started talking. I don't know how long the shooting lasted, but he's had at least twenty minutes to reach the target I offered up to him to save myself.

Ike's body lies behind his cruiser, where I dragged it in that last furious rush. His eyes are open but unseeing. I feel his carotid artery to be sure, then hold my hand over his mouth.

Nothing.

Climbing into the Maxima, I start the engine and dial Tuscany on the cell phone. While it rings, I floor the accelerator and make a wide squealing turn on the cement floor, then roar through the main loading door. The phone clicks as I hit Canal Street and nearly skid into the curb on the other side.

'Liv Marston,' says a clipped voice. 'If you're a reporter—'

'It's Penn.'

'What do you want?' The voice hasn't warmed even one degree.

'I know you don't want to listen to me, but you've got to.'

'Is it about the trial?'

'No. You've got to get out of the house.'

'What?'

I hesitate before I reply. Some savage part of me wants to get Livy away and leave her father to face the retribution of his past. Poetic justice, if ever there was any. But I can't do it.

'Ray Presley's on his way to Tuscany. He's going to try to kill your father. He could already be at your house. Or on the grounds somewhere.'

Silence.

'Did you hear me, Livy?'

'I heard you.'

'Tell your father to call the police. They'll send an army out there to protect him.'

'Are we done now?'

Are we done? 'Did you understand what I just told you? Presley is coming there to *kill* your father.'

'I hope he comes here.'

'You what?'

A police car tears around the corner of Main and Canal, lights flashing, heading in the direction of the pecan-shelling plant. In fifteen minutes every cop and deputy in this town will be combing the downtown streets.

'You're playing in things you don't understand, Penn. I tried to tell you the other day. You were a fool to involve yourself in any of this.'

'I understand more than you think. I know now why you did the things you did in the past. The choices you made.'

'Such as?'

'I don't want to discuss it on the phone. It has to be face to face.'

'We don't have anything to say to each other.'

'I'm begging you, Livy. Meet me one last time. For the sake of whatever it is that's bound us together all these years. If you will. I think it will change both our lives. Maybe forever.'

This time she hesitates. 'It's not about the trial?'

'I don't give a damn what happens at the trial. Name a place. Anywhere, I don't care. I'll even come to Tuscany.'

'No. Jewish Hill.'

'Jewish Hill?' Yet another landmark from our past. 'In the cemetery?'

'That's about as private as you can get.'

'Isn't it locked at night?'

'Park at the foot of the hill. By the wall. It's not like we've never done it before.'

'Do you still have the gun you had in the motel?'

'Yes.'

'Bring it. And drive fast leaving the house.'

'What time?'

'I'm five minutes from the cemetery. Leave now.'

'All right.'

Livy's borrowed Fiat is parked at the foot of Jewish Hill when I arrive, next to the low stone wall of the city cemetery. She got here first because I took a wide circle through town to avoid the police. I park behind the Fiat and shove Ike's pistol into my waistband, then get out and walk up to the Spyder.

Livy is not in the car.

To my left, across Cemetery Road, stands the dark silhouette of Weymouth Hall, an antebellum mansion that marks the two-hundred-foot drop to the river, its widow's walk silhouetted against the stars. To my right is the low wall and the nearly vertical slope of Jewish Hill. One mile south along the bluff, the police are taping off the pecan plant as a crime scene.

I climb the wall and push through the shrubbery, then dig my hands into the face of the hill and begin climbing. As I near the top, a ghostly figure appears at the edge, looking down at me.

It's Livy. Her hair is flying behind her, caught in the wind blowing up the bluff from the river. She's wearing a white blouse, a fitted jacket, and slacks tapered to the ankles. She bends and catches my hands, then pulls me up to the flat plateau of gravestones, statuary, and mausoleums.

'Did you call the police?' I ask.

She brushes a strand of hair from her eyes. 'Daddy called some off-duty cops. They got there before I left.'

'How did he react when you told him Presley might be coming to kill him?'

'What do you want, Penn?'

'It scared him to death, didn't it? Livy, your father gave the cops what they needed to send Presley to Parchman when we were kids.'

'Really?' A hard smile tightens her mouth. 'Good.'

'What I don't understand is why my call didn't scare *you*.'

She walks past me to the edge of the hill. The lights of Vidalia, Louisiana, a mile away, outline her like another marble angel among the stones. 'Why are we here, Penn? What's the big mystery?'

'You are.'

She turns back to me. 'I'm the mystery?'

'You're the mystery of my life. But I understand you now.'

Something flickers in her eyes. I can't tell if she's intrigued or afraid. 'Do you? Enlighten me, then.'

'I know who Jenny's father is.'

Even in the dark I can tell she has gone rigid. She turns away from me, then back, her chin held high. 'How do you know? Did he tell you?'

'Tell me? God, no. He hates me. Why would he tell me?'

She shakes her head. 'I can't believe this. I can't believe you know this. It's so pathetic.'

'I know it's bad, Livy. I realize I can't ever understand what it was – what it is – to be in your position.'

'How could you possibly know unless he told you? No one knows. *He* doesn't even know. Not as far as I—'

'Your father doesn't know about Jenny?'

She blinks. 'My father? Of course he knows. But he doesn't know, you know . . . who the father is.'

My mind reels, trying to parse the semantics. 'Livy, who is Jenny's father?'

'You just said you knew.'

'Pretend I don't.'

Suspicion now. 'If you don't know, I'm not telling you.'

'Livy—'

'Who do you think it is?'

I take a step toward her, but she moves back, nearer the

edge of the hill. As though she knows what I am about to say. As though she could fly from the edge of the hill if I dare speak the truth. 'I think Jenny's father is your father.'

She stares at me like she hasn't heard correctly. Then she closes her eyes and lowers her head into her hands.

'You don't have to say anything,' I say softly. 'You–'

'Shut up, Penn. Please just shut up. You might say something even more asinine than you already have.'

'What?'

She takes her hands away from her face. She is not crying. She is staring at me with what looks like morbid curiosity. 'Did you actually think my father raped me?'

Her voice is strong, but that could be the strength of denial, not truth. 'I still think so. What I can't figure out is how he forced you when you were eighteen.'

A bitter laugh. 'That's easy. He didn't. Christ. First you accuse my father of murder. Now incest? Could you possibly be more sick?' She holds her palms out to me. 'Have I done something to deserve this?'

'I'll tell you what you did to deserve this. You told me you wanted a future together and then disappeared. You let your father try to destroy mine without lifting a finger to stop him, and went on with your life as though none of it ever happened.'

'My God, Penn. We were just kids! Haven't you grown up yet? After twenty years?'

'Have you? You've been chasing me around like the lost love of your life, trying to relive our past, pulling me into bed every chance you got. Was all that heat manufactured to distract me from going after your father?'

At last she gives me an unguarded look. 'No.'

'If my incest idea is so off the mark, why did you treat that poor girl like you did? You gave Jenny up for adoption, which is understandable. But she had a pretty shitty life, and when she showed up at your door looking for a little information, maybe an explanation, you treated her like dirt. And your father did worse.'

'How *dare* you judge me. You don't know anything about it.'

'You're right. Why is that?'

Her eyes flash in the dark. 'You want an explanation? All right. Remember the week after graduation? The week you went touring battlefields with your dad?'

'I remember.'

'I had two weeks before Radcliffe. The senior parties were still going on. Everybody was getting as drunk as they had been before graduation, maybe drunker. Someone from South Natchez threw a party on one of the sandbars past the paper mill. It was wild. Trucks driving all over the sand, people shooting guns, skinny-dipping. One car even went into the river. You were out of town, so guys were hitting on me all night. Ray Presley was there, watching me for Daddy, like he always did. At some point the police showed up. Ray put me in his truck and talked to one of the cops, got me past the roadblock.'

She turns toward the river, and the wind carries much of her voice away. 'I was as drunk as I'd ever been, and I decided to play a little game. Ray was always watching me, making me nervous, hanging around like some malevolent shadow. And I'd always heard these stories . . . how he'd killed people, been in prison, other stuff. Anyway, I started teasing him. I asked if he'd ever killed anybody, and he admitted that he had. I asked him what it was like, what prison was like, stuff like that. Then I told him I'd always heard this story about how he had the biggest thing in town. You know, his equipment. He kept driving, but I could see I was getting to him, he was gripping the wheel so hard. So I said, Hey, is it true or what? And he said, Only one way to find out. It was like a dare, you know? So I said, Okay, let's see it.'

The knowledge of what's coming hits me like a blow to the solar plexus. 'Livy . . .'

She holds up her hand; she means to tell this story no matter what. 'So, he unbuckles his belt and takes it out. While he's driving. And it was. I mean, the stories were true. I know this sounds gross – Ray Presley, right? What a creep. But he was only thirty-five or so then. Younger than we are now. So, I took the dare further. I thought I'd drive him a little crazier, to get back at him for all the times he'd ogled me. It was the stupidest thing I ever did. He pulled off Lower Woodville Road, right into the woods. I knew then things were slipping out of control, but I wasn't sure how to get out of it. I figured, you know, just be calm, let him kiss me, touch him enough to get it over with and get out of there. The next thing I knew my dress was around my chest and he was raping me.'

'You don't have to tell me this.'

She turns to me, her eyes bright with pooled tears. 'A little too real for you? I think I passed out the first time. I woke up later and it was happening again, outside the truck. I started screaming, so he stuffed my dress into my mouth. It was like being simultaneously strangled and bludgeoned to death from the inside. When it was over, we got back into the truck, but he wouldn't leave. He was completely freaked out. I think he thought my father was going to kill him, so he just sat there, trying to figure out what to do. He sat there for twenty minutes with me screaming at him, trying to get out and run, going crazy. Then he did it *again*. I knew then that he was crazy. I mean, three times in an hour, that's just not normal for a thirty-five-year-old man.'

The déjà vu is almost too powerful to endure. Livy and I once sat in the dark while she told me the story of being raped by a high school football player during a date. Twenty years later, only the context has changed.

'I'm sorry. I had no idea. I couldn't even have imagined that.'

'But isn't it such a touching little story?' Her tears are rolling down her cheeks now. 'Ray Presley, proud father of my first and only child.'

I want to hold her, but I think she would probably hit me if I touched her.

'I couldn't believe I even conceived,' she says, wiping her face. 'But I did. And you think I should have welcomed Jenny with open arms.' She modulates her voice into a hysterical exaggeration of a TV mom: *'Hello, sweetheart! Where have you been all my life? Give Mama a hug!'*

The delirium in her voice sends chills through me. 'Jenny had nothing to do with what Presley did to you that night.'

'She *is* that night to me! Don't you get that? Do you think I could ever look at her without reliving every second of those rapes?'

I shrug and stay silent. I am not a woman. I can't know. 'When I told you Presley was coming to kill your father, you said you hoped he would come.'

'I'd kill him in a minute,' she says in a flat voice. 'Like stepping on a cockroach.'

'I knew it was something like this. Something dark.'

'Dark? The whole thing is so *Sally Jessy Raphael* it makes me want to vomit.'

'You didn't tell your father Presley had raped you?'

A shadow of shame crosses her face. 'No. I'd started the whole thing, hadn't I? I suppose I could have lied and said he attacked me out of the blue, but my father is pretty hard to lie to. He's scary that way. He sees dishonesty in people.'

'Maybe because he's so dishonest himself.'

'Don't, Penn.'

'But he knew you were pregnant. Eventually, I mean.'

She nods. 'My sister told him. She'd gotten pregnant three years before, and Daddy made her get an abortion. It really messed her up. Our great Catholic parents practically forcing her to terminate her pregnancy. You'd think that when I turned up pregnant, she would have done all she could help me hide it. But she'd felt inferior to me her whole life. I was the special one, the adored one. She just had to tell them that I'd screwed up as badly as she had.'

'Livy, why in God's name did you have the baby? Under the circumstances—'

'Under the circumstances, I wasn't thinking rationally, okay? After the rape I was so upset, I went to Radcliffe a week early. Two months later, when I found out for sure I was pregnant, I thought about terminating it. But then my sister blabbed, and the next thing I knew, my father was in Cambridge trying to force me to have an abortion. You know how he and I are. The simple fact that he tried to force me was enough to make me refuse, especially after all the lip service he'd paid to Catholic dogma. But more than that, the pregnancy gave me a chance I'd never had before. An absolute excuse to break the pattern laid out for me before I was born. I didn't know what I wanted, but I knew I didn't want to spend four years at Ole Miss in a sorority full of girls majoring in fashion merchandising and looking for husbands.'

'Thanks for telling me in time to change my plans.'

A momentary look of penitence. 'I'm sorry about that. I never told you to go there.'

'No. You just talked about how wonderful it would be if we were both there. What I can't believe is that you let your parents think I had gotten you pregnant. You did, didn't you? That's the root of all the pain that came after.'

She takes a deep breath and sighs. 'I suppose I did.'

'Suppose, nothing. You didn't have the guts to admit you teased Ray Presley into raping you, but you didn't mind letting me take the blame for knocking you up.'

'Penn, you don't understand. When Ray took me home that night, he threatened me. He said that if I told my father what had happened, he'd kill my mother.'

'Your mother?'

'He knew I wouldn't care about myself. Ray said my father might kill him for hurting me, but he'd thank him for killing my mother. And on some level . . . I felt like he might be right. Daddy was such a bastard to Mother back then.'

A wave of shame rolls through me, shame for thinking Livy was so selfish and shallow that she would let my family pay for something that was someone else's fault without any excuse. But the shame passes quickly. Livy is twisting the truth even now.

'You're lying. I don't mean about the threat. I'm sure Presley threatened you. But you've *always* cared about yourself. More than anything else. And I don't think you would have bought Ray's threat, not for long. He was scared shitless of your father. He still is, in some ways. And when Leo decided to go after my father out of revenge, you could have spoken up. You could have said, Daddy, it wasn't Penn. But you didn't. You knew why he took that suit, and you never said a damn word to change his mind.'

'It was too late by then. I was at Virginia and–'

'I flew up there to see you! And you said nothing. You're gutless, Livy. I never knew that about you until now.'

'I suppose I am. About the big things.'

'Just like your father. He wanted a man dead, but he didn't have the balls to do it himself. He was district attorney, and he arranged to have an innocent man killed for profit.'

'That is such bullshit.'

'You think so? You'll find out different tomorrow. Your father and Ray Presley set up one of the most heinous murders I've ever come across, and J. Edgar Hoover covered it up to keep your grandfather happy. To keep them pulling for Nixon in the sixty-eight election.'

'What are you babbling about?'

'Never mind.'

Her face has taken on a strange cast. 'I met him once, you

know. Hoover. When I was a little girl. Up in Jackson with my father.'

'Oh, they were big buddies. And the root of their friendship was the murder of Del Payton.'

She shakes her head as if I'm hopelessly insane.

'By sundown tomorrow your father will be indicted for murder, unless he can kill my witnesses. And he's trying hard, believe me.'

'What are you talking about?'

'Your father and John Portman tried to kill me last night.'

She shakes her head. 'You're lying.'

'When have you known me to lie, Livy? Ever? Your father killed for money and power in 1968, and he'll do it now to cover his ass. That's all he's ever been about. He's played every angle and skimmed every deal, from factory locations to backroom adoptions. Everything's money to him.'

Livy has gone still. 'What do you mean, backroom adoptions?'

'Come on. That can't be news to you. I saw a record of the private adoptions he handled over the years. He did about twenty of them, and yours was one. Jenny's, I mean. For big money too. Big for those days, anyway.'

She reaches out and touches my arm. 'Tell me what you're talking about.'

'You really don't know? Remember those records you and Leo took out of his office last week? The ones he tried to burn?'

'Yes.'

'There was a scrap of paper in there, a record of income from adoptions. He pocketed thirty-five grand off of yours. One of the highest prices paid for any baby on the list. I guess he wanted top dollar, since the baby came from his gene pool.'

The blood has drained from her face.

'Look at it, if you don't believe me. I've been carrying the list around in my wallet since the day Jenny told me her story. I thought it was a record of our child being given away.'

'Let me see it.'

I pull out my wallet and fish the scrap of yellow paper from the bill compartment. Livy snatches it away and holds it up in the blue glow of the streetlight across the road, trying to read in the dark. Her face is in shadow, but after a few moments the paper starts to quiver in her hand.

'That son of a bitch,' she murmurs. 'That son of a *bitch*.'

'You still think I'm lying?'

'That he would *profit* from my pain like that . . .'

'I doubt he gave it a second thought. Making money was his habit. Everything that passed through his hands had to turn a profit. You should know that better than anyone.'

She looks up at last, her eyes empty of everything but desire for the truth. These are the eyes I knew in high school. 'Do you really believe my father ordered Del Payton's death?'

'It's not a question of belief. I know.'

'You can prove it?'

'If my witnesses reach the courtroom alive.'

She folds the paper slowly. 'I'm going to do something you may not believe. I'm going to do it because I don't believe my father killed Del Payton. I *can't* believe that. But if it should turn out that he did, I won't protect him.'

'What are you talking about?'

'The papers you requested under discovery. Business records, all that?'

'Yes.'

'You got sanitized versions. There's another set of files. One that nobody sees. Not the IRS, not anybody.'

My heart jumps in my chest. 'You realize that withholding those papers from the court—'

'Is a felony? I'm not telling you this to hear the Boy Scout oath repeated back to me. Before I tell you where those files are, I want a promise from you.'

'What?'

'Any evidence of illegal activity that doesn't directly pertain to the death of Del Payton, you'll forget you ever saw.'

'Livy—'

'That's non-negotiable.'

'All right. Agreed. Where are these files?'

She bites her bottom lip, still resisting the deeply bred urge to protect her family's secrets. 'Ever since I was a little girl, Daddy kept his sensitive papers in a big safe under the floor of his study. He called it his potato bunk, whatever that means. If he's hiding anything from you, it's in there.'

'How can I get a look in there? He's home tonight. Isn't he?'

'He's probably upstairs by now. Mother's been flipping in and out for the past few days. He's probably up there feeding her Darvocet and Prozac cocktails.'

'What about the off-duty cops he called?'

'They won't look twice at you if I drive you in.'

She looks sincere. But it's anger that's driving her now. Her relationship with her father has always been one of extremes, love and hate commingling in proportions that change too fast to be assayed. To see the secret safe in Leo Marston's study, I'll have to go back to Tuscany. And at Tuscany, on this night, Leo could kill me and tell the police anything he wanted. He could even have one of his cops kill me. My only real protection would be the woman standing before me.

'Are you sure you want to do this?' I ask.

She folds the paper in half, then twice again, into a tiny rectangle which she slips between the buttons of her blouse and into her bra. Her eyes shine with utter resolution.

'I've never been more sure of anything in my life.'

Chapter 38

The grounds of Tuscany are dark. I parked my mother's shot-up Maxima at a gas station a quarter mile up the road from Tuscany's gate, then got into Livy's Fiat for the ride to the estate. As we approached the gate, she took a remote control from her purse, touched a button, and the barred fence slid back into itself. That was twenty seconds ago. We should have seen the lights of the mansion well before now.

'Livy—'

'I know. I've never seen it like this. The floodlights are always on.'

'I told you he was scared of Presley.'

'Look,' she says, pointing at a dim light high in the trees. 'They're on the third floor. Mother's room.'

I close my hand around the butt of the gun in my waistband. Ike's gun.

A thin beam of light slices through the darkness and comes to rest on the windshield of Livy's car. I start to pull the gun, but then our headlights sweep across a black police uniform.

Livy slows to a stop.

The cop walks around to her window and shines his light onto her chest, sparing her the direct glare of the beam.

'Evening, Miss Marston. Everything okay?'

'Yes. My friend and I are going in for a drink. Have you seen anything suspicious?'

'No, ma'am. Not a thing.'

'Why are all the lights off?'

'Your daddy said he didn't want nobody taking potshots through the windows.'

'I see.'

'Don't you worry. Billy and me are on the job.'

'I feel so much better knowing that.' She gives him a synthetic smile, then rolls up her window and drives on.

Tuscany materializes suddenly, like a spectral palace in the moonlight, ringed by towering oaks and dark magnolias. Livy pulls around to the back of the mansion and parks in a small garage.

'There's a new entrance here,' she says. 'To the pantry.'

She unlocks the door, then takes my hand and leads me quickly through the enormous house: pantry, kitchen, breakfast room, parlor, living room. The interior is shrouded in darkness, but the sense of space, of high ceilings and broad doorways, communicates itself through the sound of our footsteps and the way the air moves. Livy stops me by putting her hand against my chest, then opens a door, peeks inside, and pulls me through.

Leo's private study looks as though it had been surgically removed from an English manor house, shipped to America, and meticulously reconstructed inside Tuscany. The paneling alone must be worth a hundred thousand dollars. Livy sets her purse on the desk and points to a Bokara rug on the floor before it.

'There.'

There's a club chair sitting on the rug. As I start to move it, she takes my arm and looks into my eyes. 'Remember your promise.'

'Have you known your whole life that your father was a crook?'

She gives me a look of disdain. 'My father made a science of walking the line between what's legal and what's not. So have a lot of other businessmen. That's the way you get rich.'

'Like those adoptions?' I say softly. 'Let's not forget why we're here.'

'You're so damned self-righteous. You must have cut a few corners in a decade of practicing law.'

'I was a prosecutor, Livy. I stayed on the right side of that line you're talking about.'

'You never conveniently misplaced a piece of exculpatory evidence to keep it from the defense?'

'Never.'

'I suppose you never cheated on your wife either.'

'Sorry. Why don't we look at those files?'

She studies me a moment more, then drops her hand and pulls the club chair off the Bokara. I roll up the rug and prop it against Leo's desk.

Where the rug had lain, discolored floorboards outline a trapdoor three feet square. Livy goes to the desk and brings back a small metal handle with a hook on one end. Kneeling, she slips the hook into an aperture I cannot see and folds back the trapdoor, exposing the steel door of a floor safe.

She bends over the combination lock, thinks for a moment, then spins it left, right, and left again. 'He hasn't changed the combination in years,' she says, getting to her feet.

I crouch to turn the heavy handle of the safe, but the butt of Ike's gun digs into my stomach. After setting it on the desk beside Livy's purse, I get down on my knees, turn the handle, and pull open the heavy door.

Inside is a hoard of velvet-covered jewelry boxes, stock certificates, cash, gold coins, manila envelopes, and computer disks. Nine square feet of paydirt.

'How much time do we have?' I ask, reaching for the manila envelopes.

'Maybe five minutes. Maybe all night.'

'Maybe you should go upstairs and talk to your parents. Then I could be sure—'

'I'm staying here.'

The envelopes are thick and marked with handwritten labels. The handwriting is Leo's. After wading through the mountain of discovery material, I recognize it as easily as my own. One label reads: FEDTAX '94/NOT TO BE SHOWN AT AUDIT. Another: THIRD-PARTY HOLDINGS (LAND). A third reads: GRAND CAYMAN TRUST ACCOUNT.

'That's got nothing to do with Del Payton,' Livy says over my shoulder.

Maybe not. But it could probably put Leo Marston in jail for a few years, and cost him a considerable portion of his fortune. Reluctantly I set these envelopes aside and continue searching. There are more offshore accounts, records of hidden shares in oil fields, a dozen other ventures. I am about to abandon the files for the computer disks when a label jumps out at me as though written in neon. It says only: EDGAR.

Inside this folder is a thick sheaf of personal letters, all signed *Yours, Edgar*. The first begins, *Dear Leo, In the matter of the Nixon funds, please be assured that I consider your work in this area to be exemplary, and also a direct favor to me. He has his idiosyncrasies, yes, but he is a sound man, and we understand each other. The possibility of a Muskie or McGovern in the White House cannot be contemplated for one moment—*

The woodwind *oomph* of a wine bottle being uncorked draws my gaze away from the safe. Livy has taken a bottle of red from Leo's cherrywood bar and opened it with a silver corkscrew.

'Pretend it's our lost bottle,' she says in a cynical voice.

She takes two Waterford goblets from the bar and fills them to the rim, then lifts one to her lips, drinks a long swallow, and passes it to me. Her upper lip is stained red, but she doesn't wipe it. She simply watches me drink. I can't read anything in her expression. The wine is tart on my tongue, acidic. She takes back the glass, drains it, then sets it beside the bottle and lifts the second glass to her lips. Half the wine disappears in three swallows.

She is more upset than I thought.

I turn back to the safe and quickly flip through the Hoover letters, searching for any mention of Del Payton, John Portman, or Dwight Stone. Most of the letters date from the seventies, after the secret relationship was well established, and deal with political matters.

'Is there a computer in here?' I ask, glancing at the 3.5-inch floppies.

'There's a PowerBook in the bottom drawer of the desk.'

I'm reaching for the disks when Livy's wineglass shatters on the floor beside me.

'Someone's coming!'

As quickly as I can, I slide the manila envelopes back into the safe – all but the Edgar file – and shut the steel door.

'The rug!' she hisses.

While I unroll the rug, Livy shuts the trapdoor and jumps clear. I slide the rug into place just as someone begins jerking at the doorknob.

'Who's in there?' says a muffled voice.

It's Leo.

Livy thumps the envelope in my hands. 'If you want that file, you'd better do something with it. Quick.'

Leo bangs on the door. 'Who's in there?'

'It's me, Daddy. I'm coming.'

Unbuckling my belt, I shove the envelope down the back of my pants, retuck my shirt over it, then zip up and rebuckle the belt. As I do this, Livy unbuttons the top three buttons of her blouse and musses her hair.

'Let's make it look real,' she says, and pulls my face to hers. Her kiss is passionate, desperate even, fueled by anger and wine and God knows what else. In the few seconds that it lasts, it flushes my face and brings sweat to my skin. My senses are still buzzing when she walks to the door and unlocks it.

'What are you doing in here with the door locked?' Leo asks.

'I'm not alone.'

He pushes his six-foot-four-inch frame through the door and swings his head around to me. His hard features go slack with amazement.

'What the hell's going on here?'

'Penn and I were talking.'

'Talking.' Leo is still wearing a suit, though he has untied his necktie. 'Button that blouse, Olivia.'

Livy does not button the blouse. She steps away from her father, leaving no obstacle between him and me.

'I can't believe you brought this bastard into our house,' he says, his eyes locked on mine. 'I want an explanation.'

'Make one up. Anything you like.'

Her defiant tone draws Leo's gaze away from me for a moment. 'Don't take that tone of voice with me, young lady.'

'I'll take whatever tone I please.'

Leo looks off balance. Livy is not playing the role of favorite daughter. 'What's going on here?' he asks. 'What's Cage been telling you?'

'What could he tell me? Have you been keeping things from me?'

'Of course not.'

'No?' She reaches into her blouse and brings out the scrap of legal paper, which she unfolds and hands to him without a word.

Leo stares at it for several seconds, then looks up blankly. 'What's this?'

'Think about it,' she says, her arms folded over her chest.

His face shows only confusion. He looks like he might have had a couple of drinks since receiving the warning about Presley. 'Why don't you save me the trouble?'

'The adoption,' Livy says in a dead voice.

'Your adoption?'

'Yes.'

'What about it?'

'You took money for it?'

Leo shrugs. 'So?'

'Thirty-five thousand dollars?'

'That paid a full year of your tuition at UVA.'

Her mouth falls open. 'Paid . . . you sold my baby to pay my college tuition?'

'"My" baby?' Leo's face softens as he senses the hurt in his daughter. 'Honey, you didn't want that child. I tried to get you to terminate the pregnancy, but you were against it. Given that adoption was your choice, I don't see what's wrong with–'

'Selling your own flesh and blood?' Her eyes are blazing now. 'Like you *needed* the fucking money?'

'Profanity doesn't become you, Olivia.'

'Profanity? Try obscenity. Selling my misery for money. That's about as obscene as it gets. I was just another profit-loss entry, I guess. Offset the liability of college tuition with the asset of unwanted babies. What the hell, right?'

Leo reaches out to her. 'Honey–'

'Don't even try to justify it,' she says coldly, backing away.

His look of sympathy evaporates. 'I don't have to justify anything. You made a mess, I cleaned it up. It was the only big one you ever made, but it damn sure ruined most of what came after.' He swings back to me. 'Thanks to this punk.'

'Leave me out of this,' I tell him. 'You've had the wrong idea about me for twenty years.'

'How so?'

Livy looks at me and shakes her head.

'Ask her.'

'Livy?'

'I don't know what he's talking about.'

Leo's eyes roam over the study, taking in the wine bottle on the bar, his bookshelves, and finally the desk, where his gaze settles on the Sig-Sauer lying beside Livy's purse. He is nearer the gun than I, and he knows I'm thinking that.

'It was you who said Ray Presley was coming here to kill me, wasn't it, Cage?'

That's right. I was doing you a favor.'

'I think you were lying.' He stabs a finger in my direction. 'I think you broke in here looking for some kind of evidence. And I think I'd be within my rights to blow your goddamn head off.'

He picks up the Sig-Sauer, cycles the slide, and walks around the desk.

'Presley killed Ike Ransom tonight,' I say quickly. 'He tried to kill me, but I got clear by sending him after you. I told him you gave him up to the FBI as part of your deal with Hoover.'

Something twitches in Leo's cheek. 'You're still lying. You're using my daughter to try and get at me.' He turns to Livy. 'The trial's tomorrow, and he's desperate. He's using you.'

A dark light shines in Livy's eyes. 'The way you used me against him?'

Leo isn't much of an actor; his feigned surprise is almost comical.

'Once I got here,' she says, 'I realized why you'd asked me to come. What you wanted me to do. The sad thing is, I wanted to do it. I thought Penn could wipe away all the mistakes I'd made. I thought his wife's death was fate. That we were being given a second chance.'

'That's only natural,' Leo says in a soothing voice. 'But he took advantage of you, honey. What did he ask you to do for him?'

'Nothing. He loves me. He always has.' Her smile is full of

irony and self-disgust. 'And he has more integrity than both of us put together.'

Leo snorts. 'Spare me the wine and roses. Did you have to bring him here? Couldn't you have checked into a motel?'

'The way you always did?'

'Olivia—'

'Don't say anything. Just go back to your room. Go upstairs and take care of Mother. Better late than never.'

Instead of walking to the door, Leo gives me the superior stare I've received in the private chambers of a dozen judges. 'The trial's tomorrow,' he says in a peremptory voice. 'I'm going to give you one last opportunity to save face, and to help this town. Call your little tart at the newspaper and get her to print a public apology for the remarks you made about me. A full apology from you, and a retraction from the paper. If that's printed tomorrow I'll dismiss the suit.'

His offer leaves me dumbfounded. There can be only one reason for it. He's running scared.

'I don't see your lips moving,' Leo says. 'You'd better jump while you can. The offer's good for sixty seconds.'

'Dwight Stone is alive,' I think aloud. 'And neither you nor Portman can find him.'

His face remains impassive. 'Fifty seconds.'

A wicked elation flows through me. 'You can stick that offer right up your ass. Tomorrow—'

All of us turn at the sound of the door.

Ray Presley is standing in the study, aiming a revolver at Leo's chest. It looks like a .357 Magnum. He's abandoned his pajamas in favor of Levis, Redwing boots, and a black western shirt. Only the John Deere cap remains the same. The vulpine eyes burn from beneath its bill just as they did the day I bought my father's .38 back from him.

'Evening, Judge,' he says.

Presley looks like he's lost ten pounds since I saw him last.

He's still ropy and tough, but he seems diminished somehow. Imagining him raping Livy is almost beyond me, he looks so much older than she now. Yet Livy has backed against the wall opposite me like a frightened girl, like she's trying to become her own shadow.

'I'm not armed, Ray,' Leo says from behind his desk, but I see that he's holding Ike's Sig-Sauer behind him.

'Throw that Sig on the floor, Judge,' Presley says like a chiding parent. 'I saw it in your hand when I come in.'

Marston knows better than to try to raise the gun and fire before Ray can pull his trigger. He tosses Ike's gun onto the floor at Presley's feet.

'I saw the boys outside too,' Presley says, his voice almost friendly. 'You knew I was coming, didn't you?'

'Ray—'

'Anybody makes a move. it's their last,' Presley says, glancing at me. 'I hit what I aim at.'

'Like Ike Ransom?' I say.

He smiles. 'That nigger talk any before he died?'

'Enough.'

'You lookin' to get killed too, college boy?'

'Fuck you, Ray.'

The smile disappears. 'I came here to kill one, but I can kill three just as easy and damn near as quick.' He motions toward Livy and me. 'You two come here. Stay right in front of me, backs to me.'

I move slowly, gauging my chances of getting to Livy's purse – and gun – before Ray shoots me. Less than zero at this point. But if I can get closer . . .

Livy and I stand shoulder to shoulder, facing Leo across the desk with Presley behind us. Presley's hand pats its way up my legs, around my waist, up my torso.

'*Don't you touch me,*' Livy says in a voice that could freeze alcohol.

But he must have touched her, because she suddenly spins

into his gun and slaps him hard enough to rock him back on his heels.

'Livy!' shouts Leo. 'Don't be stupid!'

Presley's harsh laugh fills the room as Livy backs away from him, panting with outrage. If she grabs for her purse, I'll have to stop her. Presley might endure a slap with a laugh, but he'll recognize a lunge for a gun.

'Ray?' Leo says in a careful voice. 'This boy's got nothing on us. He can't connect us to Del.'

A snort from Presley. 'He can't connect *you*. But he's got me nailed down tight as a tick. Don't make no never mind, though. This visit's got nothing to do with that dead nigger. This is about you and me, Judge.'

Leo affects puzzlement. 'I don't understand, Raymond.'

Presley jerks up his gun at this use of his Christian name, what must once have been a gesture of friendship. 'Yes, you do. You gave me up to the Feds while you kept raking in the money. You made me your goddamn scapegoat.'

Marston's eyes flick toward me, not in anger, but with purpose in them. He's prodding me to think. Leo is first and foremost a survivor, and he intends to live through this. If that means a short-term alliance with me to neutralize the most immediate threat, he won't hesitate.

'Nobody in this room but me knows what five years of prison means,' Presley says. 'Five years I'll never get back. And I need them years now. You got to pay for 'em, Judge.' He fingers the trigger of his gun, raises his aim to Leo's head. 'And there ain't but one way to do it.'

Marston remains calm. 'Ray, you shot at those FBI boys on your own hook. Hoover demanded a price, and you were it. Cost of doing business, son. You understand that. You were sentenced to seven years, and I got you out in five. It cost me to do that. You want to kill me for it?'

Presley's chin quivers with rage, and the gun trembles in his hand. 'It *cost* you? You could pass out half a million bucks and you wouldn't feel it. You'd make it back in a couple of months. But time? You don't never get that back. Make your peace with the Lord, Judge. And be quick.'

'Ray!' I shout, trying to hold his attention. 'If you shoot him, you'll spend every hour you have left behind bars.'

Presley laughs. 'If I stick around to get arrested. Which I ain't. Tomorrow night I'll be in Mexico, and nobody in this world can stop me getting there. I know ways in and out the wets ain't even thought of.'

'I can see why you'd want to shoot him,' I go on. 'I'd like to shoot him myself. But the way I figure it, you two are already square.'

He gives me an uncertain look. 'What do you mean?'

'I mean, I just found out what you did to him in seventy-eight.'

'What you talking about?'

I nod at Livy. 'Well, to her, I mean. That's the same as to him, isn't it? It damn sure gives him the right to shoot you, if anything gives a man that right.'

'Shut up,' Livy hisses.

Presley starts to turn the gun on me, but he steadies himself and holds it on Marston.

'What's that, Cage?' Leo asks. 'What are you talking about?'

'Tell him, Ray.' Keep tapping on the pressure point.

Presley takes a step closer to Marston, but he doesn't fire. I think he wants Marston to know the truth before he dies.

'Do you know a girl named Jenny Doe?' I ask Leo.

'Please,' Livy begs.

'I've met her,' Leo says.

'Do you know who her father is?'

His eyes flash with anger. 'You are, you pissant.'

'Sorry, Judge. I never knew that girl existed, and I am most definitely not her father.'

'Then who is?'

'The man holding the gun on you.'

Leo blinks three times quickly. Livy has gone white. But Presley's face is a strange mix of wonder and defiance. He obviously knew nothing about Jenny Doe until this moment.

'You and me got a kid?' he says, his eyes on Livy.

'Olivia?' Leo says quietly.

'Tell him, Livy,' I urge her.

'He raped me,' she says simply. 'When I was eighteen, Ray raped me three times one night and got me pregnant.'

'That's a goddamn lie!' Presley bellows. 'She give it to me, Judge. Teasing me with it all the time, prissing around like a bitch in heat, grabbing my privates. She told me she wanted it that night.'

'Livy?' Leo says again.

The mere fact that he's asking tells me Leo believes Presley's story could be true. Livy knows this too. Her lips are pressed tightly together, her nostrils flared. She stares into the middle distance for a few moments, alone with her demons. Then she looks at her father with absolute sincerity.

'He raped me, Daddy. I should have told you when it happened, but I was too afraid. He told me he would kill Mother if I did. All these years I let you think Penn was the father. He wasn't. It was *him*.'

Leo's face goes through a dozen different emotions, only a small number of them readable. But the one that finally settles in his features is rage. Pure, unalloyed rage. This is the natural reaction of any father, but there is more here. Ray Presley served Leo for more than thirty years, performing deeds too dirty for his master to soil his hands with. But whatever bond this forged between them, Presley was always a servant. A hired man. The realization that he transgressed this class boundary – trespassed into the very flesh of the Marston family line – probably offends Leo more than the act of rape itself. His jaw muscles are working with enough force to grind his teeth to nubs if he keeps it up, and his blue-gray eyes burn with a fearsome light.

'You *white-trash bastard*,' he says, each word dripping with contempt. 'You touched my little girl? I'll snap your neck like a stick.'

Presley shakes his gun in front of him like a man waving a crucifix before a vampire.

'You're the one, goddamn it! Ratting me out after all I did for you? So I fucked your slut daughter. You think I was the first? She handed it out like candy in school, and God knows what she did after she left this town. Like father, like daughter, I guess.'

To my surprise, Leo does not explode at this but instead seems to calm down. He drops his hands to his desk drawer. 'How much will it take to buy you off, Ray? To make you go to Mexico and never come back?'

'More than you got, Judge.'

'I've got a lot.'

'That's the Lord's truth. But you ain't got enough to buy your life. Not this time.'

Leo reaches into the drawer and feels around inside. His mouth goes slack.

Presley smiles darkly and takes a step forward. 'What you lookin' for, Judge? You lose something?'

Leo freezes, his hand still in the drawer. His face has lost all color. It's the face of an animal, a predator backed into a corner by a larger one.

Presley reaches into his pocket with his left hand and removes the derringer Leo pulled on me the day Kelly backed him down. 'You're too predictable, Judge.' He points the derringer at Livy, who's standing to his left, and straightens the arm pointing the .357 at Leo's head.

He means to shoot.

I have only one weapon to hand, the half-empty wine bottle on the bar behind me. Presley's attention is divided between what he perceives as the most immediate threats. He probably figures I won't even mind him shooting Leo. Visualizing the bottle as I saw it last, I reach back with my right hand, relaxing my fingers so that I won't knock it off the bar by mistake.

My fingertips touch cool glass.

I close my hand around the neck of the bottle. Now it's a matter of peripheral vision. If Ray would glance at Livy again, I could swing without him seeing the bottle until it's too late. Focusing on Livy, I concentrate the full power of my will on communicating to her what I need. Her eyes search mine, trying to read my thoughts. As she stares, I incline my head very slightly toward Ray.

Presley cocks the hammer of his .357, and Leo at last gives in to terror. 'Ray, I'm begging you. Please don't do it.'

Presley wrinkles his lips in disgust.

Livy says, 'Our daughter looks just like you, Ray.'

Presley's profile vanishes as he looks toward her, and in a single fluid motion I swing the bottle in a sweeping arc that terminates at the base of his skull. The impact of the heavy glass club slams him forward, and he falls over the front of the desk.

Somehow he still has both pistols in his hands. I leap forward and hammer at his head with both fists, thinking of Livy lying under him with her dress stuffed down her throat. As I flail away, I see Leo's huge hands take hold of Presley's IV-scarred wrists and pin them to the desktop like brittle sticks.

Presley pulls the trigger of the derringer.

Leo flinches as though stung by a hornet, but he looks less hurt than pissed off. He rakes a huge right hand down Presley's left wrist, stripping the derringer from the smaller hand and tossing it on the floor. With his other hand he yanks the .357 out of Presley's right, which is still pinned to the desk.

Presley tries to raise himself off the desk, but all my weight is on him.

Leo presses the .357 to Presley's forehead.

'Let him go, Cage.'

I smack Presley once more for good measure, then heave myself off him. Despite the blows to his head, he straightens up, like a punch-drunk boxer who can remember only one thing: *stay on your feet.*

Leo pulls open his jacket long enough to reveal a blood-stain on the right side of his shirt, but he doesn't examine the wound any more closely than that. 'This creates a problem,' he says, the anger gone from his voice. Already he is computing the calculus of how Ray's actions will affect tomorrow's trial. 'Cage, you and I should try to–'

He stops at the sound of Livy's voice. I'm not sure, but I think she said, '*Ray?*' in the intimate voice of a lover. She must have, because Presley turns from the desk to the sound of her voice, his eyes glassy but still curious.

'I wanted you to see this,' she tells him.

Then she brings up Ike's Sig-Sauer and shoots him in the chest.

Ray sits down on Leo's desk as though he has decided to have a think there. Then his eyes bulge as he looks down at the red river flowing from his upper chest with a depressingly regular rhythm.

Livy stands with the automatic held stiffly before her, smoke drifting from its barrel, exactly the way it looks in old westerns. She doesn't look the slightest bit upset. She seems, in fact, to be contemplating a second shot. Before she can fire again, I jump in front of her and grab her wrist. She doesn't resist as I pull the gun from her hand.

'Lock the door, Cage,' Leo orders from behind his desk. 'Hurry.'

I obey without hesitation, though I'm not sure why.

'The guards will be here any second,' he says. 'I shot Ray.

Do you understand? He broke in, tried to kill me, and I shot him.' Leo's eyes are full of paternal concern. 'Will you back me up?'

'Are you kidding? You can't lie about something like this. Not these days.'

His eyes glow with hypnotic intensity. 'Listen to me, Cage. We can tear each other to pieces at trial tomorrow. But if you've ever cared for my daughter, help me protect her now.'

'You can't pull it off. Not nowadays. There are nitrate tests . . . a hundred things.' I look at Ray, who, despite horrific blood loss, is still sitting on the desk. 'Besides, he's *still alive.*'

Leo walks around his desk and takes the Sig-Sauer from my hand. Before I can ask what he means to do, he backs three feet away from Ray, aims at his head, and blows his brains out. Presley flips backward over the desk and lands with his head in the corner.

'Now he's dead,' Leo says, giving me a look so matter-of-fact that it makes a psycho like Arthur Lee Hanratty look like a Cub Scout. 'So much for your nitrate tests.'

The study door shudders under a sudden barrage of rapping.

'Judge Marston!' shouts a male voice. 'Judge! Are you all right?'

'Cage?' Leo asks calmly, the Sig-Sauer still in his hand. 'Are we agreed?'

I look at Livy, who seems to be undergoing some sort of delayed shock reaction. Then at Ray Presley, the man who engineered the murder of Del Payton and the living death of Ike Ransom . . . who killed Ike in the end and probably killed Ruby Flowers. Who raped the girl I loved at eighteen, dooming us to lose each other forever.

'Agreed,' I say softly.

The off-duty cops are still rapping and yelling at the door.

Leo crosses the study, opens it, and waves the officers in. Two uniforms step into the room, guns drawn.

'You're a little late, boys,' Leo says, pointing at the body behind the desk. 'He got past you.'

The cops gape at the corpse on the floor. Without his John Deere cap Presley looks like a hundred-year-old man with three eyes.

'Goddamn,' says one of the cops in an awed voice. 'Ain't that Ray Presley?'

'I'll be damned if it ain't,' says his partner. 'You were right, Judge.'

'It's a good thing I was ready for him,' Leo says. 'He got off a shot, hit me in the gristle. But I nailed him. You'd better call the chief, Billy, so we can get this mess straightened out. I've got to be in court tomorrow.'

The cop called Billy starts around the desk to examine Ray more closely, but Leo says: 'Why don't you use the hall phone?'

Billy stops. 'Sure thing, Judge.'

'When you're done talking to the chief, y'all come back and drag this piece of trash out of here for me.'

Billy bites his lip. 'Well . . . it's a crime scene, Judge. We can't move anything. You know that.'

'It's more of a crime to have this bastard bleeding all over my Bokara rugs.'

'Um,' says Billy's partner, the one who stopped Livy and me outside. 'Is your daughter okay?'

'She's fine,' says Leo, though Livy is standing like a statue near the door. 'A little squeamish. All the blood, you know.'

An absurd laugh escapes my lips. Livy is about as squeamish as a fur trapper.

After Billy and his partner leave the study, Leo walks back behind his desk and sits in his chair. 'Penn,' he says, using my Christian name for the first time in two decades. 'I was wrong to blame you all those years for what happened to Livy. I see that now.'

'That's why you went after my father?' I ask, making sure. 'Because of me?'

He nods. 'I was wrong to do that too. It's a hard thing to accept after all this time. I guess Livy bears the ultimate responsibility.' He gives me a fatherly look. 'You call your girl at the newspaper and tell her to run that apology. We'll end this thing like gentlemen, and save the town a hell of a lot of misery.'

'I might do that,' I say quietly. 'If you were a gentleman.'

His eyes narrow.

'But since you're an amoral, hypocritical, heartless bastard, I won't. Tomorrow you're going to be indicted for capital murder in the death of Del Payton.'

I turn away from him and walk toward the door.

'Goodbye,' I say, touching Livy's hand. 'Don't think twice about Presley. You did the world a favor. I'll tell it just the way your dad wants it.' I squeeze her hand, then pause and kiss her lightly on the cheek.

She says nothing at first, but as I move away she says, 'Penn, I can't let you take that file.'

'What?' Leo says, his voice instantly alive with suspicion. 'What file?'

'I showed him your safe. I was angry. Penn, please give me the envelope. I can't help you destroy my father. Not like that. Not after all that's happened.'

I reach for the doorknob, wondering how far she'll go to stop me.

'She won't shoot you, Cage. But I will.'

I don't know if he'd shoot me in the back or not. But I have a daughter waiting for me at home. And I will not bet our future on the honor of Leonidas Marston.

Turning to face him, I untuck my shirt, slip the Hoover file out of my pants, and toss it toward him. There's a flutter of papers as the letters scatter across the desk and floor. I start to leave, but then I bend down and lift the fallen wine bottle from the Bokara. It survived the impact with Presley's skull, though most of the wine has spilled out. Glancing back at Livy, I invert the bottle and pour the remaining wine onto the desk, splashing the red fluid across Hoover's personal missives to Leo.

'Pretend it's our lost bottle,' I tell her. 'You two were made for each other.'

I reach for the brass knob, open the door, and walk out into the hall. The last thing I hear is Leo's voice floating after me:

'See you in court.'

Chapter 39

An hour before jury selection in the slander trial of Penn Cage, the police blocked motor-vehicle access to the streets surrounding the Natchez courthouse. The television vans had already been let through, at least eight, despite the fact that only crews from CNN and the black-owned Jackson station would be allowed inside the courtroom.

Judge Franklin's decision to allow cameras in her court was a landmark in Mississippi jurisprudence, and she had carefully defended it in her pretrial order. Besides stating that *Marston v. Cage* was a civil case and that both parties to the suit had agreed to have the proceedings televised, Franklin observed that community interest in the Payton murder – which was the central issue of the trial – was at such a pitch that the 'window into the court' provided by the news camera could go a long way toward fostering the perception of fair and impartial justice.

The police roadblocks did nothing to limit the crowds outside the courthouse. Caitlin's newspaper account of the deaths of Ike Ransom and Ray Presley had electrified the city. Black families laid out blankets beneath the oak trees on the north lawn, and endured without complaint the de-sultory showers that had fallen since dawn. The whites stood mostly on the south lawn, huddled under umbrellas with Calvinist stoicism. The division was not solely racial; there was intermingling at the edges of each crowd, but for the most part a natural segregation had occurred. Police officers milled through the throngs, watching for verbal altercations that could all too easily spark violence under the circumstances.

None of this concerned me as I entered the courthouse flanked by two sheriff's deputies. All I could think about was Dwight Stone. Except for the strange call Caitlin had received yesterday, saying that Stone's dead FBI partner would be at the trial, I'd heard nothing. This morning Caitlin picked up a story off the AP wire saying that four unidentified men had been found dead in the mountains near Crested Butte, Colorado. This buttressed my hope that Stone had at least survived our encounter by the river, but many hours had passed since then. I tried calling his daughter several times but had no luck. Dwight Stone seemed to have vanished from the face of the earth.

In a city with over six hundred antebellum buildings, more than sixty of which are mansions, one might expect the courtrooms to be marvels of architectural splendor, spacious and high-ceilinged, paneled with oak and smelling faintly of lemon oil. In fact, while the original Natchez courthouse was built in 1818 and has been expanded several times since, its second-floor courtrooms are small compared to those in Houston, and surprisingly functional in character.

The circuit court has seven rows of benches for spectators, with another six in an upstairs balcony at the rear, several of which have been co-opted today by the cameras of CNN and WLBT. Viewed from the rear door, the jury box stands against the right wall, with the door to the jury room in the far right corner. The witness box stands to the right of the judge's bench and, awkwardly, a little behind it, attached to the rear wall. The judge's bench is set on a dais at the center, with desks for the court reporter and circuit clerk extending forward into the room at right angles to the bench. The reporter sits on the right, the clerk and his deputy on the left. Beyond the clerk's desk on the left is a large, open space for the presentation of exhibits. The lawyer's tables stand just beyond the bar, not far separated from the clerk's and reporter's desks, with the podium beside the table on the right. The only touches of Southern atmosphere are the white capitals of the Doric columns visible through the windows behind the judge's bench, and the intertwining oak branches beyond them, which give an unexpected airiness to the otherwise close room. And then there is the clock on the wall. Symbolically enough, it has no hands, and I am reminded of Carson McCullers's dark and poignant novel. She would feel right at home in the midst of the strange and tragic case that has brought us here today.

Walking up the aisle toward my table to begin the voir dire phase of the trial, I receive one of the greatest shocks of my life. Seated at the plaintiff's table alongside Leo Marston and Blake Sims is Livy Marston Sutter. She doesn't look up at me, but any fleeting hope that she might be here for moral support is quickly banished by her appearance. From her pulled-back hair to her tailored navy suit and Prada shoes, she is every inch a lawyer. Every movement precise, every glance measured, Livy radiates a self-assurance that draws the eyes of everyone in sight of her, producing in both men and women a desire for her attention and approval.

Blake Sims looks dowdy beside her. He wears the traditional uniform of the Ole Miss lawyer: blue blazer, white pinpoint button-down, striped tie, dress khakis, and cordovan wing tips. His face is pink and fleshy, the face of a student council president, with sandy blond hair and blue eyes. The more I think about Sims, the more obvious it becomes why Leo wants Livy here.

Leo himself sits facing the bench with imperious detachment. He is a head taller than Blake Sims, and his close-cropped silver hair and chiseled features give him the look of a wise but austere judge, which he was. Four decades spent roaming the corridors of power have served him well.

His tailored English suit was made for the television cameras, and no one looking at him this morning would suspect that he executed a man last night.

Moving toward my table, I scan the faces of the spectators who have managed to get into the packed courtroom. This morning I arranged with the bailiff to make sure that my parents be allowed in, with Sam Jacobs escorting them, and also Althea and Georgia Payton, with Del Jr. All are seated in the second row on the right, behind my table. The first row was roped off for city officials, who have turned out in force. Mayor Warren and District Attorney Mackey shoot me glares whenever I look their way. Beyond them are many faces from my youth and, peppered among these, the characters who have populated my life for the past two weeks. Ex-police chief Willie Pinder. Reverend Nightingale. Some of the neighbors who helped search for Annie on the day of the fire. Charles Evers. What sobers me is my awareness of those who aren't here. Ruby. Ike. Ray Presley. Dwight Stone.

I shake hands with my father over the bar, then take my seat. As I begin reviewing the notes I made last night about questioning potential jurors, someone touches my shoulder. It's Caitlin Masters. For the first time since the cocktail party, she has abandoned her informal uniform of jeans and button-downs for a dress. A blue sleeveless one that emphasizes her lithe body. The effect is so profound that I simply stare at her.

'I do own dresses,' she says, obviously pleased by my reaction.

'You look very nice. Any word from Stone?'

She bites her lip and shakes her head, then pats her pocket. 'He has the number of the paper. They'll call me the second he or his daughter calls in.'

'*If* he calls. Is Portman here?'

'They've got him in a room upstairs with five FBI agents.' She reaches out and touches my forearm. 'Hold on to your hat. They've got the governor up there too.'

'The governor of what?'

'Mississippi. He's here as a character witness for Marston.'

I feel my face flushing. 'He's not on the witness list.'

She gives me a 'get real' look. 'Do you think Judge Franklin is going to tell the governor to go back to Jackson without letting him take the stand?'

'Damn.' I fight the urge to tear out a handful of my hair.

'Take it easy. African Americans hate the governor. Did you get any sleep?'

Sleep. Last night, after the police and the sheriff's department took turns grilling me for hours over the shootings at the pecan plant and at Tuscany, I met with Betty Lou Beckham and her husband. Mr. Beckham is totally against his wife testifying, but she promised my father she would, and she means to go through with it. Considering the embarrassment she will suffer when the circumstances that allowed her to witness the crime come to light, she is doing a brave thing indeed. After meeting the Beckhams I went to the Eola Hotel and woodshedded with Huey Moak and Lester Hinson, whom Kelly had delivered safely from Baton Rouge. When we finished, I spent the few hours before dawn trying to build a convincing case against Marston that did not rely on the testimony of Dwight Stone.

I failed.

'Hang on as long as you can,' Caitlin says, squeezing my hand. 'If Stone is alive, he'll be here.'

'Do you think Portman would be here if he thought there was any chance Stone would show? With TV cameras?'

'Don't second-guess yourself. You've got a murder to prove, and that's what you're good at. Pick your jury and forget the rest.'

She gives my hand a final squeeze and walks back to the benches.

Judge Franklin enters the court wearing a black robe with a white lace collar, looking very different than she did the night she confiscated Leo's files from Tuscany. She's obviously had her hair done, and her makeup looks television-ready. She takes her seat on the bench, and the bailiff calls the court to order.

Blake Sims rises and informs the judge that Livy Marston Sutter has been retained as co-counsel and with the court's permission will occupy the second chair at the plaintiff's table during the trial. Judge Franklin makes a show of asking if I have any objection, but she clearly expects me to go along. I could point out that Livy is not licensed in Mississippi, but with her considerable trial experience and Sims acting as lead counsel, I don't really have a leg to stand on.

Livy meets my eyes only once during the entire voir dire process, which turns out to be a surprise in itself. I had always assumed I would enjoy the advantage of a largely black jury. White professionals tend to use their jobs and influence to avoid jury duty, but this morning that tradition goes out the window. Not one white in the first group taken from the venire, or pool of potential jurors, tries to evade his civic responsibility. The usual excuses about job and health problems are not voiced, nor are distant blood relations to trial principals invoked. Every juror in the pool wants a front-row seat.

Blake Sims handles voir dire for Marston, pacing before the jury box in a rather annoying fashion while he questions the potential jurors about their backgrounds and what they've read in the newspapers. Most admit that they've read about the case (how could they have avoided it?) but claim they have formed no opinion as to the guilt or innocence of either party. Most of them are lying, of course. That's the way these things go. You can't keep human nature out of a human process.

As the voir dire progresses, I notice that Sims is avoiding direct questions about racial views. At first I thought this was circumspection; with cameras in the courtroom, he would want to avoid any hint of racial bias. But as he exercises his peremptory challenges, his strategy becomes clear. He has seen that he has a shot at a predominantly white jury, and he means to get it, even if it means breaking the law.

After Sims rejects the fourth black juror, I stand and make my first objection of the day, citing *Batson v. Kentucky* and the line of subsequent cases extending the prohibition against excluding potential jurors on the basis of race to civil cases. Judge Franklin immediately sustains my objection, and Livy finally turns in my direction. Her eyes hold nothing for me. They are merely the eyes of opposing counsel, acknowledging my small victory in a war that will see many more skirmishes before the issue is decided.

After this the voir dire passes more quickly than any in my career. I judiciously exercise my peremptories, culling on the basis of instinct. When my mental radar picks up echoes of blue-collar or rural backgrounds combined with religious fundamentalism, I pull the trigger. I challenge some whites for cause after tripping them up on questions about prejudice, but most racists quickly figure out how to conceal their true beliefs. Nearly every potential juror admits knowing Leo Marston to some degree, so many that I cannot realistically disqualify them on this basis. By eleven-forty-five a.m., we have empaneled twelve jurors (seven white, five black) and two alternates. Judge Franklin recesses for lunch and instructs the lawyers to be ready for opening statements at one.

I eat a quick lunch with Caitlin in an empty conference room near the chancery court, gobbling deli sandwiches from Clara Nell's between calls to the newspaper to see whether they've heard anything from Stone or his daughter. They haven't. Then I hurry downstairs through a crowd of courthouse employees and rubbernecking lawyers to give my witnesses one last pep talk, paying particular attention to Betty Lou Beckham, who looks as though she might come apart at any moment. Admitting on the stand that she was fornicating in a car with a married man must be akin to donning a scarlet letter in the village square. If it weren't for my father's influence, Betty Lou wouldn't be coming near this courthouse today. After holding her hand for a few minutes, I return to the crowded courtroom, sit at my table, and wait for one o'clock to tick around on the clock without hands.

Judge Franklin brings her court to order with a stern look, and Blake Sims rises from the plaintiff's table and walks to the podium to make his opening statement. Sims is the son of Leo Marston's former law partner (now deceased) and was raised in Greenville because of a divorce. He speaks with a cultured Delta accent rarely heard in Natchez, and though Greenville – the home of Hodding Carter's *Delta Democrat-Times* – was perhaps Mississippi's most liberal city during the civil rights era, Sims's accent might evoke some negative responses in the black jurors.

'Ladies and gentlemen of the jury,' he begins. 'My client needs no introduction. But allow me to say a few words about him. Leo Marston is one of the most distinguished figures in Mississippi jurisprudence. He is a former attorney general of Mississippi and former justice of the state supreme court. He is a friend and adviser to Mississippi congressmen, and has been for more than thirty years. He's a powerful business force for the city of Natchez, bringing industry and jobs to Adams County. He is also a pillar of the Catholic church, and a major supporter of charities in our area.'

Sims leaves the podium and walks halfway to the jury box, testing Judge Franklin's formality. She makes no objection to his move. 'With that in mind,' he goes on, 'I want to ask you a question. What is a man's name worth? The defendant in

this case, Mr. Penn Cage, has signed an agreement stipu-
lating to certain facts. First, that he uttered the vile charges
in question. Second, that he uttered them in the full knowledge that they would be published in a newspaper. And
third, that my client's reputation has been severely damaged
by his charges. That being the case, I won't waste your valuable time trying to prove damages. Mr. Cage has publicly
called my client a murderer. What more malicious charge
could anyone make against another human being? Child
molestation perhaps.' Sims slowly bobs his head as though
weighing this issue.

'My client does not contest the fact that a tragic murder
took place in May of 1968. Mr. Cage may even have
evidence against the man who committed that crime. But
what he does not have – what he cannot possibly have – is
evidence that *Leo Marston* had anything whatever to do with
that crime. Leo Marston was, in fact, the district attorney
at that time. The chief law enforcement officer of the county.
Mr. Cage may present some sort of *circumstantial* evidence,
which he may try to weave into a web of deception to fool
you good people. But my client and I know that you will not
be fooled. Del Payton was a civil rights worker murdered to
stop him from doing his noble work. And Leo Marston is
demonstrably one of the most racially progressive leaders in
this town, and has been since he was a young man.'

Sims lists various pro-civil rights statements Leo made
during the sixties, his friendships with black leaders, dona-
tions to black causes. He cites testimonial letters he will enter
into evidence, attesting to Marston's contributions to
Mississippi's economy: letters from John Stennis and Jim
Eastland (both deceased), Trent Lott, Mike Espy, and five
former governors.

'What we have here,' Sims concludes – giving me a
theatrical look of disdain – 'is an irresponsible and sen-
sational attack carried out by a man who has had a personal

vendetta against my client for more than twenty years. Before this trial is over, you will understand why. And I want you people to know something else. The money involved in this case is of secondary importance to my client. What he wants, and what he deserves, is the *vindication of his good name.*' Sims folds his hands with the apparent probity of a deacon. 'But if you good people should see fit to teach Mr. Cage a moral lesson about the price of such irresponsible action, so be it. We leave that to you. Thank you.'

Sims is unable to conceal his self-satisfaction as he takes his seat, but if he was hoping for congratulations from his client or co-counsel, he is disappointed. Leo stares sullenly ahead like a truck driver in the eleventh hour of a drive, while Livy sits with the cool composure of a pinch hitter waiting to be called to the plate.

In the restless silence of the crowd, I rise from my table and walk slowly toward the jury box. Their faces are expectant, as they always are at the beginning of a trial. Before boredom has set in. Before resentment against vain attorneys who love to hear themselves talk has settled in their veins. I lay my hands on the rail and speak directly to them.

'Ladies and gentlemen, my name is Penn Cage. I am a writer. Before I wrote books, I was a prosecuting attorney. I spent every day of my life putting violent criminals behind bars. I put more than a few on death row.

'I was born and raised right here in Natchez, but like a lot of our young people, I had to move away to earn my living.'

Several jurors nod their heads, probably those with adult children.

'I earned that living as a prosecutor in Houston, Texas. Now, if you were to go to Texas and ask about Penn Cage, you might find some people willing to speak ill of him. If you went to the penitentiary at Huntsville, you'd find a lot of them.'

General laughter from the gallery.

'What you would *not* find is a single person who would describe me with the word Mr. Sims just used. *Irresponsible.* Because when you are prosecuting murderers and asking for the death penalty, irresponsibility is not a weakness you can afford. It's not a trait that my former boss, the district attorney of Harris County, would tolerate for one minute. Folks, you are looking at a man who says what he means, and means what he says.'

From the rapt faces of the jury, I can see that I haven't lost the old touch. It's a good feeling, like climbing onto a horse after ten years away and feeling him respond without a moment's hesitation. It's a pity that I have no case.

'When I called Leo Marston a murderer,' I say evenly, 'I meant it. Together with a brutal and crooked cop named Ray Presley, Leo Marston engineered the death of a young father, army veteran, and civil rights worker named Delano Payton. And contrary to what Mr. Sims suggested – and what the citizens of our town have believed for thirty years – that murder had nothing to do with civil rights. No, Leo Marston had Del Payton killed for *profit.*' I glance back at Livy, but she refuses to look at me. 'The same reason he does everything else. And despite what Mr. Sims told you, money is *never* of secondary importance to Leo Marston.

'Mr. Sims also mentioned the term "circumstantial evidence" in a rather derogatory tone. After all the television lawyers we've seen, a misconception has grown up that circumstantial evidence is somehow inherently weak. But that is simply not true. Circumstantial evidence is merely *indirect* evidence. Let's say a woman is shot to death at midnight with a thirty-eight caliber pistol. When the police arrive, they learn from one neighbor that the woman and her husband were in the middle of a messy divorce, and from another that the husband sped away from the house at five past midnight. The next day the police discover that the husband has a thirty-eight revolver registered in his name.

Everything I just told you is circumstantial evidence. But I think a pretty clear picture of what happened is emerging in your minds. I'm not saying it's conclusive evidence. I'm saying this is evidence that *cannot be ignored.*'

More nods from the jury, especially from the women.

'Mr. Sims asked what a man's name is worth. I'll tell you.' I turn and point at Leo, the man who acted with such shocking dispatch last night. His blue-gray eyes burn with the subzero cold of liquid nitrogen. 'After this trial that man's name won't be worth the price of a cup of coffee. He ordered one of the most terrible crimes in the history of this city, and by so doing stained the name of Natchez, Mississippi for thirty years. And with the help of J. Edgar Hoover, he sabotaged the investigation that followed that crime. The cold-blooded details of this premeditated murder will sicken you, just as they did me. But you must hear them. For the time has come to remove the bloody stain from the name of our fair city. Thank you.'

The jury seems a bit flabbergasted by the passion of my indictment, but it's been my experience that juries like passion – to a point. And in my present situation, passion is better than nothing.

When Blake Sims rises to present his case, he does just as he promised: he ignores the question of damage to Leo's reputation. He accomplishes this by a neat reversal, calling three character witnesses whose combined testimony is designed to canonize his client, making the image of Leo Marston as a cold-blooded murderer one that jurors will feel guilty for even entertaining.

The first is Governor Nunn Harkness, a Republican with a two-fisted, shoot-from-the-hip style that has won him two terms despite his methodical gutting of social programs. Playing to the balcony TV cameras, Harkness praises Leo to the skies, lauding his success in bringing industry and gaming to Mississippi and lamenting that, while Marston is a bit too liberal for his taste on issues like affirmative action, he is morally beyond reproach. It's a pitch-perfect performance by a master, and the jury is visibly impressed. When Sims tenders the governor to me for cross-examination, I don't ask a single question. Best to get Nunn Harkness offstage as soon as possible.

Sims's second character witness is Thomas O'Malley, bishop of the Catholic diocese of Jackson. Once the priest of St. Mary Cathedral in Natchez, O'Malley has moved up the hierarchy. For fifteen minutes O'Malley waxes poetic about the multitudes of poor children whose Christmases Leo Marston brightened with toys. Then he moves on to the church itself. To hear O'Malley tell it, Leo single-handedly restored the cathedral to its present splendor, donating over half a million dollars to the restoration effort. As the bishop speaks, I am reminded of Michael Corleone being honored by the pope in *The Godfather III*. I shudder to think what sins O'Malley must have heard Leo confess during his years as a priest in Natchez, but none of that will ever pass the bishop's lips. When Sims tenders O'Malley to me, I let him go without a word. Unless you're dealing with questions of sexual molestation or mismanagement of funds, a Catholic bishop is bulletproof.

Sims's third witness is another matter. As Bishop O'Malley leaves the courtroom, pausing in the aisle to shake the hands of a half dozen former parishioners, Sims calls FBI Director John Portman.

Portman enters the courtroom with two bodyguards, who take up posts at the door as their master walks up the aisle. Lean, tanned, perfectly coiffed, and attired in a dark blue suit, the FBI director is clearly accustomed to television. He ascends to the witness box with the air of a medical expert about to hold forth on matters beyond the understanding of a lay audience.

This time it is not Blake Sims but Livy who rises from the

plaintiff's table and approaches the box. Judge Franklin gives Sims a questioning look, but Sims says nothing.

'You will be handling this witness, Ms. Sutter?' asks Franklin, using Livy's legal surname.

'With the court's permission, Your Honor.'

Franklin turns to me. 'Any objection, counselor?'

'No, Your Honor.'

Livy walks past the podium and up to the witness box. Though Portman is much older than she, both emanate a sense of confidence and ease to which lesser mortals should not begin to aspire.

'Mr. Portman, what is your current position?' she asks.

'I'm the director of the Federal Bureau of Investigation. The FBI.'

'Do you know the plaintiff in this case?'

'I do. I've known Leo Marston for thirty years.'

'How did you meet?'

Portman purses his lips like he's thinking back. 'Leo was the district attorney in Natchez in 1968. I was serving here as an FBI field agent at that time, investigating the death of Delano Payton. Mr. Marston gave the Bureau valuable assistance during that investigation.'

My heart lurches.

'Why do you think he did that?' Livy asks.

Portman opens his hands, palms upward, as though the answer were obvious. 'Leo Marston believed in the necessity of civil rights legislation. At no small risk to himself, he worked to help us enforce that. The man was a hero.'

Livy nods thoughtfully. 'How did you first become aware of the charges made by Penn Cage against Leo Marston?'

'Leo contacted me in Washington by telephone on the day the charges were printed in the local newspaper. We spoke at length at that time, and several times subsequent.'

So much for the phone records. Livy's strategy is all too

clear. She plans to undercut what little documentary evidence I have before I can present it.

'What was the substance of those conversations?' she asks.

'Judge Marston expressed anxiety that this sensitive case was being dragged through the media, and that his reputation was being damaged.'

'You called the Payton case a sensitive case. Why is that?'

Portman adopts a pose of paternal concern. 'I'm afraid I can only speak indirectly to this issue. As I've stated to the press, our file on Delano Payton is sealed on the grounds of national security interest. It has been for thirty years. Earlier this week the Senate Intelligence Committee voted to maintain the sanctity of that file.'

'Please tell us anything you can about the case.'

Portman nods agreeably. 'The Payton case involved a veteran of the U.S. Army, a man who served in Vietnam. J. Edgar Hoover, the FBI director at that time, felt that the details involving this man, if released during the Vietnam conflict, might damage national morale, particularly the morale of line troops in Vietnam, where racial problems had become an issue.'

He has to be talking about Ike Ransom.

'But the Vietnam War has been over for more than twenty years,' Livy points out. 'Why is the file still sealed?'

'As I said, I can't speak as fully to this issue as I would like. I'm sorry Mr. Cage has seen fit to exploit this case in his bid for publicity or revenge, or whatever it is.'

Livy pretends to be intrigued by this aside. 'Have you had experience with Mr. Cage in the past?'

'I had some dealings with him when he was an assistant district attorney in Houston, Texas. I found him to be highly partisan, and indeed an unstable sort of man for that type of job. He actually killed the brother of a man he tried for murder, and the facts of that incident were never satisfactorily explained. I think the citizens of Texas were well served when he left that job to pursue a career in which a vivid imagination is an asset, not a liability.'

I feel like throwing my pen at Portman, just to break up the rhythm. He and Livy are like tennis pros giving an exhibition match, sleek and practiced, the volleys perfectly timed, every shot a winner.

'One final question,' she says. 'As one of the agents who originally investigated the Payton murder, what do you think of the allegation that Leo Marston was somehow involved in that crime?'

A superior smile touches Portman's lips. God, he's enjoying this. 'I find the notion utterly preposterous. The fact that we are sitting here today discussing it is a travesty of justice.'

'Thank you, Mr. Director. Your witness.'

I would prefer to cross-examine Portman after I have presented my case, but I cannot let his slurs against me stand unchallenged. Nor can I be sure that Portman will even stick around Natchez after he leaves the stand. I rise but remain at my table.

'Mr. Portman, you and I were involved in a jurisdictional dispute over the extradition of a murderer from Texas to Los Angeles, California, where you were a U.S. attorney. Is that correct?'

'Broadly.'

'Where was that murderer ultimately tried and convicted?'

'Houston, Texas.'

'Thank you. You also stated that I killed the brother of a man I tried for murder. That trial ended in a conviction, did it not?'

'Yes.'

'And wasn't the man I convicted also the subject of our jurisdictional dispute?'

'He was. But—'

'Was I charged in the shooting of his brother?'

'Not to my knowledge.'

'Your Honor, I have further questions for this witness, but I would prefer to examine him during the presentation of my case.'

Seeing Franklin gearing up to explain to me why the director of the FBI cannot be expected to sit around at my beck and call, I add, 'I hope to recall Mr. Portman before the end of the day.'

Judge Franklin turns to Portman with a solicitous smile. 'Will that impose an undue hardship on you, Mr. Director?'

'I can be available until the end of the day, barring an unforeseen emergency.'

'Very well. You are temporarily excused.' Franklin turns to the defense table. 'Mr. Sims, does the plaintiff intend to call further witnesses?'

Blake Sims leans across Leo's massive chest and holds a whispered conference with Livy. She listens, then shakes her head. They want this show to close as quickly as possible.

'Your Honor,' says Sims. 'Reserving the right to call rebuttal witnesses, the plaintiff rests.'

Judge Franklin looks at her watch. 'This phase of the trial has taken much less time than I anticipated. Let's take a ten-minute break, and then Mr. Cage will present his defense.'

As the jurors file out, I turn and look for Caitlin. She's sitting with my parents. She slides along the bench, then comes up to the bar behind my table. I can tell by her face that she doesn't have good news.

'No word from Stone?'

'Nothing. I'm sorry. You'd better drag out the testimony of every witness you have.'

'I hate to do that. Juries always sense it.'

'I don't think you have a choice.'

What a comfort. The ten-minute recess lasts about two minutes, and then I'm on my feet again, doing what I have done countless times in my life: presenting a murder case. I do not stall for time. I do not equivocate. I present it just as I'd planned.

My witnesses come and go like commentators in a documentary. Frank Jones admits he lied about being alone in the Triton parking lot; his ex-wife describes finding the soiled stockings in their car; Betty Lou tearfully places Ray Presley at the crime scene (earning points with the jury for testifying against her own interest) then describes Presley's subsequent threats and brutal harassment; Huey Moak's expert testimony establishes that Payton's car was destroyed by C-4, proving the evidence 'discovered' by Presley was planted; and Lester Hinson testifies that he sold C-4 to Ray Presley in April 1968. All this testimony runs like a Swiss watch.

And therein lies the problem.

Neither Blake Sims nor Livy rise once to cross-examine my witnesses. They don't even challenge Huey Moak's credentials. Every time I tender a witness, Sims waves his hand from the table and says, 'No questions, Your Honor.' Their strategy is simple. They'll happily let me prove Ray Presley guilty of murder. And they will probably let me draw connections between Presley and Ike Ransom, if I can. As long as I can't link Presley or Ransom to Leo Marston, I am fulfilling the scenario painted in Sims's opening statement. The Payton murder was a race crime, committed by a racist. In his closing argument Sims will probably laud my efforts to find justice in this terrible tragedy. But to suggest any nefarious link between such men and Leo Marston must indicate some secret malice toward Marston on my part.

My dilemma is simple. Either I begin the long, laborious task of building circumstantial links between Presley and Marston, which will last well into tomorrow and bore the jury to tears (not to mention sabotage my opportunity to cross-examine John Portman in this lifetime), or I can question Portman now, do what damage I can, and pray that Dwight

Stone descends from the heavens like the deus ex machina of my dreams. Without Stone's testimony as a fulcrum, I can't force Portman to help my cause. But by forcing him to lie, I can set him up for a later fall on perjury charges. And for the director of the FBI, that could be a very long fall.

'Call John Portman,' I say loudly.

'Bailiff,' says Judge Franklin. 'Call John Portman.'

Portman returns to the courtroom wearing the same confidence with which he left it. He takes his seat in the witness box, shoots his cuffs, and gives me a serene smile.

'Director Portman,' I begin, 'in your earlier testimony you stated that Leo Marston rendered valuable assistance in the investigation of Del Payton's death. What was the nature of that assistance?'

He pretends to agonize over this question. 'He provided certain information to us.'

'In other words, he acted as a federal informant.'

'Yes.'

A couple of the white jury members frown.

'I'm going to ask you a direct question. Please answer yes or no. Did the FBI solve the murder of Delano Payton in 1968?'

Portman takes a deep breath but says nothing. We have come down to the nut-cutting, as we say in the South. If he lies now, he is laying himself open to perjury charges.

'Director Portman, I asked whether the Bureau learned the identity of Del Payton's murderer in 1968.'

'Yes. We did.'

A gasp goes up from the spectators.

'Order,' snaps Judge Franklin.

'Why didn't the FBI arrest or charge anyone in connection with that murder?'

'For reasons of national security.'

'Let me be sure I understand this. The FBI preserved the national security by protecting the identity of a man who had murdered a veteran of the Korean War?'

Portman shifts in his seat. 'Director Hoover made that decision. Not me.'

'Did you agree with his decision?'

'It wasn't my place to agree or disagree.'

'You were just following orders.'

'Yes.'

'Like a good German,' I remark, recalling Stone's phrase.

'I strongly resent that.'

'Mr. Cage,' Franklin warns. 'Don't push me.'

'Withdrawn. Director Portman, did you—'

The loud clearing of a throat behind me breaks my train of thought. I start to ignore it, but something tells me to turn.

Caitlin Masters is crouched at the bar behind my table, urgently beckoning me with her hand.

'Your Honor, I beg the court's indulgence.'

I walk back behind my table and kneel so that Caitlin can whisper to me. Her lips touch the shell of my ear. 'I just talked to Stone's daughter,' she says. 'She and Stone were both at the newspaper. Two of my people are bringing them over now. They'll be on the courthouse steps in two minutes.'

Relief and elation flood through me.

'Mr. Cage?' Judge Franklin presses. 'We're waiting.'

I squeeze Caitlin's arm, then rise and walk back toward the witness box with a briskness Portman cannot fail to notice. Caitlin's news has galvanized me.

'Director Portman, was there only one person responsible for Payton's death? Or more than one?'

'More than one.'

A murmur from the spectators.

'How many? Two? Three? Ten?'

Portman folds his arms across his stomach. 'I decline to answer on grounds that it might damage the national security.'

'But you did say more than one. So, a minimum of two.

Was one of those conspirators a Natchez police officer named Ray Presley?'

He gives me the great stone face. 'I decline to answer on grounds that it might damage the national security.'

'Did you work the Payton case alone, Director?'

'I was part of a team.'

'Did that team include a veteran agent named Dwight Stone?'

Portman's eyes track me as I move, trying to read the source of my new-found confidence. 'Yes.'

'Was the Payton murder your first major case as a field agent?'

'It was.'

'Had Agent Stone wide experience in working civil rights cases for the Bureau?'

'Yes.'

'Did you admire and respect Agent Stone?'

Portman hesitates. 'At the time, yes.'

'Did you, earlier this week, order the assassination of Agent Dwight Stone, who is now retired?'

'Objection!' shouts Blake Sims, with Livy close behind.

Franklin bangs her gavel in a vain attempt to silence the gallery. 'Mr. Cage, you'd better be prepared to substantiate that statement.'

'I intend to do just that, Your Honor.' I turn back to Portman. 'Did you also order the assassination of Sheriff's Deputy Ike Ransom, the man murdered at the old pecan-shelling plant last night?'

The spectators collectively suck in their breath as Portman turns to Judge Franklin for help.

Franklin looks hard at me, then says, 'The witness will answer the question.'

'I did not,' Portman says in an indignant voice.

'Did you last week order the assassination of former Natchez police officer Ray Presley?'

'Mr. Cage,' Franklin interrupts, 'I'm losing my patience.'

'One final question, Your Honor. Director Portman, if Special Agent Dwight Stone walks through that door back there and takes the stand, will you remain in Natchez to be recalled as a witness by me?'

He looks right through me. 'I will.'

'No more questions, Judge.'

'Director Portman, you are excused,' says Franklin.

Portman glances up at the TV cameras, then stands, shoots his cuffs again, and leaves the witness box. As he passes on the way to the aisle, I say: 'Call retired Special Agent Dwight Stone.'

The hitch in Portman's walk is momentary, but for me it occurs in slow motion. His eyes flit instinctively to the main door, searching for his old enemy. Then they return to me, the fear in them tamped down, varnished over with the go-to-hell defiance of a man who has survived every threat to his monumental egotism.

'Call Dwight Stone,' Judge Franklin orders.

The bailiff opens the back door. A tall, wiry man wearing a Denver Broncos windbreaker and leaning on the shoulder of a much younger woman limps through with a cane in his left hand. Even from my table I can see the steely resolve in Stone's eyes. But he is not looking at me. As his daughter squeezes in beside Caitlin, he limps up the aisle using the cane, his eyes never leaving the face of John Portman, the man who threatened his daughter's life, and who tried to kill us two nights ago. I have a feeling that a lot of dead Koreans and Chinese saw the look that is on Stone's face right now. I would not want to be John Portman at this moment. But when I turn back to Portman, what I see unsettles me.

He looks surprised but unafraid.

Chapter 40

When Stone finishes his slow journey to the witness box, he pauses for a few deep breaths, then turns to Judge Franklin. 'May I stand during my testimony, Your Honor?'

'Do you have a physical malady that prevents you from sitting?'

'I was shot two nights ago. In the left buttock.'

Predictably, some spectators snicker in spite of Stone's obvious pain.

'You may stand,' says Franklin, glaring at the crowd.

I move slowly toward the podium, running through memories of everything Stone told me two nights ago in Colorado. He lied to me then – by omission – leaving Ike Ransom completely out of his story. I need the truth today, the whole truth. Stone must be made aware that Ike the Spike no longer needs his protection. Instead of stopping at the podium, I adopt Livy's tactic and continue right up to the witness box. In a voice barely above a whisper, I say:

'Ike Ransom was shot to death last night.'

As Judge Franklin orders me to speak at an audible level, Stone winks, and my heartbeat rushes ahead.

'Mr. Stone, were you ever an agent of the Federal Bureau of Investigation?'

'I was a field agent for sixteen years.'

'Did your duties ever bring you to Natchez, Mississippi?'

'Yes.'

'In what capacity?'

'In May of 1968, I was assigned to investigate the death of Delano Payton. I arrived here the day after he was murdered.'

'Who gave you that assignment?'

'J. Edgar Hoover.'

'Personally?'

'Yes.'

'Did you succeed in that assignment? Did you solve the murder?'

'I did.'

Even though Portman said the same thing during his testimony, the crowd buzzes in expectation. It's plain that Dwight Stone does not intend to hold anything back.

'Could you briefly describe how you went about doing that?'

'Objection,' says Livy, rising to her feet. 'Judge, this man is testifying to information that has been sealed to protect national security. His willingness to break the law or even to commit treason is no reason to allow him to divulge protected information in front of television cameras.'

I try not to let my anxiety show on my face, but Livy may have just stopped this trial dead, at least until government officials are brought in to decide what Stone may and may not say.

Judge Franklin looks at me. 'Ms. Sutter raises a serious issue, Mr. Cage. You have argument on this point?'

I could argue for an hour, but I would probably lose. 'Perhaps we should hear Mr. Stone on this point, Judge. He's an attorney himself.'

Franklin gives Stone an inquisitive glance. 'Mr. Stone?'

Stone shakes his head like a soldier pondering a heavily defended hill he has just been ordered to take. 'Judge, the heart of my testimony goes to the justification of that national security classification. After sixteen years working for J. Edgar Hoover, I can tell you this. No man more readily abused such classifications for his own personal ends than Hoover. He sealed the Del Payton file *solely* to mask evidence of criminal activity. It had nothing to do with the national interest. If you allow my testimony, you'll know beyond a shadow of doubt that you've done the right thing.' He looks Franklin square in the eye. 'Have the courage of your office, Judge.'

She regards him thoughtfully. 'My dilemma, Mr. Stone, is that once you've spoken, your words cannot be taken back.'

Stone sighs. 'With all respect, Judge, I'm going to tell my story regardless of your decision. I've been silent too long. I can tell it here on the stand, or outside on the steps.'

Franklin tilts her head back, shocked by Stone's frank threat. 'I have a third choice. I can have you jailed for contempt.'

Stone doesn't even blink. 'You can jail me, Judge. But you can't stop me from speaking. That is the one thing you cannot do.'

Eunice Franklin studies Stone for a long time. What does she see in him? He is ten years her senior, but from another era altogether. Is he a veteran cop with a conscience? Or an unstable and dangerous has-been, as John Portman would portray him? Livy opens her mouth to argue further, but Franklin stops her with an upraised hand.

'No additional argument, Ms. Sutter. If Mr. Stone has the courage to risk jail, I will risk censure. If he strays into what I feel is dangerous territory, I'll stop him. Continue with your story, Mr. Stone.'

'Under protest,' Livy says in a cold voice.

'Noted. Mr. Cage?'

I turn to Stone with as much gratitude as I can bring to my eyes. 'Mr. Stone, could you describe how you went about solving the Delano Payton murder?'

In clear and concise language, the former agent gives a chronological account of his investigation up to the point that he nailed Ray Presley. His story mirrors exactly the testimony given by my earlier witnesses, from Frank Jones to Lester Hinson, and he confirms that John Portman worked with him every step of the way. Their discovery that Lester Hinson had sold C-4 to Ray Presley, Stone says, prompted a 'rather intense' meeting with Presley, during which Presley stated that he'd merely acted as a middleman in the deal, purchasing the plastic explosive for a young Natchez black man, an army veteran. This brings us just past the point at which Stone began lying to me in Colorado.

'What was that young black man's name, Mr. Stone?'

'Ike Ransom.'

'Are you aware that a sheriff's deputy by that name was murdered last night?'

'Yes.'

'Was he the same man you interviewed in 1968?'

'Yes.'

'John Portman stated that the FBI file on Del Payton was sealed because of the involvement of a certain Vietnam veteran. Was Ike Ransom that man?'

'Yes.'

'What did you do after Patrolman Ray Presley told you he'd bought the C-4 for Ike Ransom?'

'Portman and I interviewed Ransom at his apartment. Two minutes after we were inside, he confessed to the murder of Delano Payton.'

Livy jumps to her feet, but her objection is drowned by the explosive reaction of the crowd. Judge Franklin bangs her gavel, but it takes some time for order to be restored. Even the jury is gaping at Stone.

'Your Honor,' says Livy, 'I object. This witness's testimony is hearsay.'

Franklin nods and looks at me. Under the Mississippi rules of evidence, Livy is right. But all rules are proved by exceptions. As I come to my feet, I troll my memory for the details of exceptions under Mississippi law, which I scanned less than six hours ago in the office of the chancery judge, an old high school friend.

'Your Honor, this qualifies as a hearsay exception under Rule 804 (b)3. Deputy Ransom was on my witness list specifically to testify to this information. His murder last night has made that impossible. Since the declarant is unavailable due to death, Mr. Stone's statement should be admitted.'

Franklin looks surprised by my knowledge of Mississippi law.

Livy says, 'Your Honor, Mr. Cage's exception is—'

'Sidebar,' Franklin cuts in. 'Approach the bench.'

Livy and I meet before Franklin and lean toward her.

'Judge,' says Livy, 'this is patent hearsay, and no exception should be made.'

'Judge, Ike Ransom's confession was a statement made against interest. A murder confession so obviously subjected him to criminal liability that great weight must be accorded to it.'

Franklin taps her pen on a notepad as she considers my argument. 'Given the totality of the circumstances, I'm going to allow it.'

'His entire statement?' I press.

'Let's see where it leads. I may stop him.'

Livy starts to argue, then thinks better of it. She returns to her table as I approach Stone.

'Please continue, Mr. Stone.'

He lifts his cane from the rail and leans heavily upon it. 'Ike Ransom was a mess. Suicidal probably. He was living in squalor that would be difficult to believe by today's standards. There was drug paraphernalia in plain view. What we called "heroin works" back then. He was literally dying to tell someone his story.'

'What was his story?'

'He had recently separated from the army after a tour in Vietnam. He'd served as a military policeman there, as I recall. He'd tried to find work with the local police department but was turned down. Desperate for money, he'd turned to drug dealing.'

'He admitted this to you?'

'Yes. Two weeks before Del Payton was murdered, Ransom was stopped on a rural road by Patrolman Ray Presley. Presley discovered a large quantity of heroin in Ransom's trunk. He offered to overlook this if Ransom agreed to kill a man for him.'

'Objection!' Blake Sims cries.

'On what grounds?' asks Judge Franklin.

But Livy has taken hold of Sims's jacket and pulled him back down to his seat.

'There's no objection,' she says.

Franklin gives them an admonitory look. 'Continue, Mr. Stone.'

'Patrolman Presley also promised Ransom that if he carried out this murder, Presley would ensure that he was eventually hired by the police department. Presley had told the truth about Ike Ransom asking him to get the C-4. Ransom was afraid of dynamite, but he'd had experience with C-4 in Vietnam.'

'Did you report Ransom's confession to Director Hoover?'

'I did.'

'What was his reaction?

'I would describe it as glee.'

'Glee. Could you elaborate on that?'

'Mr. Hoover was being forced to aggressively pursue a civil rights agenda. This did not reconcile with his personal feelings. He particularly hated Martin Luther King and Robert Kennedy. My revelation that the murder of Del

Payton – a crime which Robert Kennedy considered a civil rights murder – had in fact been carried out by a black man gave the director obvious enjoyment. He remarked that he would dearly enjoy telling Bobby Kennedy that Payton's death had been nothing but another "shine killing." Those were his words.'

'Did Hoover in fact report this to Bobby Kennedy?'

'Not to my knowledge.'

'What did he do?'

'He authorized me to wiretap the home of Ray Presley, and also the pay phones within a two-mile radius of his home.'

'Did you learn anything from those wiretaps?'

'A few days later Presley called Leo Marston, the local district attorney, and asked for a private meeting.'

'Objection!' cries Sims, to Livy's obvious displeasure.

It looks to me like Sims may be objecting on the order of his client. Leo's face has grown steadily redder during Stone's testimony.

'Grounds?' asks Judge Franklin.

When Sims hesitates, Franklin says, 'I want no more frivolous interruptions of this testimony. You can object from now till doomsday, but Mr. Stone is going to tell his story. Is that clear?'

Sims sighs and takes his chair, while Leo sets his jaw and glares at Franklin.

Stone relates the story of wiretapping Tuscany, and of Hoover taking personal control of the investigation because of its political sensitivity. 'The meeting between Presley and Marston took place in the gazebo outside the Marston mansion. It became clear in the first ten minutes of that conversation that Ray Presley had arranged the death of Delano Payton at the specific request of the district attorney, Leo Marston.'

Judge Franklin is so engrossed by Stone's testimony that it takes her several seconds to realize that the spectators are out of order. She furiously bangs her gavel.

'I'll clear this court!' she vows, pointing her gavel at the balcony for emphasis.

I would have expected Livy to leap to her feet at Stone's last statement, but she seems as engrossed in the story as Judge Franklin.

'How did that become clear, Mr. Stone?' I ask.

'Marston knew every detail of the murder, right down to Ike Ransom's request for the C-4.'

'Did their conversation shed any light on the possible motive for this crime?'

'Yes.' Stone lucidly lays out the pending land deal between Marston and Zebulon Hickson, the carpet magnate from Georgia. He explains Leo's secret ownership of the land, Hickson's concern with black labor problems, and his insistence that an 'example' be made of a black union worker before committing to purchase Marston's property.

'Mr. Stone, I'm sure everyone in this courtroom is wondering why, since you solved the murder, no one was arrested for it. Can you explain that?'

'Yes. After Director Hoover had all the evidence and reports in his possession – including the audiotapes – he set up a meeting with Leo Marston at the Jackson field office of the FBI. After this meeting took place, I was instructed to stand down my Natchez detail and report to Tuscaloosa, Alabama, for other duties. I was told that no arrest would be made because that was in the best interests of the Bureau and the country.'

'What did you make of that?'

Stone shakes his head. 'I'd seen it before. Hoover liked having leverage over people. Particularly people in government. Leo Marston came from a powerful political family. His father had tremendous influence in both Mississippi and

Washington. Over the next year, I learned that Hoover used the leverage of the Payton murder to force Leo's father to influence the 1968 presidential election by trying to swing Mississippi's electoral votes away from George Wallace to Richard Nixon, who was a protégé of Hoover's. It was also clear in 1968 that Leo himself was destined for higher office. Director Hoover and Leo Marston developed a mutually beneficial relationship that flourished from Payton's death in 1968 until Hoover's death in 1972.'

Judge Franklin is shaking her head in amazement.

I can't believe that Livy or Sims did not object to Stone's last statements, but they probably assumed – rightly, I suspect – that Judge Franklin meant to hear him out no matter what.

'So,' I summarize, trying to bring it all into perspective for the jury, 'J. Edgar Hoover was willing to bury conclusive evidence of a civil rights murder in order to strengthen his own political influence. How did you react to this?'

'Not well.'

'Please be specific.'

'I began drinking. It affected my work. I cheated on my wife. She divorced me, took my daughter from me. I was eventually dismissed from the Bureau.'

A fragment of Ike's confession in the pecan shelling plant comes to me from the ether. 'Did you ever make any attempt to right what you considered the terrible wrong that had been done in the Payton case?'

Surprise flashes in Stone's eyes. 'Yes.'

'How?'

'I had retained a copy of the incriminating tape. About a year after the murder, when I knew no official action would ever be taken against the killers, I called Ike Ransom. He'd been hired as a police officer by then, just as Presley had promised.'

'What did you tell him?'

'Nothing. I played him my copy of the tape. Then I hung up.'

'What did you think Ransom would do after hearing that tape?'

'I don't know. I suppose I hoped that he might take direct action.'

'You hoped he would kill Presley and Marston?'

Stone's face remains impassive. 'The thought entered my mind.'

'Mr. Stone, when you described these events to me two days ago, you didn't mention Ike Ransom. Why?'

He looks at the rail, his eyes filled with something like grief. 'I felt some sympathy for Ike Ransom, despite what he'd done.'

'Sympathy for a murderer?'

'Ransom was a combat veteran. I was one myself. Del Payton too. Ransom had a bad time in Vietnam, I could tell that right off. When Presley caught him with that heroin, his choices narrowed down to nothing. Parchman prison or commit murder. That may not mitigate his act, but when I interviewed the man, he was paralyzed by remorse. He was the only one of the three who ever showed any, and to this day, I'm surprised he lived through those weeks.' Stone rubs his free hand over the one holding the head of the cane, then expels a lungful of air. 'Presley and Marston were *arrogant* about what they'd done. And why not? The system rewarded Marston for it.'

I ask Stone to briefly explain the Presley angle of the Marston–Hoover deal (Marston's betrayal of Presley to the FBI), my goal being to show the jury that even last night's attempt by Presley to kill Marston had its roots in the Payton murder. When Stone finishes, Judge Franklin looks overwhelmed by the implications of the case.

'One last question, Mr. Stone. Why, knowing all that you did, did you wait so long to come forward with the truth?'

He looks past me, but I doubt he sees anything of the court-room. 'Cowardice,' he says. 'Plain and simple. Hoover used John Portman to threaten my family if I caused a scandal. After my ex-wife died, I thought about coming forward. But by then my daughter had graduated law school and against my advice joined the FBI. She was subject to the will of the Justice Department, of which John Portman was a major part. The murder had happened so long ago. I just tried to put it behind me.'

'Did you succeed?'

'No. It's haunted me my whole life.'

'Thank you, Mr. Stone. I tender the witness, subject to redirect.'

Judge Franklin lays both hands on her desk and sighs. 'I'm going to take a recess here. I'd like to think for a bit, and I'm sure Mr. Stone would like to rest his legs.'

Livy stands abruptly. 'I'd prefer to cross-examine now, Your Honor.'

Franklin frowns and looks at me. 'Mr. Cage?'

I should probably opt for the recess, to give Stone time to decompress. But something pushes me in the opposite direction. Something in me is driven to witness Livy's perfor-mance. How far is she willing to go to protect her father? How far, now that Stone's testimony has destroyed any re-maining illusions she might have had about Leo's innocence?

'No objection, Your Honor.'

'Proceed, Ms. Sutter.'

Livy squeezes Leo's shoulder in a gesture that looks genuine. Then she approaches Stone at an oblique angle, walking slowly with a burgundy Montblanc pen in her hand, not looking at him but at the jury. Every man and woman in the box watches her with fascination.

'Mr. Stone, what year were you dismissed from the FBI?'

'1972.'

'Were you summarily dismissed, or were efforts made to help you stop drinking?'

'I wasn't fired for drinking.'

'Your record states that you were. But I'm interested. Why do you *think* you were fired?'

'For drawing my service weapon on Leo Marston in the lobby of the Watergate office complex.'

Livy doesn't bat an eye. 'There's no mention of such an incident in your record. Were there any witnesses to it?'

'My partner, Henry Bookbinder.'

'Will he corroborate your story?'

'He would if he were alive.'

'Any other witnesses?'

'Not that I know by name. Only Marston himself.'

Leo actually smirks from his table. He loves seeing Livy perform this way. This is what he fantasized about before she ran off to Virginia and then Atlanta.

'Let's return to your dismissal,' she says. 'I admired the candor of your earlier testimony. Being honest about things like losing your wife and child must be very hard. I know, because I'm going through a divorce myself.'

Livy wins instant points with the jury for this personal revelation, one with stratospheric value in the Natchez gossip market. Stone stands with a resigned frown on his face, like a soldier being court-martialed, one who knows something bad is coming and that he has no choice but to endure it.

'I wonder,' Livy says with false spontaneity, 'were you *completely* honest about your dismissal?'

Stone just waits.

'Do you know a woman named Catherine Neumaier?'

His face sags.

'Would you like some water?'

Stone's jaw clenches. He is clearly offended by Livy's feigned concern. 'I did know Catherine Neumaier. She's dead now. Dead twenty-five years.'

'Did Miss Neumaier have a profession?'

'She was a dancer.'

'A dancer. She had no other profession?'

'Not to my knowledge.'

'FBI records indicate that Miss Neumaier was a prostitute.'

'I don't know anything about that.'

'How did you meet Miss Neumaier?'

'I was working an organized crime task force. I was assigned to try to compromise her as an informant.'

'Because she had ties to organized crime?'

'She danced in a club owned by Sam Giancana.'

'The mafia boss of Chicago?'

'Yes.'

'Did Miss Neumaier become your informant?'

'Yes.'

'Was she an alcoholic?'

'No.'

'FBI records indicate that she was. Also that she took drugs.'

Stone sighs. 'She had a severe health problem. Lupus. She took pills to help her stay awake for work. Pills to help her sleep.'

'Did you have a sexual relationship with Miss Neumaier?'

His eyes don't waver. 'Yes.'

'Wasn't it this relationship that caused the breakup of your marriage?'

'Yes.'

'Were you reprimanded for unprofessional conduct because of this sexual relationship with Miss Neumaier?'

'Officially. And only after the fact. Unofficially, Hoover encouraged it from the start.'

'You were encouraged by the director of the FBI to have an affair with a Mob prostitute? I find that difficult to believe.'

Stone's eyes are burning now, all patience gone from his face. 'Lady, the total tonnage of what you don't know about federal law enforcement would sink a damned oil tanker.'

Livy is already smiling in triumph when Judge Franklin reprimands Stone for his language.

'Did you feel,' she goes on, prodding a different nerve, 'that John Portman had anything to do with your dismissal from the FBI?'

'I know he did.'

'How do you know?'

'Portman had known since the Payton case that I didn't go along with what Hoover had done.'

'Allegedly done.'

'Keep telling yourself that.'

'I'm warning you, Mr. Stone,' Franklin cuts in.

'How did Mr. Portman influence your dismissal?' Livy asks.

'He reported all my conversations and movements to Hoover after the director took over the Payton case.'

'Why would he do that?'

'Because he sensed that I wasn't going to toe the line. He sensed my sympathy for Del Payton and Ike Ransom. Hoover's standard procedure would have been to tell Portman to keep a close eye on me and report back. This was Portman's first major case. He would have kissed Hoover's— He'd have done whatever Hoover told him to without question.'

'What else did Portman do?'

'Two days before I was fired, evidence pertaining to the Payton case was stolen from my apartment. Portman took that.'

'I thought you told us that Director Hoover requested that all the Payton evidence be forwarded to Washington.'

'I kept copies of certain things.'

'Against direct orders?'

'Yes.'

'Why do you think it was Portman who allegedly stole this material?'

'He left me a calling card.'

'A business card?'

'No. A map.'

Livy looks less certain here. 'What kind of map?'

'My evidence was hidden behind a wall panel. After the theft the panel was purposefully left out of place. When I looked inside the wall, I found a map of Natchez, Mississippi. There'd been no map there before. That was Portman's calling card. That was the only place we'd ever served together. I suppose he thought it displayed a certain wit.'

'How do you feel about Mr. Portman personally?'

'Since he sent four men to kill me last night, I don't feel too well disposed toward him.'

'The jury will disregard that statement,' Judge Franklin cuts in. 'Confine yourself to the question, Mr. Stone.'

'All right. I think John Portman is a rich, spineless bureaucrat who didn't get spanked enough when he was a kid.'

Franklin turns red, but Livy is ecstatic. Stone is giving her exactly what she wants. Before Franklin can reprimand him, she turns to face the jury box.

'Mr. Stone, did you enter into a conspiracy with the author Penn Cage to ruin the careers of John Portman and Leo Marston?'

He blinks in surprise. 'What? Absolutely not.'

'But you see the symmetry of the suggestion?

'I do not.'

She turns back to him with a knowing smile. 'Come, now. You're a smart man. I'm suggesting that you and Mr. Cage made a deal of sorts. Mr. Cage hated Leo Marston, you hated John Portman. Alone, neither of you could do much to destroy those men. But together—'

'Objection,' I say at last.

Livy smiles. 'I withdraw the question, Your Honor. And I have no further questions for this witness.'

I can't understand why she's releasing Stone so soon until

she says, 'If this is Mr. Cage's final witness, I would very much like to call Mr. Cage at this time as a rebuttal witness.'

Her suggestion stuns me. All I can think to say is, 'Ms. Sutter is out of order, Judge.'

'Just a moment,' says Franklin. 'You are excused, Mr. Stone. But don't leave the courthouse.'

Stone makes no move to leave the witness box. He looks down at Livy with contempt and says, 'You're not worth a hangnail on Catherine Neumaier's little finger. Your father is a murderer, and you know it. But you stand there—'

'Mr. Stone!' snaps Franklin. 'Leave the stand, or I'll be forced to hold you in contempt.'

Stone looks away from Livy like a man looking away from a dead enemy, then limps off the stand with his soldier's bearing. As he passes me, he stops, shakes my hand, and leans close.

'I told you you didn't want me as a witness.'

I squeeze his hand and whisper, 'Bullshit. I wanted the truth, and you gave it to me. The question is, was the jury ready for it?'

As Stone passes the spectators' benches, his cane rapping on the hardwood floor, his daughter rises, takes his elbow, and helps him toward the doors.

'Ms. Sutter,' says Judge Franklin. 'This is an unusual request. Whose testimony are you calling Mr. Cage to rebut?'

'Mr. Stone's, Your Honor.'

Franklin considers this for a few moments. 'Mr. Cage, do you plan to call additional witnesses?'

I had planned to recall Portman, but now that Livy has undercut everything Stone said by making him look bent on revenge, I'm not sure what to do. And now she wants to question me? I suppose she is finally answering the question of how far she is willing to go.

'I have no more witnesses, Your Honor.'

'Does the defense rest, then?'

A strange sense of sadness flows through me, not for myself but for Althea Payton, sitting out there in the benches. She nods at me as though to say, *At least we tried.* 'Subject to calling rebuttal witnesses, the defense rests.'

'Very well. Please take the stand, Mr. Cage.'

Without looking at Livy, I mount the steps to the witness box and seat myself. Everyone in the room is watching me. My parents. The Paytons. Austin Mackey, who looks like he's in shock from the revelations he's heard in the past half hour. High in the back of the court, more faces watch from the balcony, and among them the larger gleaming eyes of the CNN and WLBT cameras.

One pair of eyes is not watching me. Livy Marston's, and it's a damn good thing. If she had the nerve to look me in the eye while playing out this obscene charade, I might decide to stand up and announce her sins to the world. But I won't do that. And she knows it. It's not in me to do something like that. But maybe it is in her.

'Mr. Cage,' she says, facing the jury. 'Did you and I have a romantic relationship when we attended the St. Stephens Preparatory School?'

'Yes.'

'Was it a serious relationship?'

'Define serious.'

'An extended relationship of a sexual nature.'

She has guts, I'll give her that. 'Yes.'

'When did that relationship finally end?'

Two minutes ago. 'Our freshman year of college.'

'Did it end that year because my father, Leo Marston, handled a malpractice suit against your father, Thomas Cage?'

'Yes.'

'In the course of that lawsuit, did your father suffer a near-fatal heart attack?'

'Yes.'

'Did you blame my father for that?'

'Yes.'

'Did that lawsuit effectively end any chance of you and I getting married?'

'Yes.'

At last she turns to me, but her eyes look opaque, as though she has closed them against all my feeling for her, steeling herself against mercy. 'Did you blame my father for that as well?'

Does she want me to tell the truth? Does she want me to say, *No, I blame you? The whole goddamn thing happened because you got yourself pregnant by a stupid redneck murderer and couldn't deal with it.*

'For a long time, I did.'

'And did you conspire with former Special Agent Dwight Stone to destroy my father and John Portman?'

'I did not.'

She holds my eyes a moment longer, as though waiting for me to counter-attack with everything I know about her.

I say nothing. What would it accomplish, besides convincing Livy that I'm willing to sink as low to destroy her father as she is to protect him? Would it convince the jury that Marston and Portman are guilty? If Stone's testimony didn't do that, the Marston family's dirty laundry certainly won't.

'No further questions,' Livy says, turning away at last.

Judge Franklin looks at me as though I have fulfilled the assertion she made on the day we met in her office. I have a fool for a client. 'Mr. Cage,' she says, 'I find myself in the curious position of asking if you would like to cross-examine yourself.'

I almost laugh out loud. Here it is, my chance to say anything I want. And curiously enough, I have no inclination to say anything. Without Ike Ransom or Ray Presley to confirm Stone's story, I can add nothing that will sway the twelve people in the jury box.

'No questions, Your Honor.'

'You're excused, Mr. Cage.'

Excused. My parents are watching me with agony in their faces. Althea Payton nods, her lips tight. Caitlin's black veil of hair frames her porcelain face among all the others. She's looking at me with something like pity in her eyes. She thinks I'm unable to turn Livy's sword against her, not trapped in a situation where my conscience is forcing me to endure humiliation without fighting back. As I walk back to the defense table, I turn toward the jury. I do not give them my lawyer's look – full of confidence, certain of victory – but a simple human look, an unstated question.

Their faces are hard to read. Stone's testimony resonated with the black jurors, but even they cannot help but connect the simple dots Livy held up before them. I blamed Leo Marston for making my father ill and ruining my prospects with his daughter. Stone hated Portman for his dismissal from the FBI. Once the two of us were brought together, a conspiracy was almost inevitable. Factually, this theory has at least one major hole. But emotionally it makes sense. It plays. And some of the jury members are bound to buy into it.

As I reach the table, the door at the rear of the courtroom opens, and a young woman walks in. It's Jenny Doe. She looks toward the judge's bench, then pans her eyes until they settle on me.

I nod to her and take my seat just as Judge Franklin says: 'Ms. Sutter? Does the plaintiff rest?'

Any lingering illusion that Blake Sims is leading Leo Marston's legal team crumbles into dust.

Livy nods. 'The plaintiff rests, Your Honor.'

As Franklin turns to me, someone pulls at my elbow. 'Mr. Cage?'

It's Jenny, crouching at the bar behind my table.

'Mr. Cage?' says Judge Franklin. 'Does the defense rest?'

581

Jenny grabs my arm above the elbow and jabs her thumb into a nerve. I jerk my elbow away.

'Mr. Cage?' says Franklin. 'Is that young lady bothering you?'

'May I have a moment, Your Honor?'

'If you must.'

I twist in my chair until I'm face to face with Jenny. 'What the hell are you doing?'

Her eyes are glittering with excitement. 'I have something for you,' she whispers. 'I think I have what you need to win your case.'

'What are you talking about?'

'I tried to get in here this morning to watch the trial, but it was too crowded. And it's a good thing for you. Because I went back to my apartment and watched it on TV. I didn't realize what I had until I heard that Mr. Stone talking about J. Edgar Hoover. I ran—'

'Mr. Cage,' Judge Franklin presses. 'I'm ready to give this case to the jury.'

I hold up my hand. 'Jenny, for God's sake, get to the point.'

'It's the tapes.'

I blink in bewilderment. 'Tapes?'

She reaches into the pocket of her jeans and pulls out a black Maxell cassette tape. 'This,' she says. 'It's one of the tapes I stole from Clayton Lacour's office. Remember? The mobbed-up lawyer who handled my adoption? When I stole all the files relating to Marston, I stole his phone tapes too. Lacour's conversations with Marston. Twelve tapes. And on this one he's talking about your case. About Del Payton. He never actually says the name, so I never realized what I had. But when that poor Beckham woman started saying the name Ray Presley, something zinged in my mind. I couldn't place it until Mr. Stone started talking about J. Edgar Hoover. I had to fast-forward through eight different tapes before I found it. I sprinted the three blocks over here.'

'Jenny, what *is* it? What do they say?'

She shakes her head, her eyes brimming with secret joy. 'Just get the judge to play it. You won't believe it.'

I close my eyes, thinking furiously.

'Mr. Cage, I've had enough,' says Judge Franklin. 'Does the defense rest?'

I take the tape from Jenny, get to my feet and lay my hands on the table. 'No, your Honor. I request a conference in chambers. Critical new evidence has just come to my attention. I believe it will be conclusive evidence, and—'

'Objection!' Livy cries, shaking her head. She has already seen the tape in my hand. She probably thinks it's Dwight Stone's recording of her father and Ray Presley talking in the gazebo of Tuscany. 'No such evidence was disclosed to us!'

'Your Honor, I didn't know about it myself until a moment ago. The young lady behind me just brought it to my attention.'

Livy looks at Jenny with dread in her face.

'Who is that person?' Franklin asks.

Livy closes her eyes.

'Her name is Jenny Doe, Judge. Who she is, is less important than what she has.'

'What does she have?'

'A tape of Leo Marston discussing the Payton murder with a New Orleans attorney named Clayton Lacour.'

Judge Franklin looks to Livy for an objection, but Livy is still standing with her eyes closed, as though she can no longer stand the schizophrenic nature of what she is being called upon to do today. Prodded by Leo, Blake Sims gets to his feet.

'Judge, I object to the introduction of this surprise evidence on the grounds of—'

Eunice Franklin stops him with an upraised hand. 'I'll

hear argument in my chambers.' She stands in her black robe and looks down at me. 'Mr. Cage, this had better not be desperation grandstanding.'

'The tape will speak for itself.' I assure her, praying that Jenny knows evidence when she hears it.

'Counsel in my chambers,' says Franklin. She points at Jenny. 'You too, young lady.'

Chapter 41

We stand like human islands in Judge Franklin's chambers, an archipelago of attorneys situated around the mainland of her mahogany desk. Blake Sims to the left. I'm in the center with Jenny behind me. Livy stands to the right, apart and alone, reading the spines of the books in Franklin's shelves.

'Ms. Sutter, are you with us?'

Livy half turns to the judge but doesn't come close to eye contact with me or Jenny. 'Yes, Your Honor.'

The judge looks up at me, her eyes hard. 'All right, Mr. Cage. What exactly is on this tape?'

Blake Sims is shaking his head, but he doesn't speak.

'I haven't heard it myself, Judge. But this woman claims that it refers directly to the murder of Del Payton, and I have reason to believe she's telling the truth.'

Franklin transfers her glare to Jenny. 'How did you come by this tape, young lady?'

'I worked for Clayton Lacour. The lawyer who made the tape. I went to work for him to try to find out the identities of my birth parents. I'm an adopted child, and I knew that Lacour had handled my adoption.' Jenny glances at Livy, who is pointedly ignoring her. 'While working for Lacour, I found out Leo Marston had been involved in my adoption. When I quit that job, I took all the files and tapes pertaining to Judge Marston with me.'

'You mean you stole them?'

'Yes, ma'am.'

Judge Franklin looks like she wants a cigarette or a drink, and probably both. 'I don't understand. Why were there tapes at all?'

'Mr. Lacour taped most of his phone calls. He was connected with the Marcello family in New Orleans. You know, Mafia. He was seriously paranoid.'

Franklin sighs and holds out her hand. 'Let me have the tape.'

I hand over the cassette. The judge studies it for a few moments, then speaks without looking up. 'Did you learn who your birth parents were?'

'Yes, Your Honor.'

'Who are they?'

Livy goes rigid beside the shelves.

'At least one of them is in this room right now, Judge. Do you want me to say more?'

Franklin shakes her head in amazement. 'Not at this time.' She looks up at me. 'I don't know exactly what's going on behind this lawsuit, but I don't appreciate having my court used as an arena to play out private vendettas. Is that clear?'

'Absolutely, Your Honor.'

'I want counsel back at their respective tables. You' – Franklin points at Jenny – 'stay with me. I'm going to listen to this tape. Then I'll make my decision as to admissibility. If I walk back into that courtroom and announce that the tape will be played, I don't want to hear a single objection. If I don't mention the tape, the same holds true, and I will give this case to the jury. It's late, and there's too much craziness surrounding this trial to drag it into tomorrow if we don't have to.' She claps her hands together. 'Everybody out.'

As I walk back to my table, Caitlin nods in encouragement from the bar. I take my seat and slide back within earshot of her.

'What do you have?' she whispers.

'I'm not sure. A tape of Marston and a New Orleans lawyer. Jenny says it will nail Marston.'

'You haven't heard it?'

'No. Franklin's listening to it now. She's going to rule on admissibility.'

'I'm praying here,' Caitlin says. 'I'm actually praying.'

The wait is almost impossible to bear. Two minutes stretch to five, then ten. The spectators are silent at first, but as the minutes drag on, they begin to whisper. Without Franklin to intimidate them, the whisper grows to a hum, then a dull roar. It reminds me of students assembled in a gymnasium. Twice I look across the aisle to Marston's table, but Leo and Livy stare straight ahead, their faces set in stone. Only Blake Sims looks worried. Sims looks, in fact, like he would rather be getting a root canal than sitting at his client's table.

At last Judge Franklin's chamber door opens, silencing the court. Jenny Doe walks through first and heads for the spectators' benches, her head bowed. Franklin emerges carrying a cassette tape player, a cheap jam box with a silver antenna sticking up off of it.

At Marston's table, Blake Sims actually covers his eyes.

'*Yes*,' whispers Caitlin from behind me.

Judge Franklin takes the bench, sets the tape player before her, then turns to the jury box. 'Members of the jury, I am about to play a tape recording of two voices having a telephone conversation. One, I am told, belongs to a lawyer in New Orleans. The other, I am convinced, belongs to the plaintiff in this case, Leo Marston. I have instructed counsel to make no objections to the playing of this tape. The supreme court might disagree with my decision, but this is not a murder trial, and I suspect that it will never see an appeals court.'

A murmur of anticipation ripples through the crowd.

'The language on the tape is profane,' Judge Franklin goes on, 'as language spoken between men in private sometimes tends to be. I will play only that portion of the tape I believe relevant to this case. I want no displays of emotion. I want *absolute silence*. I will eject anyone who disobeys that order.'

She rubs the bridge of her nose and sighs. Then another liver-spotted hand emerges from the black robe. It presses a button on the machine and turns the speakers toward the jury.

Static fills the courtroom. Then an unfamiliar male voice comes from the speakers, the New Orleans accent plain: Brooklyn with a little crawfish thrown in. This must be Clayton Lacour.

'*. . . and this problem, Leo, it's, you know, one of those things you could earn a lot of gratitude by fixing.*'

'*I'm listening.*'

A collective intake of breath by the crowd as it recognizes the resonant voice of Leo Marston.

'Order!' demands Judge Franklin.

'*This goddamn new guy they got at the field office here,*' Lacour goes on, '*Hughes, his name is, he's not playing by the old rules. This is the new SAC I'm talkin' 'bout. He's stoppin' by for coffee at Carlos's office at the Town and Country, for God's sake, got surveillance on him around the clock. Uncle C is gettin' ulcers. You gotta help me out here, cher.*'

'*I'm not sure what you want.*'

'*What I want? It's not me, Leo. I'm just passing a message from the man.*'

'*From Marcello?*'

'*Yeah. Elvis was down here a few months ago, and he told Carlos you were tight with Hoover. He said—*'

'*Elvis?*'

'*Yeah. Presley. That, ah . . . what's his first name? Ray. Carlos's guys call him Elvis.*'

A pause on Marston's end. Then: '*I thought Frank Costello greased the skids with Hoover for Marcello.*'

'*Well, you didn't hear it from me, okay? But Carlos and Frank are on the outs just now. Not a good time for Carlos to call New York for a favor. So anyway, Elvis was down here, and he told the man you guys cooled out a nigger down there two or three years back and Hoover let it slide for you –'* A gasp from the jury box.

'– said you call him Edgar, like he's your uncle or something.' Lacour laughing now. *'Anyway, Carlos wants you to talk to the old queen and get this Harold Hughes off his back. This fucking guy don't know how it works down here.'*

'Does Marcello understand how things work with Hoover?'

'What do you mean?'

'Hoover expects a quid pro quo.'

'Hey, there's always a quid pro quo, right? That's business. But look, Elvis wasn't just talkin' shit about this nigger, was he?'

'No. Hoover grew up in Washington, D. C., when it was still a Southern town. This business you're talking about was in sixty-eight. Hoover would have traded twenty nigras for one electoral vote for Nixon. It was that close. You tell Marcello I'll speak to Edgar, but remember . . . quid pro quo. That goes for me as well.'

'Hey, do I know you or don't I? Now, what about those gas leases where they're dredging down by Houma–.'

Judge Franklin switches off the machine.

The silence is total. I'm not sure anyone in the courtroom is breathing. The jury appears to be in shock, particularly the black jurors, who are staring at Leo Marston as they might at a dangerous wild animal. Blake Sims gets to his feet to start listing objections, but Franklin stops him with a gesture.

A chilling screech of chair legs rips through the courtroom. As all heads turn toward the source of the sound – the plaintiff's table – Livy rises from her chair, puts her purse over her shoulder, and without looking at her father or anyone else walks around the table and down the aisle to the door at the back of the courtroom.

This act is probably more damning to her father than the tape. To me it suggests a chance for the possibility of redemption. At least she draws the line somewhere. I suppress the urge to go after her, even though I know that at this moment she might do something truly desperate. I must play my part in this grotesquerie to the end. As I turn back toward the bench, Austin Mackey stands and hurries after Livy. I'll have to wait to find out what he's up to.

'Mr. Sims,' Judge Franklin says from the bench. 'I know what you're going to say. First, that the voice on this tape is not Leo Marston's. Second, that if the voice *is* Marston's, it has been spliced together using some miracle of modern technology. Third, you want to request a continuance while your experts examine the tape.'

Franklin drums her fingers on her desk. 'Mr. Sims, that is not going to happen. I am not going to recall this jury three weeks from now just to hear your experts denounce the tape and Mr. Cage's experts argue that it's genuine. I've known Leo Marston for twenty-five years, and *I* believe the tape is genuine. Mr. Sims, I am giving this case to the jury.'

Most of the heads in the jury box are nodding.

'Does the plaintiff rest?' Franklin asks.

'Under protest,' Sims says weakly.

'Noted.' Franklin turns to me. 'Does the defense rest?'

'Your Honor, the defense rests.'

Franklin is about to begin instructing the jury when Leo Marston rises from his chair and walks toward the aisle as though to follow Livy out.

'Judge Marston?' Franklin says from the bench.

He gives the judge his broad back and starts down the aisle.

'Leo?' she calls.

Marston ignores her. He is nearly to the doors, his enormous shoulders rocking with purposeful motion.

'Bailiff,' says Franklin, her voice quivering with what sounds like fear. 'Please restrain Mr. Marston.'

The bailiff, a middle-aged black man, stands in front of the door and lays a hand on the butt of his holstered gun. Leo looks prepared to make the poor man use it.

'You will stay to hear the verdict of this jury, Mr. Marston,' Franklin says in a firmer voice. 'Unless you're dismissing this suit.'

Leonidas Marston finally stops and turns back to Judge Franklin, his face a mask of contempt. 'I'm entitled to a jury of my peers,' he says, his voice booming through the courtroom. 'I won't be judged by that rabble sitting up there.'

Franklin's face reddens to the point that I fear she might stroke out. 'Leo, I'm holding you—'

'I'm dismissing the suit,' he growls. Then he turns back to the door as though he could as easily dismiss the consequences of this proceeding from his life.

As the bailiff looks to Judge Franklin for guidance, the door behind him is yanked open and Austin Mackey walks through, followed by two large deputies. The deputies block the door while Mackey walks far enough up the aisle to make sure the TV cameras capture the full range of his limited charisma.

'Judge Franklin,' he says in the deepest voice he can muster. 'Regardless of the verdict of this jury, I am ordering the arrest of Leo Marston for the crime of capital murder.'

Pandemonium erupts in the courtroom.

'Order!' Franklin shouts. 'Quiet in this court!'

'The grand jury will be convened in two weeks,' Mackey goes on, 'and I intend to bring the case before them at that time.'

Judge Franklin shakes her head and gives the district attorney a sarcastic smile. 'Let me state for the record, Mr. Mackey, that you are a day late and a dollar short. Since Mr. Cage has proved your case for you, I suggest you forward your salary for the month to him.'

Mackey blushes from his neck to the top of his head, but

he recovers quickly and turns back to the deputies blocking the door. 'Place Mr. Marston under arrest. The charge is capital murder.'

It must gall Mackey to have to get the deputies to make this arrest. But even with his overarching ambition, Mackey hasn't the nerve to try to arrest Leo Marston. It would be like a rabbit confronting a Bengal tiger. I half expect Leo to fight the deputies to the floor, but he allows himself to be quietly handcuffed.

'Judge Franklin,' says Blake Sims. 'I request that Judge Marston be taken out through a side door, to spare the embarrassment of a mob scene. He's done great service to this city and this state, no matter what else he might have done.'

Technically, Leo is Mackey's prisoner now, but this is Eunice Franklin's court. He defers to her.

Franklin stares at Leo, who is looking indifferently ahead, as though bored by the events around him. His problem has become one for the criminal courts, and he knows that particular jungle better than most.

'Take him out the front door,' Franklin says.

As the deputies escort Marston out, Judge Franklin looks to the jury box. 'Ladies and gentlemen, you have done your duty. I apologize for the incompleteness of the process. At least it only took one day. You are discharged.' She turns to the gallery. 'This court is dismissed.'

A wild roar erupts from outside the building, undoubtedly prompted by the appearance of Leo Marston in handcuffs. I have no desire to be in that crowd of jubilant blacks and confused whites, people who still know nothing of the facts of this case, and who probably won't fully absorb them for several days. As the spectators rise from the benches in a rush, I am surrounded by people slapping my back and trying to shake my hand.

The first hand I take is my father's. His grip is firm and

strong, his eyes filled with pride. 'You did a fair job, son.' He breaks into a smile.

My mother is in tears beside him. She reaches out and hugs me, while behind her Charles Evers and Willie Pinder give me brief salutes, then turn and move toward the door. As I stare after them, Caitlin materializes out of the crowd, smiling with relief.

'Well, I guess we won,' she says. 'Right?'

'You're damn right,' Dad agrees.

'I'm thinking of Ruby,' my mother says quietly.

'Me too,' I tell her.

She takes my hand. 'You had to do it. I see that now.'

Before I can say anything else, Caitlin steps up to me, stands on tiptoe, and kisses me on the cheek. 'I've been wanting to do that all day.' She turns to my parents. 'I hope you don't mind public displays of affection.'

My mother surprises the hell out of me by saying, 'That's quite all right.'

I punch Caitlin's shoulder. 'Can you win the Pulitzer if you're personally involved in the story you're covering?'

She waves her hand as though swatting a fly. 'To hell with the Pulitzer. I'll take it if they offer it, but I'm not chasing it anymore.'

My father grips my right shoulder and turns me in place. Judge Franklin is standing behind me in her black robe. She extends her hand and shakes mine. 'That's the first time I've ever seen a slander case hijacked into a murder trial,' she says.

'I couldn't figure any other way to do it. I apologize.'

'Don't. Sometimes you have to go the long way around to get justice.'

'I appreciate what you did. The hearsay exception . . . letting the tape in.'

A hint of a smile comes to her lips. 'The truth will out. Good-bye, Mr. Cage.'

I nod thanks and turn back to Caitlin, who takes my hand, pulls it behind her back, and squeezes it tight.

Out of the swirl of my parents' friends, Althea Payton steps forward wearing a dark blue dress. Behind her stands Del, looking very uncomfortable in a Sunday suit.

'I can finally get on with living,' Althea says softly. Her liquid brown eyes meet mine, and for a moment there is no one in the courtroom but us. 'I think you know what I'm talking about,' she adds.

An image of Sarah flashes behind my eyes, but too much has happened today to let it in. 'I do.'

Del reaches over his mother's shoulder and shakes my hand. 'Thanks, man.'

I shake his hand, nod thanks, then prepare to accept the congratulations of all the others waiting behind him. But my thoughts are already far away. Somewhere outside this building Livy Marston is walking or driving alone, pondering the wreckage of her life. Her father is right where I hoped he would be, but Livy isn't. Despite all I have seen of her – the coldness and dishonesty and manipulation – part of me longs to be with her now. The bottle of wine we sank twenty years ago still waits at the bottom of that cold, clear pool, buried under mud and sand and time, but there all the same. And God help me, I wish I were going to her bed tonight.

But I'm not. I will not.

The past is dead.

Epilogue

I am standing in line for It's A Small World at Walt Disney World in Florida. Annie is in my arms, but this time we are not alone. Caitlin stands beside us, smiling as the line snakes toward the boats filled with parents and wide-eyed children. We are not a family, the three of us, not legally, but we are very happy together in this moment. Caitlin takes my hand as the line moves forward, not looking at me but simply being with me, with the comfort of familiar lovers.

I hardly ever think of Livy now, and when I do it is only with sadness for her, not for us. She flew back to Atlanta the day after the trial, but whether to conclude her divorce or to reconcile with her husband, I have no idea. Before she left, I had coffee with her at the Eola Hotel. In the awkward silence between us, I made three requests. First, that she inform Jenny Doe that her father was a boy who is now married and does not want his identity revealed. Second, that Livy provide funds for Jenny to attend the college of her choice, and establish a trust fund that will provide a livable income for the rest of Jenny's life. And third, that she make no fuss over Jenny using the Marston family name, should she elect to do so. I suspect that Jenny will elect not to, but I want her to have the choice. The threat of what could happen should Livy not live up to these conditions did not need to be stated. My knowledge of the contents of Leo's secret safe could decimate her family fortune.

The remaining fallout from the trial happened quickly.

Less than forty-eight hours after portions of Dwight Stone's testimony began running on CNN, John Portman was asked by the President to resign as director of the FBI. One week later it was announced that he had accepted a position with the DeTocqueville Trust, a conservative think-tank based in Alexandria, Virginia.

Four days after Portman's resignation, Special Agent Peter Lutjens's transfer to North Dakota was rescinded, and he resumed his duties in Washington, D.C. Dwight Stone's daughter also resumed her Bureau duties, but Stone has confided to me by telephone that she plans to resign soon. She seems to have some crazy idea about practicing country law with her father in Colorado.

Two weeks after Stone mounted the witness stand in Natchez, a grand jury indicted Leo Marston on capital murder charges. He is scheduled to go to trial in two days, with Austin Mackey prosecuting. The consensus of the Natchez legal community is that he will be found guilty and receive life imprisonment. When the masses finally turn on a tyrant, they turn viciously.

In the mayoral election, Wiley Warren defeated Shad Johnson by a percentage margin of 51–49. Shad did not win the votes of those 'good whites' he needed to push him over the top, and the ill feeling stirred up by my pursuit of the Payton case may well have been the cause of that. Such is life. Wiley Warren has not been a bad mayor. And if Shad means business, he can stick around four more years and become a true citizen of the town. I may do that myself.

The cool November air has thinned the crowds at Disney World, and we've had our run of the park. Some popular rides have no lines at all. Yet the Fantasyland rides – Dumbo and Alice's Tea Party and It's A Small World – are always backed up at least to the end of the chute. Some parents have the stupefied looks of ride hypnosis, but most of the faces are alight with joy. The longing for that kind of innocence never quite fades.

As we near the magical grotto, the syrupy sweet chorus of 'It's A Small World After All' envelops us, and I think again of Jenny Doe. As a foster child, she never set foot in a place like this. She never had the chance to believe it was real, or to return later and laugh about how corny it is. Jenny was not my child. But she could have been. She could have been. In the dreadful moment that she told me she thought she was, my fear had testified to the possibility. Our actions have consequences that last long after us, entwining the present with the future in ways we cannot begin to understand. I have resolved a simple thing: I will do those things which make me happy today, and which I can also live with ten years from now.

As Caitlin helps Annie into the flat-bottomed boat, she turns back and looks at me, her green eyes sparkling. My mind is a thousand miles away, and she knows it. She kisses me anyway, pulling me gently back to reality with a warm and promising gesture of love. Caitlin is not a substitute for the wife I lost. She is a different person. Her own person. Sarah will always be the secret sharer in my heart, and in Annie's too. But Annie no longer walks the streets of Disney World with haunted eyes, searching for a face she will never see in life again. And when I make love with Caitlin, holding her tenderly in the dark as Annie sleeps, I push not into the past but into the future.

As the little boat jerks forward off the rollers and settles into the water, I put my arms around Caitlin and Annie and hug them to me with all my strength and soul. Their laughter is like lamplight in the dark.

I can live with this.

24 HOURS

Chapter 1

'The kid always makes it. I told you that.'

Margaret McDill had not seen the man in her life until yesterday, but he had dominated every second of her existence since their meeting. He had told her to call him Joe, and he claimed it was his real name, but she assumed it was an alias. He was a dark-haired, pale-skinned man of about fifty, with deep-set eyes and a coarse five-o'clock shadow. Margaret could not look into his eyes for long. They were dark, furious pools that sucked the life out of her, drained her will. And now they carried knowledge about her that she could not bear.

'I don't believe you,' she said quietly.

Something rippled deep in the dark eyes, like the flick of a fish tail. 'Have I lied to you about anything else?'

'No. But you . . . you let me see your face all night. You won't let me go after that.'

'I told you, the kid always makes it.'

'You're going to kill me and let my son go.'

'You think I'm going to shoot you in broad daylight in front of a freakin' McDonald's?'

'You have a knife in your pocket.'

1

He looked at her with scorn. 'Jesus Christ.'

Margaret looked down at her hands. She didn't want to look at Joe, and she didn't want to chance seeing herself in one of the mirrors. The one at home had been bad enough. She looked like someone who had just come out of surgery, still groggy with anesthesia. An unhealthy glaze filmed her eyes, and even heavy makeup had failed to hide the bruise along her jaw. Four of her painstakingly maintained nails had broken during the night, and there was a long scratch on her inner forearm from the initial scuffle. She tried to remember exactly when that had happened but she couldn't. Her sense of time had abandoned her. She was having trouble keeping her thoughts in order. Even the simplest ones seemed to fall out of sequence by themselves.

She tried to regain control by focusing on her immediate environment. They were sitting in her BMW, in the parking lot of a strip mall, about fifty yards from a McDonald's restaurant. She had often shopped at the mall, at the Barnes & Noble superstore, and also the pet store, for rare tropical fish. Her husband had recently bought a big-screen television at Circuit City, for patient education at his clinic. He was a cardiovascular surgeon. But all that seemed part of someone else's life now. As remote as the bright side of the moon to someone marooned on the dark half. And her son, Peter . . . God alone knew where he was. God and the man beside her.

'I don't care what you do with me,' she said with conviction. 'Just let Peter live. Kill me if you have to, just let my son go. He's only ten years old.'

'If you don't shut up, I might take you up on that,' Joe said wearily.

He started the BMW's engine and switched the air conditioner to high, then lit a Camel cigarette. The cold air blasted smoke all over the interior of the car. Margaret's eyes stung from hours of crying. She turned her head to avoid the smoke, but it was useless.

'Where's Peter now?' she asked, her voice barely a whisper.

Joe took a drag off the Camel and said nothing.

'I said—'

'Didn't I tell you to stop talking?'

Margaret glanced at the pistol lying on the console between the seats. It belonged to her husband. Joe had taken it from her yesterday, but not before she had learned how useless a gun was to her. At least while they had Peter. Some primitive part of her brain still urged her to grab it, but she doubted she could reach the pistol before he did. He was probably waiting for her to try just that. Joe was thin but amazingly strong, another thing she'd learned last night. And his hard-lined face held no mercy.

'He's dead, isn't he,' Margaret heard herself say. 'You're just playing games with me. He's dead and you're going to kill me, too—'

'Jesus *Christ*,' Joe said through clenched teeth. He turned over his forearm and glanced at his watch. He wore it on the inside of his wrist so that Margaret couldn't see the time.

'I think I'm going to be sick,' she said.

'Again?' He punched the number into the BMW's cell phone. As he waited for an answer, he muttered,

3

'I do believe this has been the worst twenty-four hours of my life to date. And that includes our little party.'

She flinched.

'Hey,' he said into the phone. 'You in your spot? . . . Okay. Wait about a minute, then do it.'

Margaret jerked erect, her eyes wide, searching the nearby cars. 'Oh my God. Peter! *Peter!*'

Joe picked up the gun and jammed the barrel into her neck. 'You've come this far, Maggie. Don't blow it now. You remember what we talked about?'

She closed her eyes and nodded.

'I didn't hear you.'

Tears rolled down her cheeks. 'I remember.'

A hundred yards from Margaret McDill's BMW, Peter McDill sat in an old green pickup truck, his eyes shut tight. The truck smelled funny. Good and bad at the same time, like just-cut grass and old motor oil, and really old fast food.

'You can open your eyes now.'

Peter opened his eyes.

The first thing he saw was a McDonald's restaurant. It reassured him after his night of isolation. The McDonald's stood in the middle of a suburban strip mall parking lot. As Peter panned his eyes around the mall, he recognized the stores: Office Depot, Barnes & Noble, the Gateway 2000 store. He'd spent hours in that store. It was only a few miles from his house. He looked down at his wrists, which were bound with duct tape.

'Can you take this off now?'

He asked without looking up. The man behind the wheel of the truck was hard for him to look at. Peter had never seen or heard of Huey before yesterday, but for the last twenty-four hours, he had seen no one else. Huey was six inches taller than his father, and weighed at least three hundred pounds. He wore dirty mechanic's coveralls and heavy plastic glasses of a type Peter had seen in old movies, with thick lenses that distorted his eyes. He reminded Peter of a character in a movie he'd seen on the satellite one night, when he sneaked into the home theater room. A movie his parents wouldn't let him watch. The character's name was Carl, and the boy who was Carl's friend in the movie said he sounded like a motorboat. Carl was nice, but he killed people, too. Peter thought Huey was probably like that.

'When I was a little boy,' Huey said, peering thoughtfully through the windshield of the pickup, 'those golden arches went all the way over the top of the restaurant. The whole place looked like a space-ship.' He looked back at Peter, his too-big eyes apologetic behind the thick glasses. 'I'm sorry I had to tape you up. But you shouldn't of run. I told you not to run.'

Peter's eyes welled with tears. 'Where's my mom? You said she was going to be here.'

'She's gonna be here. She's probably here already.'

Through the heat shimmering off the asphalt, Peter scanned the sea of parked cars, his eyes darting every-where, searching for his mother's BMW. 'I don't see her car.'

Huey dug down into his front coverall pocket.

Peter instinctively slid against the door of the pickup truck.

'Look, boy,' Huey said in his deep but childlike voice. 'I made you something.'

The giant hand emerged from the pocket and opened to reveal a carved locomotive. Peter had watched Huey whittling for much of the previous afternoon, but he hadn't been able to tell what Huey was working on. The little train in the massive palm looked like a toy from an expensive store. Huey put the carving into Peter's bound hands.

'I finished it while you was sleeping,' he said. 'I like trains. I rode one once. When I was little. From St Louis, after Mamaw died. Joey rode up by hisself on the train and got me. We rode back together. I got to sit in the front with the rich people. We wasn't supposed to, but Joey figured a way. Joey's smart. He said it was only fair. He says I'm good as anybody. Ain't nobody no better than nobody else. That's a good thing to remember.'

Peter stared at the little locomotive. There was even a tiny engineer inside.

'Whittlin's a good thing, too,' Huey went on. 'Keeps me from being nervous.'

Peter closed his eyes. 'Where's my mom?'

'I liked talking to you. Before you ran, anyway. I thought you was my friend.'

Peter covered his face with his hands, but he kept an eye on Huey through a crack between his left cheek and palm. Now that he knew where he was, he thought about jumping out. But Huey was faster than he looked.

Huey dug into his coveralls again and brought out his pocket-knife. When he opened the big blade, Peter pressed himself into the passenger door.

'What are you doing?'

Huey grabbed Peter's bound wrists and jerked them away from his body. With a quick jab he thrust the knife between Peter's forearms and sawed through the duct tape. Then he reached over and unlocked the passenger door of the truck.

'Your mama's waiting for you. In the playground. At the McDonald's.'

Peter looked up at the giant's face, afraid to believe.

'Go see her, boy.'

Peter pushed open the truck's door, jumped to the pavement, and started running toward the MacDonald's.

Joe reached across Margaret McDill's lap and opened the passenger door of the BMW. His smoky black hair brushed against her neck as he did, and she shuddered. She had seen his gray roots during the night.

'Your kid's waiting in the McDonald's Playland,' he said.

Margaret's heart lurched. She looked at the open door, then back at Joe, who was caressing the BMW's leather-covered steering wheel.

'Sure wish I could keep this ride,' he said with genuine regret. 'Got used to this. Yes, sir.'

'Take it.'

'That's not part of the plan. And I always stick to the plan. That's why I'm still around.'

As she stared, he opened the driver's door, got out, dropped the keys on the seat, and started walking away.

Margaret sat for a moment without breathing, mistrustful as an injured animal being released into the wild. Then she bolted from the car. With a spastic gait born from panic and exhaustion, she ran towards the McDonald's, gasping a desperate mantra: '*The Lord is my shepherd, I shall not want. . . . The Lord is my shepherd, I shall not want. . . . The Lord is my shepherd . . .*'

Huey stopped his green pickup beside his cousin Joe with a screech of eroded brake pads. Two men standing under the roofed entrance of the Barnes & Noble looked over at the sound. They looked like bums hoping to pass themselves off as customers and spend the morning reading the papers on the sofas inside the bookstore. Joe Hickey silently wished them good luck. He'd been that far down before.

When he climbed into the cab, Huey looked at him with the relief of a two-year-old at its returning mother.

'Hey, Joey,' Huey said, his head bobbing with relief and excitement.

'Twenty-three hours, ten minutes,' Hickey said, tapping his watch. 'Cheryl's got the money, nobody got hurt, and no FBI in sight. I'm a goddamn genius, son. Master of the universe.'

'I'm just glad it's over,' said Huey. 'I was scared this time.'

Hickey laughed and tousled the hair on Huey's great

unkempt head. 'Home free for another year, Buckethead.'

A smile slowly appeared on the giant's rubbery face. 'Yeah.' He put the truck into gear, eased forward, and joined the flow of traffic leaving the mall.

Peter McDill stood in the McDonald's Playland like a statue in a hurricane. Toddlers and teenagers tore around him with abandon, leaping on and off the foam-padded playground equipment in their sock feet. The screeches and laughter were deafening. Peter searched among them for his mother, his eyes wet. In his right hand he clutched the carved locomotive Huey had given him, utterly unaware that he was holding it.

The glass door of the restaurant opened, and a woman with frosted hair and wild eyes appeared in it. She looked like his mother, but not exactly. This woman was different somehow. She looked too old, and her clothes were torn. She pushed two children out of the doorway, which his mother would never do, and began looking frantically around the playground. Her gaze jumped from child to child, lighted on Peter, swept on, then returned.

'Mom?' he said uncertainly.

The woman's face seemed to collapse inward upon itself. She rushed to Peter and crushed him against her, then lifted him into her arms. His mother hadn't done that in a long, long time. A terrible wail burst from her throat, freezing the storm of children into a still life.

'Oh, dear Jesus,' Margaret keened. 'My baby, my baby, my sweet baby . . .'

Peter felt hot tears rolling down his cheeks. As his mother squeezed him, the little wooden train dropped from his hand onto the pebbled concrete. A toddler wandered over, picked it up, smiled, and walked away with it.

Chapter 2

ONE YEAR LATER

Will Jennings swung his Ford Expedition around a dawdling tanker truck and swerved back into the right lane of the airport road. The field was less than a mile away, and he couldn't keep from watching the planes lifting over the trees as they took off. It had been nearly a month since he'd been up, and he was anxious to fly.

'Keep your eyes on the road,' said his wife from the seat beside him.

Karen Jennings was thirty-nine, a year younger than her husband, but much older in some ways.

'Daddy's watching the airplanes!' Abby chimed from her safety seat in the back. Though only five-and-a-half years old, their daughter never hesitated to interject her comments into any conversation. Will looked at his rearview mirror and smiled at Abby. Facially, she was a miniature version of Karen, with strawberry-blond curls, piercing green eyes, and a light dusting of freckles across her nose. As he watched, she pointed at the back of her mother's head.

Will laid his right hand on Karen's knee. 'I sure wish my girls would come along with old Dad.' With Abby present, he often referred to himself as 'Dad' and Karen as 'Mom', the way his father had done. 'Just jump in the plane and forget about everything for three days.'

'Can we, Mom?' cried Abby. 'Can we?'

'And what do we wear for clothes?' Karen asked in a taut voice.

'I'll buy you both new wardrobes on the coast.'

'Yaaayy!' Abby cheered. 'Look, there's the airport!'

The white control tower of the terminal had come into sight.

'We don't have any insulin,' Karen pointed out.

'Daddy can write me a subscription!'

'*Pre*scription, honey,' Will corrected.

'She knows the right word.'

'I want to go to the beach!'

'I can't believe you started this again,' Karen said under her breath. 'Daddy won't be spending any time at the beach, honey. He'll be nervous as a cat until he gives his lecture to all those other doctors. Then they'll spend hours talking about their days in medical school. And then he'll tear up his joints trying to play golf for three days straight.'

'If you come,' Will said, 'we can beat the bushes around Ocean Springs for some undiscovered Walter Anderson stuff.'

'*Noooo*,' Abby said in a plaintive voice. She hated their art-buying explorations, which usually entailed hours of searching small-town back streets, and some-times waiting in the car. '*You* won't be playing golf, Mom. You can take me to the beach.'

'Yeah, Mom,' Will echoed.

Karen cut her eyes at him. Full of repressed anger, they flashed like green warning beacons. 'I agreed to chair this flower show two *years* ago. It's the sixtieth anniversary of the Junior League, and I don't know whose brilliant idea it was to have a flower show, but it's officially *my* problem. I've put off everything until the last minute, and there are over four hundred exhibitors.'

'You got everything nailed down day before yesterday,' Will told her. There wasn't much use in pressing the issue, but he felt he should try. Things had been tense for the past six months, and this would be the first trip he had made without Karen in a long time. It seemed symbolic, somehow. 'You're just going to agonize until the whole circus starts on Monday. Four nights of hell. Why not blow it off until then?'

'I can't do it,' she said with a note of finality. 'Drop it.'

Will sighed and watched a 727 lift over the treeline to his left.

Karen leaned forward and switched on the CD player, which began to thump out the teen dance groove of Britney Spears. Abby immediately began to sing along. '*Hit me baby one more time . . .*'

'Now, if you want to take Abby by yourself,' Karen said, 'you can certainly do that.'

'What did you say, Mom?'

'You know I can't,' Will said with exasperation.

'You mean you can't do that *and* play golf with your med school buddies. Right?'

Will felt the old weight tighten across his chest. 'This is once a year, Karen. I'm giving the keynote speech, and the whole thing is very political. You know that. With the new drug venture, I'll have to spend hours with the Searle people—'

'You don't have to explain,' she said with satisfaction. 'Just don't try to make me blow off my obligations when you won't do the same.'

Will swung the Expedition into the general aviation area. Lines of single- and twin-engine planes waited on the concrete apron, tethered to rings set in the cement, their wheels chocked against the wind. Just seeing them lightened his heart.

'You're the one who encouraged me to be more social,' Karen said in the strained voice she'd used earlier.

'I'm not joining the Junior League when I grow up,' Abby said from the backseat. 'I'm going to be a pilot.'

'I thought you were going to be a doctor,' said Will.

'A flying doctor, silly!'

'Flying doctor sure beats housewife,' Karen said *sotto voce*.

Will took his wife's hand as he braked beside his Beechcraft Baron 58. 'She's only five, babe. One day she'll understand what you sacrificed.'

'She's almost six. And sometimes I don't understand it myself.'

He squeezed Karen's hand and gave her an understanding look. Then he got out, unstrapped Abby from her child seat, and set her on the apron.

The Baron was ten years old, but she was as fine a piece of machinery as you could ask for, and Will owned her outright. From the twin Continental engines to the state-of-the-art avionics package, he had spared neither time nor expense to make her as safe and airworthy as any billionaire's Gulfstream IV. She was white with blue stripes, and her tail read *N-2WJ*. The 'WJ' was a touch of vanity, but Abby loved hearing the controllers call out *November-Two-Whiskey-Juliet* over the radio. When they were flying together, she sometimes made him call her *Alpha Juliet*.

As Abby ran toward the Baron, Will took a suit bag and a large leather sample case from the back of the Expedition and set them on the concrete. He had driven out during his lunch hour and checked the plane from nose to tail, and also loaded his golf clubs. When he reached back into the SUV for his laptop computer case, Karen picked up the sample case and suit bag and carried them to the plane. The Baron seated four passengers aft of the cockpit, so there was plenty of room. As they loaded the luggage, Karen said:

'You're having pain today, aren't you?'

'No,' he lied, closing the cabin door as though the fire in his hands did not exist. Under normal circumstances he would have canceled his flight and taken a car, but it was far too late now to reach the Gulf Coast except by air.

Karen looked into his eyes, started to say something, then decided against it. She walked the length of the wing and helped Abby untether it while Will did his preflight walkaround. As he checked the aircraft, he glanced over and watched Abby work. She was her mother's daughter from the neck up, but she had Will's lean musculature and length of bone. She loved helping with the plane, being part of things.

15

'What's the flight time to the coast?' Karen asked, joining him behind the wing. 'Fifty minutes?'

'Thirty-five minutes to the airport, if I push it.' Will was due to give his lecture at the Beau Rivage Casino Hotel in Biloxi at seven P.M., which would open the annual meeting of the Mississippi Medical Association. 'I'm cutting it a little close,' he conceded. 'That aneurysm ran way over. I'll call you after my presentation.' He pointed to the beeper on his belt. 'If you want me during the flight, use the SkyTel. It's new. Digital. Hardly any dead spots.'

'Mr High-Tech,' Karen said, making clear that she wasn't impressed with what she considered boy toys. 'I just type in the message at home and send it like e-mail?'

'Right. There's a special Web page for it. But if you don't want to fool with that, just call the answering service. They'll get the message to me.'

Abby tugged at his hand. 'Will you wiggle the wings after you take off?'

'You mean *waggle* the wings. Sure I will. Just for you. Now . . . who gets the first kiss?'

'Me! Me!' Abby cried.

As Will bent down, she turned aside his kiss and whispered in his ear. He nodded, rose, and walked to Karen. 'She said Mommy needs the first kiss today.'

'I wish Daddy were as perceptive.'

He gently took her by the waist. 'Thanks for giving me time last night to finish up the video segment. I'd have been laughed out of the conference.'

'You've never been laughed at in your life.' Her face softened. 'How are your hands? I mean it, Will.'

'Stiff,' he admitted. 'But not too bad.'

'You taking anything?'

'Just the methotrexate.' Methotrexate was a chemotherapeutic agent developed for use against cancer, but, in much smaller doses, was used against Will's form of arthritis. Even small doses could damage the liver.

'*Come on,*' she pressed.

'Okay, four Advil. But that's it. I'm fine. Good to go.' He slipped an arm around Karen's shoulder. 'Don't forget to turn on the alarm system when you get home.'

She shook her head in a way that conveyed several emotions at once: concern, irritation, and somewhere in there, love. 'I never forget. Say good-bye, Abby. Daddy's late.'

Abby hugged his waist until at last he bent and picked her up. His sacroiliac joints protested, but he forced a smile.

'I'll be back Sunday night,' he said, and kissed her on the forehead. 'You take care of Mom. And don't give her any trouble about your shots.'

'But it doesn't hurt as much when you do it.'

'That's a fib. Mom's given a lot more shots than I have.'

He set her down with a muffled groan and gently pushed her toward her mother. Abby walked backward, her eyes locked on Will until Karen scooped her up.

'Oh!' Karen said. 'I forgot to tell you. Microsoft is going to split again. It was up twelve points when I left the house.'

He smiled. 'Forget Microsoft. Tonight starts the ball

17

rolling on Restorase.' Restorase was the trade name of a new drug Will had helped develop, and the subject of his presentation tonight. 'In thirty days, Abby will be set for Harvard, and you can start wearing haute couture.'

'I'm thinking Brown,' Karen said with a grudging laugh.

It was an old joke between them, started in the days when they had so little money that a trip to Wendy's Hamburgers was a treat. Now they could actually afford those schools, but the joke took them back to what in some ways had been a happier time.

'I'll see you both Sunday,' Will said. He climbed into the Baron, started the twin engines, and checked the wind conditions with ATIS on the radio. After contacting ground control, he waved through the plexiglass, and began his taxi toward the runway.

Outside, Karen backed toward the Expedition with Abby in her arms. 'Come on, honey. It's hot. We can watch him take off inside the truck.'

'But I want him to see me!'

Karen sighed. 'All right.'

Inside the Baron, Will acknowledged final clearance from the tower, then released his brakes and roared up the sunny runway. The Baron lifted into the sky like a tethered hawk granted freedom. Instead of simply banking to his left to head south, he executed a teardrop turn, which brought him right over the black Expedition on the ground. He could see Karen and Abby standing beside it. As he passed over at six hundred feet, he waggled his wings like a fighter pilot signaling to friendly ground troops.

On the concrete below, Abby whooped with glee. 'He did it, Mom! He did it!'

'I'm sorry we couldn't go this time, honey,' Karen said, squeezing her shoulders.

'That's okay,' Abby reached up and took her mother's hands. 'You know what?'

'What?'

'I like arranging flowers, too.'

Karen smiled and lifted Abby into her seat, then hugged her neck. 'I think we can win the three-color ribbon if we give it half a try.'

'I know we can!' Abby agreed.

Karen climbed into the driver's seat, started the Expedition, and drove along the line of airplanes toward the gate.

Fifteen miles north of the airport, a battered green pickup truck with a lawn tractor and two weed-eaters in back rattled along a curving lane known for over a hundred years as Crooked Mile Road. The truck slowed, then stopped beside a wrought-iron mailbox at the foot of a high wooded hill. An ornamental World War One biplane perched atop the mailbox, and below the biplane, gold letters read: *Jennings, #100*. The pickup turned left and chugged slowly up the steep driveway.

At the top, set far back on the hill, stood a breathtaking Victorian house. Wedgwood blue with white gingerbread trim and stained-glass windows on the second floor, it seemed to watch over the expansive lawns around it with proprietary interest.

When the pickup truck reached the crest of the drive, it did not stop but continued fifty yards across the St Augustine grass until it reached an ornate playhouse. An exact replica of the main house, the playhouse stood in the shadow of the pine and oak trees that bordered the lawn. The pickup stopped beside it. When the engine died, there was silence but for birdcalls and the ticking of the motor.

The driver's door banged open, and Huey Cotton climbed out. Clad in his customary brown coveralls and heavy black eyeglasses, he stared at the playhouse with wonder in his eyes. Its roof peaked just above the crown of his head.

'See anybody?' called a voice from the passenger window of the truck.

Huey didn't take his eyes from the enchanting playhouse. 'It's like Disneyland, Joey.'

'Christ, look at the real house, would you?'

Huey walked around the playhouse and looked across a glittering blue swimming pool to the rear elevation of the main house. Peeking from two of the four garage bays were a silver Toyota Avalon and the white nose of a powerboat.

'There's a pretty boat in the garage,' he said distractedly. He turned back to the playhouse, bent, and examined it more closely. 'I wonder if there's a boat in this garage?'

As Huey studied the little house, Joe Hickey climbed out of the truck. He wore a new Ralph Lauren Polo shirt and Tommy Hilfiger khakis, but he didn't look natural or even comfortable in the costume. The lower half of a crude eagle tattoo showed on his biceps below the band of the Polo's left sleeve.

'Look at the real house, Buckethead. See the third downstairs window from the end? That's it.'

Huey straightened and glanced over at the main house. 'I see it.' He laid one of his huge hands on the playhouse's porch roof. 'I sure wish I could fit in *this* house. I bet the whole world looks different from in there.'

'You'll never know how different.' Hickey reached into the truck bed and took out a rusted toolbox. 'Let's take care of the alarm system.'

He led Huey toward the open garage.

Twenty minutes later they emerged from the back door of the house and stood on the fieldstone patio.

'Put the toolbox back in the truck,' Hickey said. 'Then wait behind the playhouse. As soon as they go inside, you run up to the window. Got it?'

'Just like last time.'

'There wasn't any freakin' Disneyland playhouse last time. And that was a year ago. I don't want you fooling around back there. The second you hear the garage door close, get your big ass up to that window. If some nosy neighbor drives up in the meantime and asks you a question, you're with the lawn service. Act like a retard. It shouldn't be much of a stretch for you.'

Huey stiffened. 'Don't say that, Joey.'

'If you're waiting at the window when you're supposed to be, I'll apologize.'

Huey smiled crookedly, exposing yellowed teeth. 'I

21

hope this one's nice. I hope she don't get scared easy. That makes me nervous.'

'You're a regular John Dillinger, aren't you? Christ. Get behind the playhouse.'

Huey shrugged and shambled across the patio toward the tree line. When he reached the playhouse, he looked around blankly at Hickey, then folded his giant frame into a squat.

Hickey shook his head, turned, and walked into the house through the back door.

Karen and Abby sang at the top of their voices as they rolled north on Interstate 55, the tune one from *The Sound of Music*, Abby's favorite musical. The Jenningses lived just west of Annandale in Madison County, Mississippi. Annandale was the state's premier golf course, but it wasn't golf that had drawn them to the area. Fear of crime and the race problems of the capital city had driven many young professionals to the gated enclaves of Madison County, but Karen and Will had moved for a different reason. If you wanted land, you had to move north. The Jennings house sat on twenty acres of pine and hardwood, twelve miles north of Jackson proper, and in evening traffic it took twenty-five minutes to get there.

'*That will bring us back to doe, oh, oh, oh. . . .*'

Abby clapped her hands and burst into laughter. Breathing hard from the singing, Karen reached down and punched a number into her cell phone. She felt guilty about the way she'd spoken to Will at the airport.

'Anesthesiology Associates,' said a woman, her voice tinny in the cell phone speaker.

'Is this the answering service?' asked Karen.

'Yes ma'am. A-1 Answer-all. The clinic's closed.'

'I'd like to leave a message for Dr Jennings. This is his wife.'

'Go ahead.'

'We already miss you. Break a leg tonight. Love, Karen and Abby.'

'With sugar and kisses on top!' Abby shouted from the backseat.

'Did you get that last part?' asked Karen.

'With sugar and kisses on top,' repeated the bored voice.

'Thank you.'

Karen hit END and looked at her rearview mirror, which was adjusted so that she could see Abby's face.

'Daddy loves getting messages from us,' Abby said, smiling.

'He sure does, honey.'

Fifty miles south of Jackson, Will settled the Baron in at eight thousand feet. Below him lay a puffy white carpet of cumulus clouds, before him a sky as blue as an Arctic lake. Visibility was unlimited. As he bent his wrist to check his primary GPS unit, a burning current of pain shot up the radial nerve in his right arm. It was worse than he'd admitted to Karen, and she'd known it. She didn't miss anything. The truth was, she didn't want him flying anymore. A month ago, she'd threatened to tell the FAA that he was 'cheating' to pass his flight physicals. He didn't think she would, but he couldn't be sure. If she thought Will's arthritis put him – and thus the family – at risk while flying, she wouldn't hesitate to do whatever she had to do to stop him.

If she did, Will wasn't sure he could handle it. Even the thought of being grounded put him in a black mood. Flying was more than recreation for him. It was a physical expression of how far he had come in life, a symbol of all he had attained, and of the lifestyle he had created for his family. His father could never have dreamed of owning a three-hundred-thousand-dollar airplane. Tom Jennings had never even *ridden* in an airplane. His son had paid cash for one.

But for Will the money was not the important thing. It was what the money could buy. Security. He had learned that lesson a thousand times growing up: money was an insulator, like armor. It protected people who had it from the everyday problems that besieged and even destroyed others. And yet, it did not make you invulnerable. His arthritis had taught him that. Other lessons followed.

In 1986, he graduated from LSU medical school and began an obstetrics residency at the University of Mississippi Medical Center in Jackson. It was there that he met a surgical nurse with stunning green eyes, strawberry-blond hair, and a reputation for refusing dates with physicians or medical students. After three months of patience and charm, Will persuaded Karen to meet him for lunch, far from the hospital. There he discovered that the cause of her dating policy was simple: she'd seen too many nurses put medical students through school only to be cast aside later, and others caught in messy triangles with married doctors and their wives. In spite of her policy, she dated Will for the next two years – first secretly, then openly – and after a year-long engagement, they married. Will entered private practice with a Jackson OB/GYN group the day after his honeymoon, and their adult life together began like a storybook.

But during the second year of his practice, he began experiencing pain in his hands, feet, and lower back. He tried to ignore it, but soon the pain was interfering with his work, and he went to see a friend in the rheumatology department. A week later he was diagnosed with psoriatic arthritis, a severe, often crippling disease. Continuing as an obstetrician was impossible, so he began to investigate less physically rigorous fields like dermatology and radiology. His old college roommate suggested anesthesiology – his own specialty – a three-year program if the university would credit Will's OB experience and let him skip the internship year. It did, and in 1993, he began his anesthesiology residency at UMC in Jackson.

The same month, Karen quit her nursing job and enrolled at nearby Millsaps College for twenty-two hours of basic sciences in the premed program. Karen had always felt she aimed too low with nursing – and Will agreed – but her decision stunned him. It meant they would have to put off having children for several more years, and it would also force them to take on more debt than Will felt comfortable with. But he wanted Karen to be happy. While he trained for his new specialty and learned to deal with the pain of his disease, she racked up four semesters of perfect grades and scored in the ninety-sixth percentile on the Medical College Admissions Test. Will was as proud as he was surprised, and Karen was luminous with happiness. It almost seemed as though Will's disease had been a gift.

Then, during Karen's freshman year of medical school – the third year of Will's residency – she got pregnant. She had never been able to take the pill, and the less certain methods of birth control had finally failed. Will was surprised but happy; Karen was devastated. She believed that keeping the baby would mean the death of her dream of being a doctor. Will was forced to concede that she was probably right. For three agonizing weeks, she considered an abortion. The fact that she was thirty-three finally convinced her to keep the baby. She managed to complete her freshman year of med school, but after Abby was born, there was no question of continuing. She withdrew from the university the day Will completed his residency, and while Will joined the private anesthesiology group led by his old roommate, Karen went home to prepare for motherhood.

They made a commitment to go forward without regrets, but it didn't work out that way. Will was phenomenally successful in his work, and Abby brightened their lives in ways he could never have imagined. But Karen's premature exit from medical school haunted her. Over the next couple of years, her resentment began to permeate their marriage, from dinner conversations to their sex life. Or more accurately, their lack of one. Will tried to discuss it with her, but his attempts only seemed to aggravate the situation. He responded by focusing on his work and on Abby, and whatever energy he had left he used to fight his slowly progressing arthritis.

He treated himself, which conventional wisdom declared folly, but he had studied his condition until he knew more about it than most rheumatologists. He had done the same with Abby's juvenile diabetes. Being his own doctor allowed him to do things he otherwise might not have been allowed to, like flying. On good days the pain didn't interfere with his control of the aircraft, and Will only flew on good days. Using this rationale, he had medicated himself to get through the flight physical, and the limited documentary records of his disease made it unlikely that his deception would ever be discovered. He only wished the problems in his marriage were as easy to solve.

A high-pitched beeping suddenly filled the Baron's cockpit. Will cursed himself for letting his attention wander. Scanning the instrument panel for the source of the alarm, he felt a hot tingle of anxiety along his arms. He saw nothing out of order, which made him twice as anxious, certain that he was missing something right in front of his eyes. Then relief washed through him. He reached down to his waist, pulled the new SkyTel off his belt, and hit the retrieve button. The alphanumeric pager displayed a message in green back-lit letters:

WE ALREADY MISS YOU. BREAK A LEG TONIGHT. LOVE KAREN AND ABBY. WITH SUGAR AND KISSES ON TOP.

Will smiled and waggled the Baron's wings against the cerulean sky.

Karen stopped the Expedition beside her mailbox and shook her head at the bronze biplane mounted atop it. She had always thought the decoration juvenile. Reaching into the box, she withdrew a thick handful of envelopes and magazines and skimmed through them. There were brokerage statements, party invitations, copies of *Architectural Digest*, *Mississippi Magazine*, and *The New England Journal of Medicine*.

'Did I get any letters?' Abby asked from the backseat.

'You sure did.' Karen passed a powder blue envelope over the front seat. 'I think that's for Seth's birthday party.'

Abby opened the invitation as Karen climbed the long incline of the drive. 'How long till *my* birthday?'

'Three more months. Sorry, Charlie.'

'I don't like being five and a half. I want to be six.'

'Don't be in too much of a hurry. You'll be thirty-six before you know it.'

When the house came into sight, Karen felt the ambivalence that always suffused her at the sight of it. Her first emotion was pride. She and Will had designed the house, and she had handled all the contracting work herself. Despite the dire warnings of friends, she had enjoyed this, but when the family finally moved in, she had felt more anticlimax than accomplishment. She could not escape the feeling that she'd constructed her own prison, a gilded cage like all the others on Crooked Mile Road, each inhabited by its own Mississippi version of Martha Stewart, the new millennium's Stepford wives.

Karen pulled into the garage bay nearest the laundry room entrance. Abby unhooked her own safety straps but waited for her mother to open the door.

'Let's get some iced tea,' Karen said, setting Abby on the concrete. 'How do you feel?'

'Good.'

'Did you tee-tee a lot this afternoon?'

'No. I need to go now, though.'

'All right. We'll check your sugar after. Then we'll get the tea. We're going to have some fun today, kid. Just us girls.'

Abby grinned, her green eyes sparkling. 'Just us girls!'

Karen opened the door that led from the laundry room to the walk-through pantry and kitchen. Abby squeezed around her and went inside. Karen followed but stopped at the digital alarm panel on the laundry room wall and punched in the security code.

'All set,' she called, walking through the pantry to the sparkling white kitchen. 'You want crackers with your tea?'

'I want Oreos!'

Karen squeezed Abby's shoulder. 'You know better than that.'

'It's only a little while till my shot, Mom. Or you could give me that new kind of shot right now. Couldn't you?'

Abby was too smart for her own good. Conventional forms of insulin had to be injected thirty minutes to an hour before meals, which made controlling juvenile diabetes difficult. If a child lost its appetite after the shot and refused to eat, as children often did, blood sugar could plummet to a dangerous level. To solve this problem, a new form of insulin called Humalog had been developed, which was absorbed by human cells almost instantly. It could be injected right before a meal, during the meal, or even just after. Physicians like Will were some of the first to get access to the drug, and its convenience had revolutionized the daily lives of families with diabetic children. However, Humalog also tempted children to break their dietary rules, since they knew that an 'antidote' was near to hand.

'No Oreos, kiddo,' Karen said firmly.

'*Okay*,' Abby griped. 'Iced tea with a lemon. I'm going to tee-tee.'

'I'll have it waiting when you get back.'

Abby paused at the hall door. 'Will you come with me?'

'You're a big girl now. You know where the light is. I'm going to fix the tea while you're gone.'

'*Okay*.'

As Abby trudged up the hallway, Karen looked down at *The New England Journal of Medicine* and felt the twinge of anger and regret she always did when confronted by tangible symbols of the profession she'd been forced to abandon. She was secretly glad that the flower show had given her an excuse to miss the medical convention, where she would be relegated to 'wife' status by men who couldn't have stayed within fifteen points of her in a chemistry class. Next month, Will's drug research would be published in this very magazine, while she would be entangled in the next Junior League service project. She shoved the magazine across the counter with the rest of the mail and opened the stainless-steel refrigerator.

Every appliance in the kitchen was a Viking. The upscale appliances were built in Greenville, Mississippi, and since Will had done the epidurals on two pregnant wives from the 'corporate family,' the Jennings house boasted a kitchen that could have been featured in the *AD* that had come in today's mail – at a discounted price, of course. Karen had grown up with a noisy old Coldspot from Sears, and a clothesline to dry the wash. She could appreciate luxury, but she knew there was more to life than a showpiece home and flower shows. She took the tea pitcher from the Viking, set it on the counter, and began slicing a lemon.

Abby slowed her pace as she moved up the dark hallway. Passing her bedroom, she glanced through the half-open door. Her dolls were arranged against the headboard of her tester bed, just as she'd left them in the morning. Barbies, Beatrix Potter bunnies, and Beanie-Babies, all mixed together like a big family. The way she liked them.

Five more steps carried her to the hall bathroom, where she stretched on tiptoe to reach the light switch. She pulled up her jumper and used the commode, glad that she didn't tee-tee very much. That meant her sugar was okay. After fixing her clothes, she climbed up on a stool before the basin and carefully washed and dried her hands. Then she started for the kitchen, leaving the bathroom light on in case she needed to come back.

As she passed her bedroom, she noticed a funny smell. Her dolls all looked happy, but something didn't seem right. She started to walk in and check, but her mother's voice echoed up the hall, saying the tea was ready.

When Abby turned away from the bedroom, something gray fluttered in front of her eyes. She instinctively swatted the air, as she would at a spiderweb, but her hand hit something solid behind the gray. The gray thing was a towel, and there was a hand inside it. The hand clamped the towel over her nose, mouth, and one eye, and the strange smell she'd noticed earlier swept into her lungs with each gasp.

Terror closed her throat too tightly to scream. She tried to fight, but another arm went around her stomach and lifted her into the air, so that her kicking legs flailed uselessly between the wide-spaced walls of the hallway. The towel was cold against her face. For an instant Abby wondered if her daddy had come home early to play a joke on her. But he couldn't have. He was in his plane. And he would never scare her on purpose. Not *really*. And she was scared. As scared as the time she'd gone into ketoacidosis, her thoughts flying out of her ears as soon as she could think of them, her voice speaking words no one had ever heard before. She tried to fight the monster holding her, but the harder she fought, the weaker she became. Suddenly everything began to go dark, even the eye that was uncovered. She concentrated as hard as she could on saying one word, the only word that could help her now. With a great feeling of triumph, she said, 'Mama,' but the word died instantly on the wet towel.

Huey Cotton stood outside the Jennings house, nervously rubbing his palms against the legs of his coveralls and peering through Abby's bedroom window. *Abby*. Unlike most names, he could remember that one without trouble. His mother had once read letters to a woman named Abby out loud to him. *Dear Abby*, she would drawl in her cigarette-parched voice, sitting at the kitchen table in her hair-rollers and house-coat. The people who wrote to that Abby never signed their real names. They were embarrassed, his mother said. They signed big words instead of names, and sometimes they signed places, too, like *Bewildered in Omaha*. He always remembered that one.

Huey heard the scuff of a heel on wood. He looked up to see his cousin walking through the pink bedroom with the little Abby in his arms. She was fighting, kicking her skinny legs to beat the band. Joey held her at the center of the room so that her feet wouldn't hit the furniture or the tall bedposts. The kicks got weaker and weaker until finally they were just little jerks, like a hound's legs when it dreamed of hunting.

The little girl looked like another of the hundred or so dolls that lay around the room like the sleeping occupants of some fairyland, only bigger. Joey walked to the open window and passed her through it. Huey accepted Abby as gingerly as he would a wounded bird, his mouth open in wonder.

'You're a genius,' Joey said, a crooked grin on his

face. 'I apologize, okay? She'll be out for two to four hours. Plenty of time.'

'You're going to call me, right?' Huey asked.

'Every thirty minutes. Don't say anything but "hello," unless I ask you a question. And shut off the cell phone when you get there. Just cut it on for the check-in calls. And remember the backup plan, right?'

'I remember.'

'Good. Now, get going.'

Huey turned away and started to walk, then stopped and turned back.

'What's wrong now?' Joey asked.

'Can she have one of her dolls?'

Joey leaned back inside the window, snatched up a gowned Barbie off the bed, and handed it out. Huey took it between Abby's hip and his little finger.

'Don't crank the truck till you hit the road,' Joey said.

'I know.'

Carrying Abby with maternal care, Huey turned and lumbered toward the playhouse and his concealed pickup truck, the gold-lamé gown of the Barbie fluttering behind him like a tiny flag.

Karen stood at the kitchen counter, thumbing through the *NEJM* in spite of her resentment. Two sweating glasses of iced tea stood on the counter beside her, bright yellow lemon rinds hooked over the rims. Beside the glasses lay a plastic device for pricking Abby's finger; it looked like a ballpoint pen. Without taking her eyes from the magazine, Karen called: 'Abby? You okay, sweetie?'

There was no answer.

She took a sip of tea and kept reading, thankful for a few moments of silence before the maddening last-minute details of the flower show would have to be dealt with.

Beneath the tall, sweet-scented pines behind the play-house, Huey opened the driver's door of his pickup and slid Abby's unconscious body across the bench seat to the passenger side. She lay still as a sleeping angel. Huey watched her for a while. He liked standing on pine needles. They were cushy, like deep carpet. He wished he was barefoot.

Suddenly, an image of his cousin filled his mind. Joey would be really mad if he messed up. He reached into the truck, shifted it into neutral, and pushed it backward around the playhouse like a normal-sized man pushing a motorcycle. After the truck cleared the playhouse, he stopped, shifted his weight forward, and began pushing again, steering the pickup across the yard toward the steep driveway. The yard had a pitch to it, for drainage, and gravity soon began to help him.

When the wheels hit concrete the truck gathered momentum, and Huey tried clumsily to climb inside. He got one foot up on the step, but as he tried to pull himself through the open door, his boot slipped. He stumbled forward, trying to keep his feet under him as the old Chevy raced down the hill. Only the strength in his huge hands kept him and the truck joined as it careened down toward Crooked Mile Road.

Three quarters of the way to the bottom, Huey

flexed his wrists with enough power to snap the tendons of a normal man and dragged himself into the cab by main strength. He hit the brakes just before the truck shot into the road, and the vehicle shuddered to a stop. Abby was thrown forward against the dash, but she did not wake up. Huey pulled her back across the bench seat, her head pillowed on his thigh, then put his hand to her mouth to make sure she was breathing.

After his nerves settled a little, he pulled his door shut, cranked the engine, and turned onto Crooked Mile Road, which led to Highway 463, and from there to Interstate 55. He had a long night ahead.

Karen's ears pricked up at the rumble of a starting engine. It seemed out of place at this time of day. Her neighbors' houses were too far away to hear that sort of thing. She glanced through the kitchen window but saw nothing, as she'd expected. Only one curve of Crooked Mile Road was visible from the house, and the height of their hill hid the intersection of the road and the driveway. Maybe it was a UPS truck running late, making a turn in the drive.

She looked back at the hall door and called, 'Abby? Do you need help, honey?'

Still no answer.

A worm of fear turned in Karen's stomach. She was compulsive about controlling Abby's diabetes, and though she hated to admit it, panic was always just one layer beneath the surface. She put down the magazine and started toward the hall. Relief surged through her as she heard footsteps on the hardwood. She was laughing at herself when a dark-haired man of about fifty walked through the hall door and held up both hands.

Her right hand flew to her heart, and in some sickening subdivision of a second, her mouth went dry, her throat closed, and sweat broke out from the crown of her head to her toes. Almost as quickly, a desperate hope bloomed in her brain. Hope that the stranger's presence was merely a mistake, some crazy mixup, that he was a workman to whom Will had given a key.

But he wasn't. She knew it the way you know about the lump in your breast, an alien thing that shouldn't be there and isn't going anywhere soon except by very unpleasant means. Karen had lost a sister that way. And her father – a Korean War veteran – had taught her very young that this was the way fate came at you: out of the blue, without warning, the worst thing in the world appearing with a leer and a ticking clock.

'Stay calm, Mrs Jennings,' the man said in a reassuring voice. 'Abby's fine. I want you to listen to me. Everything is *o-kay*.'

At the word 'Abby,' tears filled Karen's eyes. The panic that lived beneath her skin burned through to the surface, paralyzing her where she stood. Her chin began to quiver. She tried to scream, but no sound came from her throat.

Chapter 3

As Karen stood gaping, the stranger said, 'My name's Joe, Mrs Jennings. Joe Hickey. I'm going to help you through this thing. And the first thing to remember is that Abby is *absolutely fine.*'

The temporary paralysis caused by seeing a strange man where she had expected Abby finally broke, and Karen jerked as though she had taken a physical blow.

'Abby!' she screamed. 'Come to Mama!'

'Calm down,' the stranger said softly. 'Look at me, not the door. I'm Joe Hickey, okay? I'm telling you my real name because I'm not worried that it's going to matter later. You're never going to report this, because Abby's going to be fine. Everybody's going to be fine. Abby, you, me, everybody. The kid always makes it through. That's my rule.'

Absurdly, Karen flashed onto the movie *The Jungle Book*, which she had watched at least fifty times with Abby. Listening to this man was like listening to Kaa the cobra, who hypnotized you with his voice while he waited for the perfect moment to strike. She shook her head and fixed her mind on Abby's face, and her fear dissolved in a violent rush, replaced by a fury beyond any she had known. The man before her stood between her and her child. If he wanted to keep them apart, he would have to kill her.

Hickey seemed to sense this. 'Abby's not here, Mrs Jennings. She's—'

Karen charged, batting him aside like an old man as she raced into the hallway. She yanked open the bathroom door and, though she found it empty, cried, 'Abby! Abby? Where are you?'

She stood blinking for a moment; then she tore through the ground floor, checking every room and closet. With each empty space that greeted her, dread settled deeper into her bones. She raced up the back stairs and began searching the second floor. Every room was empty. She ran into the main upstairs guest room, picked up the nearest phone, and dialed 911. Instead of a dispatcher's voice, she heard a man speaking in a deep piney woods drawl: '. . . *Preacher Bob's Fount of Life Church is a Full Gospel church, with no wishy-washy bending of the Word, no newfangled editions of the King James—*'

She clicked the disconnect button, but the voice droned on. Hickey must have dialed the prayer line from the kitchen phone and left it off the hook. She slammed down the phone, ran around the bed and picked up the private line. This time a female voice that sounded like an android was speaking.

'. . . *the satellite farm forecast is made possible by a grant from the ChemStar corporation, maker of postemergent broad-spectrum herbicides—*'

Karen dropped the phone and stood staring at herself in the bureau mirror. Her eyes were frantic, blanked out like those you saw in the ERs after motor vehicle accidents. Relatives. Victims. Walking wounded. She needed to calm down, to try to think rationally, but she couldn't. As she struggled to gain control, an image came into her mind with the power of a talisman.

She ran to the back stairs again, but this time she crept down the carpeted steps. When she reached the first floor, she swept up the hallway on tiptoe and darted into the master bedroom, locking the door behind her.

Her heart thumped as though to make up for the beats it had skipped when the stranger first appeared. She put her hands on her cheeks, which felt deathly cold, and took three deep breaths. Then she walked into the closet and stood on the inverted wooden box that gave her access to the top shelf.

Her hand barely reached over the edge, but she felt what she wanted: Will's .38 revolver. She had pleaded with him a hundred times not to keep the pistol in the house with Abby. Now she thanked God he hadn't listened. She pulled down the gun and opened the cylinder, as her father had taught her long ago. *A gun is just a tool, hon, like an axe or a drill . . .* The .38's hammer rested on an empty chamber, but five rounds filled the others.

Karen snapped the cylinder home and walked to the bedroom door, steeling herself with each step, clenching the pistol's checked grip like a lifeline. She was about to face the man who had taken Abby, and she would do whatever was necessary to make him give her back. There was no room for hesitation. Or for mercy.

She quietly opened the door, then edged along the hallway toward the rectangle of light that was the kitchen door. Her breath coming in little pants, she stopped just outside the door and peered into the kitchen.

Joe Hickey was sitting calmly at the kitchen table, drinking from one of the glasses of tea. The realization that she had made that tea for Abby brought a lump to Karen's throat. She stepped into the kitchen, raised the gun, and aimed it at his face.

'Where's my daughter?'

Hickey swallowed some tea and slowly set down the glass. 'You don't want to shoot me, Karen. Can I call you Karen?'

She shook the .38 at him. 'Where's my little girl!'

'Abby is perfectly safe. However, if you shoot me, she'll be stone-dead within thirty minutes. And there won't be a thing I can do about it.'

'Tell me what's happening!'

'Listen carefully, Karen. This is a kidnapping for ransom. Okay? It's about money. M-O-N-E-Y. That's all. So, the last thing I want is for anything to happen to your precious little girl.'

'Where is Abby *right now*?'

'With my cousin. His name's Huey. Right after you got here, I passed her outside and Huey drove her off in his pickup truck. He's got a cell phone with him. . . .'

Hickey kept talking, but Karen couldn't make sense of the words. She couldn't get past the image he'd just described. Abby alone with a stranger. She'd be whimpering in terror, crying for her mother. Karen felt as though she had been pushed from a great height, her stomach rolling over and over as she went into free fall.

'Are you listening, Karen? I said, if I don't call Huey every thirty minutes, he'll kill her. He won't want to, but he will. That's rule number two. So don't get any crazy ideas about calling the police. It would take them an hour just to get me fingerprinted and into lockup, and by the time I saw a pay phone, Abby would be lying dead beside the highway.'

Karen snapped out of her trance.

'But that's not going to happen,' Hickey said, smiling. 'You're a smart girl. And Huey's a good boy. Loves kids. He's practically a kid himself. But he's a little slow. Since I'm the only person who was ever nice to him, he alway does exactly what I tell him. So you want to be real careful with that gun.'

Karen looked at the weapon in her hand. Suddenly it seemed more of a threat to Abby than to the man in front of her.

'You pick things up real quick, I can tell,' Hickey said. 'So keep paying attention. This is a kidnapping-for-ransom, like I said. But it's not like you've seen on TV or in the movies. This isn't the Lindbergh baby. It's not some Exxon executive, buried-alive bullshit. This is a work of art. A perfect crime. I know, because I've done it five times before and I haven't been caught yet. Not even a whiff of Johnny Law.'

Karen pointed to Hickey's left arm, where a poorly inked needlework showed below the band of his sleeve. An eagle holding an iron cross in its talons. 'Isn't that a prison tattoo?'

Hickey's face tightened, then relaxed. 'They busted me for something else. How'd you know that was done in the joint?'

'I don't know.' Karen had seen several tattoos like it on surgical patients in the OR. 'I just know.'

'You're smarter than the average June Cleaver, aren't you? Well, it won't help you any. I own you, lady. And your little girl. You need to remember that.'

Karen forced back fresh tears, unwilling to give Hickey the satisfaction of seeing them. The gun wavered in her hand. She steadied it.

'I know what you're thinking,' he said. 'What happened to the kids those other five times, right?'

She nodded slowly.

'Right this second, every one of them is living a care-free life, watching *Barney* or *Rugrats* or swimming in their private freakin' swimming pool. You know why? Because their mamas didn't shoot me and their daddies were calm and methodical after the first few minutes. Just like you're going to be.' He took another slow sip of tea. 'Needs sugar. I can tell you weren't raised in the country.'

Karen had been raised on rural army bases, but she saw no reason to correct Hickey's impression.

'If that gun happens to go off by accident,' he said, 'Abby will be just as dead as if you shot her. The bullet in that chamber will kill two people, Karen. Something to think about.'

She didn't want to put down the gun, but she saw no choice. She tossed it onto the table beside Hickey, cracking one of the white tiles of its surface.

'Good girl,' he said, leaving the .38 where it had fallen. 'Yes, ma'am, that's exactly what a good mother does in a situation like this. I hope your husband's as smart as you are.'

New fear gripped Karen. 'Where's Will? What have you done with him?'

Hickey made an elaborate show of looking at his watch, which he wore on the inside of his wrist, like certain military officers, as though time were his province alone, and not to be shared with anyone else. 'Right about now, hubby's winged most of his way to Biloxi's *beautiful* Beau Rivage Casino Resort.'

Hickey said this with the exaggerated enthusiasm of a game show huckster, but it was the level of his knowledge that crystalized the fear in Karen. He knew their lives, their plans, their exact schedules—

'After hubby gets checked in, we're going to let him shower up and give his little speech. Then he's going to get a visit from a partner of mine, and he'll find out where things stand. The way you just did. Then we're all going to wait out the night together.'

Terror ballooned in Karen's chest. 'Wait out the night? What are you talking about?'

'This operation takes exactly twenty-four hours. I'm talking from the time Huey and me cranked up this afternoon. A day's work for a year's pay.' Hickey chuckled. 'We've got about twenty hours left to go.'

'But why do we have to wait?' The old panic had come back with a vengeance. 'If you want money, I'll get it for you. All you want. Just bring my baby back!'

Hickey shook his head. 'I know you would, Karen. But that's not the way this operation works. Everything's set up according to a timetable. That way there's no surprises.'

'But we *can't* wait twenty hours!'

'You'd be surprised what you can do for your kid.

This is a nice place. We'll get to know each other a little, have supper, pretend everything's fine. Abby can watch Huey whittle. Before you know it, I'll have my money and you'll have Abby back.'

'*Listen to me, you stupid son of a bitch!*'

Hickey paled. 'You want to watch what you're saying there, Mom. It's not smart under the circumstances.'

Karen tried to keep her voice under control. 'Sir – Mr Hickey – if we wait until tomorrow, Abby is going to die.'

His dark eyes narrowed. 'What are you talking about?'

'Abby's a diabetic. A juvenile diabetic. She'll die without her insulin.'

'Bullshit.'

'My God . . . didn't you *know* that?'

'Talk's cheap. Let's see some proof.'

Karen went to a kitchen drawer and pulled out a plastic bag full of orange-capped syringes with 25-gauge needles. She threw the bag onto the table, then opened the refrigerator, where a dozen glass vials waited in compulsively organized rows. She took out a vial of long-acting insulin and tossed it at Hickey.

He caught it and stared at the label. It read: *Humulin N*. PATIENT: Abigail Jennings. PRESCRIBING PHYSICIAN: Will Jennings, M.D.

'Damn,' Hickey said under his breath. 'I don't believe this.'

'Please,' Karen said in the most submissive voice she could muster. 'We *must* get this medicine to my daughter. She – My God, I didn't check her sugar when we got home.' Karen felt herself falling again, as though the floor beneath her feet had vanished. 'Abby's due for her shot in an hour. We've *got* to get this to her. How far away is she?'

'We can't go,' Hickey said in a flat voice.

Karen grabbed the .38 off the table and pointed it at his chest. 'Oh, yes, we can. We're going right now.'

'I told you about that gun.'

She cocked the revolver. 'If Abby doesn't get her insulin, she's going to die. Now you *do what I say*!'

Something flickered in Hickey's eyes. Amusement. Perhaps surprise. He held up his hands, palms toward Karen. 'Take it easy, Karen. I meant we can't go *yet*. Abby's being transported to a safe place. Maybe we can go later. Tell me about her condition. How critical is it?'

'How critical? She could *die*.'

'How long before she's in trouble?'

Karen did the math in her head. If Abby ate only normal food before falling asleep – if she could sleep at all – she could make it through the night. But Karen had no intention of taking that risk. What if Hickey's cousin fed her candy bars?

'Juvenile diabetics are very unstable,' she said. 'If Abby eats too much sugar, she could get in trouble very quickly. She'll get dehydrated. Then comes abdominal pain and vomiting. Then she'll go into a coma and die. It can happen *very* fast.'

Hickey pursed his lips, obviously doing some mental math of his own. Then he reached over the little built-in desk where Karen paid the household bills, hung up the cordless phone, and punched in a new number.

Karen stepped up to the desk and hit the SPEAKER button on the phone. Hickey looked down, trying to figure out how to switch it off, but before he could, a deep male voice said: 'Joey? Has it been thirty minutes?'

'No. What happened to "hello"?'

'Oh, yeah. I'm sorry.' The man's voice had an incongruous sound, like the voice of a fifty-year-old child. *He's practically a kid himself*, Hickey had said.

'How does the kid look?'

'Okay. She's still sleeping.'

Karen's heart thudded. She jerked the gun. 'Let me talk to her.'

Hickey warned her back with a flip of his hand.

'Who was that, Joey?'

'Betty Crocker.'

'Give me the phone!' Karen demanded.

'Abby can't talk right now. She's sedated.'

Sedated? 'You son of a bitch! You—'

Hickey half rose and slugged Karen in the stomach. The breath left her in an explosive rush, and she dropped to the kitchen floor, the gun clattering uselessly in front of her.

'Touch the kid's chest, Huey. She breathing okay?'

'Kinda shallow. Like a puppy.'

'Okay, that's fine. Look, don't give her any candy bars or anything like that. Okay? Maybe some saltines or something.'

'She needs fluids,' Karen gasped from the floor. 'Plenty of water!'

'Give her some water. Plenty of water.'

'Saltines and water,' Huey echoed.

'I may be coming out to see you tonight.'

Karen felt a surge of hope.

'That'd be good,' Huey said. 'I wouldn't be so nervous.'

'Yeah. Drive slow, okay?'

'Fifty-five,' Huey said dutifully.

'Good boy.'

Hickey hung up and squatted before Karen. 'Here's the deal. Before we do anything, we have to let my partner make contact with your husband. We've got to make sure old Will's on the same page with us before we move. Nobody knows that better than you, right? And with this diabetic thing, he might just flip out. I hope not, because if he does, all the insulin in the world won't save Abby.' Hickey stood. 'We'll take care of your little girl. It's just going to take a couple of hours. Now, get up off that floor.'

He offered his hand, but Karen ignored it. She got her knees beneath her and used the edge of the table to pull herself to her feet. The gun remained on the floor.

He walked past her to the opposite wall of the kitchen, where a four-foot-wide framed silk screen hung. It was a semi-abstract tendering of an alligator, brightly colored like a child's painting, but with the unmistakable strength of genius in it.

'You've got paintings by this guy all over your house,' he said. 'Right?'

'Yes,' Karen replied, her thoughts on Abby. 'Walter Anderson. He's dead.'

'Worth a lot of money?'

'That silk screen isn't. I colored it myself. But the

watercolors are valuable. Do you want them?'

Hickey laughed. 'Want them? I don't give a shit about 'em. And by morning, you're going to hate every one. You're never going to want to see another one again.'

He turned from the painting and smiled.

Forty miles south of Jackson, a small, tin-roofed cabin stood in a thick forest of second-growth pine and hard-woods. An old white AMC Rambler rested on cinder blocks in the small clearing, blotched with primer and overgrown by weeds. A few feet away from the Rambler stood a rusting propane tank with a black hose curled over the valve mechanism. Birdcalls echoed through the small clearing, punctuated by the rapid-fire *pock-pock-pock* of a woodpecker, and gray squirrels chased each other through the upper branches of the oaks.

The animals fell silent. A new sound had entered the woods. A motor. An old one, its valves tapping from unleaded gasoline. The noise grew steadily until the green hood of a pickup truck broke from beneath the trees into dappled sunlight. The truck trundled down the rutted lane and stopped before the cabin porch.

Huey Cotton got out and walked quickly around the hood, the Barbie still sticking out of his pocket. He opened the passenger door and lifted Abby's limp body off the seat. Cradling her like an infant in his massive arms, he closed the truck's door with his hip and walked carefully up the porch steps.

The old planks groaned beneath his weight. He paused before the screen door, then bent at the waist, hooked his sausagelike pinkie in the door handle, and shuffled backward until the screen opened enough for him to thrust his bulk between it and the main door. The main door yielded to one shove of his size-16 Redwing boot. He carried Abby through it, and the screen door slapped shut behind him with a bang.

Will landed the Baron behind a vintage DC-3 he would have loved to get a look at, but today he didn't have the time. He taxied to the general aviation area and pulled into the empty spot indicated to him by a ground crewman. The Gulfport-Biloxi airport housed units of the Army and Air National Guard. There were fighter jets and helicopters stationed around the field, and the resulting high security always gave Will a little shock.

He had radioed ahead and arranged to have his rental car waiting at US Aviation Corp. which handled the needs of private pilots. As soon as the props stopped turning, he climbed out and unloaded his luggage from the cabin. Hanging bag, suitcase, sample case, notebook computer case, golf clubs. Schlepping it all to the blue Ford Tempo made his inflamed sacroiliac joints scream, even through the deadening layer of ibuprofen.

A security guard told him that Interstate 10 East had been closed due to a jackknifed semi-truck, so he would have to take the beachfront highway to Biloxi. Will hoped the traffic was not too bad between the airport and the casino. He had less than an hour to reach the meeting room, and he needed to shower and shave before he took the podium before five hundred physicians and their wives.

It took him five minutes to reach US 90, the highway that ran along the Gulf of Mexico from Bay Saint Louis to the Alabama border and Mobile Bay. The sun was just starting to fall toward New Orleans, sixty miles to the west. It would still be light when he began his lecture. Bathing-suited families walked and flew kites along the beach, but Will saw no one in the water. There were no waves to speak of, and the 'surf' here had always been brown and tepid. The gulf didn't turn its trademark emerald green until you hit Destin, Florida, two hours to the east.

Will didn't particularly like the Mississippi Gulf Coast. He never had. The place had a seedy, transient air. A peeling, tired-out atmosphere that drifted over the trucked-in sand and brown water like a haze of corruption. In 1969, Hurricane Camille had torn through the beachfront communities at two hundred miles per hour, and after that things were the same only worse. There was a pervasive sense that the best times had come and gone, never to return.

But two decades after Camille's fearsome passage, casino gambling changed everything. Glittering palaces rose off the beach like surrealistic sand castles, employing thousands of people and pollinating all sorts of service industries, particularly pawn shops and 'Cash Quick' establishments where you could cash your social security check or hock your car title for money to blow at the craps table. But at night you didn't see all that. You only saw the line of sparkling towers, their Vegas-style signs blazing over the night waters of the gulf as thousands of cars crawled up the coast highway, filled with the desperate and the gullible.

Will felt strange being by himself, away from home. Having the simple freedom to stop anywhere he chose, to take an unplanned turn without having to explain or to answer to anyone. Of course, that freedom was illusory. There were people waiting for him, and he was late already. He pressed down the accelerator, figuring it was worth the risk of a ticket.

As he neared the casino, traffic slowed to a crawl, but he was already in sight of the words BEAU RIVAGE glittering high in the fading sunlight. He turned off the highway and pulled up into the tasteful entrance of the casino resort, thankful for the bellboys who stood waiting to take his bags. Keeping the computer and sample cases for himself, he gave his keys to a valet and walked through the massive doors.

The interior of the Beau Rivage was built on the colossal scale of post-mafia Las Vegas casinos. A fantasy recreation of the ante-bellum South, with full-size magnolia trees growing throughout its lobby, the casino hotel struck Will as a cross between Trump Tower and Walt Disney World. He picked his way through the gamblers in the lobby and walked over to the long check-in desk. When he gave his name, the hotel manager came out of an office to the left and shook his hand. He was tall and too thin, and his name tag read: GEAUTREAU.

'Your colleagues have been getting a little nervous,

Doctor Jennings,' he said with a cool smile.

'I had a long surgery this afternoon.' Will tapped his computer case. 'But I've got my program ready to go. Just get me to a shower.'

Geautreau handed over an envelope containing a credit card key. 'You've got a suite on twenty-eight, Doctor. A Cypress suite. A thousand square feet. Dr Stein instructed me to give you the red carpet treatment.' Saul Stein was the outgoing president of the Mississippi Medical Association. 'Are you sure I can't have a bellman take those cases up for you?'

Will strained to maintain his smile as he realized that his privacy had been violated. He could hear Dr Stein telling the hotel manager about his arthritis, warning Geautreau not to let Will carry a single bag upstairs. All with the best of intentions, of course.

'No, thanks,' he said, tapping his case again. 'Sensitive cargo here.'

'Our audio-video consultant is waiting for you in the Magnolia Ballroom. You'll find the VIP elevators past the jewelry store and to the right. Don't hesitate to call for anything, Doctor. Ask for me by name.'

'I will.'

As Will crossed the lobby, making for the elevators, a heavyset man in his forties shouted from an open-air bar to his left. It was Jackson Everett, an old medical school buddy. Everett was wearing a Hawaiian shirt and held an umbrella drink in his hand.

'Will Jennings!' he boomed. 'It's about damned time!' Everett shouldered his way across the lobby and slapped Will on the back, sending a sword of pain down his spine. 'I haven't seen you since the scramble at Annandale, boy. How's it hanging? Where's Karen?'

'She didn't make it this trip, Jack. Some Junior League thing. You just get here?'

Everett laughed. 'Are you kidding? I flew in two days ago for some early golf. You're giving the speech tonight, I hear.'

Will nodded.

'Hey, without Karen, you'll have to hit the casino with me. High rollers, stud!'

'I'd better pass. I had a long surgery, and then the flight. I'm whipped.'

'Pussy-whipped, more like,' Everett complained. 'You gotta live a little, son.'

Will gave an obliging laugh. 'Let's get a beer tomorrow and catch up.'

'How are your hands? Are you up for eighteen holes?'

'I brought my clubs. We'll just have to see.'

'Well, I hope you can. Hey, don't put us to sleep tonight, okay?'

'But that's my specialty, Jack.'

Everett groaned and walked off gulping his drink.

As Will waited for an elevator, he saw a few more faces he recognized across the lobby, but he didn't make an effort to speak. He had twenty-five minutes to get dressed and down to the meeting room, where he would still have to set up the notebook computer for his video presentation.

On the twenty-eighth floor, he opened the door to his suite and found his bags and golf clubs waiting for him. The manager had not exaggerated. The suite was large enough for permanent residence. He set his cases on the sitting-room sofa, then walked into the marble-floored bathroom and turned on the hot water. As the bathroom filled with steam, he unzipped his suit bag, hung a blue pinstripe Land's End suit in the closet, and unpacked a laundry-boxed shirt, which he laid out on the coffee table. Then he stripped to his shorts and lifted his sample case onto the bureau beside the television. From it he removed a bound folder and laid it on the desk. The title on the cover read: 'The Safe Use of Depolarizing Paralyzing Relaxants in the Violent Patient.' The paper summarized three years of work in the laboratory and in clinical trials, as well as in the conference rooms of pharmaceutical companies. The culmination of that work – a drug that would trade under the name *Restorase* – represented potential profits on a vast scale, enough to make Will a truly wealthy man.

Nervous compulsion made him check the other contents of the sample case: a video-adapter unit, which would allow his computer to interface with the hotel convention room's projection TV; several drug vials, some of which contained prototype Restorase; and some high-tech syringes. Will counted the vials, then closed the case and hurried into the steamy bathroom, pulling off his underwear as he went.

Hickey and Karen sat facing each other across the kitchen table. A few moments before, Karen had picked up the .38, and he had made no move to stop her. She pointed it at his chest as they talked.

'That gun makes you feel better?' Hickey said.

'If you tell me we're not taking the insulin to Abby, it's going to make me feel a lot better. And you a lot worse.'

He smiled. 'The Junior League princess has guts, huh?'

'If you hurt my baby, you'll see some guts. Yours.'

Hickey laughed outright.

'I don't understand why we have to wait until tomorrow,' she said. 'Why don't you just let me empty our accounts and give you the money?'

'For one thing, the banks have closed. You can't come close to the ransom with automated withdrawals. Even if the banks were open, just pulling out the money would cause a lot of suspicion.'

'What will be different tomorrow morning? How do you plan to get the ransom money?'

'Your husband is going to call his financial advisor here – Gray Davidson – and tell him a great little story. He's just discovered the missing centerpiece of Walter Anderson's largest sculpture. It's a male figure with antlers called *Father Mississippi*. Only one photograph of it exists, and many people believe it was stolen from Anderson's house. The value is—'

'Higher than any painting he ever did,' Karen finished. 'Because he didn't do much sculpture.'

Hickey grinned. 'Pretty good, huh? I do my homework. These goddamn doctors, I tell you. Every one of 'em collects something. Cars, boats, books, whatever. Look at this kitchen. Every gadget known to man. I bet you got eighty pairs of shoes upstairs, like that Filipino hog, Imelda Marcos. You can't believe the money these guys piss away. I mean, how many freakin' gall bladders can you take out in a month?'

'Will's not like that.'

'Oh, no, he doesn't spend more money on paintings every year than he pays all his employees put together. These guys . . . a slip of the knife, somebody dies, and it's "Gee, sorry, couldn't be helped. Wish I could stick around, but I've got a two o'clock tee time."'

Karen started to argue, but she sensed it wouldn't help her situation. Hickey knew a lot about their lives, yet there were huge gaps. Abby's diabetes. Will's work. Will didn't even use a scalpel. He was an anesthesiologist. He used gases and needles. She watched Hickey closely, trying to get a handle on the man beneath the bluster. One thing she knew already: he carried a chip on his shoulder the size of the Rock of Gibraltar.

'Anyway,' Hickey said, 'tomorrow morning, Will's gonna call Davidson and tell him he needs two hundred grand wired to him in Biloxi. He's got a one-time opportunity to buy this statue, and the owner wants cash. And just in case Mr Tight-Ass Gray Davidson is suspicious, Will's lovely wife Karen is coming down to the office to authorize the wire. It isn't strictly required, but it's a nice touch. Then you and I are going to drive down to Davidson's office. I'll wait outside while you go in and bitch a little. "That Will, he goes absolutely off his head when he makes a discovery, but what can you do? Boys will be boys." Then you sign off on the money, and the two hundred grand is off to Biloxi at the speed of light. My partner drives Will to the bank in Biloxi, Will goes in, comes out with the cash, and hands it to my partner. And that's all she wrote.'

'You're doing all this for two hundred thousand dollars?'

Hickey laughed and shook his head. 'See? That's what I'm talking about. To you, two hundred grand is nothing. A down payment on a house. You won't even *feel* two hundred. And that's the point. The money's liquid. You can get it easy, and you don't feel any pain when it's gone. You're happy, I'm happy, and your kid's back safe at home. What more could you ask for?'

'Abby here now! Why can't she stay with us? Or us with her? That won't hurt your plan a bit.'

Hickey's smile vanished. 'This whole little machine runs on fear, Karen. Your fear for Abby. Will's fear for you, and for Abby. Fear is the only thing keeping you from pulling that trigger right now. Right?'

She didn't answer.

'Most kidnappers are brain-dead,' he said. 'They get busted the minute they go for the ransom. Or right after. They try all kinds of complicated shit, but the truth is, no ransom pickup method is safe from the FBI. Not even wiring the money to Brazil. The technology's just too good now. You should see the statistics. Damn near *zero* kidnappings-for-ransom succeed in this country. Why? The drop. Picking up the ransom. But I'm not picking up any ransom. Your husband's doing it for me. You're sending it, he's picking it up. I'm not even *involved*. Is that beautiful or what?'

Karen said nothing, but she saw the merit of his plan. Like all great ideas, it had the virtue of simplicity.

'I'm a goddamn genius,' Hickey went on. 'You think

your old man could've dreamed this up? Fucking gas-passer's all he is. Pass the gas, pick up the check. And a fine wife like you waiting at home. What a waste.'

She forced herself not to look away as Hickey appraised her body. She would not let him believe she was intimidated by anything but his control of Abby.

'The other way people screw up,' he said, 'is taking the kid off with them and sending a ransom note. That leaves the parents at home, alone and scared shitless. Then they get a note or a call – both traceable – asking for more ransom money than they could raise in a week. What else are they going to do but call the FBI? My way, nobody calls anybody but me and my partners, every half-hour like clockwork. And as long as we do that, nobody gets hurt. Nobody goes to prison. Nobody dies.'

'You like listening to yourself talk, don't you?'

He shrugged. 'I like doing things right. This plan is as clean as they come. It's run perfectly five times in a row. Am I proud of that? Yeah. And who else can I talk about it to but someone like you?'

Hickey was talking about kidnapping the way Will's partners bragged about inside stock trades. 'Don't you have any feelings for the children involved?' she asked. 'How terrified they must be?'

'A kid can stand anything for twenty-four hours,' Hickey said softly. 'I stood a lot worse for *years*.'

'But sooner or later you'll make a mistake. You're bound to.'

'The parents might. Not me. The guy I got keeping these kids? He loves 'em. Weighs about three hundred fifty pounds. Looks like goddamn Frankenstein, but he's a giant teddy bear.'

Karen shut her eyes against the image of Abby being held prisoner by a monster. The image did not vanish but instead became clearer.

'Don't worry,' Hickey said. 'Huey's not a child abuser or anything. He's too slow. Only . . .'

Her eyes flew open. 'What?'

'He doesn't like kids running away from him. When he was little, kids at the regular school treated him pretty bad. When he got bigger, they just yelled things and ran. Then his mama put him in a retard school. Kids are pretty damn cruel. When Huey sees kids run, it makes him lose his head.'

Hot blood rushed to her face. 'But don't you think it's natural for a child being held prisoner by a stranger to try to run?'

'Your kid the panicky type?'

'Not usually, but . . . God, can't we please spend the night wherever they are?'

'I'm getting hungry,' Hickey said. 'Why don't you see about fixing some supper? I'll bet you were a natural with an Easy Bake oven.'

Karen looked at the gun in her hand. A less useful thing she could not imagine. 'When can we take Abby the insulin?'

'Food,' Hickey said, rubbing his flat belly. 'F-O-O-D.'

Chapter 4

Will ate a bite of redfish and looked out over an audience of close to a thousand people eating the same dish. To his right, at the podium, Dr Saul Stein was giving a rather digressive introductory speech. At last, like a man making a sudden left turn, he veered back onto the point.

'Ladies and gentlemen, we are very lucky to have with us tonight a physician of the first caliber. A man whose pioneering work on the clinical frontiers of anesthesiology will be published in next month's *New England Journal of Medicine.*'

A burst of applause stopped Stein for several moments, and he smiled.

'Tonight, we will be treated to a précis of that article, which describes fundamental work carried out at our own University of Mississippi Medical Center. What's amazing to me is that our speaker – a native Mississippian – entered his field as a second specialty, out of unfortunate necessity. We are very lucky that he did, because—'

A high-pitched beep stopped Stein in midsentence. Five hundred doctors simultaneously reached for their belts, Will included. General laughter rolled through the huge room as most of the physicians remembered that they were on vacation, and their pagers back in their hometowns. Will was wearing his, but it had not produced the offending beep. Still, he moved the switch on the SkyTel from BEEP to VIBRATE.

'Who the hell's on call down here?' Stein barked from the podium. 'There's no getting away from those damn things.' As the laughter died away, he said, 'I could easily talk about our speaker for another hour, but I won't. Dessert is coming, and I want to let Will get started. Ladies and gentlemen, Dr Will Jennings.'

Applause filled the darkened ballroom. Will rose, speech in hand, and walked to the podium, where his notebook computer glowed softly. He sensed the expectation in the crowd.

'They tell me you should begin a speech with a joke,' he said. 'My wife tells me I'm not much of a comedian, so I shouldn't risk it. But flying down here today, I was reminded of a story an old paramedic told me about Hurricane Camille.'

Everybody thought about Camille when they came to the coast. You could still see trees that had been twisted into eerie contortions by the mother of all hurricanes.

'This guy was driving an ambulance down here in sixty-nine, and he was one of the first to go out on call after the storm surge receded. There were dead animals everywhere, and it was still raining like hell. On his second call, he and his partner saw a young woman lying beside the road in a formal dress. They thought she might be one of those fools who tried to ride out the hurricane by throwing a party. Anyway, he figures the girl is dead, but he doesn't want to let her go without a fight, so he starts CPR, mouth-to-mouth, the whole bit. Nothing works, and he finally gives up. The next day, they're hearing who died in the hurricane, because relatives of the missing are coming back to view the bodies in the morgue. The EMT asks about the girl he tried to save, but nobody's come forward to identify her. A week goes by, and he still can't forget her. Then the word comes down from the morgue. The girl's mother finally ID'ed her. She'd been dead for two years. The hurricane had washed her up from the cemetery.'

Squeals of revulsion were drowned by a wave of male laughter. No one appreciated morbid humor more than a bunch of docs with a couple of drinks under their belts.

'My presentation will be brief and to the point. The emergency physicians and anesthesiologists should find it provocative, and I hope the rest of you find it interesting. I'm going to try something new tonight, a bit of high-tech wizardry I've been toying with.' Will had videotaped his past year's clinical work on a Canon XL-1, a broadcast-quality digital video camera that Karen had tried to talk him out of buying. He'd worked dozens of hours on his computer, editing it all down to the program that would accompany tonight's talk. The finished product was seamless. But any time you worked with hard drives and video, glitches lurked in the wings. 'If it doesn't work,' he added, 'at least nobody dies.'

More laughter, wry this time.

'Lights, please.'

The lights dimmed. With a last flutter of nerves, Will clicked a file icon with his trackball, and the 61-inch Hitachi television behind him flashed up a high-resolution image of an operating room. A patient lay unconscious on the table as the OR team prepared for surgery. Wonder lit the faces in the crowd, most of them doctors with minimal computer knowledge. Their ages varied widely, with couples in their sixties seated beside others in their thirties. Some of the younger wives looked a lot like Karen.

Will glanced at his large-font script and said, 'This patient looks thoroughly prepped for surgery, doesn't he? Twenty minutes before this picture was taken, he assaulted a doctor and two nurses with a broken coffee carafe, causing serious injuries.'

The image on the Hitachi smash-cut to a jiggling, handheld shot that looked like something out of a Quentin Tarantino film. A wild-eyed man was jabbing a broken coffee carafe at whoever was behind the camera and screaming at the top of his lungs. '*Satan's hiding inside you, motherfucker!*'

The audience gasped.

The man in the video swung the jagged carafe in a roundhouse arc, and the camera jerked wildly toward the ceiling as its operator leaped back to avoid being slashed. Only Will knew that the cameraman had been himself.

'*It's the end times!*' the man shrieked. '*Jesus is coming!*' In the background, a nurse cried, 'Where the hell is security?' The man with the carafe charged her and began weeping and howling at once. '*Where's my Rhelda Jean? Somebody call Rhelda, goddamn it!*'

Suddenly the video cut back to the man lying prostrate and prepped in the OR.

'If I were to tell you that this man was subdued in the ER not by police, but by me – using a drug – you might guess this was accomplished with a benzodiazepene, a barbiturate, or a narcotic. You would be wrong. No doctor can hit the vein, or even the muscle, of a PCP-crazed man who is trying to kill him with a coffee carafe, not without grave risk to himself and other staff. The ER docs among you might make a more experienced guess and assume that it was done with a paraylzing relaxant like pancuronium bromide, curare, or succinylcholine. And you'd be right. Nowadays, emergency physicians routinely resort to the use of these drugs, because they sometimes offer the only means of compelling violent patients to accept lifesaving treatment. And though they won't talk about it much, they sometimes use paralyzing relaxants without first administering sedatives, as a sort of punishment to "repeat offenders" – violent addicts and gangbangers who show up in the ER again and again, causing chaos and injury to staff.

'All of you know how dangerous the paralyzing relaxants are, both medically and legally, because they leave patients unable to move or even breathe until they're intubated and bagged, and their breathing done for them.'

The Hitachi showed a nurse standing over the patient in the ER, working a breathing bag. Will glanced into the crowd. At the first table, a stunning young woman was staring at him with laserlike concentration. She was twenty years younger than most of the women in the audience, except the trophy wives escorted by those doctors who had ditched the loyal ladies who put them through medical school, in favor of newer models. This woman wore a tight black dress accented by a diamond drop necklace, and she seemed to be alone. Older couples sat on either side of her, framing her like bookends. Since she was sitting in front of the first table, Will had an unobstructed view, from her tapered legs and well-turned ankles to her impressive décolletage. The dress was shockingly short for a medical meeting, but it produced the desired effect. She was distracting enough that he had to remind himself to start talking again.

'Tonight,' he said, 'I'm going to tell you about a revolutionary new class of drug developed by myself and the Searle pharmaceutical company, and tested in my own clinical trials at University Hospital in Jackson. This drug, the chemical name of which I must keep under wraps for one more month, can completely counteract the effects of succinylcholine, restoring full nerve conductivity in less than thirty seconds.'

Will heard murmurs of disbelief.

'Beyond this, we have developed special new compressed-gas syringes that allow the safe injection of a therapeutic dose of Anectine – that's a popular trade name for succinylcholine – into the external jugular vein, with one half second of skin contact.'

The Hitachi showed the screaming man with a broken carafe again. This time, as he charged a female nurse, a tall man in a white coat stepped up behind him with something that looked like a small white pistol in his hand. The white-coated doctor was Will. As the patient jabbed the glittering shard at the brave nurse who had agreed to distract him, Will moved in and touched the side of his neck with the white pistol, which was in fact a compressed-gas syringe. There was an audible hiss, and the man's free hand flew up to his neck. The dramatic fluttering of his eyelids and facial muscles was hard to see in the handheld camera shot, but when he threw up both arms and crossed them over his chest, the audience gasped. As he collapsed, Will caught him and dragged him toward a treatment table, and two nurses hurried over to help.

The ballroom was silent as a cave.

On screen, two nurses restrained the patient with straps. Then Will stepped up and injected him in the antecubital vein with a conventional syringe.

'I am now injecting the patient with Restorase, the first of these new drugs to be approved by the FDA. Now, if you'll look at your watches, please.'

The camera operator moved up to the treatment table and focused on the patient's face. His eyes were half closed. Every doctor in the audience knew that the man's diaphragm was paralyzed. He could not move or breathe, yet he was fully conscious of what was going on around him.

Will heard shuffles and whispers as the seconds ticked past. At twenty-five seconds, the patient's eyes blinked, then opened. He tried to raise his hand, but the arm moved with a floppy motion. He gasped twice, then began to breathe.

'What's your name, sir?' Will asked.

'Tommy Joe Smith,' he said, his eyes wide.

'Do you know what just happened to you, Mr Smith?'

'Jesus Lord . . . don't do that again.'

'Are you going to try to stab anyone else, Mr Smith?'

He shook his head violently.

The image cut to a shot of drug vials – Anectine and Restorase – sitting beside a compressed gas syringe on a soapstone surface.

'I know how shocking that footage can be,' Will said. 'But remember the scene that preceded it.'

On the Hitachi, Tommy Joe Smith charged the nurse again with the shard of glass.

'The potential applications are limited, thank God, but their necessity cannot be argued. In emergency rooms, psychiatric wards, and prison infirmaries, healthcare workers are suffering grave injury at the hands of violent patients. Now their safety can be insured without resorting to greater violence to restrain the out-of-control patient. Very soon, physicians will be able to use depolarizing relaxants without fear of fatal outcomes or costly lawsuits.'

A collective murmur of approval swept through the darkened room, followed by a wave of applause. Will had known the video would disturb them – as it should have – but he also knew they would recognize the enormous potential of the drug. He glanced to his left and saw Saul Stein grinning like a proud parent.

'As you know,' he said, checking to be sure that the Hitachi showed an anatomical diagram of a hand, 'the relaxants work primarily at the myoneural junction, interrupting the normal flow of impulses from the brain to the skeletal muscles. . . .'

He continued almost without thought, thanks to the rehearsals he had done with Karen and Abby. The woman in black was still staring from the front table. She wasn't smiling exactly, but there was a suggestive curve to her lips that signaled interest in more than drug therapy. He tried to make eye contact with several other audience members, but every few seconds his gaze returned to the young woman. And why not? It was natural for a lecturer to pick out an individual and speak directly to him – or her. It eased the nerves and gave the voice an undertone of intimacy. Tonight he would speak to the woman in black.

Whenever he turned back from pointing out something on the Hitachi, she was watching him. She had large eyes that never seemed to blink, and a mane of blond hair that fell to her shoulders in the style of Lauren Bacall in *To Have and Have Not*. With the exception of Karen, blondes had never done much for Will, but this one was different. What struck him – even in the dim spill of light from the big Hitachi – was her remarkable symmetry. His eyes followed the curve of her long legs as they rose to feminine hips, the hips curving into an hourglass waist. Her breasts were not too large, but almost too perfect. The strapless black dress revealed fine collarbones and strong shoulders. Her neck was long and graceful, her jaw defined, her lips full. But what held him was her eyes. They never left his face, even as he studied her from head to toe.

He turned to the Hitachi to check the video feed, and when he turned back, she shifted in her seat, uncrossed her legs, then recrossed them with the languid grace of a lioness stretching her flanks. The shortness of the cocktail dress gave him a brief but direct sight line between her legs, even from the podium. He felt blood rush to his face. It wasn't quite Sharon Stone in *Basic Instinct* – this woman was wearing panties – but she had made sure he could see everything but the brand name on the silk. Those dark panties were a far cry from the white cotton 'granny' panties Karen had taken to wearing the past couple of years. As Will dropped his gaze to look at his speech, he realized that he had fallen behind the video. He looked back up and skipped ahead to the proper cue line.

The ghost of a smile touched the woman's lips.

Huey Cotton stood on the cabin porch, looking into darkening trees as the sun sank behind them. Tiny flashes of greenish-yellow light floated beneath the branches like phosphorescent sparks from an unseen fire.

'Lightnin' bugs,' he said, his voice filled with pleasure. 'I wonder if there's a mason jar in the kitchen.'

As he watched the little flares winking in the shadows, a soft groan came from inside the cabin. Huey's smile vanished, replaced by something like fear. He took a deep breath, then turned slowly and looked at the door with trepidation.

'I wish you was here, Mamaw,' he said softly.

The groan came again.

He reached out and opened the screen door, then pushed open the main door and walked inside.

Hickey sat at Karen's kitchen table, eating a huge muffaletta sandwich and drinking iced tea.

'Damn, that's good,' he said, wiping his mouth. 'You got the dressing just right. Reminds me of New Orleans. That grocery store down in the Quarter.'

'Are you from New Orleans?' Karen asked. She was standing at the island, opposite the refrigerator, packing syringes and insulin into a small Igloo ice chest.

'You hear a New Orleans accent?'

'Not really.' She couldn't classify Hickey's speech. There was some Mississippi in it, but other inflections, too. He had to have spent some time outside the South. In the service, maybe.

'We'll just skip over my biography for now,' he said, chewing another bite of the big sandwich. 'Maybe we'll get into it later.'

Karen was closing the ice chest when the garage doorbell rang.

Hickey was instantly on his feet, Will's gun in his hand. 'Who's that?' he asked, his eyes flicking around the room as though a SWAT team might burst in. 'You expecting somebody?'

Karen shook her head. She had no idea who it could be.

'Don't answer it. We'll just let them go on their merry way.' He took a step toward the pantry. 'Which door are they at?'

'The garage,' she whispered, shocked by the sense of conspiracy she felt with Hickey. But the last thing she wanted was someone disrupting his carefully organized plan while Abby was under his control.

The bell rang twice more. The urgency of the ringer was like a finger poking Karen in the side.

'How come I didn't hear a car?' Hickey asked.

'Sometimes we don't.' As she spoke the words, she realized who the visitor might be. Stephanie Morgan, the co-chair of the Junior League flower show. Stephanie drove a Lexus that ran so quietly Karen never heard it pulling up the driveway. And of everyone she knew, Stephanie had the most reason to drop by over the next couple of days.

She and Hickey jumped when the kitchen window rattled. Karen turned and saw Stephanie Morgan's face pressed against the glass. She was shaking a reprimanding finger, and beside her was the little moon face of her eleven-month-old son, Josh.

'Open the door,' Hickey said in a flat voice.

'*Hide*,' Karen told him.

'I can't. She's looking at me right now.' He slid the gun behind his right leg. 'Go open it.'

Karen didn't want to invite Stephanie into her nightmare, but if she refused to open the door now, Steph would throw a fit, and Hickey's plan would come apart. She held up her hand and motioned toward the garage. Stephanie nodded and disappeared from the window.

'Let me handle this,' Karen told him. 'Please.'

He looked skeptical. 'Let's see if you can.'

When Karen opened the door, Stephanie pushed right past her with Josh in her arms, talking as she went. 'Karen, you've *got* to come down to the Coliseum in the morning. I mean *first thing*. I've been down there all day, and the place is a wreck. They were supposed to have those livestock people out of there by lunch today, but there are still cows on the floor. *Cows*, Karen.'

Stephanie had reached the kitchen. 'Hello,' she said to Hickey. 'Are you Karen's secret lover? I always knew she had one. It's the quiet ones you have to watch out for.'

Karen stepped into the kitchen and rubbed Josh's arm. The little guy was obviously exhausted from his day at the flower show venue, and he was resting his head on his mother's shoulder. Or had he sensed something frightening in Joe Hickey?

'Stephanie, this is Joe, my second cousin. He's from Washington State. Joe, Stephanie Morgan, Junior League soccer mom.'

'Puh-*lease*,' Stephanie said, giving Hickey a little wave and turning back to Karen. She obviously hadn't seen the gun. 'I want to know why you didn't answer that doorbell.'

Hickey was watching Karen over Stephanie's shoulder. His eyes had gone dead the moment she turned away from him. 'I had some Mormons around before,' Karen said. 'I thought they'd come back for another try.'

Stephanie pulled a wry face. With her overdone makeup, it made her look like a circus clown. 'Likely story. *I* know what you're doing. Hiding from me. But I've got news for you, honey. You *can't*. You're the queen bee of this show, and I need you. When I saw those cows on that floor, I said, "There's only one woman in the Junior League for this job, and that's Karen Jennings. She'll have those damn bovines out of here before another cow patty hits the floor."'

Karen didn't know what to say. The only thing in her mind was getting Stephanie and Josh out as quickly as possible. She felt a frightening energy radiating from Hickey, a sort of survival desperation. It was in his eyes, in the set of his shoulders and mouth. Something he'd developed in prison, maybe. If he perceived Stephanie as a threat, he would kill her. And eleven-month-old Josh? Karen didn't want to think about that.

Josh began to cry. Stephanie gave his back a perfunctory pat and began rocking on the balls of her feet.

'I'll be down there in the morning,' Karen promised. She took Stephanie by the arm and began walking her back toward the pantry. 'But Joe's father passed away recently, and he's down here to work out some estate problems with me. We only have tonight and the morning to do it.'

'*Karen.*' Stephanie planted her feet at the kitchen door. 'You know how important this is. Lucy Childs is just waiting for us to screw this up.'

Good God, Karen thought. *Junior League politics. Could anything in the world be less important?* She kept moving Stephanie toward the door. 'I'll take care of the cows. You take Josh home and get him some supper. Where's Caroline?'

The second she asked, she wished she hadn't. Because Stephanie would now ask where Abby was.

'With my mother,' Stephanie replied. 'Which is another reason I'm so stressed. Mom was all set to get her highlights done this afternoon, and then she had to cancel to keep Caroline. Guilt trip from hell, of course. Where's Abby?'

'With Will's mother, in the Delta.' They had reached the laundry room. Karen looked back and saw Hickey silhouetted in the kitchen door. Her eyes searched for the outline of the gun.

'Nice meeting you, Joe!' Stephanie called.

'Yeah,' he said.

Karen pushed her into the garage. Sure enough, Stephanie's white Lexus was parked just behind the Expedition.

'Your cousin looks interesting,' Stephanie said, her eyes twinkling. 'A little rough, maybe, but interesting. You sure I didn't just stumble onto *tryst*?'

Karen forced a laugh. 'Positive. Joe can't stand me. He's just here to settle the estate.'

'Well, I hope you get some money out of it.' She pointed at the Avalon parked beside the Expedition. 'You need to upgrade your transportation, girl.'

'I'll see you in the morning, Steph. I may be a little late.'

Stephanie had leaned down to strap Josh into his car seat. 'Don't you *dare*. I cannot handle cow shit, okay? This is *not* in my contract.'

Karen forced another laugh. Stephanie got into the Lexus, started it, and back around to go down the hill.

Something brushed Karen's shoulder. Hickey was standing beside her, and she hadn't even realized it. He waved at the Lexus. Stephanie honked her horn in reply, then disappeared over the lip of the drive.

'Not bad, Mom,' Hickey said. 'That skinny bitch owes you her life, and she doesn't even know it.'

Karen realized she was shaking.

Hickey slapped her lightly on the behind, exactly the way Will would have. 'Let's get back inside. My muffaletta's getting cold.'

*   *   *

Will's lecture was nearly done. The first susurrant sounds of dresses shifting on seats had reached his ears from the floor of the darkened ballroom. He had timed the program just right. Behind him, the Hitachi showed a maternal-fetal medicine specialist injecting Restorase into a fetus still in the womb. The fetus had been paralyzed before undergoing a blood transfusion to save its life. Restorase would bring it out of paralysis in a tenth of the time it would normally take.

'And while this particular injection required a good deal of comment,' Will said, 'I think this last shot is pretty self-explanatory.'

The pregnant woman's belly was replaced by a wide-screen sequence of Will teeing off at the Annandale golf course, one recognized by most doctors in the audience. With creative editing, he had made his perfect drive appear to conclude with a stunning hole-in-one. When the ball hit the pin and dropped into the cup – to the accompaniment of Tex-Mex music from Kevin Costner's *Tin Cup* – a wild whoop went up from the dark (probably from the throat of Jackson Everett) and enthusiastic applause followed. The lights came up and revealed a laughing, exhilarated audience.

'I'll be at the Searle booth for two hours tomorrow afternoon,' Will said. 'I've brought samples of Restorase with me, as well as some of the gas-injection systems I've discussed tonight. I look forward to speaking with all of you.'

This time the applause was more sedate, but also more sustained. Saul Stein stood and patted him on the back. Will shook Stein's hand, then began disconnecting his computer while the MMA president waited for the applause to die. Stein gushed over the presentation, then moved on to announcements regarding the next day's seminars. Will zipped up his computer case and stepped down from the podium.

He was immediately swallowed by a congratulatory mob that swept him out of the Magnolia Ballroom and into the atrium area. A visual echo of the woman in black remained in his mind, but he saw no sign of her among the smiling faces. For fifteen minutes he shook hands and accepted compliments, but before the real gabbers could trap him, he made for the escalators.

Like all casino hotels, the Beau Rivage made sure its guests had to pass through a carnival of slot machines and gaming tables on their way to and from the meeting rooms. Will's joints were giving him trouble, but he walked briskly. He wanted to get up to the room and take some more Advil.

He had planned to use the VIP elevators, but as he passed the main elevators, Jackson Everett reached out and pulled him into the waiting area. Everett had another drink in his hand, and the smell of rum came off him like Caribbean perfume. He opened his mouth to say something to Will, but just then an elevator opened and disgorged an elderly woman holding a cigar box full of quarters.

'Take 'em to the cleaners, Grandma!' he yelled. 'Break the bank!'

The woman grinned and hurried toward the lobby. Everett pushed Will into the elevator, then followed him. Two more doctors wearing name tags stepped in after them, and the door began to close.

'Hold the door!' cried a female voice.

Will's right arm shot out to stop the sliding door, despite the pain the sudden move caused him. As the door retracted, the blond woman in the black dress stepped into the elevator.

'Thanks,' she said. Her cheeks were flushed as though she had been running.

'You're welcome,' Will replied.

The woman immediately turned and faced the closing doors, leaving him to study the wave of Lauren Bacall hair. The elevator was lined with mirrors and burled wood. Will looked to his right and studied her reflection in profile. The first thing he noticed was Everett and the other two doctors staring at her behind. She clutched her small handbag and looked at the floor, seemingly oblivious to the men behind her. Everett's gaze was openly lascivious.

'Did you set up that video display, Jennings?' asked one of the docs, whom Will vaguely recognized. 'Or did you get some talented secretary to do it?'

'Karen probably did it,' interjected Everett.

'No, I did it. It's easier than you think.'

'Maybe,' said the first man. 'But where do you get the *time*?'

'I don't have Jack's bad habits.'

'Ha,' said Everett. 'That from the guy who just developed the ultimate date-rape drug.'

The men fell uncomfortably silent, and the elevator stopped on the eighth floor. The doctors waited, giving the woman time to exit first, but she didn't move. The one who'd spoken to Will excused himself and brushed past her. Everett reached down and made as if to squeeze her exquisitely round derriere, then laughed and followed the other man out. Instead of walking to his room, he turned back to the elevator and pointed at Will.

'Come on to the casino with us! You'll love it. And even if you don't, we're going to take in a little *dancing*, later. Know what I mean?'

The woman stiffened.

'I've got to call Karen,' Will said, before Everett could get more explicit. 'And I'm getting up early for golf. You guys knock the walls out.'

'We always do.' Everett smirked and flicked his eyebrows up and down like Groucho Marx.

Will leaned forward and hit the CLOSE DOOR button.

'Thanks,' the woman said as the doors slid shut.

'He's okay, really. Just a little drunk.'

She nodded and gave Will a look that told him she was used to such things. The elevator began to ascend. Between floors, Will caught himself staring at her trim figure again. When he looked up, her reflected face was watching him. He blushed and looked at the floor.

Someone behind Will cleared his throat. He'd forgotten the other doctor was still aboard. The elevator stopped again, this time on the thirteenth floor. The stranger got out, but the woman stayed put.

'What's your floor?' she asked.

'I'm sorry?'

'There's no floor button lit.'

'Oh. I forgot to hit it. Still nervous, I guess. Twenty-eight, please.'

'You've got a Cypress suite? So do I.' She half-turned

to him and smiled. 'Your program was great, by the way. I can't believe you were nervous.'

'Are you a physician?' he asked. He didn't like to think he believed in stereotypes, but he'd never met a woman doctor who looked like this.

'No, I'm with the casino company.'

'Oh. I see. Hey, what's your floor? There's no button lit but twenty-eight.'

'I'm twenty-eight, too. Most of the Cypress suites are up there.'

He nodded and smiled politely, but when the woman turned away he gave her a hard look. *A hooker?* he wondered. The desk manager had told him Saul Stein had said give him the red carpet treatment. Did that include a beautiful call girl?

The elevator opened on twenty-eight.

'Bye,' the woman said. She got off and walked briskly down the hallway to the left. Will got off and watched her seductive motion, then turned left and counted the numbers down to suite 28021. He was inserting his credit card key when a female voice called, 'Dr Jennings?'

He looked up the long corridor. The blonde in the black dress was walking hesitantly toward him, gripping her small handbag in front of her.

'Can I help you?' he asked.

She fidgeted with her bag, then stopped as a door opened opposite Will. A heavyset man wearing a plaid sport coat came out and hurried toward the elevators.

'My key doesn't work,' the woman said, after he'd passed. 'Could you try it for me?'

'I doubt I can do any better than you. I'll give it a shot, though.'

'No pun intended?'

Will laughed, then put his computer case inside his room and followed her past the heavyset man waiting for the elevators.

The elevator bell dinged as Will inserted her card key and watched for green LED lights. But when he removed the key, only one LED flashed – red – and there was no click of tumblers. He tried again, seating the card squarely and firmly, but no matter what he did, the lock refused to open.

'I think you're out of luck,' he told her.

'Looks like it. Would you mind if I used your phone to call the desk?'

He started to say he didn't mind, but something stopped him. A sense of something out of place, not quite logical. 'I think there's a house phone by the VIP elevators. I'll be glad to wait with you.'

She looked momentarily confused, but after a moment she smiled. 'That's right. I appreciate you waiting with me. You never know who's creeping around the casino. My name's Cheryl, by the way.'

Will accepted her proffered hand, which was cool, almost to the point of coldness. It felt like the hand of an anxious patient, someone terrified of needles. He dropped her hand and escorted her back toward the elevators, walking a little ahead.

The heavyset man was gone. Will glanced into the waiting area and saw what he was looking for: a cream-colored house telephone.

'Here it is,' he said, turning back to her. 'They'll have a new key up here in no—'

The words died in his throat. Cheryl was pointing an automatic pistol at his chest. She must have taken it from her handbag. Her eyes were resolute, but there was something else in them. Fear.

'What is this?' he asked. 'I've only got a few bucks on me, but you're welcome to it. Credit cards, whatever.'

'I don't want your money,' she said, looking anxiously at the elevators. 'I want you to go in your room.'

'What for?'

'You'll find out. Just hurry up.'

Something in Will's mind hardened to resistance. He wasn't going to start blindly obeying orders. If you did that, the next thing you knew, you were lying face-down on some dirty bathroom floor while they shot you in the back of the head.

'I'm not going anywhere. Not until you tell me what's going on. In fact—' he stepped toward the phone – 'I'm going to call the front desk and have them call the police.'

'Don't touch that.'

'You're not going to shoot me, Cheryl.' He picked up the telephone.

'If you call the police, Abby is going to die. And there's nothing I can do to stop it.'

His arm froze. 'What did you say?'

'Your daughter was kidnapped two hours ago, Doctor. If you want her to live, take me into your room right now. If you call the police, she'll die. I'm serious as a heart attack.'

A paralyzing numbness was spreading from deep within Will's chest. It was disbelief, or perhaps the brain's attempt at disbelief in the face of knowledge too terrible to accept.

'What are you talking about?'

Cheryl glanced at the elevator again. He sensed the fear inside her metamorphosing into panic.

'Doctor, if somebody gets out of that elevator and sees me with this gun, the whole thing's going to come apart. Abby's going to die, okay? And I don't want that to happen. I'll tell you everything you want to know, but you'd better get me into your goddamn room right now.'

Will heard a squawk and realized the phone was still in his right hand. He brought it slowly to his mouth.

'Talk, and you put a bullet in Abby's brain.'

He hung up.

'Hurry,' she said. 'If I don't make a phone call soon, she's going to die anyway.'

He stared at her for another few seconds, looking for options. He had none. He walked down to his door, unlocked it, and held it open for her.

Cheryl walked past him, holding the gun close against her, as though she expected Will to try to take it. Once inside, she walked all the way across the sitting room and into the bedroom. He closed the door and followed her.

Cheryl put the bed between herself and Will. She was still pointing the gun at him, but he walked to the edge of the bed anyway. His fear for Abby was burgeoning into an anger that would brook no delay.

'Get back!' she cried. 'Stay back until I explain!'

'Tell me about my little girl!'

'This is a kidnapping-for-ransom,' she said, like a grammar-school girl reciting from memory. 'Right now my partner is with your wife, at your house in Madison County. Someone else is holding Abby at a third location. This is what's going to happen from this point on . . .'

Will listened like a man being given a clinical description of a disease that would shortly kill him. His disbelief quickly gave way to horror at the way his family's lives had been studied and deconstructed, all in preparation for a plan designed to separate him from two hundred thousand dollars.

'Listen to me,' he interrupted. 'We don't have to wait twenty-four hours. I'll get you the money right now—'

'The banks are closed.'

'I'll find a way.' He tried to keep the panic out of his voice. 'I can make it happen. The casino has money. I'll call down—'

'No. It doesn't work that way. It has to be tomorrow. Now, let me finish.'

He shut up and listened, his brain working frantically. Whoever was behind this plan knew his business. He – or she – had turned the normal mechanics of a kidnapping inside out, creating a situation in which any aggressive response was impossible. Cheryl's gun was only there to control Will's initial panic. The real coercion was Abby. He could pick up the telephone and call the police right now. But if they came and arrested Cheryl, and she didn't call her partner on their thirty-minute schedule, Abby would die.

'If I do what you want,' he said, 'what guarantee do I have that we'll get Abby back?'

'No guarantee. You have to trust us.'

'That's not good enough. How are we supposed to get her back? Tell me the details. Don't think! Tell me right this second.'

Cheryl nodded. 'Abby and your wife will be driven to a public place and set free within sight of each other.'

She sounded like she believed it. And she'd told him they'd carried out the same plan five times before. He thought back over the past few years' headlines in Mississippi. He didn't remember hearing about any kidnapped children who were found murdered. Not kidnappings-for-ransom, anyway. And that would definitely have made headlines across the state.

'What's to keep me from going to the police after you let Abby go?'

'The fact that two hundred thousand dollars is nothing to you. And because if the police start looking for us, we'll know. We'll know, and my partner will come back and kill Abby. In the playhouse in your backyard, at her school, after church . . . anywhere. Believe me, he'll do it. We've done this to five other doctors just like you, and none of them have reported it. Not one. You won't, either.'

He turned away from her in frustration. Through the bedroom's picture window, he saw the lights of a freighter out on the darkening gulf, playing its way westward. He had never felt so impotent in his life. One simple dictum had carried him through many life-or-death situations: *There's always a way. Another option. Drastic, maybe, but there.* But this time there didn't seem to be one. The trapped feeling made him crazy with rage. He whirled back to Cheryl.

'I'm supposed to just sit here all night while some stranger holds my little girl prisoner? Scared out of her mind? Lady, I will rip your head off before I let that happen.'

She jerked the gun back up. 'Stay back!'

'What kind of woman are you? Don't you have any maternal feelings?'

'Don't you say anything about my feelings!' Cheryl's face reddened. 'You don't know anything about me!'

'I know you're making a child suffer pure terror.'

'That can't be helped.'

He was about to respond when a thought burst into his mind like a starshell. 'Oh Jesus. What about Abby's insulin?'

Cheryl's face was blank. 'What?'

'Abby's a juvenile diabetic. You didn't know that? You didn't *plan* for that?'

'Calm down.'

'You've got to call your partner. I've got to talk to him right now. Right now!'

The telephone beside the bed rang loudly.

They stared at it. Then Cheryl walked to the phone and laid her free hand on the receiver.

'You want to talk?' she said. 'Here's your chance. But be cool, Doctor. Very cool.'

Chapter 5

Will took the phone from Cheryl and held it to his ear.

'This is Will Jennings.'

'*Doctor* Will Jennings?' said a male voice.

'That's right.'

'You got some unexpected company down there, Doctor?'

Will looked over at Cheryl, who was watching intently. 'Yes.'

'She looks hot in that black dress, doesn't she?'

'Listen, I need to explain something to you.'

'You don't explain anything, college boy. *I'm* in charge tonight. You got that?'

'I've got it, but—'

'But nothing. I'm going to ask you a question, Doc. Kind of like the *Match Game*. Remember that one? That freakin' Richard Dawson; what a fruitcake.'

Will heard an eerie laughter.

'Anyway, we're going to see if your answer matches your wife's. This is really more like the *Newlywed Game*, I guess. *Uhh . . . that would be the butt, Bob.*' The man broke up again.

Will breathed deeply, his entire being concentrated on understanding with whom he was dealing.

'The question is . . . does your child have any serious medical condition?'

A trickle of hope flowed into his veins. 'She has juvenile diabetes.'

'That's a match! You just won the all-expense paid trip to *beautiful* Puerto Vallarta!'

The man sounded like Wink Martindale on speed. Will shook his head at the surreal horror of the situation. 'Abby needs that insulin, sir. Immediately.'

'Sir?' The man laughed darkly. 'Oh, I like that. This is probably the only time you'd ever call me "sir." Unless you had to tell me I was dying or something. *Sir*, I'm afraid you've got terminal pecker cancer. Stand two steps back please.'

'I'm an anesthesiologist. I don't handle things like that.'

'No? You never told anybody they were dying?'

Will hesitated. 'When I was an OB/GYN, I did.'

'Ahh. So, no means yes. You ever kill anybody, Doc?'

'Of course not.'

'Really? Nobody ever died on the table while you were passing the gas?'

'Well, of course. But not as a result of my actions.'

'No? I've got to wonder how honest you're being about that. I really do.'

'Would you mind telling me your name?'

'Joe Hickey, Doc. You can call me Joe.'

'All right, Joe. Are you a former patient of mine? Or a relative of a patient?'

'Why would you ask that? I mean, you never killed anybody, right?'

'It's just that you seem to have a lot of animosity toward me personally.'

'You feel that? Huh. Could be, I guess. Well, let's leave that for now. 'Cause I'm about to show you what a nice guy I am. I'm about to set it up so your little princess gets her insulin.'

'Thank God.'

'God's got nothing to do with this. Let me talk to my partner.'

'Joe, could I speak with my wife for a moment?'

'Put Cheryl on, Doc.'

Will held out the phone.

'Get in the bathroom while I'm talking,' she said.

'Your partner didn't tell me to go in the bathroom.'

She shook the automatic at him. 'Get in the goddamn bathroom!'

Will held up his hands and backed into the spacious cubicle of white marble and gold fixtures. He kept the knob turned as he closed the door, and after he heard Cheryl's voice resume, opened it a couple of inches and put his ear to the crack.

'Why didn't we know about this medicine thing?' she asked. 'Well, I don't like it. Getting on the road with her is dangerous. What if a cop stops you? . . . Okay . . . I'm all right, I guess. But this guy isn't like the others, Joey. . . . I don't know how. His eyes are on me every second. He's like a wolf, waiting for his chance. . . . I know. I *know*. Okay. Thirty minutes.'

Will put his eye to the crack and saw Cheryl grimace as she hung up.

'All clear?' he asked, pushing open the door.

'Yeah.'

'What did he say?'

'He's taking the medicine to your little girl. I mean, he's taking your wife to give her the shot. See? If we didn't care what happened to her, would we take the risk to get her medicine to her?'

'Yes. Because you know if anything happened to Abby during the night, you wouldn't get your money.'

'You wouldn't know whether anything had happened to her or not.'

'If I don't get confirmation that Abby's gotten her insulin within seven hours, I'll assume she's gone into ketoacidosis. And you'll talk then. You'll talk if I have to break every bone in your body, one at a time.'

The threat seemed to have no effect on Cheryl. From her expression, he got the feeling she'd heard such things before. Maybe she thought he wasn't capable of such barbarity. Or maybe she knew he wasn't.

'You think Joey hasn't thought of that?' she asked. 'I don't even know where your kid is. But even if I did, and you tortured it out of me, the police couldn't possibly get there in thirty minutes. I know that for sure.' With the gun still in her right hand, Cheryl rubbed both arms as if she were cold. 'And you don't want to start making threats to Joey, Doctor. He could do a lot of things to your little girl besides kill her, you know? You're not holding any cards here.'

Will closed his eyes and fought a nauseating rush of terror. 'Who the hell is this Joey?'

Cheryl looked at him like he was an idiot.

'He's my husband.'

*　　*　　*

Abby lay sleeping on an old sofa in the cabin. A crocheted comforter lay over her. Huey sat on the floor beside her, whittling slowly at a piece of cedar. Huey was nervous. He knew the little girl was going to be scared when she woke up, and that scared him. He wished she was a boy instead of a girl. Boys were easier. Three of the five times they had taken boys. Girls made him think too much, and thinking made him sad. He barely remembered his sister now, but he remembered some things. Coughing, mostly. Long, terrible coughs with wheezing whistles between them, whistles with every breath. Thinking of those whistles made him cringe. Huey had slid Jo Ellen's little bed over by the wood stove to keep her warm, but it hadn't done any good. His mother and the first doctor kept saying it was just a bad cold until it was too late. By the time they got her to the city doctor in a neighbor's pickup, she was stone dead. She looked like a little china angel lying across the seat, bluish white, one of God's chosen, just four years old. Diphtheria, they said. Huey hated the word. Someone had said it on TV once, years afterward, and he'd picked up the TV and smashed it to kindling. Joey had never known Jo Ellen. He was living in Mississippi then.

Abby groaned again, louder this time, and Huey picked up the Barbie doll Joey had passed him through the window.

'Mama?' Abby moaned, her eyes still closed. 'Mama?'

'Mama's not here right now, Abby. I'm Huey.'

Her eyes popped open, then went wide as she focused on the giant sitting before her. Tears pooled instantly in her eyes, and her lower lip began to quiver.

'Where's my mama?' she asked in a tiny voice.

'She had to go somewhere with your daddy. They asked me to baby-sit you for a while.'

Abby looked around the dilapidated cabin, her cheeks turning bright red. 'Where are we? Where is this place?'

'A cabin in the woods. Not very far from your house. Your mama will be back soon.'

Her lip quivered harder. 'Where *is* she?'

'With your daddy. They're both coming soon.'

Abby closed her eyes and whimpered, on the edge of panic now. Huey took the Barbie from behind him and set it gently before her. When her eyes opened again, they locked onto the doll, drawn to the tiny piece of home.

'Your mama left this for you,' Huey said.

She snatched up the Barbie and clutched it to her chest. 'I'm scared.'

He nodded in sympathy. 'I'm scared, too.'

Abby's mouth opened. 'You are?'

He nodded again. His eyes were wet with tears.

Abby swallowed, then reached out and squeezed his little finger as if to reassure him.

Forty miles northeast of the cabin, on the outskirts of Jackson, Joe Hickey drove Karen's Expedition southward on Interstate 55. Karen sat beside him, the small Igloo in her lap. Hickey reached into his pocket and pulled out a long silk scarf he'd taken from the Jenningses' laundry room.

'Put this over your eyes.'

Karen tied the scarf around her head without argument. 'Are we getting close?'

'Less than an hour. Don't ask me anything else. I might change my mind about the insulin.'

'I won't talk at all.'

'No, talk,' he said. 'I like your voice. It's got class, you know?'

Though blindfolded, Karen turned to him with amazement.

In the heart of Jackson, in the elite subdivision of Eastover, a white-columned mansion stood gleaming in the beams of spotlights fixed to stately oak trees. On the circular driveway before the house sat a yellow 1932 Duesenberg, the dazzling cornerstone of a vintage car collection of which its owner had spent the better part of the last year divesting himself.

Inside the mansion, Dr James McDill, owner of both the Duesenberg and the mansion, sat across the dinner table from his wife, Margaret. He felt a deep apprehension when he looked at her. Over the past twelve months, she had lost twenty pounds, and she'd weighed only one hundred twenty-five to start with. McDill wasn't in the best shape himself. But after weeks of personal struggle, he was about to speak his mind on a very sensitive matter. He knew the reaction that would follow, but he had no choice. The closer the convention got, the more convinced he became that he was right. Time and reflection had brought it all back to him, particularly the things they had said in passing.

He put down his fork. 'Margaret, I know you don't want me to bring this up again. But I've got to.'

His wife's spoon clattered against her bone china plate. 'Why?' she asked in a voice that could have shaved glass. '*Why* do you have to?'

McDill sighed. He was a cardiovascular surgeon of wide experience, but he had never approached any surgery with the trepidation with which he now faced his wife. 'Maybe because it happened exactly a year ago. Maybe because of the things they told us. I couldn't get it out of my mind in the OR this morning. How this thing has affected our lives. Poisoned them.'

'Not mine. Yours! *Your* life.'

'For God's sake, Margaret. The convention started tonight on the coast. We're not there, and for one reason. Because what happened last year is still controlling us.'

Her mouth opened in shock. 'You wish you were there now? My God!'

'No. But we were wrong not to go to the police a year ago. And I have a very bad feeling now. That woman told me they'd done it before, and I believed her. She said they'd done it to other doctors. They took advantage of the convention . . . of our separation. Margaret, what if it's happening again? Right now?'

'Stop it!' she said in a strangled whisper. '*Don't you remember what they said?* They'll kill Peter! You want to go to the police now? A year after the fact? Don't you know what would happen? You're so naive!'

McDill laid both hands on the dinner table. 'We've got to face this. We simply cannot let what happened to us happen to another family.'

'To *us*? What happened to you, James? You sat in a hotel room with some slut for a night. Don't you ever think for one minute of anyone but yourself? Peter was traumatized!'

'Of course I think about Peter! But I refuse to let another child go through what he did because of our cowardice.'

Margaret wrapped her arms tight around herself and began rocking back and forth in the chair, like schizophrenics McDill had seen in medical school. 'If only you hadn't left us here alone,' she murmured. 'All alone . . . Margaret and Peter . . . alone and un-protected.'

McDill fought the stab of guilt this produced. 'Margaret—'

'Medical convention, my foot,' she hissed, her eyes going narrow. 'It was that goddamned *car* show.'

'Margaret, please—'

He fell silent as their eleven-year-old son appeared in the dining room door. Peter was a pale, thin boy, and his eyes never settled in one place long.

'What's the matter?' he asked timidly. 'Why are you guys yelling?'

'Just a misunderstanding, son. I had a tough surgery today, and we were discussing some tax problems. I lost my temper. Nothing for you to worry about. What time are you going over to Jimmy's?'

'His dad is picking me up in a minute.'

Margaret took a gulp of wine and said, 'Are you sure you want to spend the night over there tonight, darling?'

'Yeah. Unless . . . unless you don't want me to.'

'I like having my baby under this roof,' Margaret cooed.

'Nonsense,' said McDill. 'Go have some fun, son. You've been studying too hard this week.'

A car horn sounded outside.

Peter looked uncertain. 'I guess that's them.'

'You'd better run, son. We'll see you in the morning.'

Peter crossed the room and kissed his mother. Over his shoulder, Margaret glared at McDill.

'We'll be right here if you need us for anything,' she said. 'Just call. We'll be right here. *All night.*'

McDill stared dejectedly at his plate. He had lost his appetite.

The Expedition jounced and jumped along rutted ground beneath black trees, Hickey sitting stiff behind the wheel. Karen gripped the handle on the windshield frame, the ice chest cold between her legs. She was terrified that Hickey would wreck the Expedition before they reached Abby. He had let her remove the blindfold after the last turn, but she felt like she was still wearing it. He refused to use the headlights, and with only the running lights on, she was astonished that he could pick his way through the dense trees. Wherever this place was, Hickey must have spent a lot of time there.

'We're going to meet Huey on this road,' he said. 'You and I will walk forward with the ice chest. You will not get emotional. You will not freak out. You hear? You can hug your kid long enough to calm her down.

Then you take her blood sugar and give her the shot. After that, one last hug, then we go.'

'I understand.'

'Be sure you do. She's going to go crazy when you start to leave, but you'd better tough it out. Just like the first day of school. Huey's told her he's baby-sitting her for one night. You reinforce that. Tell her everything's okay, we're all friends, and you're going to pick her up in the morning. If you flip out . . .' Hickey turned to her for an instant, his eyes hard as agates. 'If you flip out, I'll have to hurt you right in front of her. She'll have nightmares all night. You don't want that.'

A pair of headlights flashed out of the dark and speared Karen's retinas. As she thew up her hand to shield her eyes, Hickey stopped the Expedition and blinked the headlights twice. Then he left them on, creating a long tunnel of halogen light that merged with the dimmer headlights pointing at them.

'Come on,' he said, shutting off the engine. 'Bring your stuff.'

Karen picked up the ice chest and climbed out. When she got to the front of the Expedition, Hickey grabbed her arm and said, 'Start walking.'

Night mist floated through the headlight beams as they walked along them, and the humidity was heavy on Karen's skin. She was straining for a sight or sound of Abby when a giant form blotted out the other pair of headlights.

The silhouette was about thirty yards away, and it looked like the outline of a grizzly bear. Karen stopped in her tracks, but Hickey pushed her on. Suddenly a squeal cut through the night.

'Mama? *Mama!*'

Karen rushed forward, stumbling in the ruts, picking herself up, going on. She fell to her knees and embraced the tiny shadow that had emerged from behind the massive one.

'I'm here, honey!' she said, squeezing Abby as tight as she dared and choking back a wave of tears. 'Mama's here, baby!'

Abby keened and cried and screeched all at once. She wanted to speak, but each time she tried, her little chest heaved and caught, and she kept repeating the same syllable over and over.

'Wh – wh – wha—'

Karen kissed her cheeks and nose and forehead and hair. Abby was almost hyperventilating, mucus and tears running down her face, sheer panic in her eyes.

'It's okay, baby. Take your time. Mama's here. I can hear you, baby.'

'Wh – why did you leave me here, Mama? Why?'

Karen forced herself to appear calm. She couldn't let Abby see how terrified she was. 'I had to, honey. Daddy and I have an important meeting. One we forgot about. It's only for grown-ups, but it won't last long. It's only for tonight.'

'Are you *leaving* again?' The confusion in Abby's eyes was the most wrenching sight Karen had ever seen. Terror of abandonment was something she had known herself, and seeing it in her daughter made her bones ache.

'Not for a while yet,' she said. 'Not for a while. We need to check your sugar, baby.'

'*Nooooo,*' Abby wailed. 'I want to go home!'

'Is Mr Huey being nice to you?' Karen looked fearfully at the huge shadow standing a few yards away.

Abby was too upset to answer.

Karen opened the ice chest and took out the spring-loaded finger-stick device, which she had already loaded with a needle. Abby halfheartedly fought her, but when Karen took firm hold of her hand, she let her middle finger be immobilized. Karen pressed the tip of the pen to the pad of the finger and popped the trigger. Abby yelped, though the pain was negligible, and Karen wiped off the first drop of blood and forced out another. She wiped that against a paper test strip, which she fed into a small machine containing a microchip. After fifteen seconds, the machine beeped.

'Two hundred and forty. You need your shot, sweetie.'

Karen drew three units of short-acting insulin from one vial, then, using the same syringe, added five units from the long-acting vial. This was more than usual, but she suspected that Abby would sleep little during the night, and would probably be given food of some kind.

'Has Mr Huey fed you anything, sweetie?'

'Just some crackers.'

'That's all?'

Abby looked at the ground. 'And a peppermint.'

'Abby!'

'I was hungry.'

Karen started to pull up Abby's jumper to inject the insulin into her stomach, but with Huey standing so near, she decided to inject it right through the material. She pinched up a fold of fat and shot the insulin into it. Abby whimpered softly and locked her arms around Karen's neck. Karen threw the used syringe into the woods and lifted Abby into her arms. There, on her knees in the dirt, she rocked her daughter back and forth like an infant, singing softly Abby's favorite childhood rhyme.

The eensy-weensy spider climbed up the water spout. Down came the rain and washed the spider out. Out came the sun and dried up all the rain, and the eensy-weensy spider climbed up the spout again.

'I love you, punkin,' she murmured. 'Everything's going to be all right.'

She felt Hickey brush past her as he walked forward to speak to Huey.

'Keep singing, Mama,' Abby said.

Karen started the song again, but as she sang, she tuned her ears to the male voices drifting back to her on the night air.

'You doing okay?' Hickey asked.

'Uh-huh,' said a much deeper voice. Deeper but more tentative. 'She's nice.'

Hickey took out a cigarette and lit it. The match flared like a bonfire in the blackness.

'I thought you quit, Joey.'

'Give me a freakin' break.'

The orange eye of the cigarette waxed and waned like a little moon. Karen knew Hickey was watching her, transfixed in the headlight beams with her child, as vulnerable as a deer under the hunter's gun. She put her mouth to Abby's ear.

'Do you remember what I taught you about calling the police? What numbers to call?'

'Nine?' Abby thought aloud. 'Nine-nine-one?'

'Nine-*one*-one.'

'Oh. I know. When I'm nervous I forget. I know our phone number.'

'Good, honey. Don't be nervous, now. Mr Huey has a cell phone. If he goes to the bathroom, he might forget it. If he does, you use it to call nine-one-one. Run and hide outside with it, tell them you're in trouble, and then hide the phone. Don't hang it up. If you can do all that, people will come and bring you home to Mommy and Daddy early. Do you understand?'

Abby's eyes were wide. 'Will the policeman hurt Huey?'

'No, baby. But don't even try it unless you can call without him knowing. Okay? It's like a game.'

Tears shone in Abby's eyes. 'I'm scared, Mom. I want to go home with you.'

'Listen to me, honey. If you have to do number two, you wipe yourself. Don't ask Mr Huey for help. Even if he's nice. You don't know him well enough.'

Hickey dropped his cigarette and stubbed it out with his foot. 'Old home week's over,' he called. 'Let's mount up.'

Abby screamed and grabbed Karen's neck.

'Let's go,' said Hickey, walking toward her. 'Tell princess bye-bye.'

'Nooo!' Abby wailed. '*Nooooooo!*'

Karen looked over her shoulder at Hickey, her eyes pleading. 'I'm *begging* you. Let me stay here with her until morning. What can it possibly matter?'

'I told you about this crap.' He held out his arms. 'Hand her over.'

Karen backed away, clutching Abby in her arms. She knew it would do no good, but the decision was not hers to make. Two million years of evolution would not let her voluntarily give up her child. Hickey lunged forward and grabbed Abby under the arms, then yanked at her as if pulling on a sack of feed. Abby shrieked like she was being flayed alive.

'Stop!' Karen yelled at Hickey. '*Stop it! You're hurting her!*'

'Then let go, goddamn it!'

With a cry of desolation, Karen let go.

A heart-wrenching scream burst from Abby's lips.

Karen snatched up the ice chest, then ran to Huey and hooked the handle of the Igloo around his huge fingers. There were more syringes inside, and five vials of insulin, including one of Humalog. 'Please keep this! If Abby gets sick or passes out, call me and I'll tell you what to do!'

The giant's face was a mask of bewildered fear. 'Yes, ma'am. I—'

'Shut up!' Hickey shouted. 'Get the kid back inside, retard!'

Karen laid both hands against Huey's chest. 'I know you're a good Christian man. Please don't hurt my baby!'

Huey's mouth fell open, exposing his yellow teeth. 'Hurt your baby?'

Hickey thrust Abby into Huey's arms, then grabbed Karen by the elbow and dragged her toward the Expedition.

'I'll be back in the morning, Abby!' Karen promised. 'I'll be the first thing you see tomorrow!'

Abby continued to shriek with air-raid intensity, so loudly that Karen finally put her hands over her ears to blunt the agony of hearing her child's terror. But even that didn't work. Ten yards from the Expedition, she slammed her right elbow into Hickey's head and charged back toward the other pair of headlights.

She was halfway there when Hickey cracked her on the back of the head with what felt like a hammer, sending her sprawling onto the hard dirt. She heard a door slam, then the squeal of a loose fan belt as Huey's truck backed slowly down the road.

High in the Beau Rivage Hotel in Biloxi, the phone rang in suite 28021. Will grabbed it before Cheryl could.

'Joe?' he said. 'Is this Joe?'

'Will?' said an uncertain voice.

'*Karen!*'

The sound of weeping came down the line, and it nearly unmanned him. It took a lot to make Karen Jennings cry.

'Did you see Abby?' he asked through the lump in his throat. 'Did you get her the insulin?'

'Will, she's so scared! I gave her eight units and left some extra vials and syringes. It was awful—'

Karen screamed; then her voice was replaced by Hickey's. 'You can calm down now, college boy. Your kid got her medicine. It's sayonara for now.'

'Wait!'

Will was shouting at a dead phone. He exhaled slowly, trying to control the wild anger swelling in his chest. It was simply not in his nature to endure anguish and frustration without acting.

'Hey,' said Cheryl. 'Everything's gonna be okay. It is.' She reached out to touch his shoulder.

Will slammed the phone into the side of her head. As she fell across the bed, he tried to wrench the gun from her hand, but she held it tight. They wrestled over the bedspread, clawing and fighting for the weapon. Will's joints shot fire through his limbs and trunk, but they kept functioning. Cheryl was clutching the gun beneath her breasts with both hands. Abandoning caution, he grabbed it blindly with both hands and yanked as hard as he could.

Something ripped, Cheryl screamed, and the gun came away in his hands. He jumped up and pointed it at her. She was cradling her bloody right hand.

'What the hell?'

Cheryl's dress had torn, exposing her from the waist up. She wore a sheer black bra, but Will wasn't looking at her breasts. He was staring at a blue and green montage of bruises that covered her abdomen and ribs like stains, one of which continued up into the bra.

'What happened to you?'

She backed against the ornate headboard, the movement instinctive, animal-like. 'Nothing.'

'That's not nothing. That's a beating.'

She picked up a pillow and covered her chest. 'It's nothing. And you just screwed up big-time.'

After venting his rage in the attack, Will found

himself puzzled about what to do next. 'I want to ask you something, Cheryl.'

'Fuck you.'

'Are you committed to this kidnapping?'

She said nothing.

'Because I have a feeling you're not. I have a feeling this kind of thing is what Joe gets off on, but not you. I think you tried to talk him out of it. That's why you got the beating, isn't it?'

Her face was as closed as a tribal mask. 'Don't need no reason for a beating,' she said, all her earlier elocution gone. 'Ain't never no reason.'

Will flashed back to his days as a resident, working the Jackson ERs. He'd seen more physical abuse in six months than he'd thought existed in the world at the time. And many of the responses he got from women sounded exactly like Cheryl's. Sullen, angry, resigned. But he couldn't solve her marital problems in one night. He couldn't even solve his own. With that thought, a new idea entered his mind. And with it a new fear.

'Why are you here with me?' he asked.

Cheryl looked blank.

'I mean, why isn't Joe here with me? He obviously resents the hell out of me. If he was here, he could piss on me all night, beat the hell out of me. I'd have no choice but to take it. But he passed up that chance.' Will lowered the gun and stepped closer to the bed. 'It doesn't make sense, Cheryl. Why not man-man, woman-woman? You know? A man has a lot more chance of controlling an angry father than a woman does. Has Joe done it this way every time? Is he always with the wife?'

She wiped her bloody hand on the pillow. 'Putting me with the husband avoids the whole macho thing. A Type-A jerk like you doesn't feel threatened by a woman. You're less likely to blow up and do something stupid.' She gingerly tested her right wrist. 'Only you just did. You hurt me, you bastard.'

'What do you expect? You kidnapped my daughter. Don't worry about your hand. I can fix it.'

'You stay the hell away from me.'

'Whatever you say.' He walked over to the window and looked out over the gulf. There were more lights now, ships making steady headway, oblivious to the drama unfolding in the glittering tower on the beach.

'That's Joe talking,' he said, thinking aloud. 'About who stays with whom, I mean. I've talked to him less than five minutes, but I know one thing about him. He *loves* the macho thing. He'd like nothing better than to be here rubbing my face in it. That's half the point of all this. So, if he's not here . . . he's somehow rubbing my face in it *more* by being there.' Will turned back to Cheryl, who jerked up the pillow. 'How could he be doing that?'

'You think he's tearing up all your precious paintings or something? That's not Joey.'

Will pulled a chair over beside the bed. 'I want you to tell me everything you know that *is* Joe, Cheryl. Start talking.'

'I'm telling you shit. You'll find out more than you want to know when he calls back and I tell him what you did.'

Another black wave of rage rolled through him. 'If you *can* talk.'

She laughed outright. 'There's nothing you can do to me that hasn't been done before, Doctor. I mean, *nothing*.' She tossed the pillow aside, exposing her breasts and the relief map of bruises. 'Face it, Joey's got you beat, right down the line.'

In an upstairs bathroom of the McDill mansion, Margaret McDill sat at a vanity table, taking off her makeup with cold cream. She looked into the mirror at her husband, who hovered in the door behind her like an accusing ghost.

'I refuse to discuss it,' she said. 'How many times do I have to tell you that?'

Dr McDill gave a long sigh. 'I just want to—'

'What? Drive me back to a bottle a day?' She threw a mascara-stained Kleenex onto the floor. 'I can't stand this, James. It's sadistic!'

'Margaret, for God's sake. I'm just trying to understand.' He took a deep breath and pushed into forbidden territory yet again. 'Is there something more? Something I don't know about?' He'd asked this before and been rebuffed. Tonight he would press it. He had to. 'Did this man hurt you?'

'Hurt me?' Her lips tightened to white. 'Did he *hurt* me?'

'I'm your husband, Margaret. I only want to help you.'

She whirled from the mirror, her eyes wild. 'All right! All *right*! You want to know why I won't report it? Because he raped me.'

McDill flinched.

'He raped me, James. Do you feel better now? Is that what you wanted to hear? What you want to tell the police? All the gory details?'

McDill stared openmouthed at his wife.

'He told me to take off my clothes and I did. He told me to kiss him and I did. He told me I'd have to do things I'd never done before—' She covered her face with her hands – 'and I did. I *did*. And I'd do it again! All I could think of was Peter. *They had my baby!*'

She exploded into unintelligible screams, thrashing her head and arms until McDill rushed forward and, oblivious to the blows he was taking, hugged her so tightly that she couldn't move. He spoke in a reassuring voice as she continued to shriek.

'It's all right, Margaret. . . . It's going to be all right. You didn't do anything wrong. You did nothing wrong.' Tears stung his eyes. 'God help me, I thought it might be something like this. It's all right. . . .'

As her screams subsided, Margaret descended into a near catatonic state.

'Can you hear me?' asked McDill. 'Margaret?'

She nodded like an Alzheimer's patient.

'I'm afraid the same thing is happening again. Do you understand? To another family. Another mother. Another child.' He took her firmly by the shoulders and peered into her eyes. 'We can't let that happen. It wouldn't be Christian. Would it?'

Margaret slowly shook her head, her eyes glassy.

'I'm going to call the FBI,' McDill said. 'But we don't have to tell them anything about what happened to you. You understand? It's irrelevant to the situation.'

His wife's only response was fresh tears sliding down her cheeks.

'I love you, sweetheart,' he assured her. 'More than I ever have.'

McDill pulled her close. When he squeezed her shuddering body, something inside him came loose. Something came loose and a fearful darkness poured out. James McDill read the Bible every night, no matter how tired. He went to church every week, taught Sunday school to his son's class. He spent every day but Sunday bringing people back from the edge of death with his hard-earned skills. But when he thought of the faceless man who had brutalized the girl he had loved since high school – the mother of his child – something deeper than reason spoke from within him. Something deeper even than God. When he opened his mouth, what emerged was a whispered vow.

'I am going to kill that son of a bitch.'

Chapter 6

Being forced to leave Abby behind had shattered Karen. She sat in the Expedition in a sort of detached haze, like a disembodied brain floating in ether. She was wearing the blindfold again, but she sensed that there was little traffic. The whooshes of cars passing were far apart.

'You taken a vow of silence or what?' asked Hickey.

Karen let her mind reach into the starless night beneath the blindfold.

'Hey. I'm talking to you.'

The voice was like a face obscured by fog.

'You're upset, I know. But it had to be that way. You'll get over it.'

'I'm not sure I will.'

'See? You can talk.'

She heard him light another cigarette. The smell of burning tobacco filled the air.

'You can take off the blindfold now.'

'I prefer it on.'

'I prefer it off.'

Karen unwrapped the scarf. The dash lights shone like a coastal city viewed from the sea. Glancing up, she saw that the digital compass between the visors read 'E' for east. That was information she could use. They were on a two-lane road, and she knew by the speed and sound of the outgoing trip that they had driven on an interstate for at least half an hour after leaving Jackson. That left two options: I-55, which ran north and south, or I-20, which ran east and west. That meant Abby was being held somewhere south of Jackson and west of I-55, if Hickey had taken that interstate. If he'd taken I-20, it was harder to make assumptions. But if he left the blindfold off, she might soon know for sure. She decided to make an effort to keep him in a good mood.

'Thank you for letting me give Abby the shot.'

Hickey rolled down his window a crack and blew cigarette smoke outside. 'That's what I like to hear. Gratitude. You don't see much of it these days. It's a forgotten courtesy. But you're an old-fashioned girl. I can tell. You know how to show appreciation for a good deed.'

Karen waited a moment, then looked left. Hickey's profile was like a wind-eroded boulder. Heavy brows, the nose a bit flat, the chin like an unspoken challenge. It looked like a face that could take a lot of punishment, and probably had.

'We've got a whole night to kill,' he said, glancing away from the road long enough to find her eyes in the dark. 'Why make it like breaking rocks, you know? Let's be friends.'

Her internal radar went to alert status.

'You're a beautiful woman. You got that red hair, but not the coarse kind, you know? Strawberry blond, I guess they call it. And I'm not a bad-looking guy, am I?'

'Look, I don't know what you've done in the past, but—'

'I want to see that bush, girl.' Hickey's eyes glinted in the dash lights. 'I *know* you got a good one.'

The words shocked and frightened Karen more than she would have believed possible. She didn't want to show fear, but she had already pressed herself against the door.

'You got some good tan lines, too, I bet. With that pool out back.'

She stared straight ahead, her cheeks burning.

'I've got something for you, too, Karen. A lot more than you're used to, I bet.'

With every remark she left unanswered, she felt Hickey's confidence growing. 'I wouldn't count on that,' she said. 'My husband got lucky with those genes.'

Hickey gave a self-assured laugh. 'That right? Somehow I don't picture old Will having the goods. Seems like the tennis player type to me. Mr Average in the showers. See, that's why I never back off. On that elemental level, I got what it takes.' He threw his cigarette butt out of the window and pressed the dashboard cigarette lighter. 'I heard this story about LBJ once. During the Vietnam thing, MacNamara was giving him some shit about how Ho Chi Minh has this, Ho Chi Minh has that. LBJ unzips his fly, whips out his Johnson and says, "Has old Ho got anything like *this*?"'

He broke up laughing.

'Right there in the freakin' Oval Office. Hey, I wonder if that's why they call it a Johnson?'

115

'LBJ lost that war, didn't he?'

Hickey stopped laughing. 'Get those jeans off. You're gonna be walking bowlegged for a week.'

A ball of ice formed in Karen's chest.

'You think I'm kidding? We've done this gig five times, and every time the wives and me had a little party. A little bonus for the executive in the operation, and nobody the wiser.'

'No party tonight, Joe.'

'No?' He laughed again. 'In thirty minutes I'm gonna be banging on your tonsils, lady. Get those jeans off.'

'Here?'

'Like you never done it in a car before?'

She sat rigidly in the seat, refusing to acknowledge the remark.

Hickey shook his head and tapped a finger on the cell phone. 'Lose the jeans. Or I reach out and touch your precious princess.'

Karen held out for another few seconds. Then she unsnapped her jeans, arched in the seat, and pulled them off.

'Happy now?'

'Getting there. Keep going.'

A cold trickle of sweat ran down her rib cage. 'Not in the car.'

He looked down and punched a number into the Expedition's cell phone.

'Don't!'

He cut his eyes at her. 'Still dressed?'

She folded her jeans and laid them in her lap, then slid the panties off and put them on top of the jeans.

116

Hickey laughed and hit END on the phone, then picked up the cotton panties and knocked her jeans to the floor. 'Not exactly Victoria's Secret. You trying to discourage interest with these things?'

She felt an irrational prick of guilt. As Hickey laughed, she arranged the tail of her blouse so that it fell into her lap. But no sooner had she done this than he reached up and hit the passenger light switch, flooding her side of the interior with yellow light. She felt as she had as a little girl, playing hide-and-seek with her older male cousins. She'd hidden in the basement once, at the house at Fort Leavenworth, and as she heard them approach, she backed deeper and deeper into the dark recesses of the mildewed room. Yet no matter how far she went, the footsteps followed. And in the dark basement, far from the adults, she knew what they would do to her. Pressure her into 'show-me' games, whether she wanted to play or not.

'Nice legs,' Hickey said. 'Far as they go.'

She shivered in the air conditioning. 'Why are you doing this?'

He sniffed and reached down for the cigarette lighter, then shook another Camel from the pack in his shirt pocket and ignited the tip. A stream of smoke clouded the windshield like dissipating fog.

'Does there always have to be a why?'

'Yes.' She felt his gaze on her lap like the heat from a lamp.

'We've got time for all that. Slide that shirttail over.'

She wanted to refuse. But how could she? She breathed slowly and deeply, trying not to let him rattle her. 'Are you going to leave the light on all the way back? It seems dangerous.'

'I gotta admit, I'm tempted. But it wouldn't be too smart, would it?' He reached out and traced a finger-nail along her outer thigh. 'Like I said, we've got all night. What the hell.'

He flicked off the light, and the protective blanket of night closed around her again. But she was not safe. Nowhere close. Of course, *safe* didn't really matter, not in the usual sense. What mattered was survival. For once in her life, it was that simple. There was only one priority: Abby. Other mothers had walked through fire for their children; she could do the same. She could endure the worst that an animal like Hickey could dish out, and be there to hug Abby when it was over. But that didn't mean she would stop looking for a way to fight back. Because Hickey was arrogant. And arro-gant men made mistakes. If he did make one, God and all his angels wouldn't be able to help the son of a bitch who made Abby Jennings suffer pain.

Another hope burned in her heart, small but steady. Wherever Will was, he was thinking. And not the way Karen was. She had outscored her husband by five percentile points on the MCAT test, and she could balance a checkbook twice as fast as he could. But there was another kind of intelligence, and Will had it in spades. It was speed of thought, and not just down one pathway, but several simultaneously. Karen thought logically, examining each option from begin-ning to end, then accepting or rejecting it before moving on. Will could look at a situation and see the endpoints of a dozen possible choices in the blink of an eye, then from instinct choose rightly. He wasn't always able to explain his choices, but they were almost inevitably correct. He told her once that they weren't correct in any objective sense. Sometimes, he said, simply *making* a choice – any choice – and following through with absolute commitment *made* it the right choice.

That's the kind of brain I need now, she thought.

At that moment, Will was staring at the telephone in the bedroom of his suite. It had just rung, and though he was holding Cheryl's Walther in his hand, he knew it was useless. If she told Hickey he had assaulted her, anything could happen. Yet if he didn't let her answer, Hickey would assume things were not as they should be, and he might retaliate against Abby.

The phone rang again.

'What are you going to do now, smart-ass?' Cheryl asked. She was leaning against the headboard of the bed, her torn dress around her waist, the road map of bruises on her torso left exposed like a silent 'go to hell.'

He tossed the gun into her lap.

She laughed and picked it up, then answered the phone. After listening for a few moments, she said, 'It is now. The doc flipped out. . . . He hit me and took my gun. Just like the guy from Tupelo. . . . Okay.' She held out the receiver to Will. 'He wants to talk to you.'

Will took the phone. 'Joe?'

'Doc, you screw up again, and the biggest piece you find of your little girl will fit in a thimble.'

119

'I hear you, Joe.'

'You hit my old lady?'

'It doesn't look like I was the first.'

Silence. Then, 'That ain't your business, is it?'

'No.'

'You remember what I said about your little girl.'

'I understand. I made a mistake. I just want my daughter back.'

The phone went dead.

'You're pathetic,' Cheryl said. 'Like some kid stopped by a highway patrolman. Totally submissive.'

'You know all about that, don't you? Submission.'

She shrugged. 'So he smacks me around sometimes. You never smacked your wife?'

'No.'

'Liar.'

Will saw no point in arguing. 'Those bruises weren't caused by a couple of smacks. I see signs of systematic abuse.'

'You don't argue with your wife?'

'We argue. We don't hit each other. What did you and Joe argue about last? Was it about going through with his kidnapping?'

'Hell, no. We've done this lots of times.'

'Maybe you're tired of it.' He let that simmer for a few moments. 'I can see how you would be. Realizing how much pain you're putting people through. Especially the kids.'

She looked away. 'Talk all you want. You know what I was doing before Joe found me?'

'What?'

'I was a bar girl in a truck stop. A full-service bar girl.'

120

'You mean like—'

'Yeah, like that.'

'How did you end up there?'

'You sound like some frat-boy john. "Oh, Cheryl, you're so sweet, how'd ever you end up doing this?" Well, I ain't blaming nobody. My stepfather, maybe, but he's dead now. My mother had it worse than I did.'

'Being a whore is a lot more respectable than what you're doing now.'

'You ever been a whore?'

'No.'

'Then you don't know. Every time I see a hooker in a movie, I want to throw something at the screen. When I saw *Pretty Woman*, I wanted to puke. You know the part in that movie when Richard Gere's friend tries to make Julia Roberts do him? The guy from *Seinfeld*? It's like the only uncomfortable part of that whole movie.'

'I remember.'

'That's what being in the life is like all the time. Except no movie star busts in to save you from his friend. He probably bought you for his friend.' Her eyes burned into Will's with disturbing intensity. 'Think about sitting somewhere all day, all night, available to any scummy, shit-breath, disease-ridden son of a bitch who walks in the door with the price of admission. That's being a hooker.'

'You didn't have any choice about clients?'

'Clients?' She barked a little laugh. 'I wasn't a lawyer, okay? It's *johns*. And, no, I didn't have any choice. 'Cause if I said no, I didn't get the good thing.'

'The good thing. Cocaine?'

'My pimp used to say we were just trading crack for crack.'

'Joe got you out of that life?'

'That's right. He got me clean. It was the hardest thing either of us ever did. So, if you think you're gonna talk me into betraying him, or bribe me into it, think again. If he smacks me around now and then, you think I care?'

'Yes, I do. Because you know that's not love. You don't owe Joe a life of servitude because he got you off crack. You deserve to be as happy as anybody else.'

She shook her head like someone listening to a salesman. 'My stepfather always said everybody gets what they deserve.'

'He sounds like an asshole.'

A bitter laugh. 'You got that right. You ever go to a hooker?'

'No.'

'What guy admits it, right? I believe you, though. You're one of those one-in-a-million guys who were meant to be husbands, aren't you?'

'And fathers.'

She winced.

'You never had a child of your own?' Will asked.

'I'm not talking about that.'

'Why not?'

'Let's just say I've been pregnant enough times that I can't have kids.'

What did that mean? Multiple abortions? One bad one? 'Are you sure? I was an obstetrician before I was an anesthesiologist. There are lots of new therapies for—'

'Don't ask me any more about it,' Cheryl said in a desolate voice.

'All right.'

He turned and walked over to the picture window. There wasn't much moon over the gulf. It was hard to see where the dark water ended and the sky began. Far below him, the lighted blue swimming pool undulated at the center of the plaza, with the paler Jacuzzi beside it. To his right lay the marina, with its stylized light-house and million-dollar cabin cruisers. A few bright stars shone high in the sky, but the glare from the casino sign drowned the rest. Changing focus, he saw Cheryl reflected in the glass, sitting on the bed with the gun in her lap, looking as lost as anyone he'd ever seen. He spoke without turning.

'I don't want to beat a dead horse here. And I don't want to pry. But I would really like to know how you ended up in prostitution. I mean, you just don't look like one. You look too fresh. You're beautiful, for God's sake. How old are you?'

'Twenty-six.'

'How old is Joe?'

'Fifty.'

Twenty-four years' difference. 'Where are you from?'

Cheryl sighed. 'Do we have to play *Twenty Questions*?'

'What else is there to do?'

'I could use a drink.'

Will walked over to the phone.

'What are you doing?' she asked, laying a hand on the gun.

'Ordering you a drink. What do you like?'

She looked suspicious. 'I guess it won't hurt anything. I like rum and Coke.'

He called room service and ordered a bottle of Bacardi, a two-liter bottle of Coca-Cola, and a pot of tea for himself.

'You English or something?' asked Cheryl.

'I just like tea.' What he wanted was caffeine, enough to get him through whatever was going to be required of him in the next twelve hours. He needed a pain pill, too, for his joints, but he wasn't going to take anything that might dull his mind. He needed his edge tonight.

'So, where are you from?' he asked again.

'Nowhere. Everywhere.'

'What does that mean?'

'My dad was in the army. We moved a lot when I was a little girl.'

'My wife grew up in the same way. Moving from base to base.'

She gave him a skeptical look. 'I doubt much was the same about it. She was probably the colonel's daughter or something.'

'No. Her father was a master sergeant.'

'Yeah? My father was a captain. Or so I'm told. He screwed up some way, so they never let him go to Vietnam. He took it out on my Mom for one too many years, and she finally left him. We went back to her hometown, little nothing of a place in Marion County. Then she hooked up with my stepfather.' Cheryl's eyes glazed. 'That was a whole new thing. I was about ten, I guess. After he got tired of Mom in the sack, he turned to me. She was so scared he'd leave us, she wouldn't listen to anything I said. When I turned sixteen, I got the hell out of there.'

'Where'd you go?'

'I had a girlfriend who'd gone to Hinds Junior College. She had an apartment in Jackson with two other girls. I crashed with her for a couple of weeks, got a job waiting tables. I was barely making enough to help with the rent, and her roomies got mad. One of them was dancing at this club in Jackson. She was making three hundred bucks a night. Straight, you know? Just lap dances and stuff, no tricks out back. A couple of nights, just for kicks, a bunch of us went in there and watched her dance. It wasn't at all what I thought. I mean, some of the men were pathetic and all that, but it wasn't humiliating. The girls were in control. For the most part, anyway. Or that's what it looked like.'

'You started stripping?'

'Not right away. But my girlfriend got pregnant, and her boyfriend ran offshore. She went back home to Mayberry RFD, and suddenly my share of the rent went up. So, I gave it a try. And it worked. I was a natural, they said. Plenty of nights I made six hundred bucks. Of course, I had to kick half of that back to the club.'

'That sounds like enough money to eventually move up to a different kind of job.'

'That's not how it works. See, stripping is like any night job. Musician, whatever. You've got these long shifts. You sleep all day, so you don't really meet normal people. You get tired as hell. I mean, have you ever danced for eight hours straight? Drinking beer and mixed drinks? Plus, you find out it's not exactly what you thought. You've got your lap dances, which are fine. But then you've got sofa dances. A sofa dance is a little more involved. The guys want to make it, you know? It's hand jobs on the outside of the pants, or dry humping till they get off. What you try to do is get them almost there just as the song ends. Then they'll come across with another thirty bucks to get off at the start of the next song. You do that for eight hours, you start needing something to keep you going. To keep you from sinking too far down, you know?'

'Cocaine.'

A hint of a smile animated her lips, like a ghost smiling from within her. 'The sweet thing.'

'And once you got on coke, they had you.'

'Yep. Pretty soon you're only breaking even on the dancing, just to keep up your habit. Then you're into *them* for money. Dancing eight hours a day, just to pay the vig on what you owe. And that's when they hit you. There's ways to pay off the principal.'

'Turning tricks.'

'Blow jobs in the bathroom. Half-and-half in the cars out back. Around the world in the motel up the street, after your shift.'

'Jesus.'

Her eyes looked ancient in her young face. 'Girls don't last long doing that, Doc. These are people, you know? Single mothers trying to raise kids. Girls working through junior college.'

'And Joe got you out?'

A cynical smile. 'Sir Galahad to the rescue. That's Joe. One night he paid for a trick at the motel, packed me into his car, and hauled me all the way down to New Orleans. He had a house in Gentilly. He put mattresses on the walls, boarded up the windows, and locked me in.' She shuddered at the memory. 'Cold turkey. He cleaned up the vomit and brought me soup. Talk about a nightmare.'

Will tried to imagine how Joe saw this drama in his mind. He probably did see himself as some sort of knight, rescuing the fair damsel from the dark castle. And Cheryl was fair, all right. It was difficult to believe that she had endured the ravages of the life she described. Working the ERs as a resident, Will had seen twenty-six-year-old whores who looked fifty. Cheryl looked like a sorority girl from Ole Miss, poised in that bloom of youth between college and marriage. Maybe a little hard around the jaw and eyes, but otherwise unmarred.

'How the hell did you wind up kidnapping kids? Is that what Sir Galahad rescued you for?'

'It wasn't like that. Not at first. But we needed money. Joe tried some straight things, but they never seemed to work out. And I knew how to strip. He put me in a club in Metairie, just outside New Orleans. Nice club. He stayed every night watching over me. No drugs, no drinking. I was making so much money, we couldn't believe it. Everybody said I was better than the featured dancers who came through, you know. Penthouse pets, girls like that. So I got into that for a while.' Cheryl's eyes suddenly lit up, the way Abby's did when she was telling someone about her doll collection. 'I had a dozen different outfits, props, the whole works. I had a Jeep Grand Cherokee, and we'd drive around the country, following my club tour. Texas, Colorado, Montana . . . man, it was something.'

'But?'

She looked down at the gun in her lap. 'Joe got jealous. I was good enough that people started talking to me about other things. Movie people. Not like Sandra Bullock, you know, but still Hollywood. Soft porn stuff, like you see on Cinemax. And Joe got nervous about that. He didn't . . . He—'

'He didn't want you out from under,' Will said. 'He wanted you all to himself, all the time.'

She nodded sadly. 'Yeah.'

'You couldn't break loose?'

'I owed him, okay? I owed him in a way only me and him understood.'

'For getting you off crack?'

'Not just that, okay?'

'What do you mean?'

'Where's my damn drink?'

As though in answer to her question, a knock sounded at the door. Will walked through the sitting room of the suite and accepted the tray from a young Mexican girl. He tipped her liberally, then hung out the DO NOT DISTURB sign and carried the tray in to Cheryl.

'How did you owe Joe?' he asked, pouring Bacardi and Coke over the small hotel ice cubes.

She took the glass and drank a long sip of the sweet mixture. Then another. She clearly meant to finish the drink before continuing. Will poured himself a steaming cup of tea, added sugar and lemon. The scent of Earl Gray wafted through the bedroom.

Cheryl finished her rum-and-Coke and held out the glass for a refill. Will mixed another – stronger this time – then took a sip of tea and sat on the edge of the bed.

'How did you owe him, Cheryl?

'You don't just walk away from the kind of work I was doing at the club in Jackson,' she said quietly. 'I owed them money, and they wanted me working it off. When I started dancing in Metairie, they heard about it. They sent a couple of guys down to me. Joe offered to pay my debts, but they wouldn't go for it. They wanted me back at the club. The guy who owned the place . . . he had a thing for me.'

'So what happened?'

A little laugh rippled the bruised flesh of her abdomen. 'Joe convinced the guys to change their minds.'

'How did he do that?'

'Convincingly.'

'And they left you alone?'

'Those guys did.'

'And?'

'The owner sent another guy for me. To bring me back. A really bad guy.'

'And what happened?'

Another swallow. 'Joe punched his ticket.'

'You mean he killed him?'

Cheryl looked Will right in the eye. 'That's what I mean. Messy, too. So that anybody else they sent would know what he was getting into. You know? And it worked. Nobody else came. I was free.'

'You weren't exactly free. You'd just traded one master for another.'

'Hey, I ain't nobody's slave.'

'Who are you trying to convince?'

'Shut up.'

'You carry a lot of pain around, don't you?'

'Don't we all?'

'Yes. But I don't think Joe understands that. He thinks he's got a monopoly on suffering. That everything's stacked against him from the start.'

'How do you know it wasn't? You sit up there in your perfect little house, with your money and your kid and your paintings and your swimming pool and your cars. Everything laid out just right since the day you were born. Well, some people don't have it that way.'

'Is that what you think? You think I started rich? My father worked in a mill for eighteen years, Cheryl. No college degree. Then the mill shut down. He put his life savings into his dream, a music store. Every dollar he had went into Wurlitzer organs, Baldwin pianos, and brass band instruments. Five months after he opened it, the store burned to the ground. His insurance had lapsed two days before.' Will reached out and took a shot from the Bacardi bottle. 'He drove off a bridge a week later. I was eleven years old.'

Cheryl shook her head. 'You must have inherited something. You're silver spoon all the way.'

Will laughed bitterly. 'My wife's mother was a waitress. Karen was the first woman in her family to go to college. Then nursing school. Then medical school, but she had to drop out because she got pregnant.

And her father died before he could see how well she did. She fought for everything she has. So did I.'

'The American dream,' Cheryl mumbled. 'Get out the violins.'

'I'm just pointing out that Joe seems to have a personal problem with me. Some kind of class thing. And he's way off base.'

She looked up, her eyes alert. 'How much money do you make a year?'

'About four hundred thousand dollars.'

'He's not that far off.'

Will had understated his income, and he doubted Cheryl had any concept of the kind of royalties he would earn from Restorase. 'I can give you a lot more money than that, Cheryl. If you'll help me save Abby, I mean. Enough to get you away clean. Really free. Forever.'

A faint flicker of hope lighted her eyes, then died. 'You're lying, sweetie. You'd rat me out the first chance you got.'

'Why would I? I'd have nothing to gain.'

'Because it's the nature of things. I'd do the same. If you had my kid, I'd be over there right now giving you the sofa dance of your life. I'd take you to bed and give you around-the-world like you never imagined it before.' A note of professional pride entered her voice. 'I can do things for you that your wife never even heard of. That your wildest old girlfriend never heard of. When was the last time you got off four times in one night?'

Will treated this as a rhetorical question.

'I thought so. But you could. I could make you. And

131

if you had my kid, I would. Gladly. But as soon as I had my kid back, I'd rat you out.'

He started to argue, but there was no point. She would not be persuaded.

Cheryl held up her drink in a mock toast. 'Don't feel bad, Doc. Like I said, it's just the nature of things.'

Will had stopped listening. He was thinking about what Cheryl had said she would do to save her child, if she had one. And about why Hickey had chosen to spend the night with Karen rather than with him. And what Karen would or would not do to save Abby.

Chapter 7

Hickey pulled the Expedition into the garage and shut off the engine. In the ticking silence, with the leather seat clammy against her backside, Karen felt dread settle in her limbs like cement.

'Party time, *cher*,' Hickey said. He opened his door and climbed out, then waited in the glow of the dome light. 'You're not doing anybody any good sitting there. You or me.'

She folded her panties into her jeans and got out. As she walked to the laundry room door, she could feel the tail of her blouse covering her behind, and she was thankful for that. At the door she stopped and waited for Hickey to open it, but he walked up and handed her the key ring.

'You do it,' he said. 'Your house.'

She tucked her jeans under her arm, then bent and took hold of the doorknob with her left hand. When her palm touched the brass, a mild shock went through her. Before this house existed, she had drawn it on a piece of paper. Every room. Every window. She had chosen the knob in her hand. Worked with the architect on the blueprints. Badgered the sub-contractors. Mortared the patio bricks. Painted the

133

interiors. If any place on earth belonged to her, personified her, this house did. And now it was about to be violated. In point of fact, it already had been when Abby was taken. But the violation to come would be more profound. She could read the thoughts in Hickey's mind as though no border of flesh and bone concealed them. He wanted her body, yes. But his intent was more complex than that. He wanted more to desecrate her marriage.

'Come on,' he said. 'Meter's running.'

A desperate thought flashed through her mind. She could shove open the door just far enough to slip inside, then lock it behind her. Lock it and call the police. But what would that accomplish? Nothing but pain or death for Abby. Hickey had his pocket cell phone, and he could be talking to his giant of a cousin in seconds. No. There was no choice but to obey.

She turned the key and walked inside, right through the laundry room and pantry to the kitchen. Every instinct told her to pull her jeans back on, but that might prompt Hickey to retaliate. She simply stood there, on the oven side of the island, waiting for a command.

He walked up slowly and smiled. 'Up the hall. To your bedroom.'

She turned and walked up the hallway, heavy-footed as a zombie. She was walking in Abby's tracks, in the last footsteps her child had taken in this house. That knowledge infused her with guilt, but also hardened her will to resist. The scent of Abby's room was strong here, even with her door closed. The comforting smell of toy animal fur and little girls' makeup kits.

'Stop,' Hickey said.

Karen stopped. He reached around her left side and opened Abby's door. Faint moonlight shone through the window, falling upon the countless inhabitants of the room.

'Take a good look, Mom. This is why we're not going to have any trouble being friends tonight.'

Karen looked. Here was the justification for whatever she would have to do to get through the night. To bring Abby back to this sanctuary.

Hickey's cupped hand flashed under her shirttail and slapped her flank, hard. He laughed when she jumped, then poked her between the shoulder blades, pushing her until she reached the master bedroom.

Not wanting to enter it in the dark, she reached out and rotated the dimmer switch on the wall. The sight of the bedroom startled her. Everything was in its proper place, yet nothing seemed familiar. Not the antique sleigh bed. Not the overstuffed chair and ottoman. Not the matched Henredon dressers or the cherrywood cabinet that held the television. Not even the Walter Anderson watercolors on the walls. All struck her as furnishings in some nameless hotel, not objects she had chosen with the greatest care.

'The lap of luxury,' Hickey said. 'Looks like a nice place to pass an evening.'

He walked past her, fell back into the oversized chair, and kicked his feet up on the ottoman. His Top-Siders were so new that there were no marks on the soles. Only dirt from the trip to the cabin.

'I could use a drink,' he said. 'Bourbon. Kentucky bourbon, if you got it.'

The bourbon was kept on a sideboard in Will's study. Karen laid her jeans on the foot of the bed and went back up the hall, thankful for a chance to postpone what seemed inevitable. Had five other mothers submitted to this?

In the study, she saw Will's computer glowing softly. For a moment she considered trying to send a message to his pager via the SkyTel, but she had never used it before. And besides, what could she say? I'm about to be raped? If she did, Will would probably do something heroic and stupid, and get Abby killed. As she poured a shot of Wild Turkey, she realized that bourbon might accomplish what defiance could not. If Hickey drank enough whiskey fast enough, he might not be able to perform. It was probably a long shot, though. Karen thought the old saying about alcohol increasing desire but decreasing ability was exaggerated. Some of the best sex she and Will ever had was consummated when they were drunk. Of course, that had been a while back, when Will was in his midthirties. This thought disturbed the deep well of guilt inside her, but mixed with it was enough resentment to force the guilt down.

She picked up the Wild Turkey bottle and walked back toward her bedroom. Unexpected images flashed in her mind, scenes from a film she had seen long ago and forgotten until now. It starred Nicole Kidman. She couldn't remember its name, but Nicole and her husband had been blue-water sailing and had rescued a man in a life raft. The man turned out to be psychotic, and sailed off from Nicole's husband with her aboard. To go back and save her husband, Nicole had to get control of the boat again. But the psychopath had the gun. Before long, he decided to rape her, and what Karen remembered about the film – what had stayed with her long after – was that Nicole had let it happen. She had known it was the wrong moment to resist, and she had endured the rape in the hope of surviving until the right moment came. And it had arrived, finally, proving her sacrifice worthwhile.

As Karen neared the bedroom, words from her dead mother rose in her mind. A genteel woman speaking of rape in the language of older generations of Southern women. The 'fate worse than death,' they called it. But they were wrong. Pride had bred a lot of wrong notions, and that was one. Karen had lived long enough to know that. Rape could scar forever, but it was not death. *Where there's life, there's hope*, her father had always said. And whatever it cost, she and Abby were going to live through this night.

Hickey was smiling when she stepped through the door. 'Wild Turkey!' he cried. 'I'll be damned. Bring that here!'

She crossed the room and gave him the bottle, then took three steps back.

'Scared I'll bite?' He unscrewed the cap and drank liberally from the wide glass mouth, then set the bottle between his legs. 'I'll tell you a little secret. I *do*.'

She looked away.

'Put your pants back on,' he said.

What should have been a welcome command only made her more anxious. She went to the bed and slipped her panties on, then slid her jeans up and snapped them.

'Look at me,' Hickey said.

She looked.

His black eyes seethed. 'You know what a lap dance is?'

Lurid images from HBO movies went through her mind. Scantily clad women hunching over bar patrons in chairs, wiggling their silicone-enhanced breasts in the faces of bachelor party boys and rheumy-eyed older men.

'No,' she replied.

'You're lying. You know what one is. What you don't know is, my wife had to do them for a living for a while. That bugged me, Karen. That she had to do that.'

So why didn't you get a decent job? she thought. But what she said was, 'I'm sorry she had to do that.'

His face went sullen. 'All those bastards feeling her up, slobbering all over her. Your husband was probably one of them. She danced right here in Jackson.'

'Will doesn't go to those places.'

Hickey's eyes glinted. 'Who do you think you're kidding? You think hubby never had a lap dance?'

'No. At least I don't think so.'

'You're living in a dream world. Ten to one, he'd have gotten one tonight on the coast, if this thing hadn't come up. Hell, a weekend away from the old lady? Even one who looks like you do . . . a man needs a little variety.'

'That's your wife with Will right now?'

'That's right.'

Every time Hickey confided another detail, Karen became more convinced that he didn't intend to let her live through this ordeal.

'What's going on in that little head of yours?' he asked. 'Trying to think your way out of the box?'

'Your wife doesn't see anything wrong with kidnapping?'

'She doesn't see anything wrong with anything I do. And if she does, she keeps quiet about it. Get the picture?'

'I think so.'

He took another slug of Wild Turkey. 'We need some music. You got a stereo in that TV cabinet?'

Karen walked over and switched on the CD player. 'What do you want to hear?'

'Something with a steady beat. You need a good beat for a lap dance. Not too fast, but not too slow either.'

With a growing sense of unreality, she scanned the CD rack. Will collected everything from classic rock to country and New Age. There was music here that made her feel sexy, but she didn't want to taint it by being raped to its accompaniment. At a loss, she finally chose a *Best of the 80s* compilation. The first song was 'Every Breath You Take' by the Police. The bass and drums began to pulse sinuously from speakers Will had mounted in the ceiling. When she turned, Hickey was nodding to the beat.

'That's it,' he said. 'Yeah. Come over here.'

She took a step closer to the ottoman.

'Dance.'

She would have laughed, were the situation not so desperate. It was like the old Westerns her father had loved so much, where the black-hatted gunfighter said the same line to the frightened homesteader.

'I said *dance*,' Hickey repeated.

Karen began to sway to the music, but she felt awkward. She had never been a good dancer. Will claimed she was, but she knew she lacked the effortless grace of some girls she had known growing up. Long-limbed creatures who, through some physical alchemy, absorbed sound waves and transformed that energy into purely sensual motion.

'Closer,' Hickey said.

Karen danced nearer the chair, but jerked back as Hickey's hand reached towards her.

'It's just money,' he said.

He was telling the truth. In his hand was a folded one-dollar bill.

'Come over here.'

She danced closer, and he stuffed the bill into the front pocket of her jeans.

'That means you gotta take something off,' he said, as though explaining the rules of the game.

She hesitated, then slowly unbuttoned her blouse until it hung from her shoulders.

'Shake it off.'

She did. Goose bumps raced across her back and shoulders.

'Those aren't half bad,' Hickey said, staring at her bra.

Karen focused on the wall and kept swaying to the music, but her mind was spinning. How fast could the Wild Turkey dull his senses? How long could she distract him from what he really wanted?

'Lean over,' he ordered.

She bent slightly at the waist, and he rose up and stuffed a dollar bill into her bra.

'You know what that means, babe.'

She unsnapped her jeans, but Hickey shook his head. 'The bra. The bra next.'

She almost stopped dancing. Part of her – the part that took no nonsense from anyone, man or woman – wanted to scream. *If you're going to rape me, just get it over with!* But a wiser part of her knew that would be a mistake. Anything could happen between now and the moment he actually forced himself on her. Miracles could happen. Her bra hooked in front. Dancing a little more enthusiastically, she reached up and undid the catch, then threaded her fingers under the shoulder straps and slid off the cups with exaggerated sensuality.

'That's better,' Hickey intoned. 'Jesus, you look good. For a mother, I mean. You ought to get some implants, though.'

I don't want any damn implants! she screamed silently. But she let the music penetrate further into her, and gave more of herself to it.

'Yeah,' he encouraged, holding up another bill. A five this time. She danced closer, close enough for him to slide the five into her pocket, but he shook his head.

'Lean over. And don't use your hands.'

It took her a moment to figure out what he wanted, but it was simple enough. She bent over and used her upper arms to bring her breasts together, creating a soft niche for Hickey to stuff his five-dollar bill into. He immediately made use of it.

'Now the jeans.'

She unzipped the jeans but left them on. As she spun slowly, he took another slug of Wild Turkey and stared mesmerized at her chest. The effect was almost comical, one that Karen had never really understood. Men stared at naked breasts the way LSD trippers stared at the sun, as though mammary glands held the secret of the universe. As Hickey stared, she saw that his dazed fascination gave her a certain amount of control. Instead of removing her jeans, she licked her forefinger and brought it down to her right nipple, then traced a small circle around it. When it responded, Hickey's nostrils flared and his eyes widened. He took another long pull from the bottle.

She raised both arms and began swaying to 'Hold Me Now' by the Thompson Twins. She thought she must look like a go-go girl in one of those hanging cages from the sixties. Hickey was nodding in time to the beat, gripping the bottle by its neck and drinking from it every few seconds. His eyes looked darker than before, if that was possible. No longer bottomless pools, but flat disks of slate. Shark's eyes. No knowledge in them, only hunger. A vast, insatiable appetite.

'Come on,' he rasped. 'Let's see the goods.'

She didn't want to take off her jeans. The vulnerability she had felt without them was dehumanizing. But she couldn't afford to make him truly angry. Then she would lose any semblance of control. She had to keep him drinking, convince him that she was going along. She let the jeans ride down her hips, then lifted her knees one at a time and kicked her feet out of them. That she managed this without falling on her butt was a miracle in itself – she hoped not the only one of the night.

That thought evaporated as Hickey slid down in the chair so that his legs were fully extended, his hips and thighs stretched like a bridge between the chair and ottoman. 'Stand over me,' he said. 'Then you sit down and dance. That's called a sofa dance.'

Sofa dance?

'Hurry,' he said insistently. 'Right here.'

He meant his lap. Karen was nearing the limit of her tolerance. She stepped over his outstretched legs but did not sit down. She could no longer dance in any real sense, only sway from the waist up. But Hickey seemed content for the moment.

'Turn around,' he said.

She thought she detected a slur in his pronunciation. She stepped over his legs, then back over them so that she was facing his feet. She had never been more thankful for underwear. She focused on the 'L' of light that was her almost-closed bathroom door.

'Damn,' Hickey said softly. 'That's a work of art. Bend over. Slow.'

Karen shut her eyes and bent toward his feet, knowing she was fully exposed now, terrified that he would touch her.

He did. But with paper, not his hand. Another bill. This one slid between her panties and her skin. She shuddered with disgust, thinking of where that money might have been, who might have touched it. Then she realized that her disgust was not even a fraction of what she would feel when he violated her.

'Turn around again.'

She obeyed. To her horror, Hickey had laid a hand in his lap and began rubbing himself. Her stomach turned a somersault. She was thankful she hadn't eaten in a while. Or perhaps it would be better if she had.

She'd heard that vomiting was a good defense against rape, but she'd never understood how you could do it at the right time. If Hickey touched her now, though, she just might manage it.

'That was a twenty,' he said. 'Twenty for the panties.'

She couldn't do it. She could not remove the last barrier between herself and total nakedness. 'We've got all night,' she said. 'Don't rush it.'

'Sit!' Hickey commanded, as he would a dog.

Karen tried to steel herself to obey, but it was no use.

He took hold of her hips with powerful hands and yanked her down against him. In the first instant of contact, a torrent of emotions raced through her. Terror first, because now it was real. Whiskey wasn't going to keep this man from performing. Nothing was, except death, and if she somehow managed to kill him, Abby would die, too. With the terror came dazed disbelief. She had not felt any other man but Will in that place for fifteen years, and only two before him. To be touched there by someone she had not chosen was an affront to her most secret self. But most deeply she felt guilt, for allowing it to go this far. Even though logic told her she had no alternative, her insecurity said there had to be one. One that a braver or more moral woman would have seen without thought. But the only alternative she could see was death for Abby.

As Hickey groaned in rapture, a cold certainty crystallized in Karen's brain. No matter what Nicole Kidman had done in the movies, she could not endure being raped by this man. By any man. For any reason. Her answer to the eternal female question – would I fight or submit – was an unequivocal *fight*.

Hickey groaned again, and this time the sound pierced her to the marrow. Will sometimes made exactly the same sound during sex. The thought that there was any connection between her marital love-making and what was happening now nauseated her. But of course there was. Will was as human as any man, and he wanted sex all the time. Much more often than she did, anyway. And not just lovemaking. He wanted physical sex, an outlet for his drives and frustrations, and she resented that. There had been a time, just before and after their marriage, when she had felt a powerful urge to make love. But that had slowly faded with time. Not that she loved him less. But after she was forced to give up medical school, her desire flatlined. She couldn't voice the reason to Will, but the fact was that submitting to his sexual desires seemed the ultimate expression of the terrible sacrifice she had made. Because it was sex, at bottom, that had made that sacrifice necessary. And just because Will got an erection every morning and night was no reason she had to wait at his beck and call like some nineteenth-century *hausfrau*—

'Get up!' Hickey ordered. 'That's enough foreplay.'

She practically leaped off him and retreated toward the TV cabinet.

He thrust himself to his feet and carried the bottle of Wild Turkey to the bedside table. Then he walked back toward her, pulling off his Polo shirt as he came, revealing a pale, wiry torso. Only his neck was tanned, and his arms from the elbows down. A farmer's tan, her father had called it. When he reached for his belt, Karen looked at the carpet.

'Watch,' he said, his voice full of pride.

She took a deep breath and looked up as Hickey's khakis hit the floor. A tingling numbness began to creep outward from some place deep within her. The act would be bad, she knew, but the anticipation was worse. The knowing – while you were still intact – that absolute suffering was inevitable. That the place you had protected all your life was about to be violated. That no help would come. There was only Hickey. And Abby. Abby hanging over her head like a sword, enforcing every command he gave.

The numbness continued to spread through her, and the temptation was to let it come, like a freezing person giving in to the cold. *Let it penetrate into my bones,* she thought. *Into my heart and soul, so that whatever happens will be unfelt, a crime committed upon another person, an insensate body. A cadaver.* And yet, if she let the numbness that far in, could she ever get it all out again?

As Hickey stared at her with his stupid schoolboy grin, something stirred deep within her. Not quite a thought, but the seed of one. A tiny spark of awareness, smoldering and darkly feminine. A ruthless, chthonic knowledge of male vulnerability.

Her moment would come.

Chapter 8

Huey sat across from Abby on the linoleum floor of the cabin, whittling slowly. He had dragged an old saddle blanket in from the bedroom and set her on it, so she wouldn't have to sit on the bare floor. She clutched the Barbie in her little hands like a talisman.

'Do you feel better now?' asked Huey.

Abby nodded. 'A little bit.'

'Are you hungry? I'm hungry.'

'Kind of. My tummy hurts.'

A knot of worry formed in Huey's stomach. 'What do you like? I got baloney. You like Captain Crunch? I love Captain Crunch.'

'I have to eat Raisin Bran.'

'You can't eat Captain Crunch?'

'No.'

'How come?'

Her lips puckered and moved to one side as she thought about it. 'Well, when you eat, the food puts sugar in your blood. And you've got stuff in *your* body to make the sugar go away. But I don't have any. So, the sugar gets more and more until it makes me sick. And if I get too sick, I'll go to sleep. Sleep and maybe never wake up.'

Fear passed into Huey's face like a shadow falling over a rock. He rubbed his hands anxiously across his puttylike cheeks. 'That happened to my sister. Jo Ellen. I wish I could give you some of my blood to make your sugar go away.'

'That's what's in my shots. Stuff to make the sugar go away. I don't like needles, but I don't like being sick, either. It hurts.'

'I hate needles,' Huey said forcefully. 'Hate, hate, hate.'

'Me, too.'

'*Hate* needles,' Huey reasserted.

'There are big ones and little ones, though,' Abby said. 'My shots have the littlest kind. Some shots have really big ones. Like when they take your blood. And sometimes my dad has to stick people in the back. In the spine cord. Or in the nerves sometimes. That hurts the worst. But he does it to make a bigger hurt go away.'

'How do you know so much?'

Abby shrugged. 'I don't know. My mom and dad are always telling me stuff. People at school say I talk grown-up all the time.'

'Are you going to be a doctor when you get big?'

'Uh-huh. A flying doctor.'

Huey's eyes got bigger. 'You can't fly, can you?'

'In an airplane, silly.'

'Oh.'

'My tummy still hurts.'

Huey's mouth fell open. 'You just play here with your doll. I'm gonna make you the biggest bowl of Captain Crunch you ever saw!'

Before Abby could remind him that she couldn't eat Cap'n Crunch, the giant got to his feet and walked toward the kitchen. After three steps, he stopped and put his hand to his head as though he had forgotten something.

'Dumb, dumb, dumb,' he said.

He came back to Abby, bent down, and picked up the Nokia cell phone he'd left beside her. 'Joey said, take this with me everywhere. Don't leave it anywhere. He gave me a extra battery, too.'

Abby looked forlornly at the phone. She was thinking about what her mother had said about calling the police.

'I'll be right back,' Huey promised. 'You just wait.'

He walked into the kitchen, leaving Abby alone in the front room with his whittling knife and his shapeless chunk of wood. She could see his back as he opened a cabinet. Then he moved out of the doorway, and she couldn't see him anymore. She heard a sucking sound. A refrigerator door.

She turned to the cabin window. It was pitch-black outside. She hated the dark, but her mother's voice was playing inside her head. *Take the phone and hide. . . .* She wouldn't have said that if she wanted Abby to stay with Huey. But if she went outside, what could she do? She didn't know the way home, or even how far away home was. And without the phone, she couldn't call anybody.

She heard a clink, then Huey humming something. She liked Huey. But he was a stranger, and her daddy had told her over and over how strangers could be bad, even when they seemed nice. She felt sorry for him, but whenever she looked up and saw him watching her, she felt something funny in her stomach. Like a big bubble pressing up against her heart. In a moment he would walk through the door with a bowl of cereal that could kill her. Abby closed her eyes and pictured her mother's face. *What would she say if she could talk to me now?*

Run.

Abby stood up with her Barbie and took a tentative step toward the door. Looking back toward the kitchen, she saw Huey's shadow moving on the floor. She walked very fast to the front door, picked up the small ice chest her mother had left, and slipped outside without a sound.

Joe Hickey took two steps toward Karen, a lopsided grin on his face. She kept her eyes on his and tried to keep the fear out of her voice as she spoke.

'Will you please wear a condom?'

'Sorry, babe. Not tonight.'

A shudder of revulsion ran through her. God only knew what diseases Hickey carried. He had been in prison, and the HIV infection rate behind bars was astronomical.

'Please,' she implored. 'I don't want to—'

'I ain't worn a rubber since junior high, and I ain't starting now.'

She fought down a wave of nausea. 'I need to use the bathroom.'

'I'll go with you.'

'For God's sake. Give me that much privacy.'

'What's in the bathroom? Another gun?'

'My diaphragm, okay? I don't want to get pregnant.'

Hickey's grin returned. 'Well, now, I don't know. You look like you got good genes. Maybe you and me should *pro*-create. Do the global gene pool a favor.'

She closed her eyes, praying he wasn't serious. 'May I please use the diaphragm?'

'What the hell.' He waved his hand. 'Hey, maybe I should put it in for you.'

She struggled to keep her face impassive.

'Fine. Go do whatever. But when you come out of there, I don't want to see those panties. It's Lady Godiva time.'

As she walked toward the bathroom, he picked up the Wild Turkey bottle and stretched out on the sleigh bed, his face glowing with anticipation.

Huey came out of the kitchen carrying a bowl of Cap'n Crunch as big as a colander in his left hand and his cell phone in his right. He looked down at the saddle blanket Abby had been sitting on and blinked in confusion. Then he peered around the room. After several seconds, a grin lighted his face.

'Are you playing hide-and-go-seek? Is that what you're doing?'

He carried the cereal and the phone into the bathroom. Finding it empty, he checked the bedroom. He had to set the bowl on the mattress and lie prone to look under the old iron frame bed, groaning as he squeezed his oversized body between the side rail and the wall. There was nothing under the bed but what his mother used to call 'slut wool.'

151

He got to his feet again, picked up the cereal bowl, went to the bedroom door, and stared at the empty saddle blanket again. Then he cocked his head and listened hard.

'Abby?'

His voice sounded lonelier than it had when she was in the room. The silence just swallowed it up.

'*Abby?*'

The screen door banged softly in the wind.

Huey looked to his right and saw the door hanging open. His face went slack. After a long sequence of thought, doubt, and realization, he dropped the bowl and the cell phone and charged onto the porch.

The second Karen closed the bathroom door, her survival instinct kicked into overdrive. She turned on the sink taps, then opened the cabinet behind the mirror, revealing bottles of vitamins, drugs, facial cleansers, gauze bandages, and all the other sundries of a doctor's home medicine cabinet. On the bottom shelf was a stack of Lo-Ovral birth control pills. She grabbed them and threw them into the cabinet under the lavatory, so Hickey wouldn't see them if he came in.

She scanned the drugs in the cabinet. Zithromax, an antibiotic. Naproxen for Will's arthritis. Methotrexate. Stuck behind the gauze bandage pack was a small brown prescription bottle. Her heart quickened as she picked it up and read the label: *Mepergan Fortis*. Demerol. But when she opened it, she saw only two red pills in its bottom. Not enough to put Hickey out quickly, even if she found a way to slip them into the Wild Turkey bottle. Raking frantically through the cabinet, she saw nothing that could help her. As she closed the door, she caught her reflection in its mirrored surface. She looked like a ghost of herself.

Splashing water on her face, she reached down for a hand towel and froze. Standing in a ceramic cup by the sink were three toothbrushes. But beside their blue and orange handles, a different sort of handle stuck up. A thinner one. She reached down and lifted it out of the glass. It was a disposable scalpel, its thin blade shielded by a plastic sheath. As she studied it, an arc of instinct closed, completing the circuit begun when Hickey dropped his pants.

'*Christ, how long can it take?*' he complained.

Hickey sounded like he was right outside the door. Dropping a washrag over the scalpel, Karen yanked off her panties, sat on the commode, and watched the doorknob.

It didn't move.

She got up and took the scalpel from beneath the rag, then removed the clear protective sheath from the blade. Its edge was twice as bright as its side, honed to a sharpness that could lay open the human dermis like the skin of a peach. She straightened before the mirror and looked at herself. Was the scalpel conceal-able? After a moment's thought, she raised it point-first toward her forehead and slid it neatly into her hair.

It vanished.

She turned her head right and left, to see whether the scalpel was visible. It wasn't. She felt her hair to see how obvious it was. Too obvious. If Hickey held her head for any reason, he would instantly discover the blade.

She pulled the scalpel from her hair and looked at it again. Six inches of plastic and surgical steel, flatter than a key and lighter than a pencil. The Papillon solution was not an option. She turned away from the mirror and looked back over her shoulder. She could see down to the upper cleft of her buttocks. For the first time in her life, she was glad to be carrying a few extra pounds. Using the mirror as a guide, she slid the scalpel, handle first, down between her cheeks. It felt cold and alien, but only the silver tip of the blade was visible at the base of her spine.

It would have to do.

All she could hope for now was to stack the odds a little in her favor. She opened the dirty clothes cabinet and stood on tiptoe. In the top section were two shelves she used to store clothes she rarely wore. She reached up and dug through them with feverish intensity.

There.

She wriggled into a claret-colored teddy Will had bought at the mall last year, a garment she'd never even tried on. The top half must have been designed by Wonder Bra, because it lifted and pressed her modest breasts together until the cleavage reminded her of the beach bunnies on *Baywatch*. The bottom half was ridiculously tight, with a sheer lace triangle over the crotch, leaving her fully exposed.

She looked like a French whore.

Perfect.

*   *   *

Crouching in a lightless thicket, Abby watched Huey lumber past her in the moonlight.

'Abby?' he called. 'Why did you run away? You're scaring me.'

She looked down at her doll, which she had laid across the ice chest to keep it out of the briars. She was trying hard not to make a sound, but her shins had already been scratched bloody, and they stung like a thousand paper cuts. She hadn't wanted to go far from the lights, but she knew Huey would find her if she didn't get into the dark.

He paused twenty feet to her left, looking into the wall of trees. 'Abby? Where are you?'

She wondered how long she could wait here. The woods didn't scare her. Not usually, anyway. Their house was in the middle of the woods. But she'd never spent the night in them, at least not alone. Only with her dad, at the Indian Princess camp-out. Already she'd heard sounds that made her shiver. Scuttling in the undergrowth, like armadillos, or maybe possums. There was a possum that kept eating the cat's food at Kate Mosby's house up the road. Abby had seen the cat fight it once, and the long, needlelike teeth of the possum as it hissed at the cat. If a possum came close now, she wouldn't be able to sit still.

The other thing was her sugar. She felt like it was okay, but her mother wasn't there to measure it, and if she started to 'go south,' as her daddy put it, she would need a shot. She had never given herself a shot before.

'Come out!' Huey yelled, sounding really mad now. Abby watched him pick up a big stick and poke some bushes with it. Then he moved off farther to her left, going along the line of trees.

She looked at the cabin, the lovely yellow light streaming from the windows. She wished she could wait inside, where there were no animals or bugs. Huey's voice floated back to her on the wind.

'There's bad things in the woods at night! Wolves and bears and things! You need Huey to look out for you!'

She hugged herself and tried not to listen. There might be bears in these woods, but she didn't think so. And certainly not wolves. There weren't any more wolves.

'There's snakes, too,' Huey called. 'Creepy crawly snakes looking for warm bodies in the dark.'

A chill shot up Abby's spine. There were snakes in Mississippi, all right. Bad ones. She'd learned about them at Indian Princess. Copperheads and cotton-mouths and ground rattlers and coral snakes. They'd seen a coral snake on one camp-out, sunning itself on a rock by the creek. The fathers didn't even try to get close enough to kill it. They said if it bit you, you could die before you got to the hospital. Her dad had taught the Princesses a rhyme to help them tell the difference between a coral snake and a scarlet king snake, which looked almost exactly like it: *If red touches yellow, it can kill a fellow.*

'If the snakes get you, it won't be my fault!' Huey yelled, beating the bushes off to her left.

Abby shut her eyes and tried not to cry.

* * *

When Karen emerged from the bathroom wearing the teddy, she saw Hickey lying under the covers in the middle of the bed. The only light came from the lamp on the end table. He gave a long, low wolf whistle.

'Man *alive*. That's better than naked. Talk about getting with the program.'

As Karen moved toward the bed, she saw Will's .38 lying on the floor by the dust ruffle. That was how confident Hickey was in the diabolical cage of circumstance he had constructed.

He patted the side of the bed.

As she moved toward him, she slid the gun under the bed with her foot, then turned her back to him and slipped under the covers, being careful to keep her legs together as she moved. She tried not to stiffen as her hip and shoulder touched Hickey's side, but she knew that her tension would be transmitted to him in a thousand subtle ways.

'Damn, you're cold,' he complained.

'Sorry.' He smelled like a stale ashtray. She stared up at the ceiling as though she had nothing in her mind but enduring what was to come with stoicism. 'What do you want me to do?'

'You're not gonna whine about it?'

'Not if it keeps you from hurting Abby.'

'Thank God for small favors.' He turned sideways and propped himself on an elbow, and she felt him press against her hip. A deep shudder rippled through her.

'Are you ready down there?' he asked.

Unbelievable. How could he possibly think that an impending rape could arouse a woman? She had to distract him from his immediate goal. 'Is that what you want first? Straight to business? I thought you'd want something else.'

'Like what?' He reached up and cupped her left breast with a sweaty hand.

Every fiber of instinct told her to jerk away from the offending touch, but she forced herself to lie still and turn her face toward his. 'Something you fantasize about when you see women like me in the grocery store.'

He squeezed the breast. 'Like what?'

'Lie back and relax. You'll see.'

A slow smile spread his lips. 'Oh, man . . .'

She rolled onto her stomach, pulled the covers over her shoulders, and slid down toward Hickey's midsection. She hoped he would leave the comforter where it was, but he lifted it so that he could watch what he believed was to come. She was foolish to have expected anything else.

'I'm cold,' she said, looking up.

'You'll warm up.' His black eyes were bright. 'And don't think you're going to get out of anything by doing this.'

She swallowed her revulsion, then straddled his legs and took hold of him with her left hand.

'Mmm,' he moaned.

She had to get him to look away. Closing her eyes, she worked her left hand a little, the way Will liked it. Hickey groaned but did not look away. He wouldn't, she realized, until she progressed much further. This was what he got off on: watching a 'society' woman pleasure him.

'Good,' he murmured. 'Good girl.'

She slid her right hand down beneath her stomach.

'Yeah,' he said. 'I want to see you do that.'

'After you finish,' she said, feeling sweat break out on her face. It was hot in the bedroom, but it was fear, not the temperature that had brought moisture to her skin.

He groped for the back of her head.

Panic shot through her. 'I know what to do. Lie back and relax. You don't want it to be over too fast.'

'Yeah.' After a moment, his head lolled back, and his eyes rolled up toward the ceiling.

She quickly slid her right hand around her hip. Her forefinger touched the scalpel blade. Very carefully, she felt her way down the plastic handle, which was slick with perspiration. Closing her first and second fingers around the handle, she drew the scalpel from its place of concealment and set it firmly in her fist, the flat of the blade wedged between the pad of her thumb and her forefinger.

'Come *on*,' Hickey urged, his voice brimming with impatience.

She brought the blade smoothly along her right side and underneath her right breast. When it was beneath her chin, she slid her knees up under her chest, as though to position herself for oral sex.

'Finally,' he grunted.

She had to get between his legs. Straddling him this way, he could easily buck her off in the initial moment of panic. Without breaking her rhythm, she lifted one knee and wedged it between his thighs, then followed with the other.

'Go for it,' he said.

Karen gripped him as hard as she could with her left hand and pressed the blade against his urethra with her right, anchoring the point in a few millimetres of skin. It would take several seconds for him to register the pain of the puncture.

'Look down, Joe,' she said in a cold voice. 'And don't make any sudden moves.'

'What?'

'If you move, you're going to lose this organ you're so proud of.'

She felt his abdomen tighten as he raised his head to look. 'What? Hey, whatever you're doing, it hurts.'

'I'm holding a scalpel against your penis, Joe.' She prepared herself for a reflex jerk of panic. 'You *really* don't want to move, okay?'

His eyes went from blank confusion to shock in less than a second. At last he had seen and understood the scalpel. His whole body went rigid, but his pelvis didn't move an inch.

'*What the—*' he blurted in a stage whisper.

He raised his hand to strike her, but didn't have the courage to do it. Karen looked straight into his eyes. Fear crackled there like electricity. The power was intoxicating. She had gone from helpless supplicant to total dominance in seconds. If she had held the gun to Hickey's head, he would have laughed in her face. But the threat to his manhood paralyzed him. She could almost feel his heart squirming in his chest.

'This is a Bard-Parker Number Ten scalpel,' she said. 'We keep them around to take out splinters, stuff like that. But it'll take off your equipment just as easily. I

160

bet you'd hardly even feel it. Just a quick sting.'

'I'm gonna kill you,' he said in a matter-of-fact voice. 'You and your kid.'

She pushed the scalpel point deeper, drawing blood.

'*Stop!*' he shouted, his face contorted in terror. His skin had gone as white as that of a man on his deathbed.

'You're bleeding, Joe. So listen very closely. You're going to pick up that telephone, call your cousin, and tell him to bring my daughter back here.'

Hickey's eyes flicked from the blade to her face. 'You won't do it. If you do, your kid dies.'

'Oh, I'll do it.' Karen's heart felt like it was beating at random, firing off drum rolls between dangerous silences. She had to hold her nerve. 'I'll do it, and if you live through it, you'll be peeing through an indwelling catheter for the rest of your life. No more making women walk bowlegged for a week. No more banging tonsils.'

She thought she saw a flicker of fear, but Hickey covered it quickly.

'Your hand's shaking,' he said. 'Feel it?'

'*Pick up the phone!*'

'Goddamn women. You ain't got the guts.'

Something in his voice ignited an anger so deep that Karen had never even attempted to express it. She squeezed him with all the power in her left arm, and his skin went purple.

'I was a surgical nurse for six years, Joe. I'll castrate you with no more regret than slicing a chicken neck. And it won't be like that Bobbitt guy. No sewing it back on. Because while you're spurting blood all over my percale sheets, I'll throw it in the garbage disposal and flip the switch. Now *pick up that fucking phone!*'

'Take it easy!' Hickey grabbed the phone off the bedside table. 'I'm dialing!' He punched wildly at the keypad. 'What do you want me to say?'

Karen struggled to rein in her anger. The fierce pleasure she felt at seeing him broken had her muscles twitching like they did after four sets of tennis. Some primal part of her *wanted* to cut him.

'Tell him you already have the ransom money. Tell him to put Abby in the truck and drive her back here.'

'He won't do it. We've never done it that way. He'll know something's wrong.'

'You told me he always does everything you say!'

Puzzlement came into Hickey's face. 'He's not answering.'

'You didn't dial it right!'

'I swear to God I did!'

'Then why hasn't he answered?'

'How do I know?'

'Dial it again!' She pressed the blade deeper. There was a steady stream of blood now.

'*Shit! Wait!*' He hung up and redialed the number, then waited for an answer.

Karen's nerves were fraying fast. Despite her immediate control over Hickey, she had put herself in an untenable position if Huey didn't answer the phone.

'He's not picking up,' Hickey said, looking worried enough for it to distract him from his immediate peril. 'What the hell?'

'He hasn't missed a call yet! Why this one?'

Hickey shrugged. 'How do I know? He's a damn

retard. Now get that knife away from me, will you? We've got to figure out what's happening up there.'

'Shut up,' Karen snapped. 'Let me think.'

'What are you going to do? You can't sit like that all night.'

'I said, Shut up!'

'Okay. But why don't you go ahead and give me that blowjob while you're deciding?'

Karen blinked in amazement, and Hickey slammed the telephone into the side of her head.

Huey had circled back around the cabin, poking at bushes and trying to scare Abby, but now his voice had faded to almost nothing as he worked his way along the dirt road leading away from the cabin.

She crouched in the dark, her head filled with images of snakes curling and uncurling like whips in the weeds around her. During the last few minutes, beetles had crawled over her feet, and fat mosquitoes had feasted on her exposed arms and face. She was afraid to swat them, because Huey might hear the sound and come running back. Part of her wanted to find a tree and climb it, but that would surely make too much noise. Besides, snakes could climb. She didn't think they *slept* in trees, though.

As she squashed a mosquito bloody against her forearm, a faint ringing sounded in her ears. She tried to focus on it, but it disappeared. Then it came again – louder, she thought – or maybe it must seemed louder because she was listening for it. Her heart thumped.

It was a telephone.

The ringing was coming from the cabin. Huey must have left his phone inside when he went looking for her! She got up to run to the cabin, then stopped. What if he had gone back to the cabin without her seeing him? What if he was inside now? No. The phone was still ringing, and if Huey was inside, he would have answered it. She grabbed her doll and the ice chest and raced out of the trees toward the glowing windows.

White light exploded in Karen's brain. As her thoughts scattered into meaningless electrochemicals, her cerebellum executed the impulse her cerebral cortex had been holding in check for the past minute. Like a frog's leg touched by an electrode, the hand holding the scalpel jerked back toward her stomach.

Hickey shrieked like a hog having its throat cut.

The white light shattered into stars, then faded to an unstable image of a screaming man. Karen looked down.

All she saw was blood.

Abby couldn't find the phone. It wasn't on the table or the broken old couch. But it was still ringing.

She looked at the floor. There was a big puddle of spilled milk and Cap'n Crunch by the bedroom door. The phone was lying half under the upside-down salad bowl Huey had put the cereal into. Abby darted to the puddle and reached for the wet cell phone, but even as she did, she knew something wasn't right. The phone's numbers and window were dark. She pressed SEND and put the phone to her ear.

She heard only silence. '*No*,' she keened, terrified that her mother had hung up.

The phone rang again.

'Hello? Hello! Mama?'

The ringing bell sounded again. It wasn't coming from the cell phone. It was coming from the bedroom. She ran in and looked around. An old-timey black phone sat on the floor on the far side of the bed. It rang again.

She grabbed the receiver. 'Hello? . . . Hello!'

She heard a dial tone.

'*Hello!*'

The phone did not ring again. She stared at it in disbelief. How could her mother stop ringing, just when she was about to pick up? Shaking with fear, she stared at the rotary dial and spoke softly as she tried to remember. 'Nine-nine-one? Nine . . . nine-*one*-one. Nine-one—'

'Abby?' Huey's voice floated into the bedroom. 'Don't run away from Huey! You're going to get me in trouble. Big trouble.'

She froze.

The voice sounded close, but she didn't hear footsteps. She was too afraid to peek outside the bedroom door. She grabbed the Barbie and the cell phone off the bed and ran flat-out for the back door.

Outside, she ran past a small shed and crouched beside a tree. There was just enough moonlight to see the POWER button. 'Nine-one-one,' she said with certainty. She switched on the phone, carefully punched in 911, pressed SEND, and put the phone to her ear.

'Welcome to CellStar,' said a computer voice. 'You are currently in a nonemergency-service zone. Please—'

'Is this the police?' Abby cried. 'I need a policeman!'

Tears formed in her eyes as the voice refused to acknowledge her. She hit END and began to dial the only number she could think of: home.

'Six-oh-one,' she whispered. 'Eight-five-six-four-seven-one-two.'

She hit SEND again.

A man's voice answered this time, but it was a computer, too. 'We're sorry,' it said. 'You must first press a one or zero before making this call. Thank you.'

'Press one first?' Abby echoed, feeling panic in her chest. 'Press one first. Press one first. . . .'

Karen and Hickey knelt three feet apart on the bed. Karen was holding the scalpel up defensively; Hickey clutched a pillow to his groin. His face was a mask of rage and agony.

'You've got to get to a hospital!' she told him. 'You could bleed to death.'

He lifted the pillow away from his skin and looked down, then laughed maniacally. 'You missed! You *missed*. Look at that!'

He lifted the pillow higher, and his smile vanished. His right thigh had been laid open from groin to knee. Blood was pulsing out at an alarming rate.

'Oh God,' he whispered. 'Oh God.'

'You did it!' Karen told him. 'You hit me with the phone!'

'Your kid is dead, bitch. *Dead!*'

Her heart turned to stone. She had gambled and failed. As Hickey tried to stanch the flow of blood with the pillow, she jumped off the bed and scrabbled under it for the gun. She had to keep him from bleeding to death, but she didn't want to be at his mercy while he was in a fit of rage.

'Go in the bathroom!' she said, getting to her feet with the pistol. 'Tie a towel just above the laceration. You've got to slow the arterial flow.'

'*Look what you did!*' he screamed, his eyes wide with shock.

She was going to have to tend to the wound, but she didn't think she could bring herself to touch him yet. She didn't even want to get close to him.

'Get a towel!' she yelled. 'Hurry! Make a tourniquet!'

Hickey hobbled into the bathroom with the pillow pressed to his thigh, groaning and whining and cursing at once. Karen grabbed the bedsheet and wiped his blood off her thighs, then pulled her discarded blouse over the teddy, went to the bathroom door, and held the gun on Hickey while he tied a towel around his thigh. He was doing a fair job, good enough to slow the bleeding away.

'Why didn't Huey answer?' she asked. 'Why aren't they at the cabin? Has he taken Abby somewhere?'

Hickey looked up, his face red with strain. 'You don't need to worry about that. No point at all. You just bought yourself a world of pain, lady. A *world* of pain.'

'What do you expect? You steal my child and try to rape me, and I'm supposed to lie down and take it?'

He shook a bloody washrag at her. 'Look at this

goddamn leg! I'm bleeding to death here!'

'You need a hospital.'

'Bullshit, I need a hospital. I need some stitches is all. You were a nurse, you said. You do it.'

'It would take fifty stitches to close that.' She was exaggerating. A butcher could bring the edges of the wound together with ten.

'So get the stuff! Your husband's got a black bag or something, right? To take care of the neighborhood brats?'

Will did keep a bag at home for Abby's soccer games, but Karen didn't want to get it. She didn't want to hold the gun or look at Hickey's nakedness or anything else any more. She just wanted Abby locked tight in her nurturing arms.

'*Why are you doing this?*' she screamed. '*Why my little girl? It's not fair! It's not right—*'

Hickey slapped her. Then, his jaw set tight against the pain, he said through clenched teeth: 'Lady, if you don't get your shit together and sew me up, Huey will snap your little girl's spine like a twig. One phone call will do it. One fucking call.'

'You can't even get him on the phone!'

'I'll get him.'

Karen stood shaking in the aftermath of her fit. Blood was soaking through her blouse from the teddy beneath, and Will's gun quivered in her hand. She had to keep herself together. Or Abby wouldn't make it.

'Move your ass!' Hickey yelled. 'Get the bag!'

She nodded and hurried out of the bathroom.

*   *   *

Abby thought she'd heard Huey outside again, so she crept into the little shed behind the cabin. There was a tractor in it, like the one her daddy used to cut the grass at home, only bigger. She climbed up onto its seat and started pressing numbers on the cell phone's lighted keypad. She began with '1' then moved on to the area code of Mississippi. 'Six-oh-one,' she said as she dialed. Then she pressed the other seven numbers, hit SEND, and prayed that the answering service wouldn't answer.

The phone began to ring.

Karen was rummaging through Will's medical bag when the phone rang on Will's side of the bed. Hickey was still in the bathroom, loosening the towel tourniquet as she had advised. Though the caller was almost surely Hickey's wife, Karen answered, hoping against hope that her desperate act had somehow paid off.

'Hello?'

'Tell her to give me a minute,' Hickey called from behind the half-closed bathroom door.

'*Mama?*'

Karen's hands began to shake as if with palsy. 'Abby?'

'Mama!'

Karen had to swallow before she could continue. 'Honey, are you all right? Where are you?'

Abby's voice disintegrated into sobs before she could answer. Karen heard her hiccupping and swallowing, trying to control herself enough to speak.

'Take your time, baby. Tell me where you are.'

'I don't *know*! I'm in the woods. Mama, come get me! I'm *scared*.'

Karen glanced at the bathroom door. 'I'm going to come, honey, but—' She paused, unsure what to say. How much reality could a five-year-old absorb and still function? 'Baby, Mama doesn't know how to get to where you are. Are you still at the place where I gave you the shot?'

'Uh-huh. I ran outside the cabin. I was hiding in the woods and Mr Huey yelled that there's snakes and bears. Then I heard the phone inside.'

'Listen, honey. Do you remember how to call nine-one-one? If you do that, the police can come get—'

'I already *did* that. The lady wouldn't listen! Mama, help me.'

'*What the hell are you doing? Give me that goddamn phone!*' Hickey was coming through the bathroom door, trying to move quickly but not wanting to put too much weight on his injured leg.

'Mama?' cried Abby.

'Give me the phone!' Hickey roared.

Karen grabbed the .38 off the bed, pointed it at him, and fired.

Hickey hit the floor like a soldier under incoming artillery and covered his head with both hands.

'TELL ME WHERE MY BABY IS, YOU SON OF A BITCH!'

'*Mama? Mama!*'

Hickey didn't speak or move. Karen fired into the floor, missing him by inches. 'ANSWER ME, GODDAMN IT!'

'Stop shooting!' he screamed. 'If you kill me, your kid is dead!'

'RIGHT ALONG WITH YOU! GET IT?' Karen tried to speak calmly into the receiver. 'Stay on the phone, baby. Mama's fine, but she's busy. Are you in the cabin now?'

'I'm in a little shed outside. I'm on a tractor.'

Abby's captor was certain to focus on any structures as he hunted for her, no matter how simpleminded he was. It was like looking for your car keys under the streetlight.

'I want you to go back outside, Abby, into the woods. Make sure Mr Huey isn't around, then sneak out of the shed, get down in some bushes, and stay down.'

'But it's nighttime.'

'I know, but tonight the dark is your friend. Remember Pajama Sam? No need to hide when it's dark outside?'

'That's on the computer. That's not real.'

'I know, baby, but the woods are the safe place for you now. Do you understand?'

'I guess so.'

'Do you think your sugar's okay?'

'I guess.'

'Don't you worry, sweetie. Mama's going to come get you.'

'You promise?'

'I promise. Now, I want you to look outside, and then run into the woods. Take the phone with you, and stay on the line. Don't hang up, okay? *Don't hang up.*'

'Okay.'

Karen covered the phone with her hand and pointed the gun at Hickey's head. 'Get up, you bastard.'

He looked up, his eyes bright with anger. Maybe with surprise, too, she thought.

'I SAID, "GET UP!"'

Hickey flattened his hands on the floor and raised himself slowly, then leaned against the frame of the bathroom door for support.

'What the hell do you think you're doing?' he asked.

She gave him a cold smile. 'I'm changing the plan.'

Chapter 9

Dr James McDill and his wife sat across from Special Agent Bill Chalmers, a bland-faced, sandy-haired man in his early forties. Agent Chalmers's tie was still neatly tied despite the fact that it was 11:30 p.m. McDill had called the Jackson Field Office of the FBI a few minutes after Margaret's mini-breakdown, and that call had resulted in this meeting.

He had planned to come to the Federal Building alone, but Margaret had insisted on accompanying him. Chalmers met them in the empty lobby, escorted them through the unmanned security post and up to the FBI floor. They arrived to find most of the office complex empty and dark: a government-issue cube farm lit by glowing computer screens. Chalmers led them back to the office of the SAC, or Special Agent-in-Charge. A nameplate on the desk read: FRANK ZWICK.

The Jackson FBI office had a distinguished or notorious history, depending on what part of the country you were from. It had been established by J. Edgar Hoover himself during the terrible civil rights summer of 1967.

'I'm not quite clear about some of the things you said

on the phone,' Chalmers said from behind his boss's desk. 'Do you mind if I ask some questions?'

'Fire away,' said McDill.

'We're talking about a kidnapping-for-ransom, correct? And wire fraud, it sounds like.'

'Yes, to the first question. To the second, I imagine so.'

'And this happened one year ago today?'

'Give or take a few days. It happened during the same annual medical convention that's going on right now in Biloxi.'

Chalmers pursed his lips and gazed through the window, toward the old Standard Life Building, illuminated now by cold fluorescent light. After a few moments' thought, he looked the heart surgeon directly in the eye.

'I've got to ask this, Doctor. Why did you folks wait a whole year to report this kidnapping?'

McDill had rehearsed his answer during the drive over. 'They threatened to come back and kill our son. We'd paid the ransom. It was a hundred and seventy-five thousand dollars, which, frankly, isn't much money to me. Especially weighed against the life of my son.'

'But didn't you tell me the kidnappers told you they'd done the same thing before?'

'Yes.'

'So you must have feared from the first that they would do it again, to another child. Another family.'

McDill looked at the floor. 'That's true. The hard truth is, I'm more selfish than I'd like to think. If I had to do it again—'

'I was raped,' Margaret said quietly.

McDill froze with his mouth open, but Agent Chalmers settled back into his boss's chair, as though the situation was at last becoming clear.

'I see,' he said. 'Could you tell me a little more about that?'

McDill laid a hand on his wife's forearm. 'Margaret, you don't have to do this.'

She waved off his arm, then gripped the arms of the chair. It was clear that she meant to tell the truth, no matter what it cost her. As she spoke, she did not quite look at Chalmers, but into some indeterminate space beyond him.

'I wouldn't let James report what happened. I was alone with the man who was running the kidnapping, and my son was being held at another location. Peter was at the mercy of these people. My husband was also. The man with me . . . he was in telephone contact with his partners. He could have told them to hurt or kill either Peter or James. He made very sure that I understood that, that I believed he was capable of it. Then he used that fact to extort sex from me.'

McDill tried to comfort her, but she shrunk away and kept talking. 'Very painful, dirty sex,' she said. 'I was terrified that would be made public. I know now that I was wrong to keep it quiet, but—' She wiped one eye but kept going, like a marathon runner forcing herself to reach the finish line. 'Combined with the threat to come back and kill Peter, I simply couldn't deal with the idea. I couldn't take that risk. But I couldn't stop thinking about it, either. I haven't thought about anything else since it happened. I can't even make love with my husband. I – I'm going to pieces, I think.'

McDill took her hand and squeezed it hard. This time she didn't pull away.

Agent Chalmers picked up his pen and tapped it on the table. He suddenly seemed much more convinced by their story.

'The truth is,' said McDill, 'it was just easier for us to try to forget it. To pretend it never happened. But it did.'

'And now you think it's happening again.'

'Yes.'

'Tell me why.'

McDill took a deep breath and marshaled his thoughts. 'I have no objective evidence. I admit that right up front. But the woman holding me at the hotel said they'd done the same thing before, more than once. I believed her. She also said no one had ever reported them. And knowing what I know now about the leader's tactics, I believe that, too. I mean, *we* didn't report it. The man who conceived of this damned scheme – Joe, or whatever his real name is – is clearly a psychopath. He kidnaps children to get money, and to commit rape as some sort of bonus. And so far he's gotten away with it. I guess what I'm saying is, what reason does he have to stop?'

Chalmers put down his pen and laid his hands flat on the desk. McDill had the sense that the agent was deciding whether to engage the full resources of the FBI in the middle of the night, or to take a more conservative approach.

'Mrs McDill, you were with this man for a considerable period of time. Did you have a feeling about whether the name he used was his real name?'

Margaret had begun weeping softly. McDill and Chalmers waited.

'I think Joe was his real name,' she said. 'I think it was some perverse point of pride with him. Like he could do all this to us without any fear that we would report him. The fact that he used his real name demonstrated his superiority. That's what I think, anyway.'

'Did he say anything about where he was from? What state, for example?'

'No.'

'Did he say the other kidnappings had taken place in Mississippi?'

'No. But I assumed they had.'

'Did you have any feeling about what part of the country he might be from?'

'The South,' Margaret said. 'Definitely the South. I won't say Mississippi for sure, because the accent was . . . too hard. Like he was from the South but had been away for a long time. Or maybe the reverse. A man who was from someplace else but had spent a lot of time in the South. Does that make any sense?'

'Yes,' Chalmers replied. 'What about you, Doctor? Did the woman you were with say where she was from? Something about family, anything like that?'

'Nothing useful. She seemed frightened by the whole experience. But she was obviously committed enough to go through with it. I had the feeling she was dominated by this Joe character. I also thought – a couple of times anyway – that the two of them might be married. She never said it in so many words, but the way she spoke about him gave me that impression.'

'How old was she?'

'Early to mid-twenties.'

'Really?'

'She was quite attractive, to be honest.' McDill gave his wife an uncomfortable look. 'I mean, you wouldn't have expected someone who looked like her to be involved in something like that. She looked like a Junior League wife, or even a model. Swimsuit model, anyway.'

Agent Chalmers turned to Mrs McDill. 'What about Joe? The leader. How old was he?'

'Fifty. Somewhere around there.'

'Could you give a good description of him?'

'Yes.'

'Recognize him from a photo?'

'Yes.'

'Any distinguishing marks?'

Margaret covered her face. 'He had a tattoo on his arm. An eagle. Very crudely done.'

'Do you remember which arm?'

'Left. Yes, the left.'

'And the girl?' Chalmers asked McDill.

'I'd know her anywhere. If you want to put me on a plane and fly me down to the coast, I'll go through that whole hotel looking for her.'

'I'm not sure that's the most efficient way to go about it. If she is in the hotel, she's probably in a room by now. We can't go through every room in the place looking for someone we don't even know is there.'

'Not even for a kidnapping?'

'The Beau Rivage has eighteen hundred rooms. No

judge would give us a warrant for that. Not without more evidence.'

'What about a bomb threat?' McDill asked.

'What do you mean?'

'You're the FBI. You could say you had a bomb threat on the casino. They'd have to evacuate the hotel. I could stand outside, watching as you bring the people through the front door. You could videotape them.'

Chalmers looked at McDill with a combination of surprise and respect. 'You're talking about a felony, Doctor. And violating people's civil rights.'

McDill shrugged. 'Desperate times, desperate measures.'

'I wish it worked that way sometimes. We'll start by going through the Jackson police department mug books. And the NCIC computer.' He ran his tongue over his lips and glanced away from the McDills. Somehow this action telegraphed his next question.

'No,' the surgeon said.

'No, what?'

'No, we're not going to involve our son at this point. The third member of this group was a semiretarded giant who claimed to be the leader's cousin. He called himself Huey. He kept Peter in a cabin in the woods, somewhere within two hours of Jackson. He called the leader Joey. That makes me think Joe was the leader's real name. From what my son described, the retarded man might have had trouble remembering an alias. He spent all night whittling. But that's all Peter could tell you. We don't want him involved.'

'Not even to look at mug books?'

'Not at this point.'

'But, Doctor—'

'If you try to involve our son, I'm going to call my attorney and break off contact with you. I've already spoken to him tonight, and he urged me not to speak to you without him present. I disregarded that advice. However, if you try to involve Peter, I will call him. He's awake at home, waiting for just such a call.'

Chalmers started to respond, then apparently decided that McDill was not the sort to be intimidated by threats.

'Well, then. The next step is to go over to the JPD and go through some of their mug books. There'll be a homicide shift working, and I know some of the guys over there. I can access NCIC from there, as well. Are you two ready to look at a hell of a stack of pictures?'

'We're prepared to do anything you require, short of involving Peter. The sooner the better. I really think there are people in danger as we speak.'

Chalmers nodded. 'From all you've told me, I'd say we have a few hours before they try to wire and collect the ransom. I'm going to wake up my boss and outline the situation. We can alert the coastal banks to flag all wire transfers of any size coming in tomorrow morning. We can have agents from the New Orleans office ready to respond the moment a suspicious wire comes in. We can also have a tactical squad here in Jackson, ready to hit whatever bank is the source of the wire, and arrest the leader while the wife is inside trying to send it. There are lots of ways to come at this thing—'

'Just a minute,' McDill interrupted. 'You're forgetting something.'

'What? The hostage?'

'Yes. If you arrest any of these people, the schedule of thirty-minute telephone calls they keep will be broken, and the man in the woods will kill the child.'

'Doctor, a minute ago you were talking about calling in a bomb threat to ID the woman involved.'

'Yes, but only to confirm that it's really happening again. And they use cell phones, so that wouldn't break their schedule.'

'What exactly do you expect us to do with the information you've given me? Nothing?'

'I'm not sure. But you can't just ride into the middle of this thing like the Seventh Cavalry. You'll get people killed.'

'That's not how we operate, Doctor. We might follow them from the ransom pickup at the bank, using a helicopter. We could put a GPS tracking device on the doctor's car while it's parked at the bank. The leader and the woman are eventually going to meet somewhere with the money. Maybe even at the same McDonald's restaurant where your wife got your son back.'

A disturbing current of anxiety was flowing through McDill. 'Agent Chalmers, my child lived through his kidnapping precisely because I did *not* attempt to involve the police. I've come forward now to try to prevent another family from going through the same experience we did. But the fact is, they're probably going through it already. And if your people attempt to intervene, you could cause the death of a child who otherwise would probably live. And please don't start talking to me about "acceptable risk." Because I'm old enough to remember Vietnam.'

Chalmers blew air from his cheeks in frustration. 'You're saying we should let these kidnappers get away in order to be absolutely sure the hostage makes it. But if they get away with it again, they'll simply keep doing it. If you're right about any of this, I mean. And sooner or later, they'll make a mistake. Or some parent will crack under the pressure, and their child will be murdered. It's got to stop here, Doctor.'

McDill wrung his hands, a gesture he despised but at this moment was powerless to stop. 'I understand that. It's just . . . I know the potential for human error. If you involve a large number of people in any process, you exponentially increase the risk of mistakes. The kind of surveillance you're talking about, planting bugs, following cars with helicopters—'

'We're the FBI, Doctor,' Chalmers said. 'We're professionals.'

McDill sighed heavily. 'No offense, but that doesn't exactly fill me with confidence.'

Chapter 10

'Go to the other side of the bed,' Karen ordered. 'Move.'

Still rattled by the gunshots, Hickey edged around the foot of the bed, leaving her between the bathroom and Will's side of the bed.

'Pick up that phone,' she said, pointing at the cordless beside Hickey. 'That's the private line.'

'Who am I calling?'

'Pick it up!'

Hickey obeyed, but his eyes had a manic gleam that kept Karen's finger on the trigger.

'Call my husband's hotel room.'

'You're making a mistake, Karen.'

She raised the gun until it was pointed at his face, then spoke into the phone in her left hand. 'Abby, are you outside yet?'

'Yes.'

'Good. Get down out of sight.' She shifted the phone into the crook between her right shoulder and cheek. Now she could keep the pistol in her right hand while taking the private line from Hickey with her left. The phone on which Abby waited – Will's phone – handled both lines, but she didn't want to put Abby on hold unless she absolutely had to. 'Are you down in some bushes?'

'Uh-huh. They're itchy.'

'You sit tight right there. I'm calling Daddy, and we're going to straighten this out and come get you. Don't hang up, remember?'

'I'm not.'

'Have you got Will yet?' she asked Hickey.

He raised his hands as though to negotiate. 'I'm bleeding to death here. Can't you stitch up my leg first?'

'The sooner you get Will on the phone, the sooner you stop bleeding.'

Hickey dialed a number and asked for suite 28021.

'Throw the receiver onto the bed.'

He did. She picked it up with her left hand and heard the phone ringing. Then a female voice said, 'Hey.'

'Put Dr Jennings on the phone.'

'Who is this?'

'This is Mrs Jennings. And if you don't put him on the phone, I'm going to shoot your husband in the head.'

There was a stunned silence. Then the woman said, 'You can't do that. We've got your little girl.'

'Your husband's bleeding pretty badly right now, missy. You'd better get a move on.'

She heard a fumbling with the phone. Then Will said, 'Karen?'

'Will, thank God.'

'What's going on? Is Abby all right?'

'She's free. I mean—'

'*Free?*'

'She got away from the man guarding her. She's hiding in the woods with a cell phone. I'm talking to her right now.'

'My God! Where's the man now?'

'Hunting for her. But she's hunkered down in some bushes.'

'Where's Joe?'

'I'm holding a gun on him. And I'm very tempted to blow his goddamn head off.'

'Don't do that, Karen.'

'I know. But what can we do? If we call the police, can they trace the cell phone Abby's using? Can they find her?'

'I think they can triangulate cell phones pretty well. But if she's out in the country somewhere . . . I don't know. I don't know if they use towers or trucks or what. How far away from Jackson do you think she is?'

'An hour. Maybe more, maybe less.'

'It won't work,' said Hickey.

'Sixty miles,' Will mused.

'It won't work,' Hickey said again. 'What you're thinking won't work.'

'Shut up!' Karen snapped.

'What's the matter?' asked Will.

'Hickey says tracing the phone won't work.'

'To hell with him. Look, I know the guy who runs CellStar. I did a gall bladder on his wife, and I played in a golf tournament with him.'

'Call him! He'll know what the police can do.'

'We need to know what cellular company Hickey's people are using. CellStar is the biggest, and he might have picked it for anonymity. Tell him to give you his cell phone.'

Karen gestured at Hickey's pocket with the pistol. 'Give me your cell phone.'

'What for?'

'To keep me from shooting you! I'm losing my patience here.'

Hickey took a small Nokia from his pocket and tossed it across the bed.

'I've got it,' she told Will.

'Turn it on and dial – Wait. Is it already on?'

Karen used the barrel of the .38 to flip the phone over. The lights of the LED display were dead. 'No, it's off.'

'Damn. Okay. Dial star-eight-one-one and see who answers.'

'I'm doing it right now.'

'Mama?' Abby said in her other ear.

'Hang on, baby, I'm talking to Daddy.'

Karen used her trigger finger to switch on the phone and punch the keys. Hickey watched her with a puzzled look in his eyes.

'Welcome to the CellStar customer service line,' said a computerized voice.

Karen hit END. 'It's CellStar.'

'Yes!' Will exulted. 'We finally caught a break. Stay on the line. I'll use Cheryl's cell phone to call my guy.'

'Don't worry. I'm too scared to hang up.'

She heard Will tell Hickey's wife to call directory assistance for the home number of a Harley Ferris in Ridgeland, Mississippi. Then he said, 'Karen, ask Hickey why he thinks we can't trace the phone.'

'Why can't we trace Huey's phone?' she repeated.

Hickey's eyes glowed with a strange sort of amusement. 'You're about to kill your kid,' he said, 'and you don't even know it. You'd better let me talk some sense into that husband of yours.'

'He wants to talk to you,' she told Will.

'Fine. Just be careful passing the phone.'

Karen tossed the phone onto the bed. Hickey picked it up.

'Doc? You there?'

Karen said to Abby: 'I'm going to put you on hold for a few seconds, honey. I'm not hanging up, I'm just going to listen to Daddy for a minute. Okay?'

Abby's voice rose to a frantic whisper. 'Don't hang up, Mama!'

'I'll be right back.' She hit the button that switched that phone to the private line.

'You're screwing up, Doc,' Hickey said to Will. 'All you had to do was follow the rules, and you'd have got your kid back in the morning. But now you're trying to pull a fucking John Wayne. And your old lady thinks she's Wonder Woman.'

'Sometimes I think she is, too. The simple truth is that I don't trust you to keep your word.'

'Let me explain something to you, Doc. In some ways tracing a cellular phone is easy. 'Cause a cell phone ain't nothing but a radio. Right?'

'Right.'

'And you can triangulate a radio just like in the old World War Two spy movies. That's what you're thinking. You look at the relative signal strengths between towers and figure a location down to yards.

The problem, Doc – for you, I mean – is that not many towers are equipped to measure that stuff yet. All this is under legislation right now. People *want* cell companies to be able to do that kind of tracing, so people making nine-one-one calls can be found before they bleed to death. Great idea, right? The problem is the equipment. And Mississippi's five years behind the rest of the country. As usual, right? That's why I feel okay using cell phones in this operation. So, if you think the cops are gonna find your kid before Huey does, you're out of your mind. And if you're wondering why I'm telling you this, it's simple. I still want this thing to work. I still want my money. But if you bring in the cops or the FBI, you're taking control out of my hands. It's like bringing divorce lawyers into a marriage. It's the irrevocable step. There won't be anything I can do. I've got to cut my losses and run. That means when Huey finds the kid, he kills her.'

'But we know who you are,' Will pointed out. 'If you kill Abby, you're opening yourself to murder charges.'

'You're not thinking, Doc. Kidnapping alone is a death penalty offense. So I've got nothing to lose by killing her. And by killing her, I kill any chance that she can identify Huey.'

'My wife saw him, too.'

'Did she? Gee, I don't recall that.' Hickey smiled at Karen. 'You starting to get the picture?'

There was a hissing silence as Will considered his options. Karen was about to switch back to Abby when he said, 'Screw you, Joe. Put my wife back on.'

'I'm here,' said Karen. 'Abby's on hold. Let me get

her back.' She switched her phone back to the main line. 'I'm back, baby. Are you okay?'

'No! I was scared. Don't get off anymore.'

'I won't.' She motioned for Hickey to toss his phone back to her. When it landed beside her, it was smeared with dark blood. She wiped it on the comforter, then held it to her mouth. 'Go ahead, Will.'

'I already called my guy on the hotel phone. I'm getting an answering machine.'

'No. Oh God.'

'It is after midnight. And they may not have a phone in their bedroom. I'll keep calling back till they wake up.' He fell silent for a moment. 'Look, you saw the guy who was holding Abby, right?'

'Yes.'

'Do you think he would kill her if Joe told him to?'

Images of a giant standing in the dark flashed through Karen's mind. The startled eyes as she shoved the ice chest into his hands and begged him not to hurt her baby. *Hurt your baby?* Huey had echoed, as though the idea had never entered his head. But what had he really meant? Had the idea of hurting Abby been so alien that he'd been shocked by the suggestion? Or was Huey just too simple-minded to do anything but repeat what was said to him?

Karen covered the mouthpiece of the phone that connected her to Abby. 'I can't answer that. He's huge, and he's simpleminded. Hickey says he gets angry when children run from him, something about the way he was treated growing up. And Abby just ran from him.'

'Jesus. Do you think Abby could hide from him until dawn? Or maybe walk to a road?'

'It's the middle of nowhere, Will.'

'But you left some insulin with her, right?'

'Yes. Hang on.' She uncovered the mouthpiece of the other phone. 'Abby? Do you have your ice chest with you? The one I left with Mr Huey?'

'No. I picked it up when I first ran. But when I went back inside for the phone, I forgot it.'

'That's all right. You're doing great. I'm talking to Daddy.'

'Are ya'll coming to get me?'

'Yes. We're figuring it out right now. Where's Mr Huey?'

'I'm still getting the answering machine,' Will said.

'I don't know,' said Abby. 'He stopped yelling.'

A shiver ran through Karen. 'Don't make a sound, baby.' She covered the phone again. 'She doesn't have the insulin. She doesn't know how to inject herself even if she had it.'

'I think she could do it if she had to. I just don't know if she'd know she was in trouble in time.'

'She's only five years old, Will. Do we have any alternatives?'

'Abby gives herself up and we trust Joe to give her back after he gets the money.'

Karen looked across the bed at Hickey's glittering eyes, his prison tattoo, the bleeding leg. 'No. We've got to try to save her now.'

'Let me talk to him again,' Hickey said.

Karen threw the phone across the bed.

'Doc? Let me tell you a quick story. Me and Huey are cousins. We grew up in different states, but our mamas were sisters. They both married sons of bitches, only Huey's daddy was the leaving kind of son of a bitch, and mine was the ass-whipping kind. After Huey's little sister died, he had to move down to Mississippi with us. He'd got in some trouble up there trying to talk to little girls after that. Hurt some of their parents. Anyhow, my old man could be okay when he wasn't drunk – which wasn't often. He was nice to Huey, but when he was loaded he'd lay into him over being useless. Then he'd whale on me, just for kicks.'

Karen wanted to hear Will's responses, but she knew Abby might break down if she was put on hold again. She hoped Will was still ringing the president of CellStar.

'So, Pop takes us deer hunting one day,' Hickey said. 'We didn't let Huey carry a gun, of course, but we always took him. You couldn't beat him for hauling dead deer out of the woods. Anyhow, I was climbing through this bobwire fence, and my gun went off. Pop was drunk, and he started yelling how he'd felt the bullet pass his cheek. He threw down his rifle and started whalin' on me right there in the woods. I was about thirteen. Huey was twelve. He was a big boy, though. So, Pop whales on me till he runs out of wind, then he stops to rest. I try to go for my rifle on the ground, but soon as I do, he gets between me and it. Then he takes a sip from his flask and starts whalin' on me again. Huey has this funny look on his face. Then, real slow like, he walks up behind Pop and grabs him around the arms, like he's hugging a tree. And he just holds him there. Pop goes crazy. He's kicking and screaming how he's gonna kill us both when he gets loose. I pick up my rifle and point it at him. I know when he gets loose he's gonna tear me to pieces. But I can't shoot him too easy with Huey holding him, except point-blank in the head, which wouldn't look right.'

Karen made sure her palm was sealing the phone Abby waited on.

'So Huey gets this scared look on his face and says, "I just wanted him to stop hitting you, Joey. I don't want to hurt him none." I say, "He ain't ever gonna stop. Not till he's dead. You kill him, Buckethead, and we'll be done with it. We're blood brothers, boy, you gotta listen when I tell you something." So Huey thinks for a minute. Then he picks Pop up where his legs won't touch the ground and carries him over to this big rock and lays him down and smashes his head against it till he stops wiggling. He carries the body the top of a ridge, just like I tell him to, and drops him down onto the creek rocks. Like he fell there.'

Karen closed her eyes, praying for Abby with all her being.

'Now, Huey didn't *want* to do that, Doc. But he did it. He won't want to hurt your little girl, either. But if I tell him to, he will. 'Cause he can't envision a world without cousin Joey in it. And if he thinks your little girl living means me going to Parchman, she'll die sure as old Pop did.' Hickey winked at Karen as he spoke into the phone. 'He could break Abby's neck without even meaning to. Like dropping a china vase.'

Hickey listened to whatever Will said, then laid the phone near the middle of the bed, a confident smile on his face. Karen picked it up.

'What are we going to do?' she asked.

'While Hickey was telling his story, I called CellStar and tried to find out if Ferris is even in town. I told them it was a medical emergency. Their security department said he should be at home.'

'But you're still getting the machine?'

'Yes, but I'm going to keep ringing it. Somebody's bound to wake up eventually. I want to talk to Abby right now. I need to hear her voice. Can you hold the phones together?'

Karen raised the gun to Hickey's face. 'Sit on the floor by the wall.'

'Why?'

'*Sit!*'

He backed to the wall and slid down it, keeping both hands pressed to his lacerated thigh. Karen laid the .38 on the comforter, then inverted one of the phones and held them together.

'Punkin?' Will said, sounding like a transistor radio. 'This is Daddy. Are you all right?'

Karen heard Abby sobbing. It made her want to pick up the gun and blow a hole in Hickey's heart.

'I'm coming to get you, baby,' Will said, his voice cracking with emotion. 'But what I need now is for you to stay hidden. It's just like the Indian Princess campout. Just another game. It may take a little while, but Daddy's going to be there. Do you hear me?'

'Yes.' The voice sounded tiny and alone.

'I want to ask you a question. Has there ever been a time when you really needed me and I didn't come?'

'No.'

'That's right. And there never will be. I swear that on the Bible.'

'You're not supposed to swear on the Bible.'

'If it's real important, you can. I'm coming to get you, baby. If you get scared, you just remember that. Daddy's coming.'

'Okay.'

'I need to talk to Mom again. I love you, baby.'

'Please hurry, Daddy.'

Karen separated the phones. 'Will?'

'It would be good if we could get Abby to shut off that phone for a while,' he said, 'to conserve the batteries. But I don't think she could handle it. Just keep her calm and quiet. I'm doing everything I can.'

'Hurry, Will.'

Huey Cotton paused in the rutted road leading to the cabin and looked up at the sky. His heart was full of sadness, and his eyes felt fuzzy from staring into the dark trees. Huey experienced much of the world as colors. A doctor had questioned him about it once. Like the woods. The woods had a green smell. Even at night, when you couldn't see the green, you could smell and taste it. The clean green of the oak leaves overhead. The thick jungly green of the vines tugging at his pant legs.

Joey was two colors. Sometimes he was white like an angel, a guardian who floated at Huey's shoulder or walked in his shadow, ready to reveal himself when needed. But there was red in Joey, too, a hard little seed filled with dark ink, and sometimes it burst and bled out into the white, covering it completely. When Joey turned red, bad things happened, or had already happened, or were coming down the road. When Joey turned red, Huey had to do things he didn't like to do. But by doing them, he helped the red fade away, like blood on a shirt in a wash bucket.

Sometimes he couldn't see color at all. There was a shade between brown and black ('no-color,' he called it) that hovered at the edges of everything, like a fog waiting to blot out the world. He saw it when he stood in line to order a hamburger and heard people whispering behind him because he couldn't make up his mind about what he wanted. The order-taker seemed to float in a tiny, faraway circle at the center of his vision, and all he could keep in his head was what the people behind him were saying, not whether he wanted pickles or onions. He knew they said mean things because they couldn't see inside him, past how big he was, but whenever he tried to explain that, he scared people. And the more afraid they got, the more the no-color seeped in from the edges.

School was the worst. He had tried with all his might to forget the things children had said to him at the school in Missouri. But he couldn't. They lived inside his head, like termites in the support beams of a house. Even when he got so big that teenage boys wouldn't stand toe-to-toe with him, they teased him. Teased him and ran before he could make them pay for it. Girls teased him, too. *Retard, retard, retard.* In his dreams they still ran from him, and he never caught them. In real life, though, he caught one once. A teenage boy. That was one reason he'd had to come to Mississippi to live. His mother never told his aunt about it. She was afraid her sister wouldn't take him.

But Huey had told Joey. And Joey had understood.

Huey lowered his head and breathed deep. He could smell people sometimes, the way he smelled animals. Some smelled bad, others nothing special. Abby smelled like a towel fresh out of the clothes dryer. Cleaner than anything he'd ever smelled. And she sparkled. He didn't understand why he couldn't find her in the dark, because she was silver and gold, and should be reflecting the moonlight.

Maybe the no-color was hiding her. It had been seeping into his eyes since the moment he'd realized she'd run away. He had tried hard not to be scary, but he'd seen the fear in her eyes. Maybe she couldn't help it. She was so tiny. Joey said she was six years old, but her head was smaller than Huey's hand.

'Abby?' he called halfheartedly.

Nothing.

He walked back toward the cabin, sniffing and listening, but nothing registered. Cutting around the cabin, he looked into the tractor shed. The clean smell hovered around the tractor. He leaned down and sniffed the seat.

Abby had sat there.

He crept out of the shed and looked into the dark mosaic of foliage, straining his eyes. Some greens looked gray at night. The tree trunks looked silver-black. Moonlight dripped down the black leaves and hanging branches. He relaxed his eyes, which was a trick he had learned while hunting with Joey. Sometimes, if you let your eyes relax, they picked up things they never would if you were *trying* to see. As he looked into the shadows, something yellowy and far dimmer than a lightning bug winked in the darkness.

His heartbeat quickened. He focused on the spot, but the yellowy light was gone. He relaxed his eyes again.

The light winked and disappeared.

He was close. The light was important, but something else had stirred the blood in his slow veins. The green smell had changed.

Twenty yards from the tractor shed, Abby crouched in the sweltering darkness, clenching the cell phone as hard as she could. The thick branches of the oak above blocked the moonlight. She couldn't see anything beyond the bushes that shielded her. She wished she was still up on the tractor seat. It was dry and safe there, not itchy like the briars clawing at her now. She had no idea where Mr Huey was. There were too many noises around her to tell anything. Only the reassuring glow of the phone's readout panel kept her from bolting toward the lights of the cabin. It was like looking at the kitchen window of her house when she was playing outside after supper.

A soft squawk from the phone startled her, and she put it to her ear.

'Abby?' said her mother.

'What?' she whispered back.

'Are you okay?'

'I guess so.'

'Where's Mr Huey?'

'I don't know.'

'You haven't heard him?'

'He stopped yelling a while ago. Maybe he's gone.'

'Maybe. But we don't know that for sure. You have to stay down.'

'I'm sitting on my knees.'

'That's good. Daddy's calling a man right now who's going to help us find you. Do you know how he's going to do that?'

'No.'

'The phone in your hand is like a radio. As long as it stays on, the police can find you. It's the same as if you were standing there yelling, "Mama, Mama."'

'Do you want me to stand up and yell? I can yell loud.'

'No! No, honey. The phone is yelling for you, okay? People can't hear it, but computers can.'

'Like a dog hearing a whistle?'

'Exactly like that. Now – Hang on, Daddy's talking to me.'

'Okay.'

Abby held the phone against her ear so hard it hurt. She wanted to hear her father's voice again.

Hickey was still sitting against the bedroom wall. Despite his wounded leg, he watched Karen like a hyena waiting for its chance to strike.

'You going to sew me up or what?' he asked, holding up his bloody palms.

'I haven't decided.'

'I'm getting exactly nowhere,' Will said in her ear, his voice tight with frustration. 'Goddamn answering machine. I can't believe the president of a cellular phone company doesn't have a service.'

'Maybe we should call the police. Or the FBI.'

'I don't think we can risk that. If Huey—'

'Mama?' Abby said in her other ear.

'What is it, baby?'

'I think I heard something.'

Karen's heart fluttered. 'Whisper, honey. What did you hear?'

'I don't know.' Abby's voice was a thin filament stretched over a vast chasm of fear. 'How long till you get here?'

'Not long. Has the noise stopped?'

'I don't hear it right now. I'm scared it's a possum.'

Karen felt a hysterical relief. 'It's okay if it's a possum. They won't hurt you.'

'They won't bite me?'

'No. They're more scared of you than you are of them.'

'One bit Kate's cat last week.'

'That's different.'

'What if it's a snake?'

'It's not a snake,' Karen assured her, even as she panicked at the thought. 'Snakes are sleeping right now.'

'Uh-uh. Snakes hunt at night. I saw it on Animal Planet.'

Jesus. 'That's just in other countries, like India. And Sri Lanka. Cobras and things. We don't have cobras here.'

'Oh.'

'Our snakes sleep at night.'

'Mom, I heard it again.' Her whisper was barely audible now. 'Like somebody sneaking up.'

Karen fought a surge of panic. 'You have to be *quiet*. I want you to stop talking.'

'I feel better when we talk.'

'I know, sweetie, but—'

'*Mama*—'

In two nearly silent syllables, utter terror traveled from child to mother. Karen squeezed the phone tight enough to bruise her hand. 'Abby? Say something!'

There was only silence. Then she heard breathing, and she understood what was happening. Abby was sitting motionless in the dark, scared out of her mind. Huey was close. Praying that Abby still had the phone to her ear, Karen whispered, 'I'm with you, honey. I'm here. Sit very still. You're going to be fine. Remember what Daddy said.'

She listened with every fiber of her nervous system.

Out of the breathing, she heard a whimper, so soft that Abby had to be fighting a heroic battle to suppress it. Karen was about to reassure her again when a crash like breaking branches came down the line and Abby screamed.

'I found you, didn't I?' Huey said loudly.

Karen's heart turned to ice. '*Abby?*'

'I saw the light,' Huey said, his voice exultant. 'Why did you run, Abby?'

'ABBY!'

'What is it?' Will shouted in her ear.

'Joey?' said Huey.

'Put Abby back on!' Karen demanded. 'Please!'

'Where's Joey?'

'Well, well,' said Hickey. He pressed his bloody palms against the carpet and stood. 'The worm has turned.'

Karen grabbed the .38 and pointed it at his chest. 'MAKE HIM PUT ABBY BACK ON!'

Hickey walked fearlessly around the bed. 'If you shoot me now, she's as dead as a hammer. Give me the phone.'

'*Get back!*'

He brushed the gun aside and slapped her face, then stripped the phone from her hand.

'Huey? This is Joey. If you hear a shot, strangle that brat. Don't even wait to ask me a question, because I'll be dead. This bitch already stabbed me. She tried to kill me.'

Hickey's face hardened as he listened to his cousin's reply. 'You goddamn retard. I give the orders and you follow them. Period.' He grabbed Karen's wrist and squeezed until her hand opened of its own accord and she dropped the .38. He bent and picked it up. 'Tie the kid and gag her, Huey. I'll call you back.'

Without warning, Karen snapped. She flew at Hickey's face, meaning to claw out his eyes, but before she reached them, he slammed his fist into her sternum. The blow drove the wind from her lungs and dropped her to the floor. As she lay there gasping, he picked up the phone that had connected her to Will and spoke in a savage voice.

'Huey just found your kid, Doc. I hope you haven't talked to anybody yet, because if you have, Abby won't ever see second grade. . . . Calm down. I don't

201

want you to stroke out on me. I just hope this wildcat you're married to has learned her lesson.'

'Please,' Karen pleaded, struggling to her knees. 'Don't let him tie her. Don't let him hurt her. She—'

'Shut your mouth.' Hickey hung up. 'And stitch up this goddamn leg already.'

She stared up at him, panting like a winded runner. Tiny points of light danced at the centers of his eyes.

'I own you,' he said in a quiet voice. 'You know that now, don't you?'

'I just want my little girl safe. Whatever that takes.'

'That's a good answer. But first things first.' He pointed at his lacerated leg. 'Get to work.'

Karen tried to put Abby out of her mind. If she didn't, she wouldn't be able to function. Bracing her hand on the bed, she got to her feet, then picked up the forceps she'd dropped earlier and opened Will's black bag.

'No needles,' Hickey said, as she removed a vial of lidocaine and a syringe. 'I don't trust you as far as I can throw you.'

'Fine with me. Forty stitches without anesthetic will burn like the hinges of hell.'

Hickey laughed. 'You should enjoy it, then. But don't worry, babe. I'm gonna pay you back for every stitch.'

Chapter 11

Huey stumbled through the dark with Abby in his arms and fear bubbling from his heart. The no-color was all around, flooding in from the edges of his sight, leaving only the glowing cabin windows swirling in the dark. Abby shrieked endlessly, so long and so loudly that he didn't know how she was breathing. He wished to God he could put his hands over his ears, but he needed them to carry her.

Her screams were like water he had to run through. And the fear in them was the same fear he had known as a little boy. It set something vibrating in his chest, like a bell struck with a hammer. Joey had said to tie her up, but Huey didn't want to tie her up. Joey said to strangle her if he heard a shot, and Huey thanked Jesus he hadn't heard one. The only way he could hurt Abby was if he saw another face on top of her face, some other girl's face. An older girl had once taken him into the woods and showed him things, then asked him to pull down his pants. After he did, she yelled to a dozen boys who came running out of the trees, laughing and jeering at him. He wanted to twist that girl's head around and around until it came right off, like a chicken's.

Huey had never felt so twisted up inside, but he knew one thing. He couldn't live without Joey. Life before Joey was a fearful blur, and the idea of life without him would not even fit into Huey's head. Creatures like Abby were like lanterns in the dark, but he could never keep them. In the end, Joey was all he had.

Midnight had passed, and the Jennings' Victorian house stood dark and silent on its hill. Crickets cheeped in the pine trees: a truck droned out on the interstate; but the house itself was silent.

A scream pierced the night.

Inside the master bedroom, Karen crouched over Hickey's wounded thigh on the sleigh bed. Naked but for a towel she had lain across his midsection, Hickey held the bottle of Wild Turkey in his left hand and a halogen lamp from Will's study in his right. He aimed the light wherever she told him to, keeping silent during most of the work, but occasionally yelling when the needle pierced his unanesthetized flesh.

Karen worked the U-shaped suture needle with almost careless speed, mating the edges of the wound, tying knots, moving on. It was amazing how much damage one slash with a good scalpel could do. Hickey hadn't lost enough blood to threaten his life, but he'd bled enough to scare the hell out of someone unused to trauma. Karen was grateful to see that she had in fact nicked the base of his penis with her panicked stroke (a wound that required two stitches) and hoped this would discourage him from trying to force her to finish what she'd begun earlier.

'How many to go?' he asked in a taut voice.

'We're only half done. You should have taken that lidocaine.'

He gulped another slug of Wild Turkey as she jabbed the needle through his skin. 'This is all the shot I need. Just hurry it up.'

She sewed five more stitches, then paused to stretch her wrists. As she did, something that had been bothering her from the beginning slipped out. 'Why us?' she said softly.

'What?'

'I said, why us?'

Hickey reached out with the bottle and forced her chin up, so that she was looking at his face. 'Are you that dumb? Are you that fucking dumb?'

'What do you mean?'

'Why *not* you? Huh? You think because you live out here in this suburban palace, you're immune to pain? My mother had throat cancer. That's the worst, man. "*Why me?*" she'd rasp all the time. "*Dear Jesus, why me?*" I'd ask the same thing. Why my mother? Why not my shit-for-brains old man? I'd look at the ceiling like God was up there listening and ask why. Then I finally figured it out. The joke was on me.' Hickey shook his bottle, spilling amber fluid on Karen's knee. 'The joke's on you, too, June Cleaver.'

'Why?'

'You're a human being, that's why. So why not you, okay? Why *not* you?'

Karen bit her lip and grazed intently at Hickey.

Bitterness was etched in every line of his face, and his eyes were like black wells with a film of oil floating on them. 'It must be awful to be you,' she said.

'Sometimes,' he conceded. 'But tonight it's worse to be you.'

Will stood at the picture window of the bedroom, staring out over the Gulf of Mexico. The Cypress suite, despite its luxurious appointments, had begun to close around him like a prison cell, and the knowledge that the dark gulf stretched south to the Yucatan somehow calmed him.

The first seconds after he realized that Huey had recaptured Abby had been hellish. Even armed with a pistol, Cheryl had felt compelled to lock herself in one of the marble bathrooms for protection, so terrible had been his rage. He could have killed Hickey at that moment, if the man had appeared before him. But of course he hadn't. Hickey had designed his Chinese box precisely so that this scenario would never occur.

Even as Will's rage dissipated, his frustration grew. There was so much he didn't know. How had Karen gotten the drop on Hickey? Probably by sneaking the .38 from the top of their closet. But even so, why would Hickey respond to her threat? He had control over Abby, and so long as he did, a gun would do Karen no good. But apparently it had. Or *something* had. Before Hickey hung up the telephone, Will had heard him yell something about being stabbed. Had Karen stabbed him? Had she snapped under the stress and tried to kill him? No. Karen never lost control.

That was axiomatic. Her father, the master sergeant, had drilled into his daughter a self-discipline that was unnerving. Whatever had happened, Will had no way to discover it. He would just have to wait.

The only lights on the gulf now belonged to a lone freighter sailing west, probably to off-load coffee or bananas or God-knew-what-else in New Orleans. There were men sleeping on that ship, a full crew less than three miles away, men who knew nothing of his problem and could do nothing to help him if they had. There were several hundred doctors in this very hotel, many of whom Will knew personally – yet none could help him. He was trapped in an unbreakable cage constructed by a madman named Joe Hickey.

No, he thought. *Madman is probably inaccurate.* True madness was rare, if you barred disorders caused by organic disease. During his psychiatry rotation in medical school, Will had treated patients at the state mental hospital at Whitfield, several of them classified as criminally insane. After a while, he had come to the conclusion that some of the men were quite sane. They had pursued their goals and desires with the single-minded drive of men who succeeded in business or the arts or politics. It was simply that society found itself unable to admit that their chosen goals could be the goals of sane men. But Will knew different. All men had atavistic desires, sometimes savage ones. Some were merely better at suppressing them than others. And Hickey did not belong in the first category. He acted on his impulses, regardless of law or danger. His overt motive was simple enough: money. But it seemed to Will that if a man was willing to flout the law, there were easier and less risky ways to steal large amounts of money. Hickey's plan was constructed to satisfy deeper urges than money. And Will needed to figure out what those were. Very soon.

He was having trouble keeping his mind on track. He remembered the ride to the airport that morning, when he'd asked Karen to bring Abby to the convention at the last minute. He'd had a bad feeling about her refusal. A premonition. Nothing melodramatic, just a feeling that if Karen wasn't with him on this trip, their lives might skew farther apart than they already had. In his wildest flights of paranoia, he could not have imagined something like this. But he *had* imagined that without Karen at his side this weekend, he might find himself in one of those situations he'd experienced many times before. Situations in which he had always chosen to spend the night alone rather than accept an offer of female company. But during the ride to the airport, something had been whispering below the level of consciousness, a voice born during long months of miscommunication and silent rejections, whispering that a channel for release was presenting itself. And a part of him had heeded that voice. That knowledge now ate like acid at his heart.

It was a cliché of a cliché. You never knew what you had until it was gone. The idea that Abby could be murdered was so paralyzing that Will did not allow himself to consider it a real possibility. He would get her back, no matter what it cost him. Money. Blood. His life. But even with the best possible outcome, something irrevocable had already occurred. He had left his wife and child alone. Exposed. It was nothing that millions of fathers didn't do every week, but in this case, some part of him had *wanted* to be alone on this trip. He could have pushed Karen harder – and earlier – really convinced her that he wanted her with him on this weekend. But he hadn't. It wasn't solely his fault. Organizing the Junior League's sixtieth anniversary flower show was comparable to planning double-blind trials for a new drug, and missing the event itself would be Junior League suicide for the chairperson. But deep down, Will suspected, Karen *wanted* to commit Junior League suicide. And he had not done enough to help her.

'What are you thinking about over there?' asked Cheryl.

She came out of the bathroom and climbed back into the bed, using the oversized pillows to prop herself against the headboard. The torn cocktail dress was tied around her waist. She wore the black bra as though it were a Madonna-style bustier. Will supposed that to a girl who had turned tricks in cars behind a strip club, wearing only a bra in front of a stranger was no big deal.

'Not speaking to me?' she asked.

Cheryl was the kind of person who couldn't tolerate silence. Will shrugged and turned back to the lights of the freighter.

'Look, you're going to get your daughter back,' she said. 'It's just a waiting game. You pay some money – which you don't give a shit about compared to your little girl – and you get her back in the morning. You ought to try to sleep. I've got to take the calls from Joey, so I have to stay awake. But you should crash. I'll wake you when it's time.'

'You think I can sleep with this going on?'

'You need to. You're going to be a basket case in the morning if you don't.'

'I can't.'

'Yes, you can.'

'Leave me alone, okay?'

'Look, you're standing there blaming yourself and trying to figure out a way to rescue your little girl. That's what they all do. But you can't. You're not Mel Gibson, for Christ's sake. Mel Gibson isn't even Mel Gibson, you know? You save your little girl by paying Joey the money. It's that simple.'

'I should trust Joe?'

'Joey's got a motto on this deal, Doc. You know what it is?'

'What?'

'The kid always makes it.'

Will turned from the window.

'I'm serious,' she said. 'He's said it a hundred times. That's how we've managed to keep on doing this. That's how we made all our money.'

'And every child you've done this to has lived? Been returned to its parents?'

'Good as new. I'm telling you, you've got to chill.' She barked a laugh that gave lie to the classic beauty of her face. 'You gotta *chill*, Will!' she sang out, delighted by the rhyme. 'You're going to give yourself a stroke.'

He turned back to the window. Cheryl's reassurances didn't mesh with the voice on the other end of the phone. There was hatred in Hickey's voice, a resentment so deep that Will could not see it stopping short of the maximum pain it could inflict. Yet in the other cases, it had. If Cheryl and Hickey could be believed.

'You want me to help you calm down?' Cheryl asked.

He looked at her reflection in the window. She had taken a brush from her purse and was pulling it through her blond hair. 'How?' he asked. 'Drugs?'

'I told you, I'm clean now. But I can chill you out. Whatever, you know. Back rub?'

'No, thanks.'

'Front rub?'

He turned to her, unsure he had heard correctly. She stopped brushing her hair.

'It's no big deal,' she said. 'You'll sleep like a baby. All guys do.'

'Are you kidding?'

She smiled knowingly. 'Don't worry. Wifey won't ever know about it.'

'I said no, okay? Jesus.'

'I was just trying to help you relax. I know you're upset.'

'What's the deal here, Cheryl? Is sex the only way you know how to relate to men?'

She turned to the television, her lower lip pooched out like an angry child's. 'Not quite, Oprah.'

'A while ago you gave me your sob story about how terrible it was to be a whore. Now you're acting like one.'

'Hey, I was just trying to make this easier on you.'

'Do you make the same offer to all your victims?'

The word 'victim' didn't sit well with her. 'I saw you looking at me during the speech, and I knew you were interested.'

'Bullshit.'

She cut her eyes at him, and they held a disturbing knowledge. 'My mistake, I guess. What do I know? I'm just a dumb stripper, right?' She picked up the remote and flipped through some channels, finally settling on the Home Shopping Network.

Will turned back to the window. As he searched for the tiny lights of the freighter, he saw movement in the reflection of the room. Focusing on it, he saw Cheryl remove her bra. He didn't turn, but he saw her settle deeper on the pillows and begin slowly stroking her breasts. He tried to watch the freighter, but couldn't concentrate. It was absurd. This woman had helped kidnap his daughter; now she was coming on to him as if they'd just met in the casino downstairs. Cheryl moaned softly, drawing his eyes to her reflection again. Her movements were impossible to ignore.

'Why are you doing that?'

'To show you you're no different than the rest. And that it's okay.'

'Put your bra back on.'

She didn't stop moving her hands. 'You're saying that, but you'd rather I left it off.'

'Put it back on, Cheryl.'

'They look good, don't they?'

He turned toward the bed at last. 'If you like implants.'

She laughed. 'Sure they're implants. But they're

good. Not like the local junk you see around here. Joey flew me out to LA to have it done, when I was a featured dancer. I got the same doctor that did Demi. He said mine looked just as good.' She cupped them in her palms. '*Just* as good.'

They did look like perfect male fantasies, but they did not look natural. As a doctor, Will had seen more breasts than he cared to think about, and Cheryl's *Penthouse*-style showpieces had almost nothing in common with the female form in its natural state.

'Cover yourself,' he said.

'Are you sure?'

'I don't care what you do.' He turned back to the window.

'Why don't you at least face the truth about something, Will?'

It was the first time she had used his Christian name. He didn't like it. 'What?'

'When you were first giving your speech, and you saw me down there watching you, you were fantasizing about me.'

'You're wrong.'

'You can't lie about that. You checked me out from head to toe. Then you stared at my panties when I uncrossed my legs.'

'You made them too obvious to ignore.'

'But you were interested. A lot more interested than you were in your speech. And if it wasn't for the reason we're in this room together now, we might be here for another reason.'

'You're wrong,' he said again, annoyed by the accuracy of her instincts.

'Am I?'

'Yes.'

'What I saw in your face tonight I've seen in lots of guys' faces. Decent guys, I mean. I know you. For a few years now, you've been wishing you had someone like me to sleep with. You love your wife, you wouldn't trade her for anything, but she just doesn't do it for you. She doesn't understand what you need. How you need it, and how often. Nothing, really. She's making a nest, adding twigs, thinking about the little chickadees. You're helping with the nest, but you miss hunting.'

'Where'd you get that? *Cosmo?*'

'I don't remember. But it's on the money, isn't it?'

He turned back to the bed, where Cheryl was enacting a fifteen-year-old boy's dream of paradise. 'This isn't going to happen. You don't want sex. And you don't want to "relax" me. What you really want is to somehow make me culpable in what you're doing.'

'What's culpable?' She looked genuinely confused.

'You want to make me part of this. To involve me, to pull me down to your level, so that what you're doing doesn't seem so horrible. But it *is* horrible. And you know it.'

Cheryl jerked the bra up over her breasts and stared at the television.

He turned and laid his palms flat on the window-pane. The thick glass was cool from the air conditioner, but he knew there was a warm wind blowing outside. Cool compared to the stagnant air hanging over the scrub and stunted pines growing inland from the beach, but warm compared to the frigid air in the casino suite.

'We never finished our conversation from before,' Cheryl said.

'What are you talking about?'

'When you asked how I wound up doing this. Kidnapping kids.'

'You told me your story.'

'I left out a few things.' She looked the way Abby did when she was trying to conceal some surprise. 'After Joey made me stop being a featured dancer, he put me back into Jackson. New Orleans and Jackson. Sometimes the club down in Hattiesburg, but that was down-market. Mostly college kids, lining up to get off in their pants.'

'You should go on Howard Stern.'

'Maybe I should. But you should listen to me, Doc. There's a lesson here for you.'

'I'm on pins and needles.'

'Joey put me back in the clubs, but not really to dance. He started coming in every night I was on, but not to watch me. He came to talk to the people. The owners, the bouncers, the customers. He bought rounds for everybody. Bought them sofa dances. Pretty soon he got a handle on who was coming in there. And it would blow your mind, Doc. Lawyers, doctors, stockbrokers, aldermen. *Ministers*, for Christ's sake. Ministers sneaking in there to get a sofa dance. What a crazy kick. Anyway, Joey got a handle on all these guys. And then we started up a little business on the side.'

'What business was that?'

'Blackmail. These guys got addicted to me, see? I mean, I may not like doing it, but I can *give* a sofa dance. I took those guys places they'd never even dreamed about. They're dropping fifty bucks a pop for three minutes, and happy as pigs in slop. Pretty soon they're offering lots more and asking if I do any after-hours dancing.' She wrinkled her nose. 'Dancing, right? So, to the right ones – the rich, married ones – I said, Sure, honey. And I let them take me to a motel after work. A motel run by a guy who was tight with Joey, who had special cameras set up in a certain room. Once we got inside that room, I got those guys to do things they would die before they let their wives or bosses see. They left there with their minds blown and their lives in Joey's pocket. And you know something? I never felt sorry for them. Not once. Every one of those bastards left his wife and kids at home to come into that club. They took me back to that room to screw me senseless, not giving a damn if I lived or died after. Every one of them begged me to do it without a condom, and most of them wanted . . . God, I don't even want to think about it. And these were pillars of the community, you know? So, when you stand there acting like you're above it, I know it's bullshit, okay? You play your little game, but I *know*.'

'I'm not above it,' Will said. 'No man is. Or woman, for that matter. It's called human frailty. It's pathetic, but it's the story of life. You don't have any special knowledge. I think my wife knows everything you just told me, even without experiencing it. She just chooses not to let it touch her.'

'So, she's above it, huh? Maybe that's why she isn't doing it for you in the bedroom.'

'You still haven't told me how or why you switched from blackmail to kidnapping.'

Cheryl drank off what was left of her rum-and-Coke. 'Blackmail gets messy. You can't predict what guys will do when you hit them with the pictures. The reality of it. The end of life as they know it. Most of them can't wait to pay, of course. But you never know. One guy wanted copies to give to his wife and everybody at his office.' She smiled at the memory. 'But some of them freak. They run home and confess to their wives, or try to kill Joey, or . . .'

She trailed off, and in the moments of silence that followed, Will knew what she had not said. 'Some of them kill themselves,' he finished. 'Right?'

She squinted at the television. 'One guy did. It was bad. He left his copy of the tape playing on the VCR when he shot himself. His wife found him. Can you imagine?' She poured more rum into her glass, straight this time. 'The cops nearly got us for that one. After that, Joey decided we were going about it the wrong way. The thing to do, he figured, was a small number of jobs, but get the maximum bang for the risk.'

'Kidnapping?'

She nodded. 'When he was working the blackmail gigs, he saw that what these guys were most scared of – way more than hurting their wives – was their kids. They couldn't take the idea that their kids would lose all respect for them. Their kids were what they lived for. So, the way to get the most money was to make the guys pay for their kids.'

'That's a hell of a lot riskier than blackmail.'

'It is if you do it the way everybody else does it.

217

That's like asking the FBI to stomp on you with a SWAT team. Joey's smarter than that. But I don't have to tell you that, do I?'

Will stepped to his left and collapsed into the chair by the window. After all that had happened, it was Cheryl's last story that brought the full weight of reality crashing down upon him. He wasn't special. He was merely the latest in a long line of fools victimized by a man who specialized in exploiting human weakness. Hickey had made a profession of it, an art, and Will couldn't see any way to extricate himself or his family from the man's web.

'Tell me one thing.'

'What?'

'Did any of the other fathers take you up on your offer?'

Cheryl intertwined her fingers and put her hands behind her head, which showed her implants to best advantage. A strange smile touched her lips. 'Two out of five. The others tortured themselves all night. Those two slept like babies.'

Despite his speech about human frailty, Will couldn't believe that fathers whose children were in mortal danger would have sex with one of their kidnappers. It seemed incomprehensible. And yet, he knew it was possible. 'You're lying,' he said, trying to reassure himself.

'Whatever you say. But I know what I know.'

Special Agent Bill Chalmers thanked a black homicide detective named Washington and closed the door of the police interrogation room. Dr McDill and his wife had followed the FBI agent's car the few blocks from the Federal Building to police headquarters, and what they had come for now lay on the metal table in front of them. A stack of mug books two and a half feet high.

'I know it's not great,' Chalmers said. 'But it's more private than the squad room.'

'There must be thousands of photos here,' McDill said.

'Easily. I'll be outside, accessing the National Crime Information Center computer. I'll check all past records of kidnappings-for-ransom in the Southeast, then hit the names "Joe," "Cheryl," and "Huey" for criminal records under actual names and aliases. "Joe" is common as dirt, but the others might ring a bell. Also, I talked to my boss by cell phone on the way over. We may see him down here before long. Right now he's waking up some bank officers to set up flags on large wire transfers going to the Gulf Coast tomorrow morning.' Chalmers looked at his watch. 'I guess I mean this morning.'

McDill sighed. 'Could we have some coffee or something?'

'You bet. How do you take it?'

'Black for me. Margaret?'

'Is it possible they might have tea?' she asked in a soft voice.

Chalmers gave her a smile. 'You never know. I'll check.'

After he went out, Margaret sat down at the table and opened one of the mug books. The faces staring up from the page belonged to people the McDills used all their money and privilege to avoid. The faces shared many features. Flash-blinded, dope-fried eyes. Hollow cheeks. Bad teeth. Nose rings. Tattoos. And stamped into every one as though dyed into the skin, a bitter hopelessness that never looked further than the next twenty-four hours.

'Are we doing the right thing?' Margaret asked, looking up at her husband.

McDill gently squeezed her shoulder. 'Yes.'

'How do you know?'

'The right thing is always the hardest thing.'

Abby sat scrunched in the corner of the ratty sofa, crying inconsolably, her Barbie held tight against her. Huey sat on the floor six feet away, looking stricken.

'I didn't mean to scare you,' he said. 'I just did what Joey told me to. I have to do what Joey says.'

'He stole me from my mom and dad!' Abby wailed. 'You did, too!'

'I didn't want to! I wish your mama was here right now.' Huey squeezed his hands into fists. 'I wish *my* mama was here.'

'Where is she?' Abby asked, pausing in mid-wail.

'Heaven.' Huey said it as though he didn't quite believe it. 'How come you ran away? It's because I'm ugly, isn't it?'

Abby resumed crying, but she shook her head.

'You don't have to say it. I know. The kids in my school ran too. Nobody liked me. But I thought we was friends. All I wanted to do was be nice. But you ran. How come?'

'I *told* you. You stole me away from my mom.'

'That's not it. You don't like me because I look like a monster.'

Abby fixed her swollen eyes on him. 'What you *look* like doesn't matter. Don't you know that?'

Huey blinked. 'What?'

'Belle taught me that.'

'Who?'

Abby rubbed her eyes and held out her gold lame-gowned Barbie. 'This is Belle. *Beauty and the Beast* Belle. She's my favourite Disney princess because she reads books. She wants to be something someday. Belle says it doesn't matter what you look like. It only matters what you feel inside. In your heart. And what you do.'

Huey's mouth hung slack, as though he were staring at a magical fairy risen from the grass.

'You never saw *Beauty and the Beast*?' Abby said incredulously.

He shook his head.

'Let's pretend I'm Belle, and you're Beast.'

'Beast?' He looked suddenly upset. 'I'm a beast?'

'*Good* Beast.' Abby wiped her runny nose. 'Beast after he turns nice. Not mean like at first.'

She slid off the couch and held Belle out to him. 'Say something Beast says in the movie. Oh, I forgot. You missed it. Just say something nice. And call me "Belle," remember?'

Huey was at a loss. Tentatively, he said, 'I'm not going to let anything happen to you, Belle. I'm going to keep you safe till morning comes, and your mama comes to get you.'

Abby smiled. 'Thank you, Beast. And if the villagers come and try to kill you, me and Mrs Potts and Chip will make them go away. They won't get you!'

Huey swallowed, his eyes bright.

'Now you say, "Thank you, Belle."'

'Thank you, Belle.'

Abby petted the doll's hair. 'Do you want to brush her hair? Just pretendlike.'

Huey reached out shyly and petted Belle's hair with his enormous hand.

'Good, Beast,' Abby murmured. 'Good Beast.'

Chapter 12

Karen watched the digital clock beside her bed flash over to 2:30 a.m. She was sitting in the overstuffed chair in the corner, hugging her knees; Hickey lay on the bed, his injured leg propped high on some pillows. The Wild Turkey bottle sat beside him, along with Will's .38. His eyes were glued to the television, which was showing the opening credits of *The Desperate Hours* with Humphrey Bogart and Fredric March. She was glad he hadn't yet realized there was a satellite dish connected to the bedroom television; she didn't want him flipping through to Cinemax and getting more ideas from the T&A movies they seemed to run all night.

'Bogey's good,' Hickey drawled, sounding more than half drunk. 'But Mitchum was the greatest. No acting at all, you know? The real deal.'

Karen said nothing. She had never known time to pass so slowly. Not even when she was in labor, screaming for Abby to be born. It was as though the earth itself had slowed on its axis, its sole purpose to torment her family. She had entered that realm of time-lessness that exists in certain places, a few of which she had visited herself. Prisons were like that. And monasteries. But the ones she knew most intimately were the waiting rooms of hospitals: bubbles in time where entire families entered a state of temporal suspension, waiting to learn whether the heart of the patriarch would restart after the triple bypass, whether a child would be saved or killed by a well-intentioned gift of marrow. Her bedroom had now become such a bubble. Only her child was not in the hands of a doctor.

'You alive over there?' Hickey asked.

'Barely,' she whispered, her eyes on Fredric March. March reminded her of her father; he was a model of male restraint and dignity, yet he would do whatever was required when the going got tough. She still cried when she saw *The Best Years of Our Lives*, with March and that poor boy who'd lost both hands in the war trying to learn to play the piano—

'I said, are you alive over there?'

'Yes,' she replied.

'Then you ought to feel lucky.'

She sensed that Hickey was looking for a fight. She didn't intend to give him one.

''Cause a lot of people who ought to be alive aren't,' he said. 'You know?'

She looked over at him, wondering who he was thinking of. 'I know.'

'Bullshit you know.'

'I told you, I was a nurse.'

He glanced at her. 'You proud of it? People in agony waiting for pain medicine while nurses sit there painting their fucking fingernails, watching the clock, waiting for their shift to end.'

She could not let that pass. 'I am proud I was a nurse. I know that happens. But nurses are stuck with doctors' orders. If they break them, they get fired.'

Hickey scowled and drank from the Wild Turkey bottle. 'Don't get me started on doctors.'

Karen thought she remembered him saying that all the previous kidnappings had involved children of doctors. He'd said something about doctors collecting expensive toys. But that couldn't be the only reason he targeted them. Lots of people collected expensive things. Somehow, doctors were part of a vein of suffering that ran deep in Hickey's soul.

'When did your mother pass away?' she asked.

He turned his head far enough to glare at her in the chair. 'What the fuck do you care?'

'I am a human being, as you so eloquently pointed out before. And I'm trying to understand what makes you so angry. Angry enough to do this to total strangers.'

He wagged a finger at her. 'You're not trying to understand anything. You're trying to make me think you actually give a shit, so I might feel enough for you that I won't hurt your kid.'

'That's not true.'

'The hell it's not.' He drank again, then let his eyes burn into her. 'I'll let you in on a little secret, Sunshine. You ain't strangers.'

'What?'

He smiled, and a wicked pleasure came into his face. 'The light dawning up there?'

A shadow seemed to pass behind Karen's eyes, a flickering foreknowledge that made her shudder in the chair. 'What do you mean?'

'Your husband works at University Hospital, right?'

'He works at several hospitals.' This was true, but University provided the facilities for Will's drug research. He also held a faculty position, and did quite a bit of anesthesiology there.

Hickey waved his hand. 'He works at University, right?'

'That's right. That's where we met.'

'How romantic. But I have a little different feeling about the place. My mother died there.'

The transient fear that made her shudder before now took up residence in her heart.

'She was in for her throat cancer,' he said, almost to himself. 'They'd cut on her a bunch of times before. It was no big deal. But they were supposed to put some kind of special panty-hose things on her during the operation. STDs or something.'

'SCDs,' Karen corrected him. 'Sequential compression devices. Along with TED hose, they keep the blood circulating in the legs while the patient is under anesthesia.'

'Supposed to, anyway,' Hickey said. 'But they left them off, and she got some kind of clot. Sounds like Efrem Zimbalist.'

'An embolus.'

'That's it.'

'Will was the anesthesiologist?'

'Fuckin'-A right he was. And my mother died right there on the table. They told me nothing could be done. But I went back later and talked to the surgeon who'd done the operation. And he finally told me. It's the gas passer's job to make sure those SCD things are on the patient.'

'But that's not true!' Karen cried. 'The anesthesiologist has nothing to do with that.'

'Oh, yeah. What else are you going to say?'

'That's the job of the circulating nurse – *if* the surgeon has written the proper orders. The surgeon himself should check to be sure they're on.'

'The cutter told me there's some kind of box under the table, and the gas passer's supposed to check for it.'

'He was probably scared to death of you! He was shifting the blame wherever he could.'

A dark laugh from Hickey. 'He was scared, all right.' He leaned up on his elbow. 'Don't worry. That asshole paid, too. In full.'

'You sued him for malpractice?'

'Sued him?' Hickey laughed. 'I said he paid *in full*.'

'What do you mean?'

'What do you think I mean?'

'You killed him?'

Hickey snapped his fingers. 'Just like that. No telling how many people I saved by wasting that butcher.'

Struggling to keep her anxiety hidden, Karen tried to remember Will mentioning a case like the one Hickey had described. But she couldn't. And it didn't surprise her. Her resentment about leaving med school made her a poor listener when Will wanted to discuss work. 'When exactly did this happen? I mean, when did your mother pass away? Will—'

'She didn't *pass away*, okay?' Hickey sat up in the bed. 'She was murdered. By doctors who didn't give a shit. Your old man wasn't even in the room when she started to go. He was there at the start and the end. Some assistant was in there the rest of the time.'

Nurse anesthetist, Karen thought, her heart sinking. More and more, nurse anesthetists were handling the bulk of routine operations. It lowered the cost to the patient and freed up time for the doctor to concentrate on difficult cases. But the custom had always worried her. In an empirical sense, there was no such thing as a routine operation.

'Probably talking to his fucking stockbroker through most of it,' Hickey said, lying back on the pillows. 'Yapping on his cell phone while my mother was croaking. The bottom line is, your husband murdered my mother. And that's why we're here tonight, babe. Instant karma.'

Karen tried to think of a way to convince him of Will's innocence, but it was useless. His mind was made up. She shook her head, trying to resist the change that had already taken place within her, the instant reappraisal of Abby's chances. Until now, Abby's kidnapping had seemed a stroke of fate, terrible but random, like being blindsided by a bus. But this was infinitely worse. Because every moment of the crime, from the moment it was born in Hickey's fevered mind to the conclusion waiting out there in the dark, was suffused with malice, driven by hatred, and focused on revenge.

'How long have you been planning this?' she asked softly. 'I mean, you said you've done this to other doctors. Were they all involved in your mother's case?'

'Nah. I picked doctors for the reason I told you.

They collect expensive toys, go off to meetings all the time. They're perfect marks. It's strange the way it happened, really. Your husband was already on my shortlist when he killed my mother. He just went to the top of the list.'

Karen hugged her knees tighter. Hickey had already returned his attention to the movie. He seemed enthralled by the paranoia and hatred crackling off of Humphrey Bogart, an inchoate anger that quite by chance had found a target in the family of Fredric March, a man whose loving family Bogie's character had never known and never would. She recalled Hickey's story of the death of his father. Hickey had ordered his cousin to kill the man who brought him into the world, and Huey had obeyed him. A man capable of that was capable of anything.

'You just want the money, right?' she said, watching his face in the light of the television.

Hickey glanced away from the screen. 'What?'

'I said, you just want the money, right?'

'Sure.' He smiled, but his eyes were dead. 'What else?'

Karen kept her face motionless, but her soul was falling down a dark shaft. Abby wasn't meant to survive the kidnapping. She would live until Hickey's wife got the ransom money. Then she would wind up a corpse in a ditch somewhere, waiting for the inevitable deer hunter to stumble across her body. Hickey's other victims might have lived, but this time was different. This time it was not about money.

He wants to punish Will, she thought. *That's why he wanted to rape me. And how could he be sure Will would know he'd done it? By killing me. Because when the medical examiner performed the required autopsy, he would find Hickey's semen—*

It was hard to believe that a simple chain of thoughts could incapacitate a person, but Karen felt her mind and body shutting down as surely as if Hickey had cracked her skull with a hammer. She had to keep functioning. She had to shed her fear for herself. Hickey meant to kill Abby: that was the critical fact. That alone had to determine her actions from this moment forward. The first thing to do was to warn Will. He had to know that waiting out the night and paying the ransom wasn't going to bring Abby back to them. She wasn't sure how to warn him yet, but she knew one thing absolutely: if morning dawned without them any closer to saving Abby, she would have to kill Hickey. If he wasn't alive to give the death order, the giant in the forest might just falter at the brutality of his appointed task. But first she had to get out of the bedroom.

Alone.

Will lay on the sofa in the sitting room of the suite, a hot towel over his face. He was tired of looking at Cheryl in her bra. Tired of listening to her street analysis of his marriage and his present situation. He had paced out a couple of miles on the sitting room carpet, circling the furniture groups, trying to burn off the desperate energy produced by his inability to help Abby. That exercise, combined with his earlier wrestling match with Cheryl, had aggravated his joints to the point that he had to take a powerful painkiller that he kept for emergency situations. The drug and the hot towel had tamped down the pain, but his brain was humming like an overloaded circuit. The QVC shopping network babbled incessantly from the bedroom, where Cheryl lay drinking her rum-and-Cokes.

His mind was working strangely, like the jump cuts he saw whenever he flipped through MTV on the way to VH1 or CNBC. He saw himself walking into the bedroom, jamming Cheryl's gun underneath her jaw, and forcing her to tell him where Abby was, the way Clint Eastwood would do it. But Cheryl had hit the nail on the head before. This was no movie. As long as Abby was under Hickey's control, Will could yank out Cheryl's fingernails with pliers and it would get him nowhere. When the thirty-minute check-in call came, Abby would suffer horribly or die.

For a while, he'd tried to view his situation as an exercise in problem-solving. It was like a chess game, with only six pieces. But the stakes were so high that he couldn't make a move. He couldn't even *see* a move. Cheryl claimed she didn't know where Abby was being held. Will wasn't sure he believed her, but even if she did know – and he somehow forced her to tell him – she claimed it was impossible for police to reach the location within the thirty-minute window. He did believe that. It only made sense – from Hickey's point of view – and it dovetailed with what Karen had said about where Abby was being held. So, in order for Will to save Abby, Cheryl would not only have to know where Abby was – and tell him – she would also have to pretend to Hickey that everything was fine while the state police or the FBI raced to rescue her.

What could convince her to do that? Fear? He doubted it. Any torture he was capable of inflicting would almost certainly fall short of what Cheryl believed Hickey would do if she betrayed him. A bribe? It was an option, but one he'd have to be careful with. The previous fathers had undoubtedly tried it. Yet they had failed. Why? Why should Cheryl remain loyal to Hickey? A man who, by her own admission, still beat her? What would it take to erode that perverse loyalty? A million? Will could get a million dollars cash. It would take a few days, though. Which killed the idea. To be effective, bribe money would have to be in his hands before the ransom pickup tomorrow morning. Or simultaneously. Karen was supposed to wire the ransom to a bank on the coast. There were branches of Magnolia Federal – the main state bank – all over Biloxi and Gulfport, and the odds were that Hickey would pick one of them to handle the receipt of a large wire transfer. Most of Will's money was in the stock market, but he had $150,000 in CDs at Magnolia Fed. But would the promise of $150,000 – plus the $200,000 ransom – be enough to turn Cheryl against her husband? Unlikely. The other fathers had probably suffered from the same lack of liquidity.

The towel had gone cold on Will's face. He got up and went to the bathroom, then ran the tap as hot as it would go and held a washrag under it. The reflection that stared back from the mirror was not the one he saw every morning; it was the face of a lab rat trapped in a maze, forced to jump through hoops laid out for it by an unreachable adversary.

He wrung out the washrag, then returned to the sofa and laid the cloth across his eyes. Images of Abby in pain rose in his mind, but he forced them down. Why had he and his family been targeted? Had his art collection really been the determining factor? All Hickey's victims had supposedly been doctors who collected things, all of them hit on occasions when they left their families for more than forty-eight hours. Cheryl wouldn't reveal how they knew when these physicians were traveling, but Will assumed Hickey had a mole in one of the hospitals, a nurse or an aide, probably. Someone who heard the chitchat around the ORs and doctors' lounges. Not that it mattered. They were in the eye of the storm now, and everything hung in the balance. Will had seen enough parents lose children to know what it did to families. The death of a child was an emotional Hiroshima, leaving utter devastation in its wake. The world became a shadow of itself. Marriages failed, and suicide began to look like sweet release, a path back to the one who was lost.

As a doctor, Will had often speculated about the worst disease. Was it ALS? A lingering cancer? Soldiers pondered wounds the same way. Was it a Bouncing Betty in the balls? A disfiguring facial wound? But in truth there was no worst wound, or worst disease. The worst wound was the one *you* got. The worst disease was the one that got you.

But among all the evils of the world, there was one worst thing, and he had always known what it was. It grew out of a single image: a child hunched alone in the dark, alone and in pain, whimpering for help where no help would come. That child had a thousand faces, plastered on bulletin boards in the entrances of Wal-Marts, on milk cartons, on desperate flyers in the mail. *Have you seen this child?* The abandoned. The kidnapped. Runaways. But worse than being that child crying in the dark was being the parent of that child. Pondering forever the moment you let your attention wander in the mall, or that you'd said yes to that out-of-town trip, conjuring scenes of cruelty beyond Goya himself, living and reliving them in the everlasting torment of self-inflicted damnation.

Lying on the couch in his luxury suite, Will knew he was one step away from that eternity of guilt. He could not have known, of course, that someone like Hickey waited in the wings to take away everything he had during a convention weekend. Yet on some level, he had. He had always known. Yeats had said it long ago: *things fall apart*. It was the human version of the entropy that powered the universe as it ticked down toward cold death. Just as some people always built things, organized, nested, and planned, there were those serving the function of chaos: stealing, tearing down, killing. It was a paranoid worldview, but at the deepest level Will had always embraced it. Only recently had he become soft. Complacent. Lulled by material success. He had let down his guard, and now chaos had ripped into his life like a tornado.

He had to respond, and forcefully. He had never believed that by simply letting events take their course, things would work out for the best. That view was held by people who accepted whatever fate handed them and called it 'the best' in a pathetic attempt to cope. Will

Jennings *made* things come out for the best. His father's failures had taught him the necessity of that attitude.

He had to detach himself from the situation. Karen always said that his instinct was his most valuable asset. But instinct, he believed, was integrally bound up with emotion. And emotion had no place in solving a problem like this one. What he needed now was logic. Pure reason.

Of course, there *were* situations in which doing nothing was the wisest response. Any doctor could tell you that. But when doctors chose the option of 'inaction,' they were actually choosing to get out of the way of an immune system perfected over millions of years. For Will, on this night, doing nothing meant relying on a system created by Joe Hickey, a man he did not know or remember, yet who harbored a deep resentment of him and all he stood for. He could not do that. In spite of Cheryl's assurances that waiting out the night was the way to get Abby back, he was certain she was wrong. He would trust his instinct that far.

The washrag on his eyes had gone cold again. The QVC hawker's voice floated in from the bedroom, where Cheryl was watching a presentation on 'faux sapphires,' whatever they were. He threw the cloth on the floor and sat up on the sofa. He needed more information. Cheryl claimed this kidnapping was exactly like all the others, but it wasn't. What made it different? Was it something Cheryl herself did not know? Or something she did not know she knew? With a groan of pain, Will got up and walked into the bedroom.

*   *   *

In downtown Jackson, Dr James McDill was working his way through police mug books, sliding his hand down each page to isolate the lines of photos. Tired of the claustrophobic interrogation room, he and Margaret had moved out to the squad room, with the late homicide shift. Agent Chalmers had been working the NCIC computer but hadn't come up with anything yet. The number of 'Joes' who had committed crimes in the South was astounding, and most had compound names. Chalmers had shown Margaret photos of Joe-Bobs, Joe-Eds, Joe Dees, Joe Jimmys, Joe Franks, Joe Willies, and even a Joe DiMaggio Smith. But none brought even a flicker of recognition to Margaret's eyes. McDill had asked his wife to lie down on the Naugahyde sofa by the wall, but she refused. She sat at another empty desk, doggedly searching through book after book. Her eyes had a strange glint, and McDill was glad to see it. Perhaps, after the long year in purgatory, that light signaled a return to the world of the living.

He took a sip of cold coffee and looked down at the book before him. Female offenders, harshly lit. The smug grins of check kiters. The gaunt, pocked faces of coke whores. None was nearly as attractive as 'Cheryl.' In his memory, the woman who had forced him to sit all night in the Beau Rivage looked like a high school prom queen. He knew he must be exaggerating her beauty, yet his mental picture was as clear as the room he was sitting in now. He was sure of one thing. If 'Cheryl' was in one of these books, she would stand out like a rose in a field of garbage.

He rubbed his eyes and turned another page. As he

scanned the photos, Agent Chalmers's voice intruded into his concentration. The FBI agent was talking to a black JPD detective named Washington about the McDills' experience. Chalmers had enough tact not to mention the rape with Margaret in the room, but he seemed very impressed by the kidnappers' plan.

'There *is* no ransom drop,' he was saying. 'Not in the classic sense. See? The ransom is low enough so that it's liquid. The target can get it without any trouble. Two, the husband's out of town when it goes down. The kid vanishes, poof, and the mother finds herself stuck with one of the kidnappers for the night. A female member of the team hits the husband on the coast, while the kid's with a third member at an unknown location. From then on, the thirty-minute check-in calls work like an unbreakable net. It wipes out the classic model. I mean, it *neutralizes* the risk. In the morning, pretty as you please, the wife goes down to her bank and wires the ransom to her own husband. Ba-da-bing, it's over. Jackpot.'

Detective Washington nodded thoughtfully. 'You're dealing with a smart son of a bitch. What you gonna do if you find out who he is? That thirty-minute thing has you boxed. Anything you do could kill the hostage before you even figure out where he is.'

'We have to go high-tech, all the way. If we can confirm that this thing is going down, Frank Zwick is going to get a chopper, GPS homers, the works, everything by dawn.'

'Do you think it's going down?' Washington asked.

Chalmers nodded. 'I've never known a criminal to stop something that was working for him. They always push it till they get bit. That's their nature.'

'You're right about that much.'

'We just need to catch a break. If we still don't know who they are when that ransom wire hits the coast in the morning, we'll be way behind the curve.'

McDill closed his eyes and tried to shut out their conversation. In Chalmers's voice, he recognized the sound of a man who believed he could impose his will on the world. McDill knew how illusory that belief was. Every day he cut into the thoracic cavities of human beings, and it was difficult enough to impose his will on simple human tissue. When you brought large numbers of people into a dangerous situation – each acting independently – the best you could hope for was that nobody would die. McDill didn't just remember Vietnam, as he'd said before. He had served there as a medical corpsman. And he had seen more situations go to hell in a handbasket because of the good intentions of men like Agent Chalmers than he cared to recall. Chalmers was the classic second lieutenant, green and hungry for action. His faith in technology also struck a dark resonance with Vietnam. McDill hoped that the Special Agent-In-Charge had been tempered by more experience.

He opened his eyes and looked down at the rows of unfamiliar women, then wearily turned another page. His breath caught in his throat. Staring up from the mug book like a graduation portrait was Cheryl's innocent face.

'Agent Chalmers! This is her!'

The FBI agent stopped in midsentence and looked over. 'Are you sure?'

'Positive.'

Chalmers walked over and looked down at the photo beneath McDill's index finger.

'Who is she?' McDill asked.

Chalmers took the photo out of its plastic sleeve and read from its back. 'Cheryl Lynn Tilly. I'll be damned. She *did* use her real name. Maybe the others did too. I wonder why she didn't pop up on NCIC?'

He walked over to the computer he'd been using and began typing in the information off the photo. The JPD detective stood behind him with his arms folded. After several seconds, data from Washington began flashing up onto the CRT.

'She's got some small-time collars,' Chalmers said. 'Passing bad checks, forgery. One prostitution arrest. She did thirty days in a county jail. Nothing violent. You're positive it's her?'

'Absolutely.'

'I'll make a copy of this photo and fax it down to the Beau Rivage. Maybe someone on the staff down there has seen her.'

'What will you do if they have?'

Chalmers raised his eyebrows and took a deep breath. 'Call in the troops. If she's down there this weekend, we have to assume you're right. There's a kidnapping in progress. And that is a major situation. Right now, we need to see whether known associates can lead us to the man behind all this.'

Chalmers turned to Margaret McDill, who was watching them with a look of apprehension. 'Are you awake enough to keep helping us, Mrs McDill?'

'Whatever you need,' she said softly.

McDill walked over and put his hands on his wife's shoulders.

Chalmers picked up a telephone, then paused. 'These people have some nerve. To repeat the same crime in exactly the same place, a year after the fact?'

'You didn't talk to them,' McDill said. 'They think they're invincible.'

The FBI agent smiled. 'They're not.'

Karen rocked slowly but ceaselessly in her chair, her arms around her shins, her chin buried between her knees. Hickey was still lying on the bed, his eyes glued to Bogart and Fredric March as they played out the final minutes of *The Desperate Hours*. Karen sensed that she was close to a breakdown. She had been pulling hairs from her scalp, one at a time. Externally, she could maintain calm, but inside she was coming apart. The knowledge that Hickey meant to kill Abby to punish Will was unendurable.

She had to warn him.

Food was her best excuse to get out of the bedroom, but there was no guarantee that Hickey wouldn't follow her into the kitchen. For a while she had entertained the hope that the whiskey might put him to sleep, but he seemed immune to its effects. He'd gone into the bathroom twice during commercials, once to urinate and once to check his stitches, but she hadn't felt confident enough to risk using the phone, much less to try to reach the computer in Will's study.

She stopped rocking. She had the feeling that Hickey had said something to her and that she'd been concentrating so hard that she missed it.

'Did you say something?' she asked.

'I said I'm starving. Go fix something.'

She wanted to jump out of the chair, but she forced herself to sound peeved. 'What would you like?'

'What you got?'

'A sandwich?'

Gunshots rang from the television. Bogey fell to the ground. 'Goddamn it,' Hickey said. 'I don't know. Something hot.'

'There's some crawfish étouffée I could heat up.'

'Yeah.' He glanced over at her, his eyes bleary. 'Can you put it in an omelet?'

'Sure.'

'What was I thinking? I got Betty Crocker here. Weaned on an Easy Bake oven, right?'

Karen tried to laugh, but the sound died in her throat. She got up from the chair and walked toward the door. 'Anything else?'

'Just hurry it up.'

She nodded and went out.

As soon as she cleared the door, she sped to a silent run. In the kitchen, she slid a skillet onto the Viking's large burner, switched the gas to HIGH, then opened the refrigerator and took out three eggs, a bottle of Squeeze Parkay, and a Tupperware dish half-filled with seasoned crawfish tails in a roux. The eggs went into the pocket of her housecoat, the étouffée into the microwave, and a glob of margarine into the skillet.

Then she grabbed the cordless phone off the wall and punched in the number of Will's office.

'Anesthesiology Associates,' said the answering service operator.

'This is Karen Jennings. I need to—'

'Could you speak up, please?'

She raised the volume of her whisper. 'This is *Karen Jennings*. I need to get a message to my husband on his SkyTel pager.'

'Go ahead, ma'am.'

'You've got to do something, they're going to . . .'

'Just a second. Is that the message?'

'Yes – no, wait.' She should have thought this out more carefully. She couldn't simply state the situation to a stranger. The operator was liable to call the police herself. With shaking hands she broke the three eggs and dropped the yolks into the skillet. 'The message is, "You've got to do something before morning. Abby is going to die no matter what. Karen." Do you have that?'

'Yes, ma'am. This sounds like a real emergency.'

'It is. Wait. I want to add something. Add "Confirm receipt by e-mail."'

'I don't take many messages like this, Mrs Jennings. Shouldn't you maybe call nine-one-one?'

'No! I mean, that's not appropriate in this case. This is a little girl with liver cancer. Will's working with the transplant team, and things are very dicey right now.'

'Lord, lord,' said the operator. 'I know about livers. I got a brother with Hepatitis C. I'll get this entered right away.'

'It's got to go to his SkyTel. It's a brand new pager.'

'I've got that noted on my screen. Don't you worry. If he's got the pager on, he'll get the message. I think those SkyTels can even access missed messages.'

'Thank you.' Another thought struck Karen. 'If he doesn't call you to confirm that he's received this message, would you call his room at the Beau Rivage in Biloxi and give it to him?'

'Yes, ma'am. The Beau Rivage. Half our doctors are down there right now.'

'Thank you. Thank you so much.' Karen hung up the phone, her hand shaking. The concern in the operator's voice had been like salve on a burn. She'd wanted to pour out the whole horrible story to her, tell her to call the police and—

'That doesn't smell half bad.'

Karen froze.

Hickey was standing in the kitchen door in his bloody towel. He looked into her eyes for a moment, then past her. His eyes went cold. 'What are you doing by that phone?'

She felt a fist crushing her heart. To avoid Hickey's gaze, she turned and looked at the phone. Tacked and taped around it were greeting cards, photographs, and Post-it notes. She reached into the midst of them and pulled a small photo off the wall.

'I was looking at Abby's school picture. I still can't believe this is happening.'

The microwave beeped loudly. She went to it and took out the étouffée, then spooned it into the rapidly firming omelet. She sensed Hickey moving closer, but she didn't look up. With shaking hands she folded the egg over the crawfish.

His fingers fell on her forearm, sending a shock up her spine. 'Look at me,' he said in a hard voice.

She did. His eyes were preternaturally alert, the eyes of a predator studying its prey.

'What?' she said.

Hickey just stared, registering each movement of her facial muscles, every pulse beat in her neck.

'It's going to burn,' she said, pulling her arm away and reaching for the spatula. As she slid it under the omelet, he slipped his arms around her waist, as though he were a loving husband watching his wife make breakfast. His touch made her light-headed, but she forced herself to continue the motion, lifting the omelet from the pan and turning to drop it onto the plate. Hickey stayed with her as she moved.

After the omelet hit the plate, he said, 'You're a little wildcat, aren't you?'

She did not reply.

'I still own you. Don't forget that.'

She looked him full in the face at last. 'How can I?'

His expression hardened, and she had a sudden premonition that he was going to push her to her knees. She didn't know what she would do if he did.

'Bring the food back to the bed,' he said finally. Then he let his hands fall. 'And bring a bottle of Tabasco with it.'

He turned and limped up the hallway.

She had no idea how long she'd been holding her breath, but it must have been a while, because after she exhaled, she couldn't seem to get enough oxygen. Her legs became water. She gripped the counter to hold herself up, but it wasn't enough. She had to lie across the Corian and grab the top of the splashboard to keep from falling.

Chapter 13

Will sat in the chair by the bed, facing Cheryl. She was still propped against the headboard – gun beside her, QVC chattering in the background – but she had finally slipped on one of Will's white pin-point button downs. For an hour he had probed her about Hickey, but to no avail. She had given him all the biography she felt safe giving, and beyond that she would only discuss her own interests, such as aromatherapy and Reiki.

Cheryl had somehow got it into her head that the jump from sofa dancing and prostitution to the laying on of hands required in Reiki energy therapy was a natural one. Will tried to lull her into carelessness by telling her about the success of certain alternative therapies with his arthritis, but once he had got her on that subject, he couldn't turn her back to what mattered.

He changed his tack by asking about Huey instead of Joe, but suddenly something buzzed against his side. He jumped out of the chair, thinking it was a cockroach, but when he looked down he realized it was the new SkyTel. The pager was still set to VIBRATE mode from the keynote dinner.

'What's with you?' Cheryl asked.

'Something crawled over me.' He made a big show of looking under the chair cushion. 'A damn roach or something.'

She laughed. 'I wouldn't be surprised. Hey, this brochure over here says they close the swimming pool at eight P.M. That's kind of cheap, isn't it?'

'They don't want you swimming, they want you gambling in the casino downstairs.'

'Yeah.' Her eyes brightened. 'You like gambling?'

Will was dying to check the pager. He wasn't on call, so the message had almost certainly come from Karen. The only other people who would be able to persuade his service to page him at this hour would be his partners, most of whom were at the convention. 'Not really,' he said, trying to remember the thread of the conversation. 'Life's uncertain enough without that.'

'Party pooper.'

'Do you mind if I use the bathroom?'

Cheryl shrugged and returned her attention to a display of Peterboro baskets on QVC. 'Hey, if you got to go . . .'

Will walked into the bathroom with the Jacuzzi and closed the door, then whipped the pager off his belt and punched the retrieve button. The green backlit screen scrolled:

YOU'VE GOT TO DO SOMETHING BEFORE
MORNING. ABBY IS GOING TO DIE NO
MATTER WHAT. KAREN. CONFIRM BY E-MAIL.

He scrolled the message again, staring in shock at the words as they trailed past. *Abby is going to die no matter what.* What did that mean? Was Abby having some sort of diabetic crisis? Karen had given her eight units of insulin in the early evening, and that should hold her until morning. Had Karen learned something new about Hickey's plan?

You've got to do something before morning. What the hell could he do without risking Abby's life? But the answer to that question was contained within the message. *Abby is going to die no matter what.* Karen *had* learned something. And her meaning was clear: he would have to risk Abby's life to save her life.

He looked around the bathroom as though something in it could help him. The only potential weapon he saw was a steam iron. As he stared at the thing, the phone beside the toilet rang. He looked at his watch. 4:00 A.M. Hickey's regular check-in call. He heard Cheryl's muffled voice through the bathroom door. A few words, then silence again. Or rather the droning chatter of the television. He turned on the hot water tap and waited for steam to rise from the basin.

Wetting another washcloth, he wrung it out and pressed it to his face. As the blood came into his cheeks, something strange and astonishing happened. His mental perspective simultaneously contracted and expanded, piercing the fog that had blinded him for the past hours. He suddenly saw three separate scenes with absolute clarity: Abby held hostage in the woods, Karen trapped in their house at Annandale, and himself standing in the marble-floored bathroom. He saw these scenes like a man in the first row of a theater, yet at the same time he saw the relationships between them as though from satellite altitude: visible and invisible filaments connecting six people in time and space, a soft machine with six moving parts. And burning at the center of his brain was awareness of a single fact: he had exactly thirty minutes to save Abby. That was all he would ever have. The thirty minutes between check-in calls. Whether it was this half hour or the next, that was the window of opportunity Hickey had left him.

He threw the washrag into the basin. He had to know what Cheryl knew. *Everything* she knew. There was a chance that she'd lied before, that she knew exactly where Abby was being held. But probably she didn't. None of the previous fathers had dragged it out of her, and he was sure some had tried. How would they have tried? The gun was the obvious tool. But Abby gave Cheryl immunity to the gun, and to everything else. Because the effectiveness of any threat – torture with a steam iron, say – lay in the victim's belief that his tormentor would follow through. And while they had the children, no one could.

Even if he somehow broke Cheryl, it wouldn't be enough for her to spill what she knew. She would have to cooperate until Abby was found. Play her role for Hickey during the check-in calls – at least three of them, probably more. What could possibly persuade her to do that? The bruises on her body proved she could take punishment, and God alone knew what horrors Hickey had visited upon her in the past. Yet she stayed with him. She felt a loyalty that Will would never understand. And yet . . .

Her eyes had shone when she told him about the contract she'd had with Hollywood producers, the contract Hickey had acted so decisively to terminate. And she hadn't tried to make it more than it was. She admitted the potential roles were soft-core porn, late-night cable stuff. But that had been fine with her. It was a step up, and Cheryl had known it. It was also a step away from Joe Hickey, and on some level she must have known that, too. Known it, and believed she'd been born for more than prostitution and crime.

But to betray Hickey, she would have to believe she could escape him. And that would take money. Enough to not merely run, but to vanish. To become someone else. She might like that idea. Leaving Cheryl the sofa dancer in the ashes of the past. But by the time Will got his hands on that much money, the final act would be playing itself out, and by Hickey's rules. Earlier, while Cheryl made a trip to the bathroom, he had called downstairs and asked about cashing checks. The casino used TelCheck, and that company had a $2,500 limit over ten days. Given his credit rating, he could probably persuade the casino manager to take a promissory note for a larger cash advance, but only if he intended to gamble that money in the casino.

'You okay in there?' Cheryl called.

'Fine.' Maybe he could take the $2,500, max out his credit cards at the ATM, and then parlay that stake into the kind of money he needed—

'Dumb,' he muttered at his reflection. The only games he knew how to play were blackjack and five-card-stud, and he hadn't played either since medical school.

His right eye suddenly blurred, and a pain like the sharp end of a poker woke to life behind it. The

prodromal phase of a migraine. The euphoric clarity
he'd experienced moments ago began to evaporate
like drunken insight in the haze of a hangover. His
thirty-minute window was ticking away. *Abby's going to
die no matter what . . .*

He had never felt such desperation. A paralyzing
mixture of terror and futility that cornered animals
must feel. Abby was his flesh, his blood, his spirit. Her
survival was his own. Will had never seen Joe Hickey's
face, but it floated just beyond his blurred vision,
dancing like the hooded head of a cobra. The pain
behind his eye ratcheted up a notch. He reached into
his dop kit and gobbled four Advils. Then he flushed
the toilet and opened the bathroom door.

Cheryl didn't bother to look away from the television.

'Was that Joe?' he asked.

'Yeah. Everything's cool, just like I said it would be.'

Will looked at her there, wearing his button-down
and the remains of her black cocktail dress. The gun
lay beside her.

Sensing his eyes upon her, she glanced over at him.
'What are you looking at? You changing your mind
about getting calmed down?'

'Maybe.'

She gave him a strange look. A hurt look. 'Maybe I
changed my mind, too. You said some mean things
before.'

Mean things. This woman had helped kidnap his
daughter. Now she was talking about meanness on his
part.

Will walked into the bedroom, his eyes on the gun.

But as he neared the bed, something made him continue around it. Past the chair, past the window where he watched the gulf, into the spacious sitting room. Here was the sofa, the wet bar, the desk, the dining table. He looked at his notebook computer on the desk. Eight hours ago he had been running video clips from the hard drive on that machine, proud and self-satisfied, dreaming of stock options and the royalties he would realize on the drug he had worked so hard to develop. What a pathetic joke. What would that money be worth if Abby lay in a coffin beneath the ground? How much time had he spent away from home, away from her, working on the trials for Restorase? How many hours wasted thinking up the stupid name? Fighting with the Searle marketing people over it? *Restorase, Neurovert, Synapticin—*

His rambling train of thought crashed to a halt like a locomotive hitting a wall. His eyes went from the computer case to his sample case. *Restorase.* He had four vials of the prototype drug inside the case. But more importantly, he had two vials of Anectine. It was all part of the display for the Searle booth. Doctors would recognize Anectine, which was the trade name for succinylcholine, the depolarizing relaxant Will had developed Restorase to counteract. There was also a package of syringes: two conventional, and two of the special contact syringes the Searle engineering people had manufactured to Will's specifications. The compressed gas syringes could deliver a therapeutic dose of Anectine in a half second of skin contact.

'Succinylcholine,' Will murmured, and a strange chill went through him. With the chill came visions from the clinical trials of the past year, images that would scare the living hell out of a layman.

'What are you doing in there?' Cheryl called from the bedroom.

'Thinking.'

'Don't strain your brain.'

He opened the sample case and made sure everything that was supposed to be there *was* there. Then he closed his eyes and summoned Abby from memory, bringing her to center stage in his mind. Her smiling face and sturdy little body, her beyond-her-years determination, forged during her constant battle with juvenile diabetes. She lived on the knife edge of disaster, yet considered herself far luckier than most children. Will's pride in her was boundless. Abby was the nourishing flame that burned at the center of his soul. And the woman in the next room had put her life at risk. Dropped her down a black hole of terror. Whatever disadvantages fate had handed Cheryl, she had chosen to help Hickey of her own free will – not once, but six times, by her own admission. Six children put through hell. Twelve parents. Whatever she had to endure now was only what she had asked for.

He walked back into the bedroom as though everything was fine. But instead of stopping at the chair, he walked to the edge of the bed and looked down at Cheryl, much as he might have at Karen when he wanted to make love with her.

She looked up, her eyes curious. 'What?'

'I want to kiss you.'

Her cheeks went pink. 'You what?'

'I want to kiss you.'

'I don't do that,' she said in a flustered voice. 'That's too personal.'

'But I want to.'

She bit her lip. 'No kiss.' But then she undid the top four buttons of the dress shirt and slid down a cup of her bra. 'You can kiss here.'

He smiled and bent toward her breast.

'What changed your mind?' she asked in a softer voice.

As his cheek brushed her skin, he put his hand across her as though to prop himself on the bed, then closed his hand around the butt of her Walther. When he rose up and pointed the automatic at her face, she blinked with incomprehension.

'What are you doing?'

'Pull up your bra.'

She did.

Will took the pager from his belt and handed it to her. 'Read the last message.'

'What?'

An ex-hooker would know all about pagers. 'Hit the RETRIEVE button!'

She fumbled with the device, then she found the button. He could see the words scrolling on the LCD screen, her eyes narrowing as she read them.

'I just got that message from my wife. Do you understand what it means?'

She shook her head.

'Joe is going to kill my little girl. No matter what I do. Whether he gets the ransom or not.'

'He is not!'

'If Karen says he is, he is.'

'Joey would never let her send this message. This is some kind of mistake.'

'No mistake, Cheryl. Karen is smarter than Joe, and she found a way. It's that simple. Now, you're about to tell me where Abby is.'

She blinked at him. 'I can't. I don't know where she is.'

'For your sake, I hope you do.'

Confidence suddenly returned to her face. 'Are you going to shoot me? Come on, Doc. We've been over this.'

'I'm not going to shoot you. Not with a bullet, anyway.'

Something in his eyes must have gotten through, because a shadow of fear played over her face. 'What do you mean?' she said in a higher voice. 'I told you before. Even if I did know, and you made me tell, the cops couldn't get to her in time. Joey's going to call back in twenty-five minutes. If I don't answer, Abby's dead. It's that simple. And if I do, and I say one word, the same thing. And you don't know what that word is. So give me back my gun, and let's forget this happened.'

A surreal sense of detachment was settling over Will. 'Remember when you said there was nothing I could do to you that hadn't been done before?'

She gave him a blank look. 'Yeah?'

'You were wrong about that. Do you remember my presentation last night?'

She bit her lip as she thought back.

'Stand up,' he said.

'Screw you.'

He transferred the Walther to his left hand and grabbed her arm with his right. He was surprised to feel no pain. His brain had to be pumping out endorphins at five times the normal rate.

'Unhook my belt,' he said.

'*What?*'

'Do it!'

She reached up and unfastened his belt.

'Pull it out.'

'*What?*'

'The belt, damn it. Pull it out of the loops.'

She did.

'Bring that chair over here.' He pointed not at the French chaise he had been using, but at a straight-backed chair against the wall. 'Put it here by the bed and sit down.'

'Why?'

He slapped her face.

A bitterness beyond anything he'd ever seen came into her eyes. But with the bitterness came something else. Familiarity. This was a language she understood. She climbed off the bed, picked up the chair, and brought it back.

'Sit in it.'

She did.

He put down the gun and wrapped the belt around her torso and the chair back, then buckled it. From the bathroom closet he took a terry-cloth robe belt and used it to tie her lower legs to the legs of the chair.

'I'm going to scream,' she said.

'Go ahead. Scream your head off. Then you explain to Joe why he won't be getting his money in the morning.'

'You're killing your kid,' she said, as though talking to a man who had lost his reason. 'Don't you get that?'

Will stood back and considered his handiwork. Screaming could become a problem, even if Cheryl didn't mean for it to. Fear was an unpredictable thing. He went into the other room and brought back a pair of socks with his sample case, then stuffed them into Cheryl's mouth. Her eyes went wide.

He dragged the chair against the bed, then bent and flipped Cheryl and the chair up onto the mattress. From there it was simple to rock the chair legs and move her to the middle of the bed. She lay with her legs molded in the shape of the chair, feet sticking into the air like a woman in stirrups.

'If you listened to my speech,' he said, 'you know a little about paralyzing muscle relaxants.'

Cheryl looked confused. She probably hadn't listened to his program. She had been trying to seduce him with her eyes, all the time thinking about the moment when she'd have to pull the gun upstairs. Unless she could con him into taking her into his room in the hope of sex, which had probably been her original plan.

Will removed a vial of Anectine and a conventional syringe from his sample case. Cheryl's eyes locked onto the syringe as he popped off its cap, poked the needle through the rubber seal of the vial, and drew sixty milligrams of Anectine into the barrel. Many people had an irrational fear of needles. It was something you dealt with all the time in anesthesiology.

'This is succinylcholine,' he said in a calm voice. 'Shortly after I inject it, your skeletal muscles will cease to function. The skeletal muscles are the ones that move your bones. But your diaphragm is also made of skeletal muscle. So, while you'll be able to see, hear, and think normally, you won't be able to breathe. Or move.'

There was more white than color showing in her eyes now.

'You don't have to go through this,' he said. 'All you have to do is tell me where Abby is, and I'll put this syringe back in the case.'

She nodded frantically.

He leaned over and pulled the socks from her mouth. She gasped for air, then said, 'I swear to God, I don't know! Please don't stick me with that!'

Will picked up the remote control and raised the volume of the television. The QVC huckster was selling 'limited edition' china plates ('only 150 firing days!') bearing likenesses of Ronald and Nancy Reagan. As he shoved the socks back into Cheryl's mouth, she tried to bite his hand. He climbed onto the bed and sat on her rib cage. Her upraised thighs held his back like the back of a chair.

'You can scream,' he said. 'But the sound won't last five seconds after I stick you. Listen to me, Cheryl. I first saw this drug used as an intern. An ER doctor used it to restrain a crack addict who'd stabbed a cop in the emergency room. It was awful. I've seen murderers turned into whimpering babies by this stuff. They lay there paralyzed, soiling themselves, turning blue. Then you bag them and breathe for them, but the whole time they know that if you stop pumping that bag, their brain is going to shut off like a cheap lightbulb. It must be like being buried alive.'

Cheryl fought the restraining belts like a madwoman, rocking Will and the chair in her attempt to get loose. He jabbed the point of the needle into her external jugular vein, and she stopped instantly.

'You have a choice. You can help me save my little girl. Or you can find out what it's like to be dead.'

She closed her eyes, then opened them again. Tears ran from their corners down into her ears. '*I nono!*' she choked through the socks. '*I sweahta gaa!*'

'You know something.'

She shook her head violently.

Will depressed the plunger of the syringe.

'*Helll,*' Cheryl screamed. '*Someodeee—*'

The scream died in her throat. Her eyelids began to flutter, and her facial muscles twitched far too rapidly to be controlled by conscious thought. Her arms flew up and across her chest; then her body went rigid as the signals reaching its muscle fibers became a garbled storm of misfiring electrochemicals. The smell of human waste reached him, a common side effect of Anectine. It was all familiar to Will, though the context was alien. He'd seen this happen to mice, pigs, Rhesus monkeys, and homo sapiens, but always in a controlled environment. Cheryl's eyes were frozen open, filled with limitless horror.

He pulled the socks from her mouth, then climbed off her chest and sat beside her. 'I know it's bad. Maybe you feel as scared as my little girl feels right now.'

Cheryl lay as still as a stone angel on a grave. An angel with screaming eyes.

'We're going to do this over and over until you tell me where Abby is, so you'd do well to tell me everything as soon as you can.'

Her face was going gray. He checked her fingernails for cyanosis. Hypoxia was taking its toll, and consciousness would soon wink out. In the time it took him to reach down to the sample case for a vial of Restorase, Cheryl's skin took on a bluish cast. Loading the contact syringes would take more time than he had, so he drew fifty milligrams into a conventional syringe and shot the drug into the antecubital vein at the crook of her elbow. Twenty seconds later, her eyelids fluttered. She blinked, and then her lacrimal glands began draining tears again.

'I didn't like doing that,' he said. 'But you forced me to. *Joe* forced me to.' He patted her upper arm, then used his sleeve to wipe away her tears. 'I know you don't want to go through it again. So, talk to me.'

'You buh . . . bastard,' Cheryl whispered. 'You made me mess myself. You're *worse* than Joey. Worse than any of them!'

'Where's Abby, Cheryl?'

'I told you I don't know!'

'You know more than you're telling me. You couldn't have pulled this off five times before without knowing something. Where's the pickup? Where are you going to meet Joe to give him the money?'

'A motel,' she said, 'Near Brookhaven.'

Brookhaven was fifty minutes south of Jackson.

'You see?' he said. 'That's something I didn't know before. That's a good start. Keep talking.'

'That's all I know.'

'You know a lot more than that. What's the name of the motel?'

'The Truckers' Rest.' She shook her head. '*Please* don't do it again. I'm begging you.'

Will steeled himself against pity. She sounded like a child herself, a little girl begging not to be hurt by a monster. Was he a monster? Abby might be begging the same way right now, pleading not to be hurt. And that was partly the fault of the woman before him. An image came to him from somewhere, a man waiting in an airport for a defendant to be escorted through by deputies. He stood at a pay phone, pretending to talk, then drew a pistol from his coat, a pistol that had lain in a cabinet in his home for twenty years, waiting for the day when it would be used to kill a man who had molested a little boy. Will didn't know if he could commit murder out of revenge. But he could kill to prevent a murder. He could torture to spare his daughter pain.

With the coldness of a Nazi doctor he stuffed the socks back into Cheryl's mouth and injected her with seventy milligrams of Anectine. He looked straight into her eyes as her face began to twitch and her muscles turned to stone. The terror in them predated human consciousness by millions of years. It was like watching someone drown from six inches away. He loaded another dose of Restorase and watched Cheryl's fear race up an unimaginable scale, then slow and fade as her brain cells slowly starved of oxygen. She was blue when he shot the Restorase into her arm, and when she came out of the paralysis, her entire body was shivering.

'Where is Abby?' he asked. 'Right this minute?'

Cheryl seemed to be trying to speak. He pulled the socks from her mouth.

'Wuh . . . *water*,' she croaked.

Will went to the sink and moistened a clean washcloth, then came back and squeezed a few drops into her mouth. 'Careful.'

'More,' she begged, coughing violently.

He squeezed a few more drops from the cloth.

Deep sobs racked her chest. Cheryl had seen a glimpse of hell few people ever would, and the experience had shattered her.

'If I tell you anything,' she said, 'Joey will kill me.'

'Joe is two hundred miles away. I'm right here. If you tell me where Abby is, the needle goes back into the case, and you can have all the money you need to start over somewhere else. Any place you want.'

'You've forgotten something, Doctor. When Joey calls back, I can kill your kid with one word. And I think I'm going to, for what you did.'

Will kept his face calm. 'You don't want Abby to die. I sensed that before, when we were talking about kids. About being pregnant.'

She looked away.

'And you don't want to die yourself. If you kill Abby, you will. One way or another. It's one thing to talk about death, or to flirt with it when you're depressed. But you've got a taste of it now. And it's bad. Isn't it?'

She closed her eyes.

'You think that because nothing happened to the kids those other times, nothing will happen to Abby. But you're wrong. There's something different about this time. And Karen found out what it is. That's why she sent me that message. What is it, Cheryl? What's different about this time?'

'Nothing.'

He reached out and pulled her chin over until she faced him. 'Open your eyes and tell me why this time is different. Don't make me inject you again. To be honest, it's getting dangerous.'

She opened her eyes. For the first time, he thought about their color. They were grayish blue, not the cornflower you expected to go with her hair. 'Tell me,' he said.

'You killed Joey's mother.'

Will blinked. 'What are you talking about?'

'Last year, Joey's mother died during an operation. The doctor who did the surgery told Joey it was your fault. He said you weren't paying attention. You weren't even in the room.'

'*What?*' He thought back over the past year's cases. Some were clear, others a blur. He did about eight hundred fifty a year, but he almost always remembered the death. 'Was her name Hickey?'

'No. She'd remarried. Simpkins was her name.'

'Simpkins . . . Simpkins?'

'Joey said you wouldn't remember it. That's how little it mattered to you. But it matters to him.'

'I do remember! The SCD case.'

'The what?'

'SCDs. Sequential compression devices. The surgeon operated without them, and Mrs Simpkins developed a pulmonary embolus.'

'Embolus,' Cheryl said. 'That's it. A blood clot.'

'Viola Simpkins,' Will said.

'That's her.'

It was all coming back now. The surgeon had been a visiting professor, and the accident had caused a big rift between UMC and his institution. 'I had nothing to do with that death. It was a terrible mistake, but it wasn't my responsibility.'

'The surgeon told Joey it was.'

'Well, I'll tell him it wasn't. I'll make the damn surgeon tell him.'

'That might be tough. He's dead. Joey killed him.'

Will suddenly felt cold. Hickey had murdered a surgeon because his mother died on an operating table? 'Karen must have found this out,' he thought aloud. 'That's why she sent the message. And that's why Joey is going to kill Abby. To punish me.'

'He never told me that,' Cheryl insisted.

'Because he knew you might not go along.' Will gripped her arms. 'Cheryl, you've got to tell me where Abby is. Joe's going to murder her. She's only five years old!'

She looked him dead in the eye. 'I told you – *I – don't – know – where – she – is.*'

Will drew seventy milligrams of Anectine into the syringe and climbed back onto her chest. She began to fight beneath him.

'Please, *please*,' she begged. 'Don't do it!'

Streaks of blood marked the previous puncture sites on her neck and arm. Will moved the needle toward her neck and pressed it against her flesh.

'She's somewhere west of Hazelhurst!' Cheryl cried. 'Do you know where that is?'

He kept the needle in her vein. 'Where Highway 28 crosses I-55?'

She nodded violently. 'That's it! There's a shack ten or fifteen miles up that road.'

'Ten miles? Or fifteen?'

'I don't know! I've never been there. It's not on the main road. You go down two or three logging roads before you get to it.'

'That's useless. There are a hundred logging roads through those woods. Hunting camps, everything.'

'That's all I know! For Christ's sake, I'm trying to help you!'

'How is Joe calling Huey?'

'What?'

'Is Huey using a land line or a cell phone?'

'Cellular. There's no regular phone out there.'

'What else?'

She shook her head. 'That's all I know! I swear to God!'

Cheryl was exhausted, that was plain. But there was still a private knowledge in her eyes. Something she was holding back. He considered injecting her again, but he didn't really want to risk it. He had never put a human being through three consecutive cycles, and he needed her alive and cooperative for Hickey's next call. The important thing was to get a cellular trace started around Hazelhurst, if it was possible. He took the torn sheet of hotel stationery from his pocket and dialed Harley Ferris's number yet again.

'Are you going to leave me like this?' Cheryl asked.

'I'll untie you in a second,' Ferris's phone rang four times. Then the answering machine began its spiel.

Will had expected it, but even so, it was like someone slamming a door in his face at the moment he saw a way out. He hung up and redialed, taking care to enter every number correctly.

'Joey's going to be calling in a couple of minutes,' Cheryl said.

Will's watch read 3:26 A.M. By the time Ferris's phone began ringing, he was practically hyperventilating. Three rings. Four. The answering machine clicked and began speaking. Will's finger was on the disconnect button when he heard a click, then a clatter.

'Hello?' said a male voice. 'Hello! I'm here.'

'Is this Harley Ferris?'

'Yes. Who's this?'

'Thank God. Mr Ferris, this is Dr Will Jennings. This is an emergency. I want you to listen very carefully.'

'Oh my God. Oh no. Is it one of my kids?'

'No, sir. It's not your family. It's mine.'

'What?'

'Do you remember me, Mr Ferris? I was the anesthesiologist on your wife's gall bladder surgery. She requested me.'

'I know you,' Ferris said. 'We played in that scramble at Annandale a few months back. But it's four-thirty in the morning, Doctor. What the hell's going on?'

'My daughter's in trouble. Desperate trouble. You can help her. But before I tell you anything, you've got to promise not to call the police.'

'The police? I don't understand?'

Will decided to go for broke. 'Mr Ferris, my daughter was kidnapped yesterday evening. I can't go to the police because the kidnappers will kill her if I do. Do you understand?'

There was a delay as Ferris processed this information. 'I heard you,' he said finally. 'I'm not sure I understand you.'

'I'm in a casino hotel in Biloxi right now. The Beau Rivage. My wife's at home in Annandale. One of the kidnappers is with her. My daughter is being held at a third location. Somewhere in the woods around Hazelhurst, Mississippi. Every thirty minutes, the leader of the kidnappers calls the location where my daughter's being held. I know they're using a CellStar telephone. You're the president of CellStar. Can you trace that call for me?'

'Not without a court order, I can't.'

'My daughter will be dead long before anyone gets a court order.'

'Jesus. Is this some sort of prank? Is this really Will Jennings?'

'I wish it were a joke. But it's not. On the soul of my daughter, it's not.'

'Are both parties using cell phones?'

'The man on the receiving end is using one. There's no landline where he is. He's ten or fifteen miles west of Hazelhurst, down some logging road. That's all I know at this point.'

'There's not much activity around there this time of night,' Ferris said. 'We've only got one tower down that way, an older one. Our coverage is pretty thin around there, to be honest. I'd have to get a vehicle down there to trace it, and I don't know where our vans are right now.'

'Where could they be?'

'Anywhere in the state.'

'How many do you have?'

'Two.'

'Harley, if we don't find that phone, my five-year-old daughter will be dead by morning. Even if I pay the ransom.'

'How much are they asking for?'

'Two hundred thousand.'

'That doesn't seem like much.'

'That's part of their plan. It's not really the money they want. They want to hurt me. Can you help?'

'Doctor, it sounds to me like we should call the FBI.'

'No! They've thought of that. Planned for it.'

'But for a job like this—'

'This isn't a job, Harley! This is my kid. Remember how you felt when you thought I was calling because one of your kids was in a wreck? Think back two minutes.'

More silence. 'Goddamn it. Okay. I'll see what I can do.'

'I need your word that you won't call the FBI. Your word of honor.'

'I'll keep quiet until morning. But if I get a trace on that phone, we're calling the FBI. Agreed?'

'You find that phone, I'll be begging for a SWAT team.'

'Where are you now?'

'You have a pen?'

'Just a second. Okay, go ahead.'

'I'm at the Beau Rivage Casino, suite 28021. Call as soon as you know anything, but not on the hour or

GREG ILES

half-hour. That's when the kidnappers make their
check-in calls. The next one's coming in less than two
minutes.'

'I can't do anything about that one, except maybe
confirm that they're using the tower near Hazelhurst.
I'll call as soon as I know something. Hang tough,
Doctor. We'll figure something out.'

'Thank you. Hey – why did you suddenly answer
your phone?'

'My prostate,' Ferris replied. 'We don't keep a phone
in the bedroom. I got up to take a leak and decided I
was hungry. I heard the machine in the kitchen.'

'Thank God you did. I'll talk to you soon.'

Will hung up, his heart pounding. 'Joey's going to
call any second.' He turned to Cheryl. 'What are you
going to tell him?'

'Wait and see, you son of a bitch. You'd better untie
me.'

Letting Cheryl answer Hickey's next call could be
the biggest mistake he ever made. But he had no
choice. He had crossed the Rubicon. There was
no retreat now. He could hold the needle against
Cheryl's neck as she answered, but instinct told him to
show some faith. He reached out and unbuckled the
belt that bound her chest.

'I don't think you want my little girl to die. You're
not that far gone. You were a little girl once, too. Not
so long ago, either.'

She refused to look at him.

As he untied the terry-cloth belt that held her legs,
the phone began to ring. The sound constricted Will's
chest. 'My daughter's life is in your hands. Help her,

and anything I have is yours. All the money you'll ever need.'

'You'd better answer that phone, Doctor.'

He took a deep breath, then picked up the phone, handed it to Cheryl, and leaned down to listen.

'Yeah?' she said.

'Everything okay?' Hickey asked.

She looked at Will, her eyes inches away. As he tried to read them, an old memory flashed into his mind, the eyes of a secretary to a bank loan officer. She had kept him waiting for an hour even though she knew his loan application would be denied, reveling in the only power she would ever have over someone like him. Cheryl had a thousand times that power now. Would she exercise it to pay him back for the terror he'd forced her to endure?

'Yeah,' she said finally. 'Everything's cool.'

He felt light-headed. He was squeezing her arm with gratitude when Hickey said, 'What's the matter? You don't sound right.'

The son of a bitch was clairvoyant.

Cheryl looked at Will. 'I'm getting tired,' she said.

'It's not too much longer now. Take one of the pills I gave you. I need you sharp.'

'I know. I'll talk to you in a half-hour.'

Will heard the click as Hickey hung up. With shaking hands he took the phone from Cheryl and set it in its cradle. 'Thank you,' he said. 'You just started earning your first million.'

She scowled and rolled off the bed. 'Fuck you very much. Now what?'

'Now we wait for the phone trace. And pray.'

Chapter 14

Huey Cotton sat on the floor in the front room of the cabin, whittling steadily. Behind him, Abby slept soundly on the sofa, the ratty horse blanket covering her body. She had been talking to Huey when exhaustion finally overcame her. She simply closed her eyes in midsentence and slipped down onto the cushions with her Belle Barbie in her left hand.

Huey had been whittling ever since.

He didn't always know what he was whittling. Sometimes he let his hands do the thinking for him. He'd found a good piece of cedar outside in the woodpile. He cut the firewood last fall, mostly oak, and while he was oiling his chain saw he'd spotted a young cedar that had been snapped off at the ground by a tornado. Cedar was good carving wood, and there wasn't a smell like it in the world. The chunk in his hands was starting to look something like a bear. Whatever it was, there was enough cedar left for something more to develop. His hands had never felt so good. His nervousness seemed to flow out through the knife blade and into the wood, and from the wood into the air, like power leaking from a car battery left on concrete.

Soon it would be morning, and he was glad. The quicker Joey got his money, the less chance there was that he would tell Huey to do something to Abby. Huey was glad she'd finally eaten some Captain Crunch. She was so hungry, and he had gobbled up what was left of the baloney and crackers long ago. Before the first bite, she'd asked if he knew what time her mother would be picking her up. Huey figured they would be at the McDonald's by ten in the morning, so he told her ten o'clock. A smile of relief appeared on her face, and she began chomping the cereal like birthday cake. She said her shot would hold her until ten, whatever that meant. She ate two full bowls before she was done, and even drank the left-over milk. Ten minutes later, her full stomach took its effect. Her eyes rolled up and she fell sound asleep. Huey smiled at the memory and kept peeling away slivers of cedar.

Will had set up his notebook computer on the circular dining table in the front room of the suite. He was composing an e-mail to Karen. He wanted to tell her about Ferris and the phone tracing, but he couldn't. What if Hickey came upon her while she was reading the message? For the same reason, he could not even hint at Cheryl's cooperation. If Hickey knew his wife had betrayed him, he might decide to cut his losses and run, which would almost certainly mean Abby's death.

He needed to tell her he understood her message and had taken action, but in a way that only she could understand. He needed a code. He searched his memory for some event in their past that might be applicable to the present situation, but there was nothing. It was too fantastic. But then it hit him. If their own lives did not contain a parallel he could use, other lives did. Lives on screen. He and Karen had watched thousands of movies together, some of them many times. It took him less than a minute to come up with a phrase he was sure she would understand. The message he typed was:

> **ABBY IS GOING TO MAKE IT. TRUST ME. DO YOU BELIEVE THE CONDOR IS AN ENDANGERED SPECIES?**

He could not help but smile. As cryptic as this phrase would appear to Hickey, he was sure Karen would understand it. She'd had a crush on Robert Redford for years.

'What are you typing?' Cheryl asked.

At Will's request, she lay on the sofa a few feet away, sipping from a can of Coke. She had complained when he asked her to stop drinking rum, but she seemed to realize that she needed to be clearheaded for whatever might happen in the next few hours. The question of why she seemed to be cooperating had occupied a great deal of Will's thoughts. Was it fear of more succinylcholine injections? Desire for the money he had promised, and the freedom it offered? Or had she come to believe that Hickey *did* mean to kill Abby, and wanted no part of it? The answer was probably a combination of all three, in proportions she herself did not understand.

Will plugged his Dell into the data port of the hotel phone and logged on to AOL through their 800 number. His mailbox was empty. He sent the e-mail to Karen's screen name – *kjen39* – then logged off. Seconds after the program disconnected, the phone began to ring.

It was only 4:15 – halfway between the scheduled check-in calls. Will motioned for her to answer.

She picked up, said, 'Yeah?' then handed the receiver to Will. He expected to hear the voice of Harley Ferris, but it was his answering service, making sure he'd gotten the pager message. The operator said something encouraging about 'that little girl who needs the liver transplant.' Assuming this was part of a cover story Karen had fabricated, Will made appropriate noises and hung up.

Almost immediately the phone rang again.

'That has to be Ferris,' he said, grabbing the receiver. 'Will Jennings.'

'Harley Ferris, Doctor. Our computers show a call just after four A.M., processed through the tower that serves the Hazelhurst area. It came from one of the landlines at your house.'

Will's pulse kicked into hyperdrive. 'Did you get any idea of the receiver's position?'

'No. Even if we'd had a tracing van there, it would have been tough. The call lasted less than fifteen seconds, and the phone was switched off afterward.'

'What about the phone number? Do you have the name of the person who rented the phone?'

'Yes. But without police involvement, I can't do anything with it. I can't even tell it to you. I'm assuming

276

it's an alias, but only the police could tell us that.'

'I'm not asking you to give me the name, okay? But tell me this. Was it Joe Hickey?'

'No. Look, it's time to bring the FBI in on this. Our security people have good contacts with the local field office—'

'You gave me your word, Harley. Not until morning. What about your tracing vans? Where are they?'

'They're up in Tunica County, working with the state police on a fraud operation that involves casino employees.'

Will gritted his teeth. Tunica County was practically Memphis. That meant a minimum of three hours before the vans could get to Jackson, much less Hazelhurst. 'That's eight A.M. before they could even start tracing.'

'Exactly. I told one crew to hit the road and come on, but you're right about the time. That's why—'

'No police. Could this equipment be flown down?'

'It's four-thirty in the morning!'

'I have pilot friends who'd get out of bed right now and go get it.'

'Some of this gear is hard-wired into the vans, Jennings. Listen . . . there's a guy who used to work for us, an engineer. He's retired, but he keeps his hand in. I'll give him a call. He's probably got enough equipment in his garage to do a trace from his truck.'

Will's heart surged. 'Do you think he would?'

'He's a good man. We're probably looking at an hour or more to get him and his equipment on site, but that beats the Tunica crew by a long shot.'

'Does the FBI have the equipment you need?'

'I wish I could tell you they did, because I want you to call them. But the fact is, when the Bureau needs cell phones traced in Mississippi, they call us.'

'Damn it.' Will tried to think logically, but fatigue was starting to take its toll. 'You'd better call that engineer.'

'Doctor,' Ferris said in a compassionate voice, 'you realize that we may not be able to trace this phone in time, even with a vehicle down there? If the calls don't run any longer than fifteen seconds, it's a crap shoot.'

'We've got to try. It's our only option. You've got to trust me on that. My daughter's life depends on secrecy.'

He gave Ferris the numbers of his answering service, the direct SkyTel line, and Cheryl's cell phone. 'I should be here,' he said, 'but there's no telling what could happen before morning. Call me as soon as you know anything.'

'I will,' Ferris promised. 'I hope God's paying attention tonight.'

As Will hung up, he felt Cheryl's hand on his arm. Despite what he'd done to her earlier, she was watching him with empathy.

'Do you think Huey would really kill Abby?' he asked.

She bit her lip. 'It's hard for me to imagine it. But if Joey pushed him hard enough . . . he might. He can't take pressure, you know? He sort of flips out, like Dustin Hoffman in the bathtub in *Rain Man.*'

Will felt an enormous weight descend on his shoulders. If Ferris's people traced Huey's phone, they would have to be very careful about their next move. If they responded inappropriately, Abby could die simply because a mentally handicapped man lost control of himself for a few seconds.

'How are we supposed to get her back?' he asked. 'I mean, what did Joey tell you? After you and I pick up the ransom from the bank, what are you supposed to do?'

Cheryl hesitated, still fighting some internal battle. 'I call Joey,' she said finally. 'Then we meet at the motel in Brookhaven.'

'You're supposed to bring me along?'

'Yeah.'

'Have you always brought the husband?'

She hesitated again.

'Cheryl—'

'No. This is the first time.'

Will shook his head. 'I told you this time is different. Joe thinks I killed his mother, and he wants to kill Karen and Abby in front of me.'

'That's not it.'

'Yes, it is. Only I can't believe he'd put himself, Abby, and the money in one place. If he does, he's vulnerable. He has to assume that I could torture the name of the motel out of you, which means the FBI could come down on that place like the wrath of God.'

'It's the truth,' she insisted. 'The Trucker's Rest Motel, in Brookhaven.'

'That may be what he told you. But that's not how it's supposed to go down. I've got to know where Abby is. You must know something more, Cheryl. *Think*.'

She shook her head in exhaustion. 'I think you

should just pay Joey the money. That's the way to get your kid back. That's the way the other guys did it.'

'I'm not the other guys.' He picked up her Coke can and downed what was left for the caffeine. 'I'm down for special treatment.'

'I thought you didn't like gambling. Betting against Joey is like betting against the house.'

Not with you up my sleeve, he thought. But he said, 'It's that kind of thinking that keeps you where you are, Cheryl.' He turned and arced the Coke can into the wastebasket from fifteen feet. 'When everything's on the line, you've got to go for it.'

Karen downloaded Will's e-mail at 4:25 A.M. Getting into the study to check it wasn't difficult, because Hickey had finally passed out on the bed. The combination of Wild Turkey and the étouffée omelet had proved too much for him.

She stared at the message, trying to read between the lines. The first part was clear enough. Will had received her message and understood its meaning. He promised that Abby would make it and told Karen to trust him. But the next line stumped her. *Do you believe the condor is an endangered species?* It had to be some kind of code. Will had been worried that Hickey might see the message, so he had used something only she would understand. Or that he *thought* she would understand. Did 'endangered species' refer to Abby? And what did a 'condor' have to do with anything? A condor was a type of bird. A large bird. Could Will be referring to his airplane?

'Condor,' she said softly. 'Condor . . . condor.'

And then she had it.

'Oh my God,' she said, and a smile came to her face. 'Condor' was Robert Redford's code name in the film *The Three Days of the Condor*. And the line, 'Do you believe the condor is an endangered species?' had been spoken over the phone by Redford to Max Von Sydow, who played the assassin in the movie. But the significance for Karen was that the line marked the turning point in the film, when Redford turned the tables on the men trying to find and kill him. *That* was Will's message. He had somehow turned the tables on Hickey.

But how? What action could he have taken? Had he called the police? No. Not unless he had a way to keep Hickey thinking everything was still running according to plan. Tracing Huey's phone seemed the most likely option, since Will had mentioned it before. But without Abby keeping the line open, how could it be traced? Maybe he'd gotten some information from Hickey's wife. But why should she tell him anything? Had he threatened her? Bribed her? There was no way to know. She would have to do exactly what Will had told her to do. Trust him.

She hit DELETE and watched the message vanish, then looked at the clock on the study wall. She was going to have to wake Hickey to make his next check-in call. She didn't want to do it. Letting him sleep was clearly the best strategy for her own safety. But if he failed to make even one call, Abby could die. And if Will *did* have someone trying to trace Huey's cell phone, the man would have to actually switch the thing on and use it before he could be found.

Karen stood and began the long walk back to the bedroom.

Fifteen miles south of the Jennings house, Dr James McDill and his wife sat on a leather couch in the office of the Special Agent-in-Charge of the Jackson field office of the FBI. His name was Frank Zwick, and McDill figured him for ex-Army, probably Intelligence or CID. A short, fit man in his late forties, Zwick spoke with the clipped cadence McDill remembered from certain officers in Vietnam. The SAC had been on and off the phone for the past half-hour, talking to bank presidents, helicopter pilots, other SACs, and miscellaneous officials, constantly smoothing his too-black hair as he talked.

McDill's identification of Cheryl Lynn Tilly at the Jackson police station had precipitated a storm of FBI activity. After Agent Chalmers phoned Zwick, the SAC had summoned the McDills back to the Federal Building along with eight field agents. Now they all stood or sat around his spacious office, listening to Zwick arrange the logistics of his campaign over the phone. McDill could only hear one side of the conversations, but he didn't like the way the plan was shaping up. Suddenly, the phone clattered into its cradle and Zwick began addressing them.

'Here's where we stand. One: the ransom. Every bank within thirty miles of Biloxi is set to report incoming wire transfers greater than twenty-five thousand dollars to this office. Two: tactical capability. We don't have time to bring in a hostage rescue team from Quantico, so we'll use our own special weapons team. Some of you are on it, and I know you're more than capable of handling this operation. We're also coordinating a weapons team out of the New Orleans field office, for anything required on the Gulf Coast. We've got more than enough surveillance gear on site here, and we'll have twenty agents in this office by seven A.M., ready for action. We'll have twenty more out of New Orleans for surveillance duty in Biloxi. Three: air support. We'll have choppers both here and in Biloxi, ready for aerial surveillance and/or pursuit and assault.' Zwick made a steeple of his fingers and looked each of his agents in the eye. 'Questions?'

No one had any. Or no one wanted to voice what might be viewed as dissent by his SAC. McDill had several questions, but just as he was about to voice one, Agent Chalmers said, 'Sir? I wonder if we're not jumping the gun a little on this.'

'How do you mean?' Zwick asked, looking none too pleased by the question.

'Dr McDill identified Cheryl Lynn Tilly from the JPD mug books. But that doesn't necessarily mean that the crime she took part in last year is actually being repeated this year. Does it?'

Zwick gave them a self-satisfied smile. He clearly knew something they didn't, and he could scarcely contain his excitement. 'Gentlemen, ten minutes ago, our resident agent in Gulfport showed a faxed photo of Cheryl Lynn Tilly to a bellboy in the Beau Rivage Hotel. That bellboy is positive he saw Tilly in the hotel yesterday afternoon.'

Every mouth in the room fell open.

'To quote Sir Arthur Conan Doyle – through the immortal voice of Sherlock Holmes – the game is afoot.'

In that moment McDill had a premonition of disaster. It wasn't the quote itself. It was more the way Zwick had voiced it. And the context. At the core of all this frantic activity was a kidnapped child. A child who could die at any moment. And that took the situation about as far from a game as you could get.

'Our RA and that bellboy are reviewing the casino's security tapes as we speak,' Zwick went on. 'If they spot her, they'll do a video capture and e-mail it up here for Dr McDill to look at. Until then, we have to assume that McDill is right. There is a kidnapping-for-ransom taking place. The same crime has been executed five times previously by the same group, and probably within this jurisdiction.' Zwick laid his hands flat on the table. 'Gentlemen, by tomorrow noon, those sons of bitches are going to be behind bars.'

McDill held up his hand.

'Yes, Doctor?'

He tried to choose his words carefully. 'Sir, after hearing all these preparations, I'm starting to wonder if the central fact of all this is being given the priority it should.'

'What do you mean?'

'The kidnapped child. The hostage, as you call him. Or her. Somewhere not too far from here – if things are going as they did last year – a child is being held prisoner by a semiretarded man. That man is under instructions to kill the child if he doesn't get a check-in call from the leader of his group every half hour. Given

284

that, it's difficult to see what you can accomplish with all this technology. Anything that alerts the leader to your presence could instantly result in the death of the child.'

Zwick gave McDill a patronizing smile. 'Are you suggesting we do nothing at all, Doctor?'

'No. I'm simply speaking for those who can't speak. Right this minute, a father a lot like me is probably sitting in a room in the Beau Rivage, sweating bullets over his child. He wants to pick up the phone and call you, but he knows he can't. And he won't. For good reason. I hope you can put yourself in that man's place long enough to convince you to act with prudence.'

Zwick's smile faded. 'Doctor, I fully understand the complexities of this operation. But I wonder if you do. Had you and your wife reported the kidnapping of your son last year, that father you're talking about wouldn't be sweating bullets in that hotel right now. And the man behind this kidnapping would be rotting in federal prison.'

Zwick looked as though he expected fireworks in response to this statement, but McDill simply sighed. 'You may be right,' he conceded. 'But my son is alive today, and I can live with my decision. I hope that by this time tomorrow, you can say the same about yours.'

The SAC's face went red, but before he could vent his anger, Agent Chalmers stood and said, 'Doctor, why don't you come get some coffee with me?'

McDill took his wife's hand and rose from the sofa, but he didn't look away from Zwick as he walked to the door. He had looked away from too many officers in Vietnam, walked out of too many meetings without speaking his mind. At least tonight he would not have to feel the sickening regret he had felt then.

As he passed through the door, a chorus of voices broke into a spirited discussion of tactics and equipment. He squeezed Margaret's hand, but it was not his wife who filled his thoughts. It was that father trapped in the Beau Rivage. McDill had never laid eyes on him, but he knew that man better than he knew his own brother.

By 5:56 A.M., Will was close to cracking. A steady diet of hot tea and Coke had his hands shaking like a strung-out addict's, and his overtaxed mind was running in circles, like a grayhound chasing a fake rabbit. His efforts to locate Abby by tracing Huey's cell phone had come to nothing. Hickey's 4:30 check-in call had told Harley Ferris nothing new, because Ferris's retired engineer had not been close enough to Hazelhurst to do any good. But when 5:00 ticked around, Will had his hopes up. Only the five o'clock call never came.

He waited for ten minutes, but after that he could stand no more. For all he knew, Karen had somehow provoked Hickey into killing her. An acid lump clogged his throat as he dialed home. But when the phone was picked up, it was Karen's voice, not Hickey's, on the other end of the line.

The second Will spoke, she began to sob. He was certain something must have happened to Abby, but Karen explained that her tears were simply a reaction to the stress. Hickey had missed the last check-in call because he'd passed out drunk in their bed.

'I woke him for the four-thirty call,' she said. 'He told Huey he wouldn't be calling back for another hour at least. He said he had to sleep.'

Hickey hadn't bothered to inform Cheryl of this change of plan.

'What are you doing to help Abby?' Karen asked.

'I got Ferris. We're trying to trace Huey's phone. But if Hickey isn't calling him, we can't trace it.'

'Maybe I should wake him up and tell him I have to talk to Abby.'

'Do you think he'd let you?'

'Probably not. But what choice do we have?'

'Cheryl is helping us now. To a certain extent, anyway. I'll explain why later. But tell me why you think Hickey is planning to kill Abby.'

'He thinks you killed his mother.'

'That's what I got from Cheryl. Okay . . . I guess you'd better try to wake Hickey up.'

There was a strange silence. Then Karen said, 'Will, he tried to rape me.'

A burning heat swept over Will's face, and the migraine that had receded after the torture session stabbed him behind the eyes.

'What happened?'

'It doesn't matter now,' she said, 'I cut him with a scalpel, and it stopped him. For the time being, anyway. But . . . I don't know what might happen before we leave the house. Will, if it comes to a choice between enduring that and Abby dying, I can force myself to live with it. But can you?'

He sat in the hissing silence, feeling more hatred for one human being than he had ever dreamed possible. If he came face to face with Hickey, he would kill the man without hesitation. But that wouldn't help Karen now.

'Karen . . . I know things haven't been what they used to be for us. I'm not sure why. I know it has to do with your leaving medical school.'

'Oh *God*,' she said in a hysterical voice. 'At this point that sounds so petty and ridiculous. But you're right. And all I care about in this moment is getting my baby back.'

'We're going to get her back. I swear that to you. And whatever choices you have to make to stay alive, or to keep Abby alive, I can live with. Nothing you could ever do would change the fact that I love you. *Nothing*. I just hope you can forgive me for letting this happen.'

Her reply was too choked for him to understand, but he thought he heard '. . . *not your fault*' in there.

'Let Hickey sleep until six,' he said, not wanting her anywhere close to the man now. 'But if he hasn't made another call by then, you'll have to get him up and on the phone to Huey. Throw a fit. Tell him you won't wire the money unless you have proof that Abby's okay.'

'I will.'

They sat in silence for another few moments; then Karen whispered good-bye and clicked off.

When five-thirty rolled around, the phone didn't ring.

Now it was six, and still the telephone was silent.

Had Karen tried to wake Hickey? Was she trying now? Or had she succeeded, only to find herself having to submit to him to keep Abby alive?

The black sky over the gulf had changed imperceptibly to indigo. Dawn would soon break over the shrimp boats and the deep-sea fishermen heading out past the barrier islands. Will could almost see the western hemisphere whirling eastward into the sun, like some cutting-edge CNN commercial filmed by Stanley Kubrick. Only Kubrick was dead now. And if Hickey didn't start making his check-in calls again, Abby might soon be, too.

The ringing telephone stopped his breath in his throat. He darted over to the sofa and prodded Cheryl, who was snoring softly. She rubbed her eyes, picked up the phone, then nodded to indicate that it was Hickey on the phone. She said her usual 'Everything's cool,' then signed off. Her eyes had the dull sheen of sleep deprivation. Will looked back at her without speaking, and in a few seconds her eyes closed.

Two minutes later, the phone rang again.

Like an automaton, Cheryl stirred and started to answer, but Will grabbed the receiver first. 'Hello?'

'Harley Ferris, Will.'

'What have you got?'

'The Hazelhurst target switched on his cell phone just before six. The subject in your house made a land-line call that went through the Hazelhurst tower just after six. The call lasted sixteen seconds, and the trace target switched off his phone immediately after the call.'

'Where do we stand?'

'My man down there has narrowed the search area to about seven square miles.'

'I had that before I called you!'

'No, you didn't. You said ten or fifteen miles west of Hazelhurst, on a logging road. That could describe an area as large as twenty-five square miles.'

Will groaned and rubbed his forehead. 'I'm sorry. I'm going crazy here. You haven't notified anyone official, have you?'

'No. But it's long past time we did.'

'Not yet. Please, not yet.'

'These are very short calls, Doctor. We're looking at a minimum tracing time of an hour from now. And that's if the subject keeps making these check-in calls on the half hour. What if he skips another one? What if he skips two?'

God forbid. 'Calling the FBI has to be my decision, Harley. We've still got some time. There's nothing the FBI could be doing right now that we can't. You have all my numbers.'

'I hope you know what you're doing.'

'I hope so, too.'

He hung up and sat beside Cheryl on the sofa. She slept with her mouth open, and her snores were as regular as a metronome.

'Wake up,' he said.

She opened her eyes but didn't turn her head.

'I don't think Joe would kill Abby or Karen until he knew he had his money. Do you agree?'

She swallowed like someone with a bad case of cottonmouth, then nodded and closed her eyes again.

So much for reassurances. Will got up and walked back to the window.

Dawn was coming, a lighter blue hovering in the indigo, far to his left. What he had taken for pale cloud formations was actually the diffuse light of the sun making its way between much darker clouds, and the narrow strip of beach he had watched all night was resolving itself into a thin, rocky breakwater. There was no beach here. The gulf's waves actually spent themselves against the marina beneath the casino.

'Think with your head, Joe,' he said softly. 'Not your heart. Think about the money, not your mother. The money's what you want. The money . . .'

Chapter 15

Karen felt hands on her body and screamed.

'Shut up!' snapped a male voice. 'It's time to get up.'

She blinked her eyes and saw Hickey leaning over her. He was shaking her shoulders. 'What happened?' she asked, trying to collect her thoughts.

'You fell asleep.'

Two facts registered with frightful impact. First, Hickey was dressed. Second, daylight was streaming through the bedroom curtains. 'God, no,' she breathed, unable to accept the idea that she'd fallen asleep while Abby's life was in jeopardy. But she had. 'What time is it?'

'Time to shower and doll yourself up for the Man. Fix your face.'

Her eyes went to the digital clock on her bedside table. 8:02 A.M. Two hours had passed since she last woke Hickey for a check-in call. What had happened in the interim? If Will had succeeded in finding Abby, Hickey wouldn't be standing here telling her to shower and get dressed.

'Is it time to get Abby?'

'You mean, get the money. Play your part right, *then* you get Abby back.'

'Is she all right?'

'She's still asleep. I just talked to Huey.' Hickey turned and walked into the bathroom.

Karen heard the shower go on. If Hickey had just talked to his cousin, that should have given Will's friend a chance to trace the call.

'Get a move on,' Hickey said, emerging from the bathroom. He was wearing the same khakis and Ralph Lauren polo shirt he'd worn yesterday. He didn't look any more natural in the outfit today. 'I'm going to make coffee.'

'Could I talk to Abby on the phone? Would you call her for me?'

He shook his head. 'You'd only upset her more. You'll see her soon enough.'

Before he reached the door, Karen said, 'May I speak to you for a minute?'

He stopped and turned back to her.

'I know what's supposed to happen today,' she said. 'I know . . . what you want to do.'

He looked intrigued. 'What's that?'

'You want to hurt Will. Because of your mother.'

His eyes went cold.

'I understand that anger,' she said quickly. 'And I'm not going to try to convince you that you're wrong about Will, even though I believe you are. You think you're right, and that's all that matters.'

'You got that right.'

She gathered the full measure of her feelings into her voice. 'All I'm asking you to do – no, *begging* you to do – is to take pity on a five-year-old girl. Use me instead.'

Hickey's eyes narrowed. 'Use you?'

'To punish Will. Kill me instead of Abby.'

Again she saw the disturbance in the dark wells of his eyes, as though eels were roiling in the fluid there.

'You've got sand,' he said. 'Don't you, Mom? You really mean that.'

'Yes.' It was the truest thing she had ever said. If by dying she could guarantee that Abby would grow into a woman, marry, and bear her own children – or at least have that chance – then she would die. Gladly. 'I think your mother would have done the same for you.'

Hickey's cheek twitched, but Karen's honesty seemed to overcome whatever anger she had caused him. They had entered the realm of truth, and offense was beside the point.

'She would have,' he said. 'But you don't have to. Nobody's going to die today. Let me tell you a little secret. This is the last job I'll ever pull. In a few days, I'll be in Costa Rica. A rich expatriate, like Hemingway and Ronnie Biggs.'

Ronnie Biggs? 'Who's Ronnie Biggs?'

'One of the great train robbers. You know, from England.' Hickey looked toward the window. 'Maybe that was before your time. Biggs planned a perfect crime, just like me. And he got away with it, just like me. I've got away with it five times. And today is my grand exit.'

Karen felt a sudden ray of hope, like a light blinking on in her soul. Maybe she'd read Hickey wrong. Maybe he thought twenty-four hours of hell was enough punishment. Or perhaps, deep down, he knew that his mother's death had not been Will's fault.

'Take that shower and get some nice clothes on,' he said. 'You've got to put on a good show for your broker this morning. Davidson gets to his office at eight-thirty. You'll call him at a quarter to nine. Then we'll drive over and you'll sign off on the wire.'

'What exactly am I going to tell him?'

'I've got it all laid out for you. Just get in the shower.' He chuckled. 'Or do you need me to help you?'

'I can manage.'

'That's what I figured.'

As she walked toward the bathroom, she spied a small but fresh bloodstain on Hickey's khakis, just above the knee. 'You'd better wrap that leg again,' she told him. 'There's more gauze in the cabinet under the kitchen sink.'

He looked down at the blood and grinned. 'Guess I've got a new angle on safe sex, don't I?'

His sudden levity disoriented her. There seemed no reason for it, at least none she could fathom. Maybe the impending collection of the ransom had lightened his mood. His fantasy future in Costa Rica.

She paused by the bathroom door. 'Why Costa Rica?'

'No extradition to the US.'

'Oh. Of course.'

'I've got some land down there. A ranch.'

Hickey looked about as much like a rancher as Redford and Newman had in *Butch Cassidy and the Sundance Kid*. For them the pipe dream had been Bolivia. Karen looked over at the clock again, wondering what had become of Will's efforts to trace

Huey's cell phone. Had it all come to nothing? Or was a host of FBI agents even now preparing to crash into the cabin where Abby was being held?

'Get your ass in gear,' Hickey said. 'We've got less than an hour.'

She walked into the bathroom, her limbs heavy from truncated sleep. The events of the next few hours had passed beyond her control. Possibly beyond anyone's. It was like your water breaking at the end of pregnancy. That baby was going to come, and there wasn't a damn thing anyone could do to stop it, short of killing you.

Will stood at the sitting room window, wishing for a balcony. The stink of old eggs drifted from the room-service tray Cheryl had ordered. All Will had managed to get down was some tea and a biscuit, but she had eaten a massive breakfast, dubbed the 'Natchez Plate' by the Beau Rivage marketing people. He wondered briefly if repeated cycles of Anectine and Restorase had a stimulating effect on the appetite.

The sun was shining full on the water now, turning the brown waves silver in its glare. Hickey's last check-in call had come three minutes ago – exactly eight o'clock – after which Cheryl had informed Will that they would be leaving for the Biloxi branch of the Magnolia Federal Bank within the hour. Harley Ferris had not yet reported in, but Will still held out hope. CellStar's first-string tracing team had reached Hazelhurst at 7:15 A.M., but Hickey had skipped the seven-thirty check-in call, making pointless the crew's hell-for-leather ride from Tunica County. But at least they'd been on station for the 8:00 A.M. call – if Hickey had made one to Huey, and not just to Cheryl.

Any second the phone would ring, and Ferris would tell him one of two things: they had pinpointed Huey's position, or they had not. If they hadn't, Will had a decision to make. Should he call the FBI and try to convince them to start a search of the woods around Hazelhurst? Or should he pretend to play out the endgame according to Hickey's rules, withdraw all the money he could get from Magnolia Federal, give it to Cheryl to keep her cooperating, and be wearing her gun when he came face to face with Hickey? After the nightmares of Waco and Ruby Ridge, it was too easy to envision disaster resulting from calling in the FBI. An armed search team might panic Huey into killing Abby, perhaps even unintentionally. But the alternative was hardly more appealing. There was no guarantee that Will and Hickey would ever come face-to-face. Once Hickey knew Cheryl had the ransom, he could simply order his cousin to kill Abby and flee.

The ring of the telephone floated through the spacious sitting room. Will said a silent prayer, then walked over to the end table by the sofa and picked up the phone.

'Hello?'

'Will, it's Harley Ferris. We didn't get it.'

Will stood motionless, not speaking or even thinking, the way some people reacted to the news that an emergency room X-ray had turned up lung cancer.

As if by not making any move at all they could stop the terrible reality rushing toward them with the implacable indifference of a tidal wave.

'Why not?' he asked. 'What happened?'

'The calls are just too short. We're very close in absolute terms, but we're talking about undeveloped land. Thick Mississippi woods. Waist-high under-brush. As far as the logging road you mentioned, there are dozens cut through there, all turning back on each other. And there are a hundred shacks in those woods.'

Will could imagine it all too easily: typical Mississippi backcountry.

'Doctor, what we need now is a battalion of national guardsmen to line up shoulder to shoulder and march through those woods. And an FBI Hostage Rescue Team to bring out your little girl after the guardsmen find the place.'

Will put his hand over his eyes. It would take hours to organize that kind of search. Karen would be sending the ransom wire in less than an hour. Abby's captor would almost certainly leave the cabin before then, to meet Hickey at some prearranged rendezvous. Hopefully, he would be taking Abby with him. They might have left already, Will realized, just after Hickey's last check-in call.

'Doctor?' Ferris prodded.

'I'm thinking.' The only assumption Will felt comfortable making was that Hickey would keep Abby alive until he was sure he had the ransom money. He wanted revenge, but there was no reason to risk losing two hundred thousand dollars when it was an hour from being in his possession. And if he killed Abby too soon, he would lose leverage he might need if Karen or Will balked at the last minute.

Maybe that's the only card I have left, Will thought. *Hesitate at every step until I get confirmation that Abby's alive.* It would be a game of chicken. Hickey could order Huey to hurt Abby in order to force Will to proceed, but he couldn't tell Huey to kill her. Not if he wanted the money.

'Doctor?' Ferris snapped. 'I've got to say this. I don't believe you're thinking rationally.'

'Keep your tracing team on the job, Harley. I'm going to get them another shot at that trace.'

'How?'

'Just tell them to keep their eyes and ears on their screens.'

'What about the FBI?'

Will ground his teeth and looked out at the gulf. The cool air that had settled over the land during the night was taking on the yellow density of a Mississippi summer morning, as the sun baked it and sent it skyward again. *Skyward. . . .*

'My God,' he breathed. 'Cheryl!'

'What?' Ferris asked.

Cheryl came to the wide door that divided the sitting room of the suite from the bedroom. All she wore was a towel on her head.

'What's the matter?' she asked.

'What kind of car does Huey drive?'

'An old pickup truck.'

'What make? What color?'

'Last time I saw it, it was baby-shit brown. Which is

green, I guess. With lots of primer on it. It's one of those old Chevys. You know, with the rounded cab.'

'Listen to me, Harley. If you'll make me a promise, you can call the FBI.'

'I'm tired of your conditions. I already regret—'

'She's my daughter!' Will shouted, blood pounding in his temples. 'I'm sorry. You've already done more than I had any right to expect. But I've just learned what type of vehicle the guy in Hazelhurst is driving. And the sun is up now. If the FBI could get a chopper up over that area, they might be able to find it pretty quick.'

'You're damn right they could!' Ferris cried. 'And if they can't, the state police can. They can put out a statewide APB for the vehicle, too. If that guy tries to move with your little girl, they'll be on him like you know what.'

'No state police. Highway patrolmen aren't anywhere close to trained for something like this. A hostage standoff with a five-year-old? It's got to be the FBI. A chopper out of Jackson could be on station fifteen minutes after takeoff.' Will was excited, too, but he knew the realities. ER work in small towns had taught him that while helicopters were much faster than ground vehicles, the time required to prep them for flight often meant that conventional ambulance runs were faster, even over distances of eighty or ninety miles. But Ferris's enthusiasm knew no bounds.

'I'll handle everything,' he said. 'I'm so goddamn relieved. You just leave it to me.'

'The FBI is going to ask you a hundred questions

about me. You can't answer them. That's my condition. You can't even give them my name. If you do, they'll have someone out at my house in ten minutes, and that could get my daughter killed.'

'Damn it—'

'The kidnapper is at my house right now, Harley. He can kill Abby with one phone call. The FBI's job is to find that vehicle and that cabin. That's it. In ninety minutes you can tell them all you know, but for now, nothing. Just the vehicle.'

'Jennings—'

'Don't give them my phone numbers, either. If they called at the wrong time, that could get Abby killed, too. If I think of something that can help them, I'll call you and you relay it. Understood?'

'I don't like it. But I understand.'

'Use your head, Harley. Before every step you take, remind yourself that there's a five-year-old girl out there, scared out of her mind.'

'I've got two of my own. College age now, but I remember what it's like.'

'Good. And tell the FBI to put a paramedic in that chopper. With insulin. My daughter's a juvenile diabetic.'

'Jesus. Insulin, I've got it. Well . . . I'd better make that call. Godspeed, boy.'

'Harley?'

'What?'

'You don't want to know what kind of vehicle they should be looking for?'

'Shit, I forgot. What is it?'

'A green Chevy pickup with lots of primer on it. The old kind, with rounded cab.'

'Got it. I'll talk to you soon.'

Will heard the click as Ferris disconnected.

Cheryl was still standing in the door, but at least she had wrapped the towel around her torso. Will saw the bruises on her neck and arm, where he had injected her during the night.

'How do you feel?'

'Like I woke up with the flu,' she said. 'My bones ache, and all my muscles are twitching.'

'That'll pass.'

She cinched the towel tighter around her breasts. 'Um . . . there's something I didn't tell you.'

A shiver of premonition went through him. 'What?'

'This is the last job. Joey's last kidnapping.'

'He said that?'

'Uh-huh. He's been talking about it all year. He's had his money in the stock market a long time, and he bought some land down in Costa Rica. He's never been there, but he says it's a ranch. A Spanish ranch. Like zillions of acres with gauchos and stuff. For a while I thought it was, you know, bullshit. But I think maybe it's real.'

She had held back more than he thought. But this new information only confirmed what Will had thought all along. This kidnapping was different from all the others. Hickey meant to kill Abby – and possibly Karen and himself – then vanish for good.

'You calling in the cops?' Cheryl asked.

'Not exactly.'

'Are we still going to pick up the money?'

'Absolutely. And it's all yours.'

She looked skeptical. 'Once we get it . . . are you going to let me go?'

He ran his hands through his hair. 'I need you to bluff Joe a bit longer. Over the phone, you know. Like we have been. Just long enough to get Abby.'

'I'm dead,' she said in a toneless voice.

'No, you're not. Hang with me, Cheryl.'

She covered her eyes with a shaking hand. Fear and exhaustion had brought her to the point of despair. Will could almost read her mind. In some corner of her brain she was thinking she should pick up the phone and warn Hickey. That if she told him what Will was up to, he might forgive her and call the whole thing off before everything came apart.

'Cheryl, you've got to think straight right now. I'm going to do everything I can to help you. If you somehow wind up in police custody, I'll testify on your behalf. I swear it. But you can't save Joe. It's gone past that. I know you still feel loyalty to him. But if you try to warn him, I'll have no choice but to tell him everything you've told me. He'll know I could only have gotten it from you.'

Her face closed into a bitter mask, like the face of a woman from some impoverished Appalachian hollow. 'I'll tell him you tortured it out of me with those goddamn drugs.'

'If anything spooks Joe now, he'll tell Huey to kill Abby, and then he'll run. But you won't get out of this room. The only place you'll go will be death row in Parchman. You'll spend ten years rotting there while you go through all your appeals. Shitty food, no drugs, no life. And then—'

'Shut up, okay? Just shut up!' Tears welled in her red-rimmed eyes. 'I see I got no place to go. I never have.'

'But you do. If you can keep it together for another hour, you'll get enough money to become anybody you want to be. To get free and clear for the first time in your life.'

Cheryl turned and walked back into the bedroom. Before she was out of earshot, Will heard her say, 'Nobody's free and clear, Doc. Nobody.'

Dr McDill accepted the magnifying glass that Special Agent-in-Charge Zwick offered him and leaned down over the photograph on the desk. It was a black-and-white, high-resolution digital still, captured from videotape shot by a security camera at the Beau Rivage Casino on the previous day. A time/date stamp in the corner read: *16:22:21*. 4:22 in the afternoon. That particular camera had been covering one of the blackjack tables at the time. The shooting angle was downward from behind the dealer, which yielded a perfect shot of the blond in the slinky black dress standing over the king of diamonds and six of hearts.

'Is it her?' Zwick asked.

'No doubt about it.'

McDill put down the magnifying glass and looked back at his wife, who was sitting on Zwick's sofa with her legs close together. The emotions running through him were intense enough to make his eyes sting. 'I was right,' he said. 'It's happening again. Right this minute, another family is going through the same hell we did.' He walked over to Margaret, sat beside her, and took her hand. 'We did the right thing. Thank you for coming with me. I know how difficult it was.'

She looked as shell-shocked as a war refugee. He needed to get her home.

'Has Agent Chalmers seen that picture?' he asked. McDill hadn't seen Chalmers in the past couple of hours. There were so many people moving in and out of the office now that it was hard to keep up with anybody.

'Chalmers is in the field,' Zwick replied. He was already behind his desk, dialing the telephone.

'Oh my God,' McDill cried, slapping his forehead like one of the Three Stooges.

'What is it?' Zwick pressed the phone to his chest.

'I'm scheduled to do a triple bypass in a half hour. My surgical team is probably calling the police right now.'

'Would you like an agent to drive you to the hospital? We can have a female agent take Mrs McDill home.'

'I can't operate. I haven't slept in over twenty-four hours. May I use your phone?'

'Of course. There's another line just outside.'

As McDill approached the door, a young woman burst into the room.

Zwick glared at her. 'I assume you have a good reason for this interruption, Agent Perry?'

The female agent nodded, her eyes flashing with

excitement. 'There's a man on the main line asking for the Special Agent-in-Charge.'

'Who is it?'

'Harley Ferris.'

Zwick turned up his palms. 'Who the hell is Harley Ferris?'

'The president of CellStar. And he says he's got to talk to the SAC about a kidnapping-in-progress.'

The blood drained from Zwick's face.

Huey Cotton was sitting on the porch steps of the cabin, using the point of his knife to put the finishing touches on his carving. When his cell phone rang, he put down the cedar and picked up the phone.

'Joey?'

'How you feeling, boy?'

'Okay.' Huey looked past the old Rambler to the line of trees. It stayed dark longer in the woods. He liked the way the light pushed down through the limbs in arrow-straight shafts, the way it did in churches. 'I guess.'

'What's wrong?'

'I heard something a minute ago.'

'What was it?'

'A motor.'

'Where? In the woods?'

'In the sky. I think it was a helicopter.'

Hickey said nothing for a few moments. Then, 'It was probably the Forest Service. You just heard it once?'

'No. Back and forth, like a buzzard circling.'

'Is that right. Well . . . you remember the backup plan we talked about?'

Huey reached down and picked a roly-poly from the dirt below the bottom step, delighting in the way its gray segmented body curled up in the palm of his hand. 'I remember.'

'It's time to start thinking about that.'

He felt a twinge of fear. 'Right this red-hot minute?'

'Not quite. But you be ready. I'll call you.'

'Okay.'

'How's the kid?'

'She's nice. Real nice.'

'That's not what I mean. Is she still asleep?'

'Uh-huh.'

'Maybe you better wake her up.'

'Okay.' Huey heard the gurgling sound of the commode from inside. 'She already woke up.'

'Okay. I'll call you soon. Stay ready. And keep listening for that helicopter.'

'I will. Are there bad people up in the sky?'

'Nobody to worry about. You just get ready.'

'Okay.' Huey hit END, then set the roly-poly carefully on the ground and stood to the accompaniment of creaking steps and knee cartilage. When he turned, he saw Abby standing in the cabin door. Her face was pale, her eyes crusted with sleep.

'I don't feel good,' she said.

Huey's face felt hot. 'What's the matter?'

'My head hurts. And my tootie feels funny.'

Confusion and fear blurred his vision. 'Your what?'

'Where I tee-tee. It feels funny. Something's not right.'

'What should we do?'

'I need my mom. I think I need my shot.'

Huey cringed at the memory of last night's terrifying injection scene. 'Soon,' he promised. 'It won't be long now.'

Chapter 16

Karen stood in the kitchen with the cordless phone in her hand, listening to 'hold' music that sounded like George Winston on sleeping pills. She was dressed in a navy Liz Claiborne skirt suit with a cream blouse, and her face was made up to cover the bruises she'd sustained during the night. At Hickey's insistence, she had even curled her hair. She had the feeling he was molding her to fit some ridiculous idea he had of the suburban yuppie wife. But no makeup was going to hide the hunted look in her eyes.

'Still on hold?' Hickey asked. He was sitting at the kitchen table, his sutured leg propped on its tile surface.

'Gray's getting something from his car.'

Gray Davidson was one of the founding partners of Klein Davidson, an independent brokerage firm that handled most of the money in the wealthy suburbs north of Jackson. Karen and Will went to parties at Davidson's home two or three times a year.

'You're not going to listen in?' she asked.

Hickey shook his head. 'Just stick to the script.'

'Karen?' said a male voice. 'It's Gray. Sorry you had to wait.'

'That's all right. I know it's early. Did you get a call from Will a few minutes ago?'

'Did I ever. Two hundred grand for a sculpture. That's kind of steep, even for Will.'

'It's a very important piece. But I should have gone to that convention with him. I'd have kept him at the outlet mall, instead of on his little art hunts.'

When Davidson spoke again, his voice changed subtly. 'Do you feel all right with this, Karen?'

'What do you mean?'

'Well, it seems odd, is all. I don't like that this guy selling the sculpture is in such a hurry for his money. Will says it's a competitive bidding situation. A New York art dealer discovered the piece three days ago in a workshop at an estate sale. He doesn't think Walter Anderson is any great shakes, so he took Will's bid, but he claims he's flying back to New York today and he wants cash.'

'That sounds like an art dealer.'

'But why can't we just wire the money to his account? Why does he want cash?'

'Art dealers are crazy, Gray. They carry sacks of cash all over the place. Didn't you know that?'

'All I know is that most of them are gay and all of them are crooked. There's something else. Three weeks ago, Will got nervous about the market. He sold some stock and transferred the money to various banks. He put a hundred and fifty thousand into Magnolia Federal. He could go to any branch in the state and withdraw most of the two hundred thousand he needs. Including Biloxi.'

Karen faltered for a moment, confused. Will hadn't

mentioned anything about this. 'Did you tell him that?'

'Yes. He said he put the money into CDs, so there would be penalties for an early cashout. He's got two hundred thousand liquid here in his tax-free instruments trust account. No penalty for spending that.'

'I'm sure that's it.'

'I guess so.' Davidson waited for her to say something more. When she didn't, he said, 'I guess I just hate seeing that much money leave my computer in a single morning.'

She forced herself to laugh. 'Now, that I believe. I'll be down to sign for it in half an hour.'

'Look forward to seeing you. You bringing Abby?'

She closed her eyes. Davidson was a world-class schmoozer; he knew the names of every child of every client, and it showed in his company's annual profits.

'Abby's with Will's mother today, in the Delta.'

'I know she loves that. Sorry, I'll miss her. Come on down.'

'Bye.' Karen hung up.

Hickey's chair creaked as he slid his leg off the table. 'What was that part in the middle?'

'What?'

'When you said, "What do you mean?"'

'He asked if I was all right with Will spending that much money.'

'But then you said, "Did you tell him that?"'

For some reason, Karen didn't want to mention the money in Magnolia Federal. 'He said it was odd, the seller wanting cash.'

'Then you said, "That must be it." What was that?'

When she hesitated, Hickey stepped forward and took hold of her arm. 'What was it?'

'He said the guy was probably only going to report half the sale price to the IRS. That's why he wanted cash.'

Hickey stared coldly at her as he analyzed her explanation. The levity he'd displayed before was gone. She suddenly wished she had Will's pistol, but Hickey was wearing it in the small of his back.

'Get your purse,' he said.

She took her purse from the counter, then opened the refrigerator.

'You don't have time for breakfast.'

She took two vials of insulin and some syringes from the top shelf and put them in her purse. 'I want this with me in case Abby's in trouble. You have a problem with that?'

A strange light flickered in Hickey's eyes. 'No problem. I told you nobody was going to die today.'

'I'm glad to hear it.'

'Let's go. We'll take the Expedition.'

Karen picked up her keys and led the way through the pantry and laundry room to the garage. Hickey limped after her. His leg was probably burning like fire. She hoped it was infected.

She hit the UNLOCK button on her key ring, then the garage door-opener on the wall. She had the Expedition cranked and in gear by the time Hickey got into the passenger seat. The pneumatic suspension hummed as it adjusted to their weight, and as soon as the garage door retracted to sufficient height, she started backing up.

'Easy,' Hickey said, laying a hand on her arm. 'You're going to have a wreck before we even hit the interstate.'

As Karen pulled her arm away, Stephanie Morgan's white Lexus crested the top of the hill and blocked her access to the drive. She hit the brakes with a screech.

'*Shit.*'

'Who is it?' Hickey was already reaching for the gun.

Karen grabbed his wrist. 'It's Stephanie Morgan, the same woman as yesterday.'

'What does she want now?'

'Something about the flower show, I'm sure. I'll get rid of her.'

'You do that.' He rolled down his window so that he could hear whatever transpired.

Karen got out and started toward the Lexus. Stephanie was already walking toward her, dressed more like a woman going to a cocktail party than to a weekend of volunteer work.

'I just came from the Colisseum,' she said in a tart voice. 'I didn't call because I knew you'd try to blow me off.'

'What is it, Stephanie?'

'The same as yesterday! Only worse. The cattle show people swore they'd be out by this morning and that the whole place would be cleaned up by noon.'

'And?' Karen looked past her, trying to see if either of her kids were in the car. The Lexus looked empty.

'And some *redneck* has got a pen of calves sitting in the middle of the Colisseum floor. There's hay and cow manure all over the place!'

'Calm down, Steph. It can't be that bad.'

'There's cow shit all over the floor, Karen. I don't think that's going to work wonders for a flower show. You've got to come down and light a fire under those people. They just won't take me seriously.'

Karen found that easy to believe. 'I can't come yet, Stephanie. My cousin's in the car, and he's got a plane to catch. I'll get there as soon as I can. You'll just have to handle it until then.'

'I *can't* handle it. I'm maxed out on Zoloft, and even that's not doing any good. Oh, and I left out the best part. The moving company we contracted to bring in the exhibit tables double-booked this weekend. We have no tables, Karen. *No tables.*'

Karen tried to look concerned, but she could hardly believe that yesterday she would have given a damn about exhibit tables, flowers, or even cow shit. She had to get Stephanie Morgan off her property and out of harm's way.

'Listen to me, Steph. Get on the phone and call the football coach at Jackson Academy. His name's Jim Rizzi. Tell him you've got a summer project for his football team and you'll pay real money. Tell him to get as many players he can down to the convention center with a couple of pickup trucks. Those high school boys can move those tables in half the time it would take a moving company. Okay?'

Stephanie seemed shocked by the simplicity of this solution. 'Karen, that's fantastic. But I don't know Rizzi at all. And I'm no good at asking people stuff like that. And what about the cows?'

Karen wanted to scream. *Who takes you to the bath-room and wipes your behind for you, Stephanie?* But the sound of the Expedition's door stopped her cold. She turned and saw Hickey walking toward them, a concerned look on his face.

'Everything okay?' he asked.

'Oh, hello again, Mr Hickey,' Stephanie said with a Teflon smile. 'I'm sorry to hold you up.'

'Call me Joe, please.'

Karen interposed herself between them. 'I told her we have to get right to the airport.'

Hickey looked puzzled, then he smiled. 'We *are* late for my flight. They make you check in so early now.'

Stephanie's eyes went wide. 'I've got it! *I* can run you out to the airport. That way Karen can get right over to the Colisseum. Things are absolutely falling apart over there. You wouldn't believe it.'

'No,' Karen said quickly. 'Joe and I still have some talking to do. The estate things. I told you last night. It can't wait.'

Hickey looked amused by Karen's fabrication, but Stephanie's face darkened, and her voice lost its sorority-girl veneer.

'You're the *chairman* of this show, Karen. You volunteered for it. That means it's your job to – make sure . . .'

Karen followed her gaze. Stephanie was staring at the right leg of Hickey's khakis. A bright-red blood-stain ran from above the knee down to his ankle. There was blood on his Top-Siders as well. Some of the stitches must have broken loose.

'What happened to you?' Stephanie asked.

Hickey looked down at his leg.

'Joe hurt himself,' Karen said quickly. 'Doing some work for me.'

'That looks serious.'

'It's not, really,' Karen said.

Hickey was watching Stephanie, his dark eyes glittering. Karen took her by the arm and started walking her back toward the Lexus.

'I'll get down there as soon as I can, Steph. You go back and slap those people into shape. And call Coach Rizzi about the tables. Okay?'

Stephanie looked back over her shoulder. 'Is your cousin all right? He looks . . .' She slowed down and looked into Karen's eyes. Something was stirring in her Zoloft-padded brain. 'Are *you* all right?'

'I'm fine.' Karen pushed her toward the car, but she refused to be pushed.

'You don't look fine. In fact, you look like hell.'

'Thanks a lot.'

Stephanie looked over Karen's shoulder. Whatever she saw convinced her that something was very wrong. She took hold of Karen's wrist and, in an almost comic reversal of their previous motion, began pulling her toward the Lexus.

'Keep walking,' she whispered. 'When I start the car, jump in the backseat.'

'*I can't. Get your butt out of here, Steph. Now.*'

Karen risked a glance back at Hickey. His pant leg was completely soaked with blood now, and his right hand was behind his back. She turned back to Stephanie and said in a bright voice: 'I'll see you in a few hours, okay?'

Stephanie's brow was knotted in puzzlement. Why

didn't she just *go*? Was she trying to work out if Hickey was Karen's lover after all? Whatever was occupying her brain cells, self-preservation finally overrode it. Karen actually saw Stephanie write her off. She whirled and yanked open the door of the Lexus, all pretense of normalcy gone.

Hickey shot her through the window. A crimson flower blossomed on her upper chest, and her mouth formed an almost comical 'O.' Karen screamed and leaped forward, but not in time to catch Stephanie as she slid down the rear door of the car, leaving a bright trail of arterial blood on the white paint. Her eyes were closed, and blood pulsed steadily from a hole in her sternum. Karen felt her brain clicking into crisis mode, all the skills she'd learned as a nurse infusing her mind and hands. But even before she could check Stephanie's airway, Hickey's rough hands jerked her to her feet.

'Get your ass in the truck!'

'You shot her,' Karen said, still not quite believing it.

Hickey aimed the .38 down at Stephanie's head. 'If you don't get into that Expedition, I'll shoot her again.'

His enraged eyes left no doubt that he would put a bullet in Stephanie Morgan's brain. Karen backed toward the Expedition, Hickey following with the gun.

'You said nobody was going to die!'

'She called that play. She should've handled those damn cows herself.'

'She has two kids!'

'You'd better start thinking about *your* kid, Mom.'

Karen's mouth went dry. Abby's death had

suddenly become real in a way that juvenile diabetes had not prepared her for. She climbed up into the driver's seat and sat there, trying to hold herself together. Will often joked that she could remain calm in the middle of an earthquake, but Hickey was proving him wrong. Her quest for some source of strength brought an image of her father to her mind. He had fought in Korea, then in Vietnam during the early years. God, how she wished he was here. He would know how to deal with a bum like Hickey. Hickey wouldn't know what hit him. But her father was gone, taken by cancer five years ago—

'Take hold of the gear shift and pull it over to *D*,' Hickey said, as though talking to a child.

'You lied to me,' Karen said. 'Everything you've told me was a lie. You've been planning to kill us all along. You're going to get your money and kill us.'

'Listen to me. Because your stupid gene is really showing through. Remember Costa Rica? By tomorrow night, I'll be sipping umbrella drinks in paradise. I'm not worried about who saw me shoot some airhead in a Lexus. What I *am* worried about is getting my money. And that's what you need to focus on. Are we on the same page?'

Karen took a deep breath, then reached down and punched 911 on the Expedition's cell phone.

Hickey jammed the gun into her ribs, driving the breath from her lungs. 'Your friend is dead. So hang up and start driving. Or the only mother Abby will ever know is the twenty-two-year-old Will marries after you're dead.'

The 911 line rang once before Karen pressed END.

She hated herself for being a coward, but she could not die here. Not in this truck, over an acquaintance who was almost certainly dead already. She had a child to raise. Nothing else mattered. She and Abby had to get through the day alive.

She put the Expedition into gear, backed onto the lawn, and drove around the Lexus and the body of Stephanie Morgan.

When the phone rang in the suite at the Beau Rivage, Will pounced on it. Now that he'd given Ferris the go-ahead to call the FBI, he wanted to hear the man report that a fleet of helicopters was combing the forest around Hazelhurst, flying at treetop level over every road and path, not a dog or a cow moving unseen. He jerked up the receiver, aware that his sleep-deprived brain was slowly but surely slipping off its tracks.

'Will Jennings.'

'What are you doing answering the phone?' Hickey asked. 'You expecting a call?'

'No,' he stammered. 'I'm just ready to move. Ready to get your money and get Abby back.'

'That's good, Doc. Because it's time to leave for the bank.'

'I'm ready.'

'You sound sleepy. Cheryl's got some pep pills if you need them. I don't want you messing up because you can't think straight.'

'I'm not going to mess up. But I need to talk to my daughter, Joe. I'm not going to the bank until I do.'

'Is that right? Huh. Maybe you should talk to your

wife a minute. We just had a little social call at your house.'

Sweat beaded on Will's forehead. 'Karen?'

'I'm here,' she said.

'Are you all right?'

'Will, he just shot Stephanie Morgan.'

Will blinked, certain that he'd misheard. 'Did you say—'

'You heard her right,' Hickey cut in. 'She's busy driving now. But if I hear any more bullshit about what you will and won't do, the Lexus queen won't be the only one who dies this morning. You follow?'

'Yes.'

'Now, what about this helicopter?'

Acid flooded Will's stomach. 'Helicopter?'

'You been talking to the FBI?'

Harley Ferris couldn't possibly have gotten an FBI helicopter into the air and over Hazelhurst so quickly. It had to be a coincidence. 'Joe, I'm doing exactly what you tell me. Nothing else.'

'Let me talk to Cheryl.'

Cheryl was sitting on the sofa with her purse at her feet. She had gone downstairs to Impulse, a clothing store in the casino lobby that operated twenty-four hours a day, and bought a white lycra sheath to replace the torn cocktail dress. She took the phone from Will and began her litany of one-word replies.

'Yeah. . . . No. . . . Right. . . . No, he's cool. . . . We'll be there. No problem.' She handed the phone back to Will. 'It's showtime.'

'Thank you.' He hung up the phone. 'I owe you more than I can ever repay.'

She stood and slung her purse over her shoulder. 'You just remember you said that.'

The Klein Davidson Building was an elegant stone edifice in the affluent business section of north Jackson. It looked more like a town house than an office, but Karen knew its interior thrummed with computers churning out market quotes from around the world. There were four satellite dishes mounted on the flat roof in back, but Gray Davidson had hired an architect to construct a mansard roof to conceal them. Karen pulled the Expedition into the parking lot and parked two spaces over from Davidson's Mercedes 560.

'You only want to be thinking about one thing in there,' Hickey said. 'Your kid.'

As Karen reached for the door handle, an older woman parked beside them, got out, gave her a little wave, and walked into the office.

'Gray's receptionist,' she said.

'Go on,' Hickey told her, uncovering the gun in his lap.

'I'm not taking one step until you let me call nine-one-one and report a woman shot at my address.'

Hickey held the gun against her ribs again.

'If you shoot me, you won't get your money. All I'm asking is a chance to try to save a woman's life. It won't cost you anything.'

'She's dead,' Hickey insisted. 'I shot her in the pump.'

'You don't know she's dead. She has two small

children, and I can't live with myself if I don't do all I can to help her.'

'You won't be able to live with yourself if you kill your own kid, I'll tell you that. And that's what you're doing if you don't go wire that money.'

She turned to him, unable to remain silent. 'You hate Will for supposedly killing your mother, but you just shot someone else's mother. You orphaned two children. Can you explain that to me?'

Hickey expelled air from his cheeks in exasperation. 'You're going to pay for this later.'

She closed her eyes and leaned back against the headrest. She expected to feel the gun barrel pressed to her temple, but instead she heard four beeps, one ring, and a click.

'*Nine-one-one, emergency*,' said a female dispatcher.

Hickey said, 'A woman was just shot in the chest at number one hundred, Crooked Mile Road. She's dying.'

Karen looked over at him, amazed.

'One hundred, Crooked Mile Road,' said the dispatcher. 'Are you at that address, sir? I'm not getting a location readout.'

'I'm on a cell phone. The woman is lying in the driveway.' Hickey looked at Karen as though asking if he'd done enough.

'Sir, I'm showing that we already received a call for this emergency.'

Hickey's jaw clenched. 'When was that?'

'About two minutes ago.'

'Who called it in?'

'I don't have that information, sir. But we've already dispatched an ambulance to—'

Hickey hit END. 'I think your husband has made a very big mistake. First we get a helicopter over the cabin. Now somebody's at your house reporting a shooting.'

'You were outside when you shot her. A neighbor could have heard and run over.'

'Your neighbors aren't that close.' Hickey rubbed the dark stubble on his chin. 'Get your ass in there and move the money. And remember . . . one mistake will put you in a mourning dress that you'll never really take off.'

Karen got out and walked toward the entrance, his last sentence hanging over her thoughts like a pall.

The Biloxi branch of the Magnolia Federal Bank was a two-story brick building of unprepossessing architecture. There were few cars in the parking lot, but drive-through business was brisk as Will pulled his rented Tempo into the lot and parked.

'What now?'

Cheryl shifted in the seat beside him and began tapping her fingers on the dash. She had popped two amphetamines before they left the hotel, and she was wired. Will had swallowed one, fearing that exhaustion might prevent him from making the right move if an opportunity to save Abby presented itself.

'Now we wait,' Cheryl replied. 'Joey will call after the money's on its way.'

Will took her cell phone from her lap and dialed Harley Ferris's number.

'Ferris,' said a clipped voice.

'It's Will. Anything?'

'The FBI already had a chopper in the air when I called them. It's been over the woods at Hazelhurst for a while now, but the foliage is so thick, they're probably missing buildings down there, much less a pickup truck.'

'What about the phone trace?'

'We're almost there, Will. We just had a quick call to the subject's number. Our crew is working its way down an overgrown logging road right now.'

'What will they do if they find the truck?'

'There's an FBI SWAT team en route from Jackson. The SAC there says they can seal off the cabin without the subject's knowledge.'

A chill of foreboding went through Will. 'They're not going to try an assault?'

'I think they're going to play it safe,' Ferris replied. 'But my guess is that with your little girl's life on the line, if they get a clean shot at the guy holding her, they'll take it.'

'Sweet Jesus.'

'They're pros, Will. Just like you. They know their jobs.'

'I've got to clear this line.' Will couldn't bring himself to hang up. 'Harley . . . for God's sake, tell them to be careful.'

'Have faith, brother.'

He hung up. *Have faith?* It took a supreme effort simply to sit in the parking lot while Abby's future unfolded a hundred and forty miles to the north. But he had to play the hand Hickey had dealt him. Hickey had to believe until the last second that his plan was ticking along like a Swiss watch.

'What happened?' Cheryl asked. 'What's going on?'

'Nothing,' he lied. 'Nothing at all.'

Sending the wire was just like everything Karen had ever done at Klein Davidson: a matter of paperwork, signing on various lines while Gray Davidson led her through the pages and made chitchat about kids and schools. With men, he probably talked kids and sports. Or women. Karen didn't know and didn't care. She was functioning on autopilot, tormented by images of Stephanie Morgan's chest blossoming red. The only thing that really registered was the receptionist handing her a receipt and saying, 'The money's on its way.'

'That's it? That's all we have to do?'

Gray Davidson patted her on the shoulder. 'Scary how fast you can spend two hundred grand, isn't it?'

He was wearing his trademark double-breasted English suit with a spread collar shirt and rugby tie. Five years older than Karen, Davidson hailed from Hot Coffee, Mississippi, but his pretensions rivaled those of the most dedicated Anglophiles on the Eastern seaboard. Some clients made fun of his eccentricities, but nobody joked about his market acumen.

'Very scary,' Karen replied, wondering if Will was already in the bank in Biloxi, waiting to collect what she'd sent. 'I now own a two-hundred-thousand-dollar chunk of wood.'

'You look like you're going to faint,' Davidson said with genuine concern. 'Why don't you come into my office and sit down?'

'No. I've got to run.'

'May I get you some coffee?'

'No, thanks, Gray. Really.'

'Green tea? Espresso?'

Somehow Karen conjured a smile, a feat of magic under the circumstances. 'It's just a summer cold. I'll be fine.'

The broker didn't look convinced. She touched his arm above the elbow and squeezed with an intimate pressure. 'I'm *fine*, Gray. Thanks for worrying.'

Davidson's critical faculties melted. Men were so easy to manipulate. She gave the receptionist a wave and hurried toward the door.

'Go straight home and get some rest,' Davidson called after her.

She held up a hand in acknowledgement but did not turn, and she barely slowed when she went through the varnished rosewood door and down the steps to the parking lot.

The parking lot of the Magnolia Federal Bank in Biloxi was filling up fast. People were cashing paychecks, hitting the ATM machines, and carrying in payroll bags. Will could see why Hickey had picked this branch. Cheryl sat beside him in tense silence, waiting for Hickey's go-ahead call. The temperature was rising fast in the parked car, so Will started the engine and switched on the air conditioner.

When the cell phone rang, he snatched it up, but Cheryl put her hand on his wrist and took the phone from his hand.

'It's me,' she said. 'Right. . . . Okay.' She hit END and looked at Will. 'The money's here. He said you should go in and get it.'

Will shut off the engine and looked at the double-glass doors of the bank. 'Give me the phone.'

'Why?'

'I'm taking it in with me.'

'You don't trust me?'

'I didn't say that. I just said I'm taking the phone.'

Cheryl snapped her head away from him, but she did not resist when he took the phone from her hand. He slipped it into his pocket along with the Tempo's keys, then got out and started walking toward the bank.

Chapter 17

Hickey drove south along the interstate at fifty-five miles per hour, his face wet with sweat. His right thigh was thoroughly soaked in blood.

'I think some more stitches broke,' he said. 'You aren't much of a doctor. I think you're going to have to do some repairs here.'

Karen had not given the suturing her best effort. 'I don't have Will's bag. I could probably tape it up, if you stop at a drugstore.'

'I don't want to stop.' Hickey looked in the rearview mirror, then changed lanes. 'But I may have to.'

'Are we on our way to get Abby?'

'We're on our way to a drugstore.'

'Are you letting us go when you get the money?'

'That's up to your husband. Let's see if he can follow simple instructions. Start looking for a drugstore.'

Karen glanced to her left, searching the strip malls that lined the interstate. She was pretty sure there was an Eckerd's along here somewhere.

'There's a cop back there,' Hickey said, straightening in his seat.

She started to turn, but he grabbed her knee and said, 'Don't look.'

'Cops are always patrolling this interstate,' she told him.

'This one's acting squirrelly. He's ten lengths back, but hanging on me like a trailer. He's running our plate.'

'Were you speeding?'

'You think I'm going to speed today? This is your husband, goddamn it. The son of a bitch called somebody. That's the only way they'd know what to look for.'

'What about the shooting at our house?'

'They wouldn't have issued an APB on this vehicle off that. Not yet, anyway.' He checked the rearview again. 'That SOB is still back there.'

'You're paranoid! And you're driving suspiciously.' Karen spotted the Eckerd's on her left. 'Take the next exit. Northside Drive. There's our drugstore.'

Hickey leaned toward her, then craned his neck backward and looked up through the moonroof.

'What are you *doing*? Watch the road!'

'Paranoid, huh? Take a look.'

The moonroof was tinted against the sun, but even so, Karen could see the large dot against the sky. It was a helicopter.

'That's probably the WLBT traffic chopper,' she said. But for the first time, she wondered.

'Traffic chopper, my ass.' Hickey reached down and punched a number into the cell phone. After a few seconds of silence, it began to ring.

'Joey?' said Huey.

'That's right, boy. You all ready?'

'Ready.'

'Were you born ready?'

'Um . . . yeah.'

'It's time to go to the backup.'

'Okay.'

Karen's chest tightened. 'You said that before. What's the backup plan?'

'Don't worry about it.'

'May I please speak to Abby? *Please.*'

Hickey sighed with frustration. 'Huey, is the kid right there?'

'She's in the bathroom.'

Karen's maternal radar went on alert. 'Has she been to the bathroom a lot this morning, Huey?'

'She sure has.'

'Oh God. Her sugar's going up. She needs her shot.'

'And I'm bleeding to death,' Hickey said. 'Stay cool. You've got stuff with you, and we'll be there in plenty of time.'

'*When?*'

'Here she comes!' Huey sang out.

'Abby?' cried Karen.

After a brief silence, Abby said, 'Mama?'

'Goddamn it,' Hickey muttered.

Karen's heart leaped. 'I'm here, baby. Are you all right?'

'I don't think so. I think I'm going south, like Daddy says.'

Karen fought to keep control of her voice. 'It's okay, baby. Mama's on her way to get you right now.'

'You are?'

'I'll be there before you know it.'

'Put Huey back on,' Hickey said.

'I'll be there before you know it,' Karen said again. 'Now, put Mr Huey back on, baby.'

'Okay. Hurry, Mom.'

'I'm on my way!'

'Joey?' said Huey.

'I'm here. You know what to do? Everything just like I told you.'

'I remember.'

'We'll talk when we see each other.'

'Okay. But Joey?'

'What?'

'Is everything gonna be okay?'

'You bet. Get going, now.'

'Okay. Bye-bye.'

Just before Hickey pressed END, Karen heard Abby yell, 'Bye, Mom!' and she filled with pride. Abby was hanging in there.

'Bastards,' Hickey said, looking up through the moonroof again. 'If your husband had done what he was supposed to, you'd be going straight to your little girl right now.'

Karen's heart stuttered. 'You said we were!'

'We're not going anywhere until I lose this tail.'

'You don't know it *is* a tail.'

A scornful grunt was his only comment. 'Your husband had better be getting me my goddamn money.'

'He is! You know he is.'

'He's trying to fuck me over is what I know. And I'll tell you this. If they try to stop this truck—'

'I'll say whatever you tell me to!' she promised. 'All I want to do is get to Abby.'

Hickey checked the rearview mirror again. 'The squad car dropped back out of sight. They're playing us loose. They want to follow us to the girl.'

Oh, Jesus, Karen thought. *Will, what did you do?*

Without warning, Hickey veered across two lanes of traffic and onto an exit ramp. At the bottom, he swung under the interstate and onto a wide boulevard.

'Lakeland Drive?' said Karen. 'Is this the way we went last night?'

'You just sit tight, Mom.'

'This is the road to the airport.'

'That it is.' Hickey laughed softly.

'This way, Doctor Jennings.'

Will turned down a hall that led off the bank's main lobby and followed the secretary up a short flight of stairs. Upon entering the bank, he had seen that dealing with a teller was not the way to go. There were lines at the windows, and even the loan officers in the glassed-in cubicles had customers. He walked up to a secretary, identified himself, and asked to see the senior officer at the bank. When she asked what it concerned, he told her he was receiving a wire transfer of two hundred thousand dollars and wouldn't deal with anyone but the top man. The young woman made a call, then asked him to follow her up the stairs.

The staircase ended at another hall, this one lined with doors. She led him to the one at the end, knocked, then opened it and showed him into a typical branch bank office, furnished out of mail-order catalogs. Behind a mahogany veneer desk sat a balding man in his early fifties, with shining skin and a line of sweat on his upper lip. He stood.

'Hello, Doctor Jennings. That'll be all, Cindy.'

The door closed behind Will, and the man held out a plump hand. 'I'm Jack Moore, vice president.'

Will shook the hand and looked around the office again. There was a small door on the wall to his right, partially open.

'What's that?'

'My private rest room,' Moore said.

'Oh.'

'How can I help you, Doctor? Your wire came in a few minutes ago. What would you like to do with the money?'

'I want to withdraw it in cash. I also need to withdraw some personal funds. I have a hundred and fifty thousand in CDs deposited with this bank in Jackson.'

Moore wiped his upper lip. 'You want to walk out of here with three hundred and fifty thousand dollars in a suitcase?'

'That's right.' Cheryl had retrieved a cheap briefcase from her suite as they left the Beau Rivage.

'I see. Well . . .' Moore glanced at his restroom door. 'If that's what you want, I guess . . .'

The restroom door opened, and a tall man with sandy hair and blue eyes stepped out.

Will backpedaled to the door. 'What the hell is this?'

'Doctor Jennings,' said the stranger. 'I'm special agent Bill Chalmers. I'm fully aware of your situation, and I'm here to help you.'

Will was so stunned that he simply stood where he was. 'But– How did you get here? How did you know where to go? Harley Ferris didn't know where I was going.'

Chalmers nodded. 'There's a sofa behind you, Doctor. Please sit down. We don't have much time, and we have a lot to do.'

'I only have one thing to do. Get my money and get out of here.'

'Please sit down, Doctor. I think you'll like what I have to say.'

Will backed up until his calves hit something padded. He sat.

'Do you know a cardiovascular surgeon named James McDill?'

'McDill? Sure. He's a member out at Annandale. He doesn't play much golf. Collects cars, I think.' Even as he spoke the word 'collects,' something ticked in Will's brain.

'Exactly one year ago,' said Chalmers, 'James McDill's son, Peter, was kidnapped in exactly the same way your daughter was yesterday.'

Will blinked in disbelief.

'He didn't report the crime until last night, and nobody knows why better than you. But this week he was overcome with anxiety that it might happen again. He called our Jackson field office around eleven last night. I was on duty, and we've been working ever since to piece together what's going on.'

'Have you talked to Harley Ferris? Do you know where my little girl is?'

'Mr Ferris is working with us now. We've augmented CellStar's tracing crew with a SWAT team, and we just had a very lucky break. Get a grip on yourself, Doctor. The man holding Abby just took a call on his cell phone, and he forgot to switch it off. The SWAT team estimates they're two minutes from your daughter's position.'

Waves of shock and hope buffeted Will. Even after Ferris's assurances, Chalmers's words seemed incomprehensible. 'What do they plan to do when they get there?'

Chalmers walked up to the couch and squatted, so that his eyes were level with Will's. 'We think we should go in and get her.'

'You mean, guns blazing?'

'Not quite, no. We have special entry devices. Heat sensors and video to accurately place human bodies in the structure. They'll use special stun grenades to incapacitate the tango, then—'

'Tango?' Will interrupted.

'Sorry, that's radio slang for terrorists. These guys train to rescue hostages from terrorists.'

'Can't you try to talk him out?'

Chalmers smiled patiently. 'We could do that. But it's our understanding that the man holding Abby is mentally handicapped. The leader is still loose. He could call this Huey at any time and order him to kill your daughter.'

Will felt as though he and Abby were standing in the path of a truck and couldn't move. 'Can't Ferris shut off Huey's phone?'

'Yes, but that might panic him. Or he might be under orders to kill your daughter if his communications are cut off. Right now – while Huey and Abby are isolated from the leader – we have a golden opportunity to go in. Before the situation deteriorates any further.'

After a night spent in ignorance, Will was having difficulty processing the sudden influx of information. 'I still don't understand how you got here. How you knew it would be this bank.'

'We didn't. We put an agent in every bank of any size in Gulfport and Biloxi. I requested this one because it was the largest. I flew down early this morning. The minute your wire came in, I contacted my Special Agent-in-Charge in Jackson. His name's Frank Zwick. And he wants to talk to you.'

'Is he in contact with the SWAT team?'

'Yes.'

'Please call him. And there's a woman outside in my rental car. One of the kidnappers.'

Chalmers nodded. 'Cheryl Lynn Tilly. We'll leave her alone until the team hits the cabin. If she gets suspicious and comes inside, you can tell her there's some delay with paperwork. We have more agents converging on the bank right now, but they'll be discreet coming in.'

'I can't believe all this.'

The FBI agent smiled. 'In a few minutes, your daughter will be in FBI custody, Doctor.'

Will was afraid to let himself believe it.

'You did well getting Harley Ferris involved. I only wish you would have called us earlier. Trusted us.'

'I couldn't.'

'I understand.' Chalmers got up and went to Moore's desk. The bank's vice president looked as though he didn't quite believe what was happening before his eyes. 'Would you excuse us, Mr Moore?'

'Of course.' The banker made a hasty exit.

Chalmers dialled a number on Moore's phone.

'The leader's name is Hickey,' Will said. 'Joe Hickey. He has my wife with him, and he's one clever son of a bitch. Do you know where they are now?'

'Driving toward Jackson International Airport.'

'*What?*'

'Don't worry. They're not going anywhere. We're watching them from a helicopter, and we've got men in the airport. Hang on.' Chalmers spoke into the phone. 'Chalmers here. I've got Doctor Jennings with me . . . He's on board with us . . . Yes, sir. Any word on the little girl?' Chalmers gave Will a thumbs-up.

'I want to talk to him,' Will said, standing.

'I'll tell him,' Chalmers said, and hung up. 'The SAC has a lot on his plate right now, Doctor.'

'What's happening?'

'SWAT found the cabin.'

'The green pickup truck?'

'It's parked under the trees.'

Will closed his eyes and began to pray.

Eight FBI agents in camouflage ninja fatigues and black headgear crept silently through the trees toward the cabin, their Heckler and Kock submachine guns tight against their bodies. A ninth agent was already under the structure, scanning the small floor plan with a supersensitive microphone and headphones. Their leader was Special Agent Martin Cody, and Cody was in radio contact with the agent under the house.

'Got anything?' he said into the microphone mounted inside his ballistic glass face mask.

'Not yet.' Special Agent Sims Jackson was observing the cabin through a thermal imaging camera. 'Nothing but a hot water heater.'

Cody didn't like that. The truck was there, but the people weren't? Was there a root cellar of some kind? Could the tango have detected their approach and fled into the woods? It would be tough carrying a five-year-old girl, but Cody had been told the man was big. He could also have killed the little girl and fled alone, but even if she'd been dead a couple of hours, there should still be enough heat in the corpse to register on the thermal imaging device.

'Cody to tracing van,' he said into his mike. The CellStar van was seventy yards back up the logging road. 'Has the cell phone moved?'

'Negative. Still in the same position.'

'We're going in,' Cody said into his mike. 'Prepare for explosive entry. Stun grenades through the windows, ram on the front door. It looks thin as paper, but you never know.'

A staccato burst of mike clicks answered him.

'Shoot high,' Cody reminded them, though they knew the drill already. 'This kid probably isn't much over three feet, which is a good break. Okay . . . deploy.'

What followed was a ballet the team had rehearsed hundreds of times. Men moving forward without sound, carrying weapons they could dismantle and put back together in absolute darkness. In thirty seconds the team had deployed around the cabin, grenades and HKs at the ready.

Agent Cody had a bad feeling about the assault, but he often got those just before contact. He checked to make sure his ram team was in position to hit the door. It was.

'On my five-count,' he said. 'Five – four – three – two – GO!'

The cabin windows shattered one second before the front door went down. Even in daylight, the blue-white flash of the stun grenades lit up the windows, followed by ear-shattering bangs. Cody saw his men vanish into the cabin. He charged forward and went through the front door five seconds behind them.

The raised cabin floor shuddered under the impact of boots. The interior was filled with smoke, but it cleared quickly through the broken windows. There were no cries of 'FEDERAL AGENTS!' because no one could have heard them after the stun grenades.

'Bedroom! No joy!' cried the speaker in Cody's helmet.

'Kitchen, no joy!'

'Bedroom closet's empty!'

Cody checked the corners of the front room, in case the girl was lying dead in one of them. He found nothing.

'Cell phone!' someone shouted. 'Cell phone in the kitchen!'

'Got another one!' cried someone else. 'Landline in the bedroom!'

Landline? Cody had been told there was no land-line in the cabin, and he had seen no wires outside.

Maybe there was a buried cable running to the building. He went into the kitchen and saw one of his men holding the cell phone. He was about to take it when the phone began to ring. Cody yanked off his helmet, stared at the phone for a few seconds, then took it and hit SEND.

'Yeah?' he said, hoping the caller would mistake him for whomever he had tried to call.

'Do you have Prince Albert in the can?' asked a male voice.

Cody stood dumbfounded for a moment. 'Who is this?'

He heard wild laughter; then the caller clicked off.

Cody put his helmet back on and keyed his mike. 'Tracing van, did you hear that call?'

'Affirmative.'

'Where did it come from?'

'Unknown. We're checking.'

Cody ripped off his helmet again, pulled a digital cell phone from his pocket, and dialed the private number of SAC Zwick in Jackson.

Will paced back and forth across the banker's small office. Agent Chalmers sat behind Moore's desk, speaking quietly to Zwick. Suddenly, Chalmers groaned and covered his eyes with his free hand.

'What happened?' Will asked. '*What happened, goddamn it?*'

Chalmers looked up, his face pale. 'The cabin was empty when SWAT went in. Huey and your daughter weren't there.'

'*What?*' Will searched his mind for an explanation. 'It must have been the wrong cabin.'

'It wasn't. They found the cell phone inside. And someone – probably Hickey – actually called them on it while they were there. Made a joke out of it.'

Will shook his head in disbelief.

'They also found a landline in the cabin, which means Hickey could have given Huey new instructions without anyone knowing. The phone company has no record of that line. It's probably an illegal tap.'

A landline. He should have known Hickey wouldn't let Huey operate without some sort of backup. But the truck was still there?'

'The truck was still there, but the battery had been removed. It looks like there might have been another vehicle there. They may have gotten away in it.

'*May* have? Are you kidding me? They're gone!'

'Doctor—'

'Give me that goddamn phone!'

Will snatched the phone from Chalmers's hand and shouted into it: 'Are you the guy in charge of this Chinese fire drill?'

'This is Frank Zwick, Doctor. Special Agent-in-Charge. Losing your temper isn't going to help your little girl.'

'You just tell me, what do you plan to do now?'

'I'm deciding that at this moment. You can help me. Did Cheryl Lynn Tilly mention any possible destination that would require air travel?'

'Costa Rica. She said Hickey has a ranch down there. Or some land, anyway.'

'Costa Rica? You can't fly direct from Jackson to

Costa Rica. And there's no reservation for a Joe or Joseph Hickey on any flight out of Jackson today. So, he must be flying out under an alias, with a connecting flight to South America.'

'Look, if Hickey called your men at the cabin, he knows you're involved. You may have just killed my little girl, Zwick.'

'I seriously doubt that, Doctor. Hickey wants two things: his money and his freedom. Killing your daughter won't help him get either. She's half his total leverage now.'

'You don't know what's going on! It's not about *money*. Hickey thinks I killed his mother on the operating table. This is about revenge. He *wants* to kill Abby. To punish me.'

There was a brief silence. Then Zwick said, 'That's a disturbing new perspective, Doctor.'

'You're goddamn right it is.'

'Do you know this Hickey? Do you remember him?'

Will heard another phone ringing. It was the cell phone in his pocket. Cheryl's phone. 'Hang on, I think Hickey's calling me.' He dug the phone out of his pocket and hit SEND. 'Hello?'

'What's up, Doc?'

Will nodded at Chalmers. 'I'm in the bank, getting your money.'

'You're lying. You called the FBI.'

'Joe—'

'Where's Cheryl?'

'In the parking lot. I brought the phone in with me.'

'Why?'

'So I could tell you what was happening if you called.'

345

'Well . . . the plan has changed. Your wife and me are about to take a little airplane ride. And if I see a cop or an FBI agent within a mile of me. I'm going to put one right in her ear. You follow?'

'Joe, I'm getting your money! Just tell me where you want it!'

'We'll work that out later. You just get it all ready to go. And tell your new friends to keep clear of that airport.'

'I don't know what you're talking about! Joe, where's my daughter?'

'That's the sixty-four-thousand-dollar question, isn't it?' Hickey laughed. 'Hasta luego, amigo. Just remember, whatever happens, you called the play.'

The phone went dead. Will felt as though his heart had been ripped out through his chest wall. He picked up the other phone and told Zwick what had transpired.

The SAC said, 'I'm going to pull back my men and let them get into the airport.'

'Why? Won't Hickey be harder to stop with lots of people around?'

'Yes, but it's possible that this Huey character and your daughter are already inside the airport waiting for him. If we bust Hickey outside, they might just disappear.'

'Jesus Christ. Okay. But if they are inside, what can you do? How can you stop Hickey then? What's to keep him from putting a gun to Abby's head?'

'The fact that he's dead.'

'You mean you'll shoot him on sight? Can you do that?'

'Kidnapping is an extraordinary crime, Doctor. The rules of engagement allow for a great deal of discretion. And an airport is a high-security area. I can promise you this. If your little girl is in there, and Hickey makes a move toward her with a weapon, his brain will be removed from his cranium without benefit of anesthetic.'

'Do you have sharpshooters there?'

'They'll be in position before Hickey gets inside the building. Now, I have a lot to arrange, Doctor. Put Agent Chalmers back on the phone.'

As Will handed over the phone, several thoughts came to him at once. Any logistics that Zwick had to arrange were in Jackson, not Biloxi. Right now he was almost certainly telling Chalmers to make sure Will stayed right where he was, under FBI control. But Will's primary concern was Hickey. Even now, the man was controlling the movements of everyone involved in the situation. Five times he had pulled off these kidnappings, and the FBI had never even been told about them. At the cabin he had proved he could stay two steps ahead of the SWAT team and laugh while doing it. Opposing his proven brilliance was Frank Zwick, a man Will knew nothing about. He had to assume that Zwick knew his job, but instinct told him that the events of the next few minutes would not be as easy to control as the SAC believed. The FBI did not really know where Huey and Abby were. They *might* be in the Jackson airport; they might also be sixty miles away. As Chalmers listened to his boss on the phone, Will walked quietly out of the office.

'Where are you going?' Chalmers called. 'Doctor?'

Will paused in the hall. 'To get the ransom money.'

'It's no good to you now.'

'You don't know that. Hickey said to get it, so I'm getting it. I'll be back in a minute.'

He took the stairs two at a time going down.

Five miles east of downtown Jackson, Hickey turned Karen's Expedition onto the main airport access road.

'Where are we going?' Karen asked. She was terrified that Hickey would board a flight to Costa Rica without telling her where Abby was being held.

'You just watch.'

'We've got to get to Abby, Joe. Her sugar's going up.'

'Just shut your goddamn mouth for five minutes. I got everything under control.'

Karen leaned back and looked up through the moonroof. The helicopter was still there. It had stayed practically on top of them all the way from the interstate. Hickey was right. It had to be the police. Or the FBI. She hoped to God Will knew what he was doing.

The SHORT TERM PARKING sign flashed past. Then ARRIVALS/DEPARTURES.

'Are we flying somewhere?' she asked. 'Do you have a plane here?'

'Oh, yeah. I got a whole fleet of them.' Hickey glared at her. 'You just can't be quiet, can you? I bet your husband thinks you are one big pain in the ass.'

She sat back and tried to stay calm. Despite the helicopter overhead, Hickey had not ordered Abby harmed. Unless the 'backup plan' was to kill her. Karen gripped the handle on the windshield post as

Hickey swerved into the LONG TERM PARKING lane. He stopped at the barrier, took a ticket from the machine, then accelerated into the concrete-roofed garage.

He rounded the first turn at forty miles an hour. The brakes squealed as they neared the elevator on the terminal side of the building. Hickey seemed to be looking for signs of police. Seeing nothing, he accelerated around the next curve and almost ran over a young woman in a navy blue suit, who was pulling a suitcase from the trunk of a silver Camry. He screeched to a stop, reversed a few feet, then pulled into the parking space beside the Camry.

'What are you doing?' Karen asked.

He jumped out and closed the distance to the woman in the time it took Karen to turn and look. As the woman gaped, Hickey smashed Will's .38 into the side of her head. She dropped like a stone.

'*Get out!*' Hickey shouted at Karen. '*Help me!*'

A wave of nausea nearly overcame her, but she forced herself to get out and move to the back of the Expedition. Hickey was bent over the prostrate woman, rifling through her purse.

'What are you *doing?*'

He snatched his hand from the purse with a jangle of car keys and hit the UNLOCK button on the ring. 'Get in the back seat of the Camry! Move!'

Hickey grabbed the woman under the arms and heaved her upper body into the Camry's trunk. There was blood in her hair. The blow from the pistol had torn part of her ear away from her skull. She moaned in pain and confusion, but Hickey took no notice. He stuffed her legs into the trunk, then slammed it shut. When he turned to Karen, his eyes were as cold as any she had ever seen.

'Get your ass in that car, or you'll never see Abby alive again.'

He didn't wait for her to obey. He jumped into the driver's seat, cranked the Camry, and backed out of the parking space.

Snapped from her trance by the realization that he might actually leave without her, Karen leaped forward and began hammering on the back door, which had automatically locked when he cranked the engine. Hickey looked back at her but did not open the door.

'Please!' she screamed, her heart in her throat. 'Open the door! *Open it!*'

He waited a few seconds, then unlocked the door. Karen jumped inside and pulled the door shut after her.

'Get on the floor,' Hickey ordered.

She lay stomach-down across the carpeted hump behind the front seat. Hickey drove at normal speed through the lines of parked cars.

'Are we leaving the airport?' she asked.

'Yes, we are!' he cried in his Wink Martindale voice. 'That nice lady left her parking receipt right here on the drink caddy!'

Karen couldn't believe it. Hickey was going to drive right out from under the nose of the helicopter hovering overhead. The strange thing was that she wanted him to succeed. She had seen enough of his personality to know that if he were arrested, he would clam up and smile at the police while Abby died in a diabetic coma somewhere.

Hickey stopped at the exit booth.

'How would you like to pay for that, sir?' asked a woman with a Hispanic accent.

'Cash, chiquita.'

'One dollar, please.'

Hickey had the money ready.

'Sir, the short-term parking lot is much more convenient for brief—'

'I'd love to chat,' Hickey said, 'but you've got cars waiting. Hasta la vista.'

He drove away from the booth and joined the flow of traffic leaving the airport. He drove confidently, neither too fast nor too slow. Karen raised up enough to watch him between the seats.

A sound like a muffled drum suddenly echoed through the car. She thought Hickey had switched on the radio, but he hadn't. The woman in the trunk was beating on the backseat.

'I'm glad she didn't start that shit while we were at the booth.' Hickey said.

'*Help!*' screamed the muted voice. '*I can't breathe! Please let me out!*'

Karen shut her eyes and prayed for the woman to be quiet. If she kept screaming, Hickey was liable to pull over and shoot her. The speed and intensity of his acts in her driveway and in the garage had sickened Karen. As a nurse, she had seen the effects of violence, but never the acts that produced the damage. Real violence was so unlike what she'd seen in movies that it was hard to grasp. Slashing Hickey's thigh had been a reflex, an act of self-preservation. But he acted with a merciless dispatch that made her feel worse about the whole human race. The realization of what she had avoided by stabbing Hickey suddenly came home to her with searing clarity. Those other mothers had actually been raped by the man, had suffered the horror of becoming sexual whipping posts for all his repressed anger and resentment. And they had endured that horror for twenty-four hours. It was unimaginable.

The knocking behind Karen went on, but the cries decreased in intensity until they became a keening wail, like that of a small child.

'Traffic update!' Hickey cried.

'What?'

'I thought you might like to know, that helicopter's still hovering over the airport, three miles back. Amateurs, baby. Amateurs.'

'Are we going to get Abby now?'

He laughed. 'We're going somewhere, June Cleaver. That's one thing you can count on. We got an appointment with destiny!'

Chapter 18

Despite his belief that Agent Chalmers might try to keep him a virtual prisoner in the bank, Will had returned to the vice president's office on the second floor. He had the ransom (Moore had personally packed it into the briefcase at his feet), but he could not make a decision about what to do next until he knew the outcome of the FBI's attempt to arrest Hickey at the airport. If Hickey somehow managed to escape, Will couldn't trust him to tell the truth about Abby or anything else over a cell phone.

When the call from SAC Zwick finally came, Agent Chalmers lifted the phone, listened for a few moments, then turned paler than he had when the SWAT team had found nothing at the cabin. In his mind's eye, Will saw a nightmare scenario: FBI agents drawing down on Hickey on an airport concourse, Hickey putting a pistol to Abby's head, an FBI sharpshooter shooting wide, Hickey pulling the trigger. Chalmers went on listening to Zwick, but Will couldn't wait.

'Tell me!' he demanded.

Chalmers held up his hand.

'*What happened?*'

'I'm putting you on the speaker, Frank.' Chalmers hit a button on the phone. 'Go ahead.'

'What happened?' Will asked. 'Is my wife all right? Was my daughter there?'

Zwick's voice came from the bottom of an electronic well. 'We think your wife is fine, Doctor.'

'You *think*? What about my daughter?'

'We don't know.'

'What do you mean? What *happened*?'

'Hickey and your wife pulled into the long-term parking garage, but they never came out. We found your Expedition with one door open. Right now, we don't know where they are. We're searching the airport, but it's just possible they got out of that garage in another car. We have a photo of Hickey from Parchman Prison, and we're faxing it down for the garage attendants to look at. We got a photo of your wife from the *Clarion Ledger*, and that's on its way down, too. We're also getting the parking lot security camera tapes.'

'What about your helicopter?'

'Nothing useful. A lot of cars left that garage during that window of time.'

'Jesus, you don't know anything!'

'Doctor, there's no way Hickey can—'

'Can what? It looks like he can do any damn thing he pleases!' Will stood and lifted the briefcase that held the ransom.

'What are you doing?' asked Chalmers.

'Going back to the car and waiting for Hickey's next call. And I want you to stay right here.'

'That's not an option, Doctor,' Zwick said from the speaker-phone.

'You want to bet?'

'The only way you can participate in the resolution of this situation is our way. Otherwise, we'll have to arrest you.'

'For what? I haven't done anything.'

'I'll have the Gulfport police arrest you for reckless driving. You've got a hooker in your car. How about prostitution?'

'What do you want me to do?'

'By now Agent Chalmers has some special equipment at his disposal downstairs. A tracking device, which you can carry in your pocket, and which will allow us to follow you from a very discreet distance. We can wait for Hickey to arrange an exchange, then be ready to take him down at the safest possible moment. We also have an undetectable wire. With the wire, we'll know just when that moment is, and we'll also have everything Hickey says on tape.'

'Undetectable, my ass. A wire helps you guys at trial, but it doesn't do squat for my wife and daughter. And they're my only priority.'

'This is nonnegotiable, Doctor.'

'You think so?' Will reached into his pocket and brought out Cheryl's pistol. 'Ask Agent Chalmers if it's negotiable.'

'Bill?' said Zwick.

'He's holding a gun on me, Frank. Looks like a Walther automatic.'

'You just committed a felony, Doctor,' Zwick informed him. 'Don't make this worse for yourself.'

Will laughed outright. '*Worse?* Are you out of your mind?' He backed toward the door. 'You guys had

355

your chance. Two chances. And you blew it both times. It's my turn now.'

Agent Chalmers held up both hands to show that he had no intention of going for Will's gun or his own. 'At least take the tracking device. Forget the wire. I wouldn't wear it either.'

'Shut up,' Zwick snapped.

'Where is it?' Will asked.

'I'll call downstairs and have it waiting for you.'

Zwick said, 'Agent Chalmers, as soon as he leaves that room, you will call downstairs and order the agents down there to arrest him.'

Chalmers looked into Will's eyes. 'They'll have to shoot him to stop him, Frank. I say we let him go.'

'Goddamn it.' The speakerphone crackled for a moment. 'All right, just give him the tracker. Jennings, you're making the biggest mistake of your life. But if you're dead set—'

'I'm out of here,' Will said. 'Please don't try any cowboy stuff. I'll call you if you can help.'

He aimed the gun at Chalmers all the way to the stairs. Then he gave the FBI agent a salute, turned, and bounded down the steps.

In the lobby, he made a beeline for the door. The secretary who'd led him up to Moore's office saw the gun and screamed, but a business-suited man by the front doors held up his wallet and yelled: 'FBI! Everyone stay calm! It's all right!'

As Will neared the door, the FBI man held out a small black box with a blinking red LED on it. 'GPS,' he said. 'Military grade. We can track you down to the square foot you're standing on. Don't lose it.'

Will stuck the unit in his pocket, went through the automatic doors, and raced for the Tempo. When he hit the driver's seat, Cheryl said, 'Where the hell have you been? I'm peeing prune pits out here.'

'You've got a real way with words, you know?' He cranked the Ford, backed up, then pulled out of the lot and onto Highway 90. Traffic was heavy, but he didn't see any obvious pursuit vehicles.

'Where are we going?' Cheryl asked, her voice jittery from the speed she'd taken earlier.

'That's up to Joe. Right now, we're headed up to I-10. Wherever the meet is, it's going to be north.'

Will swung into the right lane and started around a dawdling pickup truck. As he came alongside it, he rolled down his window, tossed the GPS device into the bed of the truck, and sped past.

'What was that?' Cheryl asked.

'A pig trail for the FBI to follow.'

'The FBI? Was the FBI in the bank?'

'Yes.'

'Oh shit. Oh God . . .'

'The FBI raided the cabin, but Huey and Abby weren't there. All they found was the green truck and Huey's cell phone.'

'Shit. I was right about the truck, though. I told you.'

He turned and gave her a hard look. 'They also found a regular phone. A landline. You told me there was no regular phone service at the cabin.'

'I didn't know there was! I told you I never went there.'

He lifted the briefcase from the floor and set it in her lap. 'Open it.'

'Is the money in here?'

'Yes.'

She hefted the case. 'It doesn't feel right. It's too heavy. Is there a dye pack in here or something?'

'No dye pack. Open it.'

When the lid rose high enough to reveal the neatly stacked hundred-dollar bills, Cheryl's face lit up like Abby's did when she saw a deer walk into the backyard on a cool fall morning. 'This is too much,' she said in a flustered voice. 'Isn't it?'

'That's three hundred and fifty thousand dollars.'

She picked up a stack of hundreds and ran her fingers over it, than fanned the edges like a kid playing with a deck of cards. A high-pitched noise that was almost sexual came from her throat. Will knew the effect of cash money on poor people. He had learned it the hard way.

'Talking about money and holding it in your hand are two different things, aren't they?' he said. 'I told you I'd give you enough to start over. Now you've got it. That's more lap dances than you could do in a lifetime. That's freedom, Cheryl. Mexico, Bermuda, any place you want to be.'

She turned to him, her eyes guarded. 'Can I leave now? Right this minute?'

'No. Joe is going to call any second to set up a meeting. I need you to tell him everything's still all right.'

'No way.' She shook her head like a two-year-old. 'I've already done too much. Joey will—'

'He won't do anything! You'll never even have to see him again.'

'You're lying. To bluff Joey, you're going to need me up to the very last second. Then I'll be with him. And he'll *know*.'

'He won't know anything.'

'You don't know him.' Unalloyed fear shone from her eyes. 'Joey's got this thing about betrayal. Like the mafia. He's totally paranoid about it.'

'He's going to kill my little girl, Cheryl. You don't want to believe that, but deep down, you know. If he's capable of killing you, he could kill Abby without batting an eye.'

'Would you let me go if you knew where she was?'

Will nearly slammed on the brakes. 'Do you know where Huey's going?'

'Would you let me go if I did?'

'That depends on whether I believe you.'

She pursed her lips and looked down at the money on her lap. 'I was supposed to bring you to the motel, like I said. Then Joey was supposed to pick us up. I think he was going to take us back to the cabin where Huey was keeping Abby. But if the FBI raided the cabin, and Joey knows that . . .'

'He knows.'

'Then he's going to his backup plan.'

'What's his backup plan?'

'For Huey, I don't know. I'm still supposed to go to the motel in Brookhaven. Only I don't bring you. I'm supposed to stay off the cell phone, too. Joey will call me at the motel – on a landline – and tell me what to do. I might sit tight with the money until he tells me to go somewhere, or he might pick me up.'

'Where would he tell you to go?'

She looked at the money again and swallowed. 'I don't know for sure. But I've been thinking about it. One time we were driving from Jackson to New Orleans, and Joey got all hot and wanted to do it. I told him I didn't want to do it in the car, and he said we didn't have to. About ten minutes later, he pulled off the interstate and went down this two-lane blacktop a ways and stopped at an old house. He climbed in a window and unlocked the door for me. His daddy's people owned it, I think. The house was mostly empty, but there was a bed and a stove. I think if things went to hell up Jackson way, that's where he'd go.'

This was what she'd held back during the torture session. 'Could you find that house again?'

She shook her head. 'Not by myself. It was too dark and too long ago. It's up by McComb somewhere, but that's all I know.'

'You've got to try! Huey and Abby might be there right now.'

'I have tried! Look, you've got the name of the motel and the general area of the house. Just give that to the FBI and let me go. They'll find your little girl.'

'Not in time, they won't.'

'Okay, listen. Joey calls in a minute and tells me to go to the backup plan. I'll say, "Fine, see ya soon." The motel's a hundred and fifty miles north of here. The house must be a hundred and twenty. That gives you guys plenty of time to set something up. I don't know what you're doing anyway. If you want to save your kid, why are you running from the FBI?'

Will sighed. 'The FBI wants to bust Joe, okay? And you. And Huey. I don't care anything about that. I just want Abby back alive. And my wife. The FBI already spooked Joe twice. If he sees them anywhere close again, he might tell Huey to kill Abby. If he hasn't already.'

Cheryl pulled at her hair. 'But you can't do anything by yourself. Joey's closer to both places than we are. A lot closer.'

'Not necessarily.'

'What do you mean?'

Will pointed through the windshield. A Continental Airlines 727 was settling over Interstate 10 as it landed at the nearby airport.

Cheryl's mouth fell open. 'Jesus . . . your plane. But there's nowhere to land up there. Not at the house.'

'Let me worry about that.' Will had once lost an engine over the Mississippi Delta and set down on a deserted stretch of Highway 61. To save Abby, he would land the Baron on a driveway if he had to. 'One hour of acting, Cheryl. One hour, and you're free forever.'

She covered her face with her hands. 'You're making it too complicated! I told you, I don't know where the house is!'

'You know more than you think. You might—'

The ringing cell phone silenced him. There was no more time for persuasion. He pulled onto the shoulder and shoved the Nokia toward her hand.

She refused to take it.

'Answer it,' he said.

She shut her eyes and shook her head.

'Answer it!'

* * *

Abby was walking through tall trees toward a gravel road when she saw Huey toss the flat tire into the trunk of the white car. He slammed the lid and looked up at her, then grinned and waved like a little boy waving at a train. Abby raised her hand to wave back. She felt like she was raising it through water.

She had seen amazing things in the last few minutes. When it was time to leave the cabin, Huey had picked up Belle and her ice chest and led her out to the green pickup truck. But instead of getting in, he opened the lid over the motor and lifted out a big black thing he said was a battery. It didn't look like any battery Abby had ever seen, but he carried it over to the white car sitting on the concrete blocks and set it on the ground. Then he opened the lid over the white car's motor and put the battery inside. While he was doing that, Abby had to run into the trees and tee-tee. Ever since she woke up, she'd had to go a lot, and that meant her sugar was going up fast.

After Huey got the battery into the white car, he went around to the driver's door and tried to start the motor. It didn't work at first, but he worked under the lid for a minute, and the car started, rattling and puffing smoke. He looked at Abby and laughed, then went back inside the cabin. She followed. In the kitchen, he took his cell phone from his pocket, turned it on, and set it on the counter. Then he lifted Abby like she was still a baby and carried her out to the porch steps.

The white car was still running, but it couldn't go anywhere because it was sitting a foot off the ground. Huey walked to the back of the car, put his huge hands under the bumper, and started pulling on it. His face turned red, then purple. The porch steps shook under Abby's behind when the back of the car tipped off the blocks and the tires hit the ground. Huey laughed like crazy. He helped Abby into the front seat, then put his hands on the steering wheel and drove right off the blocks in front.

The car lurched forward and stopped. Huey drove backward and forward, grinding the motor and jerking the wheel left and right until the car broke loose and started across the grass. Soon they were riding under big trees whose trunks were hardly far enough apart for the car to fit between them. Huey kept saying how 'NaNa's car' was going to save them, how smart Joey was, and how pretty soon they were going to hit a road.

Pretty soon they did. Two mossy ruts through the dirt. Then the ruts hit a gravel road, which got Huey laughing again until they had the flat. It didn't boom the way flat tires did on TV. Something just started flopping and grinding on the right side of the car, and Huey pulled over. He told Abby it wouldn't take long to change it, but it took long enough that she had to run into the trees to tee-tee again.

That was when she realized she was in trouble. Her head hurt and she felt really tired. She wanted to wipe herself with a leaf, but she was afraid of poison ivy, so she pulled up her panties and started back toward the car, her eyes on Huey as he tossed the flat tire into the trunk. He was grinning and waving. She tried to wave back, but her arm didn't seem to work.

'What's the matter?' Huey called.

She fell facedown on the dirt.

The next thing she saw was Huey's face inches from hers, his eyes bugging behind his heavy black plastic glasses. He looked more scared than she was.

'My sugar's too high,' she said, looking around. Huey must have carried her to the white car, because she was sitting in the front seat. 'I need my shot.'

'The medicine in the ice chest?'

She nodded.

Huey got the small Igloo from the backseat and set it beside her. 'Do you know how to do it?'

'I've seen Mom and Dad do it lots of times. But I've never done it. You suck some medicine up into the shot and then stick the needle in my tummy and push the plunger.'

Huey screwed his face up, as though the idea were unthinkable. 'Does it hurt?'

'A little. But I could die without it.'

He shut his eyes and shook his head violently. 'We better wait till we see your mama.'

'How long is that?'

'I don't know.'

Abby rubbed her face where it felt itchy. 'Will you give me the shot?'

Huey's lips worked all around his front teeth. 'I can't. Can't do that. I hate needles.'

'But I have to have it.'

'I can't do it, Belle.'

Abby bit her lip and tried not to be scared. 'Can you open the ice chest for me?'

Huey pressed the button on the side of the Igloo and opened it. Abby reached in and took out two bottles of insulin. She picked the bottles by the 'N' and the 'R' after 'HUMULIN.'

'One of these works quick,' she told Huey. 'And one works later. So you mix them up.'

She took a syringe from the ice chest and pulled off the cap, moving quickly so she wouldn't have to think about it long. Huey's face twisted at the sight of the needle. She drew a little clear fluid from each bottle into the syringe, making sure the medicine didn't get above the '4'.

It was time to pull up her jumper, but she didn't want to do it. At least twice every day, she sat still while her mother stuck her in the stomach, but the idea of doing it with her own hands made her feel like she had to throw up.

'What's the matter?' Huey asked. 'What next?'

'Can you do one thing for me?'

'What?'

Abby pulled her jumper over her right thigh and pinched up some skin and fat. 'Pinch up some skin on my leg for me, like this.'

After some hesitation, Huey put out his hand and pinched up the skin. 'Are you scared?' he asked.

She was. But her daddy had told her that while it was okay to *be* scared, it was better not to let other people see you were. 'I'm almost six years old,' she said in the strongest voice she could. 'I can do it.'

Huey's eyes were wet. 'You sure are brave.'

Abby wondered how a giant who could pick up a car could think she was brave, but he did. And that gave her the courage to stick the needle in. She pressed down the plunger, and by the time she felt the pain the needle was out again.

'You did it!' Huey cried.

'I did!' She laughed and leaned back in the seat, then reached up and hugged Huey. 'Let's go see my mom!'

He pulled back and looked at her, the awe in his face replaced by sadness.

'What's the matter?' Abby asked.

'I'm never gonna see you again.' His bottom lip was shaking. 'Your mama's gonna take you away, and I'll never see you.'

'Sure you will.' She patted his arm.

'No.' He shook his head. 'It always happens. Any friend I ever make gets took away. Like my sister.'

Abby felt his sadness seeping into her. She picked up Belle and pushed the doll at his hand, but he wouldn't take it.

'We'd better get going,' she said. 'Mom's waiting for me.'

'In a minute,' Huey said. 'In a minute.'

'Take it!' Will shouted, shoving the Nokia at Cheryl. 'Answer the damn phone!'

She crossed herself, then took the phone and hit SEND.

'Hello? . . . Yeah, I've got it . . . he's right here . . . No, not that I saw. No cop cars . . . We're on I-10. We turn on I-55 North, right? . . . Oh. Okay.' She cut her eyes at Will. 'How come? . . . Oh God . . . Okay. Just a second.' She handed the phone to Will.

'Joe?' Will said.

'You just had to play hero, didn't you?'

'Joe, I'm doing exactly what you told me to do. All I want is—'

'Don't piss down my boot and tell me it's raining. You called the FBI.'

'They were waiting for me in the goddamn bank! But I didn't call them. It's your own fault!'

'What are you talking about?'

'A heart surgeon named James McDill called them. Does that name sound familiar?'

This time Hickey didn't reply.

'McDill was worried you were going to do to some other family what you'd done to his last year. He called the FBI last night. That's what started all this. The helicopters, the alerts for wire transfers, the whole thing.'

'Shit. McDill? His wife was a pill, too.'

'Joe, I've got the money. I'm ready to make the trade. The FBI agent in the bank tried to make me wear a wire, and I told him to stick it. I pulled Cheryl's gun on him and got the hell out of there. He gave me a GPS tracking device and I trashed it. Ask Cheryl. I *want* you to get to Costa Rica, okay? All I want is my daughter back. That's all I ever wanted.'

There was a long silence as Hickey considered his options. 'All right, listen up. Tell Cheryl to take you back to the Beau Rivage. Give her the money and the cell phone, then go back up to your suite. You sit there till the phone rings. It'll be me. That phone's going to ring a lot during the next few hours, and you won't know when. You just keep your ass in that room and answer it. Watch a movie. Because if I call and you ain't there, your kid is dead. I get a busy signal? She's dead. Got it?'

Will sat speechless, watching the cars whizz past. Once again Hickey had done the unexpected. Instead of setting up a ransom exchange, or simply telling Cheryl to dump him somewhere and go to the backup plan, he had figured a way to pin Will down while he made his escape.

'I can't accept that, Joe. When would I get Abby back? How would I know you'd keep up your end?'

'You've just got to have faith, Doc. After I get the money, I'll let your wife and kid go at a public place. Same place for both of them.'

'That won't work, Joe. Look . . . I know you don't just want the money, okay? You want to hurt me, and you want to do it through my family. I've got three hundred and fifty thousand dollars here. It's yours. But I've got to be there when we make the trade. When I see Karen and Abby drive away in a car, I'll give you the money. You can do what you want then. You can kill me. Just let them live. That's all I ask.'

'Still trying to play hero, aren't you? The big martyr. Well, forget it. It's my way or the highway. Give Cheryl the money and tell her to drop you off at the Beau Rivage.'

'I'm not giving up the money until I see Abby.'

'You got no choice, son.'

The phone went dead in Will's hand. He sat there in shock, all the frustration of the past twenty-four hours boiling like lye in his gut.

'What happened?' Cheryl asked. 'What did he say?'

Will hammered the steering wheel with his fists.

Cheryl tried to grab his arms, but he pounded the wheel until the horn cover popped off and hit the window.

'Stop!' Cheryl screamed. 'What is it? What's wrong?'

He explained Hickey's last demand.

'I told you,' she said, sinking back in her seat. 'Joey's always three steps ahead. He doesn't make mistakes.'

'He trusts you to bring him the money. That's a mistake.'

'No,' she said with resignation. 'He knows I might think about running. But when it comes right down to it, I haven't got the nerve.'

Will grabbed her arm and squeezed it hard enough to hurt. 'Is that the best you can do? Are you that beaten down?'

She jerked her arm away. 'What about you, hotshot? He's got you beat five ways to Sunday.'

Will leaned back in the seat, his head and hands throbbing. 'I could get somebody to sit in the suite and answer my phone,' he said, thinking aloud. 'Pretend they're me. One of my friends from the convention.'

'Joe wouldn't buy that for two seconds. He knows things about you that *you* don't even know. One trick question and it would be over.'

'The hotel phones, then. I could go back and smash the junction boxes with the car. They're usually on the ground outside. A car wreck . . . that's out of my control.'

'Like that's a coincidence? Get real. You're screwed.'

Another plane roared overhead – an F-18 Hornet. As the thunder of its jet engine shook the car, an idea flashed into Will's mind with the brilliance of a flare at midnight. Something so simple . . .

'What is it?' Cheryl asked. '*What?*'

He took out his wallet, removed a card from the bill compartment, and dialed a number on Cheryl's cell phone.

'Beau Rivage Casino Resort,' said the hotel operator.

'Give me Mr Geautreau, please. It's an emergency.'

'May I ask the nature of the emergency?'

'Life and death, damn it! Get him to the phone!'

'Who are you calling?' Cheryl asked.

'This is Mr Geautreau. May I help you?'

'This is Dr Will Jennings, the keynote speaker at the medical convention. We spoke yesterday when I checked in.'

'Of course, Doctor. How may I help you?'

'You've had the FBI in this morning, right?'

Geautreau hesitated. 'That's right.'

'And they checked my room.'

'Yes, sir.'

'Are there still FBI agents in the hotel?'

'The last one left a few minutes ago.'

'Listen, Geautreau. I don't know what the FBI told you, but they were there because my daughter was kidnapped last night. She's still missing. I'm not in the hotel now, but I need someone to think I am. One of the kidnappers. Starting in about fifteen minutes, he's going to call my suite several times over the next few hours. I need all those calls forwarded to the cell phone I'm using now. Can you do that?'

'Doctor, this sounds like a matter for the FBI.'

Will had considered calling Zwick. The SAC could

have an agent at the Beau Rivage in ten minutes to handle this, if Will would share his plan with the Bureau. But that would put him back under the control of the FBI, which was the last place he wanted to be.

'Can you *technically* do it? he asked. 'Just tell me that. Can you intercept the calls and patch them through?'

'Technically? Yes, we have that capability. But it's not hotel policy to—'

'Forget hotel policy. Let's talk about your personal policy. If you make sure those calls are forwarded to my cell phone for the next three hours – *personally* ensure it – I'll pay you ten thousand dollars.'

'Ten thousand . . . ?'

He had the man's attention. Geautreau was caught between perceived legal risk and flat-out greed.

'Doctor—'

'Let's make it fifteen thousand. Fifteen grand for three hours' work.'

There was a brief silence. Then the manager said, 'Promises are easy to make.'

Will breathed a sigh of relief. All he had to do was set the hook.

'I'd need some security,' Geautreau said. 'Earnest money.'

'Would a thousand dollars cover it?'

'I think that would be sufficient.'

'Connect me to Dr Jackson Everett's room. And stay on the phone after he hangs up.'

'As you say, Doctor.'

The phone rang five times. Will sweated every ring. Then he heard a click, followed by a crash.

'Son of a *bitch*,' said a ragged voice. 'Have a little mercy on a guy.'

'Jack? Wake up.'

'Who is this? Crystal?'

Crystal? Everett's wife was named Mary. 'It's Will Jennings, Jack. Wake up!'

'Will? What's so important it can't wait till a decent hour? I've got the hangover from hell.'

'I'll tell you later. Right now I need you to go downstairs and write the hotel desk manager a check for a thousand dollars.'

'A thousand dollars? What are you talking about?'

'I don't have time to explain. I just need you to do it. It's life or death, Jack.'

'You're bullshitting me, right? What is this?'

'Jack, for God's sake, I need a thousand dollars at the front desk in five minutes. My life depends on it.'

'Your life . . . ? You must have gone gambling last night after all. Did you get into one of those unofficial poker games with this guy?'

'Damn it, Jack!'

'Okay, okay. I'll put it on my Visa.'

'That won't work. It's got to be cash or a check. This is a personal thing with the desk manager. His name's Geautreau.'

'This is a casino, Will. They're dying to give people cash to lose at the tables. I'll handle it. Let me get moving, brush my teeth—'

'*Now*, Jack! The guy's waiting. His name's Geautreau. G-E-A-U-T-R-E-A-U.'

'Are you down at the desk now?'

'I'm a long way from that desk, buddy. This is life or death, no shit. Will you do it?'

'I'm on my way. But you owe me big time.'

'Anything you want. Now hang up. Geautreau's waiting for me.'

'Hey, don't worry. I've got you covered on the money.'

The phone clicked.

'I heard,' said Geautreau.

'Fourteen thousand more where that came from. Write down the number of my cell phone. It's six-oh-one, three-three-two, four-two-one-seven. Read that back to me.'

Geautreau did; the number was correct.

'You can*not* screw this up.'

'Don't worry, Doctor. A pleasure doing business with you.'

Will hung up, threw the Tempo into DRIVE, and headed for the airport.

'Do you really think that will work?' Cheryl asked.

'I'm way past thinking.'

Chapter 19

The sign beside the chain link gate read:

> **WELCOME TO GULFPORT-BILOXI REGIONAL AIRPORT**
> **PRESS INTERCOM BUTTON FOR APPROVAL**
> **AFTER GATE OPENS, PROCEED TO STOP LINE**
> **WAIT FOR GATE TO CLOSE BEHIND YOU**

The sign on the gate itself read:

> **FAILURE TO STOP AND WAIT FOR GATE TO CLOSE IS**
> **PUNISHABLE BY A $10,000 FINE.**

Will pressed the button on the post beside his window and waited.

'Good morning,' said a male voice. 'Welcome to US Aviation Corp. How can we help you?'

'This is Dr Will Jennings. I flew in yesterday in Baron November-Two-Whisky-Juliet. I have a serious emergency. My daughter has been gravely injured in a traffic accident in Jackson, and I must get airborne as soon as possible.'

There was a brief delay. 'Understood, Doctor. We are contacting the tower. Be advised that—'

The voice was drowned by the thunder of jet engines.

'Sorry. The Air National Guard has flight operations in progress, and that might cause some delay. Please wait at the gate, and we'll get back to you ASAP.'

Air National Guard operations. Will didn't like the sound of that, but it explained all the activity in the sky as they had approached the airport.

'How long will they make us wait?' Cheryl asked.

'Shouldn't be long. They do all they can to help you in an emergency.'

The speaker on the post squawked with a sound that made Will think someone had held a telephone up to a radio.

'Doctor Jennings, this is Gulfport Tower. We understand your situation and will do everything we can to expedite your takeoff. Please be advised that the Combat Air Readiness Training Facility is in the middle of a combined operations exercise. We have F-18 Hornets taking off from runway thirty-two, and Army C-130s landing on runway thirty-six. This is a timed exercise, and it cannot be stopped. However, we should have a brief window during which you can depart. We estimate that window to be eleven minutes from now.'

Eleven minutes. They could be halfway to Hazelhurst in eleven minutes. But he had to be careful. If he sounded too upset, they wouldn't open the gate for him.

'I understand, Tower. I contacted ATIS by phone on the way in, and I have the wind conditions. I also have sufficient fuel to reach Jackson. What do you suggest?'

'When the gate opens, proceed to the white line and stop. An employee of US Aviation Corp. will escort you to your plane and assist with your preflight walka-round. We're sorry about your emergency, and will do all we can to expedite. When you reach your aircraft, contact us on 123.7.'

'Thank you, Tower. Much appreciated.'

The gate slid open.

Will pulled up to the white line and put his foot on the brake. He could see his Baron about seventy feet away, parked between a Bonanza and a KingAir.

'We just sit here?' Cheryl asked.

Eleven minutes. Evidence of military operations was all around them. The roar of the departing F-18s shook the nearby buildings like a hurricane, and two more of the sleek fighters were taxiing past only a hundred feet away, on their way to the primary runway. The Hornets lifted into the sky one after another, every thirty seconds. It was hard to believe there were enough fighters at the Gulfport airport to eat up eleven minutes doing this, but perhaps the tower intended to bring them back in just as fast. Will also saw two C-130 transports hanging in the sky to his right, preparing to land on the shorter, general aviation runway.

Ten minutes. He didn't know exactly where he planned to go, but he needed to get there fast. There was no way Hickey was hiding inside the Jackson airport, as Zwick had suggested. Hickey would want to be moving toward the money. And whether he was bound for the cabin near Hazelhurst, the motel in Brookhaven, or the house near McComb did not matter. All three towns lay on a straight line south from

Jackson. Hickey was almost certainly driving south on Interstate 55. At the speed limit, he could reach Hazelhurst in thirty-five minutes, and he could have left the Jackson airport up to twenty minutes ago. By flying northwest at max cruise – and factoring in a delay for automobile traffic in Jackson – Will could probably reach Hazelhurst before him, but it would be a matter of minutes, perhaps even seconds. How he would find Hickey and Karen – or Huey and Abby – once he got there was something he'd have to figure out on the way. What mattered now was getting airborne.

He looked toward the US Aviation Corp. building on his right, but saw no one coming his way. 'Listen,' he said to Cheryl. 'When I give the word, I want you to get out of the car and follow me on foot.'

'Where are we going?'

'To my plane.' He pointed at the Baron. 'It's right over there. If I drive past this white line without permission, all hell will break loose. But if we just walk away, they may not notice a thing.'

'You go,' Cheryl said in a tight voice. 'I'm staying here.'

'What?'

'You don't need me!'

Will started to pull the Walther, but a simpler idea struck him. Cheryl would not separate herself from the money now. He took the briefcase off her lap, got out, and walked briskly toward the plane. Before he was halfway there, he heard the door of the Tempo slam, and the sound of running feet behind him.

'Change your mind?' he said without turning.

'You bastard.'

He opened the Baron's double-wide door, tossed the briefcase between the cabin seats, then turned and helped Cheryl into the plane. She slid between the aft-facing seats and settled into the right-hand seat up front. Will sat down in the left seat, scanned the control panel, then switched on his avionics and started his engines. The twin Continentals rumbled to life with reassuring ardor.

'What's that?' asked Cheryl.

A high-pitched sound was cutting through the engine noise. A siren. Will looked up and saw a boxy airport security vehicle bearing down on them, its red light flashing.

'*Shit*,' He throttled up and pulled forward before the guard in the Cushman could blockade the Baron in the line of parked aircraft. Turning right, he started down the taxiway that paralleled the general aviation runway. The Cushman was following, but it couldn't hope to keep up with the rapidly accelerating airplane.

'Beechcraft November-Two Whiskey Juliet,' crackled the radio. 'This is Gulfport Tower. You are in violation of FARs. Return to the ramp immediately.'

Will increased speed. He had thought he might take off from the taxiway, but he saw now that was impossible. A giant C-130 Hercules transport sat astride the taxiway ahead of him like an alien spacecraft, its four props slowly turning. He would have to taxi beneath the wing of the Hercules and turn onto the next taxiway, which intersected the main runway at 90 degrees.

'Baron Whiskey-Juliet,' said the tower, 'you are

endangering the lives of military aircrew and ground personnel. Cut your engines immediately.'

Cheryl braced in her seat as they rolled toward the Hercules. The sight of the huge spinning props was sobering, but Will held his collision course.

'You're going to hit it!' she shouted. 'Stop!'

He swerved left, buzzed under the left wingtip of the C-130, then slowed for the turn that would carry him onto the next taxiway.

'Tower, this is Delta-Seven-One,' said the radio. 'Who is that crazy son of a bitch?'

That had to be the C-130 pilot. Will was halfway through his turn when another C-130 dropped out of the sky to his right and touched down on the general aviation runway.

'You're going to kill us!' Cheryl shouted.

Will completed his turn, centered the Baron on the taxiway, then stood on his brakes and ran both engines up to full power. His oil pressure looked good, and under the circumstances, that was all he cared about.

Eight hundred feet ahead of him, the F-18s took off without a pause, flashing left to right across his line of sight. They looked like sculpted birds of prey as they screamed into the sky. He had always thought it a sad irony that the most beautiful machines ever built by man were built to kill. But that rule held true in nature as well, so perhaps the 'irony' was merely sentiment getting in the way of reality.

'You can't fly through that!' Cheryl yelled above the engines.

He was going to have to time his takeoff so that the Baron would pass between two of the departing

Hornets, but he felt confident he could do it. This was the last takeoff he would ever be allowed to make from this airport, probably from any airport. It might as well be his best.

'*Is this even a runway?*'

'It is for us.'

'Baron Whiskey-Juliet!' barked the radio. 'You are not, repeat not, cleared for takeoff.'

Will took his feet off the brakes, and the Baron rolled forward with nauseating slowness compared to the jets. As they approached the intersection with the main runway, an F-18 hurtled toward the same point with a roar like a perpetual explosion. Cheryl screamed and covered her eyes, but Will knew the Hornet would be airborne before they reached the runway. He gave the twin Continentals everything he could.

Seconds before they reached the intersection, the F-18 blasted into the blue. Cheryl was still screaming, but Will let himself ride the rush of adrenaline flushing through his system. All the fatigue of the past twenty-four hours had disappeared. After hours of impotence, he was finally *doing* something.

'November Whiskey-Juliet! Cut your engines! You are not cleared for takeoff!'

They crossed the intersection at eighty-five knots.

'November Whiskey-Juliet— God*damn*!'

The Baron rocketed into the air. In seconds it was only a thin cross section against the sky.

Will was banking north at a thousand feet when he sighted the helicopter. It was a mile behind him, but it was moving to cut the angle off his turn. He increased speed and kept climbing, his eye on a bank of cumulus clouds to the northwest.

He had turned down his radio to dampen the sound of the tower, but as they plowed toward the clouds, he detected a new voice competing with that of the furious controller.

'Baron Two-Whiskey-Juliet, this is the helicopter on your starboard side. I am FBI Special Agent John Sims. Be advised that you have committed multiple felonies. Return to the airport immediately. Please acknowledge.'

'Can he catch us?' Cheryl asked.

'Not a chance. We can do two hundred twenty knots, and we've got clouds ahead. He's history.'

'Baron Whiskey-Juliet,' crackled the radio. 'I know you can hear me. I'm patching my Special Agent-in-Charge through on this channel. Stand by.'

Will kept climbing toward the cloud bank, pushing the twin engines as hard as they would go. 'Can you see the chopper?'

'Getting smaller by the second,' Cheryl reported.

'Doctor Jennings,' crackled the radio. 'This is Frank Zwick. You're putting the lives of your wife and daughter at risk by cutting us out. You're going to need backup. Without it, your family will end up dead.'

Will keyed his mike. 'That's a risk I'm prepared to take.'

'At least tell us where you're headed.'

'The best thing you can do right now is get some agents into Brookhaven, Mississippi. Put some more in McComb. I'll call you back.'

He switched off the comm radio, then the transponder, which would normally broadcast his altitude and position to air traffic controllers.

'You've got a bigger problem than that helicopter,' Cheryl said.

'What?'

'You told that guy at the hotel to forward Joey's call through to my cell phone, right? That means that whether Joey tries to call you at the Beau Rivage, or me on my cell phone, he's going to get this phone. How do we decide who answers?'

Will's face suddenly felt cold. How could he have missed it? If Hickey called Cheryl and got 'the hotel' instead, his whole plan would be blown. 'We're all right for ten or fifteen minutes,' he said, thinking aloud. 'I'll answer. I'll say we're stuck in traffic on our way back to the Beau Rivage.'

'And after that?'

'By then we'll be halfway to Hazelhurst.'

'Is that where we're going?'

'North is where we're going right now. That's all we know until Joe calls and tells you something else. Where exactly is this motel you're supposed to go to in Brookhaven?'

'Right by the main exit.'

Brookhaven was twenty miles nearer than Hazelhurst, and Will had once landed there to refuel, but he didn't remember what sort of rental facilities they had. He'd have to wing it.

The Baron shot into the clouds like a stone thrown through a waterfall, and his heart lightened instantly. The FBI chopper couldn't see him now unless it had radar. And if he dropped to treetop level, it would take an air force AWACs with look-down radar to find him. He felt a brief chill as he remembered that Keesler Air Force Base was only a few miles behind them. There might be an AWACs in the air already, on maneuvers, and after his stunt at the Gulfport field, they might be glad to shadow him for the FBI. He needed to get down into the ground clutter as soon as possible.

'What about the house Joe took you to that night?' he asked. 'By McComb. Anything else come to you?'

'No.'

'When the FBI raided the cabin, they found Huey's truck. That means Huey and Abby probably left in another vehicle. Were there any other cars at the cabin?'

'I told you, I never *went* there.'

'But you must have heard them talking.'

'There's a tractor there. I know that. Huey bush-hogs fields for part-time work.'

Will tried to picture Huey and Abby escaping from a SWAT team on a rusty John Deere. It didn't seem likely.

'What else?'

'What do you mean?'

'Think about Joe's family. Cars they've had. Come on . . .'

Cheryl shook her head in exasperation.

In the switchboard center at the Beau Rivage, a young operator sat reading the unabridged version of *The Stand*. When the hotel's main line rang, he answered the way he always did: '*Beau Rivage Casino Resort*'. But when the caller asked for Suite 28021, he punched Alt-Z on his computer, executing a macro set up at the request of Remy Geautreau, the front desk manager. A digital connection was made and a forwarding number dialed. The operator verified that the macro had executed, then went back to his Stephen King novel.

Will jumped when the cell phone rang, but he dug it quickly from his pocket and checked his watch.

'I'm going to answer,' he said. 'If it's Joe, I'll feel out what he expects and play it by ear. Hold the phone up to my ear, and hit SEND when I tell you.'

Cheryl held up the phone, but Will said nothing. He had just realized something. At maximum cruise, the Baron's engines sounded like twin tornadoes, even with the soundproofing. Telling Hickey they were stuck in traffic near the Beau Rivage wouldn't explain the roar. Hickey might even recognize the distinctive sound of airplane engines.

The cell phone kept ringing.

Will had two choices. Throttle the engines back to idle and hope they were quiet enough to be un-detectable over the cell phone, or cut them altogether. Cutting the engines was far more dangerous, but only that would guarantee that Hickey wouldn't hear them.

'Are you going to answer?' Cheryl asked.

Thankful that he had not yet dived for the ground clutter, Will pulled back to idle, feathered his props, and killed both engines. In the eerie silence, the plane began to fall.

'*Shit!*' Cheryl screamed. '*What happened?*'

'Hit SEND.'

Her face was bone-white. '*Are we going to crash?*'

'We're fine! Hit SEND!'

He heard a beep, then the hiss of the open connection. 'Joe!'

'How's it hanging, Doc? You taking a nap up there?'

Up there? Will's heart thudded. Then he realized that Hickey meant the hotel suite. He'd assumed Hickey would call Cheryl before he called the Beau Rivage, to verify that she'd gotten the money. But Hickey had clearly expected Will to answer this call. That meant Geautreau had successfully patched the call. It also meant that the 'stuck in traffic' excuse was useless.

'Where's Abby?' Will asked, trying to picture himself in the suite at the Beau Rivage rather than dropping toward the earth at a thousand feet per minute. 'I want to talk to her.'

'Everything in its season, Doc. I'll be talking to you soon.'

The phone went dead. Will dropped it in Cheryl's lap and began his midair engine-start sequence.

'Start the engines!' she screamed. 'We're crashing!'

He felt a rush of exhilaration as the Continentals kicked off. He adjusted the pitch of his props and felt the plane leap forward as the blades bit into the air.

'Jesus God,' Cheryl whispered, when the nose of the Baron finally came level. 'I almost puked.'

Will began climbing to regain the lost altitude.

'Cheryl, I've got to know what kind of car Huey's driving.'

'If you'd keep the damn engines running, maybe I could think.'

'You think like you've never thought in your life, goddamn it! We're at seven thousand feet. We can glide for seven minutes without engines before we crash. Unless Joe gets talkative, we're fine.'

'Why are you so mean?' she whined, her voice like a child's. 'I'm trying to help you!'

'Try harder.'

The cell phone rang in her lap.

'Who answers this time?' she asked.

'You. He just called me. He's calling you to make sure I gave you the money.'

'What if you're wrong?'

'If he sounds surprised, tell him you came back to the hotel.'

'Why would I do that?'

'I shorted you on the money.'

She nodded.

'And try like hell to find out what Huey's driving.'

'Okay.'

'Wait till I cut the engines.'

'Sweet Mary . . .'

Once again, Will pulled the engines back to idle, feathered his props, and starved the engines into silence.

Cheryl hit SEND as the plane began to glide earthward. 'Joey? . . . Yeah, I've got it.' She gave Will a thumbs up. 'Three hundred and fifty thousand,' she said. 'He tried to bribe me with it . . . Yeah. No problem. I think he's about wasted by the whole thing . . . I'm on 110 now, headed up toward the interstate. Am I still going to the motel?'

Will heard a squawk from the phone, but he couldn't distinguish words.

'Yeah, I remember . . . Uh huh . . . What about Huey and the little girl? . . . Joey, you're not going to hurt that kid, are you?' She jerked the phone away from her ear. 'I'm sorry . . . I know. I will. I'm on my way.'

She clicked off.

Will restarted the engines, and once again the Baron began to climb.

'What did he say about Abby?'

'He told me not to talk about it on the phone.'

'What else did he say?'

'Go to Paco's place.'

'What's that?'

'A club. It's on the county line near Hattiesburg. I danced there for a while. They've got rooms out back for the girls.'

'He said the name of the club on the phone?'

'No. The name of the club is Paradise Alley. Paco just works there. He's tight with Joey.'

Will pulled out a map. He knew Mississippi like the back of his hand, but he wanted to visualize vectors as accurately as he could. I-55 was the main north/south artery, and it bisected the state. Jackson sat in the middle, with Hazelhurst, Brookhaven, and McComb straight south of it. Hattiesburg was on a diagonal, southeast of Jackson, down Highway 49. It was much closer to their present position, but there was no way he could cover both I-55 and Highway 49. And the fact that Cheryl had been told to go to Paco's place didn't mean Hickey was going straight there, or that Huey had been given the same instructions.

'Son of a bitch,' Cheryl said.

'What?'

'The Rambler!'

'What?'

She was smiling at something. 'Joey's mom had an AMC Rambler. An old white thing with push-button gears. It was the club that made me think of it. Paradise Alley. Joey's mom got to where she couldn't drive, and one night Joey showed up at Paradise Alley in her car. When we tried to leave, it broke down. We had to hitch. It supposedly sat up on blocks for a couple of years, but I never saw it. I was with Huey once when he went to Auto Shack to buy parts for it. Maybe the Rambler was at the cabin.' She shook her head. 'I haven't thought about that car in three years!'

Will couldn't suppress his excitement anymore. At last, he had something. A white Rambler. And Abby might be in it. But where was it? 'The FBI found a cell phone and a landline at the cabin,' he reasoned aloud. 'The landline was Joe's backup for Huey. So, unless Huey had *two* cell phones, Joe can't contact him while he's on the road.'

'I'm pretty sure Huey only had one,' Cheryl said. 'But the Rambler could have a phone, couldn't it?'

'It could. Does Huey know about Paradise Alley? Has he ever been there?'

She laughed. 'Are you kidding? You can't take Huey to a titty bar. One glimpse of a naked woman, he blows a gasket. Joey brought him to see me dance once, and he jumped up on stage trying to throw his coat over me. It took four bouncers to get him down.'

'But that wasn't Paradise Alley.'

'No.'

'Has Huey ever met this Paco guy?'

'No way. Joey keeps him away from all that stuff.'

'Has he spent any time in or around Hattiesburg?'

'Not that I know of.'

'Then Huey isn't headed for Paco's place. He's probably going wherever he was supposed to go according to the original backup plan. Joe changed your instructions on the fly, but I don't think he'd do that to Huey. So, what was Huey's original backup destination? Where would Joe have told him to go if there was a problem?'

Cheryl chewed her bottom lip as she considered the question. 'Joey wouldn't want him driving too far. Not with your little girl along. Too much chance of the highway patrol stopping him.'

'Did Joe say *anything* about Huey during that last call?'

'Just that he would be fine.'

'I think Huey's going to the motel in Brookhaven. It's only twenty minutes from Hazelhurst, which makes it less than an hour from the cabin. Joe could get there from Jackson in fifty minutes, pick up Huey and Abby, then head east to Hattiesburg to meet you.'

'Makes sense to me.'

'If I'm right, Joe is driving south on I-55 right now. Huey is, too. They're probably twenty minutes apart in the southbound lanes. To hell with Highway 49.'

Will gripped the yoke with both hands and put the

Baron into a steep dive. He would turn west after he dropped below radar level. He wanted to be over I-55 as soon as possible, but he didn't want any curious air-traffic controllers to see him getting there.

Karen looked into the trunk of the Camry and put her hand to her mouth. The woman Hickey had carjacked had beaten her hands bloody in her attempts to get out of the trunk. Several fingers were broken. The left side of her head was swollen from the pistol blow, and her eyes had the dull sheen of shock. She looked up at Karen like she expected to be raped and left for dead.

'Get out,' Karen said. 'Hurry! Before he changes his mind.'

Hickey was sitting in the Camry, talking on the cell phone, checking on Will. At Karen's urging, he had pulled off the interstate at a deserted exit to let the woman out of the trunk. But the owner of the Camry clearly didn't understand the chance she was being given, because she wasn't moving.

'Come on!' Karen hissed. She reached in and pulled the woman up by the arms. Slowly, like a sleepwalker waking, the woman began to jerk her arms, but whether to assist Karen or to fight her, Karen couldn't tell. Somehow she got the woman clear of the trunk and on her feet.

She was a pretty brunette, with a hint of Asian ancestry around her eyes, and she wore a blue skirt suit much like Karen's. But her eyes were blank.

Karen pushed her toward the trees on the side of the road. 'Run! Go on! Run!'

The woman looked around. The only sign of civilization was a boarded up gas station. 'Are you going to leave me here?' she asked.

'You're safer here than you are with us. Go!'

Like a zoo-bred animal that finds its cage left open, the woman seemed reluctant to leave the familiarity of her car.

'If you don't run,' Karen told her, 'you're going to die.'

The woman began to cry.

In the switchboard center at the Beau Rivage, the operator was heavy into *The Stand*. Trashcan Man was hauling his nuclear weapon toward the Dark Man's stronghold, and trivialities like gainful employment simply could not compete. The young man answered the primary line on autopilot, and when the caller asked for suite 28021, he said, 'Just one moment' as he usually did, and made the connection.

Twenty-eight floors above him, the phones in Will's suite rang, faded, and rang again. The operator read another paragraph of Trashcan Man's journey, then blinked and raised his head from the page. He was certain that something was wrong, he just couldn't place what it was. It took a few seconds to realize his mistake, but he thought he still had time to correct it. He was reaching for the keyboard to execute the call-forwarding macro when the phones in 28021 stopped ringing.

'Shit,' he whispered. '*Shit.*'

Remy Geautreau had promised him a hundred

bucks if he'd forward the suite's calls for the next three hours. He punched a code that connected him to the desk manager's office.

Remy Geautreau was not in his office. He was standing at the front desk, listening to an irate guest who had left a camcorder battery in his room after checkout. Housekeeping had already checked twice for it, but the guest refused to believe they hadn't found it. At the first brief pause, a clerk stepped up and said, 'Mr Geautreau? You have a phone call.'

'I want to talk to the maid myself!' bellowed the guest.

Geautreau gave him a syrupy smile. 'But of course, Mr Collins. Do you speak Spanish?'

The man went purple. 'Goddamn it!' He took his wife by the arm and stomped toward the grand entrance to make his exit.

'He lost eight thousand last night,' Geautreau said with a bemused smile. 'You can always tell the losers.'

He went into his office and picked up the phone. 'Hello?'

'I screwed up,' said the operator. 'With the call forwarding thing.'

Geautreau's face darkened.

'A call came in for the suite, and before I could think, I put it through. I tried to catch it, but I was too late. They hung up.'

The manager closed his eyes and hung up. 'You just cost me fifteen thousand dollars, you incompetent ass.'

As he closed the door of his office, he wondered

whether the doctor would let him keep the thousand dollars of earnest money. Of course he wouldn't.

The Baron roared northward above Interstate 55 at two hundred knots. Will didn't think they had covered enough distance to sight Huey's Rambler yet – if in fact he was driving the Rambler – but he was flying parallel to the southbound lanes just in case. Cheryl was glued to the passenger window. The traffic below was moderate but steady, the cars and trucks humming along at seventy-five miles per hour while Will shot past them at three times that.

He was about to cut his airspeed when the cell phone began ringing again. From habit he reached for the throttles; then he stopped himself. If he cut the engines at three hundred feet, the state police would soon be hosing them off the interstate.

'Who answers it?' Cheryl asked.

'You.'

'Joey already told me where to go. He wouldn't call again.'

Will considered not answering at all, but he couldn't risk it. He pulled the throttles back as far as he dared, then picked up the Nokia and hit SEND.

'Hello?'

He heard only the open connection. Then someone said, 'Jennings?'

'Joe?'

More silence.

'Joe? Are you there?'

'You wanna tell me how I dialed Cheryl and got you, you clever son of a bitch?'

Will gripped the phone tighter but kept his voice calm. 'You must have dialed the wrong number. You thought you were dialing her, but you dialed the hotel instead.'

Hickey didn't reply.

'Joe?'

'Put Cheryl on the phone.'

Will's breath caught in his throat. 'How do I do that?'

'You hand her the fucking phone, that's how.'

The coldness of Hickey's voice was worse than any blast of temper. 'Joe, I'm telling you—'

'No, I'm telling *you*, Doc. I'm gonna let you in on a little secret. You're never going to talk to your kid again.'

Will's face went numb.

'It was always going to be that way,' Hickey said. 'It had to be. It's predestination. From the day you murdered my mother. You took what was precious to me, so I gotta take what's precious to you. You see that, right?'

'Where is she, Joe? Where's Abby?'

'You don't need to worry about that. In fact, if I was you, I'd go ahead and slit my wrists, to save myself the hell that's coming. Going down to a funeral home to pick out that tiny little casket? Facing your wife after going off and leaving her like that? What kind of father does that, huh?'

Hickey's words cut to the bone, but something more

terrible struck Will like a hammer. There was no way Hickey could speak that way if Karen were in the car with him. She would be screaming at the least, possibly even trying to kill him.

'Where's Karen, Joe? I know she's not with you. What have you done to her?'

'You don't need to worry about that either. No point at all.'

The numbness began to spread along his arms. It was like being cut adrift in space, lost in a vacuum without air or sound.

'Wherever you are,' Hickey said, 'you might as well just stay there. See if Cheryl will give you a little head while you shoot yourself. She's good at it. Oh, and tell her I'll be seeing her soon. *Real* soon.'

'Joe, you've got the wrong idea. I don't know where Cheryl is. I kept the phone because—'

The phone went dead in his hand.

Will tasted blood. He had bitten through his bottom lip.

'What's the matter?' Cheryl asked in a fearful voice. 'What just happened?'

He couldn't speak.

'He knows, doesn't he? He knows we're together.'

'I think he killed Karen. And he's going to kill Abby.'

'What? You're crazy.'

Will's hands began to shake.

Karen closed the Camry's trunk and looked back over her shoulder. The woman was moving now, making for the abandoned gas station at an ungainly trot. Karen wished she would turn toward the trees, because Hickey could easily drive over and shoot her if he changed his mind about letting her go. Hopefully he had too much on his mind to worry about that.

Karen walked to the passenger door and climbed in beside him. Hickey was off the phone. He was just sitting there, staring through the windshield.

'Did you talk to Will?'

He fished a Camel out of his pocket and lit it with the cigarette lighter. 'I talked to him.'

'What did he say?'

'It's not what he said. It's where he said it. He wasn't in his suite.'

She felt a stab of alarm. 'What?'

'He answered Cheryl's cell phone. I told you he was pulling something.' Hickey turned and let the hatred in his eyes burn into her. 'You just remember, he asked for every bit of this.'

Hickey put the Camry into DRIVE, spun it in a 180-degree turn, and sped back up to the interstate. His cheeks reddened as he drove, but his lips only grew paler.

'Call the Beau Rivage again,' Karen pleaded. 'There must be some mistake!'

'Oh, there's a mistake, all right. But it doesn't matter.'

He said this forcefully, but he didn't look like he quite believed it.

Karen reached out and touched him softly on the arm. '*Please* tell me what's happening.'

Hickey backhanded her across the face.

'Don't you touch me again.'

Will reduced his airspeed to a hundred knots. They were far enough north now that spotting Huey and Abby driving south was a possibility. It was more than that, in fact. It was his only hope. The greater part of him believed that Karen was dead. There was no way she could have sat silently by while Hickey explained why he had to kill Abby. It was possible she was tied and gagged, but he doubted that scenario. With Abby under his control, Hickey didn't need such measures to make Karen cooperate.

His prayer now was that Hickey had no way to contact Huey while he was out on the road. That Abby would remain alive for the next fifteen or twenty minutes, while Will tried to locate her from the air.

'I'm dead,' Cheryl mumbled for the twentieth time. She was hugging herself and rocking like a heroin addict going cold turkey.

'Sit up!' Will shouted. 'Look for the Rambler!'

She leaned forward and looked at her knees.

He shoved the yoke forward. The busy interstate rushed up to meet them. In seconds, power pylons and oak trees rose higher than the Baron.

'*Pull up!*' she screamed, going rigid in her seat. '*Pull up!*'

At the last instant, Will pulled back on the yoke and began skimming along beside the southbound lanes. Cars slowed as their drivers gaped at the low-flying airplane. From eighty feet you could see individual faces, chattering mouths, pointing fingers. Most of the car passengers probably thought he was a crop duster, albeit a crazy one.

'You look for that Rambler, or I'll flip this thing on its back until you vomit.'

She pressed her face to the Plexiglas. 'I'm looking!'

Will switched on his radio. He had just thought of a way in which the FBI might help him after all.

'Baron November Two-Whiskey-Juliet,' crackled the speaker. 'Baron Whiskey-Juliet, this is an emergency call. Please respond.'

It was a little too soon to be hearing from the FAA about his treetop run over I-55. He keyed his mike.

'This is Baron Whiskey-Juliet, over.'

There was a brief silence. Then a voice said, 'Dr Jennings, this is Frank Zwick.'

Will shook his head. The FBI man didn't give up easily, he had to give him that. There was no telling how long they had been making that radio call. Ever since he switched off his radio, probably.

'Doctor, we intercepted part of that last cell phone transmission. We heard what Hickey said about your daughter.'

Will didn't respond.

'Where are you, Jennings? Let us help you.'

'Where I am doesn't matter.' He kept his eyes on the interstate to his right. 'Tell me one thing. Did you ever figure out how Hickey escaped from the airport?'

'We're pretty sure he carjacked a Toyota Camry from a woman who arrived in the garage at the same time he and your wife did.'

'What color was it?'

'A silver ninety-two model. We got it off the garage security tapes. We just had the Highway Patrol put out a BOLO on it.'

'Could you answer one question for me?'

'What is it?'

Will steeled himself. 'Has my wife's body turned up anywhere?'

'No. We have no reason to believe that your wife has been injured. Doctor, we need to know where you are. We can't—'

Will switched off the radio.

'Have you seen anything?' he asked Cheryl.

'I'm looking,' she assured him. 'I've seen every other kind of car, but no Rambler.'

'Scan, don't focus. If you see anything that looks remotely like it, sing out. I'll come around with the flow of traffic.'

'Is that Brookhaven over there?'

'Where?'

She pointed east. 'Yonder way.'

'Yes.'

'Hey!' she cried. 'There's the motel! That's the Trucker's Rest! Right by the exit.'

'Can you see the parking lot?'

'We're too far away.'

Will didn't think Huey could have reached the motel yet, but he couldn't afford to pass it by without a look. He pushed the engines harder and circled back to check the parking lot. Skipping the Baron over a cellular transmission tower, he floated past the exit ramp and dropped over the parking lot of the Trucker's Rest like a seagull looking for scraps.

'No Rambler,' Cheryl said.

Will shot back over the interstate and resumed his course parallel to the southbound lanes coming out of Jackson. He saw Tauruses, Lexuses, SUVs by the dozen, semi-trucks, Winnebagos, and motorcycles. But no Rambler.

'Be right,' he said softly, holding the image of a Rambler in his mind. '*Be right.*'

'Oh my God,' Cheryl said, which sometimes seemed the sum total of her vocabulary.

'What is it?'

She was staring down at the interstate with her mouth hanging open.

'*What?*'

'I saw it.'

'The Rambler?'

She turned to him and nodded, her eyes wide.

'Are you positive?'

'It was them. I saw Huey's face. I saw your little girl in the passenger window.'

Will suddenly found it difficult to breathe. He craned his neck to look back, but the spot was far behind them now. Climbing skyward, he pulled the Baron around in a turn so tight the nose could have kissed the tail.

'What are you going to do?' Cheryl asked.

'Make another pass. You make damned sure it's them. And belt yourself in.'

'Oh my God.'

Chapter 20

'Let me tell you something about revenge,' Hickey said.

He and Karen were twenty-five miles south of Jackson, and his mood seemed to improve with every mile. She could see anticipation in the way he leaned into the wheel as he drove. She looked through her window. A long field of cotton was giving way to a field of house trailers. PREFABRICATED HOUSING! blared the banner hanging over the lot's entrance. GET A DOUBLE-WIDE DELUXE TODAY!

'You remember what you asked me this morning?' Hickey asked.

'What?'

'Would I kill you instead of your kid?'

Karen nodded cautiously. Hickey was fond of games. Like a cruel child teasing a wounded animal, he liked to probe her with a sharp stick and watch her squirm.

'You still want it that way? If somebody has to die, I mean?'

'Yes.'

He nodded thoughtfully, as though considering a philosophical argument. 'And you think that would do the trick? Your dying would hurt your husband enough to pay him back for killing my mother?'

'Will didn't kill your mother.' *But someone should have*, she thought. *Before she birthed you, you son of a bitch.*

'See, I don't think it would,' Hickey said. 'Hurt him that much, I mean. And the reason is interesting. See, you're not his blood.'

She refused to look at him.

'If you died, he might miss you for a while. But the fact is, you're just his wife. He can get another one. Damn easy, with all the money he's got. A lot newer model, too. Hell, he might be tired of you already.'

Karen said nothing.

'But your little girl, now, that's different. That's blood of his blood. That's *him*, the same way Mama and me were joined. And nearly six, that's old enough for him to really know her. He loves that kid. Light of his life.'

At last she turned to him. 'What are you telling me? Are you saying you're going to kill Abby?'

He smiled. 'I'm just explaining a concept to you. Hypothetically. Showing you what's wrong with your idea from this morning.'

'This morning you told me I didn't need to worry about that. You said nobody was going to die.' *And somebody already has*, she reminded herself, thinking of Stephanie.

Hickey tapped the wheel like a man content. 'Like I said. Hypothetically.'

As soon as Will completed his turn and settled the Baron back over the oncoming traffic, he saw the small white car Cheryl had seen. Box-shaped and splotched with primer, it was piddling along compared to the other traffic, constantly being passed on the left. Cheryl was right: it was a Rambler. Will reduced power, slowing the plane until it was practically drifting up the interstate toward the car.

Then he saw it.

A small head in the passenger compartment of the Rambler, sitting close to a huge figure behind the wheel. A figure so large that it seemed to dwarf the car itself. The child was moving in the front seat, and as the Baron closed on the Rambler, Will made out the form and face he would have known by the dimmest candle-light. A relief unlike anything he had ever known rolled through him. Abby was alive. She was alive, and nothing on God's earth would keep him from her now.

'Hello, Alpha-Juliet,' he said softly. He waggled his wings once, then again.

'What are you *doing*?' Cheryl wailed as the plane rocked left and right like a roller coaster. 'I'm going to puke!'

'Waggling my wings,' he said with a smile.

Huey and Abby were singing 'The Itsy-Bitsy Spider' when the airplane first appeared. It was flying straight toward them at treetop level, just to the right of the interstate.

'Look!' Huey cried. 'A crop duster!'

'He's not supposed to fly that low,' Abby said in a concerned voice. 'I know, because my daddy flies an airplane.'

The plane shot past them. Abby whipped her head around and watched it climb, then vanish beyond her line of sight.

'I rode a airplane once,' Huey said. 'When Joey took me to Disneyland.'

'You mean Disney World.'

'No, they got two. The old one's in California. That's the one we went to. Joey says they're both the same, but I think the one in Florida's bigger.'

'I think so, too.' Abby patted Belle in her lap. 'I met the real Belle there. And the real Snow White.'

'The real ones?'

'Uh-huh. And I got dresses just like they had.'

Huey's smile disappeared. He reached into the side pocket of his coveralls, fished around, then brought out his empty hand.

'If I made you something,' he said softly, 'would you like it?'

'Sure I would.'

'It probably wouldn't be near as nice as all the things you got at home.'

'Sure it would. Presents you make are always better than ones you buy.'

He seemed to weigh her sincerity about this. Then he reached back into the pocket and brought out what he had spent the previous night carving.

Abby opened her mouth in wonder. 'Where did you get that?'

'I made it for you.'

'You *made* that?'

What had been a chunk of cedar the day before had been transformed by Huey's knife into a figure of a bear holding a little girl on its lap. The fine detail made Abby's Barbie look like a bland store mannequin. The little girl on the bear's lap had hair falling to her shoulders like Abby's, wore a jumper like hers, and held a small doll in her hands. But what riveted Abby's attention was the bear itself. It wore no clothes, but on its face sat a pair of heavy glasses, just like Huey's. The bear was clearly watching out for the little girl.

'You really made that?' she asked again.

Huey nodded shyly. 'Beauty and the Beast. You said it was your favorite. I tried to make it as pretty as I could. I know you like pretty things.'

She took the carving from his hand. The wood was still warm from Huey's pocket. But more than that, it felt *alive* somehow. Hard and soft at the same time. As though the bear and the little girl might move in her hands at any moment.

'I love it,' she said. 'I *love* it.'

Huey's eyes lit up. 'You do?'

Abby nodded, her eyes still on the figures.

'Maybe you'll remember me sometimes, then.'

She looked up at him with curiosity in her eyes. 'Of course I will.'

Huey suddenly cried out and hit the brake pedal. Abby grabbed the dashboard, fearing they were about to smash into something.

'He's going to crash!' Huey yelled.

The airplane was back, only this time it was right over the road and zooming straight at them. The cars ahead were slowing down, some even pulling onto the shoulder. The plane skated to Abby's right, toward the trees, but it was getting larger every second. As she stared, its wings rocked up and down: first the right wing, then the left, then both again.

A strange thrill went through her. 'He wiggled his wings!'

The plane's engines began to overpower the sound of the car. Its pilot rocked the wings again, as though waving right at Abby, then rocketed over the car. She clapped her hands with delight.

'My daddy does that! Just the same way! My daddy . . .'

Her face suddenly felt hot, and she had to squeeze her legs together to keep from wetting herself. Her daddy was in that plane. She knew it. And nothing in her life had ever felt quite the way that knowing that did. She reached out and touched Huey's arm.

'I think everything's going to be okay now.'

As the Baron blasted past the Rambler, Will saw Abby's face pressed to the glass of the passenger window. Tears temporarily blinded him.

'I told you!' Cheryl cried. 'You saw them?'

'Yes,' he said, wiping his eyes with his sleeve.

'What are you going to do now?'

'I'm going to land.'

'On the *road*?'

'Absolutely.'

Cheryl's face went so white that Will thought she might pass out.

'Tighten that seat belt.'

As she scrabbled at her belt, Will climbed to five

hundred feet and took the Baron to a hundred and eighty knots.

'Where are you going? You said you were going to land. You're leaving them behind.'

'We've got something to do first. I want you to watch for a silver Camry.'

Cheryl's hand flew to her mouth. She had heard Zwick on the radio, and she knew who was driving a silver Camry.

'Keep it together,' Will said. 'Everything's fine.'

He hated to let the Rambler out of his sight for even one minute, but he could cover five miles of interstate in ninety seconds, and if Hickey was close enough to give him problems on the ground, he needed to know.

'When you land,' Cheryl said, 'what about the cars and stuff? I mean, there's eighteen-wheelers down there.'

'I'll try not to hit them.'

'Jesus Christ. How did I get here?'

'Joe Hickey put you here. It's that simple.'

'I see a Camry! It's silver. It's the old kind, the swoopy one that looks like a Lexus.'

Zwick had said the car Hickey stole was a '92 model. Will was pretty sure the '92 Camry was the 'swoopy' one, not the more generic model. He climbed quickly to a thousand feet. He would have liked nothing better than to descend and see whether Karen was in that car, but if he got close enough to see her, Hickey could spot him. The silver Camry below might not be the one Hickey had stolen – there were a lot of silver Camrys in the world – but it could be. He needed to get on the ground fast.

409

He executed a teardrop turn, pointed the Baron south at two hundred knots, and began to consider the task he had set himself.

There was really only one way to stop a car with an unarmed airplane. Land in front of it. That left him two choices. He could fly past the Rambler, then turn and land against the oncoming traffic, which would greatly increase the odds of killing himself and a lot of other people. Or he could fly along with the flow of traffic – as he was doing now – match his speed to that of the cars below, and drop down into the first open stretch he saw ahead of the Rambler.

'There it is!' Cheryl said, pointing through the wind-shield.

She had good eyes. About a mile and a half ahead, a long line of cars had backed up behind a slow moving vehicle in the right lane, while faster moving traffic shot past them on the left.

Will cut his airspeed and dropped to four hundred feet. The vehicles below were moving between seventy and eighty miles per hour. At ninety knots, he was rapidly overtaking them, but also moving into position to land in front of the Rambler. As he approached the congested line of cars, he lowered his landing gear and went to full flaps. This further reduced his speed, bringing him more in line with the speed of the vehicles below, though he was still overtaking them.

When he descended to a hundred feet, fear announced itself in the pit of his stomach. This was no deserted stretch of Delta highway. This was I-55, where cars and trucks managed to slam into each other every day without the help of rogue airplanes. He could smell the exhaust of the big diesel trucks below. From this altitude they looked like aircraft carriers on a concrete sea.

Airspeed was eighty-five knots, still too fast. He would have given a lot for a cold winter day, good dense air for the propellers to bite into and to keep his stall speed low. This was the worst weather for what he was about to do. Cheryl leaned forward, watching the concrete rise toward them and endlessly repeating Hail Marys. Apparently, if she was going to die, she wanted to see it coming. A perverse instinct, perhaps, but a human one.

'Can you do it?' she asked softly.

A brief crosswind tried to push the tail around, but Will corrected for it. 'We're about to find out.'

She pointed through the windshield. 'There they are!'

He shut everything out of his mind but the scene ahead. In the right lane: the white Rambler, moving slowly, seeming to pull an endless chain of cars along behind it, cars which were actually trying to whip into the left lane so that they could pass the cars holding them back. In the left lane: the fast movers, cars and trucks racing up and passing the sideshow in the right lane at eighty miles per hour. In front of the Rambler, where he needed to set down, were the speeding cars in the left lane and a couple of dawdlers in the right. A Mercury Sable about sixty yards ahead of the Rambler, and a minivan some distance ahead of that. An intricate ballet of mechanical dancers that would remain in their present relationships for a very brief time.

It was now or never.

He centred the Baron on the broken white line and dropped toward the roof of the Rambler at eighty-two knots. He couldn't see what was happening behind him, but he felt sure that the sight of a twin-engine plane dropping toward the road with its gear and flaps down and a wingspan as wide as the interstate had sent a lot of feet to a lot of brake pedals.

The Baron overtook the Rambler with a speed differential of thirty miles per hour. Will flew half the distance to the Mercury Sable, then eased the yoke forward and reduced power further. The Baron seemed to stutter in midair, as though he had applied the brakes to a car.

Then it fell like a stone.

Three miles behind the Baron, Hickey gaped and pointed through the windshield of the stolen Camry.

'Look at that crazy son of a bitch! If he's got to crash, the least he could do is get off the highway to do it.'

Karen said nothing. The instant the Baron had dropped out of the sky and lined itself up over the interstate, her heart had jumped into her throat. It had to be Will. It *had* to be.

'What's he doing up there?' Hickey wondered aloud. 'He's a kamikaze, this guy. He must have lost an engine.'

He looked to Karen for a response, but she sat still and silent, staring at the dashboard. If Will was risking his life to land on the interstate, that could mean only one thing. Abby was somewhere up ahead. And she was alive.

'What's with you?' Hickey said. 'You gotta see this. This'll make CNN tonight.' He punched her on the shoulder. 'You sick or something? Why are you . . .'

He faced forward again and watched the plane drop to the level of the cars ahead, then disappear.

'Son of a bitch,' he said. 'Son of a *bitch*!' He floored the accelerator and started to pass the Cadillac ahead of them.

Karen grabbed the wheel and wrenched it toward her, throwing the Camry into the right lane and driving the Cadillac off the road in a cloud of dust.

'Let go!' Hickey yelled, hammering her head with his fist.

Karen clung to the wheel like a sea captain in a gale. The Camry veered onto the shoulder, which dropped precipitously to the woods below. She didn't care if they flipped three times and crashed into the trees, so long as it kept Hickey from reaching Abby. She had made that decision hours ago.

'*Let go, you crazy bitch!*'

He slammed an elbow into her ear and yanked the car back onto the road. Karen blacked out for a moment. She knew she had, because when she came to, her hands had slipped from the wheel, and the Camry's engine was whining as Hickey streaked past the cars ahead. She saw then that he was steering with only his left hand. His right held Will's .38, and it was pointed at her stomach.

'Do it again and I'll kill you,' he said in a matter-of-fact voice.

413

She backed against the passenger door.

As the speedometer needle went to ninety, then a hundred, Karen studied the gun in Hickey's hand. It was somehow more frightening than the idea of a wreck. A wreck at this speed would certainly kill them both, but the gun might kill only *her*. And Abby was so close—

Hickey cursed and applied the brake. A long chain of flashing red lights had appeared ahead. Brake lights. Something was happening up there. And that something had to be Will's plane. Hickey swerved across the left lane onto the median shoulder and raced past the braking cars. The hatred in his face was like a sulfurous fire burning beneath his skin.

Fixing an image of Abby in her mind, Karen began to pray. The image she saw was not Abby as she was now, but as an infant, the miracle of flesh and bone and smiling eyes that Karen had given up her career for, that she would give up everything for. A profound sadness seeped outward from her heart, but with it came a peace that transcended her fear. In the silence of her mind, words from Ecclesiastes came to her, heard long ago but never quite forgotten. *There is a time to kill, and a time to die.* She closed her eyes.

'I love you, Abby,' she said softly. 'I'm sorry, Will.'

'What?' Hickey said, fighting to keep the Camry moving past the bumper-to-bumper cars.

Karen curled her fingers into claws and launched herself across the console with murder in her heart.

Hickey fired.

*   *   *

414

The Baron hit the concrete hard, and Will's plan instantly began to disintegrate. The driver of the Sable must have slowed, because the Baron was racing toward it far too fast to stop. Will hit the throttles and hopped over the car like a student pilot practising a touch-and-go landing. When the wheels hit again, he saw that the minivan which had been comfortably ahead of the Sable had also braked, probably because the vehicles ahead of it had slowed or stopped to watch the crisis unfolding behind them.

He pulled up his flaps, cut power, and applied the brakes, but he saw in an instant that he wouldn't be able to stop in time. He no longer had enough power or distance to skip over the minivan, as he had the Rambler, and his props were spinning with enough force to chop the van into scrap metal. Yet the driver wouldn't get off the damned road to avoid the crash. Like Will, he was blocked by the wooded hill of the median on the left and the steep drop into woods on the right. But either would be preferable to being hit by an airplane. Then Will saw the group of heads in the back of the van.

Kids.

He swerved left and shut off his mixture, fuel, and master electrical switch. He felt a moment of euphoria as they passed the van, but it turned to horror as his right wingtip clipped the vehicle and they began to spin.

Time deccelerated with sickening slowness. Cheryl was shrieking, and at some point in the whirling chaos Will saw a log truck barreling up from behind them. Sitting in front of the log truck like a Matchbox toy was the white Rambler. The Baron's nose gear crumpled as the plane spun, and one of the props hit the cement in a storm of sparks, sending a blade hurtling off into space. As they came around to face the Rambler again, Will saw the little car suddenly scoot forward out of the log truck's path, but his relief died as it went over the narrow shoulder and plummeted down the slope toward the trees.

'We've got to get out!' he shouted, gripping Cheryl's arm.

The plane had come to rest facing north, and the thirty-ton juggernaut of steel and wood that was the log truck was speeding toward them with the sound of burning brakes. Will unbuckled both seat belts, then leaned over Cheryl and unlatched the door.

'Get out!' he shouted.

But she didn't. She was trying to look back into the cabin. Will scrambled over her and onto the wing, then pulled her from the cockpit. She was yelling something at him, but he shoved her onto the ground and jumped off after her.

'*The money!*' she screamed. '*We left the money!*'

'Forget it!' He grabbed her arm and tried to pull her clear, but she jerked free and jumped back onto the wing.

Will ran for the edge of the road.

As the Rambler hurtled down the grassy slope toward the trees, Huey pumped the brake, but it seemed to have no effect. Abby was screaming in his ear, and he saw the screams like red paint on the air. His mind went blank for a second, but then a thought flashed like a Roman candle. He grabbed Abby with both hands and tossed her into the backseat like a sack of flour.

The Rambler tore through an old fence and crashed into a wall of saplings, hurling Huey's three-hundred-pound body forward and smashing his head against the windshield. Abby smacked into the back of the front seat and bounced backward.

She couldn't seem to get her breath, but other than that, she felt okay. She got to her knees and looked over the front seat.

The windshield was smashed to pieces. Huey was bleeding from his forehead, and he wasn't moving.

'Huey?' she said. 'Beast?'

Suddenly he moaned and held his ribs. Abby climbed over the seat and took hold of his right hand. 'Wake up, Beast.' She shook the hand again, then pinched it. 'Can you talk? Daddy didn't mean to hurt you!'

A loud boom sounded behind her, followed by a *whoomph* that made the air around the car glow for several seconds. Terror for her father went through her like a knife.

'Beast? Wake up!'

His right eye blinked, and he groaned in pain. 'Run,' he whispered.

'You're hurt.'

'Run, Jo Ellen,' he said in a raspy voice. 'I smell gas. And there's a bad man coming. Run to Daddy.'

Jo Ellen? And then she remembered. Huey's little sister was named Jo Ellen. Abby looked down at the floor. Belle and the carved bear and child lay in a mosaic of shattered glass. She picked up Belle and put her in Huey's lap, then grabbed the bear and climbed out of the passenger door. She wished she could pull Huey out, but trying to pull Huey would be like trying to pull a mountain. She turned away from the car and looked up the steep hill.

A chill of fear made her shiver.

A tall man was looking down at her out of the sun. She couldn't see his face, only his silhouette. Then the shape of the man stirred something in her.

'Daddy?' she said hesitantly.

The shadow began running down the hill.

Cheryl crawled off the shoulder and onto the grass of the median. Her knees were cut to pieces. Her hair stank of gasoline, her eyelashes were gone, and her left forearm had a big red blister on it.

But she had the money.

Behind her lay what was left of the plane, a burning mass of twisted metal in the wake of a log truck that had only managed to stop a few seconds ago. A mile-long line of cars had stacked up behind the wrecked plane, and dozens of people were coming forward, gawkers and rubberneckers in the lead.

Cheryl coughed up black smoke, and the spasm hurt like a wire brush raked over the inside of her rib cage. She thought she might have breathed fire during the explosion. What the hell. It was a small price to pay.

She flattened her hands on the grass and got to her feet, then picked up the blackened briefcase and started up into the trees.

*　　*　　*

Karen lay against the passenger door of the Camry, staring at the small hole in her upper abdomen. Hickey was gone. He'd shot her and left her for dead. She couldn't tell how badly she was wounded. Abdominal wounds were tricky. They could kill you in five minutes or put you through weeks of hell. In any case, the gunshot had been enough to knock her against the door and keep her off of Hickey while he raced after Will's plane.

Through the windshield she saw cars in front of her and cars behind. But no plane. She'd heard an explosion a few moments before, one she hoped was a car wreck and not Will's Baron. But it could have been Will. Landing on a busy interstate was Evel Knievel stuff. And if something had happened to Will, Abby might be alone up there with Hickey and the others.

Karen opened the Camry's glove box, found a wad of Kleenex, and stuffed it into the bullet hole. Then, steeling herself against the pain, she forced herself to turn and pop open the Camry's door.

Falling half onto the road, she decided to let her legs follow. After they did, she rolled onto her stomach and lay there, annoyed by the numbness of her midsection. Getting up seemed a theoretical impossibility, like surpassing the speed of light. Then the smell of burning aviation fuel reached her, and she changed her mind.

Will angled down the hill toward Abby, pumping his legs like an extreme skier in a barely controlled fall.

Abby took several steps up the shoulder, her eyes bright.

'I knew you'd come, Daddy!'

He snatched her up and hugged her as tight as he dared.

'Where's Mom?' she asked. 'Is Mom with you?'

He had no answer. 'Come on, sweetie. Let's find her.'

'Wait. Huey's hurt.'

'What?'

'He's stuck in the car. He's bleeding!'

Will didn't especially want to help Abby's kidnapper, but he moved close enough to the Rambler to see that the man was badly hurt. The tang of gasoline was in the air. If the car caught fire, he'd be burned alive.

'Help him, Daddy!'

Will set Abby down and ran to the driver's door. It had not been jammed shut in the crash, but Huey was most definitely jammed behind the wheel. He weighed over three hundred pounds, and Will could scarcely budge him.

'*Huey!*' he yelled. 'Help me! *Move!*'

The man's left forearm was like a ham. Will grabbed it with both hands and pulled with all his strength. With a groan like an annoyed bull, Huey twisted in the seat and heaved himself out onto the ground. There was just enough slope for Will to roll him down and away from the car. That was all he could do.

'Let's go find Mom!' Abby called.

He had told Abby they would do that, but he really wasn't sure what to do. The smart thing would probably be to duck into the woods and wait for the police to show up. But what if Hickey *had* been in that silver Camry? And what if Karen was still with him after all? She might be bound and gagged in the backseat, or lying wounded in the trunk. He wished he had Cheryl's pistol, but there was no point in wishing. The gun had exploded with the plane.

He scooped Abby into his arms and looked up the shoulder. A dozen people stood along the crest, looking down at him. There were probably hundreds of cars backed up already. A world-class traffic snarl. If Hickey was up there with them, so be it. Somebody up there would have a gun. This was Mississippi, after all. They might *all* have guns. He hitched Abby up on his hip and started up the shoulder.

Cheryl sat down in the trees on the ridge that divided the northbound and southbound lanes and tried to catch her breath. The scene below was like something out of a Spielberg movie. It was like watching a parade from the roof of a building. Cheryl had done that once as a child. With her real father. But this parade had gone terribly wrong.

The doctor's plane was still burning, throwing up a column of black smoke like a refinery fire. The driver of the log truck was stumbling back toward the fire, to see the damage his truck had done, she supposed. Cars were lined up behind the plane as far as she could see, and hundreds of people were beginning to get out of them. By the plane, though, there were still only a few, as if the spectators sensed that the show might not be quite over. At least the little girl was okay. Cheryl had seen the doctor carry her up onto the road.

She needed to get moving, if she wanted to stay out of jail. Her best bet was probably to go down to the northbound lanes and hitch a ride with some horny salesman. She probably looked rough after the crash, but the truth was, men didn't care. Not when you were twenty-six and had a body tailor-made for the Victoria's Secret catalog.

Cheryl was standing up when she saw Joey rise from behind a parked car and walk toward the knot of people that had gathered around Dr Jennings and his little girl.

Will was stunned by the reaction of the people on the shoulder. They all talked at once, and he could only catch fragments of their conversations. A couple of guys slapped him on the back, but another yelled, 'Where's the stupid sonofabitch who was flying that plane? Somebody needs to arrest his ass!'

Will just held Abby tight and asked someone – anyone – to call the state police and the FBI. Three men detached themselves from the crowd and trotted back toward the line of cars, presumably to use their cell phones.

'Daddy, your *plane*,' said Abby, pointing at the mangled wreck.

Will heard himself laugh. 'That old girl did what I needed her to do. That's all that matters.'

'Look at my bear, Daddy. Huey made it.'

Abby held out an intricately carved figure of a bear

holding a little girl. Will was no art expert, but he was an experienced collector, and there was something in the little figure that moved him deeply.

'EVERYBODY BACK!' screamed a male voice.

Will thought it was a cop until the men around him began to scatter, half of them sliding down the shoulder behind him, the other half running back to their cars. Among the running bodies, his eyes picked out a man standing still as a pole, thirty feet away. He had dark hair and black eyes, and one of his pant legs was soaked with blood from groin to ankle. As Will watched, he raised his arm. A revolver gleamed blue-black in the sun.

Hickey.

There was nowhere to run. He and Abby were caught between the burning plane and the steep shoulder. If he made a dash down the hill with Abby in his arms, Hickey could simply take a few steps and shoot them as they tried to reach the trees.

'Who's that man, Daddy?'

'Shh, punkin,' Will had thought he might remember Hickey from the time of his mother's operation, but the man's face was a cipher. It was hard to comprehend, facing a total stranger who hated you enough to kill you and your children.

'Where's my money, Doc?' Hickey asked, his eyes smoldering like coals.

Will pointed at the burning plane. 'In there.'

'You'd better be lying.'

'I'm too tired to lie.'

'Where's Cheryl?'

'I don't know.' He wasn't so tired that he couldn't lie

423

a little. He wasn't going to tell Hickey that his wife had burned up in the plane with the ransom money.

Keeping his gun trained on Will and Abby, Hickey backed to the edge of the shoulder and looked down.

'That's the way, Huey!' he shouted. 'Come on, boy! You can do it!'

Will looked around for signs of help, but he saw none.

'You know what happens now?' Hickey asked, focusing on Will and Abby again.

'What?'

'This.'

He fired, and Will felt his right leg buckle. He almost collapsed, but he managed to keep his feet long enough to set Abby down and move in front of her. She was screaming in terror. He considered telling her to run for it, but he doubted she would, and any such move might cause Hickey to shoot again. He felt her clutching his pants from behind.

'Shot by your own gun,' Hickey said. 'How does it feel?'

Will looked down. The bullet had caught him in the meat of the thigh, but away on the lateral side, away from the femoral artery.

Hickey yelled back over his shoulder: 'Come on, Buckethead! Train's leaving! Show me you're not a wheelie-boy!'

'Get out of here while you can, Joe,' Will said.

Hickey laughed darkly. 'Oh, I'll be gettin' on soon. But you and me got an account to settle. And that little girl behind you is the legal tender.'

He took a step closer, then another. Will was about

to snatch Abby up and try to run for it when a female voice stopped Hickey in his tracks.

'*I got the money, Joey!*'

Cheryl was standing on the far side of the road, by the median. The smile on her face was as forced as an Avon lady's on a poor street, but she was making an effort. 'Let's get out of here, Joey. Come on!'

'Well, well,' Hickey said. 'The prodigal slut.' He shook his head. 'Gotta finish what you start, babe.'

Her smile cracked, then vanished. 'There's no reason to hurt that little girl, Joey. Not anymore.'

'You know there is.'

'Killing her won't bring your mama back.'

His eyes blazed. 'He'll feel some of what I've felt!' Hickey lowered his aim to Will's legs, which hardly shielded Abby at all.

'Joey, don't!' Cheryl opened the ransom briefcase, took out her Walther, and aimed it at Hickey's chest. 'It wasn't even his fault! Let's go to Costa Rica. Your ranch is waiting!'

Hickey looked at Will and laughed bitterly. 'Turned her against me, didn't you? Well . . . she always was a stupid cow.'

He turned casually toward Cheryl and fired, blowing her back onto the median and spilling hundred-dollar bills across the grass. Then his gun was on Will again, his aim dancing from head to chest to legs. As he played his little game, a strange beating sound echoed over the slab of the interstate. Will recognized it first: the *whup-whup-whup* of rotor blades. Hickey soon understood its meaning, but instead of bolting, he took two steps closer to Will.

'What do I want with a ranch in Costa Rica? I can't stand spics anyhow. This is what I came for. What goes around comes around, Doc.'

Will felt a hard tug on his pants. 'Daddy, *look.*'

As Hickey steadied his aim, Will threw himself on top of Abby. Then, just as Cheryl had done before the crash, he turned and looked death full in the face.

He expected a muzzle flash, but what he saw was a bloody forearm the size of a ham slip around Hickey's neck and lift him bodily into the air.

'You can't hurt Abby, Joey,' Huey said. 'You can hurt Huey, but you can't hurt Abby. She's my Belle.'

Hickey's eyes bulged with surprise. He tried to bring his pistol far enough back to shoot his cousin, but the first shot didn't come close. The bloody forearm just lifted him higher, closing off his windpipe like a clamp. Hickey's legs kicked like a badly hanged man's, and his gun barked harmlessly into the sky. He somehow managed to choke out four words, but they were poorly chosen.

'*You – god – damn – retard—*'

Will watched in fascination as Huey choked the life out of his cousin, his face as placid as that of a mountain gorilla at rest. Hickey's last bullet tore off part of Huey's ear, but then the gun clicked empty. By the time the sharp snap of cervical vertebrae reverberated across the road, Hickey's face was blue-black.

His limbs went limp as rags, and his gun clattered onto the concrete. After a few seconds, Huey set him gently on the side of the road, sat beside him, and began to pet his head. Then he shook him gently, as if he might suddenly wake up.

'Joey? Joey?'

The beating of the helicopter was much louder. Will rolled off Abby and unbuckled his belt, wrapped it around his wounded thigh, and tied it off.

'Look,' Abby said in a small voice. 'Huey's crying.'

Huey had knelt over Hickey and put a hand over his mouth to feel for breath. When he felt none, he started mewling like a baby.

'Why'd you want to hurt Belle?' he sobbed. 'It's not right to hurt little girls. Mamaw told us that.'

'We've got to help him, Daddy.' Abby started across the road, but Will limped after her and brought her back.

'I need you here, baby. We've got to find Mom.'

'I'm right here,' someone said from behind them.

Will turned. Karen was standing on the median side of the road, an automatic pistol in her hand. It was Cheryl's Walther. She was pointing it at its owner, while Cheryl crawled over the grass stuffing loose packets of hundred-dollar bills back into the briefcase. Both women looked like air-raid survivors, dazed beyond reason but still trying to function, their brains pushing them down logical paths without any larger perspective.

Abby started to run to Karen, but Will caught her arm and pulled her back. Karen was not herself. If she was, she would have run to Abby as soon as she sighted her.

'Bring me the gun, Karen,' he said.

She seemed not to have heard. She kept pointing the Walther at Cheryl's head, which was only two feet from its barrel. For her part, Cheryl seemed not to notice. She just kept stuffing bills into the briefcase. Will saw blood on her shoulder, but apparently the bullet had not done major damage.

He limped to within three feet of his wife. 'Karen? May I please have the gun? I need it.'

'*She's one of them!*' Karen cried suddenly. 'Isn't she?'

'It's over,' he said, holding out his hand. 'Hickey's dead. And she's not going anywhere.'

Karen jerked the Walther out of his reach. As she did, Will saw a large bloodstain on her upper abdomen.

'What happened?'

'He shot me,' she said, still following Cheryl with the gun.

'DROP THE WEAPON!' shouted a male voice. 'STATE POLICE! DROP THE GUN AND LIE DOWN ON THE GROUND!'

Will turned and saw two uniformed state troopers pointing long-barreled revolvers at Karen.

'Hold your fire!' he yelled. 'She's in shock!'

'DROP THAT WEAPON!' one trooper shouted again.

Karen turned toward them but did not drop the gun. Will knew they might fire at any moment. He stepped forward and put his body between their guns and Karen, but even as he did, a fierce wind sprang up, driving gravel and cinders across the road in a punishing spiral.

A Bell helicopter with 'FBI' stenciled in yellow on the fuel tank flared over the road and set down near the dwindling fire that had been Will's plane. Two men in business suits leaped out of the cockpit and ran toward the state troopers, their wallets held out in front of them. A hurried conversation resulted in one of the troopers lowering his gun, but the other did not seem impressed by FBI credentials. One of the agents interposed himself between the stubborn trooper and Karen, and addressed himself to Will.

'Are you Doctor Jennings?'

'Yes.'

'I'm Frank Zwick, Doctor. I'm glad to see you alive.'

'I'm *damn* glad to see you. Can you help us? My wife has been shot, and she's disoriented.'

'Can you get her to put down the gun?'

Will turned to Karen and held up his hands. 'Honey, you've got to give me the gun. These people are here to help us. You can't—'

Karen wobbled on her feet, then crumpled forward onto the ground.

Will ran forward and knelt beside her. Her radial pulse was weak. As carefully as he could, he rolled her over and unbuttoned the blood-soaked blouse. The bullet had struck her in the left upper abdomen, probably in the spleen. He leaned over and put his ear to her mouth, listening and feeling for breath, watching her chest expansion. Her airway was open, and her lungs probably okay, but he could already see some distension in her belly from internal bleeding.

'What's wrong with Mom?' Abby wailed. 'Daddy, what's the matter?'

'She's all right,' he assured her, though the wound could be fatal if not treated quickly in an operating room.

'We've got paramedics about five miles out,' Zwick

said. 'They're coming up the shoulder in an ambulance. I'd estimate fifteen to twenty minutes.'

'I want her in your chopper,' Will told him. 'You can have her on the helipad at University Hospital in ten minutes.'

'That's not an air ambulance, Doctor. It's just a row of seats.'

'It beats waiting. Make it happen, Frank.'

The SAC nodded and ran over to talk to his pilot.

'Abby?' said Karen, her eyes fluttering.

'We're all here,' Will said.

'*Where's Abby?*' Karen struggled to rise. '*Where's my baby?*'

'Right here, Mom.' Abby knelt beside her mother.

Karen seized her hand, then raised her head, looking right and left like a lioness guarding her cubs. 'Where's Hickey?'

'Dead,' Will told her again. 'We're all safe, babe.'

It took a few moments for this to register, but at last Karen sighed and closed her eyes again. Will estimated her blood pressure by checking her various pulses, carotid, femoral, and radial. Then he checked her nail perfusion. She was going into shock. They needed to get moving.

'Daddy's going to make you all better, Mom.'

Karen smiled a ghostly smile. 'I know, baby.'

'Does it hurt a lot?'

'With you holding my hand, nothing hurts.'

Abby laughed through tears.

'All set,' Zwick said, coming over from the chopper. 'Ready to move her?'

'I'm a little under the weather,' Will told him.

'My dad got shot in the leg,' Abby said proudly. 'He was trying to save me.'

'Whose money is this?' called a state trooper from the median. He was holding up the ransom briefcase. Beside him, his partner was cuffing Cheryl's hands behind her back.

'Mine,' Will said. 'That woman was shot in the shoulder, and she was in a fire. Put her aboard the ambulance as soon as it gets here.'

'That's *my* money!' Cheryl yelled. She pointed at Will. 'Ask him!'

'Take it with you,' Will told the trooper. 'We'll sort it out later.'

'How much is in here?'

'Three hundred and fifty thousand.'

The trooper whistled long and low.

'You lying bastard!' Cheryl yelled at Will. 'I knew it!'

'I won't forget what I said,' he told her. 'I'll come to court and tell them what you did to help us.'

'Bullshit! You'll forget about me in five minutes!'

He shrugged and turned back to Zwick. 'Let's get Karen into the chopper.'

Zwick motioned for the troopers and the pilot to help.

'What about Huey?' Abby asked. 'Can he come, too?'

Will pointed at the spectacled giant, who was still trying to rouse Joey from his permanent slumber. 'That one isn't for the county jail. He needs a psychological evaluation. If you'll take him to University, I'll get him onto the ward.'

The trooper holding the briefcase nodded.

Will tried to help Zwick and the others lift Karen, but his leg buckled again. 'What's the radio frequency of the ER at University?' he asked the trooper.

'One hundred fifty-five point three-forty.'

'Thanks.'

Someone had made a pallet of blue FBI windbreakers on the floor of the chopper, and they laid Karen on it. Zwick rode up front. Will was thankful for the gesture. He knew the SAC would like nothing better than to grill him for the next eight hours, but the man was demonstrating some decency.

As the chopper tilted forward and beat its way into the sky, Will went forward and contacted the attending physician in the UMC emergency room. He outlined Karen's case, then requested a trauma surgeon that he knew had not gone to Biloxi for the convention, a crusty old Vietnam vet who knew how to clamp and get the hell out.

When he returned to the cabin, Karen's eyes were open. She said something he couldn't hear above the noise of the rotors, so he leaned down to her mouth.

'Family,' she whispered. 'Again.'

'We're a family again!' cried Abby, looking at Will with wide eyes. 'That's what she said!'

'That's what she said, all right,' he agreed. Suddenly something broke loose in him, and waves of grief and joy rolled through his heart.

'You're shaking, Daddy,' Abby said.

'I'm okay. It's been a long day.'

She smiled uncertainly, searching his eyes for the invincible father she had always known, for signs that everything would soon return to normal. Will took her free hand in his, just as she held Karen's. Together they formed a circle that he vowed would never again be broken. He had made such vows before, usually after seeing some tragic death in the hospital, but eventually the grind of daily existence dulled his awareness of the central truth of life. Chaos was working beneath everything, and death always waited in the wings, watchful as a crow. This time he would not forget how precious was the time he shared with the women who loved him. This time he would keep that knowledge close in his heart.

This time . . .

GREG ILES

MORTAL FEAR

By day, Harper Cole is a successful commodities trader working from his home in the isolated Mississippi Delta. But at night . . . at night he is a systems operator for EROS, a sexually explicit on-line service catering for the erotic appetites of an exclusive clientele.

But Harper's secret life is soon to be shattered when a brilliant, twisted serial killer uses EROS to select and stalk his female victims – and Harper finds himself a prime suspect in the eyes of the FBI. While the FBI uses the technology of the future and the psychology of the past to track the deadly 'EROS killer', Harper must clear himself by luring the real murderer into the open. Twisting himself into the mind and soul of a woman he once loved, he impersonates her on-line, placing everything he has and loves directly in the killer's path. And finally confronting a secret of his own that itself could destroy his whole world . . .

HODDER AND STOUGHTON PAPERBACKS

GREG ILES

DEAD SLEEP

When prize-winning photojournalist Jordan Glass
chances upon a portrait by an unknown artist in Hong
Kong, she is stunned. The face staring back is her
identical twin sister.

The painting is part of an exhibition entitled 'Sleeping
Women' and as Jordan studies it she realises, to her
horror, that the portraits are all of women who, like her
sister, have disappeared from New Orleans in recent
months. Jordan's discovery electrifies a case previously
paralysed by a lack of corpses. With this new evidence
the FBI's serial killer unit is spurred into action.

Teaming up with a forensic psychologist and FBI special
agent John Kaiser, Jordan follows the artist's trail. But the
FBI's use of Jordan puts her directly in the killer's sights,
and when the trail doubles back, forging a path into her
own past, Jordan is forced to confront shocking secrets in
a final stunning showdown.

CORONET BOOKS
Hodder & Stoughton

GREG ILES

SLEEP NO MORE

John Waters' world is about to be turned inside out by a single word spoken from the lips of the stunning Eve Sumner. One solitary word that takes him back a decade to another woman and the most passionate of affairs.

Mallory Gray-Chandler was the quintessential Southern Belle who loved John with a seething passion that threatened to destroy them both. Yet despite his infatuation, he ended the affair. Sometime later she was found raped and murdered on a New Orleans pier.

Two days after meeting Eve, John sees her again at a cocktail party. This time she squeezes his hand and says 'You weren't wrong about what I said, it's me, John.' Exactly who is Eve Sumner? And how does she know so much about John's past with Mallory Gray-Candler?

A swarm of secrets, lies and murder is about to explode in a novel where the boundaries between passion, obsession and love are stretched to and beyond their limits,

CORONET BOOKS
Hodder & Stoughton

GREG ILES

BLACK CROSS

An American doctor and a Jewish soldier reluctantly lead a covert mission into Nazi Germany. Their goal: to ensure a D-Day victory for the Allies. In a top secret research installation that does not officially exist, the doctor and soldier, polar opposites, meet two remarkable women crucial to the success of their nightmarish secret task.

In this terrifying crucible of war's horrors, they must find an unimaginably terrible weapon and commit an unthinkable act of destruction – all in the name of peace. In the hurricane of conflict, both men find love, a passion that utterly transforms them – killer into saviour, healer into destroyer – turning the tide of world events.

HODDER AND STOUGHTON PAPERBACKS

GREG ILES

SPANDAU PHOENIX

The Spandau Diary – what was in it? Why did the secret intelligence agencies of every major power want it? Why was a brave and beautiful woman kidnapped and sexually tormented to get it? Why did a chain of deception and violent death lash out across the globe, from survivors of the Nazi past to warriors in the new conflict now about to explode? Why did the entire history of World War II have to be rewritten as the future hung over a nightmare abyss?

'Start with an irresistible plot, add a heavy dose of historical intrigue, mix a host of shadowy characters, just a dash of terror on every page . . . and you have *Spandau Phoenix*, a scorching read'
John Grisham

HODDER AND STOUGHTON PAPERBACKS